The Best of *Jim Baen's* UNIVERSE

edited by
ERIC FLINT

Baen Books by Eric Flint

Ring of Fire series:
1632 by Eric Flint
1633 by Eric Flint & David Weber
1634: The Baltic War by Eric Flint & David Weber
Ring of Fire ed. by Eric Flint
1634: The Galileo Affair by Eric Flint & Andrew Dennis
1635: The Ram Rebellion by Eric Flint and Virginia DeMarce et al.
1635: The Cannon Law by Eric Flint & Andrew Dennis
Grantville Gazette ed. by Eric Flint
Grantville Gazette II ed. by Eric Flint
Grantville Gazette III ed. by Eric Flint

Joe's World series:
The Philosophical Strangler
Forward the Mage (with Richard Roach)

Mother of Demons

Crown of Slaves (with David Weber)

The Course of Empire (with K.D. Wentworth)

Mountain Magic (with Ryk E. Spoor, David Drake & Henry Kuttner)

With Mercedes Lackey & Dave Freer:
The Shadow of the Lion
This Rough Magic

With Dave Freer:
Rats, Bats & Vats
The Rats, The Bats & The Ugly

Pyramid Scheme
Pyramid Power (forthcoming)

With David Drake:
The Tyrant

The Belisarius Series with David Drake:
An Oblique Approach
In the Heart of Darkness
Destiny's Shield
Fortune's Stroke
The Tide of Victory
The Dance of Time

Edited by Eric Flint
The World Turned Upside Down (with David Drake & Jim Baen)
The Best of Jim Baen's Universe

The Best of *Jim Baen's*
UNIVERSE

edited by
ERIC FLINT

THE BEST OF *JIM BAEN'S UNIVERSE*

A Baen Books Original

Baen Publishing Enterprises
P.O. Box 1403
Riverdale, NY 10471
www.baen.com

ISBN 10: 1-4165-2136-4
ISBN 13: 978-1-4165-2136-5

Cover art and typography by David Mattingly

First printing, July 2007

Distributed by Simon & Schuster
1230 Avenue of the Americas
New York, NY 10020

Library of Congress Cataloging-in-Publication Data:

The best of Jim Baen's universe / edited by Eric Flint.
    p. cm.
  ISBN 1-4165-2136-4
1. Science fiction, American. 2. Fantasy fiction,
American. I. Flint, Eric. II. Jim Baen's universe (Online)

 PS648.S3B497 2007
 813'.0876208—dc22

2007009084

Printed in the United States of America

10 9 8 7 6 5 4 3 2 1

CONTENTS

SCIENCE FICTION STORIES

Dog Soldier by Garth Nix 1

The Girl With the Killer Eyes by B. B. Kristopher 19

Bow Shock by Gregory Benford 37

Decaf and Spaceship, To Go by Katherine Sanger 75

All The Things You Are by Mike Resnick 79

A Time To Kill by S. Andrew Swann 109

Local Boy Makes Good by Ray Tabler 119

The Old Woman in the Young Woman by Gene Wolfe 131

Candy-Blossom by Dave Freer 141

What Would Sam Spade Do? by Jo Walton 149

Giving it Fourteen Percent by A. S. Fox 157

Every Hole Is Outlined by John Barnes 175

Fishing by Thea Hutcheson 207

Bob's Yeti Problem by Lawrence Person 211

Brieanna's Constant by Eric Witchey 223

The Darkness by David Drake 243

FANTASY STORIES

The Cold Blacksmith by Elizabeth Bear 277

The Nature of Things by Maya Kaathryn Bohnoff 287

Sisters of Sarronnym; Sisters of Westwind by L. E. Modesitt, Jr. 309

The Opposite of Pomegranates by Marissa Lingen 347

As Black As Hell by John Lambshead 357

Benny Comes Home by Esther Friesner 395

Femme Fatale by Jason Wittman 421

A Hire Power by J. Simon 443

Poga by John Barnes 449

IN REMEMBRANCE: Jim Baen (1943-2006)

The Legacy of Jim Baen by Eric Flint 483

Why Die? by Jim Baen 493

A Genetic Model for Eternal Life as an
Evolutionary Strategy by Karl Inne Ugland 497

A Personal Remembrance of Jim Baen by John Lambshead 509

AFTERWORD 511

Dog Soldier

by Garth Nix

The seven rings of Syrene shine
Like glowing disks in a *nazdra* mine
Burning brighter than fusion fire . . .

"How long is this bullshit going to last?" Assault Sergeant Gillies whispered to his neighbor, Base Sergeant Major Traut.

"Long as it wants to," Traut muttered back. "It's the CG's poem. Lukas is just reading it."

"The golden whorl of Syrene's seas

"Swirl in torrents as they please . . ."

"Didn't Syrene take a Xene transformer bomb in '06?" whispered Gillies.

"Yeah," replied Traut. "But it was partially damped. Navy showed up just in time. Mind you, Syrene was a real dump before the trannie bomb. The xeneform went about halfway. Gave the planet dust rings and turned the oceans sort of murky yellow with sparkly bits. Killed everyone at the time, of course. But the general's from one of the later settlements. Tourist operators."

"So come to Syrene, make a start

"But be prepared to lose your heart."

"More like your wallet," Traut added in an aside to Gillies, as thunderous applause filled the amphitheatre. It wasn't actually the end of the poem, but the troops couldn't cope with any more, so they'd taken advantage of a meaningful pause to clap. Since it was officially rectime, the clapping was swiftly followed by an exodus to the low port accessway, and the fallway to the Other Ranks Club.

Gillies and Traut waited for the initial rush to subside, let the few unfortunate officers who been trapped into attending go, then made a stately exit to the topside ascensor, heading for the sergeant's mess.

As the ascensor lift gripped him, Gillies looked back at Lukas, to see whether he was still going with the poem. But the unfortunate Lieutenant Lukas, head of the Cultural Events committee, was obviously receiving some fairly harsh words over his implant com. Probably a critique from the commanding general for his stupidity in pausing long enough for the troops to applaud, Gillies thought. Just as he was wondering what it would be like to get a personal tonguelashing from Major General Orosonne, his own tongue tingled, alerting him to a communication.

"Sergeant Gillies, this is ComOp. You back on?"

"Uh, not exactly. What have you got?" Gillies subvocalized.

"Got a Navy 'at your convenience.' Report to Dock Three, navy cargo master. Logged at 2130. ComOp Out."

"Got it," Gillies affirmed. Traut, seeing the characteristic twitch of the muscles in his neck, raised her single surviving eyebrow in query—a characteristic gesture that could make junior officers and other ranks whimper, but Gillies and Traut were old comrades.

"A navy 'when you can but right now would be best if you don't want me to complain to the captain,'" Gillies explained. "Dock Three."

"Time for a drink first, then," said Traut genially, touching her ID bracelet against the sergeant's mess door. It slid back, revealing a glimpse of walnut paneling (ersatz), thick rugs (tylarn), leather lounges (havax cloth), alcoholic beverages (synthesized), and senior NCOs (not strictly human).

"No, I'd better get over there. The navy's probably caught one of my people trying to steal a cargo vessel or something. Who's cargo master on Three?"

"Berzis. Chief P.O. Rule merchant. Bit of a shithead."

"Can't be theft, then. Berzis would just call the MPs for inter-service borrowing. If it doesn't take too long, I'll take you up on that drink."

"Okay," said Traut. "But you might want an early night. The whisper is a full-sim boarding ex tomorrow for your lot. 0320 or thereabouts. A surprise."

She smiled, made an unorthodox salute in the direction of the Second Battalion HQ, topside and starboard, and disappeared into the mess. Gillies turned back to the ascensor, cursing the battalion CO. They'd only just got back from an on-planet assault exercise. Hostile environment, pulling 3Gs, in an atmosphere pretty much the same as the shit they cleaned the drains with back on the garrison station. Full-sim meant occasional live fire too, which was why Gillies was temporarily in charge of the assault engineer platoon. The lieutenant had been shuttled out yesterday, back to civilization and a hospital where they could regrow his left hand and eye, instead of the combat replacement prosthetics the garrison hospital practically bolted on before sending you back out.

Not that there was an "out" just at the moment. The Fourth Xene War had ended three years before, in a series of inconclusive engagements in the Hogawan system, resulting in an armed truce. Which was why the 203rd Marine Brigade was in garrison, on a navy-run converted battlewagon, brought out of mothballs and put in orbit around the distasteful Hogawan VI. The Xenes had a similar operation in orbit around the Earth-like Hogawan III. Needless to say, the Xenes wanted H-VI and the Terrans wanted H-III. But they weren't prepared to swap. Not for the first time, Gillies considered what might happen if the troops on both sides simply shot the politicians and did a deal on the real estate. The only problem was it took about five years to learn Xene trade talk, mostly spent in learning to operate six prosthetic feelers, simulating the ones that grew out of the lump that could loosely be described as a Xene's head. Gillies had heard that the process wasn't totally reversible, either.

The ascensor bottomed out on Deck Minus, and Gillies transferred to the ring-about that would take him in a circle halfway around the ship's hull to Dock Three. The ring-about clanked every ten meters, but that was a comfortable reminder that the old TNS Sable Basilisk had extra armor bonded on in ten-meter-wide slabs, for its next but last incarnation as a planetary bombardment station. The ring-about had been converted from the missile feeder system that ran between the old and the new armor belt.

Clank-clank-clank-clank-ping-brrrr. The *ping* was the programmed stop for Dock Three, and the *Brrr* was a gravity alert. Gillies left the capsule, pushing off for a controlled somersault to the exterior rails of the cargo master's eyrie. The dock was in zero g, though there was no reason why it should be. Except that the navy pretended to like zero g.

Gillies climbed inside the eyrie, where two vac-suited figures hung relatively upside down, their visors open, fingers flying over check-comps. Gillies spun himself, clipped on to the rail, and reoriented opposite the one with the swirling galaxies on his suit sleeves.

"Chief Berzis. Assault Sergeant Gillies."

"Oh yeah . . . Sergeant Gillies. We've got a bit of a problem."

"Okay. Who is it and what have they done?" Gillies asked resignedly. He tried to think if he'd accidentally asked the boys and girls to steal something. All it took was a slip of the tongue, like, "Okay, so those stargazing perverts might have a one-portable slipscan, but we don't. So let's see this one put together in under three minutes . . ."

"Don't worry, Sergeant. It's nothing like that. Fact is, we've got a shipment for you. Or part of one."

"A shipment?"

"Yeah. All the way from Sol. Pallas R&D, to be exact. Only there's supposed to be more of it."

"Pallas R&D? Addressed to me? I don't know anyone at Pallas."

"It's not personal, Sergeant. ComOp says you're acting OC of the assault engineer platoon of 2 Battalion, and that's who it's for. Some sort of new equipment you're supposed to trial, according to the transhipment explanation anyway. The only problem is that one cap is missing. Been missing since Syrene, four stops away."

"What's in the missing capsule?"

"If the manifest's right, you're missing all the frageware documentation. The instruction data, the specs, the familiarity program. The other cap, which we are about to present to you, lucky Sergeant Gillies, is the hardware. Only. Please tag the slate."

Gillies shook his head, but took the slate, read the details of the receipt, then pressed his ID bracelet against it. The slate didn't do anything until the cargo master tapped it briskly, then it flashed and gave a confirming beep, followed by a slow voice, "Log-ged at oh-seven-seven . . . ." The cargo master tapped it again, and the slate hiccupped, before continuing, "Correction . . . twenty-one fifty-two. Thank you."

"Piece of shit," muttered Berzis. "The cap's over there. Green decal, orafluoro stripes, number 0122. See it?"

"Got it," said Gillies. "Thanks, Chief. I think."

"Wait till he sees what's inside," Berzis muttered to his offsider, as Gillies adjusted the antigrav on the capsule and let it drag him over to the ring-about. "Pallas R&D! The *R* must be for retarded and the *D* for, uh, *D* for . . ."

"Deadheads?" suggested the offsider.

Gillies took the cap down to the assault engineers workroom, checked the hazard symbols, and opened it. Naturally, this revealed more packaging, and when he'd stripped that off, still more packaging—some sort of anodized foil with a quick release ring. Gillies pulled it, looked at what was inside, leapt back, and only just prevented himself from slapping the emergency alert panel, which would open the weapon lockers, jolt every trooper on the ship in the tongue, and alert the bridge.

There was a life-form in the capsule. A thing. It was about knee-high, had a sort of cylindrical body with a smaller cylindrical head, six legs, and a tail. It was shiny black all over, and it was alive. Its head moved. It had two eyes. They looked at Gillies, and it stretched, the six legs going from sort of rubbery multijointed stilts to stiff supports. Its mouth opened, revealing a hideously wet, yellow maw and enormous saw-edged blue teeth. It yawned, snorted, and let out a sharp, short noise.

Gillies tongued his implant and subvocalized.

"ComOp. This is Gillies in 77AE1. Get me two MPs on the double with stunzers and netweb."

"Done. Alert?"

"Local seal. Standby. Info duty officer, possible Life-form Haz."

Gillies edged around the capsule, looking for the instruction reader that he'd seen in with the life form. The thing watched him, and licked its lips. Its tongue was also yellow.

The sergeant slowly reached for the reader, which had fallen on the floor a foot away from the creature. It stepped out of the capsule and also looked at the instructions. Gillies reached again, a bit closer. The thing edged closer too. Gillies lunged. So did the creature. Blue teeth snapped on the reader, and the thing jumped back in the capsule. The sergeant jumped back too, almost colliding with the two marine police who burst through the door, stunzer and netweb at the ready.

"Stun it!" shouted Gillies, but the MPs didn't need to be told. The one with the stunzer fired. Several times. All it did was make the creature jump out of the capsule and advance on them again. Then the other MP fired the netweb, and the creature fell over in a writhing mass of rapidly ballooning threads.

It had dropped the reader to snap at its bonds. Gillies snatched the unit up and flicked it on; as the MPs watched the thing begin to successfully chew its way through the supposedly super-toughened web. One MP looked anxiously at the emergency alert panel and twitched. The other, older one was obviously subvocalizing something, but Gillies wasn't on their net. Besides, he was reading. Quickly.

"Purple Perseans . . . patrol the . . . perimeter . . . of Pair-sepol-eyes," he shouted, as the thing bit through the last strands of netweb around its forelegs. Nothing happened. Gillies looked at the reader again, keyed for phonetic, and hastily reread the sentence.

"Purple Persians . . . patrol the . . . perimeter of . . . Per-sep-olis."

The thing suddenly froze in place, three of its six legs in the air.

"What happened?" asked the nervous MP. Gillies noticed he didn't take his hand too far away from the alert panel.

"Code phrase for deactivation," replied Gillies. "Apparently Xene mockers can't pronounce alliterative series starting with *p*. That's what it says here, anyway."

"What is that thing?" asked the other MP. He'd just subvocalized something that Gillies suspected was the cancellation of an armored squad with boarding weapons.

Gillies scrolled the reader back to the introduction, and keyed it for speech. Typically, it had an accented voice that made it difficult to follow, instead of using the military standard inflections.

"This unit is a Combat Candroid DOG 01A prototype. Designed for support use with assault engineer units, the DOG 01A is a sophisticated artificial lifeform. For reasons of durability, the body is mechanical, with a high survivability in all but Class 10X environments. Lightly armored, the DOG 01A is impervious to low-powered radiant, sonic, or projectile weapons and highly resistant to Xene solvents. Its Central Intelligence Unit is based on a Sysicram 310 multiproc, with a prototype biological intelligence and personality transfer from a Terran natural life-form, the dog variant known as a collie-shepherd cross. Prototype frageware interfaces this natural personality with the special requirements of different environments and the specialized tasks of an assault engineer unit.

"This reader has further categories: Packing Instructions, Unpacking Instructions, Basic PowerUp, and Emergency Shutdown. For full specifications, run-in procedure, and operational instructions, see separate reader CCAN-DOG-01A, classified Operational Secret. This reader is classified as Restricted. Have a nice day."

"Personality transfer?" asked the nervous MP.

"It means that this thing thinks it's a live animal," replied Gillies. "A Terran dog. Whatever that is. You guys aren't from Sol are you?"

"Nephreus Prime."

"Jaminor IV," replied the older one. "I doubt there's anyone on Garrison from Terra. We've got a corporal from Sol Belt, but she's on one of the picquet ships. I'll call ComOp and see who they can come up with."

"Don't bother," said Gillies. "Our battalion quartermaster is supposed to be Terran—I'll talk to him tomorrow."

"You just going to leave that thing here?" asked the young MP. He still seemed nervous.

"Yeah," said Gillies. "I'll secure this reader, so it won't be able to PowerUp. Who knows, the other capsule might show up too, with the full order set."

"It's your responsibility," shrugged the older MP. "Come on, Nerik. Zoo tour over. Good luck, Sergeant."

"Thanks," said Gillies, eyeing the DOG with a jaundiced look. It was already 2305, and if there was going to be an alert at 0320, he wanted to be up and ready at 0250. He just hoped that neither the CO nor the company commander were aware that he was supposed to be checking out this new equipment, or they'd want to take it on the exercise.

"So where is the DOG unit you're evaluating, Sergeant?" Colonel Kjaskle asked as she marched down the first rank of the assault engineer platoon, her martinet's eye running over the armored shapes standing stiffly at attention, looking for any deviation from the standard equipment or procedures. "And why is Private Loposhin's field cutter fixed on his right sleeve?"

"Half the DOG shipment didn't come in, sir," Gillies snapped, all too aware of the gleaming capsule in the corner of the ready room. "No frageware instructions. And Loposhin's left arm rider has a malfunctioning connect, sir, temporarily US."

"Then get him out and down to Cyber," Kjaskle snapped. "Memo to adjutant: 'Check tech workshop wait times. Report by 1200.' The DOG unit works doesn't it?"

"Ah, yes, sir," Gillies replied unhappily. "But I don't know the command phrases or its capabilities."

"It has an artificial persona, I believe, Sergeant," the CO replied. "Treat it like a real dog. The exercise will be delayed till the DOG unit is ready to deploy. You have fifteen minutes, Sergeant Gillies. Copy to all OC, Bridge, BrigCom. Ex restart 0335. And we'll change it to a planetary search and destroy. All subunits deploy to drop stations. Orders Group in ten."

Gillies snapped a salute, ordered the platoon to reequip for planet action and drop, and watched the colonel's back as she marched on to the heavy weapons platoon ready room, the adjutant and RSM marching behind, catching a steady stream of orders.

"Treat it like a real dog," he muttered to himself. He'd forgotten the colonel's last assignment had been in Sol. Staff College on Mars. There were probably hundreds of dogs there. He tongued his impcom. "ComOp. Gillies. Get me BQMS Skuarren. Urgent."

Fortunately, "Sublight" Skuarren was on duty, and so it only took two or three minutes for the ComOp to convince him that he had to talk to Gillies. Sublight, being both a hundred and fifty-year veteran and a quartermaster, considered himself to be a sort of independent prince, and gave rare audiences. He probably should have been retired, but since he'd started his career back when starships were sublight and subject to temporal dilation, no one could figure out how old he actually was. It was also rumored that his retirement payout would be so huge that the Paymaster was hoping he'd die first.

"Gillies? Assault engineers, huh? I was an assault sergeant for a while, son. Back in the First War. Lost a hand when a mini-sun novaed prematurely when we were burning through the Xene flagship off Parast. Then the damned trauma seal malfunctioned and cut off my whole damn arm! Had a prosthetic one for about ten years before I could get a new one grown back. Hell of a thing, that prosthetic . . . what? Terran dogs? Yeah. A what? A collie? Nice dog, may be a bit gentle. Shepherd cross? German shepherd, that'd be. No, nothing to do with bacterial weapons. Germany is a subunit of Terra. Of course I know. I used to have a Labrador—that's another variant, son—when we were doing police work on Nightwing. Commands? The usual stuff. Sit, walk, find, retrieve, stay, attack, heel . . . no, it means follow close by your heels. On your boots. The part at the back. You call it what? Where are you from, son? Brink II! Shit, son, I was part of the relief force that recaptured Brink. More commands? Okay, I'll see what I can remember, and zap it down on the dataline. Enjoy your exercise, Sergeant. I hope it's a good dog."

Ten hours later, Sergeant Gillies was pretty sure that even if it was a good dog, he didn't like it. They'd hit the planet at 0400, deploying in squad-sized drop saucers, and the DOG had been out the hatch as soon as it opened, without waiting for a command. It had run backward and forward around him as he'd disembarked, and got in the way of the initial scans. Then, when the whole battalion had moved off toward the simulated enemy defense area, the DOG had raced out in front of the lead scouts, confusing them and everybody else. Luckily, Gillies had remembered "heel" and transmitted it at once, but to add insult to injury, the DOG communicated on one of the spare bands that Gillies had assigned as a private channel for him and the three squad leaders. Now, it was interrupted all the time by sharp, strident noises from the DOG. It seemed to make them every time it found something.

To be fair, it found things with considerable efficiency, turning up several booby traps or fixed auto weapons several minutes before Gillie's slipscan teams. But it was only a few minutes, and the sergeant didn't really think it was worth the aggravation.

The DOG had been useful in the assault too, demoralizing the defenders (from the brigade's HQ company) by digging through a frozen oxygen rampart and then springing out in a heavy weapons emplacement, blue teeth and six sets of claws scoring faceplates and shredding exterior aerials and the like. No one had been hurt by the DOG—which seemed to understand it was an exercise—but it certainly put them off long enough for a squad to gee-vault in and finish them off with low-en simulated plasma dotters.

Now, on the shuttle going back up to Garrison, Gillies noticed that the DOG must have purposefully rolled around on one of the crystalline "plant-mats" that grew on Hogawan VII, because long lines of furry crystals were now growing on its black body, giving it the appearance of long hair. The crystals were harmless, but Gillies eyed it with misgiving. Bald was good enough for marines, it ought to be good enough for an auxiliary animal. The DOG seemed to notice he was looking, because it put its head back and thrust its tongue out at him, while its tail rotated in eccentric circles. Probably an insult, Gillies thought.

Suddenly, his suit com squawked into life, and his tongue tingled with the sensation of a red alert. The troopers around him in the shuttle's shockwebs suddenly jerked upright, and the DOG sprang to its feet. Gillies felt every inch of his skin suddenly contract, like being dumped in freezing water, as the shuttle energized its protective shield. It was followed a moment later by the controlled but excited voice of the naval duty officer.

"Red! Nilsim! All hands, close up for action."

There was a pause, then Colonel Kjaskle came on the all troops channel.

"Listen up, marines! An unauthorized craft is approaching the interdicted zone. Fighters are vectoring to intercept. We're going in behind to board. The craft looks like a Xene battle barge, but it's all on its own. This is not a simulation. Nilsim. Company and platoon commanders stand by for orders."

The colonel clicked off and Gillies spoke quickly, before she came on the command channel directly.

"Pull safety tags and sim buttons and cross-check with your team."

Seconds later, the colonel spoke to Gillies directly. "Gillies. We've got an ID on the battle barge. A Xene renegade, probably a suicide run for the garrison. It's pointed straight at it on full acceleration, and the navy isn't positive they can totally vaporize it without some debris hitting the garrison and attendant craft. So we've got to clean up—and only your shuttle and 2nd Platoon, A Company are close enough for immediate intercept. That's the situation. Orders. Two-A platoon will take the bridge. Your assault engineer platoon will secure the engine room. Scan downloading now. From the schematics, it looks like a standard battle barge, but don't take it for granted, they're running a full screen. Do it by the book, exactly as you've done before. Any questions?"

"No, sir," replied Gillies, as he studied the schematics displayed just in front of his eyes on the upper part of the visor. "We'll cut in the trailing cargo hold and deploy from there."

"Sounds good to me, Sergeant," said the CO. "Take it away."

"Okay, children, listen in!" Gillies said. "We're going in to take the engine room of this battle barge. It looks like a Xene suicide ram, so we've got the important job. But I want it nice and careful, okay? Smazl, your squad will be on scan and support, Wattson, your guys'll

do the drill-in and blow. I'll go with Nreda's squad, and we'll do the
assault. The schematics look just like the sim we did last month, but
don't take it for granted. Okay. The trailing cargo bay is the cut-in,
core bulkhead the scan and blow, and then the aft hatch of that
corridor behind I'll mini-sun for the assault party. Drop in four-
thirty-two. Any questions?"

There were no questions. The DOG looked like it would ask questions if it could talk, and Gillies realized he hadn't thought about what
it would do. Stay with him, he guessed, if it had an EVA capability.

"Okay. Three minutes. Seal and energize. Weapons—ready! Load
and set! Take up boarding positions."

Gillies slapped his own faceplate down and checked the suit telltales, before arming his in-built and carried weapons and setting the
safety switches. Finally, he stood up, locked his boots into position on
the floor, and called the bridge, while his eyes ran over the men and
women of the platoon, checking the readiness telltales, which didn't
always sync up with his helmet display. The DOG, he noticed, had
automatically assumed the drop position when everyone else did.

"Platoon ready for boarding. Open boarding hatch and stand by
for drop."

"Confirmed. Okay, you marines! Boarding hatch opening, standby
for gravity alert. Two point five gees matched with the target. Good
luck!"

The floor in front of Gillies suddenly slid away, revealing open
space. He couldn't see the Xene craft because of the shield interference, but his locator beam was already on it, locking in on his chosen
drop point. It flashed a yellow warning in his helmet, and then red, as
the ejection field picked up the entire platoon and hurled them into
space.

Gravity hit like a sucker punch, more than the 2.5 g the shuttle pilot
had indicated, and the heavens wheeled around the faceplate as Gillies spun toward the enemy vessel. The suit's autopilot was firing
pulsion units to stop the spin, but Gillies assumed control and merely
slowed it, so he could get his bearings. A few seconds later, he felt his
skin crawl again, as he passed through the enemy energy field. That
made him susceptible to fire, so he upped the acceleration and started
jinking, while his suit fired chaff and tiny distorter missiles. Around
him, everyone in the platoon was doing the same, as the squads
sorted themselves into a rough formation for the landing.

The first squad hit and established a scan perimeter, taking out two enemy autoguns as they did so; Wattson's squad pancaked in and drillers flared white, sparking fountains of light. Gillies kept the other squad matched to the ship's vector, in a rough circle about twenty meters above the hull. Experience had shown that a band about four meters deep existed here, where the enemy's ship-mounted AP weapons couldn't bear. A frageware glitch probably, but one common to this type of vessel. Gillies hoped it was still current.

Down on the hull, Wattson's troops finished drilling and starting placing charges in the boreholes to finish the breach. Wattson came over the com.

"Two minutes, from my mark. Mark!"

The circle on the deck suddenly expanded, as both squads opened up the perimeter to allow room for the blast. The cutting charges were supposed to be unidirectional—inward—but it never seemed to totally work that way. Gillies, up above, opened up his perimeter too, and as Wattson said, "Three seconds!" they all flipped to take the flash and blast debris on their back armor.

Wattson's "one" was lost in the com interference from the micronukes, but the flash was clear enough. Gillies counted, "One, two," then somersaulted and jetted for what he hoped was a gaping hole through the outer hull into a cargo bay. Out of the corner of his eye, he noticed the DOG was close behind him, its crystalline hair wavering as pulsors from its legs delivered sudden changes of direction.

The breach was there, twenty meters in diameter, with molten metal still bleeding off in all directions, and the Xene's chlorine atmosphere boiling out like green steam.

"Go to wavescan," Gillies instructed the assaulting squad, and his visor suddenly cleared to show a simulated real-time view of what everything looked like without the gases. The hull was cleanly breached, revealing a large, empty cargo hold. The assault squad raced in through the breach, leapfrogging in alternate pairs along the notional floor and walls of the hold. The enemy ship was maintaining an artificial gravity of about 0.2 g, but this wasn't enough for full gravity tactics. Two marines bounced off the walls to the coreward bulkhead, the first running a deepscan across the bulkhead, the second slapping a long ribbon-shaped cutting charge on the point indicated by the scan. The bomber then went left as the scanner went right, and five seconds later there was an explosion and a door-sized hole in the bulkhead. Another marine moved up and flipped flechette grenades through, to cover each end of the corridor on the other side of the bulkhead. Immediately they exploded, two marines dived through, and plasma dotters fired, almost simultaneously with a Xene greyband. There was a muffled exclamation on com.

"One Xene down in the corridor, none in range," said Corporal Nreda. "I've taken a greyband hit on the leg, lost ablat, knee joint's immobilized."

"Okay," snapped Gillies as he bounded forward. "Stay there and cover the topside approach. I'm coming through. Smazl, stay hullside and secure. Wattson, come through when we're into the engine room."

He dived through the bulkhead hole, and cursed as the DOG dived too, almost colliding with him as he flipped to take the impact on his legs. Nreda was firing again, to the left, and the flare from the stream of microscopic plasma dots was causing part of his faceplate to polarize and the wavescan view was chopping up. The marine to his right indicated the aft hatch, then flew hullward and sticktered herself against the corridor "roof," to get a good firing position when Gillies sunned the door.

The sergeant locked himself feet first on the "wall," at right angles to the other two marines, and unclipped the black globe of the minisun from his belt. He aimed it at the hatch, thumb securely pressing the safety interlock switch, while his suitcomp downloaded the instructions that would define both the protective field and the arc of destruction. As Gillies raised his thumb, he thought of Sublight's story about losing an arm—but that had been an earlier model. Below him, the DOG unit seemed to see the weapon for the first time, and it pressed itself totally flat on the floor and tucked its head in between its front legs. Then Gillies let the mini-sun go.

It worked perfectly. The globe flew forward, and the instant before it hit the hatch, raised a protective field in a hemisphere behind it, while vaporizing everything in a hemisphere in front of it. The hatch, part of the aft bulkhead, and two Xene warriors several meters behind the hatch just disappeared. The half of the globe that had generated the field continued in its trajectory, rebounding from the far bulkhead of the room.

The marine on the roof fired as Gillies went in below her, the DOG at his reboos, or heels as Sublight called them. She missed whatever she was aiming at, and a millisecond later, she was hit by a rocket-propelled greyband capsule, the Xene organic solvent eating into her armor as she frantically activated the shedding process that would slough off her outer ablative layer.

Gillies's comp tracked the launch, and he instinctively fired back with his in-built arm dotter, taking a Xene as it dived to new cover. At that same second, Gillies realized that this room wasn't the engine control room. The schematics were wrong. He anchored himself behind a panel and called his squad leaders.

"Smazl! Get a scan team down here to me! Wattson! Report! Nreda, where's the rest of the fucking squad?"

"We're under fire, boss! Big counterattack—ambush—they're coming out of the fucking forr'd hold . . . the boat deck . . . they're everywhere!"

Gillies had to check his comp to see who was talking, the voice was almost hysterical, totally unlike Smazl. Before he could answer, Wattson came over the com, speaking fast.

"Smazl just went down, Sarge! His troopies are in hand-to-hand, I'll counter-attack up the hold rim before they're overrun. At least fifty warriors . . ."

"Okay!" Gillies snapped. "Wattson, hold your attack, there's too many of them. Get Smazl's squad to fall back if they can. Nreda, join your squad with Wattson's and establish a defensive position around the hold for a hot insertion by reinforcements. Wattson, you're in command, contact the CO and ask for some goddamn help. I'm going on for the engine room."

Gillies hardly heard the affirmatives of Nreda and Wattson. They knew as well as he did that there might not be any reinforcements if he couldn't stop or at least slow the battle barge long enough for the rest of the battalion to catch up. And in the worst-case scenario, the navy might have to try and take the barge out even with the marines still fighting onboard. Gillies would have to try and find the engine room without a scan team.

Boosting his suit scans to maximum, the sergeant moved his head from side to side, hoping that some aberrant energy emission would show up. One did, but visual observation showed it to be the DOG unit. Gillies looked at it, and suddenly wondered if the Pallas R&D people really were as stupid as everyone thought.

"Okay, DOG," he transmitted to it. "Where's the engine room?"

The DOG's ears pricked up and it moved its head sideways, as if listening, but it didn't do anything.

"DOG-01, locate engine room!" Gillies snapped. Again, the DOG looked like it was intently listening, but it still didn't do anything.

"DOG-01, search for the engine room . . ." Gillies tried, a little half-heartedly. He knew the DOG could locate things—it just needed the right command.

"Sublight!"

Gillies suddenly remembered the old codger was going to download a list of commands on the dataline. Quickly, he accessed his comp. Sure enough, there was a stored low priority send from BQMS Skuarren. He activated it, and Sublight's familiar voice filled his ears.

"I got that full list of commands, son. Would you believe it? That second capsule came to me with a batch of left-handed spinsticks. I've been scrolling it all morning, and those guys on Pallas sure have a sense of humor. Must be some old-timers there like me . . ."

Gillies hit fast-forward, as his helmet telltales showed two new casualties among Smazl's squad. Six of Smazl's ten marines were either dead or their suits were, and there five casualties among the other two squads. He had to find the engine room!

"Okay, Sergeant, the basic command menu follows. There's some real funny stuff, but it sure is a good DOG."

Gillies listened intently to the stream of one-word commands and two- or three-word groups, till he heard the one he wanted. It was incredibly obvious, but he didn't waste time worrying about that.

"DOG . . . FIND . . . ENGINE . . . ROOM."

The pauses were important apparently. Something else Xene mockers couldn't handle properly. They had no sense of rhythm.

The DOG shot up from the deck, its head went down, and it rotated through a complex sphere. Apparently finding some scantrail or trace, it then used its pulsors to head off toward the coreward hatch. Gillies followed along the wall, using his stickers, plasma dotter tracking just above the DOG's head. According to the schematics, this hatch led to a drop shaft to a drive inspection chamber, but the schematics were clearly wrong.

The DOG pawed at the hatch, and then looked back at Gillies. He nodded, and said, "Heel!" as he readied his last mini-sun. The DOG obeyed with alacrity. Gillies trained the mini-sun on the hatch, let it compute, then raised his thumb.

Something did go wrong with this one, but Gillies wasn't sure what it was, as he was knocked back across the room and momentarily stunned by the blast. Coming to, he instinctively bounced behind cover, twisting himself so he could cover the hatch. Even as he rolled, a greyband capsule struck near his feet, and the solvent spewed out, seeking marine armor. Gillies activated the mechanism that would shuck the first ablative layer, and returned fire. His dotter struck a Xene warrior who was charging through a gaping hole where the coreward hatch used to be. The alien, despite being hit through the midsection, kept on coming.

Behind him, Gillies saw the DOG unit rolling around on the ground with another Xene, and behind them, he saw the characteristic tall panels of a Xene ship's engine control room. But before he could use the com, the gut-shot Xene was on top of him, thrusting with a small trident in each of its three combat arms. Gillies jumped backward, and activated the forceblades in his gauntlets. Two bright-blue beams, each sixty centimeters long, shot out just in time for him to parry the Xene's trident attacks.

Sparks flew as forceblade met trident field. Gillies caught the two main attacks, but was too slow on the third, and a trident skewed off his blade to sink into the left side of his armor. It didn't penetrate to skin, but it didn't have to. The Xene twisted the handle, and the remaining field charge earthed itself, shorting out most of Gillies' systems. His whole left side locked up, and his sinister beam faded to nothing. Desperately, Gillies fired his back pulsors, throwing himself forward in a mad lunge with the functioning forceblade, expecting to feel the other tridents in his chest.

But the Xene toppled over, smashed into the floor, and rebounded with Gillies on top of him. Before the alien could recover, Gillies thrust his forceblade through its chest exhaust, the savage blow sending him into a spin that he couldn't control. Out of the corner of his helmet, he saw the DOG propel itself out from under the Xene's anterior limbs, where it had struck as he'd shoved.

"Well done," Gillies sent, remembering the order codes Sublight had sent down. But there was no answer: only an ominous vibration deep in his cheekbones. Quickly, Gillies flipped through the other channels, without success. He couldn't get a full damage control readout, but the emergency telltales inside his helmet told him his motor controls were shot, there was significant loss of suit environment, and the trident charge was still ravaging his suit systems. He'd probably be dead inside twenty minutes—with everyone else from his own platoon and Two Platoon as well, if he couldn't get to the drive controls and shut it down.

The controls were little more than five meters away, and there were no Xene defenders in the way. But Gillies was unable to move, his arms and legs twitching uselessly, bound in armor that had effectively lost its nervous system. He was writhing uselessly on the notional floor under 0.2 g, but even the low gravity couldn't help him.

Quickly, Gillies assessed his options. The DOG unit looked to be fully functional, but it couldn't receive his commands. He looked down at it, and it looked up at him.

"Come here!" Gillies tried, but there was no response. Desperately, he tried again. Still, the DOG just stared up at him. He tried gesturing to it to come closer, but only a few of his fingers moved. He tried again, with his other hand. No fingers, but the wrist flopped backward and forward, like a clockwork obscene gesture.

The DOG seemed to understand that, because it unwrapped its tail, and jetted up to Gillies, doing an elegant flip-over halfway that put its tail next to Gillies's helmet. He wondered what the hell it was doing, till his damage control telltales showed one restored com circuit. The DOG's tail was its antenna and input fiber, and it had just plugged into his suit phone.

"Well done!" Gillies exclaimed again. The tail wagged a little, but not too much. Praying that his message log wasn't destroyed, Gillies summoned up Sublight's message again. It worked, and this time he ran through all the codes, using up a precious five minutes of his remaining life support. But it was worth it. The DOG's command language was surprisingly sophisticated when groups of words were used, and it hinted at equally sophisticated capabilities.

"DOG! DESTROY . . . ENEMY . . . ENGINE . . . CONTROL . . . PANELS . . . IN . . . VISUAL . . . RANGE . . . AND . . . RETURN!"

The DOG detached itself, and sped over to the engine room. Gillies watched in fascination as it moved to each panel, and a cutting lance shot out of its nose, melting through the armored covers of key fiber junctions. Then, a blue claw went in, and came out festooned with broken fibers and the Xene's curious half-sentient chips, their metallic blood boiling out into vacuum. Luminescent trails on the panels died. When the second-last panel dimmed, Gillies skin crawled as the ship's screen pulsed and died. When the last panel faded into darkness, his stomach told him he was in zero g. The artificial gravity was off and the ship was no longer accelerating.

The DOG jetted back, and reconnected. Gillies smiled and nodded at it.

"GOOD . . . DOG! Very good!"

The rest of the battalion shuttles would intercept all the sooner now, maybe even soon enough to save Gillies's platoon. They could even be landing now, for all he knew. But it was too late for him. The suit said he had less than five minutes of atmosphere left, and they'd never get to him in time. Wearily, he tried to think of something he could do, something to add to the simple equation of not enough air and a broken suit. Salvage atmos tanks from one of his dead marines back in the hold? He couldn't get to them. He was too tired, and he couldn't move anyway. He might as well just go to sleep . . .

With a jerk, he twitched himself awake, and checked the telltales again. The suit had cut him to half pressure—he wasn't getting enough oxygen. He couldn't think. There was the DOG, maybe it could get him the atmos tanks, but once again, he couldn't think of the commands. His head felt like he'd just gone through a gravity flux. He couldn't remember the commands, the commands. Only the one Sublight thought was funny, though Gillies didn't know why. Maybe it was Sublight's joke, and it wasn't a real command, but it sounded like just the right thing for the situation.

Half unconscious, Gillies muttered the command that would save his life.

"Lassie. Get help."

The Girl with the Killer Eyes

By B. B. Kristopher

"Look, Roy, I'm telling you—"

"Yeah, Mike, I got it. A really hot redhead who shoots laser beams out of her eyes."

Jodie looked up from the guest register she was filling out intending to make a scathing comment about sexism in the workplace and men who treated women like sex objects, but the two men who were talking weren't even looking in her direction. One was a tall man with graying brown hair and the other was a shorter man with thick curly brown hair and olive skin. Both men seemed completely oblivious to anything but their conversation, at least if the flailing arms were any indication.

"Dude, don't start."

"Start?" the taller man said. "Mike, we've been having this same conversation for years. You can't see the future."

The shorter one, Mike, raised his index finger. "Then how do you explain Amber?"

"If that makes you able to see the future, then our entire high school qualifies. I'm the only person in the school who didn't think she'd cheat on me."

"But—" Mike said.

"And then there's football."

"Don't go there," Mike said in a warning tone.

"We've made the same bet every year for sixteen years . . ."

"Dude, this is Buffalo's year."

". . . and every year you lose."

"But—" Mike said.

"You owe me twelve hundred bucks."

"That much? Really?"

"Yes!"

"But—"

"I don't even watch football!"

The conversation trailed off as the two walked through the security checkpoint. Jodie shook her head, trying to get rid of the headache that had been building steadily through the bureaucratic nightmare that was the last two days, and turned back to the latest bit of paperwork. Once she finished signing her life away, the guard handed her a visitor's badge with a small, blurry, reddish picture of her printed on it.

"Just follow the green line, darling, and Special Agent Peterson will meet you," the guard said.

Jodie started to bristle but she stepped on it. In the last forty-eight hours, she'd been called "honey," "darling," "baby," and "sugar" more times than in the entire rest of her life, but mostly it had been by women who were either older, African-American, or who had a heavy Southern accent. Near as she could tell, it was just normal around Atlanta. Knowing that didn't do anything for her headache, however.

"Thank you," she said, doing her best to take it in the spirit in which it was offered. She picked up her purse and headed for the security checkpoint.

The checkpoint was the usual elaborate affair with thick walls, lots of guns, and even more guards. She extended the visitor's pass to an armored man who was about six foot six and built like a professional football player.

"Energy projector, huh?" the guard said as he read her badge. He pointed at the blast tank off to the side. "Try not to punch through the gizmo."

Jodie walked over and put her arm in the tube. "I'll be careful," she said. She took a deep breath and fired a blast into the tank and true to her word, she was very careful about just how much power she let out. First time she'd used a profile tank, she'd punched through the very expensive "gizmo," the bottom of the tank, the floor, and a foot of concrete foundation. The guard at the Superhuman Registry Office had been less than amused.

Unfortunately, being careful didn't stop the blast from filling the hall with the rotten egg smell of sulfur.

"She's a match," a woman said from the other side of the barricade.

The guard, his eyes watering slightly, offered her the visitor's pass back.

"Welcome to the Atlanta office, Special Agent Adan," the guard said as the door swung open.

She glanced at his badge. "Thank you, Sergeant Miller."

"Call me Frank. Everybody else does."

She was surprised at how short the wait was before a tall woman with straight black hair and a hint of Native American in her features and coloring stepped through the barricade.

"Hey, Frank," she said.

"Hey, Mary," Frank replied.

Mary turned to face Jodie. "Special Agent Mary Peterson," she said, holding out her hand.

Jodie took it. "Special Agent Jodie Adan."

"Welcome to the Atlanta office."

"Thanks."

"Well, come on. It's best not to keep HR waiting. They sign the paychecks."

"Right."

Two hours, a stack of forms, three hand cramps, a splitting headache, and two aspirin later Mary led Jodie out of the HR office.

"Your head doing any better?" Mary asked.

"No," Jodie said. "It always gets like this when I'm irritated. Airport security, movers, Superhuman Registry Office, and HR all in one week . . ."

"Yeah, that would irritate anyone. Come on." They rode the elevator down to the main office and Mary led her into the cube farm where most of the agents worked.

"Interrogation rooms for normals are off to the left," Mary said, pointing at a series of doors on one side of the farm. She turned and pointed at a massive bank vault style door that stood open off to the right. "The armored interrogation rooms are through that door for the übers."

Jodie flinched at the term and felt another throb of irritation. She hadn't heard anyone use anything other than "empowered humans" since she was about eight. Mary didn't even seem to notice, she just kept talking, so Jodie decided to let it go.

"If there's ever a breakout, stay clear of the door though. It weighs eleven tons and the rams drive it shut in about two seconds."

Jodie nodded even though she knew all about blast doors. At the academy, they'd shown her a video of an agent who hadn't gotten clear during a breakout. It had been more than enough to drive the lesson home.

"Oh, and you'll want to keep a warm coat at your desk," Mary said. "It gets really hot in the city during the summer, so you'll want to wear lightweight suits, but the office is cut into a vein of granite that shoots off of Stone Mountain, and we've never been able to keep it warm enough."

"I'll keep that in mind," Jodie said. She was honestly grateful for the tip, but it meant shopping. She only had a couple of really lightweight suits. One more adjustment to make, she supposed.

They'd gotten about halfway across the cube farm when a carefully folded paper helicopter complete with spinning rotors rose up from one of the cubicles ahead of her, sailed across the aisle, and fired a pair of paper missiles through the entrance to another cube.

"Damn it, Roy, I didn't need to know that!"

Jodie groaned as she recognized the voice. It was Mike from the lobby.

Mary sighed and called out, "Am I going to have to separate you two?"

"What?" Roy asked. "All I did—"

Mike stood up and stomped out of his cubicle. "All you did was load those stupid missiles with memories of . . ." He stopped and looked right at Jodie.

"What is it, Mike?" Roy asked. He stuck his head around the wall of his cubicle and looked at Jodie. His jaw dropped.

"Dude," Mike said.

Jodie held up her hands, "Don't say it!"

"But—"

"I mean it," she said. "I do *not* shoot laser beams out of my eyes."

Roy looked at Mike, who looked absolutely crestfallen, and started laughing. Hard. Pretty soon, other people were sticking their heads over the walls of their cubes to see what was so funny.

Mary gave Jodie an apologetic look and said, "Sorry." Then a long black tentacle stretched out from the shoulder of her suit and gave Roy a shove.

He squawked as he fell out of his chair.

It didn't do much good. Roy shut up, but Mike took one look at him lying on the floor and doubled over laughing.

Jodie reached up and started rubbing her temples, trying to ease her head. "Maybe I'll dye my hair."

Special Agent in Charge Scott Coolidge wasn't what Jodie expected. Somehow, she'd expected a man with his reputation to be taller. At five foot ten, she had a good two inches on him. Worse, he seemed perky, and one wall of his office was almost covered with photos of women in various mildly suggestive poses.

"So, what brings you to our little corner of the world?"

"Well, sir, I graduated top of my class at Quantico so I got my choice of assignments, and the chance to work with, well, you, sir . . ."

"Ah," he said. He opened a desk drawer and pulled out an old, well-worn pipe with a curved stem and slightly fluted bowl. The pipe was a dark yellow, but judging by the ivory white near where the black mouthpiece was attached, the yellow color was mostly a result of age and heavy use. He filled it from a small tin and packed it down with some kind of pocketknife-like tool.

She couldn't help but be surprised. The Bureau had a strict no-smoking policy, and as the special agent in charge, seeing that it was enforced was one of his jobs.

"You smoke, Ms. Adan?"

"No, sir."

He touched the tip of his finger to the tobacco and it glowed bright red. As the office filled with the smell of it she felt a flicker of irritation at the fact that he hadn't even asked her if she minded, but he didn't seem to notice. Instead, he took a long pull of the pipe, leaned back, and blew the smoke in the general direction of an exhaust fan.

"You shouldn't believe everything you hear, Agent," he said mildly. "Most of the stories about me are—"

The door swung open and Mary stuck her head in.

"Sir, we've got a live one."

Coolidge's chair snapped upright and he set the pipe into a shallow indentation in the ashtray on his desk.

"What is it?" he asked, suddenly all business.

"Bank robbery."

"That's a little low end, isn't it?" he asked.

"The perp tunneled into the vault, sir. Cleaned out all the safety deposit boxes and about ten million in cash. Thing is, the vault was cleared in five minutes."

"That does sound like one of ours. I take it Team Six is up in the rotation?"

"Yes, sir."

Coolidge turned back to look at Jodie.

"What about it, Agent, you feel like working a case today?"

She thought about it for a second. What she really wanted was a couple of more aspirin and a dark room where she could sleep off her headache. She hadn't been properly briefed on her teammates' abilities, or local comm procedures, or local law enforcement, or any of a dozen other things she should know before she went into the field, but Coolidge seemed to expect her to jump at the chance and she didn't want him to think she wasn't up to the job. Not only was he one of the best agents the Bureau had ever fielded, he was also the youngest Special Agent in Charge in Bureau history.

That, and he could sink her career before it even started.

"Yes, sir," she said, not entirely sure she was ready, but deciding there was no way she was going to disappoint Scott Coolidge on her first day.

"Got your badge and gun?"

"Yes, sir."

"Good girl. I hereby dub you Federal Bureau of Superhuman Investigation Enforcement Team ATL-06's official ranged attack specialist. Mary here can fill you in on the way." He turned to Mary. "And Mary . . ."

"Yeah?"

"Try to keep Tweedledum and Tweedledee in line."

She snorted. "Right. Me and what army?"

Before Jodie had time to ask what she meant, Mary turned to her and said, "Come on, kid."

The motor pool smelled faintly of diesel, but Jodie was use to that. The Bureau always used diesels. They figured the extra pollution was an acceptable trade-off for a fuel that was less explosive. After the first time she blew up a car on the training range, she had to admit they had a point.

"First time out on a case?" Mary asked.

"Yeah," Jodie answered.

"Don't worry about it. You'll do fine."

"Right. Who are the other members of . . . oh no."

Mike and Roy were standing by the black Ford Excursion Diesel.

"See what you did?" Roy said. "On the team less than a day, and she already hates you."

"Me?" Mike said. "What makes you so sure it isn't you she hates?"

"Boys," Mary said. "She hates both of you. Now, can we go before APD taints the scene for Mike?"

"Right," Mike said. "I'm driving."

"Like hell," Roy said. "I want to live until dinner."

"Fine," Mary said. "I'll drive, and Jodie here gets shotgun."

"D'oh!" Mike said.

Atlanta traffic on a Monday afternoon was different from the L.A. traffic she'd grown up with, the Boston traffic she'd dealt with during her college years, and the D.C. traffic she'd gotten used to at the academy. She'd expected it to be tamer, slower. A bit more genteel. Heck, she'd expected people to yield for the siren and the dome lights.

Instead, she'd spent the last twenty-five minutes clinging to the handle strap above the passenger door of the Excursion as Mary whipped the SUV in and out of traffic and tried to hide her amazement at the number of pickup trucks, minivans, and junkers doing eighty on the midtown connector.

And if the traffic was bad, it was nothing compared to the arguing.

"We should take the Peachtree Street exit and avoid the traffic on the connector."

"You're nuts. If we take the surface streets, the perps will be in Mexico by the time we get there."

"No, don't take the Williams Street exit, go down to the Georgia State exit."

"Dude, she's not going ten minutes out of the way so you can ogle the co-eds."

"Fine, let her get stuck in traffic."

"Both of you shut up!"

By the time they pulled up outside of Peachtree Center, Jodie was convinced she'd been assigned to the worst team in the Bureau. Mike and Roy were idiots, and Mary must have done something spectacularly stupid to get stuck with them.

She also had something close to a full-blown migraine. The light and sound sensitivity hadn't started yet, but she felt like someone was pounding on her head with a sledgehammer, from the inside.

She tried not to think about it. She just put her headset on, set her comm to the right frequency, got out of the truck, and followed them to the bank entrance.

"Sorry, folks, this is a crime scene," the uniformed officer at the entrance said.

Mike held up his badge. "Special Agent Beyer, FBSI. Special Agents Barnett, Peterson, and Adan. Who's in charge?"

"Detective Warner."

"Well, that figures," Roy said.

"Roy," Mike said in a warning tone. "Where is the detective?"

"He's in the vault, sir," the uniform said.

"Thanks."

The uniform stepped aside but his shoulder brushed up against Mike as he walked through the door and Mike stopped so suddenly Roy walked right into his back.

"Officer, do you own a Mustang?"

"Yes, sir," the officer said in confusion.

"You've been smelling gas, haven't you?"

"Yes, sir."

"I don't know much about cars, but I can't imagine a leak that's spraying hot gas on your engine block is very safe. You might want to get it towed to the mechanic."

"Yes, sir!"

Jodie was still a little stunned by Mike's behavior when they entered the vault. She'd assumed Mary was the senior agent, but the way Mike had taken charge had corrected that impression, and he'd been much more professional than she'd expected too. It was calming, both to her nerves and to the pain in her head.

"Well, well, well, if it isn't—" a man in a bad tan suit started.

"Don't say it," Roy said, cutting him off.

"Say what?" the bad suit asked.

"'If it isn't Nostradamus,'" Roy said in a mocking tone.

"Hey, you stay out of my head."

"Dick," Mary said, "he doesn't have to read your mind to know you're going to spout the same tired jokes that weren't funny the first time. He just has to smell your cheap cologne."

"What, a psychic boyfriend wasn't enough, now he's got a psychic nose too?"

"Warner," Mike said, "you want to fill us in on what happened, or should I start by ordering your people off my crime scene?"

"There's no evidence that this was done by a freak job."

"Hey," Jodie snapped, both her temper and her headache flaring. "Who are you—"

"Adan," Roy said, "leave it. 'Detective' Warner here isn't worth your breath."

Mike stepped past Warner and knelt down next to a large hole in the floor. "Tell you what," he said, "why don't we find out."

"Hey, don't contaminate my . . ." Warner never finished.

Mike touched the edge of the hole and his eyes glazed over. He stayed like that for almost a minute, then stood up.

"Three guys," Mike said. "One was a digger, one's a telekinetic, and one looks to be muscle. The digger got them into the vault. The TK picked the locks and the muscle collected the goods. All three were übers."

"And I'm just supposed to take your word for it?" Warner said.

"You know what," Mike said in an offhand manner, "I'm tired of having this argument with you, Richard. If you think your men can handle three übers, go ahead and send them out. Just don't expect us to clean them up. In the meantime, we're going to do our jobs. Mary, if you would?"

Mary nodded and her suit began to melt and shrink. The white shirt completely vanished as the black, shiny liquid that had been the suit closed up and wrapped around her neck and covered her hands. It stopped for a second while she raised a hand and waved to Warner.

"Buh-bye," she said in a cheerful tone before the suit flowed again, covering her hair and face before it finally settled into a dry, seamless matte black bodysuit with what looked like inset armor plates. Her head turned to the left, then the right, and she nodded to herself. Four thick tentacles grew out of her back, planted themselves around the hole, and lifted her up, then lowered her down into the black.

A minute later, her voice crackled over the radio.

"Looks clean. Come on down."

Mike looked at Roy.

"Roy, you're up."

Roy nodded and rose up off the ground and just floated down the hole.

"Showoffs," Warner muttered.

"How are we supposed to get down?" Jodie asked.

"TK assist," Mike said.

Jodie winced.

"You ready, Mike?" Roy asked over the radio.

"Yeah, go for it."

Mike rose up and floated down the tunnel, just like Roy had.

"Jodie," Mike's voice came over the radio, "it's about thirty feet down and the bottom's sloped. Roy's going to lift you down, but be careful when you land."

"Got it."

Jodie braced herself. TK assisted lifts were standard training at the academy, but she wasn't that fond of the experience. She felt something wrap around her like a pair of arms in a loose hug before she felt the pressure against the bottom of her feet. It was unusual. With the instructor at the academy it was like riding an elevator without walls and she always felt like she was going to fall over. Roy seemed to be focusing on holding her upright as well as carrying her down the tunnel.

Mike was right. She almost slipped on the floor.

Mary was standing up at the end of the tunnel, her tentacles gone, but looking for all the world like a ninja in body armor. Roy stood behind her and a pair of Mag-Lites floated overhead illuminating the tunnel and the spot where Mike stood, hands on the wall.

"This was well planned," he said. "They've been working the tunnel for weeks. I think . . . MARTA."

"What?" Jodie asked.

"Metro Atlanta Rapid Transit Authority," Mike said. "They abbreviate it MARTA. There's a train station under Peachtree Center, and the digger and TK both had MARTA badges."

"So they were posing as subway employees and using it as a cover to tunnel into the bank from a train station?" Jodie asked. "Wouldn't someone notice?"

Roy laughed. "Wait until you see the train station."

"Let's go," Mike said.

Mary started forward and Roy and Mike followed. Jodie noticed Mike kept his hand in contact with the wall as they walked.

"Heh."

"What is it?" Roy asked.

"They've just been dumping the rock right into the construction debris," Mike said.

Roy shook his head. "You know, I thought this kind of thing was going to stop when that idiot Campbell was voted out of office."

"What kind of thing?" Jodie asked.

"The Peachtree Center station has been under construction, constantly, for about five years," Mike said.

"Ah."

The tunnel let out into a supply closet. A large metal shelving unit had been shoved in front of the mouth of the tunnel. Mary picked it up and set it aside while Jodie and Roy covered her, ready to attack, but there was nothing in the closet but cleaning supplies. Once they were sure it was clear, Mike stepped forward and touched the door.

"We didn't miss them by much," he said. "They had to change their . . . Oh, ewww . . ."

"What?" Roy asked.

"Skid marks," Mike said in a disgusted tone.

"Okay, from now on, no one asks for details of Mike's visions," Mary said.

"Right," Roy said. "I should know better by now."

"Um, not to be a party pooper . . ." Jodie stopped when Mike and Roy both burst out laughing. Then she realized what she'd said and looked at Mary.

"Are they always like this?"

"No, sometimes they act childish," she said. "Boss, we've got a job."

"Right," Mike said, still holding his sides. "Yeah. They changed clothes and tossed the goods in one of those Rubbermaid Dumpster things."

Mary nodded and her bodysuit melted back into a black and gray pinstripe number right out of the Macy's catalogue. Jodie decided the strangest part of the process was watching her gun and badge crawl from her hip and belt up under the coat and tuck into the shoulder holster and inside breast pocket.

"That's a neat trick," Jodie said.

"Yeah," Roy said, "but it makes her a pain to shop for."

"Admit it," Mike said, "you love working with a chick who shows up to work naked every day."

Before anyone could say a word, Mike opened the door of the closet and stepped out.

They got a lot of odd looks, including one from the cop with the MARTA police patch on his shoulder. Mike waved him over as he took out his badge.

"Special Agent Beyer, FBSI," he said. "I'm looking for three men. At least two of them are in MARTA uniforms. One's a short fellow, lots of hair, swarthy with big eyes, looks kind of like a mole. The next one is tall, blond, looks kind of like a surfer dude. The last one is big and kinda dumb looking."

"The first two sound like Julio and Dave," the cop said.

"Have you seen them lately?"

"Yeah, they went up to the Dumpsters about fifteen minutes ago."

"Which way?"

"Elevators on the other end of the platform," the cop said.

"Thanks," Mike said. "That closet is now a crime scene. I need you to keep it sealed."

"Um . . ."

Mike didn't wait for the rest of his response, he just took off in the direction of the escalators and led them down a flight of stairs, across the train platform, and up another flight of stairs at very near a dead run. Sure enough, the first thing Jodie noticed when they reached the top was that end of the station was under construction and a large section was barricaded off with plywood and two-by-fours.

Mike started to turn toward the elevators but stopped. He eyed the plywood.

"What?" Roy asked.

Mike walked over to the plywood and touched it.

"There's another tunnel," he said. "Come on. I think we can beat them if we hurry." He turned away from the elevator and toward escalators that were off to the right.

Mary just shrugged. "You heard the man," she said before she and Roy took off after him. Jodie followed.

The escalators had to be the longest she'd ever seen. They were at least four stories and by the time she hit the bottom, Mike was halfway up. At the top, Mike turned right and Jodie lost sight of him.

"Slow down, Mike," Roy said over the radio.

"Dude, they're getting away," Mike said.

"Yeah, but you're not exactly combat effective are you?" Roy asked.

"So catch up," Mike said.

"Idiot."

"Heard that."

"Meant you to," Roy said.

Jodie turned the corner and ran up a couple of steps and found herself in a food court. Her stomach reminded her that she hadn't had lunch, but she ignored it and focused on catching up to Mike, Roy, and Mary.

The problem was, Mike and Roy were nowhere to be seen. Jodie skidded to a halt next to Mary.

"Which way?" Mary asked into her headset.

"The Hyatt, motor lobby," Mike replied over the radio.

Mary cornered at an Orange Julius stand and Jodie followed. They went through a short glass-covered walkway and were in the hotel.

"Where's the motor lobby?" Jodie asked.

"Four floors down," Mary said and they ran across the lobby for the escalators. "Hold on," Mary said, and before Jodie could ask what she meant, Mary picked her up and instead of taking the escalators, she jumped over the railing. Jodie screamed, but the tentacles reappeared, shooting down to the floor below and slowing their fall. Mary set her on her feet.

"This way," she said and headed for another bank of escalators. Since there was no opening around these, they were forced to take the next three flights on foot, but the last escalator put them out right by the motor lobby. They burst through the doors from the lobby into the parking garage just in time to see a van swing around the corner at speed. Roy was standing right in front of it, arms raised, while Mike stood off to the side with his gun drawn.

The front of the van crumpled as it hit an invisible wall.

"I said stop!" Roy yelled.

Mary stepped forward and her suit melted into armor again, but this time, her badge was fixed to the left side of her chest.

"FBSI," she shouted. "Step out of the vehicle with your hands raised. Any attempt to use your powers will result in charges of resisting arrest."

Jodie shoved the sleeves of her suit up to her elbows and pointed her fists at the van. No need to take chances, or ruin a good suit.

It turned out to be a good decision. The side of the van blew off and sailed toward her. She blasted it aside and started searching for targets.

A big guy with long, stringy blond hair, a mustache, and a beard who looked like a pro wrestler charged Mary and before Jodie could fire on him, Mary leapt at him and they started trading blows. She looked around and Roy was fighting the guy who could only be the digger. His hands ended in long, blunt claws that he was trying to use to gut Roy, but Roy had a telekinetic shield up and the digger couldn't get at him. That left the TK.

"Where's the third one?" she asked.

"I don't know," Mike said.

"How can you not know?" she asked.

"This place is loaded with images. It would take too long to sort them."

"Fine," Jodie said. "Roy, give him a shove."

Roy raised his hand and pushed toward the digger. The digger sailed back about ten feet and Jodie pointed her fist at him. The air rippled and slammed into the digger hard enough to knock him into the wall. He fell to the ground, out cold. She turned.

"Mary, get clear of Blondie there."

"Got it," Mary said. She rolled onto her back and slammed both of her feet into his gut, sending him sailing. Jodie gave him just enough lead and let loose with a blast. He hit the wall near where the digger had and fell to the ground, unmoving.

"Mike, we've got you covered," Jodie said.

"Good job," Mike said as he stepped back and put his hand against the wall.

"Roy," Mary said, "can you feel him?"

"Not a thing," Roy said.

"You think he's a telepath too?" Mary asked.

"Yeah, probably," Roy said.

"Look out," Mike shouted.

Jodie turned and saw the chunk of van she'd blasted earlier sailing toward her. She raised her hands and fired, blasting it aside easily.

"The perp!" Mary shouted.

Jodie turned and all three of her teammates were running for the parking garage exit. She ran after them cursing under her breath. One of the first things they'd drummed into her at the academy was to avoid street fights. Too easy to hit innocent bystanders, too many potential hostages, way too much collateral damage, the public always pitched a fit, and there were almost always letters of censure.

She didn't want a letter of censure. Her first day was going badly enough as it was.

People were screaming and running by the time Jodie hit the street. It wasn't hard to see why, either. Roy was standing in the middle of the street and a large delivery van was rising and falling on top of him like a hammer trying to drive a nail. Mary was about thirty feet up a wall, screaming in rage with tentacles flaying, but the TK obviously had her pinned. Mike was emptying a gun the size of a Cadillac at the TK, but the bullets kept flattening themselves against an invisible wall.

Jodie raised both fists, checked her line of fire, and was about to blast him when he suddenly turned on her. She was snatched up and slammed back against the wall and her hands pinned down.

The TK turned his attention back to Mike and walked right into the hail of bullets. Mike never flinched. He just fed magazine after magazine into his pistol until he shot himself dry, then pulled out a snap baton and flicked it open.

Roy kept yelling, telling Mike to run, but he couldn't get way from the delivery van. Mary screamed and a single long, spiked tentacle shot toward the TK.

He yelled and looked down when it speared his leg. He waved his hand and the spike pulled back out of his leg and Mary shot up the side of the building a good twenty stories.

He turned back to Mike.

"Time to die, little man," the TK said.

Jodie pulled against the invisible force holding her. She couldn't let this happen. She couldn't let a member of her team be killed. She couldn't let Mike be killed. She just needed to focus, to get one hand up, but she couldn't. All she could do was glare and growl.

One shot. All she needed was one shot.

The TK drove Mike to his knees.

Just one shot.

Mike's hands went to his throat.

Jodie felt the blood pounding behind her eyes, the headache she'd all but forgotten during the heat of the chase flared again, and for a second, she was sure her skull would split open.

Mike's face started to turn blue.

The world suddenly turned red and the TK folded nearly in half as two thick red beams shot out of Jodie's eyes and slammed into him, sending him sailing into the large golden sphere suspended above the fountain in front of the hotel across the street. The thing rang like a bell and Jodie, suddenly free of the invisible force holding her up, fell to her knees. She stayed there for a second, looking at the crumpled body of the TK, then passed out.

"It's no big deal," Mary said.

Jodie tried to look up at Mary and instantly regretted opening her eyes. Even with all the lights out in the interrogation room, the light getting in past the closed blinds was enough to hurt.

"I passed out during a fight," Jodie groaned.

"Come on, Jodie," Mary said, "it's not that uncommon to pass out the first time a new power manifests."

"Have you?" Jodie asked.

"No, but then I'm just a one."

Jodie groaned as she realized she'd gone from a one to a two. She'd have to get the signature of her new power cataloged and refile her registration papers.

"Roy, on the other hand, is a three."

Jodie dropped the ice pack and looked at Mary, then winced and shut her eyes as the light registered. Mary handed her the ice pack again.

"He's really a three?" she asked.

"Yeah," Mary said. "TK manifested first, but he was in the middle of a chemistry class when the telepath manifested. It was a bit embarrassing for him really. Apparently the girl sitting behind him was thinking dirty thoughts about the professor and it bled through."

Jodie chuckled, then winced as the movement upset her stomach.

"That isn't the really funny one though," Mary said.

"Really, what is?"

"Well, before he went to the Academy, Roy got his PhD. Poor boy has a thing about public speaking. Don't know why. He used to do community theater all the time, and he was one of the best teachers Georgia State ever put in a classroom, but ask the boy to present a paper and he breaks out into a cold sweat."

"Oh no," Jodie said, suddenly having a pretty good idea where this was going.

"Well, he's suppose to present a paper on the use of telekinesis to manipulate light in the optics lab, so he walks out onto the stage, looks at a crowd of about a thousand physicists, and just vanishes."

Jodie laughed, and then clutched her head.

"Oh, God," she said, not sure herself if she was referring to the pain or the image of Roy vanishing from behind a podium.

"Yeah, it gets worse. The poor guy didn't even realize it. He just stood there and presented his entire paper while he was invisible."

"Please stop," Jodie said.

"Aw, come on. Don't you want to hear the part about how it took him three weeks to figure out how to become visible again?"

Jodie laughed even harder.

The door opened and a balding man in his late thirties stuck his head in.

"Scott wants to know if she's ready to debrief," he asked.

"How about it?" Mary asked.

"Yeah," Jodie said. "Just hand me my sunglasses."

Mary handed her the sunglasses. She put them on and stood up. Mary took her arm and led her out of the interrogation room.

At which point, they ran smack into Roy and Mike.

Mike looked at her, then at Roy. "Dude, I told you. I frickin' told you . . ."

Jodie looked up at both of them and shook her head.

"Yeah, fine," she said. "I shoot laser beams out of my eyes."

"Don't forget, he thinks you're hot," Roy said.

"Please shut up," Jodie said.

Mike smiled. "Told you she hated you."

"No, Mary's right. I hate both of you."

Bow Shock

Gregory Benford

Ralph slid into the booth where Irene was already waiting, looking perky and sipping on a bottle of Snapple tea. "How'd it . . ." She let the rest slide away, seeing his face.

"Tell me something really awful, so it won't make today seem so bad."

She said carefully, "Yes sir, coming right up, sir. Um . . ." A wicked grin. "Once I had a pet bird that committed suicide by sticking his head between the cage bars."

"W-what . . .?"

"Okay, you maybe need worse? Can do." A flash of dazzling smile. "My sister forgot to feed her pet gerbils, so one died. Then, the one that was alive ate its dead friend."

Only then did he get that she was kidding, trying to josh him out of his mood. He laughed heartily. "Thanks, I sure needed that."

She smiled with relief and turned her head, swirling her dirty-blond hair around her head in a way that made him think of a momentary tornado. Without a word her face gave him sympathy, concern, inquiry, stiff-lipped support—all in a quick gush of expressions that skated across her face, her full, elegantly lipsticked red mouth collaborating with her eggshell blue eyes.

Her eyes followed him intently as he described the paper he had found that left his work in the dust.

"Astronomy is about getting there first?" she asked wonderingly.

"Sometimes. This time, anyway." After that he told her about the talk with the department chairman—the whole scene, right down to every line of dialog, which he would now remember forever, apparently—and she nodded.

"It's time to solicit letters of recommendation for me, but to whom? My work's already out of date. I . . . don't know what to do now," he said. Not a great last line to a story, but the truth.

"What do you feel like doing?"

He sighed. "Redouble my efforts—"

"When you've lost sight of your goal?" It was, he recalled, a definition of fanaticism, from a movie.

"My goal is to be an astronomer," he said stiffly.

"That doesn't have to mean academic, though."

"Yeah, but NASA jobs are thin these days." An agency that took seven years to get to the moon the first time, from a standing start, was now spending far more dollars to do it again in fifteen years.

"You have a lot of skills, useful ones."

"I want to work on fundamental things, not applied."

She held up the cap of her Snapple iced tea and read from the inner side with a bright, comically forced voice, "Not a winner, but here's your Real Fact number two thirty-seven. The number of times a cricket chirps in fifteen seconds, plus thirty-seven, will give you the current air temperature."

"In Fahrenheit, I'll bet," he said, wondering where she was going with this.

"Lots of 'fundamental' scientific facts are just that impressive. Who cares?"

"Um, have we moved on to a discussion of the value of knowledge?"

"Valuable to *whom*, is my point."

If she was going to quote stuff, so could he. "Look, Mark Twain said that the wonder of science is the bounty of speculation that comes from a single hard fact."

"Can't see a whole lot of bounty from here." She gave him a wry smile, another hair toss. He had to admit, it worked very well on him.

"I *like* astronomy."

"Sure, it just doesn't seem to like you. Not as much, anyway."

"So I should . . .?" Let her fill in the answer, since she was full of them today. And he doubted the gerbil story.

"Maybe go into something that rewards your skills."

"Like . . .?"

"Computers. Math. Think big! Try to sign on with a hedge fund, do their analysis."

"Hedge funds . . ." He barely remembered what they did. "They look for short-term trading opportunities in the market?"

"Right, there's a lot of math in that. I read up on it online." She was sharp; that's what he liked about her. "That data analysis you're doing, it's waaay more complicated than what Herb Linzfield does."

"Herb . . .?"

"Guy I know, eats in the same Indian buffet place some of us go for lunch." Her eyes got veiled and he wondered what else she and Herb had talked about. Him? "He calculates hedges on bonds."

"Corporate or municipal?" Just to show he wasn't totally ignorant of things financial.

"Uh, I think corporate." Again the veiled eyes.

"I didn't put in six years in grad school and get a doctorate to—-"

"I know, honey." Eyes suddenly warm. "But you've given this a real solid try now."

"A *try*? I'm not done."

"Well, what I'm saying, you can do other things. If this doesn't . . . work out."

Thinking, he told her about the labyrinths of academic politics. The rest of the UC Irvine astro types did nearby galaxies, looking for details of stellar evolution, or else big-scale cosmological stuff. He worked in between, peering at exotic beasts showing themselves in the radio and microwave regions of the spectrum. It was a competitive field and he felt it fit him. So he spelled out what he thought of as The Why. That is, why he had worked hard to get this far. For the sake of the inner music it gave him, he had set aside his personal life, letting affairs lapse and dodging any long-term relationship.

"So that's why you weren't . . . connected? . . . when you got here." She pursed her lips appraisingly.

"Yeah. Keep my options open, I figured."

"Open for . . .?"

"For this—" He swept a rueful, ironic hand in the air at his imaginary assets. For a coveted appointment, a heady way out of the gray postdoc grind—an assistant professorship at UC Irvine, smack on the absurdly pricey, sun-bleached coast of Orange County. He had beaten out over a hundred applicants. And why not? He was quick, sure, with fine-honed skills and good connections, plus a narrow-eyed intensity a lot of women found daunting, as if it whispered: *careerist, beware.* The skies had seemed to open to him, for sure . . .

But that was then.

He gave her a crinkled smile, rueful, and yet he felt it hardening. "I'm not quitting. Not now."

"Well, just think about it." She stroked his arm slowly and her eyes were sad now. "That's all I meant . . ."

"Sure." He knew the world she inhabited, had seen her working spreadsheets, reading biographies of the founding fathers and flipping through books on "leadership," seeking clues about rising in the buoyant atmosphere of business.

"Promise?" Oddly plaintive.

He grinned without mirth. "You know I will." But her words had hurt him, all the same. Mostly by slipping cool slivers of doubt into his own mind.

Later that night, he lay in her bed and replayed the scene. It now seemed to define the day, despite Irene's strenuous efforts.

Damn, Ralph had thought. *Scooped!*

And by Andy Lakehurst, too. He had bit his lip and focused on the screen, where he had just gotten a freshly posted paper off the Los Alamos library Web site, astro-ph.

The radio map was of Ralph's one claim to minor fame, G369.23-0.82. The actual observations were stunning. Brilliant, clear, detailed. Better than his work.

He had slammed his fist on his disk, upsetting his coffee. "Damn!" Then he sopped up the spill—it had spattered some of the problem sets he'd graded earlier.

Staring at the downloaded preprint, fuming, he saw that Andy and his team had gotten really detailed data on the—on *his*—hot new object, G369.23-0.82. They must have used a lot of observing time, and gotten it pronto.

Where? His eyes ran down the usual Observations section and—*Arecibo! He got observing time there?*

That took pull or else a lucky cancellation. Arecibo was the largest dish in the world, a whole scooped bowl set amid a tropical tangle, but fixed in position. You had to wait for time and then synchronize with dishes around the planet to make a map.

And good ol' ex-classmate Andy had done it. Andy had a straight-forward, no-nonsense manner to him, eased by a ready smile that got him through doors and occasionally into bedrooms. Maybe he had connections to Beth Conway at Arecibo?

No, Ralph had thought, *that's beneath me. He jumped on G369.23-0.82 and did the obvious next step, that's all.*

Further, Andy was at Harvard, and that helped. Plenty. But it still galled. Ralph was still waiting to hear from Harkin at the Very Large Array about squeezing in some time there. Had been waiting for six weeks, yes.

And on top of it all, he then had his conference with the department chairman in five minutes. He glanced over Andy's paper again. It was excellent work. Unfortunately.

He sighed in the dark of Irene's apartment, recalling the crucial hour with the department chairman. This long day wouldn't be done until he had reviewed it, apparently.

He had started with a fixed smile. Albert Gossian was an avuncular sort, an old-fashioned chairman who wore a suit when he was doing official business. This unconscious signal did not bode well. Gossian gave him a quick, jowly smile and gestured Ralph into a seat.

"I've been looking at your curriculum vitae," Gossian said. He always used the full Latin, while others just said "CV." Slow shake of head. "You need to publish more, Ralph."

"My grant funding's kept up, I—"

"Yes, yes, very nice. The NSF is putting effort into this field, most commendable—" A quick glance up from reading his notes, over the top of his glasses. "—and that's why the department decided to hire in this area. But—can you keep the funding?"

"I'm two years in on the NSF grant, so next year's mandatory review is the crunch."

"I'm happy to say your teaching rating is high, and university ser-vice, but . . ." The drawn-out vowels seemed to be delivering a message independent of the actual sentences.

All assistant professors had a review every two years, tracking their progress toward the Holy Grail of tenure. Ralph had followed a trajectory typical for the early century: six years to get his doctorate, a postdoc at Harvard—where Andy Lakehurst was the rising star, eclipsing him and a lot of others. Ralph got out of there after a mutually destructive affair with a biologist at Tufts, fleeing as far as he could when he saw that UC Irvine was growing fast and wanted astrophysicists. UCI had a mediocre reputation in particle theory, but Fred Reines had won a Nobel there for showing that neutrinos existed and using them to detect the spectacular 1987 supernova.

The plasma physics group was rated highest in the department and indeed they proved helpful when he arrived. They understood that 99 percent of the mass in the universe was roasted, electrons stripped away from the nuclei-plasma. It was a hot, rough universe. The big dramas played out there. Sure, life arose in the cool, calm planets, but the big action flared in their placid skies, telling stories that awed him.

But once at UCI, he had lost momentum. In the tightening federal budgets, proposals didn't get funded, so he could not add postdocs to get some help and leverage. His carefully teased-out observations gave new insights only grudgingly. Now five years along, he was three months short of the hard wall where tenure had to happen, or became impossible: the cutoff game.

Were the groves of academe best for him, really? He liked the teaching, fell asleep in the committee meetings, found the academic cant and paperwork boring. Life's sure erosions . . .

Studying fast-moving neutron stars had been fashionable a few years back, but in Gossian's careful phrasings he heard notes of skepticism. To the Chairman fell the task of conveying the senior faculty's sentiments.

Gossian seemed to savor the moment. "This fast-star fad—well, it is fading, some of your colleagues think."

He bit his lip. *Don't show anger.* "It's not a 'fad.' It's a set of discoveries."

"But where do they lead?"

"Too early to tell. We *think* they're ejected from supernova events, but maybe that's just the least imaginative option."

"One of the notes here says the first 'runaway pulsar,' called the Mouse, is now well understood. The other, recent ones will probably follow the same course."

"Too early to tell," Ralph persisted. "The field needs time—"

"But you do not have time."

There was the crux of it. Ralph was falling behind in paper count. Even in the small "runaway pulsar" field, he was outclassed by others with more resources, better computers, more time. California was in a perpetual budget crisis, university resources were declining, so pressure was on to Bring In the (Federal) Bucks. Ralph's small program supported two graduate students, sure, but that was small potatoes.

"I'll take this under advisement," Ralph said. The utterly bland phrase did nothing to help his cause, as was clear from the chairman's face, but it got him out of that office.

He did not get much sleep that night. Irene had to leave early and he got a double coffee on the way into his office. Then he read Andy's paper carefully and thought, sipping.

Few astronomers had expected to find so many runaway neutron stars.

Their likely origin began with two young, big stars, born circling one another. One went supernova, leaving a neutron star still in orbit. Later, its companion went off, too, spitting the older neutron star out, free into interstellar space.

Ralph had begun his UCI work by making painstaking maps in the microwave frequency range. This took many observing runs on the big radio antennas, getting dish time where he could around the world. In these maps he found his first candidate, G369.23-0.82. It appeared as a faint finger in maps centered on the plane of the galaxy, just a dim scratch. A tight knot with a fuzzy tail.

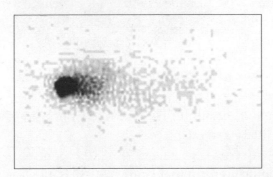

He had found it with software that searched the maps, looking for anything that was much longer than it was wide. This retrieved quite a few of the jets that zoomed out of regions near black holes, and sometimes from the disks orbiting young stars. He spent months eliminating these false signatures, looking for the telltales of compact stellar runaways. He then got time on the Very Large Array—not much, but enough to pull G369.23-0.82 out of the noise a bit better. This was quite satisfying.

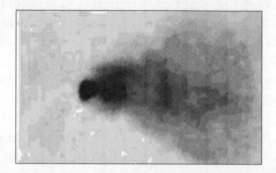

Ralph got more coffee and went back and studied his paper, published less than half a year ago. Until today, that was the best data anybody had. He had looked for signs of rotation in the pointlike blob in front, but there were none. The first runaway seen, the Mouse, discovered many years before, was finally shown to be a rotating neutron star—a pulsar, beeping its right radio beams out at the cupped ears of radio telescopes.

Then he compared in detail with Andy's new map:

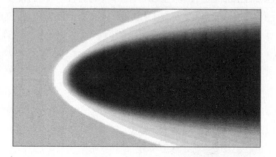

Clean, smooth, beautiful. He read the Conclusions section over again, mind jittery and racing.

We thus fail to confirm that G369.23-0.82 is a pulsar. Clearly it has a bow shock, creating a wind nebula, undoubtedly powered by a neutron star. Yet at highest sensitivity there is no trace of a pulsed signal in microwaves or optical, within the usual range of pulsar periods. The nebular bow shock cone angle implies that

G369.23-0.82 is moving with a Mach number of about 80, suggesting a space velocity ~120 km/s through a local gas of density ~0.3 per cubic cm. We use the distance estimate of Eilek et.al. for the object, which is halfway across the galaxy. These dynamics and luminosity are consistent with a distant neutron star moving at a velocity driven by ejection from a supernova. If it is a pulsar, it is not beaming in our direction.

Beautiful work. *Alas.*

The bright region blazed forth, microwave emission from high energy electrons. The innermost circle was not the neutron star, just the unresolved zone too small for even Arecibo to see. At the presumed distance, that circle was still bigger than a solar system. The bow shock was a perfect, smooth curve. Behind that came the microwave emission of gas driven back, heated, and caught up in what would become the wake. At the core was something that could shove aside the interstellar gas with brute momentum. A whole star, squeezed by gravity into a ball about as big as the San Francisco Bay area.

But how had Andy gotten such fine resolution?

Ralph worked through the numbers and found that this latest map had picked up much more signal than his earlier work. The object was brighter. Why? Maybe it was meeting denser gas, so had more radiating electrons to work with?

For a moment he just gazed at the beauty of it. He never lost his sense of awe at such wonders. That helped a bit to cool his disgruntlement. Just a bit.

There wasn't much time between Andy's paper popping up on the astro-ph Web site and Ralph's big spring trip. Before leaving, he retraced his data and got ahead on his teaching.

He and Irene finessed their problems, or at least delayed them. He got through a week of classes, put in data-processing time with his three graduate students, and found nothing new in the radio maps they worked on.

Then came their big, long-planned excursion. Irene was excited, but he now dreaded it.

His start-up money had some travel funds left in it, and he had made the mistake of mentioning this to Irene. She jumped at the chance, even though it was a scientific conference in a small town—

"But it's in *France*," she said, with a touch of round-eyed wonder he found endearing.

So off they jetted to the International Astronomical Union meeting in Briançon, a pleasant collection of stone buildings clinging to the French Alps. Off season, crouching beneath sharp snowy peaks in late May, it was charming and uncrowded and its delights went largely ignored by the astronomers. Some of the attendees went on hikes in the afternoon but Ralph stayed in town, talking, networking like the ambitious workaholic he was. Irene went shopping.

The shops were featuring what she called the Hot New Skanky Look, which she showed off for him in their cramped hotel room that evening. She flounced around in an off-the-shoulder pink blouse, artfully showing underwear and straps. Skanky certainly caught the flavor, but still he was distracted.

In their cramped hotel room, jet-lagged, she used some of her first-date skills, overcoming his distance. That way he got some sleep a few hours later. Good hours, they were.

The morning session was interesting, the afternoon a little slow. Irene did sit in on some papers. He couldn't tell if she was interested in the science itself, or just because it was part of his life. She lasted a few hours and went shopping again, saying, "It's my way of understanding their culture."

The conference put on a late afternoon tour of the vast, thick-walled castles that loomed at every sharp peak. At the banquet inside one of the cold, echoing fortresses they were treated to local specialties, a spicy polenta and fresh-caught trout. Irene surveyed the crowd, half of them still wearing shorts and T-shirts, and remarked, "Y'know, this is a quirky profession. A whole room of terribly smart people, and it never occurred to them to try to get by on their looks."

He laughed; she had a point. She was a butterfly among the astro-drones, turning heads, smiles blossoming in her wake. He felt enhanced to have her on his arm. Or maybe it was the wine, a *vin local* red that went straight to his head, with some help from the two kilometer altitude.

They milled around the high, arched reception room after the dessert. The crowd of over two hundred was too energized to go off to bed, so they had more wine. Ralph caught sight of Andy Lakehurst then. Irene noted his look and said, "Uh oh."

"Hey, he's an old friend."

"Oh? You're glaring at him."

"Okay, let's say there's some leftover baggage."

She gave him a veiled look, yawned, and said, "I'll wander off to the room, let you boys play."

Ralph nodded, barely listening. He eavesdropped carefully on the crowd gathered around lanky, broad-shouldered Andy. The man's booming voice carried well, over the heads of just about everybody in the room. Andy was going on about good ol' G369.23-0.82. Ralph edged closer.

"I figure maybe another, longer look at it, at G—"

"The Bullet," Ralph broke in.

"What?" Andy had a high forehead and it wrinkled as he stopped in mid-sentence.

"It looks like a bullet. Why not call it that, instead of that long code?"

"Well," Andy began brightly, "people might mistake—"

"There's even the smoke trailing behind it, the wake," Ralph said, grinning. "Use that, if you want it to get into *Scientific American*."

"Y'know, Ralph, you haven't changed."

"Poorer, is all."

"Hey, none of us went into this to get rich."

"Tenure would be nice."

"Damn right, buddy." Andy clapped him on the shoulder. "I'm going up for it this winter, y'know."

He hadn't, but covered with, "Well deserved. I'm sure you'll get it," and couldn't resist adding, "Harvard's a tough sell, though. Carl Sagan didn't make it there."

"Really?" Andy frowned, then covered with, "So, uh, you think we should call it the Rifle?"

"The Bullet," Ralph said again. "It's sure going fast, and we don't really know it's a neutron star."

"Hey, it's a long way off, hard to diagnose."

"Maybe it's distant, I kinda wonder—"

"And it fits the other parameters."

"Except you couldn't find a pulse, so maybe it's not a pulsar."

"Gotta be," Andy said casually, and someone interrupted with a point Ralph couldn't hear and Andy's gaze shifted to include the crowd again. That gave Ralph a chance to think while Andy worked the room.

There were nearly a thousand pulsars now known, rotating neutron stars that flashed their lighthouse beams across the galaxy. Some spun a thousand times in a second, others were old and slow, all sweeping their beams out as they rotated. All such collapsed stars told their long tale of grinding decay; the slower were older. Some were ejected after their birth in bright, flashy supernovas, squashed by catastrophic compression in nuclear fire, all in a few minutes.

Here in Briançon, Ralph reflected, their company of smart, chattering chimpanzees—all evolved long after good ol' G369.23-0.82 had emerged from its stellar placenta—raptly studied the corpses of great calamities, the murder of stars by remorseless gravity.

Not that their primate eyes would ever witness these objects directly. They actually saw, with their football-field–sized dishes, the brilliant emissions of fevered electrons, swirling in celestial concert around magnetic fields. Clouds of electrons cruised near the speed of light itself, squeezing out their waves—braying to the whole universe that they were alive and powerful and wanted everyone to know it. Passing gaudy advertisements, they were, really, for the vast powers wrecking silent violences in the slumbering night skies.

"We're out of its beam; that's got to be the answer," Andy said, turning back to Ralph and taking up their conversation again, his smile getting a little more rigid. "Not pointed at us."

Ralph blinked, taken unaware; he had been vaguely musing. "Uh, I'm thinking maybe we should consider every possibility, is all." Maybe he had taken one glass too many of the *vin local*.

"What else could it be?" Andy pressed his case, voice tightening. "It's compact, moving fast, bright at the leading edge, luminosity driven by its bow shock. A neutron star, charging on out of the galaxy."

"If it's as far away as we think. What if it isn't?"

"We don't know anything else that can put out emissions like that."

He could see nearby heads nodding. "We have to think . . ." grasping for something . . . "uh, outside the box." Probably the *vin local* talking.

Smiling, Andy leaned close and whispered through his tight, no-doubt-soon-to-be tenured lips, "Ol' buddy, you need an idea, to beat an idea."

Definitely the *vin local*, yes.

He awoke next morning with a traffic accident inside his skull. Only now did he remember that he had exchanged polite words with Harkin, the *eminence gris* of the Very Large Array, but there was no news about getting some observing time there. And he still had to give his paper.

It was a botch.

He had a gaudy PowerPoint presentation. And it even ran right on his laptop, a minor miracle. But the multicolored radio maps and graphics failed to conceal a poverty of ideas. If they could see a pulsed emission from it, they could date the age and then look back along the track of the runaway to see if a supernova remnant was there—a shell of expanding hot gas, a celestial bull's eye, confirming the whole theory.

He presented his results on good ol' G369.23-0.82. He had detailed microwave maps of it, plenty of calculations—but Andy had already given his talk, showing that it wasn't a pulsar. And G369.23-0.82— Ralph insisted on calling it the Bullet, but puzzled looks told him that nobody much liked the coinage—was the pivot of the talk, alas.

"There are enough puzzling aspects here," he said gamely, "to suspend judgment, I think. We have a habit of classifying objects because they superficially resemble others."

The rest was radio maps of various blobby radio-emitting clouds he had thought could be other runaways . . . but weren't. Using days of observing time at the VLA, and on other dish systems in the Netherlands and Bologna, Italy, he had racked up a lot of time.

And found . . . nothing. Sure, plenty of supernova remnants, some shredded fragments of lesser catastrophes, mysterious leftovers fading fast in the radio frequencies—but no runaways with the distinctive tails first found in the famous Mouse. He tried to cover the failure by riffing through quick images of these disappointments, implying without saying that these were open possibilities. The audience seemed to like the swift, color-enhanced maps. It was a method his mother had taught him while playing bridge: finesse when you don't have all the tricks.

His talk came just before lunch and the audience looked hungry. He hoped he could get away with just a few questions. Andy rose at the back and asked innocently, "So why do you think the, uh, Bullet is *not* a neutron star?"

"Where's the supernova remnant it came from?" Ralph shot back. "There's nothing at all within many light years behind it."

"It's faded away, probably," Andy said.

A voice from the left, one of the Grand Old Men, said, "Remember, the, ah, Bullet is all the way across the galaxy. An old, faint remnant it might have escaped is hard to see at that distance. And—" a shrewd pursing of lips "—did you look at a sufficiently deep sensitivity?"

"I used all the observing time I had," Ralph answered, jumping his PowerPoint slides back to a mottled field view—random flecks, no structure obvious. "The region in the far wake of the Bullet is confusion limited."

Astronomers described a noisy background with that term, meaning that they could not tell signal from noise. But as he fielded a few more quick questions he thought that maybe the jargon was more right than they knew. Confusion limited what they could know, taking their mayfly snapshots.

Then Andy stood again and poked away at details of the data, a bit of tit for tat, and finishing with a jibe: "I don't understand your remark about not jumping to classify objects just because they superficially resemble other ones."

He really had no good reason, but he grinned and decided to joke his way through. "Well, the Bullet doesn't have the skewed shape of the Duck," which was another oddly shaped pulsar wake, lopsided fuzz left behind by a young pulsar Andy had discovered two years ago. "Astronomers forget that the public likes descriptive terms. They're easier to remember than, say, G369.23-0.82." Some laughter. "So I think it's important to keep our options open. And not succumb to the sweet temptation to go sensational, y'know—" He drew a deep breath and slipped into a falsetto trill he had practiced in his room. "*Runaway star! High speeds! It will escape our galaxy entirely!*"

—and it got a real laugh.

Andy's mouth twisted sourly and, too late, Ralph remembered that Andy had been interviewed by some flak and then featured in the supermarket tabloid *National Enquirer,* with wide-eyed headlines not much different.

Oops.

Irene had been a hit at Briançon, though she was a bit too swift for some of his colleagues. She was kooky, or as some would say, annoying. But at her side he felt he had fully snapped to attention. Sometimes, she made it hard to concentrate; but he did. When he got back to UCI there was teaching to catch up on, students to coach, and many ideas to try out. He settled in.

Some thought that there were only two kinds of science: stamp collecting and physics. Ernest Rutherford had said that, but then, he also thought the atomic nucleus had no practical uses.

Most scientific work began with catalogs. Only later did the fine distinctions come to suggest greater, looming laws. Newton brought Galileo's stirrings into differential laws, ushering forth the modern world.

Astronomers were fated to mostly do astro-botany, finding varieties of deep space objects, framing them into categories, hoping to see if they had a common cause. Stamp collecting.

Once the theory boys decided, back in the 1970s, that pulsars were rotating neutron stars, they largely lost interest and moved onto quasars and jets and then to gamma-ray bursters, to dark energy—an onward marching through the botany, to find the more basic physics. Ralph didn't mind their blithe inattention. He liked the detective story aspects, always alive to the chance that just because things looked similar didn't mean they had to be the same.

So he prowled through all the data he had, comparing with other maps he had gotten at Briançon. There were plenty of long trails in the sky, jets galore—but no new candidates for runaway neutron stars. So he had to go back to the Bullet to make progress. For that he needed more observing time.

For him and Irene, a good date had large portions of honesty and alcohol. Their first night out after the French trip he came armed with attention span and appetite. He kept an open mind to chick flicks— rented and hauled back to her place, ideally—and even to restaurants that played soft romantic background music, which often did the same job as well as a chick flick.

He had returned to news, both good and bad. The department wasn't interested in delaying his tenure decision, as he had fleetingly asked (Irene's suggestion) before leaving. But: Harkin had rustled up some observing time for him on the VLA. "Wedges, in between the big runs," he told Irene.

"Can you get much with just slices of time?"

"In astronomy, looking hard and long is best. Choppy and short can do the same job, if you're lucky."

It was over a weekend, too, so he would not have to get someone to cover his classes.

So he was definitely up when they got to the restaurant. He always enjoyed squiring Irene around, seeing other guys' eyeballs follow them to their table—and telling her about it. She always got a round-eyed, raised eyebrow flash out of that. Plus, they both got to look at each other and eat. And if things went right this night, toward the dessert it might be like that scene in the *Tom Jones* movie.

They ordered: for her, the caramelized duck breasts, and for him, tender Latin chicken with plantains. "A yummy start," she said, eyeing the upscale patrons. The Golden Coast abounded with Masters of the Universe, with excellently cut hair and bodies that were slim, casually elegant, carefully muscled (don't want to look like a *laborer*), the women running from platinum blond through strawberry. "Ummm, quite *soigné*," Irene judged, trying out her new French vocabulary.

Ralph sensed some tension in her, so he took his time, glancing around at the noisy crowd. They carried themselves with that look not so much of energetic youth but rather of expert maintenance, like a Rolls with the oil religiously changed every fifteen hundred miles. Walking in their wake made most working stiffs feel just a touch shabby.

He said, "Livin' extra-large in OC," with a rueful smile, and wondered if she saw this, the American Dream Extreme, as he did. They lived among dun-colored hills covered by pseudo-Spanish stucco splendor, McMansions sprawled across tiny lots. "Affluenza," someone had called it, a disease of always wanting more: the local refrain was "It's all about you," where the homes around yacht-ringed harbors and coves shone like filigree around a gemstone. He respected people like her, in business, as the drivers who created the wealth that made his work possible. But just today he had dropped her at the Mercedes dealership to pick up her convertible, in for an oil change. Pausing, he saw that the place offered free drop-in car washes, and while you waited with your cinnamon-topped decaf cappuccino you could get a manicure, or else work on your putting at a green around the back. Being an academic scientist around here felt like being the poor country cousin.

He watched her examine all the flatware and polish it with her napkin. This was not routine; she was not a control freak who obsessed over the organization of her entire life, or who kept color-coded files, though, yes, she was a business MBA.

"That was a fun trip," Irene said in the pensive tones that meant she was being diplomatic. "Ah . . . do you want to hang out with those people all your life?"

"They're pretty sophisticated, I think," he said defensively, wondering where she was going with this.

"They—how to put this pleasantly?—work too damn hard."

"Scientists do."

"Business types, too—but they don't talk about nothing else."

"It was a specialists' conference. That's all they have in common."

"That, and being outrageously horny."

He grinned. "You never thought that was a flaw before."

"I keep remembering the M.I.T guy who believed he could wow me with"—she made the quote marks with her fingers—"a 'meaningful conversation' that included quoting *The Simpsons*, gangsta flicks, and some movie trilogy."

"That was Tolkein."

"Elves with swords. I thought you guys were scientists."

"We have . . . hobbies."

"Obsessions, seems like."

"Our work included?"

She spread her hands. "I respect that you're deeply involved in astronomy, sure." She rolled her eyes. "But it pays so little! And you're headed into a tough tenure decision. After all these years!"

"Careers take time."

"Lives do, too. Recall what today is?"

He kept his face impassive, the only sure way to not get the deer-in-headlights expression he was prone to. "Uh, no . . ."

"Six months ago."

"Oh, yes. We were going to discuss marriage again."

Her eyes glinted. "And you've been hiding behind your work . . . again."

"Hey, that's not fair—"

"I'm not waiting forever."

"I'm in a crunch here. Relationships don't have a 'sell-by' date stamped on them—"

"Time waits for no man. I don't either."

Bottom line time, then. He asked firmly, "So instead I should . . .?"

She handed him a business card.

"I should have known."

"Herb Linzfield. Give him a call."

"What inducement do I have?" He grinned to cover his concern.

She answered obliquely by ordering dessert, with a sideways glance and flickering little smile on her big, rich lips. On to *Tom Jones.*

To get to the VLA from UC Irvine means flying out of John Wayne Airport—there's a huge, looming bronze statue of the Duke in cowboy duds that somehow captures the actor's trademarked gait—and through Phoenix to Albuquerque. Ralph did this with legs jammed up so he couldn't open his laptop, courtesy of Southwest Airlines—and then drove a Budget rental west through Socorro.

The crisp heat faded as he rose up the grade to the dry plateau, where the Array sprawls on railroad lines in its long valley. Along the Y-shaped rail line the big dishes could crawl, ears cupped toward the sky, as they reconfigured to best capture in their "equivalent eye" distant radiating agonies. The trip through four-lane blacktop edged with sagebrush took most of a day. When Ralph arrived Harkin had been observing a radio galaxy for eight hours.

"Plenty more useful than my last six hours," he said, and Harkin grinned.

Harkin wore jeans, a red wool shirt, and boots and this was not an affectation. Locals described most of the astronomers as "all hat and no cattle," a laconic indictment of fake Westerners. Harkin's face seemed to have been crumpled up and then partly smoothed out—the effect of twenty years out here.

The radio galaxy had an odd, contorted look. A cloud of radio emitting electrons wrapped around Harkin's target—a brilliant jet. Harkin was something of a bug about jets, maintaining that they had to be shaped by the magnetic fields they carried along. Fields and jets alike all were offhand products of the twirling disk far down in the galactic center. The black holes that caused all this energy release were hard to discover, tiny and cloaked in gas. But the jets carried out to the universe striking advertisements, so they were the smoking gun. Tiny graveyards where mass died had managed to scrawl their signatures across the sky.

Ralph looked at the long, spindly jet in Harkin's radio images. It was like a black-and-white of an arrow. There was a lot of work here. Hot-bright images from deep down in the churning glory of the galactic core, then the long slow flaring as the jet moved above the galactic disk and met the intergalactic winds.

Still, it adamantly kept its direction, tightly arrowing out into the enveloping dark. It stretched out for many times the size of its host galaxy, announcing its presence with blaring radio emission. That came from the spiraling of high-energy electrons around magnetic field lines, Ralph knew, yet he always felt a thrill at the raw radio maps, the swirls and helical vortices bigger than swarms of stars, self-portraits etched by electrons alive with their mad energies.

At the very end, where it met the intergalactic gas, the jet got brighter, saturating the images. "It's turned toward us, I figure," Harkin said. "Bouncing off some obstruction, maybe a molecular cloud."

"Big cloud," Ralph said.

"Yeah. Dunno what it could be."

Mysteries. Many of them would never be solved. In the murder of stars, only tattered clues survived.

Harkin was lean and sharp-nosed, of sturdy New England stock. Ralph thought Harkin looked a lot like the jets he studied. His bald head narrowed to a crest, shining as it caught the overhead fluorescents. Harkin was always moving from the control boards of the ganged dishes to the computer screens where images sharpened. Jets moved with their restless energies, but all astronomers got were snapshots. Black holes spewed out their advertisements for around a hundred million years, so Harkin's jet was as old as the dinosaurs. To be an astronomer was to realize one's mayfly nature.

"Hope I haven't gotten you to come all this way for nothing." Harkin brought up on a screen the total file on G369.23-0.82.

He recognized one image from the first observations a year before, when Feretti from Bologna had picked it up in the background of some jet observations. Over the last three years came others, Andy's and Ralph's extensive maps, polarization data files, the works. All digital; nobody kept much on paper anymore.

"Y'see here?" An observing schedule sheet. "The times when G369.23-0.82 is in the sky, I've only got three slices when we're reconfiguring the dishes. Each maybe half an hour long."

"Damn!" Ralph grimaced. "Not much."

"No." Harkin looked a bit sheepish. "When I made that promise to you, well, I thought better of it the next day. But you'd already left for your flight in Geneva."

"*Vin local*," Ralph said. "It hit me pretty hard, too."

Harkin nodded at his feet, embarrassed. "Uh, okay, so about G369.23-0.82—"

"I call it the Bullet. Easier than G369.23-0.82."

"Oh yeah." Hankin shrugged. "You said that in Briançon."

But what could he do in half hour fragments? He was thinking this through when Harkin asked the same question.

"Andy pretty well showed there was no pulsar beam," Harkin said helpfully, "so . . .?"

Ralph thumbed through his notes. "Can I get good clarity at the front end? The Bullet's bow shock?"

Harkin shook his head, looking disappointed. "No way, with so little observing time. Look, you said you had some out-of-the-box ideas."

Ralph thought furiously. "How about the Bullet's tail, then?"

Harkin looked doubtful, scribbled a few numbers on a yellow lined pad. "Nope. It's not that luminous. The wake dies off pretty fast behind. Confusion limited. You'd get nothing but noise."

Ralph pointed. "There's a star we can see at the edge of the Bullet."

Harkin nodded. "A foreground star. Might be useful in narrowing down how far away it is."

"The usual methods say it's a long way off, maybe halfway across the galaxy."

"Um. Okay, leave that for later."

Ralph searched his mind. "Andy looked for pulses in what range?" He flipped through his notes from Briancon. "Short ones, yes—and nothing slower than a ten-second period."

Harkin nodded. "This is a young neutron star. It'll be spinning fast."

Ralph hated looking like an amateur in Harkin's eyes, but he held his gaze firmly. "Maybe. Unless plowing through all that gas slows it faster."

Harkin raised his eyebrows skeptically. "The Mouse didn't slow down. It's spinning at about a tenth of a second period. Yusef-Zadeh and those guys say it's maybe twenty-five thousand years old."

Twenty-five thousand years was quite young for a pulsar. The Mouse pulsar was a sphere of nothing but neutrons, a solar mass packed into a ball as small as San Francisco, spinning around ten times a second. In the radio-telescope maps that lighthouse beam came, from a dot at the very tip of a snout, with a bulging body right behind, and a long, thin tail: mousy. The Mouse discovery had set the paradigm. But just being first didn't mean it was typical.

Ralph set his jaw, flying on instinct. "Let's see."

So in the half hours when the dish team, instructed by Harkin, was slewing the big white antennas around, chugging them along the railroad tracks to new positions, and getting them set for another hours-long observation—in those wedges, Ralph worked furiously. With Harkin overseeing the complex handoffs, he could command two or three dishes. For best use of this squeezed schedule, he figured to operate in the medium microwave band, around 1 or 2 GHz. They had been getting some interference the last few days, Harkin said, maybe from cell phone traffic, even out here in the middle of a high desert plateau—but that interference was down around 1 GHz, safely far below in frequency. He need not worry about callers ringing each other up every few minutes and screwing up his data.

He took data carefully, in a way biased for looking at very long time fluctuations. In pulsar theory, a neutron star was in advanced old age by the time the period of its rotation, and so the sweeping of its light-house beam, was a second long. They harnessed their rotation to spew out their blaring radiation—live fast, die young. Teenage agonies. Only they didn't leave beautiful corpses—they *were* corpses. Pulsars should fade away for even slower rates; only a handful were known out in the two- or three-minute zone.

So this search was pretty hopeless. But it was all he could think of, given the half hour limit.

He was dragging by the time he got his third half hour. The dish team was crisp, efficient, but the long observing runs between his slices got tedious. So he used their ample computing resources to process his own data—big files of numbers that the VLA software devoured as he watched the screens. Harkin's software had fractured the Bullet signal into bins, looking for structure in time. It caressed every incoming microwave, looking for repeating patterns. The computers ran for hours.

Hash, most of it. But then . . .

"What's that?" He pointed to a blip that stuck up in the noisy field. The screen before him and Harkin was patchy, a blizzard of harmonics that met and clashed and faded. But as the Bullet data ran and filtered, a peak persisted.

Harkin frowned. "Some pattern repeating in the microwaves." He worked the data, peering at shifting patterns on the screen. "Period of . . . lessee . . . forty-seven seconds. Pretty long for a young pulsar."

"That's got to be wrong. Much too long."

In astronomy it paid to be a skeptic about your work. Everybody would be ready to pounce on an error. Joe Weber made some false detections of gravitational waves, using methods he invented. His reputation never fully recovered, despite being a brilliant, original scientist.

Harkin's face stiffened. "I don't care. That's what it is."

"Got to be wrong."

"Damn it, Ralph, I know my own codes."

"Let's look hard at this."

Another few hours showed that it wasn't wrong.

"Okay—funny, but it's real." Ralph thought, rubbing his eyes. "So let's look at the pulse itself."

Only there wasn't one. The pattern didn't spread over a broad frequency band. Instead, it was there in the 11 GHz range, sharp and clear—and no other peaks at all.

"That's not a pulsar," Harkin said.

Ralph felt his pulse quicken. "A repeating brightness. From something peaking out of the noise and coming around to our point of view every forty-seven seconds."

"Damn funny." Harkin looked worried. "Hope it's not a defect in the codes."

Ralph hadn't thought of that. "But these are the best filter codes in the world."

Harkin grinned, brown face rumpling like leather. "More compliments like that and you'll turn my pretty little head."

So Harkin spent two hours in deep scrutiny of the VLA data processing software—and came up empty. Ralph didn't mind because it gave him to think. He took a break partway through—Harkin was not the sort to take breaks at all—and watched a Cubs game with some of the engineers in the Operations room. They had a dish down for repairs but it was good enough to tip toward the horizon and pick up the local broadcast from Chicago. The Cubs weren't on any national 'cast and two of the guys came from UC, where the C was for Chicago. The Cubs lost but they did it well, so when he went back Ralph felt relaxed. He had also had an idea. Or maybe half of one.

"What if it's lots bigger than a neutron star?" he asked Harkin, who hadn't moved from his swivel chair in front of the six-screen display.

"Then what's the energy source?"

"I dunno. Point is, maybe it's something more ordinary, but still moving fast."

"Like what?"

"Say, a white dwarf—but a really old, dead one."

"So we can't see it in the visible?" The Hubble telescope had already checked at the Bullet location and seen nothing.

"Ejected from some stellar system, moving fast, but not a neutron star—maybe?"

Harkin looked skeptical. "Um. Have to think about it. But . . . what makes the relativistic electrons, to give us the microwaves?"

That one was harder to figure. Elderly white dwarfs couldn't make the electrons, certainly. Ralph paused and said, "Look, I don't know. And I have to get back to UCI for classes. Can I get some more time wedged in between your reconfigs?"

Harkin looked skeptical. "I'll have to see."

"Can you just send the results to me, when you can find some time?"

"You can process it yourself?"

"Give me the software and, yeah, sure."

Harkin shrugged. "That forty-seven-second thing is damn funny. So . . . okay, I suppose . . ."

"Great!" Ralph was tired but he at least had his hand in the game. Wherever it led.

Ralph spent hours the next day learning the filter codes, tip-toeing through the labyrinth of Harkin's methods. Many thought Harkin was the best big-dish observer in the world, playing the electronics like a violin.

Harkin was a good teacher because he did not know how to teach. Instead he just showed. With the showing came stories and examples, some of them even jokes, and some puzzling until Harkin changed a viewing parameter or slid a new note into the song and it all came clear. This way Harkin showed him how to run the programs, to see their results skeptically. From the angular man he had learned to play a radio telescope as wide as a football field like a musical instrument, to know its quirks and deceptions, and to draw from it a truth it did not know. This was science, scrupulous and firm, but doing it was an art. In the end you had to justify every move, every conclusion, but the whole argument slid forward on intuition, like an ice cube skating on its own melt.

✧   ✧   ✧

"Say, Andy," Ralph said casually into his cell phone, looking out the big windows at New Mexico scrub and the white radio dishes cupped toward the sky. "I'm trying to remember if you guys looked at long periods in your Bullet data. Remember? We talked about it at Briançon."

"Bullet? Oh, G369.23-0.82."

"Right, look, how far out did you go on period?"

A long pause. Ralph thought he could hear street noise. "Hey, catch you at a bad time?"

"No, just walking down Mass Ave., trying to remember. I think we went out to around thirty-second periods. Didn't see a damn thing."

"Oh, great. I've been looking at the Bullet again and my preliminary data shows something that, well, I thought I'd check with you."

"Wow." Another pause. "Uh, how slow?"

Ralph said cautiously, "Very. Uh, we're still analyzing the data."

"A really old pulsar, then. I didn't think they could still radiate when they were old."

"I didn't, either. They're not supposed to." Ralph reminded himself to check with the theorists.

"Then no wonder we couldn't find its supernova remnant. That's faded, or far away."

"Funny, isn't it, that we can pick up such weak signals from a pulsar that's halfway across the galaxy? Though it has been getting brighter, I noticed."

Andy sounded puzzled. "Yeah, funny. Brighter, um. I wonder if it shows up in any earlier survey."

"Yeah, well I thought I'd let you know."

Andy said slowly, "You know, I may have glimpsed something, but will get back to you."

They exchanged a few personal phrases and Ralph signed off.

Harkin was working the screens but turned with eyebrows raised.

Ralph said, "Bingo."

As soon as Irene came into the coffee shop and they kissed in greeting, he could see the curiosity in her eyes. She was stunning in her clingy blue dress, while he strutted in his natty suit. He had told her to dress up and she blinked rapidly, expectant. "Where are we going tonight?"

He said, not even sitting down, "Y'know, the only place where I can sing and people don't throw rotten fruit at me is church."

Irene looked startled. "I didn't think you were religious."

"Hey, it's a metaphor. I pay for a place to dance, too, so—let's go. To the Ritz."

Her eyebrows arched in surprise. "What an oblique invitation. Puttin' on the Ritz?"

As they danced on the patio overlooking sunset surfers, he pulled a loose strand of hair aside for her, tucking it behind her ear. She was full of chatter about work. He told her about his work on the Bullet and she was genuinely interested, asking questions. Then she went back to tales of her office intrigues. Sometimes she seemed like a woman who could survive on gossip alone. He let it run down a bit and then said, as the band struck up "Begin the Beguine," "I need more time."

She stiffened. "To contemplate the abyss of the M word?"

"Yes. I'm hot on the trail of something."

"You didn't call Herb Linzfield, either, did you." Not a question.

"No."

"Oh, fine."

He pulled back and gazed at her lips. Lush, as always, but twisted askew and scrunched. He knew the tone. *Fine. Yeah, okay, right. Fine. Go. Leave. See. If. I. Care.*

He settled into it then, the rhythm: of thickets of detail, and of beauty coming at you, unannounced. You had to get inside the drum-roll of data, hearing the software symphonies, shaped so that human eyes could make some hominid sense of it. These color-coded encrustations showed what was unseeable by the mere human eye—the colors of the microwaves. Dry numbers cloaked this beauty, hid the ferocious glory.

When you thought about it, he thought, the wavelengths they were "seeing" with, through the enormous dish eyes, were the size of their fingers. The waves came oscillating across the blunt light-years, messages out of ancient time. They slapped down on the hard metal of a radio dish and excited electrons that had been waiting there to be invited into the dance. The billions of electrons trembled and sang and their answering oscillations called forth capturing echoes in the circuits erected by men and women. More electrons joined the rising currents, fashioned by the zeros and ones of computers into something no one had ever seen: pictures for eyes the size of mountains. These visions had never existed in the universe. They were implied by the waves, but it took intelligence to pull them out of the vagrant sizzle of radio waves, the passing microwave blizzard all life lived in but had never seen. Stories, really, or so their chimpanzee minds made of it all. Snapshots. But filling in the plot was up to them.

In the long hours he realized that, when you narrow your search techniques tuned to pick up exactly what you're looking for, there's a danger. The phrase astronomers use for that is, "I wouldn't have seen it if I hadn't believed it."

The paper on the astro-ph Web site was brief, quick, three pages.

Ralph stared at it, openmouthed, for minutes. He read it over twice. Then he called Harkin. "Andy's group is claiming a forty-seven-second peak in their data."

"Damn."

"He said before that they didn't look out that far in period."

"So he went back and looked again."

"This is stealing." Ralph was still reeling, wondering where to go with this.

"You can pull a lot out of the noise when you know what to look for."

Whoosh— He exhaled, still stunned. "Yeah, I guess."

"He scooped us," Harkin said flatly.

"He's up for tenure."

Harkin laughed dryly. "That's Harvard for you." A long pause, then he rasped, "But what *is* the goddamn thing?"

The knock on his apartment door took him by surprise. It was Irene, eyes intent and mouth askew. "It's like I'm off your radar screen in one swift sweep."

"I'm . . ."

"Working. Too much—for what you get."

"Y'know," he managed, "art and science aren't a lot different. Sometimes. Takes concentration."

"Art," she said, "is answers to which there are no questions."

He blinked. "That sounds like a quotation."

"No, that was *me*."

"Uh, oh."

"So you want a quick slam bam, thank you Sam?"

"Well, since you put it that way."

An hour later she leaned up on an elbow and said, "News."

He blinked at her sleepily "Uh . . . what?"

"I'm late. Two weeks."

"Uh. Oh." An anvil out of a clear blue sky.

"We should talk about—"

"Hoo boy."

"—what to do."

"Is that unusual for you?" First, get some data.

"One week is tops for me." She shaped her mouth into an astonished O. "Was."

"You were using . . . we were . . ."

"The pill has a small failure rate, but . . ."

"Not zero. And you didn't forget one?"

"No."

Long silence. "How do you feel about it?" Always a good way to buy time while your mind swirled around.

"I'm thirty-two. It's getting to be time."

"And then there's us."

"Us." She gave him a long, soulful look and flopped back down, staring at the ceiling, blinking.

He ventured, "How do you feel about . . ."

"Abortion?"

She had seen it coming. "Yes."

"I'm easy, if it's necessary." Back up on the elbow, looking at him. "Is it?"

"Look, I could use some time to think about this."

She nodded, mouth aslant. "So could I."

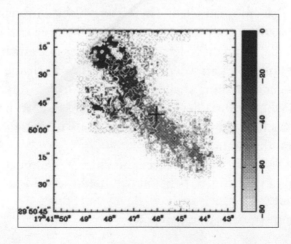

Ralph had asked the Bologna group—through his old friends, the two Fantis—to take a scan of the location. They put the Italian 'scopes on the region and processed the data and sent it by Internet. It was waiting the next morning, forty-seven megs as a zipped attachment. He opened the attachment with a skittering anxiety. The Bologna group was first rate, their work solid.

On an Internet visual phone call he asked, "Roberto, what's this? It can't be the object I'm studying. It's a mess."

On-screen, Roberto looked puzzled, forehead creased. "We wondered about that, yes. I can improve the resolution in a few days. We could very well clear up features with more observing time."

"Yes, could you? This has got to be wrong."

A head bob. "We will look again, yes."

Forty-seven seconds . . .

The chairman kept talking but Ralph was looking out his window at the eucalyptus weaving in the vagrant coastal winds. Gossian was listing hurdles to meet before Ralph would be "close to tenure"—two federal grants, placing his PhD students in good jobs, more papers. All to get done in a few months. The words ran by, he could hear them, but he had gone into that place he knew and always welcomed, where his own faith dwelled. The excitement came up in him, first stirrings, the instinct burning, his own interior state of grace. The idea swarmed up thick in his nostrils, he blinked—

"Ralph? You listening?"

"Oh, uh, yeah." *But not to you, no.*

He came into the physics building, folding his umbrella from a passing rain storm, distracted. There were black umbrellas stacked around like a covey of drunken crows. His cell phone cawed.

Harkin said, "Thought I'd let you know there's not much time I can use coming up. There's an older image, but I haven't cleaned it up yet."

"I'd appreciate anything at all."

"I can maybe try for a new image tomorrow, but I'm pretty damn busy. There's a little slot of time while the Array reconfigures."

"I sent you the Fantis' map—"

"Yeah, gotta be wrong. No source can change that much so fast."

Ralph agreed but added, "Uh, but we should still check. The Fantis are very good."

"If I have time," Harkin said edgily.

Between classes and committees and the long hours running the filter codes, he completely forgot about their dinner date. So at nine PM his office phone rang and it was Irene. He made his apologies, distracted, fretting. He knew he looked tired, his forehead gray and lined, and he asked, "No . . . change?"

"No."

They sat in silence and finally he told her about the Fanti map.

She brightened audibly, glad to have some distraction. "These things can change, can't they?"

"Sure, but so fast! They're big, the whole tail alone is maybe light years long."

"But you said the map is all different, blurred."

"The whole object, yes."

"So maybe it's just a mistake?"

"Could be, but the Fantis are really good . . ."

"Could we get together later?"

He sighed. "I want to look at this some more." To her silence he added more apologies, ending with, "I don't want to lose you."

"Then remember where you put me."

The night wore on.

Wouldn't have seen it if I hadn't believed it.

The error, he saw, might well lie in their assumptions. In his.

It had to be a runaway neutron star. It had to be a long way off, half-way across the galaxy. They knew that because the fraying of the signal said there was a lot of plasma in the way.

His assumptions, yes. It had to be.

Perfectly reasonable. Perfectly wrong?

He had used up a lot of his choppy VLA time studying the oblong shroud of a once-proud star, seen through the edge of the Bullet. It was fuzzy with the debris of gas it threw off, a dying sun. In turn, he could look at the obscuration—how much the emission lines were absorbed and scattered by intervening dust, gas, and plasma. Such telltales were the only reliable way to tell if a radio image came from far away or nearby. It was tricky, using such wobbly images, glimpsed through an interstellar fog.

What if there was a lot more than they thought, of the dense plasma in between their big-eyed dishes and the object?

Then they would get the distance wrong. Just like a thick cloud between you and the sun. Dispersing the image, blurring it beyond recognition—but the sun was, on the interstellar scale, still quite close.

Maybe this thing was nearer, much nearer.

Then it would have to be surrounded by an unusually dense plasma—the cloud of ionized particles that it made, pushing on hard through the interstellar night. Could it have ionized much more of the gas it moved through than the usual calculations said? How? Why?

But what *was* the goddamn thing?

He blinked at the digital arrays he had summoned up, through a thicket of image and spectral processors. The blurred outlines of the old star were a few pixels, and nearby was an old, tattered curve of a supernova remnant—an ancient spherical tombstone of a dead sun. The lines had suffered a lot of loss on their way through the tail of the Bullet. From this he could estimate the total plasma density near the Bullet itself.

Working through the calculation, he felt a cold sensation creep into him, banishing all background noise. He turned the idea over, feeling its shape, probing it. Excitement came, tingling but laced with caution.

Andy had said, *I wonder if it shows up in any earlier survey.*

So Ralph looked. On an Italian radio map of the region done eleven years before there was a slight scratch very near the Bullet location. But it was faint, an order of magnitude below the luminosity he was seeing now. Maybe some error in calibration? But a detection, yes.

He had found it because it was bright now. Hitting a lot of interstellar plasma, maybe, lighting up?

Ralph called Harkin to fill him in on this and the Fanti map, but got an answering machine. He summed up briefly and went off to teach a mechanics class.

Harkin said on his voice mail, "Ralph, I just sent you that map I made two days ago, while I had some side time on a four point eight GHz observation."

"Great, thanks!" he called out before he realized Harkin couldn't hear him. So he called and when Harkin picked up, without even a hello, he said, "Is it like the Fanti map?"

"Not at all."

"Their work was pretty recent."

"Yeah, and what I'm sending you is earlier than theirs. I figure they screwed up their processing."

"They're pretty careful . . ."

"This one I'm sending, it sure looks some different from what we got before. Kinda pregnant with possibility."

The word *pregnant* stopped him for a heartbeat. When his attention returned, Harkin's voice was saying, "—I tried that forty-seven-second period filter and it didn't work. No signal this time. Ran it twice. Don't know what's going on here."

The e-mail attachment map was still more odd.

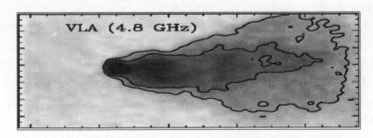

Low in detail, because Harkin had not much observing time, but clear enough. The Bullet was frayed, longer, with new features. Plunging on, the Bullet was meeting a fresh environment, perhaps.

But this was from two days ago.

The Bologna map was only fourteen hours old.

He looked back at the messy Bologna view and wondered how this older picture could possibly fit with the 4.8 GHz map. Had the Fantis made some mistake?

"Can you get me a snapshot right now?" Ralph asked. "It's important."

He listened to the silence for a long moment before Harkin said, "I've got a long run on right now. Can't it wait?"

"The Fantis at Bologna, they're standing by that different-looking map. Pretty strange."

"Ummm, well . . ."

"Can you get me just a few minutes? Maybe in the download interval—"

"Hey, buddy, I'll try, but—"

"I'll understand," but Ralph knew he wouldn't.

His home voice mail from Irene said, fast and with rising voice tone, "Do onto others, right? So, if you're not that into me, I can stop returning your calls, e-mails—not that there are any—and anyway, blocking is so dodgeball in sixth grade, right? I'll initiate the phase-out, you'll get the lead-footed hint, and that way, you can assume the worst of me and still feel good about yourself. You can think, hey, she's not over her past. Social climber. Shallow business mind. Workaholic, maybe. Oh, no, that's you, right? And you'll have a wonderful imitation life."

A long pause, time's nearly up, and she gasped, paused, then: "Okay, so maybe this isn't the best idea."

He sat, deer in the headlights, and played it over.

They were close, she was wonderful, yes.

He loved her, sure, and he had always believed that was all it took.

But he might not have a job here inside a year.

And he couldn't think of anything but the Bullet.

While she was wondering if she was going to be a mother.

Though, he realized, she had not really said what she thought about it all.

He had no idea what to say. At a talk last year about Einstein, the speaker quoted Einstein's wife's laconic comment, that sometimes when the great man was working on a problem he would not speak to anyone for days. She had left him, of course. But now Ralph could feel a certain kinship with that legendary genius. Then he told himself he was being fatuous, equating this experience . . .

Still, he let it all slide for now.

His eighth cup of coffee tasted bitter. He bit into a donut for a sugar jolt. When had he eaten last?

He took a deep breath and let it out to clear his head.

He was sure of his work now, the process—but still confused.

The earlier dispersion measure was wrong. That was clear from the broadening of the pulses he had just measured. Andy and everybody else had used the usual interstellar density numbers to get the Bullet's distance. That had worked out to about five thousand light-years away.

From his pulse measurements he could show that the Bullet was much closer, about thirty light-years away. They were seeing it through the ionized and compressed plasma ahead and around the . . . what? *Was* it a neutron star at all?

And a further consequence—if the Bullet was so close, it was also much smaller, and less intrinsically luminous.

While the plume was huge, the Bullet itself—the unresolved circle at the center of it all, in Andy's high-resolution map—need only be a few hundred kilometers long. Or much less; that was just an upper limit.

Suppose that was the answer, that it was much closer. Then its energy output—judging that it was about equal to the radiated power—was much less, too. He jotted down some numbers. The object was emitting power comparable to a nation's on Earth. Ten GW or so.

Far, far below the usual radiated energies for runaway neutron stars.

He stared into space, mind whirling.

And the forty-seven-second period . . .

He worked out that if the object was rotating and had an acceleration of half an Earth gravity at its edge, it was about thirty meters across.

Reasonable.

But why was the shape of its radio image changing so quickly? In days, not the years typical of big astronomical objects. *Days.*

Apprehensively he opened the e-mail from Irene.

You're off the hook!

So am I.

Got my period. False alarm.

Taught us a lot, though. Me, anyway. I learned the thoroughly useful information (data, to you) that you're an asshole. Bye.

He sat back and let the relief flood through him.

You're off the hook. Great.

False alarm. Whoosh!

And asshole. Um.

But . . .

Was he about to do the same thing she had done? Get excited about nothing much?

Ralph came into his office, tossed his lecture notes onto the messy desk, and slumped in his chair. The lecture had not gone well. He couldn't seem to focus. Should he keep his distance from Irene for a while, let her cool off? What did he really want, there?

Too much happening at once. The phone rang.

Harkin said, without even a hello, "I squeezed in some extra observing time. The image is on the way by e-mail."

"You sound kind of tired."

"More like . . . confused. " He hung up.

It was there in the e-mail.

Ralph stared at the image a long time. It was much brighter than before, a huge outpouring of energy.

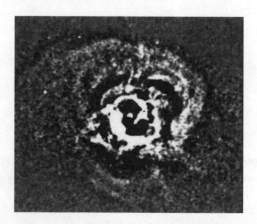

His mind seethed. The Fanti result, and now this. Harkin's 4.8 GHz map was earlier than either of these, so it didn't contradict either the Fantis or this. A time sequence of something changing fast—in days, in hours.

This was no neutron star.

It was smaller, nearer, and they had watched it go to hell.

He leaned over his desk, letting the ideas flood over him. *Whoosh.*

Irene looked dazed. "You're kidding."

"No. I know we've got a lot to talk through, but—"

"You bet."

"I didn't send you that e-mail just to get you to meet me." Ralph bit his lip and felt the room whirl around.

"What you wrote," she said wonderingly. "It's a . . . starship?"

"Was. It got into trouble of some kind these last few days. That's why the wake behind it—" He tapped the Fantis' image. "—got longer. Then, hours later, it got turbulent, and—it exploded."

She sipped her coffee. "This is . . . was . . . light-years away?"

"Yes, and headed somewhere else. It was sending out a regular beamed transmission, one that swept around as the ship rotated, every forty-seven seconds."

Her eyes widened. "You're sure?"

"Let's say it's a working hypothesis."

"Look, you're tired, maybe put this aside before jumping to conclusions."

He gazed at her and saw the lines tightened around her mouth. "You've been through a lot yourself. I'm sorry."

She managed a brave, thin smile. "It tore me up. I do want a child."

He held his breath, then went ahead. "So . . . so do I."

"Really?" They had discussed this before but her eyelids fluttered in surprise.

"Yes." He paused, sucked in a long breath, and said, "With you."

"Really?" She closed her eyes a long time. "I . . . always imagined this."

He grinned. "Me too. Time to do it."

"Yes?"

"Yes." *Whoosh.*

They talked on for some moments, ordered drinks to celebrate. Smiles, goofy eyes, minds whirling.

Then, without saying anything, they somehow knew that they had said enough for now. Some things should not be pestered, just let be.

They sat smiling at each other and in a soft sigh she said, "You're worried. About . . ."

Ralph nodded. How to tell her that this seemed pretty clear to him and to Harkin, but it was big, gaudy trouble in the making. "It violates a basic assumption we always make, that everything in the night sky is natural."

"Yeah, so?"

"The astronomy community isn't like Hollywood, y'know. It's more like . . . a priesthood."

He sipped his coffee and stared out the window. An airplane's wing lights winked as it coasted down in the distance toward the airport. Everybody had seen airplanes, so seeing them in the sky meant nothing. Not so for the ramscoop ship implied by his radio maps.

There would be rampant skepticism. Science's standards were austere, and who would have it differently? The angles of attack lived in his hands, and he now faced the long labor of calling forth data and calculations. To advance the idea would take strict logic, entertaining all other ideas fairly. Take two steps forward, one back, comparing and weighing and contrasting—the data always leading the skeptical mind. It was the grand dance, the gavotte of reason, ever mindful of the eternal possibility that one was wrong.

Still . . . When serendipity strikes . . . let it. Then seize it.

"You need some sleep." Her eyes crinkled with concern. "Come home with me."

He felt a gush of warm happiness. She was here with him and together they could face the long battle to come.

"Y'know, this is going to get nasty. Look what happened to Carl Sagan when he just argued there *might* be intelligent life elsewhere."

"You think it will be that hard to convince people?"

"Look at it this way. Facing up to the limits of our knowledge, to the enormity of our ignorance, is an acquired skill—to put it mildly. People want certainty."

He thought, *If we don't realize where the shoreline of reasonably well established scientific theory ends, and where the titanic sea of undiscovered truth begins, how can we possibly hope to measure our progress?*

Irene frowned. Somehow, after long knowledge of her, he saw that she was glad of this chance to talk about something larger than themselves. She said slowly, "But . . . why is it that your greatest geniuses—the ones you talk about, Hawking, Feynman, Newton—humbly concede how pitifully limited our reach is?"

"That's why they're great," he said wryly. *And the smaller spirits noisily proclaim the certainty of their conclusions. Well, here comes a lot of dissent, doubt, and skepticism.*

"And now that ship is gone. We learned about them by watching them die."

She stared at him. "I wonder . . . how many?"

"It was a big, powerful ship. It probably made the plasma ahead of it somehow. Then with magnetic fields it scooped up that plasma and cooked it for energy. Then shot it out the back for propulsion. Think of it as like a jet plane, a ramscoop. Maybe it was braking, using magnetic fields—I dunno."

"Carrying passengers?"

"I . . . hadn't thought of that."

"How big is it? . . . was it?"

"Maybe like . . . the *Titanic*."

She blinked. "That many people."

"Something like people. Going to a new home."

"Maybe to . . . here?"

He blinked, his mind cottony. "No, it was in the plane of the sky. Otherwise we'd have seen it as a blob, head on, no tail. Headed somewhere fairly near, though."

She sat back, gazing at him with an expression he had not seen before. "This will be in the papers, won't it." Not a question.

"Afraid so." He managed a rueful smile. "Maybe I'll even get more space in *National Enquirer* than Andy did."

She laughed, a tinkling sound he liked so much.

But then the weight of it all descended on him. *So much to do . . .* "I'll have to look at your idea, that they were headed here. At least we can maybe backtrack, find where they came from."

"And look at the earlier maps, data?" she ventured, her lip trembling. "From before . . ."

"They cracked up. All that life, gone." Then he understood her pale, tenuous look. *Things living, then not.* She nodded, said nothing.

He reached out and took her hand. A long moment passed and he had no way to end it but went on anyway. "The SETI people could jump on this. Backtrack this ship. They can listen to the home star's emissions . . ."

Irene smiled without humor. "And we can send them a message. Condolences."

"Yeah." The room had stopped whirling and she reached out to take his hand.

"Come on."

As he got up wearily, Ralph saw that he was going to have to fight for this version of events. There would always be Andys who would triangulate their way to advantage. And the chairman, Gossian . . .

Trying for tenure—supposedly a cool, analytic process—in the shouting match of a heated, public dispute, a howling media firestorm—that was almost a contradiction in terms. But this, too, was what science was about. His career might survive all that was to come, and it might not—but did that matter, standing here on the shores of the titanic ocean he had peered across?

Decaf and Spaceship, To Go

by Katherine Sanger

I always knew the world would end while I was trapped in the Starbucks drive-through. With as much time as I spent there, the odds were definitely in its favor. But it still surprised me that afternoon to see the silver, egg-shaped craft materialize in the parking lot next to me.

I placed my order at the little voice-destroying speaker box and pulled forward. The woman in front of me was already at the window. She had her door open (poor depth perception, I guessed), and I heard her complaining.

"No, no, it was an *iced* vanilla chai soy latte and a *hot* vanilla white mocha chai soy latte." She was still shaking her blond bouffant head when her Suburban vanished, taking her with it. Before I could exhale the gulp of air I had taken when the SUV had popped out of existence, something appeared in the line ahead of me.

The first word that came into my head was "alien." The second, third, and fourth were "oh my God."

I stared out my windshield, fighting the urge to rub my eyes like I'd seen people do in all the science fiction movies I'd grown up watching. The dull silver flying object sat in the brown-grey cement parking lot, not ten feet from me, taking up three and a half spots, including the handicap slot. It made a soft humming sound, kind of like one of those little vacuum cleaners that zooms around on the ground and cleans by itself.

Right in front of me stood what had to be an occupant of the craft, her head even with the top of the drive-up window. Her four legs looked like they'd come off a deer, and her two arms were longer than they should have been, giving her the appearance of one of those stick insects, a look that was further enhanced by her skin coloring.

She was the color of an iced nonfat mocha, the very drink I had ordered before the ship and the alien had appeared. What convinced me she was a woman was the fact that, over her shoulder (or the closest approximation of one that she had) was slung one of those fashionable new Tootsie Roll–looking purses. Even from my distance, I could see the little Gucci symbols all over it. Wherever this alien was from, she knew how to shop.

I fought the urge to press the button and roll my window up. Who knew if this alien woman would take that as a sign of aggression? Shopping habits aside, we might have nothing in common.

Her pencil-thin fingers opened the purse, and she dug through it. A piece of what looked like the foil that Wrigley's was wrapped in fell to the ground. Do aliens chew gum? She shook her triangular head and kept peering into the bag with those weird bug eyes. Finally, she withdrew a small booklet and flipped to one of the last pages.

Through the open window, I could hear her speaking. Her voice sounded like one of those automated machines that I heard whenever I called my bank to beg them to refund the bounce-check fees. "I would like an iced triple grande cinnamon soy no-whip mocha. I would like an iced decaf venti sugar-free vanilla chai latte. I would like a tall almond Americano—" She paused and her head whipped from side to side for a moment. I swore I heard guitar feedback, even though my radio was off. "No. I would like a grande decaf almond Americano with half and half. I would like a venti peppermint mocha frappuccino. With whip."

I couldn't hear the response of whoever was inside the window. The alien woman stood without moving. Was she breathing? Did she breathe? I could feel and hear my own breathing now. It was the only sound I heard. I couldn't tell if the outside world existed anymore. All my attention was focused on the figure in the line ahead of me.

I don't know how long I sat there. I figured this was it. After she got the drinks, I thought, the entire planet would suddenly be destroyed. It was all over. I couldn't tell if that upset me. My entire head—brain included—felt numb.

A pale, shaking hand appeared in the window, holding an iced grande drink. The alien shook her head. I waited for the planet to explode. It didn't.

"I am sorry," the alien said. "I require a cup holder. The x-Generated JVR5 does not come standard with cup holders."

The hand was withdrawn. A minute later, it reappeared, holding a brown cardboard cup holder with four cups perched in it.

I didn't see the alien move, but one second the tray sat in the disembodied hand, and the next it was floating in the air, a few inches away from the alien's purse. The alien dug through the purse, retrieved some crumpled bills, and handed them to the hand. The hand withdrew quickly.

"Please keep the change for excellent service," the alien said. She turned her head to me without moving her body. The volume of her voice increased as she addressed me. "I do apologize for cutting in your line," she said. I realized that her mouth—or the slash that I assumed was her mouth—didn't move when she spoke. "With the current atmosphere, I cannot observe proper manners. I did not mean to inconvenience you."

I nodded and smiled dumbly. Was I supposed to respond? What did she mean, anyway? The political atmosphere? Were we not alien-friendly? Or did she mean the actual physical atmosphere, the stratosphere and all that science stuff?

She turned away from me, then she disappeared, along with the drinks. The ship blinked once before it vanished. I waited, again, for the planet to explode. It still didn't. But the car in front of me did reappear, the woman still complaining.

"And when I say hot, I don't mean burn my lip and give me a blister hot." She paused and shook her head. "Never mind. Make them both iced."

I closed my eyes, giving in to the temptation to rub them. My breathing was returning to normal, and I heard ordinary noises around me again—birds chirping, cars revving on the road, tires squealing.

The hand appeared from the window again, and drinks and money were exchanged. The SUV pulled out. I exhaled and moved forward, taking my place in front of the window. The woman working the window refused to look at me while she served me my drink and took my money. I didn't know how to broach the subject of aliens ordering coffee. "So, do you get much intergalactic coffee traffic?" sounded like something you'd see written in a police report on COPS after they'd finally managed to arrest the guy who was drunk, driving on the wrong side of the road, and naked. I didn't feel like being on TV.

I lingered at the window a moment. Were they up there, sipping their coffee? I heard a honk behind me and pulled forward and out of the black BMW's way. The road before me was bumper-to-bumper, and as I waited for an opening to appear, I glanced back to the drive through and almost choked on my mocha.

In the same three and a half parking spots that the silver egg had been sitting in not three minutes ago, a blue-tinted, round craft materialized. It had orange lights encircling the bottom, and they flashed slowly, reminding me of a roadwork sign that was losing power. Before I could blink, the BMW was gone, replaced by another alien.

This alien was more humanoid than the last. It stood on what I assumed were two legs—I could see brown workboots protruding from under its satin-looking striped pants—and those were definitely hands protruding from the end of the orange and pink pineapple–covered shirt. I couldn't see how many fingers there were at this distance, but I would have bet the rest of my drink that there were a few more than five on each. The alien's octagonal head stuck out of the neckline of the shirt at a weird angle, and it was the same color as the ship.

Staring at the gaudiness on display in my rearview mirror, I tried to figure out if the alien was pure Prada or pure Wal-Mart.

Through my open window I heard it begin to order. "We wants us a solo ristretto with whip . . ."

The rest of the order—if there was one—was drowned out by the scream that escaped through the window, followed by a very loud and forceful, "I quit!"

I couldn't say I blamed her. The customers always were the worst part of working retail.

All the Things You Are

by Mike Resnick

You wouldn't think they'd be so dumb. Here they were, in the biggest spaceport in the country, with hundreds of holo cameras covering every inch of the place, and these three jerks actually think they're going to get away with robbing the currency exchange.

Okay, so they got a couple of ceramic pistols past our security devices and reassembled them in the men's room, and all right, another one managed to sneak a couple of steak knives out of one of the restaurants, but hell, did they think we were just going to sit on our hands and let them waltz out with their loot?

I hadn't seen much action during my four years in the space service, and after all those months of intensive training I'd almost been hoping for something like this. I'd been at OceanPort for three weeks, and was wondering why they even bothered with a live Security team, since their automated systems were so efficient that they discouraged anything worse than spitting on the floor.

Well, now I knew.

The men with the pistols were holding the crowd at bay, and the guy with the knife had grabbed a girl—not a woman, but a kid about twelve years old—and was holding the knife at her throat.

"Don't move on them," said the voice in my ear. "We've got to get the girl away from them unharmed, and we can't have them shooting into the crowd."

That was Captain Symmes. He was just spouting the routine and stating the platitudes: they've been identified, we can trace them wherever they go, they're dead men walking, so don't endanger any bystanders. If we don't nail them here, we'll nail them somewhere up the road. They have to eat, they have to sleep; we don't. Whatever they think they're going to escape in, we'll sugar their gas, rupture their jets, fuck with their nuclear pile. (I kept waiting for him to say we'd also put tacks in their track shoes, but he didn't.)

"Show yourselves, but don't approach him," said Symmes' voice. "If they're going to take a shot at someone, better us than the civilians."

Well, it was better us if we remembered to put on our bulletproof long johns. Most of us had, and the ones who hadn't were too frightened to say so. An enraged Captain Symmes could be one hell of a lot more formidable than a ceramic bullet from a homemade pistol.

I stepped out from my station, and found myself about fifty yards from the trio. The crowd parted before them like the Red Sea before Moses, and they slowly made their way to the door. Then something caught my eye. It was a well-dressed middle-aged man, not fat or skinny but not especially well-built. While everyone else had moved away, he had simply turned his back and taken just a step or two.

Damn! I thought. *It's too bad you're not one of us. You could just about reach the son of a bitch with the knife.*

And even as the thought crossed my mind, the man spun around, chopped down on the knife-holder's arm, and sent the weapon clattering to the floor. The little girl broke and ran toward the crowd, but I was watching the man who'd freed her. He didn't have any weapons, and he sure didn't handle his body like an athlete, but he was charging the two guys with the guns.

They turned and fired their weapons. He went down on one knee, his chest a bloody mess, then launched himself at the nearer one's legs. The poor bastard never had a chance; he picked up four more bullets for his trouble.

Of course, the bad guys never had a chance, either. The second they concentrated on him, we all pulled our weapons and began firing— bullets, lasers, long-range tasers, you name it. All three were dead before they hit the floor.

I could see that Connie Neff was running over to the girl to make sure she was okay, so I raced up to the guy who'd taken all the bullets. He was in a bad way, but he was still breathing. Someone else had called for an ambulance. It arrived within two minutes, and they loaded him onto an airsled, shoved it in the back, and took off for Miami. I decided to ride with him. I mean, hell, he'd risked his life, probably lost it, to save that little girl. Someone who wasn't a doctor ought to be there if he woke up.

OceanPort is eight miles off the Miami coast, and the ambulance shuttle got us to the hospital in under a minute, though it took another forty seconds to set it down gently so as not to do any further damage to the patient.

I'd pulled his wallet and ID out and studied them. His name was Myron Seymour, he was forty-eight years old and—as far as I could tell—retired. Still had the serial number of the chip the military had embedded in him when he enlisted. The rest was equally unexceptional: normal height, normal weight, normal this, normal that.

He didn't look much like a hero, but then, I'd never seen a real bona fide hero before, so I couldn't actually say what they looked like.

"Good God!" said an orderly who'd come out to the ship to help move Seymour to the emergency room. "*Him* again!"

"He's been here before?" I asked, surprised.

"Three times, maybe four," was the reply. "I'll swear the son of a bitch is *trying* to get himself killed."

I was still puzzling over that remark when Seymour went into surgery. He came out, heavily sedated and in grave condition, three hours later.

"Is he going to make it?" I asked the same orderly, who was guiding the airsled into a recovery room.

"Not a chance," he said.

"How much time has he got?"

He shrugged. "A day at the outside, probably less. Once we hook him up to all the machines we'll have a better idea."

"Any chance he'll be able to talk?" I asked. "Or at least understand me if I talk to him?"

"You never know."

"Mind if I stick around?"

He smiled. "You're walking around with a badge, three lethal weapons that I can see, and probably a couple of more I can't see. Who am I to tell you you can't stay?"

I grabbed a sandwich in the hospital's restaurant, called in to OceanPort to make sure I wasn't needed right away, then went up to the recovery room. Each of the patients was partitioned off from the others, and it took me a couple of minutes to find Seymour. He was lying there, a dozen machines monitoring all his vital functions, five tubes dripping fluids of various colors and consistencies into his arms, an oxygen tube up his nostrils, bandages everywhere, and hints of blood starting to seep through the dressings.

I figured it was a waste of time, that he was never going to wake up again, but I stuck around for another hour, just to pay my respects to the man who'd saved a little girl's life. Then, as I was about to leave, his eyelids flickered and opened. His lips moved, but I couldn't hear him, so I pulled my chair over to the bed.

"Welcome back," I said gently.

"Is she here?" he whispered.

"The girl you saved?" I said. "No, she's fine. She's with her parents."

"No, not her," he said. He could barely move his head, but he tried to look around the room. "She's *got* to be here this time!"

"Who's got to be here?" I asked. "Who are you talking about?"

"Where is she?" he rasped. "This time I'm dying. I can tell."

"You're going to be fine," I lied.

"Not unless she gets here pretty damned soon." He tried to sit up, but was too weak and sprawled back on the bed. "Is the door unlocked?"

"There isn't any door," I said. "You're in the recovery ward."

He looked genuinely puzzled. "Then where is she?"

"Whoever it is, she probably doesn't know you've been wounded," I said.

"She knows," he said with absolute certainty.

"Was she at the spaceport?"

He shook his head weakly. "She wasn't even on the planet," he said.

"You're sure you don't want me to ask at the desk?"

"You can't. She doesn't have a name."

"Everyone's got a name."

He uttered a sigh of resignation. "If you say so."

I was starting to feel sorry I'd stuck around. I wasn't bringing him any comfort, and his answers weren't making any sense.

"Can you tell me anything about her?" I asked, making one more attempt to be helpful before I packed it in and went home.

I thought he was going to answer, he certainly looked like he was trying to say something, but then he passed out. A couple of minutes later all the machines he was hooked up to started going haywire, and a couple of young doctors raced into the room.

"Is he dead?" I asked.

"Out!" ordered one of the doctors.

They bent over the bed, going to work on him, and I figured I'd only be in the way if I stayed there, so I walked out into the corridor. Before long they emerged from the room.

"Is he dead?" I asked again.

"Yeah," answered one of them. "Were you a friend of his?"

I shook my head. "No. I just brought him here from the spaceport."

The doctors walked down the corridor, going to wherever doctors go when they've lost a patient, and a couple of orderlies showed up with an airsled. One of them was the one I'd spoken to before.

"I told you he wouldn't last a day," he said. "Why do these guys think they can charge into a stream of bullets or lasers and come away in one piece?"

"These guys?" I repeated.

"Yeah. This is the second one this month. There was this guy, maybe three weeks back. He stumbles upon a bank robbery, and instead of calling the cops he just lowers his head and charges these four armed guys." He exhaled deeply and shook his head. "Poor bastard never got within twenty yards of them."

"Was he DOA?" I asked.

"Close to it," replied the orderly. "He was sure someone was coming to be with him, and was desperate to make sure everyone at Admissions knew where to send her."

"Her?"

"I *think* it was a her." He shrugged. "I could be wrong. He wasn't making much sense. I thought he couldn't remember his name for a couple of minutes. Turns out he was right and I was wrong. Daniel Daniels. Funny name." His companion started shifting his weight uneasily. "If you don't have any more questions, we've got to schlep this guy down to the basement for an autopsy. We were on our break, but we're a little shorthanded this week."

I stepped aside to let them go into the room, and decided it was time to return to the spaceport. But just for the hell of it, I stopped by Admissions before I left and asked if anyone had inquired about Seymour.

No one had.

✧ ✧ ✧

When I got back to my office, I was still curious, so I had the computer hunt up with what little there was on Seymour and on Daniel Daniels. Seymour was easy; born and raised in Miami, went to college here, spent nine years in the space service, honorably discharged after getting shot all to hell in a firefight on Kobernykov II, informally known as Nikita. Came back home, got a real estate license, and was selling beachfront property until two years ago, when he suddenly seemed determined to prove he was either a hero or bulletproof or both. Since then he'd tried to throw his life away three different times; the first two times the hospital made him keep it, this time they didn't.

Daniels was harder. There were actually four Daniel Daniels living in Miami at the start of the year. You'd think their parents would have had a little more creativity. Two were still around. One had died of relatively natural causes at the age of ninety-three. And then there was the one the orderly had told me about.

He was thirty-three years old. Dropped out of school at sixteen, signed a couple of minor-league soccer contracts, got cut both times, joined the space service when he was twenty, served seven years, got out on a medical discharge, and had been going from one menial job to another ever since.

I checked the medical discharge. He got it after catching some serious flak on Nikita. He recovered physically, but he'd been seeing a shrink for depression for four years before the night he tried to take on a gang of teenaged hoods and got turned into an animated cinder for his trouble. It took them a year to put him back together with a brand-new epidermis—and damned if he didn't go out and do something equally suicidal a month later. Even the police weren't sure what happened—they found him after all the shooting was over—but he was filled with so much lead of so many different calibers that he had to have taken on at least six armed men.

And that was it: two unexceptional men who had nothing in common but the town they lived in and the planet they'd served on, each willingly faced certain death for no apparent reason—and then, when they were saved, went right out and faced it again.

I was still pondering it when Captain Symmes called me into his office to give him my report. I told him what I'd observed, which matched all the other reports, and then figured I was done.

"Just a minute," he said as I was turning to leave.

"Sir?" I said.

"You accompanied him to the hospital. Why?"

"I was hoping he might be able to tell me why he willingly put himself at such risk," I answered. "I thought maybe he knew something about the men we killed."

"And did he?"

I shook my head. "We'll never know. He only regained consciousness for perhaps a minute after surgery, and then he died."

"I wonder what the hell made him do it?" mused Captain Symmes.

"I wondered, too," I said. "So I ran computer checks on him and on Daniels—"

"Daniels?" he said sharply. "Who's Daniels?"

"Another man who threw his life away the same way," I said. "But the only things they had in common were that they lived here and they both saw action on Kobernykov II."

"Kobernykov II," he repeated. "Is that the one they call Nikita?"

"Yes, sir."

"Now, *that's* interesting," said Captain Symmes.

"What is, sir?" I asked.

"About two years ago I was running security at MarsPort, and the same kind of thing happened. Four men were robbing one of the restaurants there, and this guy, he was just waiting for his flight to Titan, decided to take them out single-handed. They shot him before he got close to them. We nailed all four of them before they could harm anyone else, but the man had taken too many bullets and energy pulses. He died a few hours later." Captain Symmes paused and frowned. "I had to fill out a report, and that meant I had to find out who was killed. The reason I'm mentioning it at all is because he spent some time on Nikita."

"Medical discharge?"

"Yes," he answered. "Curious, isn't it?"

"Very," I said. "Do you know if that was the first time he'd risked his life like that?"

"No, I don't," said Captain Symmes. "I assume you have a reason for asking?"

"Yes, sir, I do."

"Give me a minute and I'll check the record. Like I said, it was two years ago."

He activated his computer, instructed it to pull up the file in question, then told it to run a biographical search on the dead man. Eleven seconds later it had the answer.

Creighton Mortenson Jr. had willingly faced what seemed like certain death on four separate occasions. Only after he'd miraculously survived the first three did Fate finally deliver on its promise at MarsPort.

"Captain," I said, "what would you say if I told you that Seymour and Daniels had also tried to throw their lives away prior to actually succeeding at it?"

"I'd say that something very interesting must have happened to them on Nikita," he said, and instructed his computer to produce a readout of Kobernykov II. He studied it for a moment, then shrugged. "It's about three-quarters the size of Earth, lighter gravity, a bit less oxygen but breathable. During the war with the Patruka Alliance we found they were using Nikita as an ammunition dump, we landed a small party, we blew the ammo dump, each side suffered serious casualties. The few survivors were scattered all the hell over; we found them over a period of maybe three weeks, and eventually they rejoined their main units. There's some plant and animal life there, but no humans and no Patrukans."

"I wonder what the hell went on there," I said. "Most men who get shot up in wartime don't ever want to experience it again—and here were three men who went out of their way to walk into enemy fire or its equivalent again."

"Have your computer hunt up the survivors and ask," he said.

When I went back to my office I filed my report, then tried to find the survivors of Nikita, as Captain Symmes had suggested. The Patrukan War was over, so all the documents and records were declassified, but it didn't help much. We'd sent in a covert team of thirty men and women. It was an exceptionally bloody action. Twenty-five died on Nikita, and the other five—which included Seymour, Daniels, and Mortenson—were wounded pretty badly. Evidently they'd become separated, and each managed to survive on his own until a rescue mission arrived a few weeks later.

I tried to track down the other two survivors. They'd both courted Death until it inevitably caught up with them.

There was nothing in any of their histories to indicate that they were either exceptionally brave or exceptionally foolish. Except for Daniels' depression, none of them was being treated for any emotional or psychiatric problems. As far as I could tell, none of them kept in touch with any of the others after they were discharged from the service.

And within six years of the firefight on Nikita, every one of them was dead, having placed themselves in what could only be termed suicidal situations until even the best surgeons and hospitals could no longer keep them alive.

I reported my findings to Captain Symmes the next day. I could tell he was as fascinated as I was.

"What do you suppose could have made them throw their lives away?" he mused. "And if they were so damned set on dying, why didn't they just put a gun to their heads?"

"There's one way to find out, sir," I said.

He shook his head. "I can't send you to Nikita," he said. "We're OceanPort security, and Nikita is more than a thousand light-years from here."

"But if there's something on the planet that caused this behavior . . ."

"Forget it. If there was anything in the food or water or air, the space service or the navy would have found it."

But I couldn't forget it. How do you forget a bunch of totally dissimilar people with one brief shared experience who suddenly act in the same, totally self-destructive manner?

Each evening when I got off work I'd go back to my quarters and try to find out more about the planet and the survivors. The problem is that there simply wasn't much to find. They'd been there for three weeks, maybe four at the outside, there were only five of them, the planet had been deserted by the Patruka Alliance after the battle, and no one had been back since.

And then I thought of the one line of inquiry I hadn't considered before. We were no longer at war, so I wrote a couple of Patrukan historians and asked them if they could supply any accounts, not of the action on Nikita, but on the whereabouts of the survivors.

It took a week before I got an answer, but finally one of them, a being called Myxophtyl—at least that's the way my computer translated his name—informed me that of the four survivors, two had died of natural causes, and two had died heroically, one saving a child who had wandered into the enclosure of a herd of vicious carnivores at a local zoo, the other trying to protect a Mollute who somehow offended a crowd of Patrukans that had instantly turned into an ugly and bloodthirsty mob.

"It didn't just affect humans, sir," I reported to Captain Symmes the day after I heard from the historian. "Whatever's on that planet affected *everyone*."

"I know that look," he said. "I'm as interested as you are, but as I told you before, I don't have the authority to send you there."

"I've got vacation time stored up," I said.

He checked his computer. "Your vacation's not for five months."

"Then I'll take a leave of absence."

"Think it through," he said. "Nothing on that planet harmed anyone. Do you really want to go there, bore yourself to tears for a week or two, come home, and then one day decide to prove that you're invulnerable to bullets and lasers?"

"No," I admitted. "No, I suppose I don't."

I thought it was the truth when I said it, but with each day I became more obsessed with what could have turned otherwise normal men into weapon-charging suicides. And in the back of my mind I kept coming back to Captain Symmes' question: if they really wanted to die, why not just put a gun to their heads, or take an overdose? And then I remembered Myron Seymour lying on his bed in the recovery room. He didn't want to die; he wanted to see this woman he was sure would somehow know he was in the hospital. Okay, he may have been fantasizing about the woman, but he wasn't fantasizing about wanting to live.

I'd never thought of myself as obsessive, but as the next three weeks sped by I found myself obsessing over the mystery of what happened on Nikita, and finally I couldn't stand it any longer. I told Captain Symmes that I was putting in for a one-month leave of absence, and that if I didn't get it I was fully prepared to quit my job.

"Don't be foolish," he said. "That's an awfully big step to take, just to chase a fantasy. Besides, I already reported your findings to the navy and the space service. I'm sure they'll look into it."

"I'm sure they will, too," I said. "Just not necessarily in our lifetimes."

"What are you talking about?"

"We've got ten or twelve minor wars going on right now," I said. "They've got more important things to do than examine a planet that nobody's set foot on in six years."

"I gave them all the details," said Captain Symmes. "If they think it's important, they'll get out there pretty damned fast."

"And if they find whatever it is that caused this behavior, they'll make it Top Secret and won't declassify it for a century," I shot back. "I want to know what happened."

"I'm not going to talk you out of this, am I?" he said after a long pause.

"No, sir, you're not."

"All right. You've got a month, starting tomorrow." He handed me a small cube. "There are no direct flights. This'll get you free passage on any ship owned by Earth or its allies."

"Thank you, sir," I said.

"The codes will vanish in exactly thirty days, so don't stay any longer than that unless you're prepared to pay your passage back."

"I appreciate this, sir."

"You're a good security man," he said uncomfortably. (Praising people always made him uncomfortable.) "I don't want to lose you."

"You won't," I promised him. "I'll be back in less than a month with the answers to what happened."

"Good health," he said.

"Not good luck?"

"I think you might be luckier if you never find what you're looking for," said Captain Symmes seriously.

The nontraveler tends to think that between FTL speeds and wormholes you can get anywhere in the galaxy in a day's time, but of course it isn't so. Wormholes go where *they* want to go, not where *we* want them to, and even when you're traveling at multiples of light speed it's still a big galaxy. It took me a day to get to Antares III, where I changed ships and proceeded to Buckingham IV. I laid over for a day until I could transfer to a ship that took me to Mickeleen, and from there I had to charter a private ship for the last leg of the journey.

"I want you to burn this location into your mind," said the pilot when the small ship touched down on Nikita. "I'll be here in exactly ten days. If you're not at this spot, I have neither the time nor the inclination to embark on a one-man planetary search, which means you'll be stranded here, probably for the rest of what remains of your life. You got that?"

"Got it," I said.

"You sure you have enough supplies?" he asked, looking at my pack.

"Food and water for twelve days, just to be on the safe side."

"If you're not here ten days from now, there won't be anything safe about it," he said. "It could be decades before another ship touches down here."

"I'll be here," I assured him.

"You'd better be," he said.

Then the hatch closed and he was gone, and I was alone, the first human to set foot on Nikita in six years.

I felt good. Hell, at 82 percent of Earth's gravity, *everybody* feels good. This was exactly the kind of world they used for recuperating heart patients. The oxygen content was a little light, but the gravity more than made up for it.

The world itself seemed pleasant enough. There was a brownish, grasslike ground cover in most places, a few clusters of oddly shaped trees here and there, and a type G sun that provided plenty of daylight without making Nikita uncomfortably hot. I saw a few small, rodent-like animals peeking at me from behind shrubs and trees, but when I turned to get a better look they ducked into their burrows.

I knew there was water on the planet. There were a pair of freshwater oceans, and a quartet of snow-topped mountain ranges that produced rivers with their runoff. My research told me that it smelled bad and tasted worse, but that it was drinkable. I had no idea if there were any fish, but I suspected there were. One thing we've learned since first reaching the stars is that life not only takes the strangest forms, but sprouts up in the oddest places.

According to my charts, I was about four miles from the site of the conflict, which is to say, the ammunition dump. I was retracing the steps of our team. They'd actually started on the far side of the planet, maybe three thousand miles away, and taken a high-speed aircar here under cover of night, but they'd gone the last few miles on foot.

I looked for signs of a camp, but then realized that a covert attack team wouldn't make a camp, but would just continue to their target before they were spotted.

The ground was level, not overgrown at all, and I just kept walking until I came to it. It wasn't hard to spot. There was a raw crater close to five hundred yards in circumference and maybe forty feet deep, the remains of the ammo dump. Evidently the rescue ships on both sides couldn't handle both the living and the dead; there were skeletons of both men and Patrukans littering the place, picked clean by small animals and even smaller insects. The Patrukans' bones had a blue-green tint to them; I never did find out why.

I walked the area. It must have been one hell of a battle. There was absolutely no place to hide, nothing to duck behind. A night attack shouldn't have made any difference: if the Patrukans had FTL ships and pulse cannons, they sure as hell had all kinds of vision aids that could turn night into day. I remember once, when I was a kid, standing at the top of Cemetery Ridge and wondering how Pickett ever got his men to charge up the long, barren slope where they were just sitting ducks; I felt the same way looking at the site on Nikita.

The other thing I wondered about was how surviving this kind of battle could give *anyone* a taste for charging men with loaded weapons or otherwise risking their lives. They should have been so grateful they lived through it that all they wanted to do was celebrate each day they were still alive.

Those were my first impressions. Then I began analyzing the site as a soldier. You wouldn't want to get too close to the dump, because you didn't know what was in it or how big an explosion it would make. And you didn't want any survivors picking your team off, so you'd have tried to surround the place so you could shoot any Patrukan who lived through it. The crater was more than a quarter of a mile across, so you'd want your men stationed perhaps a mile and a half across from each other, or given the accuracy of their weapons, maybe even farther. Say, two miles or a bit more.

I studied the area again. Okay, from a minimum of a one-mile radius, and a distance of more than a quarter mile from each other along the circumference, I saw how they could have gotten separated. If you're wounded, your first inclination is to retreat to safety, not to stay within range and seek out your teammates. Then, once you felt you were safe, you couldn't be sure all the enemy were dead, and your wounds were starting to stiffen up or worse, and the last thing you'd do is go looking for the other survivors.

So each of the five men was essentially on his own until the rescue team arrived, and it hadn't arrived for another week. Did they have a week's supply of food and water? If not, could they live off the land? Did they have any medication at all? How badly were they wounded, and how had they managed to survive? I didn't know, but I had ten days to figure it out.

Then I reminded myself that that was just the first part, the easier part, of the problem, and that I had a little less than ten days to figure *everything* out.

The sun started dropping lower in the sky—the planet had a nineteen-hour day—and I decided that I'd better make camp while I could still see. I pulled my stationary bubble out of my pack, uttered the code words that activated it, waited a few seconds for it to become a cube seven feet on a side, and tossed my pack into it after removing some rations. I ordered the door to shut, then picked up a few branches, gathered them into a pile, and set fire to them with my laser pistol. I tossed three H-rations into the flames. They'd roll out of the fire when they were properly cooked, and I decided to eat them without any water or beer, as I sure as hell didn't want to run out of drinkables in seven or eight days and have to partake of the nearby river.

I looked out across the barren plain, wondering why sentient life hadn't taken hold here as it had on so many hundreds of similar worlds. Nature always seemed to find a reason to endow one or two species with brainpower, no matter how weird or unlikely they looked. But there had been no reports of any sentience on Nikita. In fact, though the Patrukans mentioned larger animals, the human attack party hadn't seen anything bigger than the little rodentlike creatures I'd seen, but that made sense: no carnivore is willing to risk getting injured unless the odds are greatly in his favor, because an injured carnivore will usually die of hunger before he heals enough to hunt again. So when they saw the aircar, or even the men themselves, any large predator would have steered clear of them.

Or *did* it make sense? There were five badly wounded men scattered around the landscape, hardly in any condition to defend themselves, and yet they went unmolested until the rescue ship arrived. That implied that the Patrukans were wrong and there weren't any large carnivores, but I couldn't buy it, because life gets *bigger* on a low-gravity world, not smaller.

I decided it could wait for tomorrow. What lived on Nikita didn't have anything to do with what I'd come here to learn, and I certainly wasn't going to go looking for large carnivores in the dark.

My attention was taken by each of the H-rations crying "Done!", one after the other, and rolling up to my feet, where each in turn popped open.

I started on the Ersatz Stroganoff, finished it off, then attacked the Mock Parmesan. By the time I was done I was too full to eat the third one, and ordered it to close itself again.

"I will be safe for sixteen Standard hours," it announced. "After that I will self-destruct so that no one becomes ill from my contents. The self-destruction will be silent and will not adversely effect any men, even if one is holding me at the time."

It fell silent and clamped shut.

I looked up and saw Nikita's three moons, all of them quite small, racing across the sky. I'd been stationed on Earth for a couple of years, and I'd gotten used to our own large moon making its stately way across the sky. I'd forgotten how fast the smaller moons can travel.

I dictated the day's experiences, findings, and thoughts into my computer. Night fell while I was doing so, and when I was finished I decided to take a little walk to work off my dinner. I left the fire burning so I wouldn't stray too far and could easily find my way back, then headed off to my left.

When I'd gone half a mile I decided I was far enough from my makeshift camp, and began walking in a large circle around the fire. I'd circled it once, and was circling it a second time when it went out, and I figured I'd better go back and get a few more branches to start it up again. I'd covered about half the distance and was passing a thick stand of trees when I heard a hideous alien roar behind me.

I turned to face whatever it was, but something was already leaping through the air at me. The moons were on the far side of Nikita, and I could barely see its outline. I ducked and turned, and the bulk of its body sent me flying through the air. I landed about six feet away, felt my leg give way, and heard the bone snap. I rolled over once and reached for my laser pistol, but it was too quick. I still couldn't make it out, but it didn't seem to share that problem. Claws raked deep into my arm and the pistol fell from my hand. Then it was on top of me before I could even reach for my sonic weapon. Teeth raked my face and neck. I reached out, seemed to find a throat, and did my damnedest to hold it at bay, but it was a losing battle. The creature was on top of me, and I could tell it weighed at least as much as I did. It kept pressing forward, and my blood-soaked right arm was starting to go numb. I brought my unbroken leg up hard, hoping it was a male and that it had testicles, but it didn't seem to have any effect whatsoever.

I could feel hot breath in my eyes and on my cheek, and I knew I had about four seconds left before it overpowered me—and then, suddenly, it was yelping in pain and fear, and it wasn't atop me anymore.

I listened for the snarling of something even bigger—something that would turn its attention to me next—but whatever was attacking my attacker was absolutely silent.

Then there was a high-pitched screech, and I could hear the creature race off. Then my momentary savior turned to me, just as one of the moons came up over the horizon. Blood was streaming down into my eyes from a gash on my forehead, and the moon wasn't very big or very bright, but I could see something approaching me, could hear the rustle of its feet across the grass.

I finally got my good hand on my sonic pistol and held it unsteadily in front of me.

"Stay back!" I mumbled.

I fired a shot, but even in my semiconscious state I could tell it was well off target. I tried to steady my hand and fire again, but then everything went black. My last thought was: *What a stupid way to die.*

Except that I didn't die. I don't know how long I was unconscious— maybe nine or ten hours, because the sun was high in the sky when I woke up.

"Don't try to stand," said a lilting female voice in perfect, unaccented Terran. "I had to splint your leg."

I rubbed some crusted blood from my eyelashes, and noticed that my right arm was heavily bandaged. A damp cloth began dabbing at my eyes, and I was able to focus on the person who was holding it.

She was a pretty young woman, in her early twenties, certainly under thirty, with a slender body, long red-brown hair, high cheekbones, and light blue, almost colorless eyes. She looked familiar, but I knew I'd never seen her before.

"Who are you?" I asked weakly.

"My name is Rebecca," she said with a smile. "And you are Gregory Donovan."

"I thought I left my ID in my bubble."

"You did."

"Then you opened it," I said, frowning. "It's only supposed to open to my voice command."

"I haven't opened it," she said. "Now try to rest."

I was about to argue with her, for she was obviously lying, but suddenly all my energy vanished and I lost consciousness again.

It was very late afternoon when I awoke the next time. Rebecca was sitting on the ground, staring at me. I got to take another look at her, and decided that she was more than pretty—she was gorgeous. I couldn't find a single feature I'd improve.

She was dressed in an immaculate white blouse and khaki slacks that fit her like a glove, which seemed as unlikely as being cared for by a beautiful Terran-speaking girl on a planet that supposedly had no sentient life-forms.

"Welcome back," she said. "How do you feel?"

"Rested," I said. "What kind of shape am I in?"

"Your arm is badly infected, your leg is broken in three places, and you have some serious wounds around your face and neck."

"What the hell happened?" I asked.

"You were attacked by a . . . the closest I can translate it into Terran would be a nightstalker. It's the largest carnivore on Nikita."

"It can't be," I said. "Something bigger drove it off."

"Trust me, Gregory," said Rebecca. "The nightstalker is Nikita's largest carnivore."

I was too weak to argue, and it didn't make any difference anyway. *Something* had driven the nightstalker off, and I didn't much care if it was a bigger carnivore or an enraged microbe.

"How long have you been here, Rebecca?" I asked.

"With you?" she said. "Since last night."

"No, I mean on Nikita."

"All my life."

I frowned. "My computer didn't say anything about a human colony here."

"There isn't one."

"You mean you were stranded here as a child?" I asked. "Were your parents with you?"

"My parents lived here," she said.

"Are they still alive?" I said. "I've got a ship picking me up in nine days . . ."

"No, they aren't alive."

"I'm sorry. Well, at least the ship can take you and me off the planet."

"Are you hungry?" she asked.

I thought about it for a moment. "Not really. I'd like something to drink, though."

"All right," she said. "The river's just a quarter mile away. I'll be back in a few minutes."

"They say the water's pretty awful. I've got water and some electrolyte mixtures in my bubble."

"If you prefer," she said.

"See?" I said accusingly. "I *knew* you'd been in my bubble."

"I told you: I haven't entered it."

"If you're telling the truth, then you won't be able to get into it now. It's programmed only to respond to my voice pattern uttering the proper code words."

"I will get them and be right back," she said.

And sure enough, she was back just a minute or two later carrying three containers. I chose the one that would give me the quickest energy boost and tried not to think about how she got the bubble to let her in.

"I think you should eat in another hour, Gregory," she said. "You need strength to fight off the infection. I'll go through your supplies in a few minutes and see what you have." She flashed me a smile. "I'm a very good cook. Maybe I can figure out how to combine your H-rations to make them taste like duck in orange sauce."

"Why did you say that?" I asked.

"It's your favorite, isn't it?"

"Yes, it is," I replied. "How did you know?"

"You just look like a duck in orange sauce man to me."

"What the hell is going on here?" I demanded. "You know my name, you know my favorite food, you can get a voice-coded bubble to open to you, you know how to splint a leg and patch me up, and you speak without an accent."

"Why are you complaining?" she asked. "Would you rather I had left you broken and bleeding on the ground? Did you want me to bring you water that you find all but undrinkable? Should I find H-rations that you hate?"

"No, of course not," I said. "But you're not answering my questions."

"Yes, I am."

"Here's another," I said. "What the hell are you doing here in the first place? It's a big planet. How did you happen to find me just in time to save my life?"

"Serendipity," said Rebecca.

"Serendipity, hell," I said. "And while I'm asking questions, what saved me last night?"

"I did."

"You patched me up," I said. "What *saved* me? What drove the nightstalker off?"

"Is it important?" asked Rebecca. "You're alive. That's what matters."

"It's important to me," I said. "I don't like being lied to."

"I haven't lied to you, Gregory," she said. "Now be quiet and let me check the wounds on your arm and neck."

She walked over and knelt down next to me. There was a sweet smell about her, almost a perfume, that seemed to suit her exactly. She examined the gashes on my neck, and although they were badly swollen and clearly infected, her cool, sure fingers didn't hurt at all.

"It's still seeping," she said, getting to her feet. "I've treated your dressings with native herbs and leaves that promote healing. I'll change them after dinner."

"What kind of dressing are you using, and where did you get it out here in the middle of nowhere?"

She pointed to a satchel a few feet away. "I'm always prepared."

A wave of dizziness spread over me, and I spent the next couple of minutes trying not to fall over on my side. I don't remember what happened next, but when my head cleared she was sitting next to me, steadying me with her body. It felt good, and I pretended I was still dizzy so she wouldn't move away. I think she knew it, but she stayed there anyway.

"How long before I can walk?" I asked at last.

"I'll make you some crutches in three or four days," she said. "After all, you'll need some practice if you're to get to your contact point in time for the ship that's picking you up."

"So I'm stuck here for three days, maybe four," I said unhappily.

"I'm sorry," she said sympathetically. "I'll try to make you as comfortable as possible, but you're very weak and your temperature is dangerously high. I'm afraid you're not going to be able to see much of the planet."

"What makes you think I'm here to explore Nikita?" I asked sharply.

"Why else would you have come?" replied Rebecca. "I'll help you into your bubble tonight. You'll have to stay there; you're too weak to move any farther than that."

"I know," I admitted with a sigh. "It's going to be a boring few days. I wish to hell I'd brought some disks to read."

"We can discuss our favorite books," she offered. "It will make the time pass more pleasantly."

I don't know why I was surprised that she read—I mean, hell, *everybody* reads—but I was. "Who are your favorites?" I asked.

"Cisco, Jablonski, and Hedburg."

"You're kidding!" I exclaimed. "Those are *my* favorites too! At least we'll have something to talk about after dinner."

And we did. We talked for hours, and not just about books either. I'd never felt so comfortable with anyone in my life. We talked about hopes and dreams, about regrets, about everything. It was amazing: she seemed to mirror my every thought, my every secret longing. And when we'd fall silent, it wasn't an uncomfortable silence, the kind you feel you have to speak into; I was just as happy to look at her as listen to her. She'd grown up on an alien world thousands of light-years from Earth, and I knew almost nothing about her: where she lived, what she had done with her life prior to saving mine, even her last name—and yet my last waking thought was that I was already a little bit in love with her.

I don't know how long I slept. I woke up when I felt Rebecca applying some salve to the gashes on my cheeks and neck.

"Don't move," she said gently. "I'll be done in another minute."

I held still until she was through, then opened my eyes and realized that we were inside my bubble.

"I'm surprised you could drag me in here without help," I said. "I must really have been out of it, not to wake up while you were moving me."

"I'm stronger than I look," she said with a smile.

"Good," I said. "Give me a hand up, and let me hobble out into the fresh air."

She began reaching out for me, then froze.

"What's the matter?"

"I'll be back in ten minutes," she said. "Don't try to stand without me; you could damage your splint."

"What's the matter?" I asked. "Are you all right?"

But she had already run off into the nearby stand of trees, and I lost sight of her.

It was puzzling. The only logical explanation was that she'd eaten something rotten and she was going off to be sick, but I didn't buy it. She'd run too gracefully, and she'd shown no discomfort, not the least little bit, prior to leaving.

I decided to try getting up on my own despite her orders. It was a disaster. The way my leg was splinted I simply couldn't do it. As I tried to position it, I realized that the bandages were soaked and foul-smelling. I rubbed a finger against them, then held it up. It wasn't blood, just something yellow-greenish. I didn't know whether that was a good sign or a bad one.

That's some carnivore, that nightstalker, I thought. I wondered why it hadn't taken over the planet. Then I realized that except for Rebecca, who wasn't native to Nikita, I hadn't seen anything much larger than a raccoon or a possum, so maybe it *had* taken over the planet. It seemed a reasonable conclusion, but I'd served on just enough alien planets to know that reasonable and right often had very little to do with each other.

Then Rebecca was back, as immaculate as ever. She took one look at my leg and said, "I told you not to try standing up without me."

"Something's wrong with it," I said. "It smells bad, and it's wet."

"I know," she said. "I'll fix it. Trust me, Gregory."

I looked into her face and found, to my surprise, that I *did* trust her. I was alone and possibly dying a zillion miles from home, being tended with leaves and herbs by a girl I'd known for only a few days, and I trusted her. I had half a notion that if she told me to walk off a cliff I'd have done it.

"While we're discussing health," I said, "how's yours?"

"I'm fine, Gregory," she said. "But I'm flattered to know you were worried about me."

"Of course I was," I said. "You're the person who's keeping me alive."

"That's not why you were worried," she said.

"No," I admitted, "it's not."

There was a momentary silence.

"Well, are you ready to hobble outside?" she asked. "I'll help you to that tree. You can prop yourself up against it when you sit, and the branches and leaves will shade you from the sun. It can get very warm here at midday."

"I'm ready," I said.

She took my right hand in both of hers and pulled. It hurt like hell for a minute, but then I was on my feet.

"Lean on my shoulder," she said as she helped me turn toward the bubble's entrance.

I half hopped, half hobbled through it. The tree was some forty feet away. I'd gone about half that distance when my good foot went into some kind of rodent hole, and I started falling. I reached out, grabbing for her blouse, and then the strangest thing happened—instead of grabbing cloth, my fingers slid down her naked skin. I could see the blouse, but it wasn't there. She pivoted, trying to catch me, and my hand came into contact with her bare breast, slid over her nipple, down a naked hip and thigh, and then I hit the ground with a bone-jarring *thud!* The pain was excruciating.

Rebecca was beside me in an instant, positioning my leg, putting her hands under my head, doing what she could to comfort me. It took a good five minutes for the burning in my leg and arm to subside, but eventually it did, at least enough for me to consider what had happened.

I reached out to her shoulder, felt the cloth of her blouse, and ran my hand down the side of her body. The texture of the cloth changed when I got to her slacks, but there was no naked flesh—yet I knew I hadn't hallucinated it. You hallucinate *after* you're in agony, like now, not *before*.

"Are you going to tell me what's going on?" I asked.

"You fell."

"Don't play dumb with me," I said. "It's unbecoming in someone as smart and lovely. Just tell me what's happening."

"Try to rest," she said. "We'll talk later."

"You said yesterday that you wouldn't lie to me. Did you mean it?"

"I will never lie to you, Gregory."

I stared at her perfect face for a long minute. "Are you human?" I asked at last.

"For the moment."

"What the hell is that supposed to mean?"

"It means that I am what I need to be," she said. "What *you* need me to be."

"That's no answer."

"I am telling you that right now I am human, that I am everything you need. Isn't that enough?"

"Are you a shape-changer?" I asked.

"No, Gregory, I am not."

"Then how can you look like this?"

"This is what you want to see," she said.

"What if I want to see you are you really are?" I persisted.

"But you don't," she said. "*This*"—she indicated herself—"is what you want to see."

"What makes you think so?"

"Gregory, Gregory," she said with a sigh, "do you think I created this face and this body out of *my* imagination? I found it in *your* mind."

"Bullshit," I said. "I never met anyone who looked like you."

A smile. "But you wish you had." And a pause. "And if you had, you were sure she would be called Rebecca. I am not only everything you need, but everything you want."

"Everything?" I asked dubiously.

"Everything."

"Can we . . . uh . . . ?"

"When you slipped you caught me off guard," she answered. "Didn't I feel like the woman you want me to be?"

"Let me get this straight. Your clothes are as much of an illusion as you are?"

"The clothes are an illusion," she said, and suddenly they vanished and she was standing, naked and perfect, before me. "*I* am real."

"You're a real *something*," I said. "But you're not a real *woman*."

"At this moment I am as real as any woman you have ever known."

"Let me think for a minute," I said. I stared at her while I tried to think. Then I realized that I was thinking all the wrong things, and I lowered my gaze to the ground. "That thing that drove the night-stalker away," I said. "It was *you*, wasn't it?"

"It was what you needed at that instant," she answered.

"And whatever pulls the leaves down from the treetops—a snake, a bird, an animal, whatever—that's you too?"

"You need a mixture of the leaves and the herbs to combat your infection."

"Are you trying to say that you were put here solely to serve my needs?" I demanded. "I didn't think God was that generous."

"No, Gregory," said Rebecca. "I am saying that it is my nature, even my compulsion, to nurture those who are in need of nurturing."

"How did you know I needed it, or that I was even on the planet?"

"There are many ways of sending a distress signal, some of them far more powerful than you can imagine."

"Are you saying that if someone is suffering, say, five miles away, you'd know it?"

"Yes."

"More than five miles?" I continued. She simply stared at me. "Fifty miles? A hundred? The whole damned planet?"

She looked into my eyes, her face suddenly so sad that I totally forgot about the rest of her. "It's not limited to just the planet, Gregory."

"When you ran off for a few minutes, were you saving some other man?"

"You are the only man on the planet," she replied.

"Well, then?"

"A small marsupial had broken a leg. I alleviated its suffering."

"You weren't gone that long," I said. "Are you saying that an injured wild animal let a strange woman approach it while it was in pain, because I find that very difficult to believe."

"I did not approach it as a woman."

I stared at her for a long moment. I think I half expected her to morph into some kind of alien monster, but she just looked as beautiful as ever. I visually searched her naked body for flaws—make that *errors*—some indication that she wasn't human, but I couldn't find any.

"I've got to think about all this," I said at last.

"Would you like me to leave?"

"No."

"Would it be less distracting if I recreated the illusion of clothing?"

"Yes," I said. Then, "No." Then, "I don't know."

"They always find out," she said. "But usually not this quickly."

"Are you the only one of . . . of whatever it is that you are?"

"No," she replied. "But we were never a numerous race, and I am one of the very few who remains on Nikita."

"What happened to the others?"

"They went where they were needed. Some came back; most went from one distress signal to another."

"We haven't had a ship here in six years," I said. "How did they leave the planet?"

"There are many races in the galaxy, Gregory. Humans aren't the only ones to land here."

"How many men have you saved?"

"A few."

"And Patrukans?"

"Patrukans too."

I shrugged. "Why the hell not? I suppose we're all equally alien to you."

"You are not alien," she said. "I assure you that at this moment I am every bit as human as the Rebecca of your dreams. In fact, I *am* the Rebecca of your dreams." She flashed me a smile. "I even want to do what that Rebecca wants to do."

"Is it possible?" I asked curiously.

"Not while you have a broken leg," she answered, "but yes, it's not only possible, but natural." I must have looked doubtful, because she added, "It would feel exactly the way you hope it would feel."

"You'd better bring the clothes back before I do something really stupid that'll mess up my arm and leg even worse," I said.

And instantly she was clothed again.

"Better?" she asked.

"Safer, anyway," I said.

"While you're thinking deep serious thoughts, I'll start making your breakfast," she said, helping me to the shade of the tree, then going back into the bubble to find some H-rations.

I sat motionless for a few minutes, considering what I had learned. And I came to what seemed, at least at the time, a surprising conclusion. She was my dream girl. She was drop-dead gorgeous—to me, anyway. We shared dozens of interests, and she was as passionate about them as I was. I felt comfortable with her, and knowing that she was really something else didn't disturb me half as much as I'd thought it would. If she was Rebecca only when I was around, that was better than never having a Rebecca at all. And she cared for me; she had no reason to say so if it wasn't true.

She walked over and handed me a plate filled with soya products that were designed to look and taste like anything except soya products. I put the plate on the ground and took her hand in mine.

"You don't shrink from my touch," I noted, stroking her arm gently.

"Of course not," she said. "I am your Rebecca. I love your touch."

"I don't shrink from yours either," I said, "which is probably a little more surprising. I'm sitting here, touching you, looking at you, smelling the nearness of you, and I don't give a damn who you are or what you look like when I'm not around. I just want you to stay."

She leaned down and kissed me. If it felt like anything other than being kissed by a human woman, I sure as hell couldn't tell the difference.

I ate my breakfast, and we spent the morning talking—about books, about art, about theater, about food, about a hundred things we had in common. And we talked in the afternoon, and we talked in the evening.

I don't know when I fell asleep, but I woke up in the middle of the night. I was lying on my side, and she was curled up against me. I felt something warm and flat on my leg, not a bandage. It seemed to be . . . *sucking* is a terrible word; *extracting* . . . some of the infection from my leg. I had a feeling that it was some part of her that I couldn't see; I decided not to look, and when I woke up in the morning she was already gathering some firewood for warming my breakfast.

We spent seven idyllic days together at that campsite. We talked, we ate, I began walking on a pair of crutches she made. Four times she excused herself and ran off, and I knew she'd picked another distress signal out of the air, but she was always back a few minutes later. Long before those seven days were up I realized that, despite a broken leg and a shredded arm, they were the happiest days I'd ever spent.

I spent my eighth day with her—my ninth on Nikita—making my way slowly and painfully back to the spot where the ship would pick me up the next morning. I set up my bubble after dinner, and crawled into it a couple of hours later. As I was starting to drift off I felt her lie up against me, and this time there was no illusion of clothing.

"I can't," I said unhappily. "My leg . . ."

"Hush," she whispered. "I'll take care of everything."

And she did.

She was making breakfast when I awoke.

"Good morning," I said as I emerged from the bubble.

"Good morning."

I hobbled over and kissed her. "Thank you for last night."

"I hope we didn't damage your wounds."

"If we did, it was worth it," I said. "The ship is due in less than an hour. We have to talk."

She looked at me expectantly.

"I don't care what you are," I said. "To me you're Rebecca, and I love you. And before the ship arrives, I've got to know if you love me too."

"Yes, Gregory, I do."

"Then will you come with me?"

"I'd like to, Gregory," she said. "But . . ."

"Have you ever left Nikita before?" I asked.

"Yes," she replied. "Whenever I sense that someone with whom I've been linked is in physical or emotional pain."

"But you always come back?"

"This is my home."

"Did you visit Myron Seymour after he left Nikita?"

"I don't know."

"What do you mean, you don't know?" I said. "Either you did or you didn't."

"All right," she said unhappily. "Either I did or I didn't."

"I thought you were never going to lie to me," I said.

"I'm not lying, Gregory," she said, reaching out and laying a hand on my good shoulder. "You don't understand how the bond works."

"What bond?" I asked, confused.

"You know that I look like this and I took this name because I was drawn irresistably to your pain and your need, and found the name and the image in your mind," she said. "We are *linked*, Gregory. You say that you love me, and probably you do. I share that emotion. But I share it for the same reason I can discuss your favorite books and plays—because I found them where I found Rebecca. When the link is broken, when I'm not in contact with you anymore, they'll be forgotten." A tear rolled down her cheek. "And everything I feel for you this minute will be forgotten too."

I just stared at her, trying to comprehend what she'd said.

"I'm sorry, Gregory," she continued after a moment. "You can't know *how* sorry. Right now all I want is to be with you, to love you and care for you—but when the link is broken, it will all be gone." Another tear. "I won't even feel a sense of loss."

"And that's why you can't remember if you made it to Earth and saved Seymour?"

"I may have, I may not have," she said helplessly. "I don't know. Probably I never will."

I thought about it. "It's okay," I said. "I don't care about the others. Just stay with me and don't break the link."

"It's not something I can control, Gregory," she replied. "It's strongest when you need me most. As you heal, as you need me less; then I'll be drawn to someone or something that needs me more. Perhaps it will be another man, perhaps a Patrukan, perhaps something else. But it will happen, again and again."

"Until I need you more than anyone else does," I said.

"Until you need me more than anyone else does," she confirmed.

And at that moment, I knew why Seymour and Daniels and the others had walked into what seemed near-certain death. And I realized what Captain Symmes and the Patrukan historian Myxophtyl didn't know: that they hadn't tried to get themselves killed, but rather to get themselves *almost* killed.

Suddenly I saw the ship overhead, getting ready to touch down a few hundred yards away.

"Does anyone or anything need you right now?" I asked. "More than I do, I mean?"

"Right this moment? No."

"Then come with me for as long as you can," I said.

"It's not a good idea," she said. "I could begin the journey, but you're getting healthier every day, and something always needs me. We'd land at a spaceport to change ships, and you'd turn around and I'll be gone. That's the way it was six years ago, with the human and Patrukan survivors." Her face reflected her sorrow. "There is so much pain and suffering in the galaxy."

"But I need you even if I'm healthy," I said. "I love you, damn it!"

"And I love you," she said. "Today. But tomorrow?" She shrugged helplessly.

The ship touched down.

"You loved each of them, didn't you?" I asked.

"I don't know," she said. "I would give everything I have to remember."

"You'll forget me too, won't you?"

She put her arms around my neck and kissed me. "Don't think about it."

Then she turned and began walking away. The pilot approached me and picked up my gear.

"What the hell was *that*?" he asked, jerking a thumb in Rebecca's direction—and I realized that he saw her as she truly was, that she was linked only to me.

"What did it look like to you?" I replied.

He shook his head. "Like nothing I've ever seen before."

✧   ✧   ✧

It took me five days to get back to Earth. The medics at the hospital were amazed that I'd healed so quickly, and that all signs of infection were gone. I let them think it was a miracle, and in a way it was. I didn't care; all I cared about was getting her back.

I quit my job at OceanPort and hired on with the police department. They stuck me behind a desk for a few months, until my limp disappeared, but yesterday I finally got transferred to the vice squad.

There's a major drug deal going down tonight: alphanella seeds from somewhere out in the Albion Cluster, ten times as powerful as heroin. We'll be mounting a raid in about four hours. The buyers and sellers both figure to have plenty of muscle standing guard, and it's likely to get pretty hairy.

I hope so.

I've already locked my weapons away.

A Time to Kill

by S. Andrew Swann

Marine Lieutenant David Abrams was a sniper with the 3rd Force Reconnaissance Company. He had the highest operational success rate of any U.S. soldier in the Iranian theater, and coalition-wide there was only a single Scotsman with the SAS who had a better record.

And, right now, he was curled up on the floor in a dank cell somewhere in western Jerusalem where the only light came from a small opening high on one wall.

Occasionally he would cough up a mouthful of blood and phlegm from where the militia guards had battered in the left side of his chest. He was lucky to be alive; the ceramic insert in his Kevlar vest had probably kept the blows from being immediately fatal.

They had beat him, stripped him naked, and thrown him in this cell wearing only his dog tags. They had his rifle, of course. And they had the gadget.

What was left of the gadget anyway; he had heard the casing shatter when the guards fell on him. The scientists had warned him that breaching the containment isolating the strange quantum mechanism meant it would collapse into the nonspace from which it was formed . . .

No going back even if his captors meant to spare him.

He was long past going back anyway.

He coughed up more bloody phlegm, wondering exactly how he would be executed.

Light from the hallway blinded him as the door opened. David blinked up at a rough silhouette and wondered if this would be his executioner.

David's visitor spoke in a rough, almost unintelligible accent. "You speak Hebrew?"

David laughed at the incongruity.

His visitor continued in Hebrew. "Do you understand me? Do you know why you're in this cell?"

"Waiting for you to kill me."

"Do you have any conception of what you've done?"

David looked into the shadowed face and tried to see an expression. He felt dizzy. *Probably blood loss.* "One bullet, I thought. One bullet and the gadget and there could be peace . . ."

"Peace?" his captor spat, as if it was the only word he could understand.

"Lieutenant Abrams, how would you like to be the man who ends this war?"

The man asking him the question was the secretary of defense of the United States.

It was the third week of the thrust toward Tehran, and David had been called back to the States by orders signed by the president herself.

Now he sat in meeting room, deep in the bowels of an unnamed DARPA campus in the Nevada desert. He faced the chairman of the Joint Chiefs, the secretary, and a trio of scientists.

"What do you want me to do, sir?"

The secretary handed David a thick briefing book. "This is your target."

David opened the folder and saw a familiar bearded face. He looked up at the secretary. "But he's already dead."

The intel was perfect. The gadget dropped behind some sand dunes in the Afghan desert, two thousand yards from his target. It was frigid night, and the gadget was a weird weight on his back, pulling him like a gyroscope.

David staggered from the sudden change in orientation. Moments ago he had been standing on the concrete floor of an empty hangar in the DARPA complex. His feet now sank into sand, and he had the adrenaline shock of realizing that he was alone, in enemy territory.

He froze, praying his sudden appearance had gone unnoticed. It had; the desert night was quiet around him. After getting his bearings, he carefully lowered himself to his stomach and crawled with his weapon to just within sight of the impromptu camp. He brought his weapon to bear and looked through the scope, into the open tent.

The reality of what had happened didn't strike him until he saw Osama bin Laden's face in his crosshairs, laughing at something the Saudi prince with him was saying.

It wasn't until that moment that David truly believed what the scientists had told him. He really was in the Afghan desert in the year 1999. He really was here before 9/11, before the war in Afghanistan, before the invasion of Iraq. Before an unmanned drone invaded Iranian airspace to take Osama bin Laden out with a GPS-guided missile and spark the war with Iran.

In the words of the chairman of the Joint Chiefs, "The gadget gives us the opportunity to revise that particular decision and eliminate OBL at a place chosen to be of maximum advantage to the United States and our allies."

For the first time in his career as a sniper, David's hand shook.

But only after he had pulled the trigger and OBL's laughing face melted into a red mist.

The shot echoed through the desert, followed by the popcorn sound of automatic weapons fire, interspersed with the occasional shout of Arabic.

He managed to press the red button that would take him back to the DARPA testing fields, a few milliseconds later than when he left.

Of all the consequences of eliminating OBL from the historical equation, David hadn't thought of the DARPA complex itself. Somehow, an irrational part of his brain half expected to see the scientists, the chairman, and the secretary all there to greet him and to tell him what the last decade had wrought.

At first he thought that the gadget had dropped him in the wrong place and time, but his GPS locator placed him in the right area in Nevada. And the right time, a couple of seconds after he left.

But the DARPA complex was gone, and in its place was a sand-swept airstrip and a couple of dilapidated buildings that hadn't seen use since the Sixties.

"I guess the project started after 1999 . . . "

David shook his head, a little mystified why killing bin Laden would prevent development of the gadget. But it began him thinking about other consequences.

No DARPA project and he never would have gone on the mission to hit OBL. That meant there was another David Abrams out here somewhere. Someone with his name, his face, but who had a completely different history since 1999. Would he have joined the marines if 9/11 never happened? Was there any part of his life left?

David was prepared to die for his country, but somehow, this was worse.

He had to walk to the nearest town, carrying his weapon, preparing to be challenged at any moment by MPs or civilian police. He didn't know what would happen if he was picked up. He wasn't AWOL, but the only orders he had were signed by someone who might not even be president now.

He made it to a small diner, by the side of the road.

David always kept a few twenties in a pocket sewn under his vest. Never knew when American currency would come in handy. Good thing too. He was hungry.

He pushed his way into the near-empty diner.

The man behind the counter looked up and stared. "Good Lord, where'd you come from?"

David, shook his head. "Long story. Can I get something to eat?"

"Sure." The man waved away his twenty. "Your money's no good here." He turned around and called out, "Sarah, get out our best steak dinner, got a serviceman here."

David took a seat at one of the bar stools, fighting the weird gyroscope of the gadget. It was awkward, but he didn't want to set down a one-of-a-kind hundred-billion-dollar piece of equipment.

The man looked at him. "You're not the National Guard out of Vegas?" He looked a little surprised.

"No, Marines. Third Force Reconnaissance Company, out of Mobile."

"Uh huh . . . just got a truckload of National Guard, two days ago, heading for Ground Zero. That where you going?"

David shook his head, unsure of what the man had just said.

Ground Zero?

He must have taken silence as assent. "Thought so. I been telling everyone that there had to be some of those rag-head bastards running around here. How the hell else could they get a nuke into Vegas. You take a few out for me, huh?"

David could only nod.

A steaming T-bone slid in front of him.

"On the house. Anyone who puts his life on the line for his country eats free here."

"Thanks." David looked at the meal. A nuke in Vegas? How the hell could . . . Taking out OBL should have been a death blow to al Qaeda.

David looked up and saw a TV, tuned to CNN.

"Can you turn that up?"

"Sure."

David ate mechanically in silence as he listened to what a balls-up failure his mission had been.

It wasn't just Vegas.

It was Vegas, New Orleans, and Chicago. The nukes were from Iran. At least that was the excuse for leveling Tehran and a dozen other cities. And Saddam had plowed into Iran, lobbing chemical shells, with tacit approval of the U.S. Casualty figures were reaching two million. Ten times the war David had left.

Not counting the ones in the States.

No one had seen the attacks coming. Just like 9/11. But it was 9/11 with a decade more planning in the shadows of the Middle East.

The first time he saw the gadget, it was hard to believe they wanted to send something so fragile looking on a military mission. It didn't look like it, but it was the result of an effort that made the Manhattan Project look like a couple of kids working in their dad's garage.

A cube of electronics connected to a metal framework holding a sphere that resembled a silver Christmas ornament the size of a bowling ball. It would fit into a canvas envelope that would strap to David's back instead of a normal pack.

"This is really a time machine?"

"Yes, it is," said one of the scientists.

"And it can go anywhere?" David asked.

"With some limits."

"What limits?"

"The coordinates where the device coalesces cannot cooccupy a point where the probability wave has—"

"In English?" David asked.

The scientist paused, taking a moment to phrase his explanation. "Any one device can't go to a point in time between any two points it has already traveled to."

The decade between OBL's corpse falling in the Afghan desert and an Islamic nuke exploding in Vegas was now inaccessible to the gadget. But the results were so catastrophic, David had no choice but to try to fix what he had done.

But there were only so many bullets, and he had to choose wisely.

Western presence in Saudi Arabia was one of the main driving factors behind OBL and his followers. If the U.S. hadn't come to drive Saddam out of Kuwait, they would lose their focus. The U.S. would not become involved in what was really a regional conflict.

So, if Iraq never invaded Kuwait . . .

David jumped a decade before his assassination of OBL, to Baghdad in 1989. And this time it was Saddam's face that evaporated in his crosshairs.

He knew the DARPA complex would not be there. And he knew his appearance would cause alarm, especially if he had achieved his goal and there was no longer an ongoing war. So this time he appeared after nightfall, inside a library in his hometown.

He had night-vision equipment, so he was able to navigate through the green monochrome library, to the periodicals.

He picked up a newspaper and held his breath.

"Oh God. What did I do?"

He tore through more newspapers, magazines, and found the ugly history. An Iraqi civil war in the nineties, ignored by the U.S., eventually leading to an Iran-dominated Shiite theocracy that extended from Afghanistan to the Gulf; one that ignored Kuwait, and chose to invade the Saudi peninsula.

The U.S. had no choice but to repel that aggression. Now, not only was the U.S. footprint on Saudi soil, M1–Abrams tanks were rolling through Mecca.

The level of terrorism in the U.S. over the past twenty years made the Gaza Strip look like a frat party. Muslims were being herded into camps like the Japanese during WWII. Shiite clerics were disappearing into a black hole somewhere. Mosques were completely shut down, or being operated with government observers.

And over the past ten years, the casualty count rivaled that of the nuke attack.

Iran was the problem; really, the Islamic revolution there.

If there wasn't a dictator to revolt against. If a power shift happened in time to give the clerics and the students some hope that they'd have a voice in the government without a revolution. If the U.S. wasn't in a position to give the shah sanctuary and become the Great Satan.

By 1976, the shah was going to die soon anyway.

There's a law of unintended consequences . . .

The library was gone. David appeared in a lot of broken weed-shot asphalt. His old neighborhood was unrecognizable. Buildings abandoned, burnt out, boarded up, and wrapped in graffiti. The sounds of gunfire and sirens echoed in the distance.

The GPS couldn't lock on any satellites. As if they weren't there anymore.

But he knew the area. He recognized the Shell station that had been there since he'd been a kid. It was boarded up too, and spray-painted over the plywood were the words "No Gas."

David shook his head and started looking for a newspaper.

He didn't stay long enough to discover all the details, but he got enough to understand how this history went wrong. No Iranian Revolution and no hostage crisis. Jimmy Carter might have a second term. Alter the U.S. attitude to the Soviets and the U.S.S.R. puts a little more effort into their push into Afghanistan. The Russians suffer an even worse military catastrophe—after cutting a swath of destruction through an Iran weakened by a succession of military coups.

Lebanon, Iran, Afghanistan, Iraq, Chechnya—a cauldron of civil wars spread out from the Russian invasion. The Soviet Union cracked apart, but not peacefully. The Israelis now occupied Sinai, all of Lebanon, part of Jordan. They were forcefully expelling the entire Palestinian population.

No, the U.S. wasn't at war. But a third of the world was, and the U.S. was spiraling into a depression.

✧   ✧   ✧

No, the root of it was the use of terror as a political tool. If it wasn't for the PLO, and Munich, things might have been different.

The next bullet was for Arafat in 1968.

Unintended consequences . . .

Palestinian refugees, without even a vague hope of repatriation, begin revolting against the Arab governments whose land they sit on. The weak Arab governments don't allow them a place in their countries. Eventually, like a malignant pearl, a fascist pan-Arab state grows around the violence of the refugee camps.

The next Arab-Israeli war is fought with nukes.

No Nasser, no Suez War, no Six-Day War. No Israeli occupation. In 1955 the Egyptian leader is cut down by David's bullet . . .

Over half a century is too much history to glean from a newspaper, but bombs were going off in Tel Aviv, and Damascus. UN forces were in the Sinai and Jordan, and a communist regime in Syria was refusing to dismantle its nuclear program.

If the British didn't abandon control of Palestine too early . . .

If there wasn't a Holocaust or WWII . . .

If the Ottoman Empire never fell . . .

If there wasn't the split between Sunni and Shiite . . .

If . . .

"Peace," his captor spat, as if it was the only word he could understand. The guard repeated, "Who are you? Why did you do this?"

"My name is Lieutenant David Abrams, United States Marine Corps Third Force Reconnaissance Company, Serial Number . . ." David repeated the mantra in English.

"Bah. Nonsense." The man threw him down and David coughed up more blood. "The man has lost his sanity."

A third man ran into the cell. "Josephus! The Romans are here for him. What should we do?"

Josephus rubbed the bridge of his nose and a grave expression shadowed his face, as if he could see the centuries of violence awaiting them all.

"Josephus?"

"We give them what they want. We give them the man and his unearthly tools, and hope the blood of Pilate's assassin will be enough to keep them from slaughtering us all."

Josephus looked down at David, who had lapsed into unconsciousness. "Peace?" He spat the word like a curse. "You'll have yours in the grave, like everyone else."

Local Boy Makes Good

by Ray Tabler

"Somethin' smells," one of the thousand or so shock troopers milling about in the staging area said, staring straight at me. That was unfair. I'd just had a shower. Most everybody did shower right before an assault, no telling when you'd get the next chance to clean up. Days, weeks later? You never could tell.

"Just ignore him, Danny," Jenny muttered. She shot him a black look. "Stupid bastard."

Jenny didn't need to worry. This wasn't my first assault. I admit I was wound up pretty tight. Everybody was. Needed to be, to get through the chaos we were about to wade into. But, I wasn't set on a hair trigger the way I was the first two or three times.

Either this little guy was too stupid to figure out that starting a brawl in the staging area would get us all thrown in the brig, or he was smart enough to figure out that starting a brawl in the staging area would get us all thrown in the brig. He might get injured in the confusion, but he wouldn't be dropping into a fire-laced hell with the rest of the division. I looked down at the guy with the sensitive nose, flashed him a very toothy smile, and marched on with the rest of the team. The sour expression on his ugly face was a tasty treat I savored all the way across the hanger deck to our assigned drop carrier.

"Damn!" Pete complained when Sarge led us up to a scorch-marked and rust-stained old tub with the unlikely nickname *Yolanda Sue* stenciled on her grubby side, just forward of the official alphanumeric vessel designation. Nothing smaller than a frigate is supposed to have an actual name. It was one of those rules that generally got ignored after a couple of years into the war. Yolanda must have been some dead hero. You'd see that a lot. There were plenty to choose from.

"What's your problem, Kezelsky?" Sarge bellowed.

"Another sardine can, Sarge. Can't the navy spare a decent transport for us?"

Sarge rewarded Pete with a withering glare. "I'll be sure to pass that question along the next time I have lunch with the fleet admiral. Until then, get your smelly goon asses on that dropper! This is the one we're supposed to be in. It's almost showtime and *all* of these tubs are goin' to the same place! Move!"

We moved. Sarge is pretty tough for a little guy. I think I could probably take him in a one-on-one fight, but I'd end up with important pieces missing.

Pete wasn't the only one disappointed with the drop carrier. It was quite a squeeze getting all twenty-five of us into the cargo bay of the *Yolanda Sue*, DC24569 Navy designation. Sarge ordered us all to exhale and then slammed the ramp closed before anybody thought to breathe again. Sarge had a bit of free space around him at the forward end of the bay, next to the ladder up to the control deck. Everyone else, goons and little guys were jammed in so tight it reminded me of a crude joke I'd heard back in high school.

"What's so funny, Danny?" Jenny asked. Being a little guy, she could sit on one of the benches.

"Nothing." I shook my head. That was about all I could move without poking a teammate. I was sitting on the deck with my knees tucked under my chin, back up against the port-side bulkhead and my arm brushing the now vertical surface of the ramp/hatch. That meant I'd be first out once the *Yolanda Sue* skidded in, assuming she got that far. I wasn't overly concerned. It wasn't the first time.

"Danny's always smiling. Haven't you noticed?" Pete teased from the same position against the starboard bulkhead. Our combat kits were between us; lumpy with all of the toys we'd soon be playing with.

"I have, actually," Jenny confided to Pete in a loud whisper. "I don't think it's normal, if you know what I mean."

I wagged my head back and forth with a foolish grin. "Ah, duh, doyh, doyh!"

"Can that chatter, back aft there!" Sarge was on the horn, probably letting the lieutenant know we were good to go. He hung up after a minute and yelled up the ladder. "Yo. Up topside, we're all secure down here."

A swabbie stuck his head through the forward hatch to make sure we'd shut the ramp. Then he got a look at us and went forward. We could all hear him talking to the bosun's mate in charge of the dropper. The word *goons* was clear enough. Shortly, the mate appeared in the hatchway. She took a good long look at us.

The mate looked like a female version of Sarge, if you can picture that. To her credit, she may not have been pissed about being tasked with dropping a goon unit simply because we were goons. The problem was that we goons don't drop anywhere but the hottest LZs, and that could seriously shorten her life expectancy.

The mate and Sarge glowered at each other for a few seconds, and then she hustled back up to the control deck and clanged the hatch shut behind her. Sarge watched her go and shrugged. Orders were orders and grunts were grunts, goons or little guys.

A couple of minutes later we could hear the dropper's engines powering up. A few bumps as the tub skidded along the deck, and then we were outside the ship.

The bosun's mate came over the loudspeaker. "ETA, thirty-seven minutes."

Pete muttered another curse about the sardine can as he tried to get a bit more comfortable. The folded-up bench seat must have been digging into his back. Its port-side equivalent was digging into mine.

Pete had a right to be pissed. The navy did have a fair number of drop carriers designed specifically for us goons. They're nice, big, roomy tubs with seats that I could actually sit on. They usually have friendlier flight crews as well. Trouble is the enemy is smart enough to tell the difference. The Rigelians target the bigger tubs preferentially to minimize the number of goons we can get on the ground; so much for ergonomic design.

I leaned my head back against the cold metal of the portside bulkhead and closed my eyes.

"How can you do that, just fall asleep anywhere, anytime?" Jenny asked shaking her head.

"It's a goon thing," I teased.

"No, it's not," Pete commented sourly. As usual, Pete hadn't slept a wink the last two nights before the assault.

The *Yolanda Sue* pitched suddenly, engines vibrating unevenly. Shrapnel pattered the hull armor like hail. One of the other droppers must have been hit.

"Lucky shot for as far up as we must be yet," I said.

"The lieutenant said this one's well defended. The Rigies want to hold on to it," Jenny speculated. "They must be pitching a lot of plasma into orbit."

The lieutenant said a lot of things. You learned to filter out the parts that didn't have to do with the job at hand, like the name of the mudball the *Yolanda Sue* was hurtling towards. Nobody but a Rigie could pronounce it anyway. Besides, what difference does a name make?

Well, it *can* make a lot of difference. The swabbies topside sure seemed to feel a lot better about riding *Yolanda Sue* down into hell than DC24569. The Human Worlds Alliance calls us an Enhanced Capabilities Tactical Unit. That's what you see in the news and hear on the 3-D. In practice, people call us goons. We call ourselves goons. We call everybody else little guys. As long as we call each other by these convenient labels, we can all pretend that we're all humans, which, by strict definition, we goons aren't. So, now you see the problem.

We all *think* of ourselves as humans, and maybe that's all that counts. It's worked so far, and will probably hold up for the duration. After the war's over, we'll just have to see.

The tub pitched and dodged more and more as we got lower. Some guys bitched about not being issued pressure suits in case the tub got holed. The truth is a suit won't do you any good. I've seen a couple of droppers that took plasma hits. There wasn't enough left of the whole damned tub to fill a pressure suit. And those clumsy suits just get in your way once the ramp drops.

"There's the light," Sarge warned. The amber bar above the ramp flashed slowly. It was hard to hear him. The atmosphere was getting thick, wailing like an angry ghost on the hull. The amber light flashed on and off faster and *Yolanda Sue*'s main gun began to speak. It made the hull ring like a bell.

"ETA, sixty seconds." The bosun's calm voice over the speaker sounded like she was piloting a commuter shuttle from Chicago to St. Louis. The flashing amber light turned into a flashing green light.

"When the ramp drops, haul ass! Spread out, stay low, and maintain your intervals!" Sarge had to yell over the racket. We'd heard it I don't know how many times before, and he'd said it many more than that. Didn't matter. He had to say it, and we felt better for hearing it.

Pete muttered a prayer, kissed his St. Stanislaus medal, and tucked it inside his shirt. Jenny caught my eye and winked. I gave her a thumbs-up and got a good grip on my combat kit bag.

"Brace for landing," the bosun announced.

The ghost's wail changed to a deafening rumble punctuated with bone-jarring thumps.

"I think we're coming in a little hot?" I screamed into Jenny's ear.

"Naaah! This is the way the swabbies always land these tubs," Jenny mimed steering.

We *were* coming in hot. Tubs that didn't were just ordering a plasma breakfast. Then, with a final skewing to port, *Yolanda Sue* shuddered to a stop. The ramp flew open.

"Go! Go! Go! Go! Go!" Sarge thundered in the sudden silence.

I rolled out, literally. I couldn't stand up in the dropper, and standing up isn't something you want to do coming out the rear of an assault craft. I crawled at least thirty meters on my hands and knees as fast as I possibly could, which is pretty damned fast. Once the dropper is down and the payload is out it's no longer a worthwhile target. It's done its job and the deployed assault team is the greater danger. But, psychologically, it'll draw a large percentage of the enemy's fire. It's a healthy thing to get far away from it fast.

We were in a muddy field; a muddy field planted in a crop that looked a lot like purplish orange soybeans. I'd marched past enough soybean fields at the training base west of Saginaw to know what they looked like, and I would have preferred something taller like corn or even wheat. But alien soybeans were all we had. *Yolanda Sue* had plowed an ugly furrow across the land; a long, earthen arrow pointed straight at our objective.

The compound was about one hundred meters away. The dropper had brought us almost to the edge of the bean field, where the dead ground stretched to the high, razor-wire fence. Guard towers stood at each of the five corners of the layout. Rigelians are big on pentagons. Yep, this was the place.

The dropper's main gun fired again, making the air between it and the compound shimmer with the passage of the plasma bolt. The roof of the nearest guard tower seemed to blow away in a high wind. I could see other tubs skidded, or skidding, at other points around the objective. They were firing too. The Rigelians were returning fire.

"Advance by squads! Second squad, go!" Sarge's voice cut through the noise like a meat cleaver. It was time to earn my pay.

Along with the rest of second squad, I rose and dashed forward in a crouching run, firing assault rifles as we went. I wasn't trying to hit anything, just keep the Rigies' minds off of their aim. When I figured I'd gone far enough, I found some cover and dove for it. I might be ten feet tall, but I'm not bulletproof.

That cover turned out to be an agricultural robot that had the great misfortune to be tending purplish orange soybeans that particular morning. It was a big, slab-sided, gray ovoid that normally moved about on several dozen short, stout legs so it could gingerly step between the plants. The robot's AI must have dropped into self-preservation mode and directed it toward the supposed safety of the compound. A stray plasma bolt had vaporized its control module, instantly converting the robot to five or six tons of scrap metal and carbon fiber composite.

A second or two after I set my back against the lee of the robot, Pete dropped down next to me, breathing hard and cursing like he'd slammed his thumb in a door. Then Jenny jumped in between us. Damn, but she could run fast for a little guy.

"Nice place you boys have got here. How's the rent?"

Three bolts from a heavy plasma gun slammed into the other side of the robot in quick succession.

"Stiff!" I replied.

"Location, location, location," Pete commented. Greasy black smoke started pouring from vents on the top of our robot.

"Jenny, you're hit," I pointed at drippy line of red on her upper arm.

She looked at it and giggled. "I gouged my arm on the fire extinguisher on the way out of the tub."

Pete and I started laughing, too. Who knows how much lead and plasma zipping about, and Jenny had injured herself on a piece of our own safety equipment.

"Second squad, cover fire." Sarge sounded tinny and distant in my earphone. "First squad, advance!"

Jenny, Pete, and I leaned around or over the dead robot and hosed lead at the compound. *Yolanda Sue*'s gun was firing more frequently now that her thrusters were powered down and the entire output of her engine was dedicated to generating ballistic plasma. First squad swept by us at a desperate sprint and flopped down to fire prone almost at the fence line.

"Here it comes," Pete lamented.

"Second squad, breach the wire!" Sarge ordered into our earpieces.

Training is that thing that delays the perfectly natural resistance to leaving cover in a firefight until you're three steps out, screaming like a madman. Then it's too late to turn back. Momentum suffices where courage fails.

Pete and I got to the fence, and I knew without asking that he wanted to cut. You're more exposed that way, standing there severing one strand of razor wire after the other, but that's the way he is. Pete would rather be doing *something,* even a dangerous something, than waiting around for something to happen to him. I dropped to one knee and plinked away at various likely targets while Pete worked his cutter. Jenny ran up, fished a grenade launcher out of my kit bag, and made herself useful by keeping heads down in the nearest guard tower.

The last wire went *ping* and we all rushed into the compound. It's not like we were being heroic, dashing into the thick of the enemy. It just was pretty unhealthy out by the wire, with both sides firing through it.

Rigelians tend to build things with five sides, and cluster their structures in threes. Nobody's figured out exactly why yet, but then we haven't had much of a chance for cultural exchange since first contact. And that's another thing; most people don't even realize they're not from Rigel. Rigel happened to be where humans first encountered them. I don't have to remind you how that went. The war was well underway by the time we found out different. Faced with the choice of calling them what they call themselves, which nobody can pronounce, or some form of the stellar catalog number of the star their home planet actually orbits, we stuck with Rigelians. Why not? Rodriguez, in first squad, calls *me* a gringo, which I'm pretty sure I'm not.

If this had been a normal assault, one of us would have blasted a small hole in the wall of the nearest building and another would have tossed a grenade in, to insure a friendly reception as the old saying goes. This time was different. Any one of these buildings might've held what we'd come to find. So, we had to do it the hard way.

Sarge marshaled us into the lee of big concrete shed, and laid out the general plan. He or the lieutenant couldn't hope to conduct a thorough and systematic sweep and clear operation. There was too much chance the Rigies would decide to destroy what we were after. We had to strike hard and keep moving fast, until the objective was secured. Troops were pouring in through the breach in the wire behind us, but, as usual, it was goons to the front.

There was a momentary lull in the firing as something big blew up to the south. A tall cloud rose that way, above the Rigie city twenty kilometers away where the main assault was happening. It might have been the city's fusion plant going up or maybe one of our ships crashed. There was no way to tell from where we were. We never did find out. We never do.

Pete, Jenny, and I advanced farther into the compound, two moving while the third covered. Normally, two cover while the third cautiously advances. We called it our hurry-up offense, and it's dangerous as hell. But, we were running short on time and playing it safe just isn't in the job description. Our luck ran short, too, about three hundred meters in from the wire.

Jenny and Pete ran up to an ugly gray building that might have been a warehouse and dashed around the corner. I was about to jump up and follow, when they came back around the corner and threw themselves into an open doorway. Having seen this type of behavior before, I wasn't at all surprised to see five Rigies come boiling around the corner about a femtosecond later.

I opened up on full auto and two of the Rigies went down. One of the injured Rigies was good and dead, but the other made it to cover with his buddies. He'd only been hit maybe a couple of times, and that's not near enough to stop a Rigie.

I would have just loved to stick around and deal with this group of Rigies, but we were on a tight schedule. Sarge ordered forward a light plasma gun at the double quick. The plasma gun, with help from a squad of little guys, backed the three Rigies into a corner. While they were pinned down, we goons skirted around and pressed on into the compound.

There wasn't any real chance that those three Rigies would surrender. The very concept of surrender was new to them when the war started. Some little guy, a clerk in an intelligence unit, told me once they even borrowed our word for it.

Basically, the Rigies are big and mean and they never give up. That, in itself, wouldn't mean that they will win the war. The trouble is that the Rigies and the human race happen to be pretty evenly matched in resources and technology. The quantity and quality of ships and weapons are about equal. So, ironically, the edge the Rigelians have in physical strength and ferocity made a real difference in our interstellar war. For a while, they were kicking our butts. The human race needed some big, tough, mean bastards of their own.

The firefight behind us tipped off the Rigies where we were, so Pete, Jenny, and I worked our way wide to the right and continued the advance. The intensity of plasma bolts and rifle fire doubled and then doubled again. The Rigies were feeding troops into the firefight we'd touched off. This, we reasoned, would have the effect of pulling them away from the rest of the place. We decided to take advantage of the situation and sprinted along.

Pete and I pulled ahead of Jenny by a dozen meters or so. Any other time one of us would have picked Jenny up and carried her. But we needed both hands free, because who knew what could come boiling around the next corner.

It might seem silly to have little guys like Jenny in our unit at all. But, they're there to make sure we goons feel a personal connection to actual factual human beings and the human race in general. It's the same logic as having us raised by normal foster families. I think it worked. I have a soft spot in my goon heart for Jenny, or at least some impure thoughts.

Pete and I didn't even need to talk. We each could tell what the other was thinking. That's because we've been buddies so long, even before basic training. Pete grew up two blocks east of me, on Lakeshore Boulevard. I can close my eyes and imagine the way over to his house from mine, right past that big, rusty old twentieth-century tank on a concrete pad outside the library.

I think I actually smelled something different first. I stopped short of a right-hand jog in the "road" and carefully peeked around a peeling concrete wall. Ten meters away was a young Rigie standing guard in front of a door. He was alone. At that moment, I *knew* that we'd found what we'd come to get.

This guy was obviously a low-status individual. Rigies don't have a firm, organized system of rank. Leadership and status are based on a combination of fighting prowess, clan ties, and seniority. Leadership can change day to day, even hour to hour. It sounds chaotic and inefficient as hell, but let me tell you, it can work pretty damned good for them. With humans inside the wire, every warrior would charge for the sound of the guns. The fact that they left one behind, even this sad puppy, meant that there was a high-value item behind that door.

Without a moment's hesitation, I emptied a clip into the guard's blue midsection. Pete and I sprinted toward the door.

The brainstorm that eventually resulted in us goons sprang from the human race's pressing need to match, or better yet exceed, the Rigelians in physical, one-on-one combat. From what I've heard, the initial attempts at genetic modification experiments ranged from disappointing to truly horrific. It turns out that it's pretty tough to do in one generation what natural selection took maybe a million years to accomplish. They were just about ready to give up when they found the answer.

I hugged the wall on one side of the door. "Squad Two to Six. Squad Two to Six. Over," I whispered into my mike.

"Squad Two. Six. Go," Sarge roared back in my ear, making himself heard over plasma fire in the background.

"Found the cheese. Repeat, found the cheese. Coordinates charlie delta four niner." I read the glowing alphanumeric from my face shield display. "Repeat, charlie delta four niner."

"Copy. Cheese at charlie delta four niner. Hold position. Cavalry coming." Sarge killed the transmission.

Knowing Sarge, I took "hold position" to mean "secure the position." So, Pete kicked the door open and I rushed in, keeping me low and my weapon ready. There was a short corridor that opened up into a large room with a high ceiling. The smell I'd whiffed outside hit me like a brick wall. It was the smell of people who hadn't had anything close to a bath in two or three decades.

There were maybe three hundred of them sitting or lying on the bare concrete floor. This was a warehouse of some kind, not a barracks. The Rigies must have herded them in here on the spur of the moment to keep them from getting in the way, or more probably to make it easier to kill them all quickly.

This was the first batch of humans that the Rigelians had captured, way back at the start of the war. A long time ago there had been a lot more of them. I could only imagine what kind of holy hell these people had been living for decades, and, as it turned out, my imagination came up well short of reality. Freeing them was a big part of the reason we were assaulting this particular mud ball.

In fact, I guess you could say that these people were a big part of the reason that we goons exist. The initial justification for the war was to retrieve them, before we figured out that the Rigies were going to try to wipe us *all* out whether we fought back or not. So we needed to be better at fighting, which led humans to develop goons by genetic modification, which didn't work. Then it dawned on some bright boy that instead of trying to rush Mother Nature through a million years of evolution overnight to make big, mean soldiers we could just use some ready-made DNA that was lying around, if slightly scorched. Even at that point in time, cloning was a well-established technology.

The prisoners were staring at Pete and me. Of course they'd never seen a goon before and didn't know what to make of us. But we were wearing a uniform that was pretty close to what they'd worn a long, terror-filled time ago.

Then Jenny shoved her way past us. The people in the room saw her and slowly realized that she was undeniably human, and armed to the teeth. You could see it in their eyes. They were telling themselves that this was some kind of cruel joke or trick. They were trying to beat down the hope that was rising up inside of them.

Jenny looked at them, grinned a wide grin, and said, "Remain calm. We're from the government, and we're here to help you."

There was a long pause, and then a woman in the back laughed nervously at the old, old joke. Then they were all laughing, shouting, weeping, staggering forward to touch us and make sure we were real.

Outside I could hear Sarge setting up a perimeter around the place.

I turned to see one prisoner standing next to me. Unlike the others, he was calm. His hair was white as ashes. He was missing his right eye and his left arm ended in a ragged stump just below the elbow. His remaining eye burned with an icy, green fire.

He slowly reached up and tapped my name tag: Toscanelli. "Funny." He spoke in a hoarse whisper that may have had something to do with the scars on his throat. "You don't look Italian."

"Yeah, a lot of people tell me that."

"I'll bet they do."

"I'm adopted."

"Thought you might be." He paused, weighing my human uniform against my electric blue skin. "As a matter of fact, you look more like you're from Rigel."

"Well, my DNA might be from Rigel." I smiled, showing all three rows of razor-sharp, pearly white teeth. "But *I'm* from Cleveland."

The Old Woman in the Young Woman

by Gene Wolfe

He had been walking all day. Twice the wandering trails he followed had led him into ruined towns; in each case he had halted and spent an hour or so poking through such rubbish as nature had not yet buried. In neither case had he found anything worth keeping. Knives that would not rust were found in ruined towns, sometimes. Or so some said. Long Tom, who would have liked one, had never found one or even seen one.

To the people who had lived in those towns, he had given not a moment's thought. The roofs of their houses had fallen, and the walls were falling. The broad, black pavements were crumbling. The people who had made them had died long before he was born. He had never met anyone who had spoken to one of them, and he never would.

His belly was empty when he came to the village. The little buckskin pack in which he sometimes stored food held only an old pair of stockings. The slender rifle he bore was heavy on his shoulder, its weight reminding him over and over again that he had not had a

131

decent shot all day. That rifle would no longer feed a cartridge when he pulled its lever down, but he rarely needed a quick second shot.

Up the hill along a path that was a little too wide and clearly marked to be a game trail. Through blackberry brambles on which not one berry was ripe.

Then, the crest of the hill.

Long Tom put down his rifle, setting its curved brass buttplate almost carefully beside his right moccasin, and looked down at the tiny village in the valley. Six cabins, he thought, or it could be seven. Smoke rising from three chimneys. The cabins looked too poor to offer much comfort to a traveler. Too poor, although one was a trifle bigger than the rest and had an outbuilding. A little barn, or perhaps a woodshed.

Inside that larger cabin, young Emmy sat at old Miz Emily's bedside, listening. Listening, but the words came slowly, punctuated with much labored breathing. The wide spaces between those words had room for a great deal of dreaming, and Emmy was a practiced dreamer. Someday—some happy day very soon—Miz Emily would be close to young again. Miz Emily would rise from her bed and once more do all the things she now did only in her stories. She would bake bread, can, and heal.

"A brain," Miz Emily told Emmy, "spiles faster 'n a fish." She shut her eyes, and the breath whistled through her toothless old mouth. "Brain's the worst part of a man . . . Or a woman, either . . . You can't hardly never save it."

Emmy nodded, rapt.

"Ol' Sheller Shapcott . . . He wasn't hardly cold. I shot in my heart-get-up . . . Best I had. His heart . . . She galloped again . . . You see, Emmy?"

Emmy nodded as before.

"Never moved . . . Never spoke. Horse's alive, only nobody riding."

Still nodding, Emmy cocked her head, conscious of a new sound. Someone was tapping on the front door. She rose.

A faint smile touched Miz Emily's lips. "Somebody's sick. You see who."

Emmy hurried away.

Outside, Long Tom, who had been knocking with his knuckles, had changed to the handle of his knife. He was about to resume knocking when the door swung back.

The girl was young and small, with the sort of plain, smooth face that promises beauty (although not prettiness) to come. Her blue eyes widened at the sight of Long Tom, and her small lips formed an O.

Tom removed his cap. "I'm a man that needs a place to stay tonight, ma'am. There's rain comin', which you can feel if you breathe deep. Just a place out of the rain, and a bite to eat, if you can spare. Corn-pone or what you got. Tell your ma?"

"I don't have no ma." The girl's voice was scarcely audible. "Never did."

Long Tom nodded and smiled. "You the lady of the house, ma'am?"

"Miz Emily." The girl reached a decision. "She said let you in." She stood aside.

Long Tom entered, still smiling. "I don't believe we've met proper, ma'am. Tom Bright's my name. Long Tom's what most folks call me. Guess you can see why." He held out his hand.

The girl's touched it; hers was far smaller than his but just as hard, the hand of a girl who scrubbed, cooked, and swept, Tom thought, from kinsee to kaintsee. "I'm Tom Bright," he repeated, " 'cept you can call me anythin' you'd like. Long Tom or whatever."

The girl's hand had closed on his.

"Lazy, mebbe. Lazy's good. There's lots of folks call me that."

At last she smiled, and her smile stirred to life something in him he knew at once would never die.

"Hungered, Tom? Didn't you say you was? Stew for supper tonight, an' I got it on a'ready. Be fit to eat 'fore long. You could sleep by the fire, mebbe? I do, only in Miz Emily's room, you know. Case I got to git her somethin'. We got our own li'l fire in there, an' it's God's own blessin'."

"Your pa won't mind?"

The girl shook her head. "Ain't never had none, Tom. Ain't nobody here 'cept us. Miz Emily an' Emmy. I'll have to show you to Miz Emily, Tom. It's only polite. You come along. We got to see if she's wakeful."

Tom sighed. "If she don't want me, I'll go, Emmy. There won't be no trouble."

"She'll cotton to you," Emmy told him. "It's certain sure. There aplenty for us to be feared of without our bein' feared of you."

Hand-in-hand they walked through the big front room, a lofty room redolent of venison stew. A clean and orderly room that had, somehow, something of the air of the ruined towns. It might, perhaps, have been the high, stained table.

It might also have been the bags of rags, or the three lofty cabinets along one wall, locked cabinets of hardwood black with years, somber and silent.

Emmy motioned him back and opened the door of another room enough to put her head through. "Comp'ny, Miz Emily. Name's Tom Bright an' seems a well-favored man. You want to see him?"

Apparently Miz Emily did; Emmy turned and waved.

Going in, Tom saw the oldest woman he had ever set eye on sitting propped up in bed. Her white hair was almost gone, her cheeks fallen in, and her nose and chin so long they nearly touched. Only the eyes, blue eyes that seemed as young as Emmy's, remained alive in her ruined face.

"Long Tom's what they call me, ma'am." Tom touched his forehead. "I'm headed west, Miz Emily. There's land there that ain't so pizzoned as 'tis 'round here. So I hear tell. The folks is dead, mostly, like here. Only the land's better. So I'm goin' to claim a real good piece for my own."

The aged head nodded the merest fraction of an inch. For an instant, Tom thought he saw the dry lips twitch in what might have been a smile—or almost anything else.

"So I'm jest passin' through," he finished lamely. "I'd slept out in the woods like I done last night, only there's rain in the air, you know. So I seen your place here, all these houses, an' this's the biggest so I thought it'd have more room most likely. I'll work, if you got work to do, or else be gone at sunup. I'll go now, if you say to. Only Emmy said I got to talk to you."

"Goin' to farm, Tom? Know how to?"

Tom nodded. "Yes'm. My pa had a farm, an' me an' Cy, we worked it. Only us, out toward the end, you know. Then Pa passed. Cy, he said we'd split. Only there wasn't enough for it. I want a couple fields an' medders. Enough for a horse an' a milk cow fer sure."

His own eyes had sunk in dream, although he did not know it. "Corn an' a garden, too. Chickens an' mebbe a pig. Got to have a sight of good land for all that."

"Like him, Emmy?" Miz Emily's voice shook. "Can see you do. Wouldn't have brought him to me if you didn't."

Emmy nodded.

"Got a wife, Tom? Girl back home?"

Looking stricken, Tom shook his head.

"Don't let that pretty face fool you, Tom. Emmy's a hard worker."

Tom managed to say, "I know it, ma'am."

"Smart, too. Smart as a whip."

"I . . . I ain't much, ma'am. I ain't much, an' I couldn't—"

Emmy made a tiny noise.

"Well, I ain't." Tom swallowed. "An' you got to take care of your grandma, Emmy. Only I guess I could, mebbe, stay on a bit . . . If you'd have me."

Miz Emily cackled. "She ain't my granddaughter, Tom. She's me."

Tom stared at her, then at Emmy. And found he could not tear his eyes from the latter.

"'Splain, Emmy. I'm that tired."

"There's a man here . . ." Emmy groped for words. "A neighbor, you know. Pen Perry's his name. He found a real pretty bush one time. Had pretty flowers all over it, an' he wanted two. Wanted one for each side of his door."

Rain rattled the cedar shakes of the roof.

"So he dug it up an' split it. I seen that. Seen him hackin' it into two with his hatchet. He planted the halves an' had him two bushes. You know 'bout that, Tom?"

"Sure thing. We done it."

"People can do it, too. 'Cept it's way harder for us."

From the bed, Miz Emily said, "I done it once. Made me a girl folks called Emma. Only she was me, and grown from little bits of me."

Emmy said, "She's a medicine woman, Tom. Miz Emily's a medicine woman."

"Soon's she'd growed big 'nough," Miz Emily continued, "I harvested. Took the eyes and the liver and kidneys. That was what I needed, and I buried the rest proper."

Tom said nothing; he was looking at Emmy.

"You'll be wonderin' how I set my new eyes in once the old was out. There's a lady in Swinton. Miz Pris, they call her. I help her, and she helps me."

"It's her heart this time, Tom. Heart an' lungs, too." Emmy touched her chest. "I'm growin' the new in me now. 'Fore long I'll be big 'nough. Next year, Miz Emily tells."

"It don't seem right," Tom muttered, "puttin' the young woman in the old one."

"Ever'body needs Miz Emily, Tom. There's folks sick all the time, sick er leg broke er shot. They got to have her, an' she's got to have me."

Miz Emily's breath wheezed before she spoke. "Pretty soon I seen I was going to need more, so I done it again. I missed Emma, too, and she'd been a great, great help to me. So I done, and here's Emmy that's been the same. She's a good girl through and through, Long Tom Bright. Don't you never forget it. She's me, too, just like my Emma was. Don't never forget that either."

She coughed. "Emmy . . . Emmy, honey, you come here. I'm going to do something I never done before, Emmy. Going to 'cause I got to. Hold out your sweet hand."

Emmy did, and Miz Emily laid a large key in it. A brass key, green with years. "That what you got's the key to the big cab'net I never did let you into." Miz Emily paused. "You open her up. Top shelf. A-ways in back."

She paused to breathe, the close air of her bedchamber whistling in her nostrils.

"Top shelf," Emmy repeated dutifully.

"In back, Emmy honey. It's a li'l blue bottle. The best medicine I got. Back corner."

She gasped for breath. "Tom. Long Tom. You hear all this?"

"Yes'm."

"You fetch it down for her. I don't want her standing on no chair."

Together they returned to the big front room, shutting the door quietly behind them. "That's her medicine-woman cab'net," Emmy whispered. "I never did open it before. She'd have me go 'way when she got somethin' out. I never did s'pose I'd hold this key."

The antique key turned smoothly in the lock; the highest shelf was high indeed, but not so high that Tom had difficulty in seeing the bottles and boxes that stood on it.

"Li'l blue bottle," Emmy told him. "Back in the corner's what she told. Way in back."

He found it and took it out. "No writin' on this one."

Emmy nodded. "Didn't want nobody that come stealin' to know what was in there, I guess. Them medicines . . . A body can't find 'em no more. Not nowhere."

"Out west, mebbe." Tom spoke mostly to himself. "Ain't so many lookin' out there."

Emmy took the bottle, and they returned to Miz Emily.

"Not so many lookin'," she said. "That's wise. You remember what all you said this day, Tom Bright. You, too, Emmy. Don't forget, nor let him forget."

Emmy nodded silently and returned the key.

"My medicine, Emmy? What I sent you for?"

Emmy handed her the blue bottle. A tear coursed down Emmy's cheek as she did, but neither of them commented on it.

No more did Tom, although he took a half step back.

"I'm weary with talking." Miz Emily coughed. "Only I got to talk more. I'll try to get it over quick."

Lean, blue-veined fingers drew the cork of the blue bottle. "I'm not going to tell you to do your duty, Emmy. You will, I know. Do your duty by Tom or whatever man you find. Do your duty by whatever children you get."

Emmy nodded vigorously. Hearing her stifled sobs, Tom laid his hand on her shoulder.

"There's a-many a man, Tom Bright, that never finds him a good woman. You got one here. Terrible young yet, but she'll get over that. There's no man that's as wise as a wise woman."

Tom nodded. "I've heard."

"She's not. Not yet. You got to be the steady one for now."

"Yes, ma'am."

"Build you a cabin when you've got that land. Make it li'l but solid. Won't be nobody but you to protect it, so it's got to be li'l. When there's more, you can make it bigger."

"Like you said, ma'am. That's the best, I know."

Nodding, as it seemed, wholly to herself. Miz Emily raised the blue bottle to her lips.

Emmy shrieked.

Miz Emily might not have heard her; Tom watched her swallow and fall back among her pillows.

Like a rabbit frozen by the serpent's eye, Tom saw the blue bottle roll slowly to the edge of the bed. The thump as it struck the floor freed him to kneel beside Emmy and—hesitantly, awkwardly—lay his rifle aside and put his arms around her.

So they remained as second after second ticked past, until someone began knocking on the door through which Tom had entered the house.

Emmy rose, wiping her eyes with the heels of both hands. "I'll see," she gasped. "Y-you stay right here."

He did, but listened through the half-open door of the bedchamber.

"*You heard me cry out, Miz Ledbetter.*" The voice was Emmy's.

Tom could not hear the reply.

"She's tooken bad. Real bad. Asked me to fetch her medicine for her, which I done."

A woman's voice murmured, though Tom could not make out the words.

"You wait till she's better, Miz Ledbetter. She wouldn't want nobody to see her like she is now. Didn't want me to, even. Only you're gettin' soaked."

Nodding, Tom went to the bed and picked up Miz Emily's right arm. It was not yet stiff, but there was no pulse. He straightened her legs and crossed her arms on her chest.

When Emmy returned, he said, "She's gone. Reckon you knew 'fore me."

"My heart knowed." Emmy sighed. "I jus' kept sayin' no, no, no inside myself. Only my heart knowed soon's the bottle passed."

"Wasn't till that bottle fell that I did, Emmy." Tom looked for the blue bottle then, but he had kicked it under the bed.

"You didn't know her like me."

"I reckon not."

"I know the folks 'round here, too." Emmy sighed again. "They goin' to say I kilt her, Tom. They been prophesyin' it."

"You didn't."

"Don't matter now." Emmy shrugged. "It's what's said that does the work. Kill me for it, if they can."

"Have to kill me first," Tom told her.

"You sure, Tom?"

He nodded solemnly, and she embraced him, her smooth chestnut hair well below his chin.

When they parted at last he said, "We got to bury her, Emmy. Wouldn't be decent not to."

"Think you can wrap her up an' tie her tight, Tom?"

"Now?"

Emmy nodded. "Won't nobody see us carry her out back, 'cause of the rain. You want to eat 'fore we do it?"

He shook his head.

"Nor me, Tom. I'll feel better when she's been put under proper an' prayed over. Stew'll keep. It ain't but simmerin'. Where's the key?"

They found it among the bedclothes.

"Put it in her hand, Tom. She'd like it. Put it in there an' we'll tie her up."

Rolling the shriveled body in its blankets required no more than a minute. When it was done, Emmy carried in rags he tore to strips.

"Her bandages they was," Emmy murmured. "They're bandagin' her this day."

"She died for you," Tom told her.

"I died for me," Emmy corrected him.

He carried the long bundle like an infant in his arms when they left the house. Emmy, leading the way, bore the too-large spade with which she had dug Miz Emily's small garden that spring.

So it was that they passed through the clearing and into the trees, and at last entered another clearing, a place where no one lived. There, in the rain, Tom built a deep house for the dead woman, and laid her in it while Emmy wept, and heaped the sodden clay upon it.

Together they knelt and prayed aloud, their strong, young voices muted by the rain.

Back in the house that had been Miz Emily's, they hung their clothes before the fire and ate venison stew with home-baked bread. "Like seein' me like this?" Emmy asked.

He nodded, and she said, "Knew you would."

She smiled when her bowl was empty. "Don't have to wash no dishes. Been a long time since I've et an' didn't have to do up afterward. You got anything to take west 'cept your rifle an' what you got in your li'l pack?"

He shook his head.

"Have a look around. You see anything we might need, you take it." She went to the third cabinet, the one Tom knew he would never forget. Its door swung back, and she said, "I'll take from here. Much as I can carry, anyhow. I don't have much else."

"How'd you do that? Git it open?"

"You think I locked it again?" She smiled. "You git dressed, hear? I'll git dressed, too. I see what you're thinkin', Tom, plain as pikestaff. I'm thinkin' the same, only they'll say I kilt her once they learn, an' we ain't got time."

Neither of them was slow, and they got a start of a day and more; but when the little food Tom had carried away—for there had been but little in the larder—was gone, he had to hunt.

Even so, almost a week passed before they heard the distant crack of a rifle and the deathly whisper of the bullet that showered them with twigs and leaves.

Tom ordered Emmy back (a distance that she took as one and a half paces) and waited until he had a clear view of the head and shoulders of their nearest pursuer. His rifle spoke. That man's hands flew to his face, and he fell.

The shrill, cracked voice of an old woman sounded behind him while he was reloading: "You there, Pen Perry? Answer me! Slim Ledbetter? Speak up!"

There was a silence before someone called, "I'm here, Miz Em'ly."

"That man Tom shot—"

The old voice shook, and Tom himself turned back to look at Emmy.

"Through the head, is it?"

"Yes'm."

Another man said, "Ain't cold yet, Miz Em'ly."

"That don't matter. I can't help him. You bury him proper, hear? Get him under and go back where you belong."

There were no more shots. They had walked almost until dark when Tom said, "I been wonderin', Emmy. It ain't—only I hope you'll tell."

"How I talked like her?" Emmy giggled. "I been listenin' to her all my life. Be a shame to me if I couldn't sound the same."

He shook his head. "I seen that right off. 'Bout that blue bottle. You knew what 'twas."

"Not till I handed it over I didn't." The giggle was gone. "When I handed it over, I seen her eyes an' knew."

"Them medicines you got. The shiny li'l knives. I was wonderin' if you know how to use 'em."

" 'Course I do!"

Soon after, her hand found his. "She was me, Tom. An' I'm her. You got to remember it."

Candy-Blossom

By Dave Freer

I was going to run. As soon as he . . . it . . . the THING stopped looking at me. Staring a hole through my *stupid* head with its four eyes. I was going to run like the wind. I shouldn't have come here. Never. I swore to God . . . if I ever got out of here . . .

The thing opened its mouth. The wrong way, like a vertical slash. The inside was watermelon-pink, full of tombstone teeth. Orange tombstones. Glowing even in the moonlight.

"Candy-blossom?" it said. Or that is what I thought it said, anyway. It sounded like one of those wind-chime *magodies* that that *langhaar* by the beach sells. What was the word he used again? Oh, *ja*. Mellifluous. Mellifluous with just a little bit of lost-child despair.

Nothing that looks like a cross between a nightmare and train-smash should speak like that. Not even to an old poacher. My bag of illegal spiny lobster twitched where it lay on the sand.

The creature jumped like a startled rabbit. He pointed the thing in his—hand?—at the bag and backed off. I was happy he was pointing it at the bugs. I didn't know what a set of semi-see-through rods in these modern Day-Glo fashion-design colors did. But something about the thing said "gun."

A spiny lobster stuck out a feeler and went *"eerrrrrk."* A bleddy scary noise in the quiet, if I say it myself. The thing crouched and aimed the gun-goody, waiting. Hey, the bugs could make a sudden move and find out if it was a cigarette vending machine or not. Me, I was out of here.

I tensed myself to make the dash. Just a few seconds and I'd be gone behind that big gray granite boulder. And then I'd be away. I'd sneaked around these granite bricks and scrubby *fynbos* for thirty years. If the bleddy army couldn't catch me, then furry feeler-face Candy-blossom hadn't a chance.

Suddenly my ears picked up a familiar sound. One I was used to listening for.

Put-put . . . Patrol boat.

Old Candy-blossom heard it too. His four eyes nearly bugged out. And then, from up the hill, we heard a radio crackle.

Shit. Not even to save my life from this alien thing was I going to be caught here! That bleddy *magistraat* at Vredenburg wouldn't give a damn how I'd been caught this time . . .

"Candy-blossom? Enku?"

I didn't have to be a mind reader to understand the alien. It was just as scared of being caught as I was. And I'd bet *enku* meant "please."

"Oh, bugger it. *Ja.* Come." I picked up the bag.

It stood, looking bleddy pathetic.

"Man! *Heretjie-tog*, follow me, dammit."

It still didn't move, just made a miserable little "eeep!ting" sound. The patrol boat was getting closer.

"*Ag!* Candy-blossom."

"Candy-blossom?"

"*Ja*, all right then, bleddy Candy-blossom. Now come."

It did.

Down here on this patch of beach there was no cover, unless you counted the piles of half-dry washed-up kelp. I'd got myself caught once before, hiding in one of those piles. The bleddy patrol had stopped and sat down on the rock next to my pile for a smoke break. The buggers were parking off maybe three feet from where I was lying under that stinking kelp. They didn't have a clue that I was lying there with a streepsak of *perlemoen* and those damned kelp *goggas* crawling all over me. *Ai.* It still makes me *gril* just thinking about it. Eventually I just had to scratch, even if it meant getting caught.

I wasn't doing that again.

Up the slope was mostly those big granite boulders and scrubby little *renosterbossies*. Not an easy place to hide but also damned near impossible to keep a skirmish-line patrol in contact with each other.

You could hear the dumb *troeps vloek*ing their way through the bushes. Hell. There must have been a couple of hundred of them up there. This wasn't just a patrol out looking for old Piet Geel poaching in the military reserve again. They must be out looking for Candy-blossom here. Looking for him seriously.

I'd been wondering if I'd done something really stupid. Maybe I should give this monster to them. I mean he was . . . an alien. Like from The X-Files, on the TV down at Minna's place. But they shouldn't have come searching for him like that, not with half the bleddy Military Academy out after him. That got me mad. I'd had them looking for me before. Right now old Candy-blossom and me were up the same damned creek. I'd get him away, then, maybe . . .

There was a little *vlei* just up the hill in a bit of a flat patch there. The water is the color of *rooibos* tea that's been boiled for two hours, with this red-brown scum on it. At the deepest it is just over knee-deep, and it's full of *platannas* and *waterblommetjies*. I pulled old Candy-blossom out into it, and made him lie down in between the lily leaves. Then, pulled a couple of them over him and put one on his face. I lay down next to him, with a leaf on my face, too.

I heard them splash in the shallow water. Couldn't hear what they were saying, because my ears were underwater, but I know *troeps*. There hasn't been a *troep* born that is going to walk into the water deeper than half way up his boots, if he gets that wet. Not on a winter's night, that's for sure. All I had to worry about was that there'd be some *snotkop* officer watching them. A torch shone across my face. I lay still. The torchlight stopped blinding me. Moved on.

The splashing stopped. We waited.

I gave old Candy-blossom a nudge. We got up. The skirmish line was downhill from us now. On the sea I could see not one patrol boat but all four. All around where we'd been. Not, thankfully, where we were going. I poured the water and a happy little *plattie* out of my boots and led old Candy-blossom over the ridge.

Now, you leave a boat on the beach, and anyone can see it. Put it in the open water and it's pretty obvious in the moonlight. Cover it with kelp and it gets full of those damned kelp *goggas*. Me, I always leave the boat in a patch of three big gray rocks just off the beach. Who notices if there are three or four rocks? They're higher than my old boat. I put a bit of kelp on the back and just leave her there.

She stayed there three months, last time I got arrested. They thought I'd come over the fence. *Lelik is niks, maar stupid* . . . Like, I'm going to climb a ten-foot razor-wire fence when I can just row around? So the old boat just stayed there. Even in the daytime nobody noticed her. Okay, it means I get myself wet getting out to her, but what is a bit of wetness to old *smokkelaar* like me? I could see my rocks below us, and in two minutes we'd be away.

Except there was some *troepie gyppo*ing on the point. Okay. Maybe he was supposed to be on guard. Looked more like he was having a smoke and a daydream. Funny, they reckoned these black *troeps* would be different from the white ones. But a *troep* is a *troep* is a *troep*, like they say.

We couldn't wait. I'd swear blind that was a dog I heard. You can't fool dogs as easily as you can people.

"Stay here," I whispered. It didn't work. Candy-blooming-blossom followed me anyway. There were no small rocks around, but I took a couple of nice undersized *perelemoen* from my bag. There's a good thick patch of bush in the gully just other side of the headland. Couple of bat-eared foxes have their hole there, and this close to morning they're pretty near to it. I know. They nearly made me shit myself the first time I came that way. I waited till the guard had taken a nice deep pull on that smoke, and chucked the bat-eared foxes a *perelemoen* for breakfast.

Hey, I didn't expect that *troepie* to shriek like that. "*Hai! Haii!*" and then to go in shooting. Shooting, *nogal*! Shit. I felt sorry for the bat-eared foxes. They don't even eat *perelemoen*. Still, we were into my old boat faster than I can pull a *snoek*. I've been shot at once before and I didn't like it.

Quiet like mice I rowed us away between the bricks and kelp. I tied off the bag and hung it over the side, as usual. If a Sea-fisheries boat found us now, I'd just cut the rope. I wished like hell I could do that with old Candy-blossom, too. 'Cause now that we were in the boat, I was thinking, *What am I going to do with this . . . thing?* I mean, I live alone. But my grandchildren are in and out of the place. Maybe I should just—

A helicopter whopped away out of the dark with a searchlight, off towards Saldahna.

"Candy-blossom?"

Ag, so what the hell could I do? I just kept on rowing along the edge, keeping near the bricks. The moon was nearly down now, and we still had a couple of hours till sunrise. Hennie and some of his boys had been going to set some nets for *galjoen* when the moon went down. I wondered how they'd feel about that chopper? It made me laugh. I'll bet old Hennie thought the Sea-fisheries boys were getting pretty bleddy sneaky.

We slipped across, with a couple of ships shining lights around in the dark. They never shone them at us. My word, but there are a lot of little boats out there in the bay at night. All on perfectly legitimate business, I'm sure. They kept the Navy boys busy. The Academy Reserve looked like a Christmas tree with all those lights flashing around. Me, I know you see much better without a torch, but the army always knows better, *né?*

So we pulled the boat up. I'll say this for Candy-blossom. He gave me a hand. Actually, he gave me four hands, and man, was he strong. I took him up to the house. It is not much of a place, but it's my home. Just an old *strandhuisie,* but my father's, my grandfather's, and my great-grandfather's before me too. I put the spiny lobster and the *per-elemoen* down, lit the lamp, and got out a bottle of brandy and a couple of glasses. After this lot I needed a shot. Hell, I thought we both needed a *dop* or two.

Old Candy-blossom took one look at the bottle and got excited. "Candy-blossom? *Candy-blossom?* " He picked up the bottle, and tried to open it by pulling the lid off. Looked like he'd never met a screw cap and he needed a drink badly.

I grabbed it back. It was my brandy, after all.

"Hey. *Los uit.* I'll give you a drink, but you can't have it all!" I poured him a shot into the glass. A good double. And you know what he did?

He stuck that gun thing into it.

It turned blue. All of it. Bright glowing blue.

"CANDY-BLOSSOM!"

He pressed the button on the thing. I didn't end up dead, although, *ja*, I did duck behind the table. Then he picked me up. I mean right up, off the ground, like I weighed nothing. "Candy-blossom. Enku?" and he held the brandy bottle in one of the other hands.

Ja-nee, well, what could I say? "Okay. Candy-blossom. Enku enku. Whatever you like!"

"Splidzat." He put me down and with my bottle of brandy in hand he walked outside. It wasn't quite dawn . . . just gray. And the road in front of my place was full of this big thing. Long, and that same kind of blue as the thing I thought was his gun. Something spiraled out of it. Old Candy-blossom turned back to me.

For a bleddy bad minute I thought he was going to take me with him. Instead he pointed this thing that I'd thought was his finger at my doorstep. It's just a piece of the rock, that *oupa-grootjie* shaped. Candy-blossom cut that shape in it. With red light. I reckon if he could cut rocks, he could have sliced soldiers. Then he climbed into that seat-*magodie* that had spiraled out and . . . *whoop* he was up into the thing. With my bottle of dop. With not so much as a *dankie oom* or a wave good-bye.

Two seconds later he was gone. The only thing to show he'd ever been here was that twisty shape he cut in my step.

I wonder what it means. Maybe, it is like the mark the Israelites put on the door. You know, when the aliens come they won't kill me and the grandchildren.

Ja, well, maybe. But, *ag* well, it is probably just alien-hobo for "you can get a *dop* off this old *balie*."

The candy-blossom wasn't very pure. Barely good enough for the ship to run on. Two enku was a quite a price for such a little. Still, the enku glyphs should protect the aboriginal for some years. And with its lifestyle, it *needed* them.

Glossary for the Afrikaans-deprived:

(Note from the author: The language in the story is Afrikaans of the dialect used by the Cape Coloured, as their original khoi-san has disappeared. It's about as different as English in the deep South spoken among black Americans is to "proper English" spoken by someone from the upper crust of New York or Boston.)

ag = och
aslie = see log
dankie oom = thanks, uncle (*uncle* = any older male, a term of endearment and respect)
dop = stiff drink

fynbos =

galjoen = a prized reef fish that is totally illegal to net

gogga = creepy-crawly

gril = shudder

gyppo = avoiding duty, slacking

heretjie-tog = for God's sake

ja = Yeah

ja-nee = lit. "yes-no"; more or less means "well, okay"

langhaar = longhair

lelik is niks, maar stupid . . . = ugly is nothing, but stupid . . .

los uit = leave it alone.

magistraat = magistrate

magodies = thingamajigs

nogal = yet

oupa-grootjie = great-grandfather

perelemoen = abalone

platanna/plattie = lit. "flat Anna"; clawed aquatic toads, slimy, black flat, ugly as hell

renosterbossies = rhinocerous bushes; scrubby gray-leafed macchia

rooibos = red-bush herbal tea. Iron oxide red.

smokkelaar = smuggler; applies to poachers too

snoek = *thyristes atun*, long thin vicious predatory fish; caught on hand-lines, possible only by hauling so fast the fish doesn't get its head; staple local food

snotkop = snothead

strandhuisie = lit. "little beach house"; poor, Cape Coloured fisherman's cottage.

troep/troepie = trooper, now applied to infantry; basically the equivalent of "grunt"

vlei = bog

vloeking = cursing; generally swearing

waterblommetjies = lit. "waterflowers"; related to waterlilies, but growing in shallower water

What Would Sam Spade Do?

By Jo Walton

It was shaping up to be a quiet day when Officer Murtagh and Officer Garcia came knocking on my door. The PI business isn't all it's cracked up to be, especially not in Philly and especially not this week. With sniffers and true-tell and DNA logging, and most especially with the new divorce laws, I'd have been better off in home insurance. I'd have been better off, that is, if it wasn't for the glamour, and the best thing you can say for glamour is that it isn't religion. I was amusing myself that morning by rearranging the puters and phones on top of my desk and calculating how long it would be before I could afford to hire a beautiful assistant to sit in the outer office. I couldn't afford an outer office either; my door opened directly from the street. The answer had come out at fourteen thousand and seven years when the knock came. I couldn't wait that long, so I answered it myself.

They showed me their IDs straight off. I looked them over while pretending to read. Murtagh was a typical cop, solid muscle all through. His canine ancestry showed in his expression as well as his build. I'd put it at half bulldog and half terrier. Garcia, on the other hand, was thoroughly human and thoroughly female and gorgeous enough to bring an inertialess drive to a full stop. Unfortunately, I'd met her before.

They came in. I took my usual seat. Murtagh took the client's chair, which left Garcia perching on the side of the desk.

"So what can I do for you, Officers?" I asked. It's always good for people in my profession to keep on the right side of the law.

"Where were you last night at eighteen-thirty?" Garcia asked.

"Right here," I said.

"You work that late?" Murtagh asked, wrinkling his pug nose, skepticism practically oozing out of his pores.

"This is my home as well as my office."

Murtagh looked around pointedly.

Garcia took pity on me. "It's all nanogear. It doesn't always look like Sam Spade's office. The desk turns into a bed."

Murtagh looked at her like maybe he was wondering how she knew. With her long black hair and tight-fitting uniform I might just have wished that Garcia's knowledge of my bed was more than just theoretical, but as I said, I'd met her before. Murtagh decided to let it go for once.

"There's a Jesus been killed," he said, and watched me closely for a reaction.

He didn't get one. It didn't seem like front page news. Jesi get killed all the time. Goes with being pacifists, goes with being set to push a lot of buttons on a lot of religious nuts. He held the pause, so I asked: "How does this affect me?"

"You don't care?" Murtagh barked.

"Only in so far as no man is an island," I replied. "I guess the dead man was a brother, but—" I was going to say he was also a stranger. Garcia cut me off.

"Closer than a brother," she said. "More like another you, as I understand cloning."

"Still a stranger, as far as I know," I said, and shrugged.

About fifty years ago they got cloning straightened out. Nobody much bothered with it. Not as if there weren't already lots of people. Sure, some people had kids as little personal faxes to the future, but it wasn't common. It seemed a bit tacky somehow. It was more use for pandas and cheetahs who didn't get a say in it. Sure, some people mixed up superkids, and animal-ancestry kids like Murtagh, but most people just yawned and pushed the next button.

About forty years ago some idiot had the bright idea of taking some of the DNA from a bloodstained handkerchief in a church in Greece and producing a genuine certified clone of Jesus. There was uproar, as you'd expect, and the uproar was only calmed down a little when they said they'd give the clones to anyone who wanted one, free of charge, every church and every family can have their own Jesus. A lot of people did, a surprising number of people, enough so that soon having a baby Jesus of your own wasn't all that interesting or unusual. In fact, it was a fad. Being a Jesus, well, that was another thing. To start with, for the first few, everything we did was news. Jesus suffers little children. Jesus cuts hair, Jesus works in gas station. By the time I was growing up, Jesi were pretty much just like any other ethnicity, only with fewer women and no cuisine. There were hundreds of thousands of us in the U.S. alone. People argued about whether the DNA was really that of Jesus, people argued about heredity versus environment, people argued about whether we were the Antichrist or the Second Coming. Churches took positions, Jesi took positions. I tried to stand somewhere well away from all the positioning. I kept my hair short and my face shaved and me well out of it. If you have to have a personal role model, I think Sam Spade is better than Jesus Christ any day.

"You're theoretically a suspect," Garcia said quietly.

This truly surprised me. Sniffers can tell who's moved through an area for hours afterward. Tasters keep photographs and air samples, and with universal logging of DNA it's really hard to actually get away with a murder these days. "Murder suspect" seemed like a very old-fashioned concept. Crime, and detection too mostly, had moved online. Then I got it. It took longer than it should have.

"Your dead Jesus was killed by another Jesus?"

Garcia grimaced. Murtagh nodded. "You're the only Jesus on record who's ever killed anyone."

"Hell, Garcia, you know about that."

Garcia tapped her fingers on my screen and brought up a record. She shouldn't have been able to do that, but I didn't object. "Like I said," she said to Murtagh. "He did it to save himself and me. He was a split second ahead of the villain."

Villain was another old-fashioned word, but it didn't sound strange on Garcia's lips, not when referring to Kelly. Kelly, Turrow, and Li had robbed a client of mine of a large amount of money, and Garcia was working on them too. She'd come to see me and we'd agreed to cooperate. We'd worked together so well. I still didn't like to think about it.

"I had a license for the gun," I said.

"There wasn't any question," Garcia said.

We'd gone in side by side. I'd shot Kelly. She'd shot Turrow and Li without hesitation. Kelly had been coming at us with a gun in her hand. Turrow and Li were sitting at their puters. Li was off in virtual. She hadn't even moved.

"You're still the only Jesus on record who's ever killed anyone," Murtagh said. "Jesi are always getting killed. A Jesus killing is something new. So, what made you do it?"

"Save my life. Save hers," I said. I've thought about it since, but I didn't think at all at the time. I saw the gun coming up and squeezed my own trigger. What was Kelly's life compared to Garcia's, or even mine? So what if it was casting the first stone? Kelly was coming right at us. One shot, one death. I couldn't have done what Garcia did, and taken out the others.

"Well, this wasn't any case of self-defense," Murtagh said.

"There are what, a couple of thousand Jesi in Philly?" I googled around and got an answer right away: 2912. "Others could have flown in, or come by train, hell, even landed at the spaceport. I can't prove it wasn't me, but in the same way I don't see how you can prove it was." They couldn't use truth-tell unless they had a court order, or unless I volunteered. Fifth Amendment.

"It wasn't you," Garcia said. "The sniffers outside this building show that you came in yesterday and didn't leave again."

"Then why are you here?"

"We wanted your help. Your psychological insight into Jesi, the insight of a Jesus who became a private investigator and who killed in self-defense, into which of the suspects it could have been. If we had a good idea we could get a truth-tell, but we can't just ask to pump it into the lot of them. The lawyers of all the innocents would scream blue murder." Garcia crossed her legs and bit her lip. "Will you help us?"

"Will you pay my professional rates?"

"Hey—" Murtagh growled, but Garcia cut him off.

"We'll pay your professional rates. Jesus!" I couldn't tell if she was calling me by name or swearing.

"So, tell me about the suspects."

"Well, the taster records are just about useless, as the DNA all comes up as just plain Jesus," Murtagh said. There are second generation Jesi now, kids of the originals, not clones, who would show up as a Jesus-mix, same as Murtagh would show as a dog-mix. "But the sniffers let us narrow it down to six individuals who were in the street at the right time."

"Tell me about them."

"First, let me tell you about the murder. The dead man is Alambert Jesus," Garcia said. "You heard of him?"

"The writer," I said. He was a best seller, and probably Philly's best known Jesus. I hadn't read any of his books. They looked to be several gig thick, and I don't have much time for reading.

"Lots of you have writing talent. It seems to be genetic. Come to that I guess the parables are pretty good short stories," Murtagh said.

"I save my skill in that direction for writing up my cases."

Murtagh gave a little barking laugh.

Garcia went on. "Well, Alambert Jesus lived in Chinatown. He was home. He opened the door to a Jesus. The Jesus tortured him to death, slowly. Then the Jesus left."

"Tortured him? That doesn't make sense."

"Doesn't, does it?" Murtagh sighed. "Doesn't go with the pacifism and thou shalt not kill stuff."

"Maybe this one came to bring a sword," Garcia suggested, looking at me.

I had enough of that in my childhood. "Whoever we're clones of, and as far as I'm concerned Jesus is just shorthand for the person whose blood was on that handkerchief, I think there are enough of us for you to be able to tell that we're the same in some ways and different in others without getting religion into it."

"You don't think religion has anything to do with the murder?" Murtagh asked.

"Was he crucified?" I asked.

"Interesting guess," Garcia said. "But while I hear that happens a lot in the South, no. Alambert was not crucified."

"Then it probably wasn't religious."

"The suspects," Murtagh said, getting a look in his eye like he was on the trail. "These are the ones who were on the spot right after. Let me run through them quickly." As he named them he brought their faces up on my screen, one pair of soulful brown eyes after another, different arrangements of hair and clothes. All of them could have been my brothers. Or me. "Jesus Potrin, twenty-eight, local radio talk show host. Only suspect who actually knew Alambert. They weren't close friends, but he'd had him on the show. Jesus Dowell, eighteen, down and out. No known connection. Alex Jesus Feruglio, thirty-five, chef at Joseph Poon's, on Arch. Alambert ate in there occasionally. Joshua Jesus, thirty-three, minister of the Church of the Second Coming. No known connection. Karl Jesus, 26, motor mechanic, no known connection. Malcolm Jesus Zimmerman, twenty-nine, doctor from Montana, in town for a convention. No known connection."

"Jesus, they really do have nothing in common except their genes," Garcia said. This time I was sure she was swearing.

"I don't know any of them either," I said. "I've eaten in Joseph Poon's, but who hasn't?" It was the best fusion food in town.

"Nothing jumps out at you?" Garcia asked.

"Not immediately. They all had the opportunity. The method's obvious. The problem is motive. I'll poke about online and see what I can find in their biographies, but I'm not hopeful." Why would any of them kill Alambert? Why would a Jesus kill another Jesus? What could they possibly get out of it?

"Well, Jesus or not, we'll catch them, and whichever of them it was will fry for it," Murtagh said, getting up.

"Though what that will do with public opinion I don't know," Garcia said.

"It must have been Joshua Jesus," I said, as the pieces came together. "Don't execute him. That's what he wants."

Murtagh sat down again. "That's what he wants? Explain."

"That's his motivation. He's a millenarian, a religious nut, a priest of the Second Coming and he thinks he's it. He's thirty-three, the age Jesus was when he was crucified. He must have picked this as a sure way of being executed by the state."

"A nut," Garcia said. "A religious fanatic."

"True-tell will get it out of him, and you ought to be able to get an order. You can put him in a nuthouse and throw away the key," I said.

"Huh," barked Murtagh. "Coming, Garcia?"

"I'll just be a moment," she said.

Murtagh stepped outside.

"You're not a religious fanatic," she said.

"There are possibilities in the genes, not predestination," I said. "I'm not a writer or a chef either. There's more to me than my genes."

"And there's more to me than my trigger finger."

We looked at each other, a little wary, a little uncertain, but damn she was beautiful and even more than a beautiful assistant and an outer office I needed a partner. "Blessed be the trigger happy," I said, and she was in my arms.

Sometimes in this life you've just got to ask yourself: "What would Sam Spade do?"

Giving It Fourteen Percent

by A. S. Fox

He was reading a comic book when it happened. "Ombudsman." Fiona's voice buzzed over O'Malley's console. "Time to work. Level A, Main Conference Room."

O'Malley rose and put on his coat. It had been in the closet, waiting in shrink-wrap and desiccators for a good fourteen months. He rolled his shoulders, swallowed his fears, and developed the mien of a man genuinely thrilled to be working for StarDrive. Having worked less than ten full days in the past eleven years, his mastery of this skill had paid the rent for quite some time now.

"Fiona, you may be the only person here that I truly love."

"I'm a computer." The voice remained dispassionate and hollow.

"My point exactly."

O'Malley worked in the tallest building in the world—the StarDrive Tower. Management arranged workers according to rank. Each successive rank earned a seat of power in a small office one step closer to the shining beacon of progress, otherwise known as Level A, the Top, or HQ. He worked on the second floor and had never been called to an office higher than the hundredth floor.

He took an elevator down to the foyer and stopped before the Door. Above it hung an epic painting of a starship breaking the bounds of light. StarDrive's stated goal was to produce a faster-than-light spacecraft. The Chinese felt that, for form's sake, even the elite should enter and leave via the main door. It was perhaps the only vestige of their eighty-year Communist experiment. O'Malley put his hand in the fingerprint reader, half expecting to get a shock. Instead, the door opened and he entered. The Door gave one access to a special elevator, filled with sofas and upholstered chairs, which fired directly to the executive floors high above.

He sat while the elevator conveyed him to the executive entrance. Four enormous jade FooDogs guarded the corridor. O'Malley had heard rumors from his fellow Ombudsmen that StarDrive had liberated them from a failing nation-state. Beyond those lay various personal offices guarded by the Dragon Ladies of the Imperial Royal Secretarial Service: beautiful, lithe, Asian women of indeterminate age who would serve tea. Possibly they were also capable of typing, calculating particle mechanics, or killing a man with one blow. O'Malley would probably never know.

He was ushered in by one such stunning beauty, handed a cup of Irish Breakfast tea—Twining's bag still in the cup to show they cared—and plunked at the end of an enormously long and, theoretically, intimidating table.

"I am Number One," a voice announced. Ten somber, middle-aged Chinese men wearing blue pinstripe suits faced him. In the logic of the Organization, Number One actually ranked fourth in the corporate schema.

"Good day, sir." O'Malley sipped his tea. They had overbrewed it by fifteen minutes. He smiled and drank more.

"We have a problem," Number One continued. They all smoked; O'Malley could barely make out the rough vicinity of his voice. In all the time he had been working for StarDrive, he had never gone more than three sentences before one of his betters would ominously say, "We have a problem."

"That, sir . . ." He enunciated to carry across the room. ". . . is why you pay me. How may I assist?"

The men appeared embarrassed. "We have a problem with our spaceship, with achieving light speed. We need your help."

"I'm sorry." O'Malley tried not to drop his jaw. They were being polite, among other things. Politeness usually meant someone had died. "I'm not an engineer or a scientist. I work for your human resources department." He sighed and then added, "At a very low level."

"We know," a different voice answered. "But your name is O'Malley and we thought you might be able to help us with this specific problem."

He sipped his tea dry; a Dragon Lady refilled it with Jasmine White leaf. He savored its crisp sweetness and tried to be motionless. He had heard it worked for lizards and certain kinds of rabbits.

"You see . . ." a third voice spoke.

"We have men hallucinating upstairs," the leader finally spoke, pushing forward. This was Han, the actual number one of StarDrive. O'Malley had never met him, but the Chairman Mao–sized banners of him on every floor familiarized a person with his general likeness. He saw now that a wart or two had been tastefully airbrushed off the inspirational posters.

"Europeans?" O'Malley thought he caught the drift of the problem. Hallucinations would be terribly bad press.

"No." Han waved dismissively. Europeans apparently were beneath his concern. "Nationals, of course—important men, pilots and engineers."

"The nature of these hallucinations?"

"Our men . . ." Han hesitated. "These men are very trustworthy and I know many personally."

Great tension filled his voice. The message was clear. *I trust them, you better trust them too. Or else.*

"Our men believe they are seeing leprechauns."

"Leprechauns." O'Malley kept a somber face.

"Yes," one of the adjutants agreed.

It all clicked. "I'm the only Irish employee you have, then?"

One of the men nodded with obvious disdain. "It would appear so."

"And you felt that being O'Malley would give me some ethnic, some Irish-born, insight into these hallucinations?"

"Exactly." Han nodded. Silence sat upon the boardroom. Finally, Han put out his cigarette and announced with finality, "You leave immediately."

O'Malley tried not to spit. Although he understood that being in the world's tallest building also connected him to the StarDrive Space Elevator, he had never given it thought. He'd read the brochures during training. A satellite stationed many thousands of kilometers above the towers trailed a cable that linked the building itself and an ancillary ballast-weight station with a tube built like a human spine. Inside, a bubble-shaped elevator made the transit. Five hours from tower to space station, four from space back down. No bends, no discomfort, no sense of g-force or blastoff; they even had some kind of gyroscopic system that buffered it against the winds in the upper atmosphere. You could drink tea on the way up.

When they ushered him into a semisterile room, he panicked. A new set of Dragon Ladies rushed forth and disencumbered him of his outer garments; olive drab overalls and a maroon sweater with elbow patches and matching knit cap replaced them. A particularly fierce Dragon Lady grabbed him and shoved two half-slipper, half-rugby cleat contraptions over his bare feet. After that, a pale red-haired woman who proved more terrifying than the Dragon Ladies arrived. She smiled and donned similar garb. He noticed she wore a Celtic cross layered with thick Gaelic sigils and some very not-Christian iconography on its edges.

They were dumped in a chute, which turned out to be the actual elevator. It was cramped and not the luxurious ride he had been led to believe existed. He and the woman huddled as the bubble rocketed into the air, faster than his lunch could follow.

"O'Malley." He spoke between hyperventilating gasps.

"Cassie." She threw her head back, clearly exhilarated by the ride. "You're from the North." She spoke Gaelic. "I saw your file. Worked in a pub, almost got a chemistry degree from Dublin, but you come from Belfast. Moved about the same time the Troubles were erupting and all those bombs started putting holes in Buckingham Palace."

O'Malley frowned. "Where are you from?" She spoke Gaelic? She spoke fast in Gaelic?

"Kilkee, but I'm a Traveler." It explained her dark eyes. Travelers were the gypsies of Ireland, though it was disputed if they were also Rom, like their Eurasian counterparts.

"My people are actually from Ballyclare, but yah. I was from Belfast. Not anymore." He shut his mouth and ignored her until the slingshot of first acceleration slowed.

"Were you any good at chemistry, O'Malley?"

"I moved to Pontianak to tend bar at a local Irish pub." He counted to twenty. "Why do you ask?"

"Malaysia had extremely porous borders with little oversight of foreign passports at the time; that meant . . ." She shrugged suggestively.

O'Malley rolled his eyes. His lunch had returned to its proper place. "How does a Traveler end up subletting her services to a Chinese spaceship company?"

She laughed and touched his shoulder. "I was visiting my sister Ling Ling, adopted. She works for StarDrive and when word came down that they needed an Irish religious expert, I apparently was the only one in Indo-Malaysia."

"Wasn't there a panda named Ling Ling?" O'Malley tried to pry his shoulder loose.

"Mom was extremely creative." She smiled and kept her grip.

By the time they had arrived and the grim Chinese technicians lifted them from the capsule, O'Malley had discovered that Cassie liked groping men. It took him another few seconds to realize he still spoke perfect Gaelic, that his employers apparently knew what he used to do for a living, and most importantly, he did not like zero gravity one tiny bit. When they were ushered into the spinning sector with its two-thirds gravity, he breathed a deep sigh of relief.

Then a group of terrified-looking Chinese engineers confronted them with the Problem. It boiled down to this: at 12 percent lightspeed the ship began to shake and shimmy, things got a little blurry, and light got sort of fuzzy. At 14 percent, the leprechauns started appearing. That was that.

The chief pilot promised them that they would be taken to the place where the little men showed up consistently; apparently no one had thought to film the operation. O'Malley tried unsuccessfully to suggest it. Instead the captain stiffly informed them the ship would again be at 14 percent translight within the hour.

The two Irish nationals endured the preflight check and the acceleration out of the star dock. The gravitational spin of the starship's twin hulls ceased, putting them in free fall. "You don't believe in little men, do you?" He rubbed his protesting stomach.

"Cassie. And why not?"

O'Malley snorted. "Okay. First, because there are no leprechauns. Second, because if there were leprechauns, we'd have seen them somewhere other than outer space. And third, did I mention the part about there being no green bonnie men?"

"What is your first name?" She brushed his arm. He told her. She made a face. "What was your mother thinking?"

"Oh, no. Da had three jobs. First, making us, second, naming us, and third, dying early enough to leave a pension to feed us. The rest was me dear mum."

"I think I'll call you O'Malley." The ship launched into some new phase of its altogether gut-wrenching throttle through space.

"Eight percent translight," a crisp voice informed them in Mandarin.

"All women do." He tried not to grimace more than was necessary. Good thing they hadn't given him tea with cream and sugar.

"Ten percent translight." The chairs started to vibrate oddly and his feet felt numb.

"Twelve percent translight." The voice sounded dubious. It might as well have screamed "Danger! Leprechaun alert!" The light did seem a bit gooey.

"Did you know that the light in Ireland actually moves infinitesimally slower than normal light?"

"Whadya mean?" O'Malley turned his face to see her dark and clearly mad eyes.

"Scientists in County Cork proved it two years ago. The speed of light across most of Ireland is actually one eighteenth of one percent slower than the universal constant."

"So what? Do you think that proves . . . "

"Fourteen percent translight," came the terrified announcement.

POP! Something small, green, and grinning stood three paces in front of them.

"Good morning," said the leprechaun in lilting, if old-sounding, Gaelic.

"Okay." O'Malley pointed to the little man in his green suit, trimmed with gold brocade and buttons, shoes with brass buckles, and a genuine shillelagh. Dimpled and thick nosed, exactly like the pictures, the elf stood two feet tall. "That's a leprechaun."

"Told you so." Cassie smiled gleefully.

"You speak the Mother Tongue?" The leprechaun stepped closer.

"We do." Cassie addressed the tiny elf in her own Southern Traveler's Gaelic. "Hello, fey friend of Mab."

The leprechaun bowed and kissed her hand. Suddenly he turned around, as if there were something coming up behind him. "Oh."

Pop! He was gone just as the ship began to decelerate.

"Kill engines, kill engines!" Apparently the crew did not find the little men as reassuring or polite as Cassie did.

The captain reestablished gravity and raced back to the pair. Had they seen them? Yes. Now what, he demanded? It took all O'Malley's ombudsman training and quite a bit of convincing to explain that they were going to have *stay* at 14 percent translight for a while. That assumed the Chinese wanted him to actually hold a conversation—with, yes, he admitted they were obviously something—these guys who looked like leprechauns.

In the end he got the guarantee of a night's sleep in semigravity while the crew radioed HQ and received further orders. O'Malley tried a toothpaste tube of something called General's Chicken Paste Number Four and gave up trying to have an appetite. Then he padded as quietly as possible to what seemed like a secluded nook. It provided a bed contraption that folded out, an air mattress, and solar blanketing with electric toe warmers. He looked left and right, saw neither a pagan woman nor men of any height, Chinese or Irish, and tried to go to sleep.

He wasn't sure if he had been asleep or merely in that sweet dozy place right before actual sleep when he felt her slip into his bed. "Cassie?" As if some other nearly six foot, mostly naked, and highly aggressive woman with red hair would sneak under his sheets.

"It's me." She began kissing his neck quite effectively.

"You're a stranger." He squirmed away.

"Not anymore." She rubbed his back.

"Um, I'm not that kind of girl." He wracked his brain for a better line.

Cassie laughed. "When in Indonesia, do as the Indonesians."

"But we're in outer space. And I have to figure out why there are leprechauns here."

"Why not ask them?" She blithely drifted off to sleep, apparently satisfied with merely having gotten in to his bed on day one. It seemed an incentive to solve the situation before day two.

On day two they managed to do the meet and greet with the leprechaun, find out his name was Tibbles of Green Burroughs, and that Tibbles seemed astonished that they did not believe in him. Then came the hysterical screaming, the deceleration, and the heinous accusations from terrified Chinese pilots who had to call the dread Chief Han and report Complications and, worse, Delays. Cassie's suggestions gave O'Malley his first headache in a decade.

O'Malley tried barring the door using a special computer code. She apparently could hack those. Thankfully, she contented herself with merely riding the night through holding him in her arms.

By day five, he had given up hope of evading Cassie at night, Tibbles by day, and the hysteria of the entire StarDrive Corporation pretty much constantly. The woman could get through furniture, welded doors, and air locks.

"Why don't you make yourself useful?" He jabbed her when they woke up on day six, she having found him buried in the cargo section under a heap of welder's tools.

"I've been trying." Cassie pinched his cheek. "But you apparently missed a couple pages out of the manual. Goddess magic is usually sex magic and you keep avoiding me."

O'Malley scratched his head. She had a certain logic. "But there isn't any magic, Cassie." He had to admit the thought of sleeping with her seemed quite appealing, it always had. He just wasn't that kind of girl.

"How do you think I got through welded doors, silly?" She ran her fingers along his forearm.

"Um, I was wondering about that," he confessed. "But magic?"

"Magic."

"Well, if you can do magic to open my doors at night, why can't you do other magics?"

Cassie sat up from their secret bed; tools crashed as they fell off of her. A frightened mechanic jumped and ran, yelping something. "You really don't understand, do you?"

"What?" O'Malley felt very queasy.

"Didn't you have a grandmother?"

"Drank herself to death."

"Aunts, older female relatives, the little old lady down the alley?"

"Blown up or shot by the Ulster Unionists or Orangemen, except for the old lady down the street who taught me how to make pipe bombs."

Cassie shook her head and kissed his forehead. "Well, if you had a nanna, she would have told you lots of stories about the olden times and magic and the Celtic knots, the runes, the secrets of the Picts, and such, our own weavings and doings."

"I've read the books."

"Do you know the difference between blood magic and circle magic, between weavings and callings, between unions and dispersals?"

O'Malley looked her in the eye. She seemed neither mad nor gleeful. In fact, Cassie looked outrageously serious, exactly like the Chinese pilots talking about their Pulse Drive buttons. "That would be a, um, a no, I guess." He grew quiet. What if she wasn't crazy?

"I can't call forth a fairy circle without some base of power and, unfortunately, there isn't any in outer space. But I can use you, and to do that I have to use a weaving and a union. The easiest way would be to sleep together but if you're absolutely hell bent to avoid my embrace, I can probably just drain half your blood and set up some kind of kettle in the back." She gave him a wicked leer.

"Why sex, why blood? There's no logic in it." He hated the sight of his own blood. He opted against telling her his fainting stories.

She smiled. "On the contrary, if you had read your quantum physics textbooks better, you'd know that in 2011 Australians found a link between indigenous song lines, genetics, and quantum flux readings."

O'Malley rolled his eyes vigorously. "That's a joke."

She shook her head. "It really is mind over matter. But within set parameters determined by the magical systems, quote unquote, of the people involved. We're Irish, we gotta use traditional Irish protocols."

"Protocols? Cassie, you just said it was magic."

"You never took physics, did you?"

O'Malley frowned. "Since when did any textbook claim that magic had a scientific verifiable basis in quantum physics?"

Cassie didn't hesitate. "Strock and Tadeschi, *The Secret Life of Particles*, 2012, published by Springer-Verlag. Followed by about seven more knockoffs and coattail studies."

He gulped. "Well, let me think about it for the day."

By the time they rose, the usual suspects had come to the cargo hold. They informed them with hidden embarrassment that the pilot, copilot, and top four engineers had been shuttled down for psychiatric care and a new pilot would be taking them to 14 percent today. Would immediately be too soon, please and thank you? He imagined they did not want to report to Chief Han that strange Europeans sleeping in their cargo hold was their sole sign of progress.

They did the drill. Strap in, hysterical announcement, null gravity, 8 percent, 10 percent, 12 percent—everything fuzzy, witty comment from Cassie—and then fourteen percent. Pop! Mr. Tibbles arriving, obviously annoyed to be still talking to them.

O'Malley tried a new tack. "I thought you were a myth."

"Of course we're real, you idiot." Tibbles reddened. "You've been sighting us for centuries."

"Near rainbows, on the ground, not in outer-freaking-space," O'Malley spat back and Tibbles grew beet red.

"Morons," he muttered. "What is a Pulse Drive? It's a fancy laser that splits and refocuses light into thousands of fractal pieces, sort of like a mini fusion reactor . . . Forget it. I can see you know nothing about science."

"Absolutely nothing." O'Malley knew exactly what a Pulse Drive was, since he had been reading schematics all day.

"Rainbow. Splits light. Pulse Drive. Splits light. Whenever you split light, we show up. We're energy beings, you dolt." Tibbles looked ready to smack him with the shillelagh.

"What about werewolves and vampires?" O'Malley sneered.

"Out of phase, their energy signature cued to moonlight and reflected shadow. Mirrors, moonlight, everything is reflected light, it's all in the angles of reflection. Man, you're pretty stupid."

"Ghosts?" O'Malley leaned back in his seat; Mr. Tibbles' stick had begun to sway dangerously close to his head.

"Negative infrared signatures of dark matter. Your physicists have been blabbing about the stuff for decades. Why do you think they make it so cold?"

"So you're real?"

"Yep. Genuine leprechaun. Fairy. Mystical sprite. Elf. Magical being. Just like the little stories have always said. Don't you people read?"

O'Malley sighed. "Apparently not enough. What's with the stupid green suit and the hokey stick, then?"

Mr. Tibbles sighed back and looked as if he were deciding between vomiting and strangling him. "It's all local. In Hawaii, we're Menehune. In upstate New York, we're little Indians dancing in the corn."

"The Chinese claimed you were leprechauns, though." O'Malley grinned.

Mr. Tibbles drew himself up to his maximum height. "The Chinese are capable of lying, you know."

Then someone screamed and the ship jolted back into normal space as a new pilot qualified for short-term disability.

"What was that about?" Cassie gave him a puzzled look. The crew sprinted toward them shouting accusations, questions, and pleas in frenzied Mandarin.

"A hunch." O'Malley put up both hands and spoke fiercely in chopped Mandarin. *Tell Chief Han it will be done tomorrow, no sooner.* They bickered, and when O'Malley did not budge or negotiate they slunk away sullenly, obviously fearful of having to tell the chief just that.

On night six, O'Malley found the biggest, warmest room possible, commandeered extra pillows and blankets and something that resembled solid food, and made a fort of his swag. He left the door unlocked and ajar. When Cassie arrived, she did so wearing a particularly fetching gown of homemade lace.

"What's it to be, blood or me?" Her eyes dazzled in the almost lightless room.

O'Malley looked up from reading a book on Irish folklore. "You can make a fairy circle in the room before we blast off tomorrow?"

She slid the door closed and locked it, her hand waving the latch closed from ten feet away. "Oh, yes." She smiled and he felt enchanted. O'Malley shrugged and said no more.

On day seven, he lectured the pilots, warning them that if they came out of 14 percent a second earlier than he asked them to, he would personally shuttle down, resign in front of Chief Han, and blame them by family name. He advised them to take tranquilizers, rice wine, chew on wood, or simply close their damned eyes—after all, they were flying through a vacuum. Whatever it took, they must not deviate course, slow down, or interfere with his and Cassie's doings. Oh, and if they didn't like it, please feel free to call HQ right this instant and ask the chief to replace him, since they had a much better idea. Strangely, no one argued and all seemed genuinely pleased that he had finally been so mean-spirited as to threaten them.

Then he went aft. He came upon Cassie finishing the circle, which she had cleverly disguised to look like any old flooring in any old spaceship. "I'll need a kiss." She leant forward and he complied.

"For completing the circle?"

"No." She gave him an enormous smile. "I just know I'm not going to get another chance if this works." He shook his head and let the engineers strap him in.

Then the countdown, the usual rev up, and the far less hysterical achieving of 14 percent. Pop! Tibbles appeared and this time O'Malley unstrapped to greet him.

"I'm sorry, old friend." He spoke formal Gaelic. "I was wrong to be so rude last time."

Tibbles looked touched and Cassie nodded. "Well, alriiiight." Tibbles blushed, clearly pleased to be appreciated.

"I really do believe in you, Tibbles. I want you to know that." O'Malley gave him a curt bow, complicated by the lack of gravity. "I was wrong to not believe the old stories. Leprechauns do exist and I know, now, that so does magic."

"It's not entirely fancy physics, you know."

"I know." O'Malley started to pace. "It's a quantum signature from a collective genetic unconscious."

"Exactly." Tibbles beamed. "I think you have actually learned something. And I thought you were totally stupid."

"I'll take that as a compliment." O'Malley and the elf chuckled. "Shake? No hard feelings?"

Tibbles put out his tiny mitt and shook O'Malley's vigorously. "You know, I'm hoping you people stop calling me here."

"I think we've learned our lesson," O'Malley assured him. Tibbles turned to go. O'Malley pushed a button on the wall. The ship instantly dropped out of the Pulse Drive, as if the pilots had been poised over the Kill button, punch-drunk, and praying for the signal. Tibbles gave a low moaning wail.

"These are called handcuffs," O'Malley explained, demonstrating that he and Tibbles were now firmly pinioned together by a chunk of metal.

"You can't." The leprechaun struggled, his legs kicking.

"Fairy circle." O'Malley pointed to Cassie, who batted her eyelashes.

"I'm in big trouble," Tibbles said to no one in the room.

"I want my pot of gold." O'Malley eyed the elf.

"What?" The little man struggled. "Absolutely not."

"Then you stay. I've got the chairman of a very large media corporation who would love to put you in a nice glass box, shuffle you around, and make a few billion credits off you."

"You can't, you won't . . ." The elf started to shrink in horror, but he could not pull far since O'Malley had him suspended by the cuffs.

"Gold. It's in the books. I want it." O'Malley yanked the wretched leprechaun to emphasize his point.

"I can curse you," the elf countered. Cassie coughed and Tibbles suddenly blushed. "If you hadn't brought a witch with you."

"But I did bring my own witch and my own fairy circle and now I have my very own leprechaun."

"I don't, I can't get the gold right away."

"Then I get pictures and the plastic box and a touring elf show, and you get to do stupid sprite tricks for the videocasters."

"The price of gold is really, really low these days." Tibbles bit his lip.

"You haven't got anything other than that to offer," Cassie said nonchalantly.

"And if I did?" Tibbles' face lit up.

"I'll take the formula for a working Pulse Drive, one that breaks the speed of light safely." O'Malley lifted the gnome to near eye level.

"Painful." Tibbles whimpered and his eyes teared. O'Malley did nothing but yank harder. They remained that way as the little man went through six colors, ranted, threatened, switched languages, and then finally sighed. "Okay."

O'Malley handed him a notebook with an erasable pen. "Now."

"I'm right-handed," Tibbles complained.

"We've got all day, don't we, Cassie?" Cassie nodded and smiled. She crossed her legs making her little sucker-booties swish. Nobody said anything. Tibbles developed an amazing ability to write with his left hand.

When the leprechaun had covered roughly twenty pages, he handed the pen and notebook back. "Okay." He smiled wanly. "You won."

"Great. Thanks." O'Malley started reading the elf's handiwork. "Now swear by Queen Mab, on your sacred honor, and upon the sworn code of the fairies that all you have written is true and good, that you have in right faith given what is due and paid your debt."

"You read the book." Tibbles' face drooped into despair.

"I read all the books, you little creep." O'Malley yanked on his captive again. Tibbles wordlessly reached for the book, took the eraser, and fixed a dozen assorted diagrams, renumbered some formulas, and took up another three pages with previously unwritten schematics. Then he handed it back, the look on his face totally defeated.

"Swear." O'Malley prodded him.

"I so swear before Mab my queen and my sacred honor, I have done as asked and the debt is paid. One pot of gold or its equivalent." Tibble's eyes lolled. "Bastard."

O'Malley cuffed him. "Hey. Don't talk like that in front of a lady. Apologize."

"Sorry," whispered Tibbles, his left foot making a pathetic figure eight on the floor. The cuffs unlocked at O'Malley's cue.

Pop! Just like magic, the leprechaun was gone.

"You were planning this all along?" Cassie watched him closely, clearly impressed.

O'Malley shrugged as the crew began to shuffle in, looking for signs of leprechauns or explosions.

"Somewhere around the time I took to sleeping under tools and tables, it occurred to me to think of a way to capture the guy. I'm from Belfast, after all."

"After all," Cassie agreed. They tried to hold off the throng's new bout of questions, which, strangely, were devoid of accusations or threats. Apparently, the chief had either invested him with new powers or everyone's desperation had simply given him a little breathing room.

O'Malley orchestrated the group. Scanned copies of the notebook needed to be made. For their part, the engineers did something capable and swift, using things with green lights that looked like pasta rollers. Whatever they were, in one sweep all the pages were read, digitized, filed, and probably cross-referenced with footnotes.

Cassie began to ask a question, but a sudden gibbering excitement interrupted her. It appeared someone, either downstairs or on the starship, had realized what O'Malley had handed them. The engineers disappeared and the new pilot replaced them, his face stolid in resolve. He sputtered some harsh Mandarin at the pair, emphasizing the words with a hand chop.

"He said?" Cassie stepped closer to O'Malley. Did she do nervousness?

"Han wants us."

Minutes later, O'Malley and Cassie found themselves unceremoniously shoved toward another chute and toppled down the elevator towards Level A and the Grand Boardroom.

Around twenty thousand miles above the planet, she muttered, "When did you figure it out?"

"The Hwa thing."

"What's a Hwa, anyway?"

O'Malley brushed a red curl off her forehead. "The old name the Japanese used upon arriving in China. It means *dwarf* in Mandarin. Until they became a modern power, the Japanese were the leprechauns of China."

"They own half of the Moon now." She curled closer to him.

"But, in the ancient subconscious they were, and to some extent still are, dwarves."

"And . . ."

O'Malley snorted. "You never read Jung, did you?" The cabin was silent. "Protocols are individual sets of rules which have local meaning on a subconscious and thus, quantum level. That means the Faerie Contract would bind."

"I thought you read comic books all day."

"Well." The elevator passed some kind of altitude marker. The Mandarin made little sense at their speed. "I subscribe to a few regular ones, but they're monthly and that leaves me with a time lag at the end of the month."

"Hwa?" Cassie came close enough that he lowered his voice.

"Well, Tibbles is some kind of alien—that's probably a safe bet. He changes with perception. So what did the Chinese see? Hwa. They had to have sent a Japanese ombudsman first."

"Who saw Japanese leprechauns."

"The Ainu—I heard the paramedics haul Furikaki out of his office last week screaming about the Hairy Hill Men."

Cassie positioned herself on his stomach. "You could have taken the gold, Mr. Ainu."

He laughed and smoothed her hair lightly. "Price of gold's real low these days."

She jabbed him in a soft spot. "But why really?" The cabin gave a faint hum but he did not speak. She jabbed again.

"Okay." He twirled a curl of her hair. "Between us?"

"Of course." She kissed his arm.

"We're the only ones, Cassie."

"Only ones what?" She sat up.

"The only ones who have a positive relationship with faeries. The English get abducted, the Swedes get ravaged, the Japanese are contaminated, the Chinese invaded. Hence, the stretchers."

Cassie's face changed color. "Does Han know?"

O'Malley patted her leg. "One suspects he must. Pot of gold and all."

"So why not something else?"

O'Malley's eyes glittered. "The Irish invent star travel. Too good to pass up. What's your excuse?"

Cassie rubbed her chin. "How do you know I don't just like going really fast?"

He put his hands behind his head and chuckled. They fell silent. By the next altitude marker, they had fallen asleep.

When they arrived, a fleet of Dragon Ladies whisked them back into the sterile corridor and he was again outfitted with clothing, this time a terribly familiar blue pin-striped suit. Even the tie seemed standard issue. The secretariat ushered them into a small office where a beaming team of ten StarDrive executives welcomed them. Chief Han had opted for a black suit with, miracles, a cream and crimson tie.

"Sit." All present sat. O'Malley waited in silence, thinking.

"You have placed us within scheduled parameters. Seventeen minutes ago, our crew completed the first faster-than-light voyage in human history, returning safely to the star base." The other nine men beamed, clearly delighted and relieved. Han lit a cigarette and watched the smoke curl. "Explain yourself."

"Isn't that StarDrive's whole purpose?" O'Malley fiddled with his tie.

"But you are not StarDrive. You work on the second floor." Han gave them a piercing stare. "Why did you help us?"

Cassie coughed. "The price of gold really is through the floor." She shrugged and looked to O'Malley.

"She's right." O'Malley let go of his collar. "I'd probably make more with a modest raise, which I think one could reasonably expect for such work."

"We're not even paying Ms. Morgaine, although you can rest assured her sister now has extremely well-compensated employment for life."

"Morgaine?" O'Malley turned to her.

Cassie smiled. "Pagan witch, remember."

"And you, Mr. O'Malley"—Chief Han spoke as if punishment were being doled out—"we have decided to promote."

O'Malley groaned, instantly filled with regret.

One of the executives set up a tripod with a large flowchart printed with impossible to read squiggles. He coughed, consulted a set of note cards, and began, "As you can see from our corporate structure . . ."

Cassie rose. O'Malley panicked and reached out his hand.

Cassie pumped it. "I'll see you later." She started walking.

"You will?" His stomach began to act up. What if he had to wear a suit everyday?

"Magic," she whispered in luscious Gaelic. He watched in anguish as his Cassie sauntered from the conference room.

Chief Han waited until she had left, then took over for the executive, droning on in grand gestures about some new position with enormous power and responsibility. But all O'Malley heard was "suit, suit, suit." After several painful minutes it grew quiet. All the men stood. He stood. One by one the men shook his hand. Han patted him on the shoulder.

Dazed, he followed a feral-looking Dragon Lady to his new office, now on the 507th floor. He closed the door and whimpered. Some unknown lackey (the new ombudsman?) had moved his gear into a larger and far more luxurious space. He had a window view, two potted plants, and something antique in the corner. His only solace lay on the desk: an intercom box with "Fiona" handwritten on the peeling label.

"Fiona." He pushed the button, fingers crossed. "What do I do for a living?"

"You are now the head of public relations, Denial of Magic Division." Her voice had acquired a friendly purr.

O'Malley tossed his tie and coat. He sat back, put his feet on the desk, and grabbed a new stack of comics. "Fiona, I love you."

Every Hole Is Outlined

by John Barnes

The ship was at least fourteen thousand years old in slowtime and more than two thousand in eintime, but there were holes in its records and the oldest ones were in no-longer-accessible formats, so the ship estimated that it was more like eighteen thousand slowtime, three and a half thousand eintime. It had borne many names. Currently it was *9743*, a name that translated easily for Approach Control no matter where the ship went in human space.

In the last two centuries of eintime, the ship's conversation with most ports had been wholly mathematical. Synminds chattered about physics and astronomy to get the ship into a berth, and about prices and quantities and addresses afterward, and the human crew had not learned a word of the local language, despite their efforts, except such guesses as that the first things people said probably were something like "hello," and the last things something like "good-bye," and in between, perhaps, they might pick up equivalents of "may I?" and "thank you."

This had little immediate impact on the ship's operation except that mathematical worlds had no entertainment, or at least none they would sell to the ship's library; the long-run concern was that the mathematical worlds tended to begin waving off all ships and not communicating at all, after a time, though strangely some of those dark worlds would sometimes begin to talk and call for ships again, after an interval of a few centuries slowtime.

But the problem for this evening meal was both shorter-run than procuring entertainment for the ship's library, and much longer run than the gradual darkening of the worlds. They needed a new crew member, and they were having a real supper tonight, with cooked food, wine, and gravity, to discuss how to get one.

9743 needed a crew of four to work it, when it needed working, which was only for system entries and system departures because the law of space required it, and for PPDs (the business and navigation sessions held whenever predicted prices at destination shifted enough to require considering a course change) because the crew were the stockholders and synminds were required to consult them. Normally they would work the ship for half a shift for PPDs, but sometimes traffic density close to a star was high enough to engage gammor restrictions for as much as a light-day out from the port, and then 9743 had to have crew in the opsball for more than one shift.

Therefore, for the very rare case of needing more than one shift, the ship usually carried eight people: Arthur and Phlox, who were married and were the captain and first mate; Debi and Yoko, the two physicist's mates, who shared a large compartment with Squire, who was the physicist; Peter, the astronomer, who was too autistic to sleep with anyone or even to talk much, but a good astronomer and good at sitting beside people and keeping them company; and Mtepic, the mathematician, whose wife Sudden Crow, the mathematician's mate, had died two years ago in eintime.

In slowtime it had been ten and a half years ago, but ship people have a saying that no one lives in slowtime. By "no one," they mean almost everyone.

Arthur and Phlox had thought that Mtepic might be too old for another wife, but he surprised them by saying he thought he might have another twenty years of eintime left and he didn't want to spend it alone.

There was actually only one possible conclusion. They would have to buy someone from a slave world. That was a bad thing, but not hopelessly bad—rather common in fact. Debi, Peter, Sudden Crow, and Arthur had all been slaves, and at least Debi and Arthur felt strongly that buying a slave into a free life, though morally question-able, was usually good for the slave.

The others had been adopted as infants, raised to age four or five on *9743*, and then sent through slowtime on a training ship to rejoin the crew when they were adults. All seven of them, whether born slave or free, agreed that it was better to be raised as ship people right from the start.

But they had had no plans for coping when Sudden Crow had died at fifty-one, without warning, from weightless calcium heart atrophy and overweight. *9743* was at least two years eintime from anywhere with freeborn babies available. They would have had to acquire the baby, tend it till it was four or five years old—a long time for a cargo ship to put up with a child, for ship people don't like to be around other people very much, and children must have attention all the time.

It would constrain them for several voyages—first to a world with adoptable freeborns, then to a short-haul pair (two inhabited star sys-tems within six or seven light-years of each other) with a training ship orbiting one of them. That short-haul pair would need to be four to five years eintime away, between twenty-one and twenty-seven light-years distance at the 98.2 percent c that *9743* usually traveled.

At the short-haul pair *9743* would then have to hand the child over to the training ship, work a short-haul shuttle back and forth, then return, rendezvous with the training ship, and pick up the former four-year-old as a trained teenage crew member. It would add up to decades of running badly off the isoprofit geodesic.

They could have afforded that, but the nearest shorthaul pair was Sol/Alfsentary, which was nearly five years eintime away from the nearest system that sold babies. This could all add up to as much as seventeen years eintime before the teenaged crew member came back aboard to keep Mtepic company.

Mtepic was eighty-one and if he died anytime soon, they would not have a mathematician at all. Phlox and Debi, both of whom had math as a secondary, would have to cover, and the whole ship would have to assume the risk of having rusty, less-capable mathematicians filling in.

Besides, the best isoprofit geodesic available for adopting and training a freeborn baby had miserable numbers—long hauls and low profits throughout. A slave would be better, surely. And it was not so bad for the slave, they all assured each other.

The slave market at Thogmarch, the main inhabited world in the Beytydry system, was only six light-years away, and their cargo would take only a small loss there, one that *9743* Corporation could easily absorb and infinitely cheaper than the costs of dealing with a depressed mathematician. The medical synmind was confident at 94.4 percent that Mtepic was depressed. Besides, Mtepic said he was, and thought it was because of the loneliness. The synmind concurred with 78.5 percent confidence that a new mathematician's apprentice would help lift Mtepic out of it, but the crew were all sure that estimate was low—medics hate to make predictions of any kind about enfleshed intelligences.

9743 had some spare mass to feed to the shielder, and they could safely boost up to 98.65 percent c and reach Thogmarch in a little less than an einyear. If they radioed now, the message would arrive at Thogmarch almost seven weeks before the ship itself did, so that they could have a buyers and sellers ready for cargo switch on arrival, and have dealers lined up to sell them an apprentice mathematician with the sort of personality that could learn to like ship life.

"And *9743* has never bought a slave who wasn't grateful for a chance to stay on after manumission," Arthur said, finishing his long, slow reprise, which had begun with the appetizers and was now finishing in the wine after dessert. "Life here compared to what they have dirtside is a lot better."

Arthur was fond of explaining things that everyone already knew, which was utterly typical. Captains are notorious for spending much time explaining unnecessarily.

Even ship people say so, and for them to say that is saying something, for ship people are all that way. They like to let the talk be slow and affectionate and thorough. They acquire a habit of listening to things they have heard many times before, and already know by heart, just to indulge the person who needs to speak; and, so that the ears of the others stay friendly, most of them learn not to talk very much except at formal occasions.

"Mostly," Peter said, startling them all because he spoke so infrequently, "we allow them some dignity and privacy." He meant the slaves, of course, though he might have meant anyone on the ship. "And by the time the first voyage is up they don't miss home, which anyway gets far enough into the past that it becomes hard to return to." He drank off a glass of the chilled white wine; they had turned on the gammors for an extra hour this week, to enjoy a sit down meal in the conference room, because this was a matter that needed some serious attention. At 98.1% percent, with a course change imminent, a quarter g of acceleration for a few hours of sitting and talking would have little effect on anything. "I'm for," Peter said.

"We're not *at* voting *yet*," Debi corrected him, a little fussily, which was how she did everything.

Squire rubbed her shoulders; it never made her less fussy but they both enjoyed it. "We know what he means, though. This is something that has always worked so far. We find a teenager with very high math aptitude and very low interpersonal attachment. Slavers are cruel; we are merely indifferent. If she doesn't have too much need for interpersonal attachment, she may even think we are kind—you do want a girl, right, Mtepic?"

"Yes, a girl."

Squire gestured like a man who would have liked to have a blackboard. "Well, then, life on the ship is better than being beaten and used and ordered about; a bit of respect and dignity often works wonders."

Phlox was nodding, and when she did, people usually felt that the vote had already been taken, and the thing approved. Everyone, even Arthur, said she would be a better captain, once he died. She rested her hands together in a little tent in front of her, nodded again, and said, "When we manumit her, she will want to stay with us. They always do. So this plan will get us a new mathematician's mate who can eventually become our mathematician. It is not as kind as adopting a freeborn baby and having a training ship raise the baby as a free member of the ship's company, and it is not as easy as working an exchange with another ship would be if there were another ship to do it with. But it is kind enough, and easy enough. So we are going to settle on doing it. Now let us enjoy talking about it for some more hours."

Everyone nodded; ship people are direct, even about delaying getting to the point, and they like to know how new things will come out, before they start them, because they so rarely do.

In the young woman's file, Mtepic had read that Xhrina had been born a shareworker's daughter on Thogmarch, and her sale forced when she was two, by her parents' bankruptcy. Her records showed that because she had intellectual talent but great difficulty learning social skills, she had been little valued on Thogmarch. The slaver who owned her had slated her for some post where her ability to endure humiliation over the long haul would be an asset; he had in mind either an aristocrat with a taste for brutalizing women, or a household that wanted to boast of its wealth by using human beings instead of robots to scrub floors and clean toilets.

Mtepic, as not only the person who would be working and living with her, but also the most empathetic person onboard *9743* (according to the medic-synmind's most recent testing), had been sent dirtside to decide whether to buy Xhrina, and as he sat in the clean-air support tank his major thought was that he would take her if at all possible, rather than endure planetary gravity for much longer.

His bones were old and space-rotten. Though he was strapped up against the interior supports of the tank, and a small man, there was still far too much weight.

Xhrina spoke a language with a distributed grammar and numerous Altaic and Semitic roots, so the translator box worked tolerably well, and with her aptitude, she was unlikely to have any trouble learning Navish, once she was aboard. Mtepic thought her voice was surprisingly musical for someone so discouraged and unhappy. After he outlined what would happen if *9743* bought her, and made sure the translator had made it clear to her, he asked, "Do you want us to buy you, then?"

She trilled a soft trickle of sweet soprano sibilance. The translator box said, "This property had not yet realized there was any choice with respect to the subject at hand, my-sir."

"Officially there is not. Unofficially, we don't like slaving; *9743* has never carried slaves and never will. As you may know, slaving planets all enforce the Karkh Code on ships carrying slaves, so we cannot manumit you until you have performed satisfactory service for thirty years. But the Karkh Code operates in slowtime; in eintime, time as we experience it, you will be a slave for less than seven years, perhaps much less. And as much as we can manage it, within the limits of the Karkh Code, you will be a slave in the eyes of the law only. We won't ever treat you as a slave." He had to put that through the translator to her a few times, and they went back and forth again until he was sure she understood the deal.

"And my-sir still makes it have a sounding, correction, gives it an aura of, as if it were this property's choice, my-sir, and this property is trained not to make choices where my-sir has the right to choose."

He went at it a sentence at a time, forcing himself to be patient with the translator, which had the uncaring stupidity one would expect of a synmind.

The first critical sentence Mtepic communicated was, "If you ask that we not buy you, we will buy someone else."

Next, because it might matter to her, whether or not she was allowed to think it did, he spent a while explaining that, "Once you are onboard, you will be expected to share a bed with me—my demands are minor, at my age, mostly that you keep away loneliness. Other crew will probably not want sex from you, being happy as they are, but if they do you will comply; our computer must show that for the Karkh Code manumission."

She seemed to accept that too easily and he didn't want her to think that was the main issue, so then he worked on getting her to understand that "you will not be coming aboard as a bedmate. Your main job will be to learn enough mathematics so that you are qualified as a mathematician's mate by the time we reach a port where we are legally allowed to free you with a universal manumission so that you will not be in danger if you change ships, or disembark and then travel again. At that port, you can leave our company if you like, or stay in the crew as a shareholder." That was actually easier to say, because the synmind was designed to understand contracts.

Then he got back to the main point, again, and this time it seemed to go faster. "If you ask that we not buy you, we will buy someone else. We do not want you to be unwilling."

"It is forbidden for this property to consider whether this property is willing for anything my-sir wills, my-sir, and I cannot know how this property will feel if this property is ever permitted to consider it, my-sir." She smiled when she said that; perhaps to let him know that she could only speak the formulas, or that the translator would only translate into the formulas, but that she accepted what he was saying, was that it? Or perhaps something in all this appealed to her sense of humor? In either case, he liked her for that smile.

Mtepic breathed deeply and let the thousands of mechanical fingers lift him straight, and the neurostimulators sharpen his perception and ease his discomfort.

Xhrina's skin was brown; the slavers had genetically modified her for almost pure-white hair; her nose was long and slim and her jaw and teeth perfectly formed. Her eyes were dark and almond-shaped. He thought that as little as twenty years ago, he would have felt physically attracted. Now, just turned eighty-three, he was attracted by what he could get through the censoring translator: that she didn't seem to want to exaggerate or overpromise, and clearly *had* an opinion she was trying to express.

He gave her another angle on it, just to make sure. "We think, based on your psychological evaluation, that you are suited to shipboard life, and you will be living like a free crewmember as soon as we leave the dock here." That seemed to go right through.

"If this property may ask, is crew life like freeborn life, my-sir?"

"You can always accept a payout and leave at the next port. Of course you have to be on the ship until we reach a port, and if you did decide to leave the ship after your first couple of voyages, you would have to move into a hospital for rehabilitation if you wanted to move permanently to a planetary surface." That thought reminded Mtepic of how painful the high gravity was, and so he decided to press the offer a little more. He just hoped he correctly understood her quirky smile still struggling through her slavery-deadened face. "I would like you to come with us," he said. "I am asking you. I could buy you and *make* you. I prefer that you say yes." And trying to think of what else he had to offer, he said, "My first order to you, as soon as you are on the ship, will be that you address no one as 'my-sir,' but speak to us all as equals."

She grinned at him as if on the brink of outright laughter. "Then if it pleases my-sir, this property wants to be bought by my-sir, my-sir."

He was fairly sure that was not what she had said, but surely it had been some form of yes. He didn't trouble to conceal his sigh of relief.

A few hours later, at her welcome-aboard dinner on *9743*, once she had been assured that now she would never be returned to Thogmarch, she used an uncontrolled translator to explain, "I was always going to say yes, but the translator didn't want me to know I was being asked to say it because I wasn't supposed to have any choices or respond to them if anyone offered me any. Once I figured out what it wasn't translating, of course I said yes—it was such a pleasure to be asked. And I beg Mtepic's forgiveness, for having kept you upright for too long in that uncomfortable tank." And she favored him again with that extraordinary smile.

Two years eintime, eleven slowtime, on their way to the Sol system; the earlier PPDs had flipped because at Thogmarch they had acquired cargo β–Hy-9743-R56, which was forecast to be at peak value at Sol almost exactly at arrival time. Xhrina's Navish was fluent and she was already well into group and ring theory, and apter than her test scores showed. Mtepic had turned eighty-five the day before, and Xhrina had been disappointed that no one wanted to have a party for him this year (she'd only been able to get two of them to participate the year before), so she'd held one for just the two of them.

She had learned to find it comforting when his fragile body pressed against her in the sleepsack, his skin so soft and dry that he felt like a paper bag of old chicken bones, and she was pleased to indulge his liking for going to bed at the same time; when he died, she would miss his company, but he would probably live for many more years; many ship people lived to be 110.

On the rare occasions when he still wanted any sort of sex, he would gently wake her and ask very politely. She understood that he was determined that she should forget that she was a slave, but Xhrina believed in rules, and would not stop being a slave till she was manumitted, though she was delighted to be ordered to behave like a free person, because the pure autophagy of it made her laugh. They often argued about that in a good-natured way, as he insisted on knowing what she thought and she attempted to tell him only what he wanted to hear, and they enjoyed their mutual failure.

She doubted whether she would ever love anyone, but if she did, it would have been very convenient and not at all a bother or a danger to have loved Mtepic.

When his age-knobbed knuckles brushed down her naked back she turned to let him touch her where he liked, but he placed a finger on her mouth and breathed, "Come with me" in her ear.

He slipped from the sleepsack and swam to his clothes. It was dim in the compartment with only the convenience lights on. As she popped from the sleepsack, he smiled at the sight of her, as he always did, and pushed her coverall bag toward her. She caught it and dressed as she had learned to do, in one movement, like his but swifter because she was young.

He beckoned her to follow him, and opened the hatch into the main crewpipe. They swam in silence up the center of the crewpipe to the opsball. She had only been there the four times that 9743 had needed working: first while they were kerring up the gravity well of Thogmarch, second as they kerred three light-weeks up the gravity well of Beytydry, once before they picked their next destination and turned the main gammors loose to leave Beytydry orbit, and then just two weeks ago for the PPD as budgets, prices, positions, relative velocities, and predictions changed.

That last time, just two weeks ago, Xhrina had been able to follow the discussions, though not really participate in them. Still, she appreciated that Mtepic was a very good ship's mathematician. It had made her bend harder to her studies, for to be an excellent ship's mathematician seemed a very grand thing to her, partly because it was clear that all the other ship people respected it, and mostly because it was what Mtepic was.

But this fifth time in the opsball, they were the only ones. He did not turn on the lights; they sneaked in as if to steal something.

She didn't ask.

She had come, in two years eintime with him, to trust Mtepic. Sometimes she asked herself if she wasn't just being a very faithful slave, but generally she felt that she was trusting like a free person, that Mtepic and she were friends like free people, and Xhrina was secretly very proud of that.

So she didn't ask. She just floated beside Mtepic on one side of the opsball. Since he seemed to be very quiet, she tried to stay even quieter.

Presently the surfaces all around them began to glow, and then the image of the stars shone round the opsball, just as if the human crew were about to commence operation, but perhaps a tenth as brightly. For a moment the display was Dopplered, and there was a blue pole that contained a crunched-down vivid blue Cassipy with Sol and Alfsentary in it, and a red smeared-out Leyo and Viryo, but in less than a second the display corrected.

Mtepic and Xhrina floated in what looked exactly like the dark between the stars, warm and comfortable in their crew coveralls. It was so beautiful with no working screens pulled up that she wondered why the crew did not do this all the time. Perhaps she could get permission to float here among the pictures of the stars, now and then, on her off-awake shift?

She had lost count of the breaths she had slowly drawn and released as she watched the projected stars creep along the surface of the opsball when from one side of the opsball, where Leyo was crawling slowly across, a pale white glow like a broken off bit of the Milky Way burgeoned from a blurry dot to a coin of fog and thence into a lumpy fist of thin white swirl. The swirl swelled into a cloud of particles, then of objects, which surged to swallow the ship and closed around them like a hand grasping a baby bird.

The particles were now as large as people—they were people—translucent and glowing, many of them gesturing as if talking, but not to each other, more as if they had all been abstracted from some larger conversation. The vast crowd converged around the ship, and then all of them were gone except for the dozen who passed right through the wall and into the opsball.

How was that possible? Xhrina wondered. The opsball was buried deep in the center of the ship, 750 meters of holds, lifemachines, quarters, and engines in all directions around it, but the translucent figures, glowing perhaps half as bright as the brightest stars, seemed to merge directly from space outside the ship into space inside the ship.

The pallid figures, mere surfaces and outlines of people, filled the dark sphere. They all took up crew stations as if they were where they belonged, reaching for the opsball surface and calling up workscreens before them, drawing them with their fingers or spreading them with their hands just as regular crew did. The one nearest her was a woman whose strangely patterned coverall had sleeves for both legs and arms, slippers for the feet, and gloves on the hands; Xhrina wondered what sort of ship it was that necessitated so much clothing. That woman seemed to be an astronomer, by what Xhrina could see over her shoulder to her screen, but the graphics were labeled in a language that was not written like Navish.

Directly in front of her, a man who wore coat, shirt, and pants like people in prestellar Earth stories tumbled slowly, pointing and gesturing as if he were the captain. Through his dim translucent sheen, Xhrina could see a nude young woman whose head was half missing, simply gone behind the ears with brains spilling down her back. Despite that, the young woman was working at a very large screen, apparently trying to estimate a vast matrix and not liking what she saw, redoing and redoing; the screen looked like the math software that Xhrina herself used. As she watched, the naked woman beat on the screen with her fists; Xhrina wondered if the problem was what was on the screen, or the lost parts of her brain.

All round the mathematician and his apprentice, the ghosts worked their ghostly screens, seeming as unaware of each other as of the living beings. They went on working—laughing, cursing, pounding, all without a sound—until the gentle, sweet whistle of Second

Shift sounded through the ship. Then they faded through the walls of the opsball, dimming to darkness, and the stars dimmed to nothing after them.

Mtepic brought the running lights up. "Breakfast?"

"Surely," she said. "Perhaps we should nap again after?"

"We're bound to be tired," he agreed. If he was disappointed that she asked no questions, he did not indicate it.

Xhrina had twice celebrated Mtepic's birthday—the first time with Peter and Yoko who were good-natured but baffled about it, the second time just the two of them the night before they had seen the ghosts. From this, Mtepic deduced that she would like such a thing herself, and checked her bill of sale to find when her birthday was (she had never been told, and Mtepic did not think she should have to see her bill of sale unless she asked).

At one shift close, he surprised her with the news that she had just turned twenty-four, and also with the sort of gifts ship people give: her favorite meal, a small keepsake produced in the ship's fabricator, and time set aside to sit with her and watch a story he knew she'd like.

She had already known that Mtepic thought that she had a great deal of mathematical talent and believed she would one day be a fine ship's mathematician, and she knew too that he liked to have her around him. But still it was a surprise to Xhrina to realize that he also just wanted to do things that would make her happy. No one had ever appeared to care about that before, at all. It took her by surprise, put her a little off balance, but she considered the possibility that she might like it.

By her twenty-sixth birthday, after their five months of slowtime in the port orbiting Old Mars, *9743* was bound for Sigdracone, where she was to be manumitted. By now she was quite sure that she liked Mtepic's kindness and concern for her happiness, and as his health began to fail little by little, she realized that she was glad to be taking care of him, which he only needed occasionally so far, and to be there when he was afraid, which was rare but sometimes severe.

After much thought she concluded that she had been very damaged by the things the slavers had done to her, and guessed that this taking care of Mtepic might be as close to love as she would ever feel. Though she did not miss sex much, she wished he were still well enough to enjoy it; though he was sometimes crabby, and nowadays he slept a great deal, she liked to sit or float where she could have a hand on him, or an arm around him, constantly, as if he were her blanket and she were two years old.

His mind, when he was awake and not in pain, seemed as fine as ever, and she was grateful for that. She was glad she had said she wanted to come along, and everyone knew without saying that she would be staying on the ship, and would probably qualify to be ship's mathematician as soon as Mtepic died or became senile, though no one mentioned the inevitability of either of those to her. Ship people are indifferent, usually knowing nothing of each other's feelings, and not caring even when they must know, but even they could tell that she would miss Mtepic terribly and that the title of ship's mathematician would mean little to her compared to the loss of the only friend she had ever had.

Friend, she thought. *That's what Mtepic is to me. I thought he might be, and how nice to know it now, while I can appreciate it.*

They were about halfway there; it would be about two years or so eintime until they would lock themselves into the support field caskets so that every cell wall in their body could be held up against the 150-g acceleration of the gammors running flat out; three days later they would stagger out hungry and tired. Xhrina had been through all that now three times, and had no dread of it; as far as she was concerned, going from gammors down to Kerr motors meant minor discomfort followed by the most enjoyable meal and nap she was ever likely to have.

But for the moment that was still two years eintime, more than a decade slowtime, in the future. They had little to do but think and learn. Learning was fun: Xhrina had already passed her mathematician's mate's exam with highest distinction, and was well on her way to qualifying as a ship's mathematician.

As for thinking, Xhrina often thought about recursion. She thought it was interesting that she didn't always know what she liked, and she thought that everyone must have the same problem, for the only people she knew well were her shipmates, and they were impossible to know well, perhaps because they did not know what they liked, either.

She particularly liked the way that thinking about how it was possible not to know what she herself liked made her thoughts turn into circles and whorls and braids, spiraling down into the first questions about how she knew that she knew anything, as if descending into dark empty singularities; as her thoughts would vanish at the edge of those absent unthinkable thoughts, they marked the boundary as surely as the glimmers of vanishing dust and atoms at the Schwarzschild radius of a black hole.

Sometimes for a whole day she would keep track of which thought led to which thought and count how often, and by what diversity of paths, thoughts returned to the surfaces and boundaries of the unknowable. She could have flicked her fingers across any flat surface to make a workscreen, recited her data into the air, and played to her heart's content with the *grafsentatz*. But when she was working on the recursivity of her thoughts, she preferred to hang in the dark in the opsball, and bring up stars for their current position/time (she could have brought them up for anywhere/anywhen, but she always chose current position and time). She always brought them up to just bright enough to see once her eyes adjusted.

Then she would slow her breathing and heartbeat, and wait for the perfect calm when her chi settled into tan tien, and see only in her mind's eye the screens, matrices, graphs, and equations, and endlessly devise graphs to portray, and statistics to measure, the recursion and circularity of her own thoughts, and consider whether thoughts about recursion should be intrinsically, or just accidentally, more or less recursive than other thoughts, and watch as all those thoughts drifted down onto the unknown, unknowing surfaces of those first known-to-be-unanswerable questions.

When she was finally cool and beautiful inside, she would softly ask the opsball to let the stars dim out, watch them till the last star was gone from the blackness, then swim back to Mtepic's quarters, where she would often find him sleeping fitfully and uneasily, drifting all over the compartment because he had fallen asleep outside the sleepsack. Then she would bathe him and rub him till he fell asleep smiling, and curl up against him for lovely, deep, dreamless sleep. The nightmares of her childhood were mostly gone now, and no more than pale shadows when they returned.

In the Sigdracone system, she still had enough of her gravity-bone to stand up and raise her hand, down on the surface of Aloysio, and receive her freedom under the open air. She wasn't quite sure why she chose to do that. It all seemed so harsh and uncomfortable and when she returned to the ship, it felt as if she *really* received her freedom at the dinner they had for her. Though they treated her just as they always had, as an equal, it mattered to her that now they were supposed to.

She affirmed and they voiceprinted it, making Xhrina a shareholder in 9743, backvested with all the equity that she had built up in the trust fund they had kept for her, while she had not been allowed to own property in case the ship had to touch base, and face a books inspection, on a Karkh Convention world. They drank a toast.

The slowtime people at Aloysio wanted a total cargo changeover, something that only happened once in a century or so of eintime. An organization that the translators called the "Aloysio Museum of Spiritual Anger Corporation" bought the whole cargo, and sold 9743 an entirely new cargo: 1,024 cubes, sixty meters on a side, with identifier strips on every face.

None of 9743's ship people had known in a long time what ships carried, except that they never carried slaves, because they refused to, or any living thing that needed tending, because none of them wanted to learn how. So they knew the containers in the hold had nothing alive, or at least nothing actively alive, in them.

Other than that they knew nothing; over the slow correspondence of decades between ship people on other ships, there was an eternal argument about why no crew knew what was in the cargo. Some said it was because in the wars of fifteen thousand years ago, a tradition had been established that no ship people were ever to be responsible for anything they carried. Others said it was simply that the hundreds of thousands of cultures in slowtime changed so much and so fast compared with ship people that no one could have understood what the cargo was anyway. And still others said that the people on the worlds did not trust ship people not to steal it if they knew what it was, but most people said that was the silliest of all ideas, since anyone knew that the most valuable thing on a ship was hold space, and who would want to keep cargo and never be able to use the hold space again? Or who would buy or sell something when all contracts were broadcast openly, and it would be obvious to anyone that it was stolen?

Actually even if she had known, she would not have cared what was in the cargo. She did know where the cargo was going—that was what a mathematician did, after all—and she liked that very much. The ship would be making a very long haul, out into the north polar section of the Third Pulse worlds, where the inhabited stars were too distant to have ancient names because they had not been naked-eye visible from Earth, and so had been named for abstract qualities by the Second Pulse surveyors; she loved the idea that the suns all had names like Perspicacity, Charity, and Preternaturalness. And it would be six years eintime before their next system entry, perhaps more if the PPDs broke right.

On her twenty-ninth birthday, they were outbound and life had settled into the most comfortable of routines; after the small gifts and the warm feeling of attention, she rubbed Mtepic to sleep—he was just a soft, thin cover on lumpy bones, anymore, she thought—and drifted off herself, glad Mtepic had been there for her first birthday as a free person, hoping she could complete her mathematics preps and qualify for ship's mathematician while he could congratulate her for it.

Mtepic's soft palms and fingers pressed for one light instant on her shoulder blades. "It's strange how it happens on birthdays."

She glanced at the clock; she and Mtepic had been asleep for five hours since they had celebrated her birthday. Xhrina turned and held him in a light embrace; he sometimes woke up, now, talking to people he had been talking to in dreams, and she didn't like to startle him.

He embraced her in return, firmly and strongly, and now she knew he was awake, just starting in the middle as he tended to do. She waited to see what he would do or say. After a sigh—he liked holding her and she knew he might have been glad to do it much longer—Mtepic said, "There will be ghosts in the opsball tonight. I am going to watch them again. Would you like to come with me?"

"Of course," she said. "Does it happen on everyone's birthday?"

"Just mine, I thought. But now yours. Dress quickly. There's never much warning. We must be there and silent before the ghost-power lights up the opsball."

They dressed, swam through the main crewpipe, and entered the opsball.

Everything that evening was as before, except that the ghosts were different. First the Dopplered stars, and then the corrected stars, dimmer even than when Xhrina came in here to meditate. The fast-moving cloud made of ghosts zoomed silently up out of the Southern Cross to surround them in less than a minute. The ghosts in their thousands swarmed around the outside of (the ship? the opsball? But the opsball was 750 meters inside the ship, and yet the twenty or so ghosts who came inside seemed to merge directly from the projected stars to their positions in the opsball).

This time Xhrina mostly watched two young men, apparently twins, trying to solve what she thought must be an equation, though on each side of the equals sign there was only a rotating projection of a lumpy ellipsoid in several colors.

Or perhaps it was a game. They were both laughing very hard about it, whatever it was, and Xhrina liked the way they threw arms around each other and rested their heads on each others' shoulders, then went back to their game or problem or whatever it was, sitting left shoulder to right shoulder, making little blobs of multicolor swim off one blob and across the equals sign to stick to the blob on the other side. Whenever they did that, both blobs would reorganize into different colors and shapes, and the two of them would clap, together, rhythmically, silently, as if to an unheard song.

A teenaged girl that Xhrina thought might have been a daughter or some other relative to the smashed-headed woman from last time— or was it the same woman at an earlier stage of life?—was working her screen, whose language looked like some late Konglish derivative, with a gymnast's concentration.

Another woman, old and stout with jowls, thin short gray hair like velvet, and something rough and wrong with the skin of her neck, wore a military uniform that could have been Late Brazilian Empire, Old Lunar Mexico, or Old Taucetian Guinea; somewhere in the First Interpulse, anyway, around the time of the Trade and Momentum Wars, because she looked just like the characters in a story, with bank codes on her sleeves, Mahmud boots, and a vibratana in a back scabbard.

Xhrina looked more closely, flapping her hands very gently to move herself toward the older woman in the military uniform. Bank trademarks on the shoulders; an admiral, then. Skull-jewels, gold with ruby eyes, in her pierced lower lip; four of them, four battle victories. The bank's symbol had the ancient dollar and yen signs, crossed, in two pairs, on either side of a balance, which could be any of the dozens of military-and-financial-services companies in any of the three millennia of that era.

The admiral was worried, her fingers gliding over a screen that kept changing its display but always showed a cluster of white points surrounded by a swarm of red points, sometimes labeled in the blocky letters of ancient Romantisco, sometimes connected by varicolored lines, sometimes with little translucent spheres around them and clocks ticking beneath them, sometimes in a view that tumbled and rotated to show the shape that the whole formation made in space.

She kept touching the white dots like a mother cat checking her kittens. Abruptly Xhrina understood; the squadron was bunching together to try to make a run through the closing bag, and the admiral didn't want to lose any of them. It was a classic situation, so common during those wars; the red dots were ringoes, robot ships that came in at a single target at one hundred g, expending their entire magazines at the target and fuel supplies in acceleration, trying to ram just as they ran empty.

Once a ringo locked on and cranked its gammor to full power, they just kept coming, everything about them bent toward pure raw violence, game pieces intended to sacrifice at one to one, but they knew that they were too valuable to throw away on a bad risk, so they would not lock on until they decided they were close enough for a high probability of a kill. The admiral was trying to get her squadron out of a bag of ringoes, losing as few as she could manage. It did not look like that number would be zero, and it would be many hours before the brief burst of their violent escape, so she could choose to save any ship, but not all of them.

A very overweight, brown-skinned older woman dressed in a sleeveless coverall like Xhrina's own opened an application that Xhrina knew well. Xhrina gently paddled through the air to see better what the woman was doing and found that she was bumping up against Mtepic, paddling over from the other side.

He floated, reflecting the glow of the ghost in front of them. His rounded, reflecting surfaces—forehead, nose, knuckles, knees— glowed gray in the dim light; these seemed to shrink back, as if he were falling back away from the ghosts and the stars beyond them, into utterly lightless dark.

Across Mtepic's face, shoulders, and chest, a tangle of bright-glowing filaments emerged as if rising through his skin, like noodles in a colander slowly surfacing from boiling water.

The filaments broadened, stuck to each other, filled in gaps between. The dense, glowing web merged into the pale white shape of a newborn baby, like a bas relief just a centimeter or so above Mtepic's ghost-lit wrinkled old skin. The baby stretched and yawned. Its light washed over Mtepic's gray, still form and seemed to suck the color out of even his red coverall, leaving his lips blue-gray as dried mold.

The baby's tiny feet on apostrophes of legs barely reached the bottom of Mtepic's rib cage, but its head was almost as big as his. The arms, ending in hands too small to fully wrap Xhrina's thumb, reached out to fathom space around the baby but did not extend as far as Mtepic's slumped-in shoulders on either side. But the puckered face opened in a toothless, radiant smile of pure *What? How? What's all this?* Then the vast, deep eyes, clear and wide, focused on Xhrina, and the tiny soft mouth twisted and folded in the expression with which Mtepic always favored her best jokes. She could not help smiling back.

Not knowing why, she placed the palm of her right hand on the baby's chest, ever so gently, as if sure it would sink through to the sleeping Mtepic. She was surprised that the baby's chest was warm, damp, and firm under her hand for that instant.

Then she realized the baby was male, for a stream of phosphorescence poured wet and warm onto her sternum, making a glowing patch on her coverall, and she glanced down to see that the ghost baby, if that was what it was, had no more bladder control than a real one.

It was so unexpected that she giggled, carefully not making a sound but letting her chest convulse, and under her palm she felt the baby's chest pulse with the baby's giggle, sharing her delight. Her hand sank a tiny fraction forward, and the baby was gone. Her palm lightly pressed Mtepic's chest, where his heart thundered and his breath surged in and out as if he had worked too long and hard in the gym again, as he did so often despite her gentle scolding. His bony old hands closed around her strong young fingers, and he smiled at her, squeezing her hand.

For the rest of the night they held hands as they watched the laughing twins, the motherly admiral, the fat mathematician, and the rest of the ghostly crew. At last the shift chimes sounded, and the ghosts faded away, and then the stars. "Lights up slow," she said, and the opsball appeared around them, its surfaces matte gray, shut down, and inert, the same old opsball it was for months and years at a time.

"Breakfast in our quarters and a long talk?" she asked.

"Surely! And I am so pleased."

"At what?"

"You said 'our quarters,' not 'your quarters.' That is the first time in six years."

"It was important to you? I would have said it much sooner if I had known it mattered."

"It was important to me that you say it without my asking. And it was not important at all, at first, but it is now." They swam through the irising door of the opsball. "And when it became important, I began to count. You wouldn't laugh at my silly senility?"

"You are not senile and I would not laugh at you."

"Well, then, as it became important, I calculated backward to your arrival, and then began to count, and so I know that it has been 2,222 days eintime since you came aboard, and this is the first time you have said 'our quarters.'"

"Other people might find something odd in that number," she said, "all those twos."

They swam into their quarters. Mtepic flipped over like a seal resting at sea, hands on his belly. "Other people might find something odd in that number, but you and I know about numbers, eh?"

"Exactly so," she said. "In octal it is merely 4,256, and in duodecimal an even less meaningful 1,352. 32,342 in quintal is about as close as you can get to meaningful expression in any other base, and that's not *very* meaningful. And I would say that if meaning is not invariant we can ignore it."

"Except when we can't, of course?"

That struck them both as funny, for reasons that they knew no one else would understand, and they laughed as they filled out their breakfast order, and filed their official intention to serve their shifts on call in their quarters that day.

Mtepic's sweet tooth had grown ever stronger as he aged. His favorite breakfast was now a fluffy, sweet pancake spread with blueberry jam and wrapped around vanilla ice cream, and as he slowly ate that this morning, he seemed to relish it more than ever. "Well," he asked, "what would you like to know?"

"Was it real?"

He pointed to her chest; the damp spot still glowed.

She ran a finger over it; the very tip of the finger glowed for an instant, and then faded.

"How does it work?" she asked.

"I don't know," he admitted. "I don't even know why I wake up knowing there will be ghosts. Or why it was so important to show them to you, or why I want to see them, myself." He took another bite of his pancake and caressed it in his mouth until it dissolved; she waited until at last he said, "I would have gone, you know. That ghost was Sudden Crow, my wife before you—not that you are my wife, though the offer is open if you want it; it meant a great deal to her, but you've never seemed to care."

"I don't. 'Not slave' is all the title I ever wanted, and you gave me that, and you know I'll be with you as long as you live—maybe I should say as long as you want to stay. But you almost . . . left? Do you miss Sudden Crow?"

"Not very much, to tell the truth. She was bad-tempered and some- times rough with me. I wouldn't mind saying hello again but I hope I wouldn't have to spend any time with her as a ghost. Thirty years of combined time on this side was enough."

"Do you say 'this side' because it feels spatial?"

Frowning, he thought, and then at last shook his head. "More like the sides of a game or a question than the sides of a segment or a sur- face." He pondered more, then took another delighted bite of his breakfast. "Really, your friendship is one good reason to stay on this side, more than enough reason all by itself, but this breakfast could be another, and when I think of all the other things I still enjoy, I can understand why so few people want to go before they have to. It was just that seeing her there, somehow I knew *how* I could go, if I wanted to go. And the old body is such a nuisance, you know, sometimes, it gets so sore and itchy and hurty. So I did want to, just for that moment, but now I'm glad I didn't."

"Do the ghosts come aboard often?"

"You've been with me the last two times. Out of six in all. Five on my birthdays, now one on yours. And I've never told anyone else, but I knew you were the right one to see it. I've searched through all twenty-seven thousand years of star trader history, and records from more than a million ships—traders but also slavers, military, scout, and colony—and though there are many accounts of ghosts, most are just fiction, labeled as such, and many of the rest seem to be merely some bit of culture that came loose from its old moorings in some folktale and washed up in the star trader culture. And *9743* itself records the ghosts but doesn't perceive them; they are there on cam- era recordings but if you ask *9743* to look for the ghosts in all its thousands of years of recordings of the opsball, it won't see any ghosts, and it can look right at a camrec full of ghosts and does not perceive them; it only sees an empty, dark opsball."

"So they are aphysical. But they record physically. What do you suppose they are?"

"A very expressive hole in space-time?" Mtepic shrugged. "Most star traders commit bodies to space at peak velocity. Most of us run at ninety-eight percent c or higher. Once the body is outside the protection of the forward shield, the atoms and dust in interstellar space erode it, and it loses velocity, though not quickly. And of course it is far above galactic escape velocity. Except for the very few that run into stars or black holes or comets, all the bodies committed to space must still be out there, some as much as thirty thousand light-years away if you allow for burials during the First Pulse when there was little or no trade.

"You could picture each corpse as a long pathway, sweeping atoms and ions and molecules and dust out of interstellar space, shaped very much like the dead person at this end in time and space, and as the interstellar medium punches them full of holes and breaks them down, trailing off into just a cloud of nucleons at a far end somewhere way outside the galaxy and some millions of years in the future. Perhaps something aphysical flows back along the path they make, and— crystallizes? condenses? maybe just *organizes* is the word for what it does, around any passing seed or nucleus or whatever you would call a thing a ghost organizes around. Maybe where a large number of pathways run close together, they entangle like spaghetti, and express as a ghost swarm when something that can appreciate their meaning comes along. That would explain the association with birthdays. Birthdays are meaningful even though they're so drastically different in slowtime and eintime and depend completely on when you got on the ship, and where it goes, and how long an Old Earth year was at the moment they standardized it. So maybe ghosts annucleate around meaningful things like ships and birthdays. It makes a certain kind of sense. Meaning is aphysical, and ghosts are aphysical. Then again, what do physical beings like us know of aphysics?"

"But none of that would explain the baby coming out of your chest, or that the baby was you, or that we both remember it, let alone that I've got a patch of spiritual pee right over my heart."

"Was I a baby? I wondered why I felt so strangely proportioned, and so small, and had no teeth. Well, that is certainly data to add to the puzzle."

"Why should there be ghosts or spirits on a starship?"

"Why not here as much as anywhere? And for that matter, why should there be ships? Robot-only starships are just slightly less likely to reach their destinations, but it would be so easy to factor that into the price, and it would be more profitable to send containers one way and just accept some losses at the other end. As it is 9743 pays for an immense amount of space and mass to keep us alive. So why are we here? Why is there even an economy? We make everything on the ship by transmutation and molecular assembly—we never 'pick up supplies' though we sometimes buy new goods to record them for later manufacture—and we know the people in slowtime are centuries or millennia ahead of us—so why is there cargo for us to carry?"

"You think that has something to do with the ghosts," Xhrina said, not a question, just trying to stay with him; clearly he had been thinking about this for a long time, had worked out the perfect presentation in his mind, wanted to have it produce perfect understanding—it was the way he had taught her mathematics. She knew he liked it when she understood at once, and she knew this might be her only chance to understand.

"I think it's another void in space-time. Once pretty much everyone human traded, going way back to Old Earth. For some reason it paid to trade between the stars. The ships began to move. Now they just move, bodies in motion remaining in motion, and the trading just happens. Maybe. Maybe we're *all* just the ghosts of what humans used to do. Three quarters of the star systems we traded in at one time or another now just wave us off, new ones come online, and old ones reactivate after centuries of slowtime. Who can say what goes on out there?"

"Is it possible that the slowtime people on the planets are all just crazy, or perhaps playing at things because there's nothing real left?"

"The slowtime people might ask the same things about us. We could just liquidate, and move into a nice orbital resort where they'd pamper us silly for the rest of our lives."

"I would hate that."

"So would I." Mtepic smiled shyly. "Do you think it would be all right for me to have another pancake like that last one?"

"You've been losing weight," she said, "and I worry about your appetite. You can have ten as far as I'm concerned. And actually, being *very* concerned, I wish you would."

"Let's start with one, but I'll keep the offer in mind. And you're right, I haven't been taking very good care of myself, and for some reason, now I feel like I want to, at least for a while."

She prepared it for him, not because he couldn't do it himself, and not because she had to. She pointed that out as she served it to him, and he said, "You see? Part of what makes it good is all the things it's not."

She thought about that for a while and she said, "So the ghosts are not hallucinations. And they're not physical as we understand it or the machines would be able to see them, rather than just record them. And you think maybe they're where the bodies—well, the traces of the bodies—are not."

"Except that Sudden Crow destroyed that theory," he said. "She always was good at destroying theory. Part of why she was a good shipmate."

"She hurt you," Xhrina said, surprised at her own vehemence. "You said she was rough with you."

"True. But I was not as fragile then as I've become, and besides she was a valuable member of the crew. And of course so are you, and getting more valuable all the time, and you are very good to me. You fill up a space different from the one she vacated."

"I'd better," she said. "I wouldn't want to fill her place, at all." And because she had said it a bit too vehemently, and the two of them were looking at each other awkwardly, she hurried on with the first question she could think of. "Why did you say Sudden Crow destroyed your theory about the traces of the bodies in spacetime?"

"Because she was buried in space about a year and a half out of Aydee-to-Ridny, outbound. Her pathway couldn't have come anywhere near here."

"But she was on this ship. Her path before she was dead included it. What if it doesn't matter as long as you can describe the path, or the place where the path was? Suppose that, and maybe—"

"But it might be too hard if we suppose that," Mteptic objected. "It doesn't restrict things enough. Why don't we see everyone's ghost all the time?"

"'Mathematics is how we find the logical implications of the boundaries of things, and the whole history of mathematics is the story of working with fewer and flimsier boundaries,'" she said. "You said that to me the very first time I sat down to learn algebra. Maybe we don't see them often enough because there aren't enough boundaries to produce them, or because we live inside so many boundaries, or . . . well, we don't even know what the boundaries are, do we?"

"Hard to evaluate the boundary conditions," Mtepic agreed. "But as far as I can see, it's all holes and voids. There's some odd thing in the slowtime world, some place we fill, though we don't know what it is. Empty spots left in crews and on ships when people die, and the holes in space they make when we throw their bodies away, and the big emptiness of space itself, and every hole is outlined, and every outline means the hole—and, well, you must think I'm senile by now, surely."

"I don't," she said. "Oh, I *don't*. You *know* I don't. Can I make you another pancake?"

In Mtepic's last few years, they talked more. She liked that. She had received the last promotion she could get while he was alive, to mathematician's-mate-pending-mathematician. That forced her for the first time to think of the succession. She decided that however she acquired her apprentice (she rather hoped to buy one out of a slave world, she would feel good about freeing someone as she had been freed), she would consider looking for someone who would talk. Many ship people didn't, for weeks or months at a time.

That was another guess of Mtepic's, that ship society was where the surrounding slowtime societies were dumping their autistic people and those whose mathematical gifts were no longer needed because they had synminds. "Sort of a featherbedding asylum for mathematicians," he would say, coughing and laughing as she bathed, dried, and rubbed him. She would always laugh too, just because it was Mtepic and she felt how close he was to crossing over to the other side, and she expected to miss him then, and wish she could hear his jokes again.

The night after her thirtieth birthday, she awoke knowing that there would be ghosts in the opsball, and felt Mtepic waking within the circle of her arms. Xhrina dressed them both quickly and gently towed him with her, as she had had to do for the past few months, since his limbs had grown too feeble and shaky to keep him stable as he swam in the air.

It was as before, with a new swarm of ghosts, and in the middle of it, the baby emerged from Mtepic; she held the baby for a long moment, and kissed the tiny mouth tenderly, and then watched it sail off, giggling and tumbling, into the stars, until it was just a star itself, and then gone. She towed Mtepic's remainder back to their quarters; for reasons she did not understand, she didn't want to tell her shipmates that he had died in the opsball.

They might have been surprised at how dry her eyes were, and how perfect her composure, when they buried Mtepic's body in space on the next shift, but ship people are never very surprised at anything human, for they don't understand it and lose the habit of being curious about it.

Treo often floated with her in the dark opsball now. "It's a big promotion," he said, "and an honor, and you would make a good captain. I admit I'm delighted with the idea of being ship's mathematician without having to wait for you to die." That was the longest speech he had made, and Xhrina found it faintly ironic that he made it as they floated in the opsball, where normally they were most silent.

It was not a normal occasion; Phlox had chosen to die voluntarily after Arthur's death, and would be doing it after she said her goodbyes tonight, so they were replacing a captain and a first mate. The crew had chosen Xhrina as captain, with Officer-Apprentice Chang to be brevet-promoted to first mate, if they wanted the positions.

Xhrina thought Chang would be all right as a first mate; he was young and should ideally have had a few more years as an apprentice, but she reckoned that he would have them by the time she died, and would still be a young, vigorous, apt-to-be-successful captain. It was a good match all around.

They were far out in the Sixth Pulse systems now, newer worlds with more cargo to send and receive, out in the thinly populated fringes of the human sphere. So there could have been very few of those pathways of the dead that Mtepic imagined, but when they jettisoned Phlox's body, Xhrina felt something; and the next day was her fiftieth birthday, and she felt it more strongly; so that night she was unsurprised to awaken and feel that it was time to see ghosts in the opsball. It had been a long time since she had seen ghosts, only twice since Mtepic's death, and this was the first time since Treo had come aboard. She woke him, told him to dress and be quiet and to hurry.

The blue-to-red Dopplered stars became plain white stars, the swarm of ghosts arrived, and as Xhrina was just beginning to watch with wonder, and celebrate being here for such a thing again, Treo cried out in fear, having seen Phlox swim through the hull and take up her navigation station, and all of it vanished.

That settled Xhrina's mind. She took the captain's cabin, and shared it with Chang, from then on, letting him rub her back because he seemed to like to do it and it did feel good, and occasionally relieving him sexually, though he was much more attracted to the second physicist's mate, Robert, who was unfortunately not interested in sex at all, or at least not any kind that Chang offered.

Xhrina didn't exactly give up on any idea of love, but it was a long time before she trusted Chang as more than a mere colleague and convenient bed companion, so long that she got to know him too well, and settled for trust without love. It was an even longer time before she saw ghosts again.

Of the old generation, only she, Peter, and Squire were left on her eighty-fifth birthday, and Squire spent all of his time sleeping in his life-support tank now, though when roused he seemed coherent enough in a querulous sort of way. 9743, by vote of the crew (a vote Xhrina had very carefully nurtured into happening) had been renamed *Ulysses*, a name it had last had 290 years eintime before. Xhrina could not have said why she preferred that.

There was a Seventh Pulse underway, carrying the human frontier out past 150 light-years from the home system, and at great distances, now and then, they detected the sonic boom of near-light-speed bodies of a kilometer or more across, pressing so fast through the interstellar medium that their bow shock was too much for the thin trace of plasma and shook it hard enough to make microwaves. "The new colony ships move much faster than the old," Captain Xhrina observed, at the table with everyone. She had insisted on establishing a tradition of birthdays, real birthdays for everyone, even looking up some old traditions so that everyone wore funny hats, and they served fish, and sang a song called "Years and Years" in ancient Konglish.

"I would like to see one more new part of space before I pass on," she said. "There may just be time for that if we do this, and there is something in it for all of you. It will make our reputation forever as traders; the name of *Ulysses* will be known, and that would please me, and I hope it would please you.

"Sixty years ago, according to radio, the Sol and Alfsentary systems were known to be open, so we could make one stop on the way. My plan would be that we would take only half a hold of cargo—we probably can't even get that, nowadays, anyway, there doesn't seem to be much at any port—and then stuff the empty holds with extra mass, which we could feed into the shielders, and we could run at ninety-nine-four instead of our usual ninety-eight-two. That would mean eintime would be about one ninth of slowtime, instead of one fifth, and we could be back to the center in about seven years eintime. Switch cargos and pick up more mass there, head out again, and run at ninety-nine-four for a hundred twenty years of slowtime, so that we get all the way into the Seventh Pulse worlds on the other side. The corporation could afford to do it a hundred times over; I'd just like to take a chance on being there at the end of that voyage, and if we make it there, we will have made a name for ourselves, forever, among star traders. No other reason."

Treo would vote with her; he always did because he feared that she thought he was a coward, though she had never said so. And his mathematician's mate Fatima would vote yes along with him. Peter would probably vote yes just because he found all port calls distressful and would like the idea that he would probably die before they made their first stop. With her vote, that was fifty-fifty; she thought Chang had liked the idea when she explained it to him, but with Chang it was hard to tell about things. The other three tended to think that the economic models that slithered and hissed through *Ulysses'* computers, paralyzing everything with their venom of marginal returns, were gods to be propitiated.

"Call the question?" Sleeth, the second physicist's mate-pending-first, said. That was conventional because she was juniormost voting member; it also fit Sleeth, because she was young and bouncing with energy in a crew of old, tired people. Most of the crew muttered that she was annoying except Squire, who said it outright whenever he was out of the tank, and Robert, the first physicist's mate, who said it coldly, as if it were the atomic mass of oxygen or the orbital velocity of a planet.

To compensate, Xhrina made no secret that Sleeth was as much her favorite now as when she had come aboard as a too-noisy-for-ship-people two-year-old. As the captain grew older, she had felt more and more that Sleeth was the only person, besides Xhrina, who liked to get things done. So this calling the question was natural, aside from being a duty.

The vote wasn't even close—only Squire and Robert voted against. Sleeth said apologetically to her cabinmates, "I'd like to be from a famous ship, and these runs around on the surface of the Sixth Pulse are getting dull."

It seemed to Xhrina more likely that Sleeth, who was barely twenty, but had come back from the training ship when only twelve, had been living too long with an angry husk in a tank, and a cold man who never spoke (did Robert use her roughly? Xhrina had asked Sleeth, more than once, and Sleeth had said *no* in a way that Xhrina thought meant *yes, but please don't do anything*). This looked to be Sleeth's first little step to saying that she would not be pushed around by Robert and Peter, and it made Xhrina glad in a way that she had not felt in a while.

That night, when Chang crawled into the sleepsack beside Xhrina, he said, "When we approach the home system, and you wake knowing that there are ghosts in the opsball, don't wake me. I'm afraid of them and I don't want to know about them."

"All right," she said. "Have you been reading my diary?"

"Yes," he said, "it's my right as first mate to read anything you write, and I don't like to ask. And I asked Treo and he told me how frightened he was, and I went back and looked at all your birthdays, and Mtepic's, and saw the ghosts on the recordings. It made me so afraid I have had a hard time sleeping since. So don't take me with you. I don't want to see ghosts." More gently, he said, "You might talk to Sleeth about it. She's always been your little shadow, and she would face the fear just for love of you."

"Thank you," she said, "I will." And Xhrina turned her back on him, to enjoy his warmth but not to talk anymore. *I suppose I would have faced the ghosts for love of Mtepic,* she thought, *but I wanted to see them anyway, though I didn't know it until he showed them to me. I hope it can be that way with Sleeth.*

On the night of her ninety-third birthday, Xhrina rolled over and touched Sleeth, who had been her sleepsack partner for some years now. "Ghosts," she said, "finally."

"I'm glad," Sleeth said, awake at once, and they turned up the lights and dressed quickly.

She wasn't sure that she really was glad. Sleeth and the captain had talked of ghosts at least every few shifts for the last five years, and Sleeth had come to realize that her first time seeing ghosts would be the captain's last. She had forced herself to seem happy and cheerful about the impending visit of the ghosts all through the annoying too-long layover around Old Earth's moon, as well, and now that the time was here, she hadn't really had time to think through what she wanted to feel, or ought to feel, and was stuck with just feeling what she felt—which was a mystery.

She had heard so much from the captain about Mtepic, and ghosts, and all the theories about ghosts, because the captain only needed to work an hour a day or so during the layover, while they found whatever cargo they could. The synminds of Old Earth and *Ulysses* at last found a small load, but did not seem to be able to explain what was in the containers, except that it was something that it was not inconceivable that someone in the new Seventh Pulse worlds out toward the Southern Cross and Sentaru might want 120 years from now.

The captain had not cared, so Sleeth had not cared. The scant cargo meant that their holds had had that much more room for a load of U238, depleted uranium, not for atomic power as in ancient times—they might as well have taken hay, oats, and water, and would have if nothing denser had been available—but because it was a conveniently dense supply of mass to be torn to nucleons and shot out the bow by the shielder, to clear a path through the interstellar medium for them. With the extra mass, they were able to run at 99.7 percent c, which meant almost thirteen years of slowtime to one year of eintime. *Ulysses* would be some sort of legend, now, for sure.

But, Sleeth thought sadly, *the end of the legend will not be Captain Xhrina bringing* Ulysses *to the port of Summer*, the port that they had been aiming for since their last PPD and change of course about a year eintime ago.

Xhrina and Sleeth had talked of ghosts, many times, and Sleeth longed to see them, with Xhrina; but she would miss their conversations about them, and it seemed sad that she would have no one to talk about this first time with. But then apparently Mtepic had seen them five times alone, and who knew how many others saw them and never talked about it at all?

Still, Sleeth had always imagined that when at last she saw them, she would be able to talk about them with Captain Xhrina. She had been ship-raised, and because of the way the schedules had worked out, had only been on a training ship for six years, about half what was normal, so that she had spent a great deal of time following Xhrina around when she was younger, and then more time tending her later. Xhrina had always been her one real friend.

Sleeth knew she would miss the captain dreadfully, but she didn't think she should say so, with the captain's eyes alight with joy; once they were in the opsball, it was easier, waiting in the dark, because Sleeth could just let her tears quietly flow.

It was all as Sleeth had heard it told, so many times.

As the ghosts neared, Xhrina bounced and fidgeted as if she had a tenth of her years. When the slender, small ghost that had to be Mtepic—though now strong and young—swam through the wall into the opsball, the glowing baby emerged from her head and chest in just two heartbeats, formed fully in the air, and held its arms to Mtepic, who swooped in and scooped up the newborn Xhrina. *Just a few seconds, the first time I ever saw the ghosts, and it was all over*, Sleeth thought sadly.

As if he had heard her thoughts, Mtepic, still cradling the fiercely glowing ghost-baby, turned back, and smiled a warm knowing smile at Sleeth.

To everyone's surprise—even to the surprise of Mtepic's ghost—ghost-Xhrina, newborn and toothless, huge-eyed face wide with glee, in the ghost-mathematician's now-strong and young arms, waved bye-bye to Sleeth, in a way so like any other baby that Sleeth giggled, aloud, and all the ghosts but Mtepic and Xhrina fled as the stars began to fade.

Grinning, Mtepic raised a finger to his lips—*shhh!*—and so did Xhrina, and they both waved bye-bye once again before they were gone into the field of stars, which faded after them, leaving Sleeth laughing in darkness.

Fishing

By Thea Hutcheson

Maruka slid a grasping tentacle through the slit into another universe and fished around. The fluid, a mild surfactant, meant she could do without a protective sheath, allowing her to feel viscously instead of groping blindly. Her timing was perfect; the fluid was calm and the agitation cycle was some moments away.

The exploration was disappointing again. The human in the other universe had begun clipping the fashion sheaths together, rendering them too big to pull through. Doubly sad, Maruka thought, flushing green. The fashion sheaths had been paying her survival debts.

The sheaths were a perfect fit for a Cleemlik's courting appendage, creating a veil from which it glowed demurely. The humans in the other universe wore them on the ends of their lower mobility appendages, inside their exterior protectors, so they became worn and stained, but odd was as odd does and universes were odd.

That thought brought her back around to Benizeer's recent oddness. All Maruka wanted was a dark umber relationship that ultimately ran deep cobalt through parenthood. And Benizeer, like that other being, insisted on clipping things to it. Certainly they should have offspring, but why two litters, and why so quickly?

"Of course," she thought, "it's the same thing, macro and micro." She quoted her mentor, Quemish. "You're looking at the bottom side of another universe. What do you think you're seeing, Maruka?"

Her grasping tentacle had shaded to black distaste in the liquid, which, she realized, was exactly how Benizeer made her feel. "You're looking at Benizeer's bottom side," she said. "What do you think you're seeing?"

She withdrew her appendage and wiped it off. She'd worked both relationship and claim very productively until recently when they both started to go puce. Now the claim seemed played out, which also described her relationship with Benizeer. Together, these thoughts made a gadabout an appealing idea. Her timing was good, too. The universe fabric was puckered here, forming a big suck at her top right as she faced the universe's underside. Scholars theorized that pressure differential between the two sides of the universe created a low-pressure system, which sucked matter through the dimple. It was going to commence shortly and she was dangerously close.

She moved away from the claim, closed her visuals, and centered herself with a wan chi breathing ritual before spreading her awareness over the land. Drawn to face northwest, she focused and saw bluffs that were suffused red with the wealth of their slits.

Maruka felt drawn past them and concentrated. Yes, nestled two ridges over, a warm rainbow spelled an interesting community. She heard ticking. The suck-hole dimple was beginning to draw. Its strength had increased since the last interval, drawing even her toward its mouth. She had told the universe cartographers and they had promised to send someone to look. She picked up her pack and began to move away. It would open quickly and suck anything in its radius into its maw. Cleemish knew where it would end up. She felt the suck's wind pull as she hit a ground-eating stride.

Maruka gadded throughout the day, reading the geography of the land, checking the color of any slits, laying stakes and marking sucks for placement on the great universe underbelly map. She went to register two small exploratory claims at the closest community. While she waited in line, two peace sentries went by with a bedraggled male.

"Geodan have mercy, there's another that can't meet his survival debts. How they let it get that far is beyond me."

She turned to see a handsome male.

"Name's Shaderjak." His voice was rich and friendly. He offered a grasping tentacle, which glowed a lovely rust. She blushed peach and noticed his courting appendage beaming brightly through a very attractive fashion sheath. She wondered if he'd fished it near here.

"Maruka," she replied, taking the tentacle. "Why did they take him?"

"His survival debt is very high and he couldn't make his promised litters to pay it off."

Maruka barely remembered to let go of Shaderjak's tentacle. His answer made her realize that survival debt explained all of Benizeer's oddness. The geography of Benizeer's underbelly was suddenly mapped in burning white.

She looked to Shaderjak, who was preening his courting appendage. She flushed orange with appreciation, maroon with pleasure at finding this place.

But she must go back and break off with Benizeer first. If Shaderjak was still available when she got back, a relationship would be worth exploring.

"I have to go," she said when she had the claim titles. Shaderjak's courting appendage faded.

"But I'll be back." She blushed dark peach as his appendage brightened.

She loped back to her claim at an easy pace, arriving in darkest night to see Benizeer approaching it, rather stealthily, it seemed to her. She rounded on him, panting. He seemed surprised to see her.

"Maruka, I was coming to see you," he said, his courting appendage creating a dim rusty glow through his fashion sheath.

"About what?"

"About our impending union."

"Yes, about our union."

"We should do it as quickly as possible."

"Do you want this arrangement so you can provide litters for survival obligations?"

Looking down at her, he turned a queer bright yellow. "I chose you because you were such a slow thing, but sweet."

How could she have been so intent on her claim yet so blind to the folds and curves of Benizeer's deception? Maruka blanched in the bright, clean white light that revealed the map of Benizeer's plans for her. Then the thought that she had nearly succumbed turned her puce down to the tips of her mobility appendages. She was free to go back to the northwest and explore her new claims and Shaderjak with good color and a fresher eye for underbellies.

The familiar ticking began. She hitched her pack up, ready to go. "This constitutes a formal dismissal of your suit. I won't say thanks, but I will say good-bye."

"No," he said, coming at her, evidently too focused on her to recognize the danger the ticking signaled. "You'll have my two litters and as many others as I need."

She scrambled away from him and the mouth of the suck. Benizeer started to chase her. The ticking grew louder; the suck opened. Benizeer stood right in front of it. That close he had no chance. He was pulled through, flailing. Maruka stood out of range, flushing with shock at his fate.

She adjusted her pack and set off at a gallop back to the northwest. There waited the bottom side of a universe in all its wealthiest red. There was also the promise of umber to be mapped in Shaderjak's geography, and maybe a bit of parenting cobalt. She was sure there was much fishing to be done in both of them.

Bob's Yeti Problem

by Lawrence Person

One morning Bob Krusden stepped outside his cabin to discover three yeti carcasses embedded in his front yard.

He was pretty sure they were yeti rather than bigfeet, as their pelts were a handsome silver-white rather than brown. Two of them were seminaked, wearing only some sort of weird loincloth and bandoleer arrangement, while the third wore what seemed to be a dull brown uniform. All three were suffering from what Bob had learned to describe, during his three seasons writing for *St. James Street*, as "massive blunt trauma." Two were planted facedown a good half foot into the pine needle–covered loam outside his cabin, and the one in uniform seemed to have come down on top of the others. All three had broken limbs and were surrounded by copious quantities of dried blood.

Bob was, to say the least, surprised. Though it had been getting close to dusk, he was sure there had been no dead yeti in front of his cabin when he had come home from his afternoon hike the day before. From the looks of things, they had fallen from a great height sometime during the night without him waking. *That* didn't surprise him. Trish, his ex-wife, had always said he could sleep through an air-raid siren. Certainly he had slept through her loading up their down-stairs furniture and leaving divorce papers on the pillow.

When he had rented the cabin for the summer, he was pretty sure the real estate agent hadn't mentioned any yeti, dead or otherwise. Moreover, the fact that yeti were generally thought of as mythological creatures, and ones native to the Himalayas rather than the Rockies, merely heightened the odd nature of the situation.

Bob wondered what to do. He had come up to Colorado to spend time cranking out screenplays far from Hollywood's clamoring Babel, and had already finished two with a third in progress. Dealing with cyrptozoological remains wasn't part of the plan.

He finally decided to head on into town. Ed might know if any-thing like this had happened before and who he should contact. Besides, he was out of cornflakes.

Bob pulled up in front of Ed's General Store, Hunting Emporium, and Internet Café. Ed Ridley was a man of many talents, most of which involved avoiding real work. The general store portion of the business offered staples at only moderately usurious prices, while the hunting supply portion sold lures, bait, ropes, hand-warmers, ammo, etc. for a good three to five times what you would pay at your local sporting goods store. The Internet café consisted of four Formica tables with old, battered iMacs hooked up to a landline upload and satellite download for a princely ten dollar an hour (one hour mini-mum), mostly for hunters who wanted to send e-mail or check their stocks. But these days Ed's biggest cyberspace venture was swapping deer and elk leases online, leaving the store's actual grunt work to his sullen teenage son, Mike, who was busy stocking cans of beans when Bob came in.

"Hi, Mike," said Bob. "Nice day today."

"Yeah, whatever," said Mike, not looking up.

Ed nodded at him from the counter as he passed, cradling his phone with his shoulder and typing into his laptop with the other. "Three for Saturday night? Yeah, I think I can arrange that," he said.

Bob drifted around the shop, picking up a box of cornflakes, a gal-lon of milk, a dozen eggs, a loaf of bread, a can of Folgers, and a four-pack of toilet paper. By the time he brought it up to the register, Ed was off the phone.

"That'll do ya?" asked Ed, running a scanning wand over the items.

"Yeah. Say, Ed, you ever see any yeti up these parts?"

"Yeti?" he asked uncertainly.

"Yeah, you know, yeti, abominable snowmen, bigfoot . . ."

"Oh. Bigfoot! Yeah, we had ourselves a little bigfoot boom down in Silverton around 1977, 1978 or so, whenever they had that bigfoot on *The Six Million Dollar Man*. Since then I can't really recall too many sightings. Most of our crazies see saucers or black helicopters these days."

"Well, I don't think I'm crazy, but this morning I found three dead yeti out in front of my cabin."

Ed stopped scanning. "Yeti?"

"Yeah."

"Three of 'em?"

"Yeah."

"Dead?"

"Oh, yeah. Looks like they had fallen a long way before smacking into the ground."

Ed scratched his head, then finished bagging Bob's groceries. "Can't say as I ever heard about anyone finding any dead bigfoots around here."

"Well, I think these are more yeti than bigfoot. They've got silver pelts."

Ed nodded sagely, as though anyone knew what color yeti pelts were. "Well, I'd tell you call Sheriff Parker, but he's in Pueblo getting his gallbladder out. That'll be $18.46."

Bob fished a twenty out of his wallet. As Ed was making change he had another thought. "Say, do you suppose yeti are an endangered species?"

"I would suppose so, since no one ever found a dead one before."

"Well, maybe you better talk to the EPA then. I've got a card from one in Denver, a Melissa Speed. She handed 'em out when she was poking around here about that spitting tree spider thing." Ed tore off his receipt and wrote the phone number down on the back. "Here, you might give her a call and see what she thinks."

Bob laid the groceries on the floorboard and fished his phone out of the Explorer's glove compartment. He kept it there for the same reason he had erased the Internet software from his laptop: so he could actually get some work done. He deleted the waiting phone spam and dialed the number Ed had given him.

"EPA field office, Melissa Speed speaking."

"Uh, Ms. Speed, I have a problem, and I'm not sure if you're the right person to talk to." He started outlining the situation.

"Yeti?" she interrupted. "This better not be a prank call! We can trace your phone number, you know!"

"No, it's no prank! I've got three dead yetis in front of my cabin, and I don't know what to do."

After Ms. Speed warned him that she could have him in jail so fast it would make his head spin for filling a false report, she had finally agreed to drive down that afternoon.

As he drove back to the cabin, Bob felt a sense of relief that the whole incident was going to be resolved soon. It had occurred to him that he could have sold the story to the *National Enquirer,* but Bob hated the tabloids, having seen them lie about a few of his acting friends. He was also wary of any publicity for himself rather than his screenplays. Bob was short, overweight, balding, and wore glasses, and knew he looked horrible on camera. The few times he had appeared on TV (right after his first, as thus far only, Oscar nomination), he was surprised at how unpleasantly nasal his voice sounded. When you came right down to it, he was a moderately shy person, and the idea of appearing on *Dateline* or the evening news filled him with a certain low-key terror.

However, his sense of relief was short-lived. When he got back to his cabin, he saw that there were now four dead yeti in his front yard.

Speed was a frumpy, overweight woman with frizzy brown hair and the deeply ingrained frown of the Permanently Disapproving.

"This better not be a wild goose chase, Mr. Krusden!" she warned, eyeing him suspiciously. "Where are these three yeti you talked about?"

"Uh, four, actually, and—"

"Four? You told me there were three! Did you kill another one?"

"No, uh, I didn't *kill* any of them. This one seems to have fallen from the sky like the rest."

"Fallen from the sky? Do you really expect me to believe that?"

"And I dragged the bodies over here to the side of the cabin so I could get in without having to walk around them. Plus they were starting to smell."

"Don't you know what sort of—" Speed stopped, looking at the four dead yetis laid out by the side of Bob's cabin, then slowly reached down to touch one of them. After a few minutes of pulling at their hair and opening their glazed eyes, she stood up.

"They are yeti, aren't they?"

"Yeah, that's pretty much what I was trying to tell you."

"I need to take a Haldol," she said.

It took Bob a few minutes to brew coffee, during which Speed raged into her phone at various other government functionaries, barking orders and making demands. When the coffee was ready, Bob handed her a mug.

"Thanks," she said briskly, swallowing a pill and chasing it with the coffee. "Without my Haldol, I get unpleasant." She went back to her phone. "No, I don't *want* him to call me tomorrow, I want him to call me *right now!*"

After another twenty minutes of haranguing other bureaucrats and pacing back and forth across his cabin floor, Speed finally rang off and put her phone away. "Well, that's finally settled," she said. "The FBI will be here to secure the scene in an hour or so."

"Secure the scene?"

"An endangered species is being slaughtered right under my very nose!" she said. "You can be sure there's not going to be another yeti-cide on my watch! Which is why you'll have to vacate this cabin "

"*What?* I've still got more than a month's rent paid on it!"

"That's your problem, Mr. Krusden, not mine. My problem is protecting biodiversity, which is why I'm having the forest around this cabin declared a sanctioned protection zone. You should just be glad that I don't charge you as an accessory to an environmental felony. You have ten minutes to pack up and leave!"

Speed stalked out of the cabin and slammed the door behind her.

Bob looked around the cabin in dismay. How the hell was he supposed to get everything packed in ten minutes?

Suddenly, from outside the cabin, there was a deep-throated cry, soon joined by a woman's scream, both of which were cut off by a loud, wet WHUMP.

Bob opened the door to find out that Speed had been crushed by yet another falling yeti.

"Mr. Krusden, do you know what the penalty is for killing an agent of the federal government?" asked Agent Rollins.

"Look, I did *not* kill Ms. Speed. She just happened to be in the wrong place at the wrong time."

"That's what *you* say. We have not ruled out foul play in Ms. Speed's death, and we still consider you a suspect."

"She was *crushed* by a *yeti*."

"Even if that is the case, we can't necessarily rule out that you used the yeti as an instrument of murder."

"Do you think I've got a secret catapult or yeti-firing cannon out behind the cabin?"

"Never underestimate the devious byways of the criminal mind."

"Don't you think that's a little crazy?"

"Crazier than yeti falling out of the sky?"

He had a point.

Two hours after Ms. Speed's demise, two FBI agents had shown up at the cabin and had become quite perturbed at the most recent turn of events. Now Agent Hernandez was busy examining the bodies while his partner questioned Bob.

Hernandez walked up, shaking his head. "It certainly looks like she was killed by a falling yeti."

Bob spread his hands. *See?*

"And the others?" asked Rollins.

"It looks like they fell too. You can still see the indentions in the loam."

"Are you sure they're yeti?"

"Heck if I know. I've never seen one before. But they ain't guys in funny suits."

"That's *aren't* guys in funny suits. You're an FBI agent now, Hernandez. We speak proper English. And don't say 'heck.'"

"Yes, sir. Sorry, sir."

Just then another SUV pulled up and two men climbed out, one of them carrying a camcorder.

"Oh, great, just what I need," groused Rollins, moving off to intercept them.

"Tightass," muttered Hernandez under his breath.

"Rollins, FBI," he said, flashing his badge. "This is a crime scene, you'll have to leave immediately!"

"Agent Rollins, Dan Parker, Fox-31 News. Is it true that this cabin is the site of a bigfoot killing spree?"

"No, it's not, and get that camera out of here!" he said. The camera-man kept filming the FBI agent for a moment, then panned to take in the dead yeti on top of Speed.

"How many people has the murderous bigfoot killed so far?"

"Only one! No, strike that! No comment! How the hell did you hear about this anyway!?"

"Oh, you came through loud and clear on the police scanner! We were out doing a spitting tree spider story when word came across, but nine or ten other news crews are on their way."

"I said, get that camera out of here! This is a crime scene! Do you want to be arrested?"

Parker shut off his microphone for a moment. "Oh, could you? Please? That would look *so* cool on my resume!" He turned the microphone back on. "Agent Rollins, before arresting me, you should know that this audio and video is being fed live to Fox-31's Web site, but if you need to do your duty, so be it."

Rollins muttered something under his breath as he walked away and pulled out his phone.

"Sir, are you the owner of this cabin?" asked Parker, sticking the microphone in Bob's face. Bob looked uncomfortable and uncon-sciously sucked in his gut.

"Uh, not the owner, the renter."

"And your name?"

"Uh, Bob Krusden."

"And your profession?"

"Uh, I'm a screenplay writer."

"And did you witness the murderous bigfoot attack?"

"Uh, well, actually it's more of a yeti than a bigfoot."

"Yeti?"

"Yeah. You can tell by the silver pelt. And it wasn't really an attack, it just fell out of the sky."

"Fell out of the sky?"

"Yeah, like the other four."

"Four?"

Bob pointed and the cameraman bounded over to the side of the cabin to film the other dead yeti.

"Mr. Krusden, how can we believe that five bigfoots—"

"Yeti."

"That five yeti just fell out of the sky?"

"Hey, now I remember!" said Hernandez suddenly. "Bob Krusden! You wrote the script for *Autumn Light*, right?"

Bob smiled. "Yeah, actually I did! How did you know that?"

"I knew your name sounded familiar! Yeah, there's an excerpt from that in *Mastering Screenplay Basics*! I've always wanted to be a screenwriter! See, I've got this idea for a script about these two FBI agents. One of them's cool, but the other is really a tightass—"

"But back to the yeti, what the public wants to know—"

At that moment, they all heard a loud, guttural cry, and turned just in time to see another yeti plowing into the ground.

Finally, Bob had an idea. He pulled out his phone.

"Ed's General Store, Hunting Emporium, and Internet Café, how may I help you?"

"Hi Ed, this is Bob. Listen, I wanted to see if you had some things in stock . . ."

Night had fallen, but the area in front of the cabin was brightly lit by an array of floodlights. Bob, Agent Hernandez, Ed, and Mike were busy tying the last of the lines in Bob's makeshift net. Rope, bungie cord, several hunting slings, and a couple of real nets were tied to several pine trees and the top of the cabin's porch some ten feet off the ground. Between the ropes and the lights, Bob had ended up putting more than a thousand dollars on his Visa card, all of it at Ed's exorbitant prices. When Bob had pointed out that his business would probably quintuple after tourists got wind of the yeti story, Ed had generously knocked off 5 percent.

"Is that end tight?" asked Bob.

"Yeah, whatever," said Mike, already climbing down the ladder.

Bob carefully walked across the makeshift net and back, uncomfortably aware of the dozens of cameramen filming his every move. There were now a good fifty to sixty reporters milling around outside the FBI's tape barrier, all covering "The Great Yeti Mystery" and all being scowled at by Agent Rollins. Rollins hadn't been wild about Bob's idea, but hadn't been able to think of anything better.

Though it shifted alarmingly under his feet, Bob was reasonably sure the net would at least break the next yeti's fall, assuming another one came tumbling. Bob carefully climbed down, waved off a batch of shouted questions, and stepped into his cabin to grab a cup of coffee. While it was brewing he checked his phone calls. Twenty-two requests for interviews, two more friends, and an ex-girlfriend calling to say they had seen him on the news, his agent Sid calling with the latest offers for the movie rights to his story, and his mother, asking why he couldn't wear some nice pants for the cameras instead of those ratty old jeans. He called Sid.

"Bob, you're golden! Sony's upped the offer to $750,000!"

"Creative control?"

"No, they're balking at that. They say they're not sure you have the proper perspective to do the story right. They think the protagonist needs to be a beautiful, twentysomething half-Native American veterinarian who's capable of speaking to the spirits of the dead yeti."

"Of course they do. That's why you're going to tell them *no*. Call back when they're willing to offer two million and creative control."

"Well, Bob, you're the man! But are you sure they'll go that high?"

"Wait until we capture a live yeti." He rung off and stepped back outside.

Bob looked up at the net. One of the strands Mike had tied seemed to be loose. Bob picked up the ladder and moved it to the next tree, painfully aware of the cameras capturing his every move. Upon closer inspection it *was* coming loose, but there wasn't enough rope left at the end to loop it around the tree again.

"Do we have any more rope down there?" he asked.

Before anyone answered, there was another guttural scream as another yeti fell, this one straight into the ropes. The makeshift net bowed in the middle, almost touched the ground, then held and rose back up, sending the ladder tumbling to the ground in the process. Bob grabbed the edge of net nearest him, then, with some difficulty, pulled himself up.

Dozens of live camera feeds captured the sight of the new yeti scrabbling to its feet in the netting, shielding its eyes against the floodlights' glare, fearful and disoriented. It seemed to be wearing the same brown uniform as the last few yeti and it carried some sort of flashlight. It let out another long cry.

Bob got unsteadily to his feet, unsure what to do next. "Uh, hi there!" he said, raising his hands, then wondering if that would really be seen as a peaceful gesture. The yeti turned to look at him, then slowly backed away.

Bob edged closer, painfully aware of the fact that the yeti probably weighed a good two hundred pounds more than he did. "Hi there! My name is Bob," he said, lowering one hand and pointing to himself.

The yeti made no reply, its gaze darting back and forth between Bob, the ground, and the assembled crowd. It was a good thing they had moved all the dead yeti back behind the cabin.

"My name is Bob," he repeated, still pointing at himself.

The yeti zeroed in on him.

"Bob!" he said again, still pointing.

The yeti seemed to get the idea. It pointed a finger at him and growled, "Brrraaaab."

"Yes, that's right!" said Bob, nodding his head and edging closer. "My name is Bob," he said, pointing at himself again. "And your name is . . ." he said, pointing at the yeti.

"Yawragrowroh!" said the yeti pointing at himself.

"Yahhgrawow," said Bob, pointing at the yeti.

"Yawragrowroh!" said the yeti, then it stiffly mimicked Bob's nodding.

Bob nodded in return. "Nice to meet you, Yawragrowroh" he said, slowly and carefully extending his hand to the yeti. Yawragrowroh looked at the hand for a moment, then, under the glare of a hundred camera flashes, cautiously reached out and grasped it.

"Are you there, Bob?"

"Yeah, Sid, I got you on the speakerphone."

"How about the Y-Man?"

Yawragrowroh growled in assent.

"What's the score?" asked Bob.

"Sony bailed at two million, but ViaDream's willing to go two point five mil, plus a one percent contingent compensation gross kicker when it exceeds one hundred sixty million."

"Crrrrreeeeeeaaaative?" asked Yawragrowroh.

"*Wellll*, sorta," said Sid. "They're willing to give you 'substantial' script consultation, but no final cut approval."

"Did they ditch the chase scene with the nuclear warhead?"

"Yeah, that's gone."

"How about the dinosaur attack?"

"Turns out Paramount is doing a dinosaurs versus robots movie next year, so they agreed to cut that as well."

"And just to make sure: I'm still not a hot Indian veterinarian psychic, right?"

"Well, not exactly, no. You're still a male Hollywood scriptwriter, but now the half-Native American veterinarian is your girlfriend."

" I *wish*. Who's going to play the girlfriend?"

"They're talking Reese Witherspoon with dyed skin."

Bob pounded his head ever so softly against the wall. "Does she still speak to the dead yeti?"

"Yeah."

"I can live with the girlfriend. But they have to drop the psychic crap. That's a deal breaker."

"Drrrreeeealbrrrreaaaker?"

"If you can live with the girlfriend, I think they'll budge on the psychic part."

"And if we can't get a real Indian, can we at least get a real brunette?"

"See what I can do. Oh, and they're also offering 'personal casting approval.'"

"Personal casting?"

"Yeah, just for the actors to play you two."

"Who do they want to play me?"

"Jason Alexander."

Bob sighed. "Yeah, I was afraid of that. Did they try Bob Hoskins?"

"He's playing the villain in a Jet Li film."

"I can live with Jason Alexander."

"Mrrrreeeeee?"

"For you they want Ben Affleck."

"RRRRRRRRRAWWWWWWRRRRR!"

"Okay, I'm sensing a *little* resistance to the Affleck idea. Who would you prefer?"

"RRRRRReeebaaacaaa?"

"Sorry, Y. Peter Mayhew is in the hospital following a golf cart accident."

"Rrrraaaawww, crrrrraaap."

"Anyone else they have lined up?" asked Bob.

"Well, *unofficially*, they're saying George Clooney is up next after Affleck."

Yawragrowroh made his hopeful noise. "Goooood deaaal."

"No problem with the Feds?"

"Nah, now that the gate's up and running they've got dozens of live yetis to work with, and they're too busy hammering out an interdimensional trade agreement to worry about some movie deal."

"So we got it? We in agreement here?"

"Yeah, let's do it. Pull the trigger."

"Y-man?"

"Rrrrrroooock aaaand Rrrrrrrrroooollll!"

"All right! I'll get ViaDream to fax over the contracts. Hang onto your seats, gentlemen. I think this one could be a monster!"

Brieanna's Constant

by Eric M. Witchey

He redlined his black Camry into the parking lot of the Leeman Building, a four-story red-brick full of software engineers and psychologists. Dr. Alan Dickson considered parking directly in front of the main entrance in Brieanna's space—the target space. Of course, that would skew his experiment results. He swung wide.

Only Brieanna Wolfe had a 100 percent success rate. She had parked her ugly, red coffee vendor's truck in the same slot in front of the Leeman building at exactly seven-thirty every weekday morning for two years. He planned to put an end to Ms. Wolfe's impossible luck and finish his study of the influence of personal expectations on chaotic systems.

He parked on the far side of the lot and reached to the passenger seat for his briefcase.

The seat was empty.

Marg's mascara-streaked face came back to him. She'd wanted some romantic time with him before work. He couldn't be late. She'd seemed so confused. It wasn't her fault she didn't understand. Aching guilt filled his chest. He reached for the gray cell phone mounted on his dash.

His hand hovered.

Calling wouldn't help. Only success and tickets to Kauai would make her smile. The tickets were in his briefcase. He needed to create the success. He got out of the car and headed across the lot.

Brieanna gathered her waist-long, honey-and-ash hair behind her head and bound it into a ponytail with a blue scrunchie—blue because she saw a crack of clear sky in the orange-bottomed dawn clouds over the sleeping city. She and Valdez, her tiger tomcat, had just finished loading Big Red's refrigerators.

Big Red, a two-ton step van painted like a red dog, waited loyally at the curb outside her one-bedroom bungalow in the wooded hills west of the city.

Red had been very near his trip to the scrap yard when Brieanna found him stalled and dying at a county fair. He'd been primer gray then, owned by a greasy, toothless perv selling carnivore carcinogen tubes wrapped in white bread buns. It made Brieanna shiver to think about what those things did to people's chi.

She rescued Red. She brush-painted him to look like a huge dog from a kid's book she had read in her aromatherapist's waiting room. His painted ears surrounded the tall doors on both sides of the cab. She put a big black spot on his side to make the sales window look right. The square windshield panels on the front weren't exactly good eyes, but the black basketball hanging on the grill was a great nose. She loved him, and that kept him running. After all, that's what kept everything running.

She checked the paws on her Mr. Peabody watch. "Six-twenty," she said.

Valdez meowed acknowledgment and pressed his broad head against her ankles.

"We're early today." She lifted Valdez and draped him over her shoulders like a fat, striped stole. Together, they mounted the two steps into Big Red.

Valdez leaped down onto his fleece-lined bed beside the long stick shift. The van smelled of fresh-roast and eucalyptus incense. Golden tassels surrounded the windshield. The cargo area overflowed with humming propane reefers and engine-driven steamers personally decorated by Brie. Her milk cooler was black-and-white and named Bessie. Her bran muffin box had little heart stickers on the glass. Her latte machine was fire-engine red, except for the hand-painted yellow smiles and the chrome tubing. She called it "Morning Smiles," after the poem she'd written the morning after a prophetic dream told her to sell coffee.

She settled into her duct-taped bucket seat and stretched her legs until her feet met the wooden blocks taped to the pedals on the floor.

"Come on, Big Red!" she cheered as she turned the key. Big Red coughed, shuddered, lurched, and died. In her side mirror, Brie watched a cloud of blue smoke explode from the exhaust and roll across her yard, engulfing her newly emerged sweet peas and the scarlet blooms of her rhododendrons.

"Oh, Red. Why'd you do that? They didn't do anything to you. Wake up, love. The world depends on us. It's a beautiful day to give people smiles!"

Brie turned the key. Red shuddered and woke. While the engine warmed and settled into its gravelly purr, Brie threw switches to bring power to the equipment in the rear. Finally, she tuned in her favorite FM station. Dulcimer, drum, and pipe tunes filled the truck. She swayed to the tunes and let out the clutch.

For the seventeenth time in a week, Marg decided to leave her workaholic husband. She stripped off her spike heels. She'd thought she could excite him with a little leather-and-lace fantasy over breakfast.

She'd been stupid. Only work held his attention. She pulled some slack into her fishnet stockings and knelt to wipe splattered egg from the floor. A brassy flash under the kitchen table caught her eye. She peered into the shadow of Alan's chair. The shield-shaped lock of his briefcase reflected the kitchen lights.

She hoisted the bulging case to the table. The worn and ragged cowhide body strained. Its dry-leather stench made her nose wrinkle.

The case held the numbers and graphs that were more important than his wife. She tugged at the leather strap holding the case closed. It was locked.

She poked the three combo wheels until her birthday lined up. The lock held. She rolled her eyes. Of course it wouldn't be *her* birthday.

Damn him *and* his briefcase. He kept secrets from her. She was sick of his secrets, of supporting his obsessions, his delusions of Nobel Prizes.

She sat down at the table and lined up his birthday on the tiny wheels.

Nothing.

His work had seemed important to her ten years ago—more important than her happiness.

His mother's birthday?

No. Damn him.

More important than children.

His father's?

Alan closed the lab's fireproof door and threw the dead bolt to secure the experiment space. When he had leased the unfinished office space, the manager had tried to sell him carpeting for the concrete floor, a suspended ceiling for the aluminum grid overhead, and wire and drywall for the room's metal stud skeleton. Alan preferred to use his funding on more important things.

Morgan, his white, overeducated, grunge lab assistant, stared out the full-wall window opposite the door. Morgan was not an important thing. After two hundred grant proposals, only one flaky R&D firm, LURC, was willing to risk money on Alan's ideas. Unfortunately, Morgan was part of LURC's deal.

The window *was* important. It was directly over Brieanna's parking slot.

Morgan turned and flipped a dust-blond dreadlock away from his eyes. "You look like hell, Doctor Al," he said.

"You haven't washed your hair in years," Alan said, venting his morning's frustration. "You show up in a purple tee and baggy shorts, and you insult me?"

"Take a pill, Doctor Al!" Morgan held up his hands in mock defense. "Your clothes are always retro-spiff. I meant the bags under your eyes."

Alan glanced at the coffee machine on top of a small refrigerator in the corner. The carafe was empty. "It's five-fifty. Where's my coffee?"

"Sorry, Doc. I forgot." Morgan laughed. "When Brie gets here, I'll buy you a double vanilla latte."

The morning was bad and getting worse. First Marg had dressed up in leather and spikes and thrown herself over his eggs and toast in some tabloid romance makeover stunt. Then he'd left his briefcase home. Now Morgan, with his woo-woo credentials in nonlinear phenomenology, was too damn happy and assuming Brieanna would arrive as usual—and the dry-land surf bum hadn't bothered to make the coffee. "To hell with Brieanna Wolfe," Alan snapped. "I want coffee now."

"I'll make it," Morgan said. "It'll be ready in a minute, but Brie's is a lot better."

"No airheaded, coffee-selling, *as if*, earth muffin is going to screw up the most important study of my life! I'm going to finish this today, Morgan. Today!"

Morgan stared, mouth open, from behind his dreads.

Alan took a deep breath. To hide his embarrassment, he crossed the lab to a long folding table supporting two computer workstations separated by his dispatcher's radio set. He dropped his keys in his jacket pocket and hung the coat over the back of his chair.

Alan took a breath. *Stay objective. Don't let him get to you*, he told himself. To Morgan, he said, "She won't make it."

Morgan went to the coffee machine and stripped the top off a foil packet. "Anticipating results, Doc? Won't *your* expectations influence the outcome?"

Ignoring Morgan, Alan settled into his chair and turned on his workstation. Cables climbed from the back of both workstations like red and green vines strangling the galvanized wall studs. The wires stretched in bellied arcs across the ceiling grid and down the opposite wall. There, another table supported LURC's quantum computer, "Q." At a glance, the million-dollar machine looked like a child's pretend computer, a bright orange shoebox anchoring the descending cables.

Q could track a nearly infinite number of seemingly unrelated details from Alan's citywide sensor grid. Using Alan's equations, Q could calculate the effect of each detail on all other details then provide a prediction of a probable outcome for a predefined event. The predefined event was whether a certain airhead could put her truck in a certain parking slot at seven-thirty. Q could suggest adjustments to the interrelated minutiae of the causal matrix. Using the dispatch radio, Alan could order those adjustments made by teams of disciplined, stone-faced field agents.

When he heard the pop and hiss of the coffee machine, Alan turned away from his workstation. "Is Q ready?"

Morgan slipped a stained, green mug under the steaming stream in the carafe bay. "All quantum pairs have undefined, linked, super-symmetrical spin. Q's copasetic. The sensor grid's up and recording." Morgan grinned and peered through tangled dreads. "Sorry I kinda pissed you off, Doc."

Alan glared. "It isn't you, personally," he lied. "I just don't like taking money from a shady R&D firm that recruits nutcases for research in irrational sciences."

"LURC studies luck. So do you. And the correct term for the mental status of us LURC researchers is 'paradigm-free.'"

"I lied. It *is* you," he said. "You and that coffee seller are wrecking my experiment and wrecking my marriage."

"We *are* both pretty cute," Morgan said.

Alan gripped the arms of his chair and took a deep breath. "No more practice." He forced himself to speak with academic authority. "Today, we execute Brieanna's special experiment and end her influence. I'm going to pay off LURC at one hundred to one and get rid of you."

"Ouch." The coffee machine dry-sputtered. "Please don't throw me in the briar patch." Morgan laughed.

"Morgan, if you can't be ser—"

"Don't jump me! You're the one obsessing on Brie. You're all caught up in how tomorrows *should* be. I live where I am and see what I see."

Alan wanted to bash a clipboard into Morgan's *I'm a Zen kinda guy* smile. "And your superior, *paradigm-free* sight shows you what?"

"That we're part of the system you want to measure."

"Experimental controls exclude us." Alan turned to his workstation. "Run diagnostics. I want to be ready by six-fifteen."

"Your show, Doc." Morgan handed Alan the green mug, then settled into the chair at his workstation.

The Buddha-boy got that right, Alan thought. *My show.* After years refining his equations, he had used hundreds of thousands of minutia sensors, seven supercomputers, and a random sample of two thousand commuters to build his model of the effects of human expectations on causal minutia.

Every day for twenty-four months, he used covert observation profiles to identify each subject's optimum daily parking place. His extensive sensor network recorded minute environmental changes as the day's commute unfolded. He plugged the sensor data and the subject's failure rate into his equations.

After weeks crunching numbers, the computers plotted the subjects' belief influence on their success or failure.

Of course, Brieanna never failed.

Her impossible, perfect record destroyed his hypothesis. She had to fail if he were going to measure the influence of her expectations on her outcomes. To force her failure, he needed to manipulate her environment and project outcomes in real time.

He needed Q's speed and his highly trained environmental-adjustment teams.

He smiled. He'd look great at the podium in Stockholm. He straightened his tie and turned on his radio. "Let's do it," he said.

"I got zeros, Doc," Morgan said. "Q's happy. Are your spooks ready to haunt?"

"They're called adjustment teams."

"Whatever."

Adjustments had to perfectly mimic natural influences. If Brieanna suspected manipulation, her expectations would change, and her influence couldn't be measured. Alan had personally trained the adjustment teams to act without creating suspicion.

Alan put on the dispatcher's headset. "Check one?"

A deep voice answered from the headphones. "Power utilities covered."

"Two?"

"Water and sewer, confirmed."

"Three?" He continued until all teams confirmed readiness.

"For once, Morgan, *your* coffee is going to be late."

Morgan laughed. "We got no number yet. She's way off the right end of your graph. I'm thinking she's like gravity. Her influence is simultaneous. It's everywhere."

Alan launched his interface software for Q. "You know better, Morgan. Gravity's a spin two, vector gauge bozon. Everything's quantifiable, Doctor Rat Hair."

"Okay, not like gravity, but she's a statistically stable point. Maybe the universe defines variations relative to her. It needs some reference point. Why not her?"

"That statement assumes consciousness on the part of the universe."

"The universe is conscious."

"You can't prove that."

"Are you conscious?"

"That's a pointless, ridiculous question."

"If you're conscious and you're part of the universe, the universe is, by definition, conscious."

"Idiot."

"That's an ad hominem ethical, rhetorical fallacy. Do you have an actual counterargument?"

Alan shook his head. "By the numbers: we block her, do the analysis, and plot her influence. You disappear back into whatever grungy R&D cave spit you out, and I accept the Nobel." Alan poked his finger in the air at Morgan. "You got that, Mr. Paradigm-Free?"

Morgan smiled and nodded. "Relax, Doc." Studying his workstation, he said, "I'm on your program. Data feeds are go, and I got numbers for you."

Alan's monitor blossomed with calculations of probabilities for Brieanna's successful arrival.

In his headphones a voice said, "Team Three to base."

Alan checked the digital clock on his screen and initialized his log file at 06:22:57:04. "Go ahead, Team Three."

"Subject passing our checkpoint."

"Status, Morgan?"

"Clocks are synched, sensors go," Morgan said. "She's early. Maybe she knows we're trying to stop her."

Alan ignored him. "Copy, Team Three. Computing probabilities."

"Like Brie cares," Morgan mumbled. Then, in mock horror, he said, "The big red truck is alive. It's coming for us."

"Shut up, Morgan."

"I hope the men in black can stop it! Oh god!" Morgan's cackle filled the lab.

Alan muted his microphone. "She's moving, Morgan. You don't get paid for color commentary. Monitor Q."

"Q'll answer your questions." Morgan grinned mischievously. "You're *sure* you're asking the right questions?"

"Just give me simulations and predictions."

"Simulations coming up now," Morgan said.

On Alan's screen, numbers flashed in two columns. Q did its magic. Minute details from all over the city poured into the box: barometric pressure at the airport; pavement temperatures on Burnside and Third; the disposition of the pregnant Dalmatian at the fire station on Northwest 23rd. Three hundred thousand sensors pumped data at light speed, and Q turned it into a mass of possibilities colliding, canceling, and occasionally amplifying one another into statistically significant probabilities. In pico-time, all the canceling and comparing resulted in a single number.

Brieanna Wolfe had an impossible 99.999 percent chance of parking success.

Alan frowned.

"There you go, *Herr Doktor*. Same as every day for two years," Morgan chided. "Me and Q did our jobs according to spec and protocol. The parking goddess cometh."

Alan examined the column of suggested adjustments for Brie's currently predicted path. He selected a solution and sent a message. "Team Seven, release your mice on my mark."

"Affirmative, base. All seven?"

"All seven."

"On your mark."

"Three, two, one, mark."

"Mice away."

From the dashboard, Valdez played with the swaying gold tassels hanging from the sun visor. A brown mouse ran into the road. Valdez batted at the window. Brie slowed to let the mouse cross. Checking her side mirror as she continued on, she saw the mouse scurry into the azalea bushes of a garden. "That was close, little guy. Look both ways next time."

On Alan's screen, new numbers appeared. The mice had changed her timing and ruined her probability of success. He turned to Morgan and grinned in triumph. "We did it! She's got less than a one percent chance of hitting her slot on time."

"A little early to call, don't you think?" Morgan said. "I mean, Brie's not even at the end of her street. A lot of stuff can shift the causal matrix—"

"Be as negative as you want. I have my number."

"*A* number."

"*The* number. And Morgan?" Alan spun to face his assistant.

"Doc?"

"You did a good job."

"Don't be too nice. You still might need to blame someone."

Alan felt magnanimous. He laughed.

"Really, Doc. I know you don't like it, but I think you should reconsider. We're part of the system. So is Q."

"Q says a forest green Ford Explorer full of kids will arrive for family counseling just before Brieanna."

"Look again, Doc."

Alan turned. The number that had been less than one was rising rapidly.

"Damn!" He tapped his screen like it was an analog gauge and vibration would free its sticky pointer. "Her success probability's rising." Frantic, Alan wheeled on Morgan. "What'd you do?"

Morgan pushed a dreadlock out of his eyes. "Told you you'd need me."

"Check the feeds!"

"Won't help." Morgan let lose a mad scientist's maniacal laugh. "She's the parking goddess of urban legend." He lowered his voice dramatically, lifted his arm, and pointed at Alan. "She's coming for *you*!"

Alan turned on his assistant, "If you can't be professional, get out!"

Morgan frowned. "Sorry, Doc. Checking feeds." Morgan hovered over Q, touching each cable with ritual precision.

Confused, Alan watched the number continue to rise. He swiveled his chair. "Morgan?"

"Q's happy with the universe." He crossed from Q to his workstation. "So am I, by the way."

"Don't give me attitude, just give me a new simulation."

Alan swiveled back to his screen. He didn't understand what had happened. Q had given them the answer. He released the adjustment. The mice shifted the causal matrix and changed her arrival time. It all worked, but it only worked for a moment.

For the probability of success to rise so fast and so far, her influence would have had to be . . .

No.

Impossible.

That was many orders of magnitude beyond the influence of any other subject.

Brieanna's number passed 80 percent and continued to rise.

Marguerite, still in lingerie, finished her coffee. She couldn't keep her eyes off the briefcase full of secrets on her kitchen table, nor could she get it open.

God! Even when he was gone, his work made her miserable. Hadn't she had friends at Livermore too? Hadn't she warned him about how he sounded? Did he care? No! He argued funding policy in public and got them exiled. He only cared about being right. She couldn't believe she'd supported him while he wrote those stupid grant proposals. She had thought the obsession would pass, that he'd settle into a teaching job at some community college. How could she have known LURC would be stupid enough to give him money?

He thought she didn't understand his work. She understood. She understood that the probability of getting spontaneity out of Alan Dickson was zero.

Staring at his bag only fueled her anger. It was so damned important, and he'd left it under the table. He'd blame her. He'd say, "You put on that getup and attacked me." Well, screw him. She'd put the case back in the closet. She'd bury it under sweaters and let him think he missed it.

She grabbed the case. Under her assault, the aged handle broke. The case fell to the tile floor. A seam split. Photographs and plane tickets spilled onto the floor.

She stared. The photographs were of a very young, very blond woman. Long, silky hair cascaded over her broad back and teased the curve of her young rear. Her tube top barely covered breasts gravity hadn't touched. The girl couldn't have been more than twenty.

In one picture, she was beside a red truck in a sunny spring yard full of budding rhododendrons. She was bent over picking up a yellow cat. Short shorts rode up her too-smooth backside. In another shot, she was pushing her long hair up over her head and smiling like some vixen from a shampoo commercial.

The ticket jackets showed tanned women in grass skirts undulating under palm trees.

Marg picked up a photo that had landed facedown. The blond was sunbathing. Topless!

"Alan Dickson, you son of a bitch!"

Marguerite scooped up the pictures and tickets, dug her trench coat from the closet, wrapped it over her lingerie, and stormed through cool morning air to the curb and her little white Honda hatchback.

Searching for solutions, Alan organized his thoughts out loud. "I have eighty-seven adjustment teams. The sensors are fine. I designed the experiment myself." He tugged on his starched cuffs. "We're getting good, real-time data."

"That's the problem, Doc," Morgan said. "Q measures here and now. He's doing what you told him, but you think the causal matrix exists in unidirectional, linear time."

"Your point?"

"The time vector goes forward *and* backward. Your adjustments create a causal ripple, but the universe has already set its own adjustment canceling adjustments in motion; so, the number rises immediately. Your adjustments are readjusted before Q thinks of them."

"The universe can't anticipate complex future potentials."

"Why not? You think you can."

"That's different."

Morgan laughed. "Oh," he said. "That explains everything."

"We have work to do."

"Q, you, Brie, me; we're all inside this universe, not outside watching. Everywhere, every when, and everyone are part of the system."

"I'm going to make several adjustments at once."

"Let it go, Doc. You can't predict the ripples. Don't make things worse."

Alan reached for the microphone toggle.

A teat-worn beagle and three pups bolted into the street. "Whoa, Big Red!" Brie stomped the brakes to keep from flattening them. A man in a dark trench coat and silvered glasses slipped into the bushes where the dogs had appeared. "Figures," she said to Valdez. "There's a perv in their bushes. I won't run in *this* park on weekends."

When the last pup was clear, she pulled forward. At the next intersection, the traffic light was out. In fact, as far as she could see down the street, all the traffic lights were out. She checked both ways and ventured across.

A white hatchback zipped in front of her, narrowly missing her bumper.

Big Red lurched. Valdez said, "Mrower."

"I guess some people have *very* important things to do this morning," she said.

"Not enough!" Alan pressed loose hair over his bald spot. He tore at his sleeves. The number headed up again. "Get my briefcase! I need my secondary causal relationship tables."

"Where is it, Doc?"

Alan scanned the lab. Cool sweat broke out on his forehead. He remembered breakfast, setting the case beside his chair, Marg throwing herself spread-eagle over the table and saying filthy things. "No," he whispered.

"Where?" Morgan asked.

"I left it home." Alan closed his eyes, tried to visualize the numbers and corresponding actions on the secondary tables.

"We can't just make random adjustments, Doc. The results are unpredictable. Someone might get hurt."

"Most adjustment ripples are self-canceling."

"Most. Not all. Your own protocols say we shut down if something like this happens."

Morgan was right. An adjustment might ripple through the matrix and amplify into a catastrophe. He couldn't risk the damage random manipulations might cause.

Or could he?

He called his teams. "Seven?"

"Monitoring, base. What do you need?"

"Status on the mice."

"She almost hit one. One's in the sewers. Bookstore cat has one. Two disappeared. One went back in the cage. He's eating a leftover pellet. One's under a bush by the curb."

"Kill one."

"Doc!" Morgan protested. "That's just mean. It's not in the protocols. Don't mess with—"

Alan waved Morgan to silence.

"Mouse in the cage is dead," Seven said.

"Bad karma," Morgan said. "Very bad. Wouldn't want to be you when the universe sends out that bill."

Alan muted his microphone and studied the numbers on his screen. Brieanna's probability of success dipped then rose to nearly one hundred.

"It doesn't make sense," Alan said. "She was past Team Seven, and the mouse death caused a dip. The ripple of an event that should have been behind her had affected her potential—even if only for a moment."

"Dr. Dickson." The good humor was gone from Morgan's voice. "This whole thing is cruising left of center."

"Whole thing," Alan echoed. In his mind, the universe twisted, dissolved, then rebuilt itself with new clarity. He jumped up and looked out the window. Below, a small group waited for Brieanna's coffee. "Morgan, have you had your coffee?"

"You know I buy from Brie. I can't stomach the camel—"

"Get out!" Righteous white fire filled Alan's mind. He grabbed Morgan's chair and rolled him toward the door. "Get everyone in this building a cup of coffee."

"Killing mice not enough?" Morgan jumped up and faced Alan. "You want to steal Brie's business?"

"Morgan, you're right. I *was* inside the box. I missed a control! She isn't isolated."

Morgan squinted from behind his dreads.

"Customers account for the strength of her effect. They *expect* her to be in that slot at seven-thirty. They amplify her influence. Eliminate them, and she's alone." Alan opened the lab door and pushed him. "Go! Do!"

"The protocols! There's no coffee in the protocols! You can't predict—"

"Giving people free coffee is good karma! Q will record everything. We'll do the analysis after we stop her!" Alan thought he was going to explode. He screamed at Morgan. "Go!"

Morgan headed out.

Alan called Teams Eighty-five through Eighty-seven. "Get coffee! A lot of coffee. Report to the Leeman Building. Keep bringing coffee until every person in the building has a cup. Move it!"

All three teams acknowledged with a crisp "Yes, sir!"

At seven ten, Morgan entered the lab, breathless. He poured a paper cup full of black coffee into Alan's mug. "Last cup," he said. "Everyone has some, and you owe Java-Roast four hundred twenty-two dollars."

Alan stared at his numbers. "Beat that, Brieanna!"

"What?"

"We have a stable outcome. There's an EMT vehicle in her slot. It'll stay for two hours."

"Wanna bet?"

Alan spun in his chair, spilling coffee on Morgan's purple shirt. "Q gives her almost zero chance. Those EMTs are teaching CPR to the Web geeks down the hall."

"Fifty bucks and two almond-vanilla lattes."

Alan laughed. "You're on!"

Morgan flipped dreadlocks over his shoulder and smiled.

The smile made Alan nervous. He checked his screen. The number that had been steady at practically zero was rising. The right side of the decimal was a blur. "How the hell?"

"She's a force of nature, Doc. Measuring her influence is like trying to trap the position of an electron. The harder you try, the crazier things get."

"This isn't a quantum effect. She's an airheaded coffee vendor."

"Not everything makes sense within our limited perspectives." Morgan patted Alan on the back. "Before I learned to surf reality waves, I was like you. I thought I could figure it all out, nail it all down."

"Don't patronize me." Alan spoke in low tones. "Get back on your machine. We need this data point, and by God, I'll have it."

"You won't get what you want. Brie's a spooky constant."

Alan's pulse pounded against his tight tie. What if Morgan was right? He pulled at the knot then checked out the window. The EMT truck was still there. He sighed and sat down. He had a moment before the rising probability would require the EMTs to leave.

He had to get Brie's number. If he didn't, he'd be labeled a failure by every legitimate research facility in the world, he'd spend his life working with idiots like Morgan, and he'd lose Marg.

A chill shook him. He had no choice. He toggled the microphone. "Forty-seven, break the water mains! All teams—"

Morgan leapt from his chair, dove across Alan's workstation, and muted the microphone. "The ripples could screw the whole city. Hell, the whole country! Maybe the world!"

"Get off my desk!"

Morgan planted himself between Alan and the console. "If she's a constant, the ripples won't touch her, but they have to go somewhere. You don't know what'll happen."

"Get out of my way!" Alan tried to push Morgan aside, but the younger man was too strong. "Chill, Doc. She's unstoppable. She's a statistical superhero."

"You're insane!" Alan pushed hard, but Morgan held fast. Alan collapsed back into his chair, suddenly regretting years of letting Marg go to the gym alone.

Morgan swiveled Alan away from his workstation. "Hear me out, Doc."

"You're fired."

"You proved she's a negative result. She's an anomaly. Log it and let it go."

"My contract says I complete the model or pay back the funding."

"You think I'd work for a company that allowed indentured servitude? That service clause only makes sure you believe completely in what you're doing. You fulfilled the contract. LURC has more useful data than they dreamed possible."

Alan considered. Morgan might believe what he was saying. He seemed sincere. But he *was* a LURC employee.

Alan relaxed his shoulders and dropped his hands to his lap. "Of course," he said quietly. "You're right." He looked up. "I'm okay. Let me up."

Morgan stepped back. Alan stood, put a hand on Morgan's shoulder, and said, "Fifty and two lattes."

Confused, Morgan stared.

"The bet," Alan said, taking Morgan's elbow and leading him to the door. "One outlier doesn't invalidate the study." Alan unbolted and opened the door. He smiled as they passed into the hallway. "I suppose," he said. The door closed behind them. "We'll have to accept the Nobel together."

Morgan laughed. "No way, Doc. I hate flying."

Alan chuckled and patted his pants pockets. "My wallet," he said. "I'll get my coat."

Alan opened the door, stepped into the lab, slammed the door, and threw the bolt.

"Doc!" Morgan screamed from the hallway. "No!"

Alan called back. "I'm not risking my future on a LURC employee's word that their lawyers are ethical."

Morgan's muffled words came through the door. "She's a stable statistical anomaly in chaos. You can get the Nobel for just discovering her, but you can't stop her. Don't screw yourself. Don't hurt her!" Morgan pounded on the door. "Doc! Please! Don't hurt her!"

Alan went to his workstation and called his teams. "Eleven, light the matches. Twelve, open the hoses. Thirteen, hit . . ." He went through his list like a machine. Each adjustment forced the probability closer to zero.

Then, after each drop, no matter how deep, the number rose.

At seven-twenty-five, he realized he had to drive the probability so low it couldn't rise above one before seven-thirty. Frantically, he called out adjustments.

Morgan pounded on the door.

Brie swerved, just missing a shuffling old woman in a pink running suit. In the back of the truck, Bessie spit out a plastic jug of milk. It split. Brie twisted in her seat to look. Valdez headed for the treat. Brie turned back to the street. A fireman pulled a hose across the road toward a burning boat and trailer. She stomped both feet down on the brake pedal.

Valdez meowed with pleasure from the rear of the truck.

Brie looked away from the flaming boat in time to see a landslide sweep across the road in the block ahead. Someone's split-level ranch rode the moving earth like a drunken cowboy on a demon bronco.

From Big Red to the slide, brake lights flashed. Before blocked traffic locked her in, she backed up and headed down a side street. A block later, a huge sinkhole stopped her. A broken main gushed water from the hole. Brie could just make out the wrecked shape of a little white hatchback under the umbrella of spray. A man with a cell phone to his ear stood near the hole.

Brie pulled completely off the road onto a dirt lane. Valdez jumped into her lap and licked milk from his paws. "I hope everyone's okay," she said. As though he heard her, the man pointed at his phone and waved her off with a thumbs-up.

"Sweet goddess, Valdez," she said. "The whole city's having trou bles. We need to get our smiles out there." Brie looked around. The dirt lane disappeared into the shadows of a blooming cherry orchard. She inhaled fragrant air and smiled. "I know this place. This is Ida Chapman's orchard. I helped her pick during high school." She laughed, put Big Red in gear, and headed for the equipment exit at the far side of the familiar maze of pink trees and dirt lanes. "Valdez," she said, "Ida's helping us deliver smiles. Tonight, we burn a candle for her."

With a little bouncing and jostling and a few quick swerves, she and Valdez managed to reach the Leeman building. There, a crew of hard-faced street workers cordoned off her normal approach. She headed around the block to enter the lot from the other side.

Alan yelled, "More, dammit!"

Only static responded. He'd used all his adjustments. Brie's number was rising fast. He checked the window.

To his horror, two uniformed EMTs ran from the building and jumped in their truck. Lights flashed. The siren wailed, and the truck was gone.

Alan checked his screen. When Brie's number hit ninety-nine, he screamed, grabbed his keys, and sprinted for the door. He threw the bolt, ripped open the door, and rammed into Morgan. "Look out!"

"Stop!" Morgan grabbed for him. "Doc, let her go! We're part of this."

Alan twisted away and ran down the stairs. Side cramped and short of breath, Alan hit the lot running. In spite of four hundred dollars worth of coffee, a small crowd waited for Brie's truck. He shoved past them, glancing in the direction of their glassy stares. The red truck was heading for the lot entrance.

Alan ran to his car, jumped in, fired it up, and raced toward Brie's spot. The crowd scattered. Alan skidded into the parking space.

Morgan stood at his front bumper, shaking his head, dreadlocks dusting back and forth across his shoulders.

In his rearview mirror, Alan saw the ridiculous red truck with a black nose slowing to enter the lot. He could see the ditzy smile on Brieanna's oblivious face.

Morgan came around to the driver's window. Alan rolled it down.

Morgan shook his head. "You better move, Doc."

"I did it!" Alan said triumphantly. He held up his wrist to show Morgan his watch. "Seven-twenty-nine! Q has enough data. It's not precise, but an approximation is better than nothing."

"I don't know what—"

"Give it up, Rasta-boy! I win!"

"Win what?"

"I'm going back to Livermore!" Alan's laugh was shrill and giddy. "I'm calling Marg, taking her to dinner, and flying to Kauai." He reached for the phone on his dash.

It rang.

"Don't answer it," Morgan said.

Alan's hand shook. He lifted the receiver.

A woman's voice said, "Alan?"

"Marg?" He smiled and winked at Morgan. "I was about to call you."

"I've been in an accident."

His grip tightened on the phone. "Where are you? Are you all right?"

"I'm at the airport. I wanted to say good-bye."

"I don't understand."

"A water main broke. I drove into a huge hole. I had the pictures of your lover. I didn't have time to change. I was soaked. I was coming—"

"My what?"

"I didn't understand until I met Brandon."

"Who?"

"Brandon Wolfe, my EMT. He pulled me out of the car. He gave me his fire coat and a cup of coffee. His little sister makes the best coffee."

"There was a fire?"

"I can't help it. I love him. I suppose it's like you and your bimbo. Anyway, fair is fair. We're using your tickets. Got an earlier flight. We leave in a half hour."

"You what?"

"It's so romantic! He quit his job to go. He's so spontaneous, so passionate. He just seems to move with the flow of things." She paused. Wet sounds came from the phone. Then, breathless, she said, "It didn't seem right to not say good-bye. No hard feelings, Alan. I really do hope you and your . . . your whatever, are happy."

Alan's vision darkened at the edges. The phone was cold in his hand. "Marg," he whispered. "You don't understand."

"We tried, Alan. This is for the best. We're both free. Aloha." The line went dead.

Thirty minutes. He could make it. He dropped the phone, burned rubber in reverse, then floored it for the street. At seven-twenty-nine and thirty seconds, he passed a lumbering red blur and raced away toward the airport.

At Big Red's window, Morgan stroked Valdez's neck while Brie steamed milk, her smiling blue eyes twinkling with natural magic.

The steamer fell silent and she handed him his latte.

"Thanks," he said.

She slipped her hair back over her shoulder then held up a chocolate-covered coffee bean. "Free for my favorite regular, Morgan. You always smile, and you never miss a day."

"You're a constant in my life too, Brie." Suddenly shy, he asked, "Brie?"

"No bean?"

Morgan took a deep breath. The mingling scents of eucalyptus incense, coffee, and cherry blossoms braced him. "A friend's playing banjo at a club downtown. I wondered—"

"Of course," she said. "But I have to be home by ten. A lot depends on me getting up early."

"Yeah, I know." Morgan opened his mouth. Brie laughed and put the bean gently on his tongue.

The Darkness

by David Drake

"Hi, Lieutenant," someone said as he walked into Ruthven's room. "Good to see you up and around. I gotta do a few tests with you back in the bed, though."

On the electronic window, a brisk wind was scudding snow over drifts and damaged armored vehicles. Ruthven turned from it; a jab of pain blasted the world into white, buzzing fragments. It centered on his left hip, but for a few heartbeats it involved every nerve in his body.

"Your leg's still catching you?" said Drayer. He was the senior medic on this ward. "Well, it'll do that for a while, sir. But they did a great job putting you back together. It's just pain, you know? There's nothing wrong really."

Pain like this isn't nothing, thought Ruthven. If he hadn't been nauseous he might've tried to put Drayer's head through the wall; but he had no strength and anyway, there was no room for anger just now in the blurred gray confines of his mind.

He eased his weight back onto his left leg; it reacted normally, though the muscles trembled slightly. The agony of a few moments past was gone as thoroughly as if it'd happened when he was an infant, twenty-odd years earlier.

"Anyway, come lie down," Drayer said. "This won't take but a—"

Drayer noticed the window image for the first time. "Blood and Martyrs, sir!" he said. What d'ye want to look at that for? You can set these panels to show you anyplace, you know? I got the beaches on Sooner's World up on all my walls. Let me tell you, walking to my quarters across that muck is plenty view of it for me!"

Ruthven glanced back at the window, catching himself in mid-motion; his hip ignored him, the way a hip ought to do. The snow was dirty, and what appeared to be patches of mud were probably lubricating oil. The Slammers' hospital here on Pontefract shared a compound with the repair yard, a choice that probably reflected somebody's sense of humor.

"That's all right," Ruthven said, walking to the bed; monitoring devices were embedded in the frame. "I chose it deliberately."

He grinned faintly as he settled onto the mattress. The juxtaposition of wrecked personnel and wrecked equipment reflected *his* sense of humor too, it seemed.

Drayer knelt to fit his recorder into the footboard. "Well, if that's what you want," he said. "Me, I was hoping we'd be leaving as soon as the Colonel got transport lined up. The government found the money for another three months, though."

Drayer looked up, a sharp-featured little man, efficient and willing to grab a bedpan when the ward was shorthanded. But by the Lord and Martyrs, his talent for saying exactly the wrong thing amounted to sheer genius.

"Had you heard that, sir?" Drayer said, obviously hopeful that he'd given an officer the inside dope on something. "Though I swear, I don't see where they found it. You wouldn't think this pit could raise the money to hire the Regiment for nine months."

"They're probably mortgaging the amber concession for the next twenty years," Ruthven said. He braced himself to move again.

The fat of beasts in Pontefract's ancient seas had fossilized into translucent masses that fluoresced in a thousand beautiful pastels. Ruthven didn't know why it was called amber.

"Twenty years?" Drayer sneered. "The Royalists won't last twenty days after we ship out!"

"It'll still be worth some banker's gamble at enough of a discount," Ruthven said. "And the Five Worlds may run out of money to supply the Lord's Army, after all."

He lifted his legs onto the mattress, waiting for the pain; it didn't come. It wouldn't come, he supposed, until he stopped thinking about it every time he moved . . . and then it'd grin at him as it sank its fangs in.

"Well, I don't know squat about bankers, that's the truth," Drayer said with a chuckle. "I just know I won't be sorry to leave this pit. Though—"

He bent to remove the recorder.

"—I guess they're all pits, right, sir? If they was paradise, they wouldn't need the Slammers, would they?"

"I suppose some contract worlds are better than others," Ruthven said, looking at the repair yard. Base Hammer here in the lowlands seemed to get more snow than Platoon E/1 had in the hills. He'd been in for hospital three weeks, though; the weather might've changed in that length of time. "I've only been with the Regiment two years, so I'm not the one to say."

Drayer's brow furrowed as he concentrated on the bed's holographic readout. He looked up beaming and said, "Say, Lieutenant, you're so close to a hundred percent it don't signify. You oughta be up and dancing, not just looking out the window!"

"I'll put learning to dance on my list," Ruthven said, managing a smile with effort. "Right now I think I'll get some more sleep, though."

"Sure, you do that, sir," said Drayer, never quick at taking a hint. "Doc Parvati'll be in this afternoon to certify you, I'll bet. Tonight or tomorrow, just as sure as Pontefract's a pit."

He slid his recorder into its belt sheath and looked around the room once more. "Well, I got three more to check, Lieutenant, so I'll be pushing on. None of them doing as well as you, I'll tell you. Anything more I can—"

The medic's eyes lighted on the gold-bordered file folder leaning against the water pitcher on Ruthven's side table. The recruiter'd been by this morning, before Drayer came on duty.

"Blood and Martyrs, sir!" he said. "I saw Mahone in the lobby but I didn't know she'd come to see you. So you're transferring back to the Frisian Defense Forces, is that it?"

"Not exactly 'back,'" Ruthven said. He gave up the pretense of closing his eyes. "I joined the Slammers straight out of the Academy."

Sometimes he thought about ordering Drayer to get his butt out of the room, but Ruthven'd had enough conflict when he was in the field. Right now he just wanted to sleep, and he wouldn't do that if he let himself get worked up.

"Well, I be curst!" the medic said. "You're one lucky dog, sir. Here I'm going on about wanting to leave this place and you're on your way back to good booze and women you don't got to pay! Congratulations!"

"Thank you, Technician," Ruthven said. "But now I need sleep more than liquor or women or anything else. All right?"

"You bet, sir!" said Drayer said as he hustled out the door at last. "Say, wait till I tell Nichols in Supply about this!"

Ruthven closed his eyes again. Instead of going to sleep, though, his mind drifted back to the hills last month when E/1 arrived at Fire Support Base Courage.

"*El-Tee?*" said Sergeant Hassel, E/1's platoon sergeant but doubling as leader of First Squad from lack of noncoms. "*We got something up here you maybe want to take a look at before we go belting on int' the firebase, over.* "

"Platoon, hold in place," Ruthven ordered from the command car, shrinking the map layout on his display to expand the visual feed from Hassel some 500 meters ahead. The platoon went to ground, troopers rolling off their skimmers and scanning the windblown scrub through their weapons' sights.

Melisant, driving the high-sided command car today, nosed them against the bank to the right of the road and unlocked the tribarrel on the roof of the rear compartment. She used the gunnery screen at her station instead of climbing out of her hatch and taking the gun's spade grips in her hands. The screen provided better all-round visibility as well as being safer for the gunner, but many of the ex-farmers in the Regiment felt acutely uncomfortable if they had to hunch down in a box when somebody might start shooting at them.

Ruthven expanded the image by four, then thirty-two times, letting the computer boost brightness and contrast. The command car's electronics gave him clearer vision than Hassel's own, though the sergeant can't have been in any doubt about what he was seeing. It was a pretty standard offering by the Lord's Army, after all.

"Right," Ruthven said aloud. "Unit, there's three Royalists crucified upside down by the road. We'll go uphill of them. Nobody comes within a hundred meters of the bodies in case they're booby-trapped, got it? Six out."

As he spoke, his finger traced a virtual course on the display; the electronics transmitted the image to the visors of his troopers. They were veterans and didn't need their hands held—but it was the platoon leader's job, and Ruthven took his job seriously.

The Lord knew there were enough ways to get handed your head even if you stayed as careful as a diamond cutter. The Lord *knew*.

Instead of answering verbally, the squad leaders' icons on Ruthven's display flashed green. Seven troopers of Sergeant Rennie's Third Squad—the other two escorted the gun jeep covering the rear—were already on the high ground, guiding their skimmers through trees that'd wrapped their limbs about their boles at the onset of winter. The thin soil kept the trees apart, and the undergrowth was already gray and brittle; Heavy Weapons' jeeps, two with tribarrels and the third with a mortar, wouldn't have a problem either. The command car, though—

Well, it didn't matter that a command car's high center of gravity and poor power-to-weight ratio made it a bad choice for breaking trail in wooded hills. This wasn't a choice, it was a military necessity unless Ruthven wanted to take the chance that the bodies weren't bait. His two years' experience in the field wasn't much for the Slammers, but it'd been plenty to teach him to avoid unnecessary risks.

The victims had been tied to the crosses with their own intestines, but that was just the usual fun and games for the Lord's Army. Ruthven grinned. If he'd had a better opinion of the Royalists, he might've been able to convince himself the Regiment was Doing Good on Pontefract. Fortunately, Colonel Hammer didn't require his platoon leaders to maintain feelings of moral superiority over their enemies.

His eyes on the dots of his troopers slanting across the terrain display, Ruthven keyed his microphone and said, "Courage Command, this is Echo One-six. Come in Courage Command, over."

The combat car's display showed that the transmitter in Colonel Carrera's headquarters was one of half a dozen in Firebase Courage that were live, but nobody replied. Ruthven grimaced. He wasn't comfortable communicating with the Royalists to begin with, since any message that the Royalists could hear, the Lord's Army could overhear. It added insult to injury that the fools weren't responding.

The car bucked as the forward skirts dug into an outcrop with a *skreel!* of steel on stone. Ruthven expected they'd have to back and fill, but Melisant kicked her nacelles out and lifted them over the obstacle. She was driving primarily because her skimmer—now strapped to the side of the car in hopes of being able to repair it at the Royalist base—was wonky, but she was probably as good at the job as anybody in the platoon.

"Courage Command, this is Echo One-six," Ruthven repeated, keeping his voice calm but wondering if showing his irritation would help get the Royalists' attention. "Respond ASAP to arrange linkup, if you please. Over."

The car shifted back to level from its strongly nose-up attitude, though it continued to rock side to side. Ruthven had a real-time panorama at the top of his display, but he didn't bother checking it. His responsibility was the whole platoon, not the problems of weaving the car through woodland.

"*Echo One-six, my colonel say, 'Who are you?'*" replied a voice from the firebase. "*We must know who you are, over!*"

Ruthven sighed. It could've been worse. Of course, it might still get worse.

"Unit, hold in place till I sort this," he said aloud. Rennie's squad, now in the lead, must be nearly in sight of the firebase by now. "Break. Courage Command, this is Echo One-six. We're the unit sent to reinforce you. Please confirm that your troops are expecting us and won't open fire."

He hesitated three long heartbeats while deciding whether to say what was going through his mind, then said it: "Courage, we're the Slammers. If we're shot at, we'll shoot back. With everything we've got. Over."

Third Squad *was* in sight of the Royalists: the feed from Rennie's skimmer showed the firebase as a scar of felled trees on the hill 700 meters from him. Ruthven frowned; he was looking down into the firebase. The ridge by which E/1 had approached was a good fifty meters higher than the knoll where the Royalists had sited their guns.

"*You must not shoot!*" squealed a new voice from the Royalist firebase; a senior officer had apparently taken over from the radioman. "*We will not shoot! You must come in and help us at once!*"

Ruthven grinned faintly. "Courage, I'll give you three minutes to make sure all your bunkers get the word," he said. "We don't want any mistakes. Echo One-six out."

"*Hey, El-Tee?*" said Sergeant Wegelin on the command push; he was crewing the tribarrel at the end of the column. "*What d'ye mean, come in shooting with everything we got? We're not exactly a tank company, you know, over."*

"They don't know that, Wegs," Ruthven said, smiling more broadly as he examined the real-time visuals. "And anyway, I don't think we'd need panzers to put paid to this lot, over."

Fire Support Base Courage housed four 120mm howitzers with an infantry battalion for protection. Tree tunks had been bulldozed into a wall around the camp, but they wouldn't stop light cannon shells as effectively as an earthen berm. The Slammers' powerguns would turn the wood into a huge bonfire.

"Why in hell did they set up with this ridge above them, d'ye suppose?" asked Hassel. Though the platoon sergeant had his own line of sight to the firebase, the display indicated he was using Wegelin's higher vantage point. *"We could put the guns out of action with four shots, over."*

"Because I never met nobody wearing a uniform here who knows how to pour piss outta a boot, Top," said Wegelin. *"Over."*

"The ridge's too narrow for a battalion and the guns," said Ruthven. He was using text crawls to monitor the panicked orders flying across the firebase, but he didn't see any reason to wait in respectful silence for the Royalists to get their act in order. "They should've left a detachment—"

"Echo One-six, you must come in now," Lieutenant Colonel Carrera said sharply. *"Quickly, before the Dogs take advantage! Quick! Quick!"*

"Break," said Ruthven, closing his conversation with his squad leaders. "Rennie, take your squad in. Wegelin, stay on overwatch. I'll follow Rennie, then Sellars, Wegelin, and you bring up the rear, Hassel. Six out."

Again green blips signaled "received and understood." Sergeant Rennie knelt on his skimmer to lead the way down and up the wooded saddle to the firebase. His troopers were lying flat with their control sticks folded down. That wasn't a good way to drive, but it made them very difficult targets in case somebody in the garrison hadn't gotten the word after all.

Rennie wasn't the brightest squad leader in the Regiment, but he was reflexively brave and never hesitated to take a personal risk to spare his troopers. They'd have followed him to Hell.

Melisant was sending power to the fans before Ruthven'd finished giving his orders, but the command car lifted awkwardly and only slowly started to wallow forward. The grace with which the troopers flitted around him made Ruthven feel like a hog surrounded by flies, but the skimmers'd run out of juice in a matter of hours without the car's fusion bottle to recharge them. He knew he was doing his proper job here inside the vehicle, though he didn't *feel* like he was.

The gun jeep that'd been reinforcing the lead squad didn't follow Rennie's troopers. The driver/assistant gunner waved as the combat car swept past; the jeep was hunkered down in a notch on the reverse slope that gave it a line of fire to the four howitzers and most of the interior of the firebase.

Sergeant Wegelin'd probably ordered the crew to keep under cover till he came up with the other gun and mortar. That wasn't precisely disobeying Ruthven's instructions, but it came bloody close; and Wegelin was probably right in his caution, so the El-Tee would keep his mouth shut. That was a lot of what a junior lieutenant did when he had good noncoms. . . .

The infantry moved toward the firebase through the stumps and brush in a skirmish line, but Melisant swung the car onto the road as soon as she reached the swale connecting the knolls. The track'd been cut with a bulldozer rather than properly graded, but the car's air cushion smoothed the ride nicely. The deep ruts from wheeled vehicles were frozen now and had snow on their southern edges.

Royalists cheered from the top of the wall. The soldiers were male but there were scores of women and children in the compound as well, some of them waving garments.

Ruthven grimaced, thinking of what'd happen if the Lord's Army overran the place. His job was to prevent that, but if the rebels were in the strength Intelligence thought they were—well, one platoon, even a bloody good platoon like E/1, wasn't going to be able to do the job without help that the Royalists might not be able to provide.

The firebase entrance was a simple gap in the wall, but bulldozers had scraped a pile of trunks and dirt as a screen ten meters in front of it. Semi-trailers bringing in supplies would have a hard time with the angle, but Melisant should be able to guide the combat car through without trouble.

There were three strands of barbed wire in front of the wall. That gave negligible protection against assault, but maybe it'd hearten the defenders: placebo effects were real in more areas than medicine.

Ruthven grinned. It wasn't much of a joke, but in a situation like this you took any chance for a laugh that you got.

Rennie parked his skimmer beside the entrance and hopped up the front of the wall like a baboon with a 2cm gun; he stood facing inward. His troopers split to either side, four of them joining him on the main wall while the other two mounted the screen and looked back to cover the rest of the column.

"Melisant, ease off a bit," Ruthven said over the intercom as he opened the roof hatch. "We don't want to spook our allies, over."

"*You mean they'll mess their pants, El-Tee?*" Melisant said. "*Yeah, we don't want that. Out.*"

The fan note didn't change, but the driver let gravity slow the heavy vehicle as they started up the slope toward the entrance. Ruthven thumbed the lift button and a hydraulic jack raised his seat until his head and shoulders were above the hatch coaming. This way the Royalists could see *him* instead of watching forty tonnes of steel and iridium growl toward them impassively.

Ruthven tried to keep his face impassive as he eyed the barrier. It was a tangle of protruding roots and branches, no harder to climb than a ladder. Defenders firing over the top from the other side would have very little advantage over an attacking force. The common soldiers carried locally made automatic rifles, but the three blockhouses spaced around the wall mounted pulsed lasers; each weapon had its own fusion bottle.

The Lord's Army wasn't any better equipped, but the Prophet Isaiah certainly did a better job of building enthusiasm in his followers than King Jorge II did. Rumor had it that Jorge and his three mistresses had left Pontefract for a safer planet several months ago . . . and this time rumor was dead right. Ruthven'd heard that from a buddy on Colonel Hammer's staff.

The command car eased through the S-bend at the base entrance. Melisant was squaring the corners, apparently to impress the locals. Ruthven looked down at them, trying to keep a friendly smile. They were impressed, all right, waving and cheering so loudly that sometimes he could hear them over the car's howling fans.

Good Lord, they're young! he thought. It really was a war of children. Most of the Royalist soldiers were teenagers and so undernourished they looked barely pubescent, while the Lord's Army recruited ten-year-olds at gunpoint from outlying villages.

It'd go on for as long as King Jorge managed to pay the Slammers and the Five Worlds Consortium shipped arms to the Prophet. A whole generation was dying in childhood.

History was a required subject at the Academy; Ruthven had done well in it. The realities of field service had provided color for those textual accounts of revolts, rebellions, and popular movements, however. That color was blood red.

He'd expected a vehicular circuit inside the wall, but the interior of the compound was sprinkled randomly with shanties and lean-tos except for the road from the gate to a clearing in the center. The four howitzers were emplaced evenly around the open area, each in a low sandbagged ring, which again must've been built for its morale value.

"*You want us up between the guns, El-Tee?*" Melisant asked. "*Looks like they dump the resupply there and the troops hoof it back to their billets, right? Over.*"

"Roger that," Ruthven said. "Break, Unit, we'll form in the central clearing while I figure out what to do next. Six out."

Blood and Martyrs! This's looking more and more like a ratfuck. Ruthven hadn't been thrilled by the assignment from the start, but until E/1 got to Firebase Courage he hadn't have guessed how bad things really were.

He'd expected the Royalist troops to be ill trained and poorly equipped—because all Royalist field units were: the defense budget never percolated far from the gaudily dressed officers in the capital, Zaragoza. He *hadn't* expected Fire Support Base Courage to be so ineptly constructed, though. It was a wonder that the Lord's Army hadn't rolled over the position long before.

The headquarters complex was four aluminum trailers that'd been buried in the ground to the right of the gate. A tower in the middle of them carried satellite and shortwave antennas, making the identification obvious and coincidentally providing an aiming point to the Prophet's gunners. The Lord's Army had only small arms, but painting a big bull's-eye on your Tactical Operations Center still isn't a good plan.

An officer in a green dress uniform with gold crossbelts was coming up the steps from one of the trailers, steadying his bicorn hat. The three aides accompanying him were less gorgeously dressed; that, rather than the rank tabs on his epaulets, identified Lieutenant Colonel Carrera.

Ruthven dropped into the compartment again. As soon as Melisant brought the car to a halt, he swung the rear hatch down into a ramp and stepped out to meet the Royalist officers.

Carrera stopped where he was and braced to attention. A rabbity aide with frayed cuffs scurried to Ruthven and said, "Sir, you are the commander? My colonel asks, what is your rank?"

Ruthven frowned. Instead of answering, he walked over to Carrera and said, "Colonel? I'm Lieutenant Henry Ruthven, in command of Platoon E/1 of Hammer's Regiment. We've been sent to you as reinforcements."

"A lieutenant?" the Royalist officer said in amazement. "One platoon only? And where are the rest of your tanks? This one thing—" He flicked his swagger stick toward the command car. "—this is not enough, surely! We must have more tanks!"

What Major Pritchard, the Slammers Operations Officer, had actually said when he assigned Ruthven was, "to put some backbone into the garrison." It wouldn't have been polite or politic either one to have repeated the phrasing, but now Ruthven half wished he had.

"We're infantry, Colonel," Ruthven said calmly, because it was his job—his duty—to be calm and polite. "We don't have any tanks at all, but I think you'll find we can handle things here. We've got sensors to give plenty of warning of enemy intentions. We've got our own powerguns, and we have direct communications to a battery of the Regiment's hogs."

"Oh, this is not right," Carrera said, turning and walking back toward his trailer. "My cousin promised me, *promised* me, tanks and there is only this tank."

"Sir?" said Ruthven. Sellars was bringing her squad in; the jeeps of Heavy Weapons followed closely. "Colonel! We need to make arrangements for the siting of my troops."

"Take care of him, Mendes," Carrera called over his shoulder. "I have been betrayed. It is out of my hands, now."

Carrera's aides had started to leave with him. A pudgy man in his forties, a captain if Ruthven had the collar insignia right, stopped and turned with a stricken look. The Royalists didn't wear name tags, but he was presumably Mendes.

"Right, Captain," Ruthven said with a breezy assertiveness that he figured was the best option. "I think under the circumstances we'll be best served by retaining my troops as a concentrated reserve here in the center of the firebase. We're highly mobile, you see. We'll place sensors around the perimeter to give us warning of attack as early as troops there could do."

That was true, but the real reason Ruthven'd decided to keep E/1 concentrated was so that his troopers could support one another. Self-preservation was starting to look like the primary goal for this operation. The Slammers'd been hired to fight and they *would* fight, but Hank Ruthven knew the Colonel hadn't given him troopers in order to get them killed for nothing.

All elements of E/1 were now within the compound. Hassel'd put the troopers with 2cm shoulder weapons on the wall aiming northeast, toward the ridge they'd just come from. Both the tribarrels covered the high ground also.

The ten troopers with submachine guns faced in, keeping an eye on Ruthven and the babbling crowd of Royalists. They weren't threatening; just watchful. With their mirrored face-shields down they looked like Death's Little Helpers, though, and they could become that in an eyeblink if anybody gave them reason.

"We'll need the use of your digging equipment," Ruthven continued. "The bulldozer and whatever else you have; a backhoe, perhaps?"

"We have nothing," Mendes said.

Ruthven's face hardened; he gestured with his left hand toward the dug-in trailers. His right, resting on the receiver of his slung submachine gun, slipped down to the grip.

"They went back!" Mendes said. "They came, yes, but they went back! We have nothing here, only the guns; and no tractors to move them!"

Bloody hell, that was true! Ruthven'd assumed he wasn't getting signatures from heavy equipment during E/1's approach simply because nothing was running at the moment, but the shanties scattered within the compound would make it impossible for even a jeep to move through them.

"Right," said Ruthven. "Then I'll need a labor party from your men, Captain. We have a few power augers, but there's a great deal of work to do before nightfall. For all our sakes. However the first requirement is to garrison that knob."

He gestured toward the high ground. When Mendes didn't turn his head, Ruthven put his hand on the Royalist's shoulder and rotated him gently, then pointed again.

"It's not safe to give the enemy that vantage point," Ruthven said. To any real soldier, that'd be as obvious as saying, "Water is wet," but real soldiers were bloody thin on the ground on Pontefract.

And it seemed they all wore Slammers uniforms.

"Oh, we can't do that!" Mendes said. "That is too far away!"

"Together we can," Ruthven said. "I'll put a squad there, and you'll supply a platoon. We'll rotate the troops every day. Dug in and with fire support from here, they'll be an anvil that we can smash the rebels on if they try anything."

"Oh," said Mendes. "Oh. Oh."

He wasn't agreeing—or disagreeing, so far as Ruthven could tell. He sounded like a man gasping for breath.

"Right!" Ruthven said cheerfully, clapping the Royalist on the shoulder. "Now, let's get to your ops room and set up the assignments, shall we?"

He'd put Rennie's squad on the ridge the first night, though he might also take Sellars' up for the afternoon also to get the position cleared. He could only hope that the Royalists would work well under Slammers' direction; that happened often enough on this sort of planet.

"Top?" Ruthven said to Hassel over the command push as he walked Mendes toward the trailers. He'd cut the whole platoon in on the discussion through the intercom, though he was blocking incoming messages unless they were red-tagged. "Take charge here while I get things sorted with our allies."

He paused. Because Mendes could theoretically hear him—in fact the Royalist officer appeared to be in shock—Ruthven chose the next words carefully: "And Top? I know what you're thinking because I'm thinking the same thing. But this is going to work if there's *any* way in hell I can make it work. Six out."

"Good morning, Hank," a professionally cheerful voice said. "Oh! Were you napping? I didn't mean to wake you up."

"Just thinking, Lisa," Ruthven said, opening his eyes and smiling at Lisa Mahone, the Frisian recruiting officer. Apologetically he added, "I, ah . . . I haven't gotten around to the papers, yet."

He thought he saw Mahone's eyes harden, but she sat down on the side of his bed and patted his right leg in a display of apparent affection. She said, "Well, I've used the time to your advantage, Hank. I told you I *hoped* I'd be able to get Personnel to grant you a two-step promotion? They've agreed to it! I'm authorized to change the recruitment agreement right now."

She leaned forward to take the folder from the side table, her hip brushing Ruthven's thigh. "How does that sound, *Captain* Ruthven?"

"It's hard to express, Lisa," Ruthven said, forcing a smile to make the words sound positive. He slitted his eyes so that they'd appear closed. In truth he *didn't* know what he thought about the business; it seemed to be happening to somebody else. Maybe it was drugs still in his system, though Drayer'd sworn that they'd tapered his dosage down to zero thirty-six hours ago.

Ruthven watched silently as Mahone amended the recruitment agreement in a firm, clear hand. She was an attractive woman with dark, shoulder-length hair and a perfect complexion. Her pants suit was severely tailored, but the shirt beneath her pale green jacket was frilled and had a deep neckline.

The gold-bordered folder not only acted as a hard backing for Mahone's stylus, it recorded the handwritten changes and transmitted them to the hospital's data bank. There they became part of the Regimental files, to be downloaded or transmitted by any authorized personnel.

Mahone wasn't as young as Ruthven'd thought when she approached him three days earlier, though. Perhaps the drugs really had worn off.

"I have to admit that I didn't have to do much convincing," she said in the same bright voice as she appeared to read the document in front of her. "My superiors were just as impressed by your record as I am. Very few graduates in the top ten percent of their class join mercenary units straight out of the Academy."

"I wanted to be a soldier," Ruthven said. This time his wry smile was real, but it was directed at his naive former self. "I thought I ought to learn what being a soldier was really about. I wanted to see the elephant, if you know the term."

"Seeing the elephant" had been used by soldiers as a euphemism for battle from a very long time back. It might even be as old as "buying the farm" as a euphemism for death.

"And you certainly did," Mahone said. "Your combat experience is a big plus."

She met his eyes with every appearance of candor and said, "The Frisian Defense Forces haven't fought a serious war since the Melpomene Emergency fifteen years ago. You knew that: that's why you enlisted in Hammer's Regiment when you wanted to see action. I know it too, and most importantly, the General Staff in Burcana knows it. The Defense Forces are willing to pay very well for the experience that our troops haven't gotten directly."

Mahone smiled like a porcelain doll, smooth and perfect, and held the folder out to Ruthven. "You bought that experience dearly, Captain," she said. "Now's the time to cash in on your investment."

Ruthven winced. It was a tiny movement, but Mahone caught it.

"Hank?" she said, lowering the folder while keeping it still within reach. She stroked Ruthven's thigh again and said, "Is it your leg?"

"Yeah," Ruthven lied. "Look, Lisa—can you come back later? I want to, ah, stand up and walk around a bit, if that's all right. By myself."

"Of course, Hank," Mahone said, smiling sympathetically. "I'll leave these here and come by this evening. If you like you can just sign them and I'll pick them up without bothering you if you're asleep."

Mahone set the folder upright on the table, between the pitcher and water glass. Straightening she glanced, apparently by coincidence, at the electronic window.

"Thank the Lord you don't have to go back to *that*, right?" she said. She smiled and swept gracefully out of the room.

Ruthven continued to lie on the bed for nearly a minute after the latch clicked. Then he got up slowly and walked to the window. He'd been thinking of Sergeant Rennie. That, not his leg, had made him wince.

They'd met on Atchafalaya. It'd been Ruthven's first day in the field, and it was Trooper Rennie then. . . .

"Here you go, Chief," said the driver of the jeep that'd brought Ruthven from E Company headquarters. "Last stop this run."

It was raining and well after local midnight. This sector was under blackout conditions; water running down the inside of Ruthven's face-shield blurred his light-enhanced vision and dripped on the tip of his nose. It was cold, colder than he'd dreamed it got on Atchafalaya, and he was more alone than he'd ever before felt in his life.

"Sir, you gotta get out," the driver said more forcefully. "I need t'get back to Captain Dolgosh."

Besides the jeep's idling fans, the only sound in the forest was rain dripping into the puddles beneath the trees. Air-plants hung in sheets from high branches, twisting and shimmering in the downpour. Ruthven couldn't see anything human in the landscape.

"Where do I . . . ?" he said.

Two figures came out of the blurred darkness. "Hold here, Adkins," one of them said. "I'll be going back with you. It won't be long."

"If you say so, El-Tee," the driver said. In bright contrast to his resigned agreement he added, "Hey, it's captain now, right? That was sure good news, sir. Nobody deserved it more!"

"Lieutenant Ruthven?" the newcomer continued brusquely, ignoring the congratulations. He was built like a fireplug and his voice rasped. "I'm Lyauty; you're taking E/1 over from me. I thought I'd stick around long enough to introduce you to your squad leaders."

"Ah, thank you very much, Captain," Ruthven said. He'd heard the man he was replacing'd been promoted to the command of Company K. That'd worried him because it meant Lyauty must be a good officer. *How am I going to measure up?*

The trooper who'd accompanied Lyauty was looking in the direction they'd come from, watching their backtrail. He had his right hand on the grip of his 2cm weapon; the stubby iridium barrel was cradled in the crook of his left elbow. He hadn't spoken.

"This your gear?" Lyauty said, reaching into the back of the jeep before Ruthven could forestall him. *I thought the trooper would carry the duffle bag.* "Via, Lieutenant! Is this *all* yours? We're in forward positions here!"

"I, ah," Ruthven said. "Well, clean uniforms, mostly. And, ah, some food items. And the assigned equipment, of course."

The driver snickered. "He's got his own auger, sir," he said.

"Right," said Lyauty in sudden harshness. "And you let him bring it. Well, Adkins, for that you can haul his bag over to the car. I've got Sellars on commo watch. The two of you sort it out. Leave him a proper field kit and I'll take the rest back to Regiment with me to store."

"Sorry, sir," the driver muttered. "I shoulda said something."

"Come along, Ruthven," Lyauty said. "Sorry about the trail, but you'll get used to it. Say, this is Trooper Rennie. I've got him assigned as my runner. You can make your own choice, of course, but I'd recommend you spend a few days getting the feel of the platoon before you start making changes."

The trooper leading them into the forest turned his head; in greeting, Ruthven supposed, but the fellow didn't raise his face-shield. He was as featureless as a billiard ball.

Ruthven turned his head toward Lyauty behind him. "A power auger is assigned equipment, sir," he said in an undertone.

"Right," said the captain. "We've got three of them in the platoon. A bloody useful piece of kit, but not as useful as extra rations and ammo if things go wrong. The brass at Regiment can afford to count on resupply because it's not their ass swinging in the breeze if the truck doesn't make it forward. Here in the field we pretty much go by our own priorities."

The trail zigzagged steeply upward; Rennie in the lead was using his left hand to pull himself over the worst spots, holding his 2cm weapon like a huge pistol. Ruthven's submachine gun was strapped firmly across his chest, leaving both hands free. Even so he stumbled repeatedly and once clanged flat on the wet rock.

"It's not much farther, Lieutenant," Lyauty said. "Another hundred meters up is all."

"I thought—" Ruthven said. He slipped and caught himself on all fours. As he started to get up, the toe of his left boot skidded back and slammed him down again. The submachine gun pounded against his body armor.

"I thought your headquarters would be the command vehicle," he said in a rush, trying to ignore the pain of his bruised ribs.

"We couldn't get the car to the top of this cone," Lyauty said. "I've been leaving it below with three troopers, rotating them every night when the rations come up."

"The jeeps couldn't climb above that last switchback," said Trooper Rennie. "We had to hump the tribarrels from there, and that's hell's own job."

There was a tearing hiss above. Ruthven jerked his head up. The foliage was sparse on this steep slope, so he was able to catch a glimpse of a green ball streaking across the sky from the west.

"Is that a rocket?" said Ruthven. Then, "That was a rocket!"

"It wasn't aimed at us, Lieutenant," Lyauty said wearily. "Anyway, our bunkers're on the reverse slope, though we've got fighting positions forward too if we need them."

"I just thought . . ." Ruthven said. "I thought we, ah . . . I thought that incoming artillery was destroyed in the air."

"They can't hit anything with bombardment rockets," Lyauty said. "Anyway, they can't hit us. To use the tribarrel in the command car for air defense, we'd have to shift it into a clearing. That'd make *it* a target."

"We're infantry, Lieutenant," Rennie said over his shoulder. "If you want to call attention to yourself, you ought to've put in for tanks."

Ruthven opened his mouth to dress the trooper down for inso-
lence. He closed it again, having decided it was Lyauty's job properly
since he hadn't formally handed over command of the platoon.

"We can hit hard when we need to, Lieutenant," Lyauty said. "But
until then, yeah—keeping a low profile is a good plan."

"Who you got with you, Rennie?" a voice called from the darkness
above them.

Ruthven looked up. He couldn't see anybody, just an outcrop over
which a gnarled tree managed to grow. His torso beneath the clam-
shell body armor was sweating profusely, but his hands were numb
from gripping wet rocks and branches.

"Six's come up, Hassel," Rennie said. "And we got the new El-Tee
along."

"Sir?" said a man kneeling beside the outcrop. "Come on up but
keep low. If you stand here, the wops get your head in silhouette. I'm
Hassel, First Squad."

"It's Hassel's bunker, properly," Lyauty said. "I asked the other
squad leaders to come here tonight so I can introduce you."

Another man stepped into the night; this time Ruthven saw his
arm sweep back the curtain of light-diffusing fabric hanging over a
hole in the side of the hillside. "This the new El-Tee?" he said.

"Right, Wegs," said Lyauty. "His name's Ruthven. Lieutenant, Sergeant Wegelin's your heavy weapons squad leader. Come on, let's get
under cover."

"Yessir, two tribarrels and two mortars instead of three of each,"
said Wegelin as he held the curtain for Hassel, then Ruthven after a
directive jab from Lyauty's knuckles. "And if you think that's bad, then
we only got three working jeeps. It don't matter here since we off-
loaded the guns, but we'll be screwed good if they expect us to displace on our own."

Ruthven hit his head—his helmet, but it still staggered him—on
the transom, then missed the two steps down. He'd have fallen on his
face if the tall man waiting—he had to hunch to clear the ceiling—
hadn't caught him.

"Have you heard something about us displacing, Wegs?" the man
said, stepping back when he was sure Ruthven had his feet. "Because
I haven't. Talk about getting the shaft! E/1 sure has this time."

"Troops, this is Lieutenant Ruthven who's taking over from me,"
Lyauty said. "Lieutenant, that's van Ronk, your platoon sergeant,
Axbird who's got Second Squad—"

"How-do, Lieutenant," said a short woman who at first seemed plump. When she lifted her rain cape to pour a cup of cacao from the pot bubbling on a ledge cut into the side of the bunker, Ruthven realized she was wearing at least three bandoliers laden with equipment and ammunition.

"And that's Purchas there on watch," Lyauty said, nodding to the man in the southeast corner. "He's Third Squad."

Purchas was on an ammo box, using a holographic display that rested on a similar box against the bunker wall. He didn't turn around.

"We pipe the sensors through optical fibers," Lyauty explained, gesturing to the skein of filaments entering the bunker by a hole in the roof. Rain dripped through also, pooling on the floor of gritty mud. "Below the ridgeline there's a microwave cone aimed back at the command car. We need the car for the link to Central, but other than that we're on our own here."

Everybody'd raised their face-shields; Ruthven raised his too, though the bunker's only illumination was that scatter from the sensor display. *My eyes'll adapt. Won't they?*

"If you're wondering, there isn't a separate command bunker," Lyauty said. "You can change that if you want, but I feel like moving to a different squad each night keeps me in the loop better."

Everybody was looking at Ruthven. Well, everybody but Purchas. They expected him to say something.

Ruthven's lips were sticking together. "I . . . " he said. "Ah, I see."

"Well, I'll leave you to it, then," Lyauty said. "This is as good a platoon as there is in the Slammers, Ruthven. You're a lucky man."

He turned toward the curtained entrance. "Ah, excuse me, sir," Ruthven said. *How do I address the man? Oh Lord, oh Lord!* "Ah, my sleeping bag is with my other gear. Ah, in the jeep."

"No sweat, Lieutenant," said Trooper Rennie, pointing to the bag roughly folded on a wall niche. The outside was of resistant fabric; beneath were layers of microinsulation and a soft lining. This cover was torn, and from what Ruthven could see, the lining was as muddy as the floor. "There's an extra in each of the squad bunkers. You and me won't both be sleeping at the same time."

Lyauty cleared his throat. "Well," he said, "keep your heads down, troopers. I'll be thinking about you, believe me."

He muttered something else as he stepped back into the rain. Ruthven thought he heard, "I've got half a mind—" but it might not have been that.

The bunker was cold and it stank. Sweat and rainwater were cooling between Ruthven's skin and his body armor, and he was sure he'd chafed blisters over his hip bones. Another rocket screamed through the sky; this time it hit close enough to shake dirt from the bunker ceiling.

Ruthven looked at his new subordinates. Their expressions were watchful, hostile, and in the case of Purchas completely dismissive.

He wished he were back on Nieuw Friesland. He wished he were anyplace else but here.

Lieutenant Henry Ruthven wished he were dead.

There was a knock on a door down the corridor. "El-Tee, is that you?" somebody called. Ruthven, his face blanking, stepped quickly around the bed to get to the door.

Muffled words answered unintelligibly. "Sorry," said the familiar voice. "I'm looking for Lieutenant Ruthven and—"

"Axbird, is that you?" Ruthven said, stepping into the corridor. "Via, Sergeant, I thought you'd already shipped out! Come on in—I've got a bottle of something you'll like."

"Don't mind if I do, El-Tee," Axbird said. "Tell the truth, there isn't a hell of a lot I don't like, so long as it comes out of a bottle. Or a can— I'm democratic that way."

E/1's former platoon sergeant had gained weight—a lot of weight— since her injury, though that hadn't been but—well, it'd been four months. Longer than Ruthven would've guessed without thinking about it. But still, a lot of weight.

The skin of her face was as smooth as burnished metal. Her eyes had the milky look of a molting snake's, and she had an egg-shaped device clipped above each ear.

Ruthven backed into his room and rotated the chair for Axbird, primarily to call it to her attention. A buzzbomb had hit the side of the command car while she was inside with her face-shield raised. The jet from the warhead's shaped charge had missed her—had missed everything, in fact; patched, the car was still in service with E/1—but it'd vaporized iridium from the opposite bulkhead. That glowing cloud had bathed her face.

Axbird entered with the careful deliberation of a robot. She wasn't using a cane, but she held her hands out at waist height as though preparing to catch herself. When she reached the chair, she put one hand on the back and tapped the device above her right ear. "How do you like them, El-Tee?" she said with a plastic smile. "I always wanted to have black eyes. Didn't say they shouldn't be lidar transceivers, though. That's what you get for not specifying, hey?"

"You're getting around very well, Axbird," Ruthven lied. He squatted to rummage in the cabinet under his side table. There was only one glass, and the brandy was too good to pour into the plastic tumbler by the water pitcher.

"I'm still getting used to them," Axbird said. "Dialing 'em in, you know? They say I'll get so I can tell the numbers, but right now I'm counting doorways."

"There's a linen closet in the middle of the corridor," Ruthven said apologetically. He offered her the glass, wondering if she could see his expression. Probably not; probably never again.

Axbird drank the brandy without lowering the glass from her lips. "Via, I needed that," she muttered, wiping her mouth with the back of her hand. She forced another grin and said, "How are you doing, sir? I heard you guys really got it in the neck."

"It was bad enough," Ruthven agreed carefully. He'd hesitated a moment, but he took the glass and refilled it for her. "Thank the Lord for Fire Central."

"You can't trust wogs," Axbird said. Her voice rose. "We might as well kill 'em all. Every fucking one of 'em!"

"There's better local forces and worse ones, Sergeant," Ruthven said with deliberate formality. "I'd say the Royalists here were pretty middling. They'd do well enough if they got any support from their own government."

"Yeah, I suppose," Axbird said. She was trembling; she held the glass in both hands to keep from spilling. "You trust your buddies and screw the rest, every one of 'em."

A rebel sapper had gotten close enough to nail the command car with a buzzbomb because the Royalists holding that section of the perimeter had all been asleep. The car's Automatic Defense System hadn't been live within the compound; it wouldn't have been safe with so many friendlies running around.

"Sorry, El-Tee," Axbird said. She seemed to have gotten control of herself again. "Yeah, remember on Diderot where our so-called allies were trying to earn the bounties the Chartists were offering on a Slammer's head?"

"Umm, that was before my time, Axbird," Ruthven said, sitting on his bed. He held the brandy bottle but he didn't think a drink would help him right now. "I joined on Atchafalaya, remember."

"Oh, right," said Axbird. She drank, guiding the glass to her lips with both hands. "Right, Diderot was back when I was a trooper."

For a moment she was silent, her cloudy eyes staring into space. Ruthven wondered if he should say something—and wondered what he *could* say—but Axbird resumed. "They got a great spot lined up for me, El-Tee. The Colonel did, I mean: a condo right on the beach on San Carlos. It's on Mainland because, well—until I get these dialed in better, you know."

Her right hand gestured toward the lidar earpiece, then quickly closed again on her empty glass.

"And for maintenance at first, I don't want to be out on my own island," she continued in a tone of birdlike perkiness. "But I can be. I can buy my own bloody island, El-Tee, I'm on full pay for the rest of my life! That'll run to a lotta brandy, don't you know?"

"Here, I'll fill that," Ruthven said, leaning forward with the bottle. He took the glass in his own hand before he started to pour. "Are you from San Carlos originally, then?"

"Naw," Axbird said. "I'm from Camside, sir. Haven't been back since I enlisted, though, twelve years."

She stared off into space. Her eyes moved normally; Ruthven wondered how much sight remained to them. Probably no more than being able to tell light from dark, though that'd be some help when she was on her own.

"I thought of going back, you know?" she said. "My pension'd make me a big deal on Camside, leastways unless things've changed a bloody great lot since I shipped out. But I thought, who do I know there? There's nobody, nobody ever who'd understand what it means to be a Slammer. What do I care about them?"

Axbird drank convulsively, dribbling brandy from the corners of her mouth. She started to lower the glass and instead dropped it. It bounced once, then shattered.

"Oh Lord, sir!" she said, her voice rising into a wail. She lurched to her feet. Tears were streaming from beneath the lids of her ruined eyes. "What do *I* care about wogs, on Camside or any bloody place?"

She was wearing hospital slippers. Ruthven got up quickly and gripped her shoulder to keep her from stepping in the glass she probably couldn't see. Axbird threw her arms around him.

"Oh, Lord, El-Tee!" she said. "There's nobody who'll understand! There'll never be anybody!"

Ruthven held the sobbing woman. His eyes were closed. He was remembering E/1's second and last night in Fire Support Base Courage. *Nobody'll ever understand.*

"El-Tee!" said Rennie in a hoarse whisper. "Sir, wake up. The bastards're bugging out!"

Ruthven jerked upright. He'd been sleeping in the rear compartment of the command car while Rennie sat at the console with the sensor readouts and commo gear. The squad leaders each took a two-hour watch, debriefing Ruthven when they were relieved or if anything significant appeared.

As it'd done, apparently.

Melisant'd been sleeping on top of the cab; her boots clunked against armor as she slid down behind the controls. The tone of Rennie's voice through the open hatch had snapped her awake, so she was heading for her action station like the good trooper she was.

Rennie had the sensor display filling most of the holographic screen; commo was a narrow sidebar, unimportant for the time being. People—hundreds of people—were clustered at the firebase entrance. They were leaving on foot, heading eastward along the road. From the south, west, and north other groups of people were approaching.

Those coming toward the base were rebels of the Lord's Army, armed to the teeth. Judging from the lack of metal for the magnetic sensors to pick up, the Royalists had left their weapons behind.

"Them wogs're just walking outa the base!" Rennie said. "They musta been talking to the rebs, don't you guess?"

"More to the point, they're walking out on us," Ruthven muttered. "Rouse the platoon—but quiet, don't let the locals know we've tumbled to what's going on."

He uncaged and pressed the panic button that automatically copied all platoon communications to Base Hammer, through the satellite net if it was up or by bouncing off cosmic ray tracks if it wasn't. It was faster than making a separate transmission to Regiment, and there was *bloody* little time. The rebels'd be climbing over the wall in a few minutes, and when that happened it'd all be over for E/1.

Ruthven raised the platform to put his head and shoulders through the roof hatch. Using his helmet's thermal imaging, he could see that the howitzer crews were gone too. The guns hadn't been disabled: explosions or the roar of thermite grenades would've warned the Slammers. In all likelihood, the Lord's Army had offered the Royalists their lives, in exchange for all their arms and for the Slammers who'd been sent as reinforcements.

It was at best an open question as to whether the rebels intended to honor their bargain. They'd left the road clear for half a klick from the firebase entrance, but the figures concealed in the brush there to either side looked to Ruthven like a kill zone placed far enough out that the victims couldn't run back to safety.

On the other hand, the Royalists hadn't exactly delivered Platoon E/1 into the Prophet's hands either.

"Unit, listen up," Ruthven said. The troopers in the firebase were gathered close enough that his helmet intercom reached them unaided, but the command car's powerful transceivers were relaying the signal to Sergeant Sellars' squad on the knoll to the northeast. "We can't hold this place, it's too big, but we can break out and join Second Squad. All together in a tight perimeter we can hold till help comes."

Via, what was the closest friendly unit? Maybe G Troop's combat cars, based with a Regimental howitzer battery at Firebase Groening? But that was forty klicks away, and it wouldn't be safe for them to come direct by the road.

"I'm taking the car out by the entrance," he continued aloud. "We can't get over the wall or through it. Wegelin, your jeeps follow me."

Maybe a tank could push a hole in the tangle of tree trunks, but a command car couldn't and overloaded jeeps *certainly* couldn't. Nor did they have enough excess power to climb the irregular surface.

"The rest of you lift over the wall in the zero to forty-five-degree quadrant," Ruthven said. That'd spread the troopers enough that they wouldn't get in each other's way while awkwardly jumping the trees. "The skimmers can do it if you're careful. I'll call a fire mission on the rebs coming from the north. When it lands, that's our signal to roll. Any questions?"

"El-Tee, I was a redleg on Andersholz before I joined the Regiment," said Wegelin. "*I can fire them one-twenties. The wogs keep 'em loaded but powered down, you see.*"

Ruthven tried to make sense of what Wegelin had just said. He hadn't known the Heavy Weapons sergeant had been an artilleryman, but he didn't see what difference it made now. They could startle the rebs and cause casualties by firing the Royalist guns in their faces as they climbed the wall, but it sure wouldn't drive them away.

"*What I mean, sir,*" Wegelin continued, "*is a charger of five HE rounds'll give us a hole any bloody place you want to go through the wall. Not at the gate where they'll be expecting us, I mean, over.*"

"Can you manage that in two minutes, over?" Ruthven said as he dropped into the van's interior. Rennie'd vacated the console and was on his way out of the compartment, returning to his squad.

Ruthven checked the display. Rennie'd prepped fire missions on each of the four rebel concentrations; three moved as the company-sized groups advanced on the firebase.

"*We're on our way, out,*" the sergeant responded. As he spoke, icons on Ruthven's display showed the jeeps sprinting to the northernmost howitzer; the sound of their fans burred faintly through the open hatches. The big gun wasn't far from where Wegelin's squad was to begin with, but he obviously wanted them all to be able to jump into the jeeps as soon as they'd set up the burst.

"Unit," Ruthven said. He placed his right index finger on the terrain map image of the firebase wall, exporting the image to all his troopers. "Adjust the previous order. The car and jeeps will be leaving the firebase *here*. I don't know what the shells are going to do—"

One possibility was that they'd blast the existing tangle into something worse, so that the skimmers couldn't get over or through either one. It was still the best choice on offer.

"—and if you want to follow me through what I hope'll be a gap, that's fine. But *don't* get in the way, troopers, this car's a pig. We're going to be a full honk, and we won't be able to dodge. Questions, over?"

Nobody spoke, but three green icons blipped onto the top of the display. *Via, they're pros, they're the best platoon in the bloody regiment, they really are. . . .*

"*Six, we got the tube ready!*" Sergeant Wegelin said as his icon lit also. "*Five rounds, HE, and I've programmed her to traverse right fifteen mils at each round. We're ready, over!*"

The Royalist howitzers had their own power supplies to adjust elevation and traverse; they could even crawl across terrain by themselves, though very slowly. The northern weapon was now live, a bright image on Ruthven's display and a whine through the hatch as its pumps pressurized the hydraulic system.

"Fire Central, this is Echo One-six," Ruthven said, calling the Regiment's artillery controller but distributing the exchange to his troopers on an output-only channel. "Request Fire Order One—"

Targeting the rebels approaching from the northeast. They were coming uphill by now. That plus the stumps and broken rocks of the roughly cleared terrain had slowed them.

"—HE, repeat HE only, we're too close for firecracker rounds, time of impact fifty-five, repeat five-five seconds from—"

His index finger tapped a marker into the transmission.

"—*now*, over."

"*Roger, Echo One-six,*" replied a voice barely identifiable as female through the tight compression. She was so calm she sounded bored. Then, "*On the way, out.*"

"Echo One-four-six," Ruthven said. *I probably sound bored, too.* "This is Six. Take the wall down in three-five, I repeat three-five, seconds. Break. Unit, wait for our Hogs, don't get hasty. Then it's time to kick ass, troopers, out!"

The command car's fans were howling. The vehicle slid forward; forty tonnes accelerates slowly, so Melisant was getting an early start. *They'll hear us, but screw 'em. They'll hear more than our fans real soon.*

Ruthven started to close the back ramp but Melisant had already taken care of that. He went up through the roof hatch and took the tribarrel's grips in his hands.

There were a lot of reasons to stay down in the body. Communications with E/1 and Central were better inside; he could operate the gun just as well from the console and had a better display than his visor gave him; and the vehicle's armor, though light, might save him from shrapnel or a bullet that'd otherwise rob the platoon of its commander. There wasn't a trooper in E/1 who'd think their El-Tee was a coward if he stayed in the compartment.

But Ruthven himself'd worry that he was a coward in the dark silences before dawn, especially if he survived and some of his troopers didn't. And somebody was going to die. That was as sure as sunrise, even if E/1 got luckier than any veteran expected.

The long-barreled 120mm howitzer belched a bottle-shaped yellow flash toward the perimeter wall; companion flares spewed out and back from both sides through the muzzle brake's baffles. The tube recoiled and the blast slapped Ruthven. The commo helmet's active sound cancellation saved his hearing, but the shock wave pushed him against the hatch ring. Even at this distance, unburned powder grains speckled his throat and bare hands.

The wall erupted, leaking the shell burst's red flash through the tree trunks it blew apart. Royalist shanties flattened, flung outward in a cone spreading from the howitzer. A huge dust cloud rose from the shock-pummeled compound.

The command car hit the ground, plowing a track through the hard soil. The steel skirt rang, scattering sparks when it hit embedded stones as the vehicle bucked and pitched.

Either the shock wave had startled Melisant into chopping her throttles, or she'd realized it'd be a disaster to get in front of the howitzer while it was still firing. The Regiment used rocket howitzers rather than tube artillery. She probably hadn't expected the muzzle blast of a long-range gun to be so punishing.

Ruthven hadn't expected it either. Being told something by an Academy lecturer wasn't the same as being hit by what felt like a hundred-kilo sandbag in the field.

The howitzer returned to battery and slammed again, then *again*, *again*, and *again*. The interval between shots was less than two seconds. The last shell screamed toward the northwest horizon as the gun fell over on its side. Rapid fire at zero elevation had lifted the recoil spades at the end of the gun's trail.

Between the third round and the fourth, the salvo from the Hogs at Firebase Groening burst outside the encampment as a white glare that silhouetted the flying tree trunks. Central'd fused the shells to go off just above the surface instead of burying themselves before exploding.

Fragments of casing screeched across the hillside in an interlocking web more deadly than any spider's. A large chunk—maybe the base-plate of a Royalist shell—howled through Firebase Courage in a flat red streak. It didn't miss the command car by much, but it missed. . . .

"Go!" Ruthven shouted. "Go! Go! Go!"

The car was accelerating again. After Melisant'd gotten them stopped the first time, she'd gimbaled the nacelles vertical and kept the fans at maximum output. They'd been hovering at ten centimeters on a pillow of air, not exactly flying—the vehicle remained in ground effect—but shuddering to every shock wave.

The elevation, though slight, gave the car a gravity boost when Melisant shoved the steering yoke forward. They gathered speed quickly despite ticks and bounces from debris scattered across the interior of the firebase. Flames spurted beneath the plenum chamber when they crossed the former perimeter; the 120mm shells had started small fires in the wood, and the drive fans whipped them into hungry enthusiasm.

There were some larger chunks for them to kick aside, but the trees no longer formed an interlocked mass that could resist a forty-tonne battering ram. Showers of sparks and blazing torches flew ahead of the skirts. Then the car was through and heading down the slope into what remained of a company of the Lord's Army.

Ruthven snapped a short burst at what looked in his visor's thermal image like a rebel kneeling only twenty meters away. The car skidded enough to throw his bolts wide, but before he could correct he realized that he was shooting at a legless, headless torso impaled on a sapling.

Cyan bolts snapped through the night, igniting the brush. Nobody could aim accurately from a skimmer at speed, but in the corner of his eye Ruthven saw a secondary explosion. A trooper'd gotten lucky, hitting a rebel's buzzbomb and detonating the warhead.

Red tracers and muzzle flashes danced in the darkness also, but most of the rebels firing were in the companies to the south and east. The party on which the Hogs had unloaded were largely silent, dead or stunned by the 20cm shells. One rebel opened up from a gully to E/1's left front, but at least a dozen powerguns replied to the chattering rifle. Either somebody hit the reb, or he decided that huddling out of sight was a better idea than martyrdom for the Prophet after all; at any rate, the shooting stopped.

The command car reached the ground slope rising toward Second Squad. The brush and canes hadn't been cleared here; they averaged maybe two meters high, and there were occasional much taller trees.

Melisant kept moving, but she had to slow to 20kph. They'd drawn well ahead of the jeeps and skimmers on the downhill run, but now the smaller vehicles were able to slip between clumps that the car had to fight through.

For a wonder, Sergeant Sellars was keeping her Royalists from shooting down at Ruthven's force. Maybe Second Squad was holding the locals at gunpoint to enforce fire discipline . . . and then again, maybe that detached platoon'd bugged out when the shooting started. Either way, Ruthven was going to put Sellars in for both a medal and a promotion when this was over.

If I'm around to make the recommendation. If she's around to get it.

Badly aimed rifle fire had been zipping overhead since the beginning of the breakout, but now a machine gun on a fixed mount cut branches nearby. Ruthven rotated his tribarrel to the right. Bullets whanged off the car's high side. The machine gunner was part of the unit that'd been waiting down the road for the Royalist garrison. He was bloody good to hit a moving target at six hundred meters, even with the advantage of a tripod.

Ruthven fired a short burst. His tribarrel was stabilized, but the lurching car threw him around violently even though the weapon held its point of aim. His bolts vanished into the night, leaving only faintly glowing tracks on their way toward interplanetary vacuum.

Ruthven took a deep breath, letting the car bump into a small depression. When they started up the other side, into a belt of canes trailing hair-fine filaments, he fired. This time his shots merged with the muzzle flashes of the rebel machine gun. Plasma licked a white flare of burning steel.

Got you, you bastard! Ruthven thought. Three rebels with buzzbombs rose out of the swale ten meters ahead of the car.

Ruthven swung the tribarrel back toward the new targets. The rebels to left and right fired: glowing gas spurted from the back of the launching tubes, and the bulbous missiles streaked toward the vehicle behind quick red sparks.

The car's automatic defense system banged twice, blasting tungsten pellets from the strips just above the skirts. They shredded the buzzbombs in the air, killing one of the rebels who happened to be in the way of the remainder of the charge.

Ruthven shot before his gun was on target, hoping his blue-green bolts chewing the landscape would startle the rebels. The remaining rebel fired. Because the car's bow was canted upward, the third buzzbomb approached from too low to trip the ADS. The warhead burst against the skirts, punching a white-hot spear through the plenum chamber and up into the driver's compartment.

Several lift fans shut off; pressurized air from the remaining nacelles roared through the hole blown in the steel. The car grounded, rocked forward in a near somersault, and slammed to rest on its skirts.

The first impact smashed Ruthven's thighs against the hatch coaming; pain was a sun-white blur filling his mind. When the car's bow lifted, it tossed him onto the bales of rations and personal gear in the roof rack. Ruthven was only vaguely aware of the final shock hurling him off the crippled vehicle.

He opened his eyes. He was on his back with the landscape shimmering in and out of focus. He must've been unconscious, but he didn't know how long. The car was downslope from him. One of its fans continued to scream, but the others were silent. Black smoke boiled out of the driver's compartment.

He tried to stand up but his legs didn't move. *Have they been blown off? They couldn't be, I'd have bled out.* He'd lost his helmet, so the visor no longer protected his eyes from the sky-searing bolts of plasma being fired from the knoll above him. The afterimages of each track wobbled from orange to purple and back across his retinas.

Ruthven rolled over, still dazed. Pain yawned in a gaping cavern centered on his right leg. He must've screamed but he couldn't hear the sound. When the jolt from the injured leg sucked inward and vanished, his throat felt raw.

"It's the El-Tee!" somebody cried. "Cover me, I'm going to get him."

Another buzzbomb detonated with a hollow *whoomp!* on the right side of the command car. Momentarily, a pearly bubble swelled bigger than the vehicle itself. The jet penetrated the thin armor, crossed the compartment, and sprayed out the left side.

Ruthven started crawling, pushing himself with his left foot and dragging his right as though the leg were tied to his hip with a rope. He couldn't feel it now except as a dull throbbing *somewhere.*

He wasn't trying to get to safety: he knew his safest course would be to lie silently in a dip, hoping to go unobserved or pass for dead. He wasn't thinking clearly, but his troopers were on the knoll so that's where he was going.

A rebel ran out from behind the command car shouting, "Protect me, Lord!"

Ruthven glanced back. His submachine gun was in the vehicle, but he wore a pistol. He scrabbled for it but his equipment belt was twisted; he couldn't find the holster.

The rebel thrust his automatic rifle out in both hands; the butt wasn't anywhere near his shoulder. "Die, unbeliever!" he screamed. A 2cm powergun bolt decapitated him. The rifle fired as he spasmed backward.

One bullet struck Ruthven in the small of the back. It didn't penetrate his ceramic body armor, but the impact was like a sledgehammer. Bits of bullet jacket sprayed Ruthven's right arm and cheek.

He pushed himself upward again, moaning deep in his throat. He thought he might be talking to himself. A skimmer snarled through the high grass and circled to a halt alongside, the bow facing uphill. Nozzles pressurized by the single fan sprayed grit across Ruthven's bare face.

"El-Tee, grab on!" Rennie shouted, leaning from the flat platform to seize Ruthven's belt. "Grab!"

Ruthven turned on his side and reached out. He got a tie-down in his left hand and the shoulder clamp of the sergeant's armor in his right. Rennie was already slamming power to the lift fan, trying to throw his weight out to the right to balance the drag of Ruthven's body.

The skimmer wasn't meant to carry two, but it slowly accelerated despite the excess burden. Ruthven bounced through brush, sometimes hitting a rock. His left boot acted as a skid, but often enough his hip or the length of his leg scraped as the skimmer ambled uphill. A burst of submachine gun fire—a nervous flickering against the brighter, saturated flashes of 2cm weapons—crackled close overhead, but Ruthven couldn't see what the shooter was aiming at.

The skimmer jolted over a shrub whose roots had held the wind-swept soil in a lump higher than the ground to either side. Ruthven flew free and rolled. Every time his right leg hit the ground, a flash of pain cut out that fraction of the night.

A tribarrel chugged from behind, raking the slope up which they'd come. Ruthven was within the new perimeter. Half a dozen Royalists huddled nearby with terrified expressions, but E/1 itself had enough firepower to halt the rebels. They'd already been hammered, and now more shells screamed down like a regiment of flaming banshees.

Firebase Groening was northeast of Firebase Courage, so the Hogs were overfiring E/1's present perimeter to reach the rebels. Somebody—Sergeant Hassel?—must be calling in concentrations, relaying the messages through the command car. The vehicle was out of action, but its radios were still working.

Rennie spun the skimmer to a halt. "Made it!" he shouted. "We bloody well made it!"

Ruthven found his holster and managed to lift the flap. Beside him, Rennie hunched to remove his 2cm weapon from the rail where he'd clamped it to free both hands for the rescue.

A buzzbomb skimmed the top of the knoll, missing the tribarrel at which it'd been aimed and striking Sergeant Rennie in the middle of the back. There was a white flash.

The shells from Firebase Groening landed like an earthquake on the rebels who'd overrun the Royalist camp and were now starting uphill toward E/1. In the light of the huge explosions, Ruthven saw Rennie's head fly high in the air. The sergeant had lost his helmet, and his expression was as innocent as a child's.

"Good afternoon, Lieutenant Ruthven," Dr. Parvati said as he stepped into the room without knocking. "You are up? And packing already, I see. It is good that you should be optimistic, but let us take things one step at a time, shall we? Lie down on your bed, please, so that I can check you."

Ruthven wondered if Parvati'd put a slight emphasis on the phrase "one step." Probably not, and even if he had it'd been meant as a harmless joke. *I have to watch myself. I'm pretty near the edge, and if I start overreacting, well . . .*

"Look, Doc," he said, straightening but not moving away from the barracks bag he was filling from the locker he'd kept under the bed. "You saw the reading that Drayer took this noon, right? I'm kinda in a hurry."

"I have gone over the noon readings, yes," Parvati said calmly. He was a small, slight man with only a chaplet of hair remaining, though by his face he was in his early youth. "Now I would like to take more readings."

When Ruthven still hesitated, Parvati added, "I do not tell you how to do your job, Lieutenant. Please grant me the same courtesy."

"Right," said Ruthven after a further moment. He pushed the locker to the side and paused. The garments were new, sent over from Quartermaster's Stores. The gear on the command car's rack had burned when they shot at rebs trying to get to the tribarrel. The utilities Ruthven had worn during the firefight had been cut off him as soon as he arrived here.

He sat on the bed and carefully swung his legs up. He'd been afraid of another blinding jolt, but he felt nothing worse than a twinge in his back. Funny how it was his left hip rather than the smashed right femur where the pain hit him now. He'd scraped some on the left side, but he'd have said that was nothing to mention.

"So," said Parvati, reading the diagnostic results with his hands crossed behind his back. The holographic display was merely a distortion in the air from where Ruthven lay looking at the doctor. "So."

"I was talking to Sergeant Axbird this afternoon," Ruthven said to keep from fidgeting. "She was my platoon sergeant, you know. I was wondering how she was coming along?"

Parvati looked at Ruthven through the display. After a moment he said, "Mistress Axbird's physical recovery has gone as far as it can. How she does now depends on her own abilities and the degree to which she learns to use her new prosthetics. If you are her friend, you will encourage her to show more initiative in that regard."

"Ah," Ruthven said. "I see. *I'm* cleared for duty, though, Doctor. Right?"

He wondered if he ought to stand up again. Parvati always used the bed's own display instead of downloading the information into a clipboard.

"Are you still feeling pain in your hip, Lieutenant?" the doctor asked, apparently oblivious of Ruthven's question.

"No," Ruthven lied. "Well, not really. You know, I get a little, you know, tickle from time to time. I guess that'll go away pretty quick, right?"

It struck Ruthven that the diagnostic display would include blood pressure, heart rate, and all the other physical indicators of stress. He jumped up quickly. Pain exploded from his hip; he staggered forward. His mouth was open to gasp, but his paralyzed diaphragm couldn't force the air out of his lungs.

"Lieutenant?" Parvati said, stepping forward.

"I'm all right!" said Ruthven. Sweat beaded his forehead. "I just tripped on the locker! Bloody thing!"

"I see," said Parvati in a neutral tone. "Well, Lieutenant, your recovery seems to be proceeding most satisfactorily. I'd like you to remain here for a few days, however, so that some of my colleagues can check you over."

"You mean Psych, don't you?" Ruthven said. His hands clenched and unclenched. "Look, Doc, I don't need that and I *sure* don't want it. Just sign me out, got it?"

"Lieutenant Ruthven, you were seriously injured," the doctor said calmly. "I would be derelict in my duties if I didn't consider the possibility that the damage I was able to see had not caused additional damage beyond my purview. I wish to refer you to specialists in psychological trauma, yes."

"Do you?" Ruthven said. His voice was rising, but he couldn't help it. "Well, you let *me* worry about that, all right? You're a nice guy, Doc, but you said it: my psychology is none of your business! Now, you clear me back to my unit, or I'll take it over your head. You can explain to Colonel Hammer why you're dicking around a platoon leader whose troops need him in the field!"

"I see," said the doctor without any inflection. "I do not have the authority to hold you against your will, Lieutenant, but for your own sake I wish you would reconsider."

"You said that," Ruthven said. He bent and picked up his barracks bag. "Now, you do your job and let me get back to mine."

Parvati made a slight bow. "As you wish," he said. He touched the controller in his hand; the hologram vanished like cobwebs in a storm. "I will have an orderly come to take your bag."

"Don't worry about that," Ruthven said harshly. "I can get it over to the transient barracks myself. They'll find me a bunk there if there isn't a way to get to E/1 still tonight. I just want to be out of this place ASAP."

He didn't know where the platoon was or who was commanding in his absence. Hassel, he hoped; it'd be awkward if Central'd brought in another officer already. He wondered how many replacements they'd gotten after the ratfuck at Firebase Courage.

"As you wish," Parvati repeated, opening the door and stepping back for Ruthven to lead. "Ah? By the water pitcher, Lieutenant? The file is yours, I believe?"

Ruthven didn't look over his shoulder. "No, not mine," he said. "I was thinking about, you know, transferring out, but I couldn't leave my platoon. E/1 really needs me, you know."

He walked into the corridor, as tight as a compressed spring. Even before Axbird had come to see him, he'd been thinking of night and darkness and the faceless horror of living among people who didn't know what it was like. Who'd *never* know what it was like.

The troopers of Platoon E/1 did need Henry Ruthven, he was sure.

But not as much as I need them, in the night and the unending darkness.

The Cold Blacksmith

by Elizabeth Bear

"Old man, old man, do you tinker?"

Weyland Smith raised up his head from his anvil, the heat rolling beads of sweat across his face and his sparsely forested scalp, but he never stopped swinging his hammer. The ropy muscles of his chest knotted and released with every blow, and the clamor of steel on steel echoed from the trees. The hammer looked to weigh as much as the smith, but he handled it like a bit of cork on a twig. He worked in a glade, out of doors, by a deep cold well, just right for quenching and full of magic fish. Whoever had spoken was still under the shade of the trees, only a shadow to one who squinted through the glare of the sun.

"Happen I'm a blacksmith, miss," he said.

As if he could be anything else, in his leather apron, sweating over forge and anvil in the noonday sun, limping on a lamed leg.

"Do you take mending, old man?" she asked, stepping forth into the light.

He thought the girl might be pretty enough in a country manner, her features a plump-cheeked outline under the black silk veil pinned

277

to the corners of her hat. Not a patch on his own long-lost swan-maiden Olrun, though Olrun had left him after seven years to go with her two sisters, and his two brothers had gone with them as well, leaving Weyland alone.

But Weyland kept her ring and with it her promise. And for seven times seven years to the seventh times, he'd kept it, seduced it back when it was stolen away, held it to his heart in fair weather and foul. Olrun's promise-ring. Olrun's promise to return.

Olrun who had been fair as ice, with shoulders like a blacksmith, shoulders like a giantess.

This girl could not be less like her. Her hair was black and it wasn't pinned, all those gleaming curls a-tumble across the shoulders of a dress that matched her hair and veil and hat. A little linen sack in her left hand was just the natural color, and something in it chimed when she shifted. Something not too big. He heard it despite the tolling of the hammer that never stopped.

"I'll do what I'm paid to." He let his hammer rest, and shifted his grip on the tongs. His wife's ring slid on its chain around his neck, catching on chest hair. He couldn't wear it on his hand when he hammered. "And if'n 'tis mending I'm paid for, I'll mend what's flawed."

She came across the knotty turf in little quick steps like a hobbled horse—as if it was her lamed, and not him—and while he turned to thrust the bent metal that would soon be a steel horse collar into the coals again she passed her hand over his bench beside the anvil.

He couldn't release the bellows until the coals glowed red as currant jelly, but there was a clink and when her hand withdrew it left behind two golden coins. Two coins for two hands, for two pockets, for two eyes.

Wiping his hands on his matted beard, he turned from the forge, then lifted a coin to his mouth. It dented under his teeth, and he weighed its heaviness in his hand. "A lot for a bit of tinkering."

"Worth it if you get it done," she said, and upended her sack upon his bench.

A dozen or so curved transparent shards tumbled red as forge coals into the hot noon light, jingling and tinkling. Gingerly, he reached out and prodded one with a forefinger, surprised by the warmth.

"My heart," the woman said. " 'Tis broken. Fix it for me."

He drew his hand back. "I don't know nowt about women's hearts, broken or t'otherwise."

"You're the Weyland Smith, aren't you?"

"Aye, miss." The collar would need more heating. He turned away, to pump the bellows again.

"You took my gold." She planted her fists on her hips. "You can't refuse a task, Weyland Smith. Once you've taken money for it. It's your geas."

"Keep tha coin," he said, and pushed them at her with a fingertip. "I'm a smith. Not never a matchmaker, nor a glassblower."

"They say you made jewels from dead men's eyes, once. And it was a blacksmith broke my heart. It's only right one should mend it, too."

He leaned on the bellows, pumping hard.

She turned away, in a whisper of black satin as her skirts swung heavy by her shoes. "You took my coin," she said, before she walked back into the shadows. "So fix my heart."

Firstly, he began with a crucible, and heating the shards in his forge. The heart melted, all right, though hotter than he would have guessed. He scooped the glass on a bit of rod stock and rolled it on his anvil, then scraped the gather off with a flat-edged blade and shaped it into a smooth ruby-bright oval the size of his fist.

The heart crazed as it cooled. It fell to pieces when he touched it with his glove, and he was left with only a mound of shivered glass.

That was unfortunate. There had been the chance that the geas would grant some mysterious assistance, that he would guess correctly and whatever he tried first would work. An off chance, but stranger things happened with magic and his magic was making.

Not this time. Whether it was because he was a blacksmith and not a matchmaker or because he was a blacksmith and not a glassblower, he was not sure. But hearts, glass hearts, were outside his idiom and outside his magic.

He would have to see the witch.

The witch must have known he was coming, as she always seemed to know. She awaited him in the doorway of her pleasant cottage by the wildflower meadow, more wildflowers—daisies and buttercups—waving among the long grasses of the turfed roof. A nanny goat grazed beside the chimney, her long coat as white as the milk that stretched her udder pink and shiny. He saw no kid.

The witch was as dark as the goat was white, her black, black hair shot with silver and braided back in a wrist-thick queue. Her skirts were kilted up over her green kirtle, and she handed Weyland a pottery cup before he ever entered her door. It smelled of hops and honey and spices, and steam curled from the top; spiced heated ale.

"I have to see to the milking," she said. "Would you fetch my stool while I coax Heidrún off the roof?"

"She's shrunk," Weyland said, but he balanced his cup in one hand and limped inside the door to haul the stool out, for the witch's convenience.

The witch clucked. "Haven't we all?"

By the time Weyland emerged, the goat was down in the dooryard, munching a reward of bruised apples, and the witch had found her bucket and was waiting for the stool. Weyland set the cup on the ledge of the open window and seated the witch with a little bit of ceremony, helping her with her skirts. She smiled and patted his arm, and bent to the milking while he went to retrieve his ale.

Once upon a time, what rang on the bottom of the empty pail would have been mead, sweet honeyed liquor fit for gods. But times had changed, were always changing, and the streams that stung from between the witch's strong fingers were rich and creamy white.

"So what have you come for, Weyland Smith?" she asked, when the pail was a quarter full and the milk hissed in the pail rather than sang.

"I'm wanting a spell as'll mend a broken heart," he said.

Her braid slid over her shoulder, hanging down. She flipped it back without lifting her head. "I hadn't thought you had it in you to fall in love again," she said, her voice lilting with the tease.

" 'Tisn't my heart as is broken."

That did raise her chin, and her fingers stilled on Heidrún's udder. Her gaze met his; her eyebrows lifted across the fine-lined arch of her forehead. "Tricky," she said. "A heart's a wheel," she said. "Bent is bent. It can't be mended. And even worse—" She smiled, and tossed the fugitive braid back again. "—if it's not your heart you're after fixing."

"Din't I know it?" he said, and sipped the ale, his wife's ring—worn now—clicking on the cup as his fingers tightened.

Heidrún had finished her apples. She tossed her head, long ivory horns brushing the pale silken floss of her back, and the witch laughed and remembered to milk again. "What will you give me if I help?"

The milk didn't ring in the pail anymore, but the gold rang fine on the dooryard stones.

The witch barely glanced at it. "I don't want your gold, blacksmith."

"I din't want for hers, neither," Weyland said. " 'Tis the half of what she gave." He didn't stoop to retrieve the coin, though the witch snaked a soft-shoed foot from under her kirtle and skipped it back to him, bouncing it over the cobbles.

"What can I pay?" he asked, when the witch met his protests with a shrug.

"I didn't say I could help you." The latest pull dripped milk into the pail rather than spurting. The witch tugged the bucket clear and patted Heidrún on the flank, leaning forward with her elbows on her knees and the pail between her ankles while the nanny clattered over cobbles to bound back up onto the roof. In a moment, the goat was beside the chimney again, munching buttercups as if she hadn't just had a meal of apples. A large, fluffy black-and-white cat emerged from the house and began twining the legs of the stool, miaowing.

"Question 'tisn't what tha can or can't do," he said sourly. "'Tis what tha will or won't."

The witch lifted the pail and splashed milk on the stones for the cat to lap. And then she stood, bearing the pail in her hands, and shrugged. "You could pay me a Name. I collect those."

"If'n I had one."

"There's your own," she countered, and balanced the pail on her hip as she sauntered toward the house. He followed. "But people are always more disinclined to part with what belongs to them than what doesn't, don't you find?"

He grunted. She held the door for him, with her heel, and kicked it shut when he had passed. The cottage was dim and cool inside, with only a few embers banked on the hearth. He sat when she gestured him onto the bench, and not before. "No Names," he said.

"Will you barter your body, then?"

She said it over her shoulder, like a commonplace. He twisted a boot on the rushes covering a rammed-earth floor and laughed. "And what'd a bonny lass like thaself want with a gammy-legged, fusty, coal-black smith?"

"To say I've had one?" She plunged her hands into the washbasin and scrubbed them to the elbow, then turned and leaned against the stand. When she caught sight of his expression, she laughed as well. "You're sure it's not your heart that's broken, Smith?"

"Not this sennight." He scowled around the rim of his cup, and was still scowling as she set bread and cheese before him. Others might find her intimidating, but Weyland Smith wore the promise-ring of

Olrun the Valkyrie. No witch could mortify him. Not even one who kept Heidrún—who had dined on the leaves of the World Ash—as a milch goat.

The witch broke his gaze on the excuse of tucking an escaped strand of his long grey ponytail behind his ear, and relented. "Make me a cauldron," she said. "An iron cauldron. And I'll tell you the secret, Weyland Smith."

"Done," he said, and drew his dagger to slice the bread.

She sat down across the trestle. "Don't you want your answer?"

He stopped with his blade in the loaf, looking up. "I've not paid."

"You'll take my answer," she said. She took his cup, and dipped more ale from the pot warming over those few banked coals. "I know your contract is good."

He shook his head at the smile that curved her lips, and snorted. "Someone'll find out tha geas one day, enchantress. And may tha never rest easy again. So tell me then. How might I mend a lass's broken heart?"

"You can't," the witch said, easily. "You can replace it with another, or you can forge it anew. But it cannot be mended. Not like that."

"Gerrawa with tha," Weyland said. "I tried reforging it. 'Tis glass."

"And glass will cut you," the witch said, and snapped her fingers. "Like *that*."

He made the cauldron while he was thinking, since it needed the blast furnace and a casting pour but not finesse. *If glass will cut and shatter, perhaps a heart should be made of tougher stuff,* he decided as he broke the mold.

Secondly, he began by heating the bar stock. While it rested in the coals, between pumping at the bellows, he slid the shards into a leathern bag, slicing his palms—though not deep enough to bleed through heavy callus. He wiggled Olrun's ring off his right hand and strung it on its chain, then broke the heart to powder with his smallest hammer. It didn't take much work. The heart was fragile enough that Weyland wondered if there wasn't something wrong with the glass.

When it had done, he shook the powder from the pouch and ground it finer in the pestle he used to macerate carbon, until it was reduced to a pale-pink silica dust. He thought he'd better use all of it, to be sure, so he mixed it in with the carbon and hammered it into the heated bar stock for seven nights and seven days, folding and folding again as he would for a sword blade, or an axe, something that needed to take a resilient temper to back a striking edge.

It wasn't a blade he made of his iron, though, now that he'd forged it into steel. What he did was pound the bar into a rod, never allowing it to cool, never pausing hammer—and then he drew the rod through a die to square and smooth it, and twisted the thick wire that resulted into a gorgeous fist-big filigree.

The steel had a reddish color, not like rust but as if the traces of gold that had imparted brilliance to the ruby glass heart had somehow transferred that tint into the steel. It was a beautiful thing, a cage for a bird no bigger than Weyland's thumb, with cunning hinges so one could open it like a box, and such was his magic that despite all the glass and iron that had gone into making it, it spanned no more and weighed no more than would have a heart of meat.

He heated it cherry-red again, and when it glowed he quenched it in the well to give it resilience and set its form.

He wore his ring on his wedding finger when he put it on the next morning, and he let the forge lie cold—or as cold as it could lie, with seven days' heat baked into metal and stone. It was the eighth day of the forging, and a fortnight since he'd taken the girl's coin.

She didn't disappoint. She was along before midday.

She came right out into the sunlight this time, rather than lingering under the hazel trees, and though she still wore black it was topped by a different hat, this one with feathers. "Old man," she said, "have you done as I asked?"

Reverently, he reached under the block that held his smaller anvil, and brought up a doeskin swaddle. The suede draped over his hands, clinging and soft as a maiden's breast, and he held his breath as he laid the package on the anvil and limped back, his left leg dragging a little. He picked up his hammer and pretended to look to the forge, unwilling to be seen watching the lady.

She made a little cry as she came forward, neither glad nor sorrowful, but rather tight, as if she couldn't keep all her hope and anticipation pent in her breast any longer. She reached out with hands clad in cheveril and brushed open the doeskin—

Only to freeze when her touch revealed metal. "This heart doesn't beat," she said, as she let the wrappings fall.

Weyland turned to her, his hands twisted before his apron, wringing the haft of his hammer so his ring bit into his flesh. "It'll not shatter, lass, I swear."

"It doesn't beat," she repeated. She stepped away, her hands curled at her sides in their black kid gloves. "This heart is no use to me, blacksmith."

He borrowed the witch's magic goat, which like him—and the witch—had been more than half a God once and wasn't much more than a fairy story now, and he harnessed her to a sturdy little cart he made to haul the witch's cauldron. He delivered it in the sunny morning, when the dew was still damp on the grass, and he brought the heart to show.

"It's a very good heart," the witch said, turning it in her hands. "The latch in particular is cunning. Nothing would get in or out of a heart like that if you didn't show it the way." She bounced it on her palms. "Light for its size, too. A girl could be proud of a heart like this."

"She'll have none," Weyland said. "Says as it doesn't beat."

"Beat? Of course it doesn't beat," the witch scoffed. "There isn't any love in it. And you can't put that there for her."

"But I mun do," Weyland said, and took the thing back from her hands.

For thirdly, he broke Olrun's ring. The gold was soft and fine; it flattened with one blow of the hammer, and by the third or fourth strike, it spread across his leather-padded anvil like a puddle of blood, rose-red in the light of the forge. By the time the sun brushed the treetops in its descent, he'd pounded the ring into a sheet of gold so fine it floated on his breath.

He painted the heart with gesso, and when that was dried he made bole, a rabbit-skin glue mixed with clay that formed the surface for the gilt to cling to.

With a brush, he lifted the gold leaf, bit by bit, and sealed it painstakingly to the heart. And when he had finished and set the brushes and the burnishers aside—when his love was sealed up within like the steel under the gold—the iron cage began to beat.

"It was a blacksmith broke my heart," the black girl said. "You'd think a blacksmith could do a better job on mending it."

"It beats," he said, and set it rocking with a burn-scarred, callused fingertip. "'Tis bonny. And it shan't break."

"It's cold," she complained, her breath pushing her veil out a little over her lips. "Make it warm."

"I'd not wonder tha blacksmith left tha. The heart tha started with were colder," he said.

For fourthly, he opened up his breast and took his own heart out, and locked it in the cage. The latch was cunning, and he worked it with thumbs slippery with the red, red blood. Afterward, he stitched his chest up with catgut and an iron needle and pulled a clean shirt on, and let the forge sit cold.

He expected a visitor, and she arrived on time. He laid the heart before her, red as red, red blood in its red-gilt iron cage, and she lifted it on the tips of her fingers and held it to her ear to listen to it beat.

And she smiled.

When she was gone, he couldn't face his forge, or the anvil with the vacant chain draped over the horn, or the chill in his fingertips. So he went to see the witch.

She was sweeping the dooryard when he came up on her, and she laid the broom aside at once when she saw his face. "So it's done," she said, and brought him inside the door.

The cup she brought him was warmer than his hands. He drank, and licked hot droplets from his moustache after.

"It weren't easy," he said.

She sat down opposite, elbows on the table, and nodded in sympathy. "It never is," she said. "How do you feel?"

"Frozen cold. Colder'n Hell. I should've gone with her."

"Or she should have stayed with you."

He hid his face in the cup. "She weren't coming back."

"No," the witch said. "She wasn't." She sliced bread, and buttered him a piece. It sat on the planks before him, and he didn't touch it. "It'll grow back, you know. Now that it's cut out cleanly. It'll heal in time."

He grunted, and finished the last of the ale. "And then?" he asked, as the cup clicked on the boards.

"And then you'll sooner or later most likely wish it hadn't," the witch said, and when he laughed and reached for the bread she got up to fetch him another ale.

The Nature of Things

By Maya Kaathryn Bohnhoff

"Can someone explain to me what a box labeled 'cookware' is doing in the upstairs guest bath?"

Harry Ferguson looked up from the laptop perched atop the kitchen table to see his wife, Marilyn, standing in the kitchen archway rooting in her purse for her keys.

Across the table from Harry, his teenaged daughter, Kim, looked up from her last bite of Rice Krispies. "I didn't do it."

"Don't look at me." Her younger brother, Scott, had already deposited his dishes in the sink.

"Gosh," said Marilyn, still rooting. "Must've been those darned cookware fairies. Harry, honey, if you could move it back down . . . Oh, here they are." Marilyn produced her car keys with a flourish. "I'm off. In the car, kids."

Scott was already out the door with the delicate patter of size eleven sneakers. His sister followed at a more decorous pace.

"Sure you'll be okay here with Megan?" Marilyn asked Harry. "What if you have to go to the office?"

"I'll just take Meg with me. Gwen loves her."

287

"Hm. How does the DA feel about it?"

"He'll love anything that contributes to the prosecution of a case, even if it involves a five-year-old in the law library. He might even hire her. After all, she knows everything."

Marilyn laughed and kissed his cheek. "Good luck."

Good luck. He'd need it, he mused over his coffee. It was a bad time to have moved into a new house, but moving was always a pain in the wazoo, and the real-estate market did not obey human whim.

Which made his personal and professional life a matched set; the case he was working on was equally disobedient. They had a body— Marcellus Boite, owner of a downtown gun shop. They had a suspect—Ernest Combs, a small-time embezzler Boite had the misfortune to hire. They had a motive—Boite had recently reported to the police that some inventory was missing. They had opportunity— Combs had no alibi for the time of his employer's death. They had suspicious behavior—confronted with a police presence, Combs fled, though he claimed an emergency at home.

What they did not have was a murder weapon.

Boite had died of a single .38 caliber bullet to the head, but no gun had been found during the search of Combs's home and car, and no record existed that he had ever owned one. Till now, he'd been a "numbers" man—mangling accounts not people; his thefts had been confined to the virtual world. His fingerprints were everywhere at the crime scene, but then he worked there. The only place they mattered was on the conspicuously absent murder weapon.

Harry grimaced at the taste of his coffee and went to the fridge for milk. The carton was empty.

"Damn." He was in the act of putting the carton back when he caught himself and sheepishly threw it in the trash.

Returning to his makeshift laptop, he read Combs's criminal record again, slowly. A tiny sound from the foyer made him glance up expecting to see Meg. The words "How're you feeling, sweetie?" stalled on his lips when he realized there was no one there.

"Winslow, leave the ficus alone!"

There was a rustle of foliage and the soft thump of little cat feet. Harry went back to the futile task of trying to pry leads out of Combs's file.

Ernest Combs was a man without a life. A man who could be reduced to a birth date, a list of schools, a series of dead-end jobs, and a succession of unspectacular crimes. Maybe, Harry thought, he'd committed murder out of boredom, figuring that prison *had* to be more stimulating than life on the outside.

The rustle of ficus leaves repeated. Without raising his head, Harry said, "Winslow! You're cruisin' for a bruisin.'"

"What's that mean?"

Harry jumped. His youngest daughter stood in the foyer, still in her PJs, a stuffed Pooh bear tucked under one arm.

"Hi, sweetie," he said, wondering what had made him think he could work at home. "Feeling better?"

"I'm hungry," she announced and flounced into the kitchen to pull herself up into a chair across from him.

He wasn't getting anywhere with Ernest Combs anyway. He rose and began a search for breakfast cereal. "Glad to hear it. What'll it be?"

"Scrambledy eggs. *Please*, Daddy?"

He made the mistake of looking at her. The sweet heart-shaped face with its chocolaty brown eyes, the silky auburn hair, tousled from sleep. Her Pooh bear smiled amiably at him from under her chin.

"As you wish. If I can find the cookware."

They'd been in the house for about a week and had yet to cook. They'd unpacked cereal bowls and flatware and little else. Nothing was where it belonged, every available corner was piled with boxes, the furniture was half-arranged. As were Harry's thoughts. He felt guilty for not unpacking, but knew if he unpacked, the guilt of not working on the case would be just as intense.

Belatedly, Harry recalled that the cookware box was in the upstairs bathroom. He dragged it down to the kitchen, popped the lid, and rummaged for a sauté pan.

"Daddy? What sort of animal lives in a closet?"

Goody, Harry thought, *a five-year-old joke.* "I give, honey, what lives in a closet?"

"*Dad*-dy," she said in a tone of voice that suggested he had slightly less wattage than an oven light.

The phone rang and he leapt to get it before the voicemail kicked in, giving Megan the universal shush sign, finger to lips. "Fergusons.'"

"We may have a problem," his assistant Gwen said without preamble. "We've got two weeks to build a case. Not four."

"How did that happen?"

"Fortis pled personal duress. Her baby is due in a month and a half. She told the judge it might be early. Which is such bull. Merle Fortis has delivered two weeks late three times running. And, if that's not bad enough, the date change lands us with a different judge: 'Technicality' Quinn."

Harry rolled his eyes. Justice Erica Quinn had earned her nickname for an unparalleled record of throwing cases out on technicalities.

"Yeah, I know," Gwen said, as if she had heard his eyes turning in their sockets. "I have some case law for you, counselor. I know Meg's not well, and I'd bring it to you, but John's got me on the Edwards case. I'm not even getting a lunch break."

"Meg's well enough to ride in the car."

"Great. I'll leave the stuff on your desk."

Harry rang off, his mind tilting slightly at the thought of trying to mount this case in two weeks. His eyes went unfocused to the *ficus benjamina* by the front door. It seemed to have blossomed. A bright red sock was cradled among the leaves.

Damned cat. He retrieved the sock and shook out the ficus debris. A "watched" feeling made his nape hairs prickle; he turned to find Winslow regarding him quizzically from the middle of the staircase. A strange creature whose behavior was less than catlike, Winslow followed his favorite human everywhere. He allowed himself to be led on a leash. He fetched. He stole socks.

Harry shook the sock at him. "Winslow, I'm sorry we haven't found your cat toys, but . . ." He knew a moment of guilt as the tabby's dark yellow eyes gazed back at him, soulful and doggish. He decided he'd buy a catnip mouse today. A red one.

"Hey, Meg, honey, how about breakfast at Applebee's?"

"Fortis will move for dismissal due to insufficient evidence." Those were the first words out of Gwen's mouth when Harry entered the office. She smiled when she saw Megan standing in the doorway behind him. "Hi, sweetie. How're you feeling?"

"My nose is sniffly." She demonstrated.

"The case law?" Harry prompted.

Gwen ignored him. "Poor baby. Want a tissue?" She snatched one from the box on her desk.

"Gwen, the case law?"

"Oh, yeah. Here." She moved to his desk and bent to embrace a stack of legal books. A rainbow of little vinyl tags sprouted festively from the pages.

"The blue ones," Gwen said, "are cases in which the defendant worked for the victim. The red ones deal with search and seizure powers. In the yellow ones the defendant skipped bail. Purely cautionary."

"Any of them give you gooseflesh?"

Gwen swore that when she encountered items that "meant something" she felt as if someone were blowing on the back of her neck.

"Anderson versus the State of California," she said, then added, "Want me to show you how to use that tissue, sweetie?" She was smiling past Harry at Megan who was snuffling into Pooh's ear.

Gwen, he thought, *is a mother waiting to happen.* "I can arrange for you to borrow her."

"Hah. Go study your case law, counselor."

Homeward bound, Harry was jarred out of his ruminations by an irregular thudding on the back of his car seat. "Meg, please stop that."

The thudding was replaced by steady pressure.

"Megan! Stop kicking my seat." He glanced up into the rearview mirror, half expecting to catch an urchin grin; she was gazing out the window.

She faced forward. "I *wasn't* kicking your seat, Daddy."

"You were pushing it with your feet."

"No, I wasn't."

"Meg."

"I *wasn't.*"

He pulled the car into the driveway contemplating how to handle the fib. "Look, honey. I realize I wasn't paying as much attention to you as I should have at breakfast. But you really need to refrain from these little demonstrations of—"

"What's 'refrain'?"

"Never mind."

"Can I watch TV, Daddy?" Megan asked as they came through the front door.

Harry tripped over a pair of shoes left smack in the middle of the entry and hopped forward, trying not to topple over.

Meg giggled. "You look like a kangaroo."

"Thanks. Yes, you may watch TV." Chances were, she'd fall asleep and he would get some work done . . . and he wouldn't have to enforce naptime.

Harry went back to the kitchen—noting with annoyance that he'd forgotten to turn off the lights—and started weeding through the case law. As Gwen predicted, he found Anderson vs. the State of California interesting. Because the prime suspect had worked for the victim and the crime had occurred in the workplace, the judge had extended the search warrant to the home of the suspect's ex-wife, which was between his office and home. There they'd found the murder weapon.

Combs didn't have an ex-wife, or even a girlfriend. But the scenario of him dumping the weapon between work and home seemed plausible. The police had gotten to Combs's house within thirty seconds of his arrival, surprising him as he came out of his kitchen. He'd had no time to hide a weapon. Yet no weapon had been found.

Harry went over the time line: Mrs. Boite called 911; the arresting officers spotted Combs's car less than a half mile from the crime scene and tailed him back to his house. They'd lost sight of him for about twenty seconds when he ran a light. He'd had no time to take a detour. If he dropped the gun somewhere, it had to be in a direct path between the crime scene and his house.

Harry checked Combs's phone records. Prior to the murder, he'd called only two numbers with addresses in the target area. Ignoring the stentorian falsetto of Muppets filtering in from the living room, Harry e-mailed the numbers to the lead detective, tagged "urgent." Then he wandered the house, thinking, turning off lights, straightening pictures, moving things from one place to another. He mulled over Ernest Combs as he tsked over the state of the upstairs bathroom, wondering why a row of hair clips marched across the top of the toilet tank.

Combs had a motive.

He dumped the hair clips into a drawer.

Of course, it was a motive that worked for a number of people, including the victim's wife.

Combs had opportunity.

He moved mouthwash from the floor to the medicine cabinet.

Closing the cabinet, he caught movement in the mirror—someone passing the open bathroom door. Meg was too small for him to see more than the top of her head in the bathroom mirror.

He poked his head out into the hall. There was no one there. He started down the hall toward the master bedroom. An inhuman shriek greeted him at the door and Winslow shot out into the hall like a furry cannon ball. He ricocheted off Harry's knees, and skidded toward the staircase.

Heart pounding, Harry teetered on the bedroom threshold with the eerie feeling there was someone standing behind the half-open door. He sucked in a breath and barged into the room, slamming the door against the wall. No one was behind the door.

Harry shook his head, clucking ruefully at himself. He was as bad as Winslow—jumping at shadows. *Doofus.*

The phone rang, drawing him downstairs.

"Checked those numbers," Gwen told him. "Both businesses. A Blockbuster Video and a pawnshop."

"Pawnshop? Okay, let's get—"

"Done," Gwen said. "Detectives Price and Kirwan are on it even as we speak. If that's not where Combs disposed of the weapon, maybe it's where he purchased it. You coming to work tomorrow?"

"That's the plan. Marilyn got another professor to cover for her. I can't wait to get back. A half-moved-into house is . . . damned distracting."

As he rang off, the cartoon voices from the living room cut off in mid-squeak. "Daddy, Winslow and I are gonna take a nap."

He turned to find Meg standing in the foyer with the cat draped over one arm, looking singularly more relaxed than it had the last time he'd seen it. Meg padded upstairs and Harry went back to his case. He was deeply engrossed when he got an e-mail from Detective Price announcing that the pawnshop was a dead end. The owner, Bill Greeley by name, recognized Combs, but had never sold him anything. He'd done a background check on Combs the first time he tried to buy something, uncovered his criminal record, and refused service.

Which didn't keep Combs from trying, Greeley noted, though he denied that Combs had ever tried to sell him anything.

So, Combs didn't get the gun at the pawnshop nor, if the owner was to be believed, did he dump it there. Then . . . Harry called up a manifest of Boite's missing inventory. What better place for Combs to arm himself than his employer's stock? Combs's harassment of the pawnshop owner might just be a means of covering his ass.

"All *right*." Harry leaned closer to the screen. There were indeed a number of .38 caliber guns missing—five Smith and Wessons, two Colts, and a couple of Rugers.

Harry's train of thought was derailed by what sounded like a police chase being conducted at warp speed by chipmunks. "Meg, turn that down!"

The cacophony continued. Harry popped up from the table and crossed the foyer to the living room. "Meg, I asked—" He stopped. The TV blared toons into an empty room. He turned off the TV and went upstairs where he found Meg fast asleep on her bed, Winslow sitting Sphinx-like at her feet.

"I gotta get back to the office," Harry told the cat, who yawned.

Downstairs, the front door opened. "Dammit, Harry—you left your shoes in the middle of the entry!"

Harry had left his shoes neatly on the mat behind the *ficus*, but decided to let it go. He was sincerely glad Marilyn was home, because it meant he could remand stewardship of the house to her, recover his wits, and get to work.

"So now you know Combs had a weapon, right?" Marilyn asked as she settled under the covers.

"*If* he's the one who stole the guns, yeah. The murder weapon was a .38—probably a Smith and Wesson. That narrows it down to five guns in Boite's missing inventory. *If* the murder weapon came from Boite's inventory."

"But?"

"*But* if we don't find the gun, Combs may walk."

"Bummer."

"Meg's going to school tomorrow, right?" Harry asked, yawning.

"I'd rather keep her home one more day, but I've got it covered. You can return to work, counselor."

"God bless you," Harry murmured. "This house is . . . creepy."

"What?"

Reality began to recede toward sleep. "Shoes," he mumbled.

"Daddy? *Dad*-dy!" Meg was a blur in the dim light. "Daddy, some-thing's under my bed. Make it go away."

Like a well-trained dog, he rose, trailed her docilely to her room, and looked under her bed. "Nothing there, Muffin."

"I bet he went back into the closet."

He straightened. "Oh. Do you want me to chase him away?"

"No, I don't mind him being there. I just don't like it when he crawls under my bed. He wakes me up."

"Okay. Well, um, you stay in that closet then, you hear?" he said to the half-closed door.

Meg beamed. "Thanks, Daddy."

✧   ✧   ✧

The next morning, Harry packed his briefcase and escaped the house gleefully, leaving Marilyn in charge. He piled the two older kids into the car and ferried them to school, absently pondering the connection between Combs and the pawnshop; wondering if there wasn't more there than met the eye. Maybe . . .

"Hey, Scott. Stop kneeing me in the back."

"Huh?"

"You're pushing on the back of my seat," Harry complained, pulling into the turnaround in front of the high school.

Kim shot a grin back at her brother as she opened her door. "Busted. See ya, Dad."

"I *wasn't* pushing on your seat," Scott said. His door slammed.

"Yeah, right," Harry muttered. "Nobody kicks my seat. Nobody leaves the TV on, or the bathroom lights, or the water. Nobody leaves shoes lying in the entry."

He pulled away from the school trying to regain his concentration. Was the pawnshop owner witness or accomplice? If Combs was ripping off his boss, the guns had to go somewhere. It might be productive to bring the guy in. . . .

"Dammit, Scott, I said *stop!*" Harry's annoyance guttered in the realization that Scott was on his way to Algebra 101. He pulled over against the curb and craned his neck around to peer down the back of the seat, expecting to find that Winslow had snuck into the car.

No Winslow.

Great. Now I'm having back spasms.

By the time he stepped out of the elevator into the DA's office, Harry was much more chipper. He had a hunch. He told Gwen as much the moment he entered the office.

"You hide it so well," she said, straight-faced.

Not long after, Harry found himself behind a two-way mirror in an interrogation room watching Detectives Price and Kirwan question Bill Greeley, pawnshop owner. Greeley stuck doggedly to the claim that he knew Ernest Combs only as a nuisance who continued to try to buy weapons and ammo he wouldn't sell him.

"I'm a law-abiding American citizen, dammit," Greeley said for the fiftieth time. "A card-carrying member of the NRA and Neighborhood Watch. I don't sell guns to criminals. Ernest Combs was a criminal."

Detective Price looked into the two-way, rolled his eyes, and mouthed, "No go," to the invisible Harry.

"I think he's being straight," Price said later. "The way his eyes bugged out when we asked if he'd purchased arms from Combs, I thought he was going to have a coronary."

"Maybe he's a good actor," Harry said.

"Yeah, but Combs isn't. Practically the first thing he said when the question of gun ownership came up was, 'I can't *buy* a gun in this freakin' town. I tried.' Maybe he was planning all along to use this guy as a sort of alibi—you know, establish that he'd made repeated attempts to buy a gun and failed."

"I still think that gun is hidden somewhere on his property," said Detective Kirwan. "We mentioned that we'd interviewed Greeley. He seemed completely unconcerned, then asked if we'd finished tossing his house. Said we'd better have put everything back where we found it. Said he'd hold us responsible if there was any damage to the place. He seemed a little angsty about it."

"Chitra, we've turned that whole damn place over," argued Price. "The gun's not there."

Harry chewed his lip. "He was exiting the kitchen when the arresting officers entered the house."

The detectives nodded.

"So they started the search there."

"We dismantled the kitchen," Price said, "pulled appliances out from the wall, even looked for hidden compartments."

Kirwan added, "First, we thought it was in the broiler pan because the door was slightly ajar—and stuck, as if it had been closed in a big hurry. Maybe he started to stash the gun there, then changed his mind. Maybe it was a deke."

"He didn't have time to change his mind," objected Price. "And why bother with misdirection? We searched everywhere."

"Was he nervous about the search?"

"Yeah, he was. But apparently he didn't need to be."

After lunch Harry paid a visit to Combs's house. It wasn't much more than a shoebox with a peaked roof, but it had obviously just been through a major remodel. Combs had moved in a scant three months before. There were three rooms downstairs: living room, kitchen, bath. The furnishings were simple but tasteful. And they were of a quality beyond the means of most store clerks. There was a hand-knotted silk Persian carpet. The kitchen had Viking appliances.

Suppressing envy, Harry checked the broiler tray, the lettuce crisper, and the garbage disposal, knowing the detectives had already done that. Then he moved to the second floor.

Up a flight of spiral stairs he was confronted by a single, long room with a sharply peaked ceiling that ran the length of the house from front to back. The bed was cherry wood, with side table and dresser to match. A wardrobe stood at the end of the room opposite the door. A wood-burning stove hunkered halfway between in a wide gable, its pipe extending up into the ceiling. Ashes littered the floor in front of it, a souvenir of the police search. Every drawer and cabinet hung open.

Harry had bubkes. No clues, no epiphanies, not even a niggle. He went home to the joys of unpacking.

"Any idea where the cookware went?" Marilyn followed her voice into the foyer. "I'd swear it was right here by the table this morning."

"It was. I brought it down myself." Harry mounted the staircase, intent on a quick change into a sweat suit.

"Huh . . . By the way, you left every light on downstairs this morning."

He stopped halfway up the stairs. "No, I didn't. I only left the foyer light on."

"Oh. Must've been Scott."

"Wasn't me." Scott's voice floated from the living room on a raft of video game sound effects.

Marilyn gestured "never mind" and headed back into the kitchen. "If I can't find the cookware there'll be no dinner tonight—unless you want to order out."

"Pizza!" yelled Scott.

At the top of the stairs, Harry nearly collided with Kim who'd appeared on the landing cradling a box.

"Cookware?"

Kim nodded. "It was in the upstairs bathroom."

"Again? I brought it downstairs," said Harry.

"Sure, Dad." Kim gave him an indulgent smile, then carried the box downstairs.

Marilyn had come out of the kitchen again. She winked up at Harry. "Poltergeists. They also got Scott's homework." When Harry didn't laugh, she followed him up to their bedroom. "No break-throughs on the case?"

"No." He sat heavily on the bed, shaking his head. "That gun has got to be in Combs's kitchen. He flat out didn't have time to hide it anywhere else."

"But they searched the whole house."

"Thoroughly."

"Yeah? How about the turkey carcass left over from Thanksgiving?"

Harry smiled. "Checked it. No gun."

Harry Ferguson had long been accused of living in his head. At the moment his head contained an exact replica of the floor plan of Ernest Combs's house. As he padded down his own staircase to let the cat out, he recalled how many steps were in Combs's. Returning upstairs, he was disoriented by the sight of a transverse hallway instead of a right angle turn into a loft.

"Daddy?" Megan's voice issued tentatively from the semidarkness of her room.

He crossed to her door. "You're supposed to be asleep."

She was sitting up in bed, hands in her lap, watching him solemnly. "I need you to talk to him again. He won't obey me."

"Who, honey?"

"The thing in my closet. He keeps going under my bed. He snores."

Harry smiled. "He snores."

She nodded.

"Okay," Harry crossed to the closet and opened the door quickly, as if he expected to surprise something out of hiding.

Meg cleared her throat delicately. "He's under the *bed*, Daddy."

"Oh, right."

Harry got down on hands and knees and peered beneath the bed. His eyes locked on a darker patch of dark that seemed to be blocking the glow of Meg's nightlight. A frisson ran up his spine before he could chide himself for being overimaginative. Had to be a stuffed animal. He started to reach under the bed for it and was vaguely ashamed when his hand refused to move.

"You there," he said, making his voice menacingly deep. "You're upsetting my little girl. I must ask you to stop hiding under her bed. Please return to the closet."

He straightened and looked at Meg. "Okay?"

"Thank you, Daddy. You sounded mean. But could you check and make sure he's gone?"

"Oh . . . sure." He peered beneath the bed again. Odd. Now he could see the nightlight through the bed skirt. He straightened. "Gone."

Meg smiled and held out her arms. "Thanks, Daddy. You're great."

He hugged her. "Glad you think so."

He passed the closet on his way out, half of a mind to open the door and peek. He didn't.

Saturday morning Harry realized he'd dreamed about Combs's house all night. Waking in his flat-ceilinged, perfectly square bedroom was disconcerting.

After breakfast the family dispersed and the house, empty and quiet, seemed to give up a huge sigh. As did Harry. He sat at the kitchen table for a while, savoring his coffee and mulling over the case . . . for all the good it did.

Coffee exhausted, he wandered upstairs and found every light on. He made a complete round, shutting them off—bathroom, Meg's room, Kim's room, Scott's room, the master bedroom. Then he headed back toward the staircase determined to do some gardening.

The bathroom light was on. Again. He remembered turning it off.

He approached the room cautiously, nape hair at attention. The door was ajar, and he swore he saw movement through the slit between door and jamb. He slapped himself mentally. It was probably an electrical problem. Even new houses could have electrical problems.

He stood uncertainly in the doorway. Then, swearing under his breath, he thrust the door open. It impacted the wall with a padded thump.

Harry entered the room fully, turned, and swung the door shut, belatedly considering what he'd do if there were someone there. It closed with a swish and flap of the bathrobes hanging on the back.

Harry chuckled. *Alarmist.* He let the door swing half open and turned his attention to the light switch. It was in the "on" position. He flipped it on and off, then wiggled it. Out of the corner of his eye he saw a shadow slip past the bathroom door and down the hallway. He lunged at the door and flung it open.

Nothing.

He took a deep breath and stepped into the hall, looking both ways and wondering if stress caused hallucinations. Shaking his head, he turned and nudged open the bathroom door.

A thin, dark, little man with startlingly pale, protuberant eyes blinked up at him. He was wearing black pants and matching long-sleeved turtleneck sweater. He looked like a mime who'd forgotten his makeup.

"Nuts," he said in a high, nasal voice.

An understatement.

"What . . . what are you doing in my house?" Harry asked around the lump in his throat.

"Ex-*cuse* me. This is really embarrassing."

"What are you doing in my house?" Harry repeated.

"Uh . . . I work here."

"Who *are* you?"

"I'm the Thing That Hides Behind Doors. Did I scare you?"

"Hell, yes! I thought I was going to turn around and find you sneaking up behind me."

"Oh, not *me*. That would be the Thing That Sneaks Up Behind You. He's off today. Now, if you'll excuse me . . ." He started to turn away.

"No, I won't excuse you! You *work* here?"

"Yessir. Really, I oughta get going. I'm not supposed to talk to you. Wow. This is weird."

"No kidding." Harry's heart rate slowed. The guy didn't seem dangerous, just incoherent and nervous. "Who are you?"

"Didn't I say? I'm the Thing That—"

"Hides Behind Doors. I caught that. I just don't know what it means."

The guy fidgeted, his big watery eyes bobbing this way and that. "It means . . . well, pretty much what it says. I hide behind doors. I'm a—a Thing."

"A thing . . ." Harry shook his head. "What do you mean 'a thing'?"

The protuberant eyes flicked back to Harry's face. "I really shouldn't be talking to you. Can I go now?"

"Go? I find you in my bathroom and I'm supposed to just let you go?"

"Aw, c'mon. I promise to do better. Only don't tell the Boss."

"How about the police?"

He seemed puzzled. "The police? What would the police care? This isn't their jurisdiction . . . is it?"

"I'm willing to find out." Harry stepped backward into the hall.

The little fellow quivered and glanced feverishly about. "Oh, *jeez*, mister. I don't want—" His eyes darted to a spot over Harry's left shoulder and froze there. "Oops."

Harry swung around. A tall, thin, sepulchral fellow faced him across the upstairs runner. He wore a black serge suit with a long coat and string tie. Sad, dark eyes were a perfect match for the doleful set of his mouth, while graying eyebrows arched toward a distant hairline. The man inclined his head.

Harry dropped into a posture he'd seen in a Jackie Chan movie. "Stay back. I know Kung Fu."

"Of course you do, sir. But I came only to apologize."

"Apologize . . ."

"For the behavior of my staff."

"Your staff?" Harry realized he was echoing, but could think of nothing remotely intelligent to say.

"The Household Things. I am, I regret to say, the Chief Thing for this domicile. I am forced to admit, sir, that in all my years in your service, I have never had such a raw and undisciplined crew."

"You've . . . you've been in my service," Harry echoed, "for years."

"Well, not *your* service precisely, sir, but your family's. In fact, I've been in service to this family since you married and rented that quaint little cottage on Sepulveda." He said "quaint" with the same disdain Scott showed when he said "peas." "Your personal staff are quite good, if I do say so myself, but these other Things . . ." The sad eyes rolled heavenward.

"What do you mean 'things'? What *things*?"

"Well, sir, since you inquired—there are three classes of Things in your service. Personal Things (which include myself and immediate staff), Furnishings Things, and of course Household Things such as the Thing That Hides Behind Doors." Contempt curled his thin lips. "It is the last group that has caused the trouble, I fear. They are inexperienced and cocky, which I suspect comes with attachment to one of these 'designer' homes. Modern conveniences, indeed."

"They've caused trouble?"

"Oh, sir, surely you've noticed how clumsy they are. Never waiting long enough to turn on lights you've turned off, open doors you've closed, close doors you've opened. And they are too ambitious altogether. Why the Thing That Lurks in the Closet of your youngest daughter's room has been bucking for a promotion to Thing That

Hides Under the Bed since you moved in. He's disturbed the dear child a number of times. No, I fear your Household Things are utterly without experience and poorly trained."

"P-poorly trained?"

"Especially in comparison with your Personal and Furnishings crews."

"Ah," Harry said, as if he understood one word of what this odd man was telling him. "Those crews are . . . more experienced and better trained, then."

The funereal fellow drew himself up to his full height, reminding Harry of Jeeves, the quintessential butler. "I pride myself on it, sir. As I said, your Personal Things have been with your family since your first rental. And even your Furnishings Things have been with you long enough to understand your comings and goings—with the possible exception of the Thing that came with your new car."

"A Thing came with my *car*?"

"Yes sir. The Thing That Kicks the Driver's Seat. He's the newest member of the crew. But I have confidence that in a few weeks time, he'll get the hang of it."

"M-my car has a Thing."

"Yes sir. As do all your major appliances."

"Appliances . . . as in our washing machine and dryer?"

"The Thing That Hides Socks."

"Our refrigerator?"

"The Thing That Drinks the Last of the Milk and Puts the Carton Back Empty."

"I thought that was my *son*."

Jeeves beamed. "As you were meant to, sir."

"Is there a Thing That Feeds Pâté to the Cat?"

"That would be your youngest daughter. You also have a Thing That Rumples the Carpets. In some homes he would also do bedspreads, but you have a cat for that purpose. Cats are honorary Things," he added.

Harry rubbed his temples. "You and your staff work at *scaring* us?"

"Oh, *no* sir. Our purpose is to *engage* you, keep you on your toes, make your lives interesting. And of course, to give your home a personality—to make it feel lived-in."

"*Lived*-in? It feels *haunted*. And I'm not engaged, I'm frustrated."

"For which I am profoundly sorry, sir. Were your Household Things better trained, you would never have noticed us at all."

"I find that hard to believe."

"You never noticed us before."

"Wait a minute. Are you responsible for carting our cookware all over the house?"

"You see—that's exactly what I mean. That unfortunate incident was perpetrated by the Thing That Misplaces Your Belongings—a Household Thing unversed in the Protocols. No Thing under my tutelage would have made such a gross error as to move that box to the target area so quickly."

"Target area? Protocols? What are you talking about?"

"Domestic Protocols, sir. You can't run a household without them. Take, for example, your cookware. Protocol requires that the movement of such articles be made in logical increments over time so that if the movement is noticed it can be easily attributed to the natural propensity of people to displace items that are in the way. So your cookware should have been moved from the kitchen floor to the top of the refrigerator, or to the floor of an adjacent room. Then it should have been moved to sit among those boxes that are still halfway up your staircase."

Harry detected a note of reproach in that "still." "We've been busy."

"Of course you have, sir. And so, unfortunately, have your Household Things. They saw fit to take your cookware directly from the kitchen floor, under the table, to the upstairs bathroom atop the étagère."

"The what?"

"The shelved unit above the toilet tank."

"Why there?"

Jeeves shrugged as if that should be the most obvious thing in the world. "A simple case of geometry. Each house is divided into quadrants. Likewise each room. Articles are moved so as to end up in the quadrant opposite the one in which they were originally located. So, from the lowest point along the southwest wall of your kitchen . . ."

"To the highest point on the northeast wall of our upstairs bathroom."

"Precisely, sir. You have a keen grasp of the situation."

"Thanks. So, everything we own is going to be moved around like this forever?"

"Oh no, sir. Every object has a particular place in which it belongs. We move only objects that are not where they belong. The cookware was on the floor under your kitchen table. Not at all where it belonged, sir."

"Uh-huh. Does everybody have . . . Things?"

"Every man, woman, and child who inhabits a domicile built or remodeled since 1900."

"Siberian sheepherders?"

"They call them *domovoi*, sir. Siberia is not the backwater you might think it is. Now, sir, I really must go. I've broken Protocol in discussing this with you, but I felt an apology was imperative." He executed a smart little bow and said, "Good day, sir. I promise we will do better."

Harry reached out to prevent him from leaving, but the front door banged open, startling him.

"Da-ad!" Kim's voice carried up the stairs. "I brought some friends home. We're going to the den to study."

Harry took his eyes off the Head Thing for only a second, but it was enough. He was gone.

"Hey!" Harry stage whispered. Then louder: "*Hey*! Where'd you go?"

"The *den*, Dad. Why?"

Harry crossed the hall to look down the stairs. Kim had poked her head back into the foyer and was peering up at him.

"It's nothing. Just . . . have fun."

"Yeah. Right. Fun." She disappeared.

Harry made a systematic search of the second floor, but found nothing. He spent the remainder of the day in a state between credulity and denial. He considered telling Marilyn, but she'd only say he was overstressed. Was he? Undoubtedly. But he'd never heard of stress manifesting itself as a six-foot-seven Jeeves archetype who claimed he'd been working for you unseen for umpteen years. No, he couldn't tell Marilyn.

In the end, he decided there was only one person in the family who wouldn't think he was nuts if he started asking questions about Things That Go Bump in the Night, and she was at the mall.

To kill time, he ran experiments. He collected odd items—useless keys, a penlight, one of Meg's bevy of Furbees—and put them in places they definitely did not belong. Then he went into the kitchen and unpacked the remainder of the boxes there. When he went back to check on his experiments he met with uneven results. The keys and Furbee were gone, the penlight was right where he'd left it.

He embarked on a systematic search of the premises based on what Jeeves (possibly a figment of his imagination) had told him about protocols. He'd left the Furbee on the hearth in the living room; he looked for it on the bookshelf on the opposite side of the room. No luck. He moved to the foyer next. Nothing.

Okay. Cut to the chase. If our Things are extremists, then the Furbee should be . . . He sprinted upstairs to Meg's room—opposite side of the house, second floor, opposite quadrant.

The Furbee was sitting atop the window casement in Meg's room.

Next, he looked for the keys. He'd left them under the sink in the kitchen. He found them, as insanely expected, atop the étagère in the upstairs bathroom.

What did that mean? That there really were Things living in his house that misplaced toys, lurked in closets, and returned empty cartons of milk to the fridge? Or that he was coming unglued?

Marilyn arrived home with Megan at last, sporting Macy's bags. They marched through the front door and up the stairs, brushing past Harry where he hovered on the landing.

"Hi, hon." Marilyn airmailed him a kiss. "Meg, sweetie, I'm going to go put my things away, then I'll help you with yours."

"I'll help her," Harry volunteered.

Marilyn stopped and stared. "You? Mr. Wad-it-up-and-throw-it-in-the-nearest-drawer?"

"I don't—" Harry began and stopped. *He* didn't. But apparently Some*thing* did. "I'll be careful."

"Uh-huh. I'll inspect the results."

Marilyn sailed into the master suite with a rustling of bags. Harry, meanwhile, ushered Meg into her room and emptied the contents of her bag onto her bed.

"Look at this pretty dress Mommy got me," she enthused, holding up the article.

"Oooh," said Harry. "Let's hang it up." He snagged the dress and opened the closet.

"Mommy cuts the tags off, first," Megan said.

"Oh. Well, you can do that the first time you wear it, okay?"

She shrugged.

Harry made a big deal out of finding a hanger, pushing aside clothes to peer into the closet's dark corners. Nothing.

"Say, Meggie . . . about the guy who hides in your closet."

"Uh-huh." She was standing next to him holding another dress.

"Is he there all the time?"

"No. Only at night."

"You've seen him?"

"Uh-huh." She handed him the dress.

"What does he look like?"

"He looks like that guy in the funny Frankenstein movie. The one with the buggy eyes."

"He looks like Marty Feldman?"

She shrugged and went back to the bed for another outfit. "But he wears a black super-hero suit."

"When did you see the funny Frankenstein movie?"

"Only a little of it. Then I sneezed and Mom made me go back to bed."

"So you don't mind this guy being in your closet?"

"Uh-uh. He finds lost stuff. Besides, I'm kinda scared of the dark sometimes, so I'm glad he's there. But I don't like it when he hides under my bed. He snores. The other guy didn't snore. And I'm afraid if he stays there, the other guy won't come back."

Harry sat weakly on the foot of the bed. "The *other* guy?"

"Yeah. The one who's s'posed to hide under my bed."

"And what does *he* look like?"

She shrugged. "I dunno. I've never seen him. But he bumps so I know he's there. But he doesn't *snore.*"

"How long have you known about these . . . guys?"

"Well, before we moved, I *thought* they were there, but I wasn't sure. I thought they might be piglets of my imagination."

"Figments, honey," Harry corrected absently.

"Oh. Anyway, I wasn't *sure* they were there until we moved into this house. That's when I *saw* them. I think they're elves."

Elves. "Are . . . are you sure?"

She gave him a wounded look. "Daddy, I *saw* them. I wouldn't make something like that up."

No, Harry thought, she probably wouldn't.

Lying in bed that night, he went over it drowsily for the zillionth time: the Thing lurking behind the bathroom door, the Things in Meg's room, the experiments that seemed to prove Jeeves's Domestic Protocols.

Suddenly wide awake, Harry found his head galloping with wild thoughts. He rolled out of bed, pulled on a T-shirt and a pair of sweatpants, then hesitated. How do you contact someone who wants to remain hidden? Someone who may very well be, as Meg put it, a piglet of your imagination?

He tiptoed into Meg's room and poked his head into the closet. "Hey," he whispered. "You. Thing That Hides in the Closet—I need to talk to your boss."

The closet was silent. Meg mumbled in her sleep.

"Please. I really need to talk to the—the Chief Thingie, or whatever you call him."

Still nothing. But the feeling of being watched sent serious willies up his spine.

"C'mon guy. I'm not kidding. This is important!"

"Sir?"

Harry stifled a yelp and spun around. Jeeves stood behind him, his basset eyes glistening in the light from the hall. Harry hurried him out of Meg's room.

"All that stuff about protocols and procedures—that applies to *all* Things *everywhere*?"

"Well, of course, sir. Without protocols, you have chaos."

"And the protocols are always the same?"

"Naturally, sir."

"Okay. You implied that our Household things are rookies because they came with a new house."

He nodded solemnly.

"What about a house that's just been through a major remodel, new appliances, furniture, window treatments, the works? Would that have a rookie crew?"

"Indubitably."

Harry clapped a hand on the tall guy's shoulder. "Jeeves—may I call you 'Jeeves?'—you've been immensely helpful. Thanks."

"'Jeeves is fine, sir." He smiled in a way that reminded Harry of the Eeyore puppet perched on Megan's bedpost. "Is there anything else?"

"Yeah. Are you guys some kind of . . . elves?"

Jeeves looked positively morose. "We've been called that, sir. But we are Things. Nothing more; nothing less."

"Great. Thanks. I'm going back to bed now. Have a nice night, Jeeves."

"Thank you, sir. And you."

✧   ✧   ✧

"We've been over this, counselor," said Detective Price. "If Combs had a gun, he didn't hide it here."

"I think he did. Just not where we expected." Harry stood in the entry of Ernest Combs's cottage, flanked by Detectives Price and Kirwan. "You thought he'd hidden it in the broiler pan, right?"

"Right," said Kirwan. "But he hadn't."

Harry glanced through the kitchen portal to the Viking range, then made a beeline for the stairs.

"Where are you going?" Kirwan asked.

Harry didn't answer. He wanted to say something nonchalant and cocky, something James Bond might have said, but as he might be about to make a fool of himself, he stifled the urge.

On the upstairs landing, he turned and scanned the attic bedroom's left-hand wall. It was dominated by the woodstove. Heart pounding, mouth dry, Harry moved to the stove, aware of the watchers at his back. He looked up, following the stovepipe. About six feet off the floor a handle stuck out of the pipe. It looked like a tapered spring with a porcelain knob at one end. Above it, a metal cuff encircled the pipe.

"What's that?" Harry pointed at the handle.

"Flue handle," said Price. "You turn it to adjust the flow of air."

Harry turned the handle. Something rattled down the stovepipe and dropped heavily into the firebox. He opened the stove door, squatted, and peered in. There, at the bottom of the empty firebox was a handgun. Harry pulled a pen out of his coat pocket, fished the gun out, and held it up for inspection. It was a .38 Smith and Wesson.

Kirwan made a sound like a cat hocking up a fur ball.

"I'll be damned," said Price.

"I don't get it," said Kirwan, watching Harry bag the gun. "How'd you do that?"

Harry shrugged. "Just a hunch."

"Some hunch. There is no way Combs had time to come up here, slide that cuff up, and slip the gun onto the flue."

"Yeah," said Price. "And even at that I'd swear we looked there. C'mon, Harry, how'd you come to think of it, really?"

"Something a . . . a friend of mine said about what happens when you put things where they don't belong."

"Let me guess," said Kirwan. "A forensics guy?"

Harry waggled his head. "Not exactly. Just someone who knew a Thing or two."

Sisters of Sarronnyn;
Sisters of Westwind

by L. E. Modesitt, Jr.

I

The Roof of the World was still frozen in winter gray, and the sun had not yet cleared the peaks to the east or shone on Freyja when I caught sight of Fiera coming up the old stone steps from the entrance to Tower Black.

I moved to intercept her. "What were you doing, Guard Fiera?"

"I was coming to the main hall, Guard Captain." Fiera did not look directly at me, but past me, a trick many Westwind guards had tried over the years. Even my own sister, especially my own sister, could not fool me.

"Using the east passage?"

Fiera flushed. "Yes, Guard Captain."

"Assignations before breakfast, yet? When did you sneak out of the barracks?"

She straightened, as she always did when she decided to flaunt something or when she knew she'd been caught. "He kissed me, Guard Captain. Creslin did."

Oh, Fiera, do not lie to me. I did not voice the words. "I seriously doubt that the esteemed son of the Marshall would have even known you were in the east passage. It is seldom traveled before dawn in winter. If anyone kissed anyone, you kissed him. What was he doing? Why were you following him?"

Fiera's eyes dropped. "He was just there. By himself. He was walking the passage."

"You're a fool! If the Marshall ever finds out, you'll be posted to High Ice for the rest of the winter this year, and for all of next year with no relief. That would be after you were given to the most needy of the consorts until you were with child. You'd never see the child after you bore her, and you'd spend your shortened life on remote duty, perhaps even on the winter road crews."

This time, my words reached her. She swallowed. "I meant no harm. He's always looked at me. I just . . . wanted him to know before he leaves for Sarronnyn."

"He knows now. If I see you anywhere near him, if I hear a whisper . . ."

"Yes, Guard Captain . . . please . . . Shierra."

"What was he doing near Tower Black?" I asked again.

"I do not know, Guard Captain. He was wearing field dress, without a winter parka. He looked like any other guard." Fiera's eyes met mine fully for the first time.

We both knew that young Creslin, for all his abilities with a blade, was anything but another guard. He was the only male ever trained with the Guards, and yet his masculine skills had not been neglected. He could play the guitar better than any minstrel, and I'd heard his voice when he sang. It seemed that he could call a soft breeze in the heat of summer, and more than a few of those who had guarded his door had come away with tears in their eyes. Fiera had been one of them, unhappily. He'd even called an ice storm once. Only once, after he had discovered he'd been promised to the Sub-Tyrant of Sarronnyn.

Shortly, after more words with Fiera, I walked down the steps to the door of the ancient tower to check on what might have happened.

I always thought that tales of love were romantic nothings meant for men, not for the guards—or guard captains of Westwind— although I worried about my younger sister, and her actions in the east passage showed that I was right to worry. Fiera was close to ten years younger than I. We had not been close as children. I've always felt that sisters were either inseparable or distant. We were distant. Much as I tried to bridge that distance, much as I tried to offer kindness and advice, Fiera rejected both. When I attempted kindness, she said, "I know you're trying to be nice, but I'm not you. I have to do things my own way." She said much the same thing when I first offered advice. After a time, I only offered simple courtesy, as one would to any other Westwind guard, and no advice at all.

To my relief, the Tower Black door was locked, as it always was and should have been. There *might* have been boot prints in the frost, but even as a guard captain, I was not about to report what I could not prove, not when it might lead to revealing Fiera's indiscretion. Besides, what difference could it have made? Fiera had not made a fatal error, and young Creslin would be leaving Westwind forever, within days, to become the consort of the Sub-Tyrant of Sarronnyn.

II

Four mornings later, Guard Commander Aemris summoned the ten Westwind Guard Captains to the duty room below the Great Hall. She said nothing at all for a time. Her eyes traveled from one face to another.

"Some of you may have heard the news," Aemris finally said. "Lord Creslin skied off the side of the mountain into a snowstorm. The detachment was unable to find him. The Marshall has declared mourning."

"How . . . ?"

"The weather . . ."

"He wasn't supplied . . ."

"There are some skis and supplies missing from Tower Black. He must have taken them. Do any of you know anything about that?"

I almost froze in place when Aemris dropped those words, but I quickly asked, "How could he?"

The Guard Commander turned to me. "He does have some magely abilities. He coated the walls of the South Tower with ice the night after his consorting was announced. The ice is still there. None of the duty guards saw him near Tower Black recently, but he could have taken the gear weeks ago. Or he could have used some sort of magely concealment and made his way there."

Not a single guard captain spoke.

Aemris shook her head. "Men. They expect to be pampered. Even when they're not, and you do everything for them, what does it get you? He's probably frozen solid in the highlands, and we'll find his body in the spring or summer."

I tried not to move my face, but just nod.

"You don't think so, Guard Captain?"

Everyone was looking at me.

"I've seen him with a blade and on skis and in the field trials, ser. He's very good, but he doesn't know it. That will make him cautious."

"For the sake of the Marshall and the Marshalle, I hope so. For the sake of the rest of us . . ." Aemris said no more.

I understood her concerns, but for Fiera's sake, I could only hope Creslin would survive and find some sort of happiness. Despite all the fancies of men and all the tales of the minstrels, most stories of lost or unrequited love end when lovers or would-be lovers are parted. In the real world, they never find each other again, and that was probably for the best, because time changes us all.

III

For weeks after Creslin vanished, Fiera was silent. She threw herself into arms practice, so much so that, one morning, as ice flakes drifted across the courtyard under a gray sky, I had to caution her, if quietly.

"Getting yourself impaled on a practice blade won't bring him back."

"They're blunted," she snapped back

"That just means the entry wound is jagged and worse."

"You should talk, sister dearest. I've seen you watch him as well."

"I have. I admit it. But only because I admired him, young as he was. I had no illusions."

"You don't understand. You never will. Don't talk to me."

"Very well." I didn't mention Creslin again, even indirectly.

IV

Slightly more than a year passed. The sun began to climb higher in the sky that spring, foreshadowing the short and glorious summer on the Roof of the World. The ice began to melt, if but slightly at midday, and the healer in black appeared at the gates of Westwind. Since she was a woman, she was admitted.

Word spread through the Guard like a forest fire in early fall. *Creslin was alive.* He had somehow found the Sub-Tyrant of Sarronnyn, or she had found him, and the Duke of Montgren had married them and named them as coregents of Recluce. I'd never heard anything much about Recluce, save that it was a large and mostly deserted isle across the Gulf of Candar to the east of Lydiar.

Fiera avoided me, and that was as well, for what could I have said to her? Creslin was alive, but wed to another, as had been fated from his birth. No male heir to the Marshall could ever remain in Westwind, and none ever had.

That night after inspecting the duty guards, I settled onto my pallet in the private corner alcove I merited as a guard captain without a consort.

I awoke in a tower. It was Tower Black, and the walls rose up around me. I looked up, but the stones extended farther than I could make out. The stone steps led upward, and I began to climb them. Yet they never ended, and at each landing, the doorway to the outside had been blocked by a stone statue of an unsmiling Creslin in the garb of a Westwind Guard. Behind the statue, the archway had been filled in with small black stones and deep gray mortar. I kept climbing, past landing after landing with the same statue of Creslin. The walls rose into a gray mist above me. Blood began to seep from my boots. I refused to say anything. I kept climbing. Surely, there had to be a way out of the tower. There had to be . . .

"Shierra, wake up." Dalyra shook me. "Wake up," she hissed. "You'll rouse everyone with that moaning and muttering. They'll ask what you were dreaming. Guard captains don't need that."

"I'm awake." I could tell I was still sleepy. My words came out mumbled.

"Good," whispered Dalyra. "Now go back to sleep." She padded back to her pallet in the adjoining alcove.

I lay there in the darkness under the thick woolen blankets of a single guard captain. I'd never wanted a consort. Not in Westwind, and it wasn't likely I'd ever be anywhere else. Even if I left Westwind, where would I ever find one strong enough to stand up to me? The only man I'd seen with that strength was Creslin, and he'd been little more than a youth when he'd escaped Westwind, and far too young and far too above me. Unlike Fiera, I knew what was possible.

Yet what had the dream meant? The Tower Black of my dream hadn't been the tower I knew. Tower Black was the oldest part of Westwind. Its smooth stones had been cut and fitted precisely by the ancient smith-mage Nylan under the geas of Ryba the Great before he had spellsung the traitor Arylyn to free him and fled with her to the world below the Roof of the World. The great hall, the Guard quarters, the stables, the craft buildings, all of them were far larger than Tower Black. Yet none of them conveyed the *solidity* of the far smaller Tower Black that they dwarfed.

I finally drifted back into sleep, but it was an uneasy slumber at best.

The next morning, Aemris mustered all the Guards, and even the handfuls of consorts, and the guard captains, in the main courtyard of Westwind. She stood in the gusty spring wind and snowfall, the large fat flakes swirling lazily from the sky. Beside her stood the healer.

"The Marshall of Westwind has learned that Lord Creslin made his own way to the Sub-Tyrant of Sarronnyn," the Guard Commander began. "They were wed in Montgren, and, as a token of his esteem, the Duke named them coregents of Recluce. They are expanding the town of Land's End there on Recluce, and the Marshall will permit some from Westwind to join them in Recluce. The healer will explain."

Aemris delivered her speech without great enthusiasm. Even so, everyone was listening as the healer stepped forward.

"My name is Lydya. I am a healer, and I bring news of Creslin. He crossed much of Candar by himself and unaided. For a time he was imprisoned by the white wizards of Fairhaven, but he escaped and made his way to Montgren. He and Megaera are coregents of Recluce. They are building a new land, and there is opportunity for all. The land is much warmer and much drier than Westwind, but there are mountains and the sea." She smiled crookedly. "The mountains are rugged, but much lower and not nearly so cold. For better or worse, neither men nor women rule, but both can prosper, or suffer, according to ability. . . ."

Somehow that did not surprise me, not from a youth who had crossed much of Candar alone. What puzzled me was that he had married the woman he had left the Westhorns to avoid being consorted to. That suggested that Megaera was far more than he or anyone had expected.

After the healer finished speaking, Aemris added a few words. "Any of you who are interested in accompanying the healer to Recluce remain here. That includes consorts."

Perhaps forty guards out of three hundred remained in the court-yard. I was the only guard captain.

Aemris motioned for me to come forward first.

"You, Shierra?" asked the Guard Commander. "You have the mak-ings of an armsmaster or even Guard Commander in years to come."

How could I explain the dream? That, somehow, an image of Creslin kept me walled within Westwind? I could only trust the dream. "Someone must bring his heritage to him," I finally said.

Aemris looked to Lydya. The healer nodded.

"She's the most senior guard who wishes to go," Aemris said. "She should be guard captain of the detachment."

"That she will be." The healer smiled, but I felt the sadness behind the expression.

In the end, Aemris and Lydya settled on twenty-five guards and ten consorts with five children—all boys under five.

For the two days until we rode out, Fiera avoided me even more pointedly than before, walking away when she could, giving only for-mal responses when she could not. She could have volunteered, but she had not. Instead, she had asked to accompany a trade delegation to Sarronnyn. She hadn't told me. I'd discovered that from others—as I had so many things.

V

The ride to Armat took almost four eightdays. We rode through the Westhorns to Middle Vale and then down into Suthya by the road to the north of the River Arma. Until we reached Suthya, in most places, the snow beside the roads was at least waist-deep, and twice we had to help the road crews clear away new-fallen snow. In Armat, we had to wait another eightday for the ship Lydya had engaged with the letter of credit from the Marshall.

While we waited, she continued to purchase goods in one fashion or another. When the *Pride of Armat* ported, I was surprised to dis-cover it was one of the largest vessels in the harbor, with three tall masts. The ship was heavy-laden indeed by the time her master lifted sail and we departed from Armat three days later. Lydya and I talked frequently, but it was mostly about the cargo, about the guards and their consorts, and about how we would need to use all the wood-working and stoneworking tools to build our own shelter on Recluce. That bothered me little. All Guards knew something about building and maintaining structures. Westwind could not have endured over the centuries without those skills. I tended to be better with stone. Perhaps I lacked the delicate touch needed for woodwork.

After more than an eightday of hugging the northern coasts of Candar, the ship had finally left the easternmost part of Lydiar behind, swallowed by the sea. For the first two days, we'd been followed by another vessel, until Lydya had suggested to the captain that he fly the banner of Westwind I had brought. About halfway across the Gulf of Candar, the war schooner eased away on a different course.

Lydya and I stood just aft of the bowsprit, at the port railing.

"Do you know what to expect in Recluce, Shierra?"

"No, except that it will likely be hot and dry and strange. We'll have to build almost everything from nothing, and there's a garrison of savage men we'll have to deal with."

Lydya laughed. "They'll have to deal with you. None of them are a match for your least-trained Guards. That's one of the reasons why Creslin needs you, and why the Marshall permitted some of you to come."

"But she drove him out, didn't she?"

"Did she?"

The question made me uneasy, especially asked by a healer. "Why did you come to Westwind?"

"To ask the Marshall for what might be called Creslin's dowry. For obvious reasons, he cannot ask, and he would not even if he were physically where he could."

For that, I also admired him. "How did you come to know him?"

"I was a healer in the White road camp where they imprisoned him. After he escaped, Klerris and I followed him, not to Montgren, but to Tyrhavven. That is where he and Megaera took the Duke's schooner that brought them to Recluce. Klerris accompanied them, and I traveled to Westwind."

"Is he really a mage?"

"Yes. He may become one of the greatest ever. That is if he and Megaera survive each other."

"Healer . . . what is the Sub-Tyrant like?" I did not wish to ask the question, but I had to know, especially after Lydya's last words.

"She has hair like red mahogany, eyes as green and deep as the summer seas south of Naclos, fair skin, and freckles. She is also a white witch, with a kind heart, and a temper to match the most violent thunderstorms of summer."

"Is she . . ."

"She is as beautiful and as deadly as a fine dagger, Shierra. That is what makes her a match for Creslin, or him for her."

What could I say to that, except more pleasantries about the sea, the weather, and the cargo we carried?

VI

Another day passed. On the morning of the following day, a rocky headland appeared. I could see no buildings at all. There was no smoke from fires. As the ship neared land, and some of the sails were furled, I could finally make out a breakwater on the east side of the inlet between the rocky cliffs. At first, I wasn't certain, because it wasn't much more than a long pile of stones. There was a single short pier, with a black stone building behind it, and a scattering of other buildings, one of them clearly half-built. A dusty road wound up a low rise to a keep built out of grayish black stones. On one end was a section that looked to have been added recently.

The captain had a boat lowered, with a heavy rope—a hawser, I thought—attached to the sternpost. The men in the boat rowed to the pier and fastened it to one of the posts, and then the crew used the capstan to winch the ship in toward the pier. As we got nearer to the shore, I could see that very little grew anywhere, just bushes.

"Lydya . . . it doesn't look like we'll have much use for that wood-working equipment. All I see are a few bushes."

The healer laughed. "Those are trees, or what passes for them."

Trees? They were barely taller than I. I swallowed and turned back to look at the handful of people waiting on the pier. One of them was Creslin. I could tell that from his silver hair, lit by the sunlight. Beside him on one side was a black mage. On the other was a tall red-haired woman. That had to be Megaera.

Once the ship was tied past to the pier, the captain scrambled onto the pier, bowing to Creslin and Megaera. I just watched for a moment.

"Shierra . . . you're the Guard captain," said Lydya quietly. "Report to the regents."

I was senior, and I would have stepped forward sooner, except . . .

There was no excuse. I vaulted over the railing and stood waiting behind the captain. Once he stepped back, I moved forward.

"Guard Captain Shierra, Regent Creslin, Regent Megaera," I began, inclining my head in respect to them.

"Did you have any trouble with the wizards?" Creslin asked.

"No, ser. But then, we insisted that the captain fly our banner. One war schooner did follow us. It left halfway across the Gulf." I couldn't help smiling, but felt nervous all the same as I gestured to the middle mast that where the Westwind banner drooped limply.

"You seem to have a full group." Creslin smiled, but he didn't seem to recognize me. Then, why should he have? Fiera had been the one who had kissed him.

"Two and a half squads, actually."

Creslin pointed westward toward the keep. "There are your quarters, rough as they are. We'll discuss other needs once you look things over. We might as well get whatever you brought off-loaded."

"Some carts would help, ser. The healer"—I didn't wish to use her first name, and what else could I call her to a regent?—"was apparently quite persuasive . . ." I went on to explain everything in the cargo holds.

"Now, *that* is true wizardry." Creslin laughed.

The sound was so infectious, almost joyful, that I ended up laughing with him. Then, I was so embarrassed that I turned immediately to the Guards. "Let's off-load!"

I forced myself to concentrate on the details of getting the Guards and consorts and the children off the ship, and then making sure with the ship's boatswain that the holds would be unloaded in the order on the bill lading that I did not even sense Megaera's approach.

"Guard Captain?" Her voice carried, despite its softness.

I tried not to jump and turned. "Regent Megaera."

"Once you're ready, I'll escort you up to the keep." She smiled, almost humorously. "They'll have to walk. We're a bit short on mounts. It's not that far, though."

"We have enough mounts for the Guards, and some spares." I paused. "But they'll have to be walked themselves after all the time on ship."

It took until early afternoon before we had even begun to transfer cargo and to walk the horses up to the crude stables behind the keep. Once I had duties assigned to the Guards, I stayed at the keep, trying to keep track of goods and especially weapons. The wall stones of the outbuildings being used as stables were so loosely set that the stalls would have filled with ice on a single winter day at Westwind. The storerooms on the lower levels of the keep were better, but musty.

I blotted my forehead with my sleeve as I stood outside the stable in the sun, checking the contents of each cart, and directing the Guards.

After the cart I had checked was unloaded and Eliera began to lead the old mare back down to the pier, Megaera appeared and walked toward me

"Guard Captain . . . I have a question for you."

"Yes, Regent?" What could a white witch want of me?

"Recluce is a hard place, and it is likely to get harder before it gets easier. Could you instruct me in the use of blades?"

"Regent . . ." What could I say? Westwind Guards began training almost as soon as they could walk, and Megaera was nearly as old as I was, I suspected. Beautiful as she was, she was certainly older than Creslin.

She lifted her arms and let the tunic sleeves fall back, revealing heavy white scars around both wrists. "I can deal with pain and discomfort, Guard Captain. What I cannot abide is my own inability to defend myself with a blade."

But . . . she was a white mage.

"Magery has its limits." She looked directly at me. "Please . . . will you help me?"

How could I say no when she had begged me? Or as close to begging as a Sub-Tyrant could come.

VII

I was studying the practice yard early the next morning. The sun had barely cleared the low cliffs to the east, and the air was cool, for Recluce, but dusty. I wondered if I'd ever escape the dust. Already, I missed the smell of the firs and the pines, and the clean crispness of the air of Westwind. The barracks were stone-walled, sturdy, and rough. From what I could tell, so were the Montgren guards.

I heard boots and turned.

"You're Guard Captain Shierra. Hyel, at your service." As eastern men sometimes were, he was tall, almost half a head taller than I was, but lanky with brown hair. His hands were broad, with long fingers. Megaera had pointed him out the day before and told me that he was in charge of the Montgren troopers, such as they were, but with all the fuss and bother of unloading and squeezing everyone in, we had not met.

"I'm pleased to meet you." I wasn't certain that I was, but his approach had been polite enough.

"Are you as good as Regent Creslin with the blade?"

How could I answer that question? There was no good answer. I forced a smile. "Why don't we spar, and you can make up your own mind?"

Hyel stiffened. I didn't see why. "I only made a friendly suggestion, Hyel. That was because I don't have an answer to your question. I never sparred against Creslin." That was shading things, because Heldra had, and at the end, just before Creslin had ridden off, even she had been hard-pressed. I certainly would have been.

"With wands?"

"That might be best." Best for both of us. If he were a master blade, I didn't want to find out with cold steel, and if he weren't, I didn't want to have to slice him up to prove a point.

"I'll be back in a moment."

Why had Hyel immediately sought me out, and before most others were around?

In moments, he reappeared with two white oak wands that seemed scarcely used. He offered me my choice. I took the one that felt more balanced. Neither was that good.

"Shall we begin?" Hyel turned and walked into the courtyard. He turned and waited. Once I neared, he lifted the white oak wand, slightly too high. I was less comfortable with the single blade, but the shorter twin wooden practice blades were still buried in the storeroom where they'd been quickly unloaded.

His feet were about right, but he was leaning forward too far.

It took just three passes before I disarmed him.

He just shrugged and stood there, laughing.

I lowered the wand, uncertain of what to say. "Are you . . ."

"I'm fine, Shierra. Might I call you that?"

"You may."

He shook his head. "I always thought that what they said about Westwind was just . . . well, that folks believed what they wanted. Then, when Creslin slaughtered Zarlen in about two quick moves, well . . . I just thought that was him."

"No. He could have been as good as a Westwind armsmaster . . . he might even have been when he left, but there are many Guards as good as I am." That was true enough. There were at least ten others. But Creslin . . . slaughtering someone? I'd known he was determined, but somehow, I'd never imagined him that way.

"It wasn't like that," Hyel said quickly. "Creslin and Megaera came here almost by themselves. On the Duke's small schooner with no guards and no troopers. Zarlen thought he could kill Creslin and have his way with her. Creslin saw what he had in mind and asked him to spar. Creslin disarmed him real quick, and Zarlen went crazy. He attacked Creslin with his own steel. Creslin had to kill him." Hyel laughed ruefully. "Made his point."

That made more sense . . . but to see that a man wanted his wife . . . and to kill him like that? The Marshall would have acted that quickly, and Creslin was her son. I'd never thought of it that way. I lowered the wooden wand until the blunted point touched the stones.

"Can you teach me?" Hyel asked.

I could. Should I? "If you're willing to work," I answered, still distracted by what Hyel had told me.

"Early in the morning?" A sheepish look crossed his face.

"Early in the morning. Every morning."

I'd been in Recluce only two days, and I'd already committed to teaching Megaera the basics of the blade and to improving the skills of the Montgren garrison commander.

VIII

With the Regent Megaera, I had to start farther back, with an exercise program of sorts. I gave her stones of the proper weight to lift and hold and exercises to loosen and limber her shoulders. After an eight-day, she found me remortaring the stones in what would be the armory.

"Regent." I laid aside the trowel that I'd recovered from the recesses of the keep and stood.

"When can we start with blades?"

I didn't answer her, but turned and walked to the wall where I'd laid aside my harness. I unsheathed one of the blades and extended it, hilt first. "Take it, if you would, Regent."

After a moment of hesitation, she did.

"Hold it out, extended. Keep holding it." That wasn't totally fair, because no blademaster works with her weapon fully extended or with the arm straight, except for a thrust. But it's a good indication of arm strength.

Her arm and wrist began to tremble before long. She fought the weakness, but finally had to lower the blade.

"When your arms are strong enough to hold that position longer," I answered.

Her lips tightened.

"If we start before you're ready, you'll learn bad technique because you won't have the strength you'll have later, and strength and technique won't match."

Abruptly, she laughed. "Strength and technique won't match. That's almost what Klerris said about black magery."

I nodded slightly. I knew nothing about magery, but it seemed that strength and technique should match in any application.

"Did you ever see Creslin work magery?"

How was I to answer that?

"Did you?" Megaera's voice was hard.

I thought I saw whitish flames at the tips of her fingers.

"Only once. I wasn't certain it was magery. He called a storm and flung the winds against the South Tower until it was coated with ice."

"Why did he do that?"

"I could not say, Regent."

Megaera smiled. I didn't like that kind of calculating smile. "*When* did he perform this . . . weather magery?"

I could have lied, but she would have known. "After his betrothal to you was announced. He left the Great Hall as soon as he could."

"Oh . . . best-betrothed . . . if only . . ."

While her words were less than murmured, I might as well not have been there.

Abruptly, she looked at me. "I would appreciate it if you would say nothing of this."

"I will not, Regent Megaera."

"Next eightday, we *will* begin with blades."

Then she was gone.

IX

Several days later, I took one of the mounts and rode up the wind-ing road to the Black Holding. Several of the Guards had been detailed to help Creslin build the quarters for him and Megaera. I knew he'd never shirked work, but it was still strange to think of the Marshall's son and the Regent of Recluce working stone. I'd overheard remarks about his skill as a mason, and I wanted to see that, as well as check on the Guards working there.

When I reached the structure, still incomplete under its slate roof, I reined up and dismounted, and tied the horse to the single post. The stones of the front wall and the archway were of various sizes, but all edges were smoothed and dressed, and fitted into an almost seamless pattern that required little or no mortar. Had Creslin done that? I couldn't have dressed the stones that smoothly, especially not with the tools we had, and I was the best of the Guard stoneworkers on Recluce.

Hulyan appeared immediately. She was carrying a bucket. "Guard Captain, ser, we didn't expect you."

"What are you doing?"

"It's my round to carry water to the Regent. He's cutting and dress-ing stone down in back, ser."

"Where are the others?"

"They're finding and carrying rough stones to the Regent. That's so he doesn't have to spend time looking."

"You can lead me there, but don't announce me."

"Yes, Guard Captain."

We walked quietly around the north side of the building and to the edge of the terrace. There I stopped and watched.

Below the partly built terrace, Creslin stood amid piles of black stones. His silver hair was plastered against his skull with sweat, yet it still shimmered in the sun. He adjusted the irregular black stone on the larger chunk of rock, then positioned the chisel and struck with the hammer. Precise and powerful as the blow was, the stone shouldn't have split, but it did. One side was as smooth as if it had been dressed. I watched as he readjusted the stone and repeated the process.

Before long he had a precisely dressed black stone block. He only took a single deep breath, wiped his forehead with the back of his forearm, and then started on the next irregular chunk of heavy stone.

In some fashion, he was mixing magery and stonecraft, and the results were superb. At that moment, I did not want to look at another piece of stone. Ever.

After a moment, I realized that Creslin must have known that as well. Was that why he worked alone?

I watched as he cut and then dressed one stone after another. I could not have lifted the hammer so strongly and precisely. Not for stone after stone. No stonecutter I had ever seen or known could have.

Slowly, I moved forward, just watching, trying to sense what he was doing.

Despite the brilliant sunlight, there was a darkness around him, but it wasn't any kind of darkness or shadow that I had ever seen. It was more like something felt, the sense of how a blade should be held, or a saddle adjusted to a skittish mount. I kept watching, trying to feel what he did, rather than see.

For a moment, I could *feel* the stone before Creslin, knowing where the faults lay, and where chisel should be placed . . .

"Guard Captain Shierra!" he finally called, as if he had just seen me.

"Yes, ser. I was just checking on the Guards."

"They've been most helpful. We couldn't have done half what's here without them." He paused. "But if you need them at the keep . . ."

"No, ser. Not yet anyway. Thank you, ser." My voice sounded steady to me. It didn't feel steady. I turned and hurried back to my mount, before Creslin could ask me anything more.

I untied the gelding and mounted, turning him back toward the keep in the harbor valley.

Thoughts swirled through my head as I rode down the dusty road.

Was that order-magery? The understanding of the forces beneath and within everything?

What I had seen wasn't what anyone would have called magecraft. There were no winds or storms created. No one had been healed, and no keep had been suddenly created. Yet those stones could not have been cut and dressed so precisely in any other fashion. What I had also seen was a man who was driving himself far harder than anyone I had known. His body was muscle, and only muscle, and he was almost as slender as a girl guard before she became a woman.

I had thought I'd known something about Creslin. Now I was far from certain that I knew anything at all.

Back at the keep, I couldn't help but think about the way in which Creslin had turned irregular chunks of rock into cut and dressed black building stones. Could I do that? How could I not try?

I settled myself in the stoneyard on the hillside above the keep, with hammer and chisel and the pile of large chunks of broken dark gray stone. I set an irregular hunk on the granite-like boulder that served as a cutting table and looked at it. It remained a gray stone.

I closed my eyes and tried to recapture the feeling I'd sensed around Creslin. It had been deliberate, calm, a feeling of everything in its place.

Nothing happened.

Knowing that nothing was that simple, I hadn't expected instant understanding or mastery. While still trying to hold that feeling of simplicity and order, I picked up the chisel and the hammer. After placing the chisel where it *felt* best—close to where it needed to be to dress the edge of the stone, I took a long and deliberate stroke.

A fragment of the stone chipped away. It was larger than most that I had been chiseling away. That could have been chance. Without hurrying, I placed the chisel again, concentrating without forcing the feeling. Another large fragment split away.

Slowly, deliberately, I worked on the stone.

After a few more blows, I had a clean face to the stone, cleaner and smoother than I'd ever managed before, but the face was angled slightly, compared to the other, rougher faces.

I kept at it. At times, I had a hard time recapturing that deliberate, calm feeling, but I could tell the difference in the results.

Learning how to harness that feeling, and to use it effectively in cutting and dressing stone was going to take some time. I just hoped it didn't take too long. We needed dressed stones for far too many structures that had yet to be built. Creslin had also asked that some of the stone be used to finish the inn near the pier, especially the public room. That was to give the guards and troopers some place where they could gather and get a drink. I had my doubts about how that would work, for all of Hyel's efforts, and those of Creslin.

X

Exactly one eightday after she had last asked me, Megaera appeared in the keep courtyard, early in the morning, right after I had finished my daily session with Hyel.

"We're running out of time, Guard Captain," she said firmly. "Whether I'm strong enough or not, we need to begin."

"You've made a good start with the physical conditioning. But whether you can master a lifetime of training in a season or two is another question." That wasn't even a question. I doubted that she could, but she could learn to use a shortsword to defend herself against what passed for eastern bladework. In case of raiders or invaders, or even assassins, that could save her life just by allowing her to hold someone at bay long enough for help to reach her.

"There's no other choice."

The way she said the words, it seemed as though she was not even thinking of raiders.

"Creslin's not that hard, is he?" I couldn't believe I'd said that to the Regent, and I quickly added, "My sister felt he was a good man at heart."

Megaera laughed, half humorously, half bitterly. "It's not that at all. Against him, I need no defenses. Besides, from what I've seen, I'm not sure that I'd ever prevail by force of arms."

Her words lifted a burden from me. But why was she so insistent that she needed to learn the blade? She was a white witch who could throw chaos-fire. I'd even seen it flaring around her once or twice.

Megaera lifted the white oak wand. "Where do we begin?"

"At the beginning, with the way you hold the blade." I stepped forward and repositioned her fingers. "You must have firm control, and yet not grip it so tightly that it wearies your muscles." I positioned her feet in the basic stance. "And the way in which you stand will affect those muscles as well."

"Like this?"

I nodded and picked up my own wand. "You may regret this, lady."

"The time for regrets has come and gone, Shierra. There is only time to do what must be done."

"Higher on the blade tip . . ." I cautioned.

For the first few passes, breaking through her guard was almost laughably easy. Unlike many of the junior guards when they first began, once she had a wand in her hand, Megaera had no interest in anything but learning how to best use it.

Her eyes never left me, and I could almost feel that she was trying to absorb everything I said. Her concentration, like Creslin's, was frightening.

What was between the two regents, so much that they each drove themselves beyond reason, beyond exhaustion?

XI

The following morning, Hyel was waiting for me.

"You're early," I said.

"I wanted to make sure I got my time with you before the Regent Megaera appeared." He laughed easily.

"You don't need that much more work." He really didn't. He learned quickly. His basic technique had never been that poor, but no one had ever drilled him in the need for perfection. I wondered if the Westwind Guards had developed that insistence on absolute mastery of weapons and tactics because the women were both the warriors and the childbearers and every woman lost meant children who would not be born.

"I'll need to keep sparring with you to improve and hold what you've taught me."

True as his words might be, I had the feeling that Hyel was not telling me everything. "And?"

He gave me the sheepish grin. "Who else can I talk to? You're the only one who commands fighting forces. The regents are above me, and . . ."

I could understand that. I did enjoy talking to him. Still . . . "If we're going to spar before the Regent gets here . . ."

"You're right." With a nod, he picked up his wand.

We worked hard, and I had to admit that he'd gotten enough better that I had to be on guard all the time. He even got a touch on me, not enough to give me more than a slight bruise, but he hadn't been able to do that before.

When we set down the wands, I inclined my head. "You're pressing me now." I even had to blot my forehead.

"Good!" Hyel was soaked, but he was smiling broadly—for a moment.

"What's the matter?"

"Is everyone from the West like you and the Regents?"

"What do you mean?"

"You never stop. From dawn to dusk, you, Creslin, and the Regent Megaera push yourselves. Anyone else would drop. Some of my men have, just trying to keep up with Creslin on his tours of the fields and the springs. He cuts stone, looks and finds springs, runs up and down mountains—"

"Compared to Westwind," I interjected, "they're just hills."

"They're mountains to the rest of us." He grinned before continuing. "You and the Regent Megaera are just as bad. You give me and her blade lessons, drill your own guards, cut and dress stones, check supplies and weapons . . . I've even seen you at the grindstone sharpening blades."

"A guard captain has to be able to do all that. That's what the position requires."

"Stonecutting, too?"

"Not always stonecutting or masonry, but all guards have to have at least apprentice-level skills in a craft."

"No wonder Westwind has lasted so many ages." He shook his head. "That explains you and Creslin. What about the Regent Megaera?"

I shrugged. "She's more driven than Creslin, and I don't know why."

Hyel cleared his throat abruptly. "Ah . . ."

I turned. Megaera had entered the courtyard carrying a practice wand.

"Until later, Guard Captain." Hyel inclined his head, and then stepped away, offering a deeper nod of respect to Megaera.

"Can we begin, Shierra?" Megaera asked.

"Yes, Regent."

I turned and lifted my wand.

Megaera had practiced . . . or she had absorbed totally what I had taught her the day before. Once more, she concentrated totally on every aspect of what I showed her. At the end of the practice session, she inclined her head and thanked me, then left hurriedly. I couldn't help but think about what Hyel had said.

Her intensity made Creslin look calm, and I knew he was scarcely that.

After washing up a bit, I was back working on cutting stones. I couldn't match the pace that I'd seen in Creslin, but with each day I felt that I was getting more skilled. That was strange, because I'd felt no such improvement over the years before. I couldn't exactly explain what was different, except that the work went more quickly when I could hold onto the sense of calm and order.

I'd cut and dressed several larger stones when I sensed more than saw Lydya approach. She radiated a calmness that didn't interfere with my concentration. Her presence should have, but it didn't. She said nothing, and I kept working.

Finally, she stepped forward, almost to my elbow. "You're good at cutting and shaping the rough stone."

"I've been working at it."

"You're using some basic order skills, you know?"

"I watched Creslin for a time. I just thought I'd try to do what he was doing. It looked . . . more effective."

"Just like that?" Lydya raised her eyebrows.

"No, not exactly. I already knew something about masonry and stonecutting. But there was a certain feel to what he was doing . . ." How else could I explain it?

The healer laughed, softly, but humorously. "There is indeed a feel to the use of order. If you continue to work on developing that feel to your stonework, you may become a master mason." The humorous tone was replaced with one more somber. "In time, it will impair your ability to use a blade."

"But . . . Creslin . . ."

Lydya just nodded. "Order has its price, and there are no exceptions."

XII

Megaera made solid improvements. By the end of the second eight-day of practice, she was sparring at the same level as the most junior guards. At times, she made terrible mistakes. That was because she had so little experience. Each of those mistakes resulted in severe bruises, and she was fortunate not to have broken her wrist once. Even so, she continued to improve. After our sessions, I began to match her against the guards. That was as much to show her that she had improved as for the practice itself.

After one session, she forced herself not to limp, despite a slash-blow to her calf that would have tried the will of most of the guards. She did sit down on the stone bench beside me.

"That was quite a blow you took."

"I should have sensed it coming." She shook her head.

I couldn't help noticing that the circles under her eyes were darker. "You can't learn everything all at once."

"You sound like . . ." She stopped, then went on. "Do you have a sister, Shierra?"

"A younger sister. She's probably a squad leader now."

"How do you get along?"

Should I have answered? How could I not, when she could tell my very thoughts?

"I love her, but she has kept her distance from me."

Megaera laughed. It wasn't a pleasant sound.

"Do you have a sister?"

"You know I have a sister. She's the Tyrant."

She was right, but I hadn't known quite what to say. "Is she a mage, too?"

"No. Not many Tyrants have been mages, not since Saryn anyway. She is just the Tyrant. Were you ever close to your sister?"

"I tried to be. But she never wanted to hear what I had to say. She said she had to make her own decisions and mistakes."

Megaera looked away. After a moment, she rose. "Thank you. I'll see you tomorrow." Then she turned and left.

Had my comment offended her, by suggesting her sister had only meant the best for her? Did she react that way to everything, taking even harmless statements as criticisms or as slights?

Megaera said little to me for the next three mornings, only what was necessary to respond to my instructions. She avoided me totally in matters involving the upgrading of the quarters and the keep, or even the duty rosters for the guards. Creslin and Hyel discussed the duty rosters for the Montgren troopers, and Hyel and I worked out the rotations between us.

On the fourth morning, before we began, Megaera looked at me, then lowered the practice wand. "Shierra . . . you meant the best."

"I did not realize that matters were so between you and your sister." I wasn't about to apologize when I had done nothing wrong, but I could say that I meant no harm.

"You could not have known. No one here could have. Even Creslin did not know until I told him. Sisters can be so cruel."

Could they? Had I been that cruel?

Even as we sparred, Megaera's words crept through my thoughts.

XIII

Late one afternoon, Hyel found me in the stoneyard. "We need to get down to the public room."

"Now? We need more stones . . ."

"You know how the troopers and guards don't talk to each other?"

"We talk to each other."

"Our guards don't talk to each other. Even when they're drinking they sit on opposite sides of the room."

I'd seen that. "It will change."

Hyel shook his head. "I told Regent Creslin about it. He's going to do something, This evening. He didn't say what. I think you should be there."

"Frig! I don't need this." But I picked up my tools and my harness. "I'll meet you there. I need to wash up." At least, I needed to get stone dust out of my eyes and nose and hair.

I did hurry, but by the time I got to the half-finished inn and public room, the sun was low over the western hills that everyone else called mountains. The windows were without glass or shutters, and someone had propped wooden slats over several of the openings to cut the draft.

Hyel was right. The Westwind guards had taken the tables on the south side, and the Montgren troopers those on the north side. I should have paid more attention, but between keeping things going and the stonework, and the training sessions, I'd had little time and less inclination for the going to the public room.

I eased onto one end of the bench on the leftmost table. "What is there to drink?"

"Some fermented green stuff," replied Fylena, "and something they call beer."

"Doesn't anyone ever talk to the Montgren guards?"

"Why? All they want is to get in our trousers."

"Without even bathing," added someone else.

"There's the Regent."

I looked up. Megaera had taken a place at the adjoining table, and beside her was the healer. Across the room, Klerris the mage was sitting beside Hyel.

Creslin walked into the public room and glanced around. He carried his guitar as he made his way to Hyel and spoke. Hyel hurried off and returned with a stool. After a moment, Creslin dragged the stool into the open space and then recovered his guitar.

He settled onto the stool and fingered the strings of the guitar. He smiled, but it was clear he was uneasy. After another strumming chord, he spoke. "I don't know too many songs that don't favor one group or another. So enjoy the ones you like and ignore the ones you don't." Then he began to sing.

"Up on the mountain

"where the men dare not go

"the angels set guards there

"in the ice and the snow . . .

I'd forgotten how beautifully he sang. It was as though every note hung like liquid silver in the air. When he finished the first song, no one spoke, but Megaera slipped away from the other table and sat beside me.

Creslin then sang *"White Was the Color of My Love."*

"Has he always sung this well?" murmured Megaera.

"His father was supposed to have been a minstrel, but no one knows for sure."

Creslin launched into two humorous songs, and both the guards and the troopers laughed. When he halted, he stretched his fingers, then coughed, looking around as if for something to drink. Megaera left me for a moment, carrying her cup to him.

Instead of thanking her, he asked, "Are you all right?"

"Fine, thank you. I thought you might need this." After he drank she took the cup and rejoined me. For the first time, I saw that she was deathly white, and she held her hands to keep them from trembling.

Creslin sang several more songs, and then coaxed one of Hyel's troopers into singing one of their songs.

Finally, he brought the guitar to Darcyl. I hadn't even known that she played. Creslin turned, looking for a place to sit. Megaera rose, taking my arm and guiding me with her. We ended up at the one vacant table. I did manage to gesture for Hyel to join us, and Megaera beckoned as well.

"I didn't know you could sing." Megaera's words were almost an accusation.

"I never had a chance until now, and you never seemed to be interested," Creslin replied, his voice either distant or tired, perhaps both. His eyes were on Darcyl and the guitar.

No one spoke. Finally, I had to. "Fiera said that the hall guards used to sneak up to his door when he practiced."

For the first time I'd ever seen, Creslin looked surprised. "Fiera? Is she your—"

"My youngest sister." I don't know why I said it that way, since she was also my only sister. "She talked a lot about you, probably too much." I wished I hadn't said that, either, almost as soon as the words were out of my mouth, but I hadn't expected to find myself sitting at a table with just the two Regents and Hyel.

"How is she?"

I sensed Megaera bristling, but all I could do was answer. "She went with the detachment to Sarronnyn. She'll be rotated back later in the year sometime. It could be that she's already back at Westwind."

"Where did the guitar come from?" Hyel was doing his best to keep the conversation light.

"It was mine," Creslin replied. "I left it behind. Lydya—the healer— brought it. My sister Llyse thought I might like to have it."

"You've never played in public?" I was trying to do . . . something . . . to disarm Megaera's hostility.

"No. I was scared to do it, but sometimes music helps. The second song, the white-as-a-dove one, probably saved me from the white wizards."

"You didn't exactly sound scared." Megaera's voice was like winter ice in Westwind.

"That wouldn't have helped much," Creslin said slowly. "Besides no one born in Westwind shows fear. Not if they can help it."

Megaera looked at me, as if she wanted me to refute what he'd said.

"Feeling afraid is acceptable, but letting it affect your actions is not. That's one of the reasons the Guards are often more effective than men. Men too often conceal their fear in brashness or in unwise attacks. The Guards are trained to recognize their fears and set them aside. Regent Creslin was trained as a Guard until he left Westwind."

Hyel raised his eyebrows, then took a long pull from his mug.

For several songs by Darcyl, we just sat there and listened.

Then Creslin rose. He offered an awkward smile. "I'm going to get some sleep."

At the adjoining table, both Klerris and Lydya stiffened.

"I do hope you'll play again for us," Hyel said. "That really was a treat, and just about everyone liked it."

Everyone but Megaera, I felt, and I was afraid I understood why. I was also afraid I'd just made matters worse without meaning to.

Creslin recovered his guitar and looked at Megaera.

"I do hope you'll play again," I said quickly.

Megaera's eyes fixed on Creslin. "I need to talk to you."

"Now?"

"When you get to the holding will be fine. I won't be long."

Her words told me that matters were anything but fine.

Concern flooded Creslin's face.

"Stop it. Please . . ." Megaera spoke softly, but firmly.

Before Creslin could move, Klerris stepped up to Megaera. "A moment, lady?"

"Can it wait until tomorrow?"

"I think not."

As if they had planned it, the two mages separated Creslin and Megaera, Klerris leading her in one direction and Lydya guiding him in another.

"What was that all about?" asked Hyel. "I thought things were going better between the troopers and the guards."

"Between my guards and your troopers, yes."

Hyel's eyes went to Megaera's back as she and Klerris left the public room. "He was singing to her, and she didn't hear it. Was that it?" asked Hyel.

I shook my head. "He was singing to us, all of us, and she needs him to sing for her."

"She's not that selfish."

He didn't understand. "I didn't say she was. It's different." I tried not to snap at him.

"How's he supposed to know that?"

I didn't have an answer, but I knew it was so, and even Fiera would have understood that.

XIV

After the night that Creslin sang to all the guards and troopers at the public room, two things happened. The first was that Creslin and Megaera began to call Klerris and Lydya, and Hyel and me, together to meet almost daily about matters affecting Recluce. Creslin laughed about it, calling us the unofficial high council of Recluce. Usually, I didn't say too much, Neither did Hyel.

Mostly, I watched, especially Creslin and Megaera. Sometimes, I couldn't help but overhear what they said afterward as they left the hall.

" . . . don't . . ."

"I'm sorry," Creslin apologized. "I still can't believe your cousin wants to tax us . . ."

"He doesn't. It has to be Helisse . . . not any better than sister dear . . ."

Creslin said nothing.

"Sisters of Sarronnyn . . . except she never thought of us . . . just of her, of what she thought was best for Sarronnyn . . ."

"Don't we have to think of what's best for Recluce?"

"It's not the same!" After a moment, Megaera continued, her voice softer. "I'm sorry, best-betrothed. You try to ask people. You don't always listen, but you care enough to ask . . ."

Their voices faded away, and I stood there, thinking about how they had spoken to each other and what they had said—and not said.

The second thing was that, not every night, but more and more frequently, Megaera began to sleep in the keep. Then it was every night.

I didn't even pretend to understand all the reasons why she preferred to share my small room at the keep rather than stay in the Black Holding where she had a fine large room to herself. I also understood why she'd married Creslin. What real choice had she had? I could have understood why she'd never slept with him, except for one thing. It was clear to every person on the isle that he loved her, that he would have taken a blade or a storm for her. Yet she ignored that, and she also ignored the fact that she cared for him. That was what I found so hard to understand. But a guard captain doesn't ask such things of a Regent, even one who shares her chamber.

Finally, one night, in the darkness, she just sat on the edge of her pallet and looked at the wall.

"It's not my affair," I began, although it was because anything that the regents did affected all of us on Recluce, "but could you . . ." I didn't quite know what to say.

Megaera did not speak for a time, and I waited.

"It isn't your affair, Shierra. It's between Creslin and me." She paused, then went on. "We're tied together by magery. It's an evil thing. I know everything he feels. Everything. When he looks at me . . . or when he feels I've done something I shouldn't . . . or when . . ." She shook her head.

"Does he know what you feel?"

"He's beginning to know that. The . . . mage-ties were done at different times. I had no choice . . . mine to him was done even before we were betrothed. He didn't even know. That . . . it was my sister's doing. My own sister, and she said that it was for my own good. My own good. Creslin . . . he chose to tie himself to me. He didn't even ask. He just had it done." She turned. "How would you feel, to have every feeling you experienced felt by a man you never knew before you were married?"

I was confused. "Didn't you say that you know everything he feels?"

"Every last feeling! Every time he looks at me and wants me! Every time he feels hurt, like a whipped puppy, because I don't think what he did was wonderful . . . Do you know what that's like? How would you feel if you knew every feeling Hyel had for you, and he knew how you felt?" She snorted. "You've at least worked with Hyel. When I started feeling what Creslin felt, we'd met once at a dinner, and we'd exchanged less than a handful of words. Sister dear and his mighty mother the Marshall decided we should be wed, and that was that."

The idea of having every feeling known? I shuddered. I liked Hyel, and we had gotten to know each other somewhat. The idea that a complete stranger might know all my feelings . . . no wonder Megaera looked exhausted. No wonder she was edgy. Yet . . . I had to wonder about Creslin.

"What about Regent Creslin?" I asked softly.

She shook her head.

Once more, I waited.

"He does what he feels is right, but . . . he doesn't always think about how it affects others. At times, he tries to listen, but then . . . it's as though something happened, and he's back doing the same things." Megaera's voice died away. Abruptly, she stretched out on the pallet. "Good night, Shierra."

Everything Megaera had said rang true, and yet I felt that there was more there. Was that because I had watched Creslin grow up? Because I wanted to believe he was doing the best he knew how? I had watched him both in Westwind and since I had come to Recluce, and I could see how he tried to balance matters, and how he drove himself. But was I seeing what I wanted to see? Was what Megaera saw more accurate?

How could I know?

I lay on my pallet, thinking about Fiera. I'd only wanted the best for her. I'd never even thought of doing anything like the Tyrant had. I wished I could have told her that. But when I left, she hadn't let me. She'd gone off to Sarronnyn, as if to say that she could go where she wanted without telling me.

XV

The warning trumpet sounded while I was just about to begin finishing the stonework reinforcing around the second supply storehouse. I was halfway across the courtyard when Gylara called to me.

"Guard Captain! Ships! At least two warships entering the harbor. They're flying the standard of Hamor . . ."

Hamor? Why were the Hamorians attacking?

". . . Regent Megaera has ordered all squads to the pier! She's left with First Squad!"

I should have been the one to issue that order. But then, I shouldn't have properly been doing stonework, except no one else in the detachment had been trained in it, except Doryana, and two stonemasons weren't nearly enough with all that needed to be repaired and built. I was already buckling on my harness and sprinting for the courtyard.

"Second Squad! Form up! Pass the word."

Hyel rushed into the courtyard just as we were heading out. I'd hoped we could catch up with First Squad. I didn't like the thought of Megaera leading them into battle.

"Get your men! We've got invaders!" I didn't wait to see what he did, because Second Squad was already moving. The harbor was close enough that advancing on foot was faster than saddling up. Besides, there wouldn't be enough room to maneuver in the confined area, and we'd lose mounts we had too few of anyway.

Second Squad followed me in good order. I didn't bother to count the ships filling the harbor or the boats that were heading shoreward. Counting didn't solve anything when you were attacked and had no place to retreat. The first boat reached the pier before First Squad did.

First Squad tore into the attackers, but another set of boats was headed toward the foot of the pier. If they landed there, they could trap First Squad between two Hamorian forces.

"Second Squad! To the boats!"

We managed to reach the rocky shore just as the first Hamorians scrambled from the water. The leading warrior charged me with his oversized iron bar. I just stepped inside and cut his calf all the way to the bone and his neck with the other blade.

After that, it was slash and protect.

Then fire—white wizard-fire—flared from somewhere.

I took advantage of that to cut another Hamorian throat and disable two more. So did my guards.

More wizard fire flared across the sky.

Then the winds began to howl, and the skies blackened. Instantly, or so it seemed. Lightnings flashed out of the clouds. I hoped they were hitting the Hamorian ships, but we weren't looking that way, and the Hamorians who were died under our blades.

"Waterspouts! Frigging waterspouts!"

I didn't look for those, either. "Second squad, toward the water!"

The Hamorians began to panic.

Before long we held the shore to the east of the pier, and the only Hamorians nearby were wounded or stumbling eastward.

"Second Squad! Reform on me!"

Only then did I study the harbor. The water was filled with high and choppy waves, and debris was everywhere. Three ships were enshrouded in flames. A fourth was beached hard on the shingle to the east. I didn't see anyone alive on it, but there were bodies tangled in twisted and torn rigging and ropes.

Then, I turned to the pier. The guards of First Squad had been split by the ferocity of the initial attack and by the numbers, but they had reformed into smaller groups. They were standing. I didn't see any Hamorians. I also didn't see Creslin or Megaera.

"Second Squad! Hold! Dispatch anyone who doesn't surrender!"

I scrambled over and around bodies to get to the pier. Half the way toward the seaward end, I found them. Megaera lay on the blood-smeared stones of the pier, gashes in her leathers. Creslin lay beside her, an arrow through his right shoulder. One hand still held a blade. The other was thrown out, as if to protect Megaera. Both were breathing.

Creslin was more slightly built than I recalled, so wiry that he was almost gaunt. He looked like a youth, almost childlike, helpless. Despite the blood on her leathers and face, Megaera looked young, too, without the anger that sometimes seemed to fuel every movement she made. For the briefest moment, I looked from the two, looking young and bloody, and somehow innocent, to the carnage around them. There were scores of mangled bodies, and burning and sunken ships. Ashes rained across the pier, along with the smoke from the burning schooner that had begun to sink.

Hyel hurried toward me, followed by four litter bearers, two of his men and two guards.

"They're alive, but . . . they'll need the healers," I told him. "We'll need to round up the survivors. Some of them are swimming ashore." I glanced around. "Most of your men are on the west side of the pier. You take that area. The Guards will take the east."

Hyel nodded. "We'll do it. The lookouts say that there aren't any more ships near."

That was some help.

Once we finally captured all the surviving Hamorians and had them under guard, I headed back to the keep.

I trudged up the steps, only to have one of the Montgren troopers approach and bow.

"Guard Captain, the mage and Captain Hyel are waiting for you in the hall."

"Thank you." I wiped the second short sword clean and sheathed it.

Even before I stepped into the hall, Klerris moved forward. Hyel followed.

"How are they?"

"Lydya is working with them. They'll live." Klerris glanced at me and then Hyel. "You two are in charge for now."

I looked back at the mage. "Us?"

"Who else? Lydya and I will be busy trying to patch up bodies and spirits. You two get to take care of everything else."

It was pitch-dark before I felt like I could stop, and I'd made a last trip down to the pier and back because I'd posted guards on the grounded Hamorian vessel. I didn't want the ship looted. There was potentially too much on her that we could use.

"It's hard to believe, isn't it?" Hyel was sitting on the topmost step leading into the keep. "Sit down. You could use a moment to catch your breath."

"Just for a bit." I did sit down, but on the other side of the wide step, where I could lean back against the stone of the walls. "What's hard to believe?"

"People. You get two young leaders, and they start trying to make a better place for people who don't have much hope or anywhere to go, and everyone wants to stop them."

I didn't find that hard to believe. I'd already seen enough of that as a Westwind guard.

"You don't agree?" He raised his eyebrows.

I laughed. The sound came out bitter. "I do agree, but I don't find it hard to believe. People are like that."

He gestured to the north, his arm taking in the small harbor and the last embers of the grounded and burning sloop. "And all this? That's not hard to believe?"

"It's real, Hyel."

"How could two people—even if they are wizards—create such . . ."

"Chaos?" I laughed again. "Creslin's a mage, and she's a white witch. They both have to prove their worth. To the world and to each other." Proving it to each other might be the hardest part, I thought. "We all have to prove things." I stood. "I need to check on the wounded and see what changes we'll need in the duty rosters."

Hyel grinned crookedly, uneasily, as he rose from the step. "What do you have to prove, Shierra?"

"Tell me what you have to prove, Hyel, and then I'll tell you." I started to turn.

His long-fingered hand touched my shoulder. Gently.

"Yes?"

His eyes met mine. "I have to prove . . . that I was sent here wrongfully. I have to prove that I'm not a coward or a bully."

"What if you were sent here rightfully, but you're not the same man that you once were?"

His lips quirked. "You ask questions no one else does."

"I did not mean to say—"

"You didn't, Shierra. I always learn something when I'm with you." He smiled. "You'd better check those rosters."

I could have avoided Hyel's question. He wouldn't have pressed me again. He'd answered my question and not demanded my answer. After a moment, I managed a smile. "I have to prove that I didn't make a mistake in choosing to come here. I have to prove that I've escaped an image."

"The image of a Westwind Guard?"

"Partly."

He nodded, but didn't press. This time, I wasn't ready to say more. "Until tomorrow, Hyel."

"Good night, Shierra."

XVI

Over the next three eightdays, something changed between Creslin and Megaera. I didn't know what, or how, but after they recovered, they both slept at the Black Holding, and occasionally they held hands. They still bickered, but most of the bitterness had vanished.

Our meetings didn't have the edginess that they had once had. Not that there weren't problems and more problems.

A second tax notice came from the Duke of Montgren, and there was no pay chest, either, although the Duke had promised them for a year.

"What about the cargo?" I asked, looking around the table in the keep hall.

"It's paid for," snapped Creslin.

"Did you have to pay, since the ship is the Duke's?" I didn't understand why that was necessary, since Creslin and Megaera were his Regents.

"The captain's acting as a consignment agent. If he doesn't get paid now, when would we get another shipment of goods? Would anyone else trade with us?" He went on, pointing out how few wanted to trade with such an out-of-the-way place.

"So they're gouging the darkness out of us?" asked Hyel.

"That's why we need to refit the Hamorian ships for our own trading."

"We can't afford to refit one ship, let alone others," observed Megaera.

"We can't afford not to," snapped Creslin.

Then after a few more words, he stood and strode out. Megaera rose. "He's worried."

After the others left, Hyel looked to me. "He's acting like we're idiots."

"Sometimes we are," I pointed out. "He's paid for most everything we have personally, and he doesn't have much left."

"What about Megaera's sister, the Tyrant? At least, the Marshall sent you and equipment and supplies. The Tyrant hasn't sent anything. Neither has the Duke."

Why hadn't the Tyrant sent anything? Sarronnyn was rich enough to spare a shipload of supplies now and again. Did Megaera's sister hate her that much? Or did she regard her as a threat? How could Recluce ever threaten Sarronnyn?

XVII

Whether it was the result of Creslin calling the storms against the Hamorians or something else, I didn't know, and no one said, but the weather changed. Day after day, the clouds rolled in from the northwest, and the rains lashed Recluce. Fields began to wash out, and we kept having to repair our few roads. No one had ever thought about so much rain on a desert isle, and most of the roofs leaked. After nearly three eightdays, the worst passed, but we still got more rain than the isle had gotten before.

Megaera, once she had fully recovered from her injuries, and once we did not have to deal with rain falling in sheets, continued her sparring and working with me on improving her blade skills. One morning she did not bring her practice blade. Instead, she sat on one of the benches in the courtyard and motioned for me to sit beside her. Her face was somber.

"Shierra . . . something has happened . . ."

What? It couldn't have been Creslin, or Megaera would have been far more distraught. It couldn't have been Hyel, because I'd seen him a few moments before, and enjoyed his smile.

"Creslin . . . he sensed something last night. Something has happened at Westwind. He doesn't know what it is, but . . . it's likely that the Marshall and Marshalle are dead."

"Dead? What about . . . all the others?"

Her fingers rested on my wrist, lightly. "We don't know. We don't have any way of knowing, but we thought you should know what we know. You're the senior Westwind guard here. Creslin and I . . . we thought that perhaps you could tell the guards that you've had word of hard times at Westwind, and that the Marshall and Marshalle have been hurt, but that you don't know more than that."

I found myself nodding, even as I wondered about Fiera. Had she been hurt? Or killed? Would I ever know, with Westwind thousands of kays away?

"I'm sorry, Shierra." Megaera's voice was soft. "I know you have a sister . . ."

For some reason, hearing that, I had to swallow, and I found myself thinking of Megaera as much as Fiera. How could her sister have been so cruel to her?

After Megaera departed, I did gather the squads, and I told them something similar to what she had suggested.

But the eightdays passed, and we heard nothing.

I kept wondering about Fiera. Was she all right? Would I ever hear? Would I ever know?

Then, one morning at the keep, as Hyel and I waited for the Regents, Creslin burst through the door. "There's a coaster porting." He hurried past us and down the steps to the hill road that led to the pier.

Hyel looked at me. Then we both followed.

"That's a Westwind banner below the ensign," I told Hyel. "That's why he's upset."

"Upset?"

I didn't try to explain, not while trying to catch up with Creslin. "We're going to have more guards." Would Fiera be there? If she weren't, could someone tell me about her?

"More—?" Hyel groaned as he hurried beside me.

"Don't groan so loudly."

We finally caught up with Creslin as the coaster eased up to the pier and cast out lines.

"Do you want to explain?" asked Hyel.

Creslin pointed to the Westwind guards ranked on the deck.

"I still—" Hyel didn't understand.

"I hope they aren't all that's left," I said. Please let Fiera be there . . . or alive and well somewhere.

"The Marshall's dead. Llyse is dead, and Ryessa has been moving troops eastward into the Westhorns," Creslin said.

I hadn't heard about the Sarronnese troops. I wondered how he knew, but perhaps the mages or the trading captains had told him.

"If Westwind still existed, there wouldn't be three squads coming to Recluce." His words were hard.

Once the coaster was secured to the pier, the gangway came down, and a blond guard—a squad leader—stepped down and onto the pier.

My heart almost stopped. Fiera! But I had to take her report as she stepped past Hyel and Creslin and stopped before me.

"Squad Leader Fiera reporting."

"Report."

"Three full squads. Also ten walking wounded, five permanently disabled, and twenty consorts and children. Three deaths since embarkation in Rulyarth. We also bring some supplies, weapons, and tools . . . and what is left of the Westwind treasury."

Hard as it was, I replied. "Report accepted, Squad Leader." I turned. "May I present you to Regent Creslin? Squad Leader Fiera."

Creslin did not speak for a moment. He and Fiera locked eyes. The last time they had met, she had kissed him, and now everything was different.

Then he nodded solemnly. "Honor bright, Squad Leader. You have paid a great price, and great is the honor you bestow upon us through your presence. Few have paid a higher price than you . . ." When he finished, his eyes were bright, although his voice was firm.

So were Fiera's, but her voice was hard. "Will you accept the presentation of your heritage, Your Grace? For you are all that remains of the glory and power of Westwind."

"I can do no less, and I will accept it in the spirit in which it is offered." Creslin looked directly into her eyes and lowered his voice. "But never would I have wished this. Even long ago, I wished otherwise." He tightened his lips.

Even I felt the agony within him.

"We know that, Your Grace." Fiera swallowed, and the tears oozed from the corners of her eyes. "By your leave, Regent?"

"The keep is yours, Squad Leader, as is all that we have. We are in your debt, as am I, in the angels', and in the Legend's."

"And we in yours, Regent." Fiera's voice was hard as granite or black stone, but the tears still flowed.

"Form up!" I ordered, as much to spare Fiera as for anything. "On the pier."

"What was all that about?" Hyel asked Creslin.

Whatever Creslin said, it would not explain half of what had happened, nor should it.

Carts had already begun to arrive. They had to have been sent by Megaera, and at that moment my heart went out to both my sister and to Megaera, for both suffered, and would suffer, and neither was at fault. Nor was Creslin.

With all the need to accommodate the unexpected additional guards, consorts, and children, I could not find a time when Fiera was alone until well past sunset.

I watched as she slipped out the front entrance of the keep and began to walk down the road. I did not know what she had in mind, but I had to reach her.

Following her, I did not speak until we were well away.

"Fiera . . . ?"

She did not respond.

I caught up with her. "I wanted to talk to you, but not . . . not with everyone around."

She stopped in the middle of the rutted road, under a cloudy and starless sky.

"Why?" she asked. "Why did it have to happen this way?"

"You gave him his future. You gave him what will save us all," I told her, and I knew it was true. I also knew that, at that moment, it didn't matter to her.

She said nothing.

"Fiera . . . ?"

"What?" The single word was almost snapped. "I suppose you have some great suggestion. Or some reason why everything will be wonderful."

"No. I don't. I don't have any answers. For you or for me. Or for us." I rushed on. "I know I didn't do everything right, and I know what I did must have hurt you. I didn't mean it that way. I only wanted to help . . ." I swallowed. "I love you, and you are my sister, and you always will be."

We both cried, and held each other.

There were other words, but they were ours and for us alone.

XVIII

Late that night, I sat on the front steps of the keep. Fiera was sleeping, if fitfully, and Megaera and Creslin doubtless had their problems, and I . . . I had my sister . . . if I could keep her, if I could avoid interfering too much.

"Are you all right?" Hyel stood in the doorway of the keep.

"I'm fine."

He just looked at me with those deep gray eyes, then sat down beside me. For a long time, he said nothing. Finally, he reached out and took my hand. Gently.

Love is as much about wisdom as lust and longing. Fiera had loved Creslin, not wisely, but well, and out of that love, she had brought him the tools to build a kingdom. He would never forget, for he was not the kind who could or would, but he loved Megaera. So he would offer all the honors and respect he could to Fiera, but they would not be love.

Megaera had loved her sister, also not wisely, but well, while I had loved my sister wisely, carefully, I had not shown that that love, nor had the Tyrant, I thought. Unlike the Tyrant, who would never show any love to her sister, I'd been given the chance to let Fiera know what I felt, and I, for once, had been brave enough to take it.

As for the future, I could only hope that, in time, Fiera would find someone who matched her, as Creslin and Megaera had found each other, as Hyel and I might.

The Opposite of Pomegranates

By Marissa K. Lingen

The real difference between humans and fey is not the magic: there are human sorcerers, so thick on the ground some places you can hardly take a step without kicking one. (I do not advocate kicking sorcerers.) It isn't that we were born outside and they were born (or hatched or constructed) under *there*. Or maybe that is the difference, but not the crux of it, like saying a Russian is different from a Brazilian because their houses are far apart. There's always something else that's the heart of the matter.

And something else with the fey comes down to this: they only know how to make bargains. My bowl of milk for my housecleaning. Your freedom for your pot of gold. My answer to a riddle for your spell—but I get ahead of myself.

When my parents were young—and my parents were young for four hundred years under the hill—the fey got the notion that they might breed two changelings together and get from the continuing union a seemingly endless stream of changelings. Or at least an easier stream of changelings than the ones they'd gotten stealing from human cradles.

After her twenty-third month of pregnancy, my mother decided that this was not, in fact, the solution to anyone's problems. She was quite firm on that point. The Queen of Air and Darkness herself cowered when my mother yelled that day. They let her out on the hillside to finish the job in a mere three more months. In Victorian Ireland. With no money nor husband nor kin nearer than her nine-times-great-nieces, who were in Estonia. My mother spoke neither English nor Gaelic.

I'd like to attribute that lapse to them being fey, but humans sometimes turn out clueless, too.

Mother really wasn't sure which was worse: making her way as a single parent in *that* place and time or throwing her lot and mine back in with the fey. They decided not to give her a choice. After all, the point of breeding changelings had been to get more changelings. So back we came, both of us howling and red in the face.

I am told that I howled for three days running. I am told that I smiled only for three people: my mother, a fire elemental called Kezhzh, and the yeti who ended up raising me, a sweet soul named Alits. (Alits, in our 120 years together, has shared many theories of gender with me. None of them has impinged even slightly on Alits's own experience of the subject. I was sixteen before I understood that the gendered pronouns existed.)

Alits raised me in part because Alits was the only one who could do it without ear protection for the first two years, and in part because my mother had gone entirely mad. When she stopped howling, a few hours after being brought underhill, she wouldn't stop *smiling*. You can't leave a baby with someone like that. Even the fey know that much. So it was off to Alits's place for me, with tiny little mittens and a tiny little squirrel-fur hood.

They allowed my father to visit on alternate Thursdays, when they could remember it was a Thursday in the first place. Thursday was not an important concept to the High Sidhe. Kezhzh was allowed to visit whenever he could stand the cold, which was more often than alternate fuzzy Thursdays. They taught me how to negotiate with a brownie and how to call tomten and which oceans were suitable for selkies.

They never taught me how to go outside.

It wasn't for lack of asking—there was about a decade when I asked Alits every single day. It didn't feel like a decade to me, but it must have to Alits. Finally I decided that Alits had won the battle of wills, and I would have to do something else to win the war.

But it turned out Alits had gotten there before me, too. I was a favored changeling, small and winsome, and I bargained for knowledge easily, for favors, for treats and tricks and games. I cajoled my way into more than one place I shouldn't have been, and there was always Alits's looming furry presence to bail me out if I got into trouble. But that same looming furry presence made sure I was not going anywhere outside.

Finally luck was with me. I saw a rock sprite caught in a mite trap. He was a bright purple, veined with white; at first I thought that was his fury at the trap, but it turned out he was that color all the time.

"Want some help getting out of there?" I asked casually.

"*No!*" snapped the rock sprite. "Stay away from me, changeling! I do not accept your help!" He bared little white teeth at me, ready to snap if I came closer.

I shrugged and settled on the hill next to him. "Suit yourself." I watched him struggle. He glared. "I could make that go a lot faster, you know."

"I know, Alits taught you," he said, stopping to rest and think. "But I don't care to owe you a favor for it."

I shrugged again. He started to chant a spell. I whistled tunelessly.

"*Do* you *mind*?"

"Not at all," I said. "I was just thinking of the song I was going to sing tonight."

"I hope you sing better than you whistle," he said.

"I do. I'm singing at the revel Bald Obix is throwing. They're having all kinds of music and spell contests and dancing—of course dancing—and Alits is making banana enchiladas." Alits's banana enchiladas, with molé sauce and cherries, wrapped in flattened fairy cakes, are famous.

"Oh, yeah?" said the rock sprite. He was trying to feign disinterest, but I had the equivalent of five years of being thirteen. I can do disinterest like nobody's business. He didn't even seem to notice that he'd freed himself from the trap.

"Yeah," I said. "It's too bad you won't be able to be there. It's really something to see."

"Maybe I'll stop by," he said.

"Oh, I don't know. They have a door troll who'll ask you a riddle. If you don't know the answer, he won't let you in."

"I'm good at riddles," said the rock sprite.

I gave him my best skeptical look.

"How tough are troll riddles anyway?"

"The troll didn't make up the riddle," I said. "Canufiel the Brown made up the riddle."

The rock sprite looked daunted, and rightly so. You don't survive long as a High Sidhe if you can't ask killer riddles. Sometimes literally.

"I'll tell you the answer, though," I said.

The rock sprite's little purple features twisted. "For what?"

"Oh, nothing much, really," I said. "You know how generous we humans are."

He looked even more suspicious. "Tell me."

"All I want to know is how to open a door in the hill."

"Oh, no," he said hastily. "Oh, no, no no no. Alits would *kill* me."

"Alits is a big teddy bear," I said. "And Alits would never have to know."

"Forget it," he said. "Just forget it. I can make you a lovely necklace, charmed to give you the voice of a bard—"

"Bards don't know when to shut up," I said.

"To give you the seeming of any creature underhill."

"I got bored with shapeshifter games when I was a toddler. They always smell like themselves."

"To let you fly."

I rolled my eyes.

"Anything!" he screamed. "Anything but that! If Alits wanted you to leave the underhill, Alits would have taught you how! Alits has big furry white arms for ripping rock sprites to bits! Alits has pointy vicious ivory teeth for rending rock sprites' crunchy flesh from their bones! Alits has—"

"Alits has no idea that you're talking to me," I pointed out.

When he didn't immediately reply, I knew I had him.

So I whispered the answer to the riddles, and the rock sprite— glancing furtively around him—talked his way around the spell for me. They have a kind of code worked out, so that spells can be taught without being cast. This is particularly useful for battle magics. It also comes in handy when you don't particularly want to shout about what spell you're learning.

I would have to wait for the right time to open the door to the upper world. The rock sprite was a nuisance at the party, but no one knew I'd let him in, and I certainly wasn't going to tell them. He stayed well clear of me, too—not wanting Alits to have any reason to question him (or rip his arms off) when I went above, I suppose.

I finally got my chance when one of the Puck's cousins, a straggle-haired beauty called Fee, went missing. Or rather, when everyone noticed she was missing; she had been gone at least a month. No one could be sure. But they all turned out in force to find her. They suspected foul play. So did I, but what I suspected even more strongly is that they would all be distracted and wouldn't notice one more excursion outside, more or less.

I had just finished drawing the first spiral in silver dust when the rock sprite appeared. He was in such a hurry he had lost his hat. I had never seen a sprite without a hat. "Stop! Stop it! Now is not the time!"

"Now is the *perfect* time," I said, adding the first of the five runes. "Everyone is distracted."

"They'll be convinced that whoever took Fee took you, too!"

"So?" I said, drawing the second rune. "I'll be back before they notice, and if they did notice, I'd just explain to them that I wasn't abducted. End of story."

"You've never been out on the surface before, and you're not going alone!" The rock sprite leapt into the middle of my spell and spread its short, squatty limbs as far as it could reach. I sniffed and continued with the third rune. When the spell was complete, I said the word of power. The rock sprite squeaked in annoyance, but the hill fell away beneath him, and a door to the outside glowed.

He picked himself up and stood, arms akimbo, in the opening. "Go back, changeling!"

"Back? I'll go through you if I have to."

"Oh, yeah?" said the rock sprite. "Awfully tough for a human, aren't you?"

"You ready to find out?"

He deflated suddenly and mumbled something I couldn't make out.

"What was that?"

"I said, let me come with you."

I stared down at him. "I don't need a babysitter."

"It would make me feel better. Then I might have some chance of throwing myself on Alits's mercy and living through all this."

"I told you, she won't find out."

"I'll go with you," said the rock sprite in a slightly desperate voice. "Let me go with you."

If I stuck around arguing much longer, some human was going to notice a door out from under the hill, or the spell would shut down, or something. "Yeah, all right, come on," I said.

I'm not sure what I expected of the outside. Here's what I got: the colors are predictable, mostly. Under the hill, we have Sidhe ladies with eyes green as grass, but more often than not, we don't have *grass* green as grass. Things outside stay where you put them, or if they don't, you can see what happens to them instead.

Outside, things made sense in ways I didn't know I'd been missing.

"How strange," I said aloud.

"Yes, isn't it?" said the rock sprite. "And now you've seen the outside. Come on, then, back we go."

"You go ahead if you want," I said. "I'm going exploring."

"Outside isn't like under the hill!" protested the rock sprite. "You can't just *go exploring*!"

"Relax," I said. "I have a knife in my boots and an entire yeti's arsenal of defensive spells at my fingertips. What more could I need?"

Scuttling after me, the rock sprite did not reply.

We walked down a dusty road made of a drab, smelly black material. The rock sprite tried to stay in the grass, chattering at the human machines that passed us. I had no idea how much time had passed—not because it felt variable, but because it felt solid for the first time in my life—when we saw human buildings. The ones with labels said they were a bank, a church, and a diner.

"I'm hungry, sprite," I said. "You hide in the bushes. I'm going into that diner."

"Oh, no," moaned the rock sprite. "No, no, you *can't*. Really really. Alits will—"

"Kill you. You've said that part. Haven't I promised to protect you from Alits? Are you doubting my oath, sprite?"

"It's only effective if you stick around to fulfill it," said the sprite.

It dawned on me what he was saying. "Wait, so if I eat something up here—"

"Some things are fine," said the sprite hastily. "Want an apple? We can get you an apple. Or some nice cookies. Some humans do okay with cookies. The disir trained—"

"What *can't* I have?"

The rock sprite, intelligently, said nothing.

"It could be pomegranates," I mused, keeping a sharp eye on his face. "But no, pomegranates kept Persephone Underhill, not above ground."

"Hades is certainly further down than Underhill," the rock sprite sniffed. But he looked nervous.

"Not a pomegranate, then. But something related to a pomegranate. Another red fruit? No, no." I chewed on my lip. "Magic doesn't work that way. It's—the opposite of a pomegranate."

The rock sprite closed his eyes. I knew I was right. But what was the opposite of a pomegranate? What was he sure they would have in a human diner? I had never been to one, of course, but the Daughters of Ran had had a party with a diner theme a few months back, or maybe it was years. Milkshakes, burgers, fruit pies, and . . .

"French fries," I said aloud. Of course. Pomegranates grew out in the air, red and juicy and seeded and sweet. Potatoes grew under the ground, white and starchy and solid. And if Persephone had given some of her aboveground sweetness to the underworld with the pomegranate . . . yes.

I marched into the diner, the rock sprite's wail dopplering after me. I fended off a few spells from him absentmindedly. He didn't dare follow me in where my kind would see him, but he felt it necessary to put up some resistance.

"I'd like an order of French fries, please," I told the first person I encountered.

"Sure, hon," she said. "Let's just get you a table first, huh? And then your waitress can take your order."

Sheepishly, I slid into the booth she had indicated. When the waitress came, I repeated myself.

"You want something to drink with that?" said the waitress.

The rock sprite pressed his nose against the glass next to my table. I looked away. "Just water. Thanks."

"French fries and some water. Got it." She walked away shaking her head and muttering, "Kids."

The sprite kept bobbing outside the window. I could tell he was trying not to call attention to himself, but he was probably doing more harm than good, popping up and down.

The French fries were ready almost immediately. The waitress plunked them down in a red plastic basket with a layer of red-and-white waxed paper lining it. They were golden and salty and smelled so good. The rock sprite's little purple head bounced up just in time to see me bite the first one in half. He rattled down the window in despair.

I chewed slowly to make it last. And rightly so: I was only going to have one. Persephone got stuck with a whole season away from home. I just wanted a vacation every year, with the chance to get to know humans a bit better.

I slid out of the diner booth.

"One fry?" demanded the waitress. "One lousy fry?"

I took a gulp of the water to mollify her.

It didn't appear to work. "What's wrong with our fries?"

"Nothing is wrong. It was excellent. But I must return to the underworld for most of the year."

She gaped at me. Finally she found solid ground: "Don't think you can get out of paying for them. There was nothing wrong with those fries."

I handed her a gold coin and walked out. The sprite was having paroxysms of delight on the sidewalk. "You changed your mind!"

I snorted. "You didn't know what my mind was to begin with. I didn't ever mean to stay here. So you can set your mind at ease: I'll go home. I just want to look around."

"Good," said the rock sprite, "because I think we have someone else to take care of here. Oh *my*."

"Who? What?" I said.

He pointed straight ahead, barely able to keep his mouth closed. And there in the town square, pouting up a granite storm, was our missing Fee.

"Well, I'll be," I said. The rock sprite said nothing. I looked down at him. He was practically drooling gravel.

"She's so beautiful!" he breathed.

"She's been turned into a granite statue, in case you hadn't noticed."

"I know! She used to be squishy, but now—" He sighed happily.

I shook my head. Squishy. "I came with defensive spells. I don't know how to fix this. We can go back and tell Alits where she is, and then—"

"I don't want to leave her!" said the rock sprite.

"It'll just be until we can find someone to fetch her. Someone with better spells. What's wrong with her, anyway?"

The rock sprite scampered forward—precipitously, I thought, considering that we didn't know what had caused her to turn to stone in the first place. I could see why he had gotten caught in the trap when I found him. "Be careful," I called after him, feeling like Alits.

"It's a trap," he called back. "Turns things to stone. Looks old—a hundred years or more."

I opened my mouth and closed it again. Of course: he was already stone. "What can you do about it?"

He hopped back to me. It had been a miserable trip for the little beast from beginning to end. "Nothing, nothing at all. But I don't want to leave her alone! What if someone—what if they take her away somewhere? We'd never find her!"

I sighed. "I don't know how to make rock into flesh, sprite. I just don't. So unless you've got a better idea—"

"Into flesh!" His face twisted. "There's no need to be nasty."

"So . . . all you want is that she should be able to move and talk again?" I chewed on my lip. "I think I can do that."

I had a spell in my pack to animate things. I'd meant it for transportation or something of the sort, but it would do for a stoned cousin of the Puck. I thought the rock sprite would die of rapture on the spot when the statue shook her granite locks and pouted quizzically down at us.

He climbed up on her shoulder. She kissed him soundly. I thought *I* deserved a bit of thanks as well, but as I wasn't interested in kissing her, I didn't say anything about it. In fact, I tried to ignore them for most of the way home. Next time you hear someone say, "I'm not made of stone," for heaven's sake, be glad.

Everyone was glad to see Fee, though a little taken aback by her stony appearance and her diminutive new paramour. Not everyone was distracted enough by her return not to notice who had brought her back.

"You've been outside," said Alits. "And you've had human food."

I scuffed my toe on the ground and waited for the explosion. It never came.

"I wish you hadn't."

"I'm glad I did," I said. "I needed to see where I come from. I needed to see how my people live. And—" I grinned. "It was kind of fun. And I *did* bring Fee back."

"I suppose you think that makes it worth it?"

"Yes!"

"You are a stubborn little beast, do you know that?" said Alits fondly.

"I can't help it. It's how I was raised."

Alits heaved a great sigh. "You're coming home sometimes, aren't you?"

"I only had one fry," I said. "That's a month on the surface and eleven months with you every year."

"I would miss you if you were gone."

"I know, Alits." I paused. "You could come with me. It could be a surface holiday for us. We could go camping. Kezhzh could roast the marshmallows."

Alits snorted and then laughed against her will. I hesitated but went on: "I wouldn't feel comfortable up there all the time. The grass stays the same color, and the rocks never teach you new spells."

Alits was too happy to tear the sprite to bits after that. Really, it worked out for all of us.

As Black as Hell

By John Lambshead

"For I have sworn thee fair and thought thee bright, who art as black as hell, as dark as night."

—Sonnet 147, William Shakespeare

Gaston was used to waiting. The unofficial motto of the British Army was "hurry up and wait." Gaston had reached the rank of sergeant in the 2nd Battalion, the Parachute Regiment—the Queen's own Royal goon squad, not bad for the illegitimate son of a Charing Cross streetwalker. He had joined up after his mother's pimp had beaten her senseless with a red-hot coat hanger. Gaston had taken a white-hot poker to the pimp in retaliation. The local police had found the incident hilarious but a kindly bobby had suggested that Gaston should join the Queen's colors for a while to keep him out of circulation. The pimp was connected to one of the more vicious Kosovan white slaver gangs that imported teenage girls for the sex trade in Central London.

In Afghanistan, Gaston had come across something much older and far more dangerous than the Taliban, something that stalked and killed his section, one by one. Gaston had survived and even fought back. The Commission team that finally put down the beast had been impressed enough to recommend that the soldier be recruited. His mother was dead by then so Gaston was footloose and free. He was quietly discharged from the ranks on health grounds and disappeared into the Commission's tender arms.

Gaston sat on the floor in the back of a battered van with three others. "For Christ's sake stop drumming your fingers, MacDowell," he said.

"Sorry, Sarge," MacDowell said. He guiltily placed his hand in his lap.

Gaston closed his eyes again. The one thing a soldier learnt was to sleep when he could. You never knew when the chance might come again. The spearmen who followed Achilles knew this, as did the legionnaires who marched behind the Caesars. The important things never change.

The mobile vibrated in Gaston's pocket. He pulled it out and checked the message. It read simply "She's in." "Okay, boys," said Gaston. "It's on." He would have preferred to wait for daylight to deal with a Code Z but his orders were precise.

The van might have looked old and battered but the side door slid back in well-oiled silence. The four men debussed and moved purposely toward the cottage carrying bulky equipment. Two of them moved to the front door while the others knelt down in the garden. Gaston inserted a device into the door lock. A light flashed on the equipment, briefly illuminating black body armor, topped by a helmet with a reinforced visor.

The door lock opened with a noticeable click and the men froze, listening. When nothing happened, they pushed open the door and crept inside. Inside, the cottage was dark. The men opened the doors to each room with the barrels of bulky guns, scanning each room before entering. They moved confidently and silently through the darkened rooms, using the light-enhancement technology in their visors.

Eventually, they had searched all the ground floor without finding their quarry so they clustered around the base of the narrow staircase. Gaston silently designated an order by pointing at each man and indicating a number with his fingers. The men filed up the stairs behind Gaston in the indicated sequence, keeping one meter's distance apart.

Gaston stepped on a loose board that creaked underfoot. All the men stopped and waited but the cottage remained dark and silent.

Finally, they started moving again but each of the following men stepped carefully over the treacherous stair.

They stopped at the first bedroom door on the top landing and repeated their room-opening ritual. The door was ajar. Gaston and a partner stood each side of the door and pushed it fully open with their gun muzzles. When there was no reaction, they moved inside, the second two members of the team taking their place at the entrance.

The room was empty except for some basic furniture. The bed was solid and the wardrobe door open, so there was no possible hiding place. Gaston started to back out when, for some odd reason, the second team member looked up.

Chaos theory insists that a single flap of a butterfly's wing in China can change the direction of a hurricane in the West Indies, sparing one island to devastate another. This may or may not be true. Certainly Chinese butterflies continue to irresponsibly flap, giving absolutely no thought to the welfare of their relatives in the Americas.

Human beings consider themselves to be inestimably superior to mere butterflies because they have created opera, organic vegetables, and *The Oprah Winfrey Show*, but in terms of irresponsible body movements they may not have advanced much further than the Lepidoptera.

The second team member looked up, changing several lives. It certainly changed his own life. Orange streetlight leaking through the window gently illuminated a lady all in black, crouching against the ceiling. She wore black leather trousers and jacket like a biker babe. Long black curly hair trailed down over her face. Her face was starkly North European pale. She crouched, hands and feet against the roof as if gravity were reversed.

The woman dropped down on the team member before he could move. Somehow, she twisted in mid-air so that she dropped astride him as he fell to the floor. She grabbed his helmet with both hands and jerked hard. His neck broke with a noticeable crack.

Gaston hit her hard across the shoulders with his gun, driving her back. She hissed at him, opening her mouth to show impossibly long fangs. There was a great flash and crack of discharging capacitors that filled the room with indigo light and ozone. Invisible ultraviolet raked the woman's face causing her to moan in agony. The whine of recharging capacitors filled the room with high-pitched sound. As she dropped, disoriented onto her knees, Gaston stepped up to her. He had not fired yet. He placed his gun muzzle directly against her face and discharged it. The flash flipped the woman onto her back.

"Quickly, get the restraints on." Gaston spoke for the first time since they had entered the cottage. Working with polished speed, the men slapped heavy silvered restraints around her wrists and ankles. One of the team pulled a thick leather bag over her head and fastened it at the neck.

A team member knelt to check the pulse of the man down on the ground. "He's dead."

Gaston unclipped a mobile phone and triggered a number. "Send a cleanup crew. We got her. We have one friendly casualty, terminal."

The woman on the floor sat up.

A soldier walked over to her. "You killed Frank, you bitch." He kicked her in the face, as hard as he could.

"There's the Code Z," said Farley. "She's already had the preliminary treatment. Only the oaths are left."

"What do we know about her?" asked Jameson.

Farley opened a file. "We know she has been using the name Karla. We are not sure who she really is or how old she is. She can still pass as human well enough to function to a limited degree within human society. She has made at least five kills in the red-light zones. Three clients and two prostitutes have been drained to our certain knowledge over the last two years. Given that she would need regular meals, the low frequency of deaths must mean that she mostly stops short of a kill. That suggests she hasn't yet descended into animal irrationality. Frankly, I never thought that R&D would ever find a suitable candidate. It certainly took them long enough."

Jameson did not comment. Code Zs became more dangerous as they aged. Young suckers were more malleable but the old ones were the real prize for the experiment. Mental deterioration set in past a certain age though. That was why immortal Code Zs did not overrun the world. Some became twisted obsessive maniacs that were too damn dangerous to do anything but destroy—if you could. Most shut down mentally and retreated into nonsentience to become the basis for monster and demon legends.

The two men stood behind a shield of one-way armored glass. The woman in black leather was chained to a heavy steel chair that was itself bolted to a concrete floor, like it was in some demented dentist's surgery. She sat with unnatural stillness.

The interrogator pulled the hood off her head. She didn't move but blinked in the bright, artificial lights, watching him.

"Can you understand me?" the interrogator said.

She looked at him without speaking. The man sighed.

He raised his hand and a guard in body armor walked around him and pointed a weapon at her torso. It looked like an assault rifle but had a much thicker barrel and magazine.

"That is a model YR03 rail gun. The electromagnetic coils accelerate a steel-cored wooden bolt up to two hundred miles an hour. At this range it will punch clean through you."

She still did not respond so he spoke again. "You are useless to me if you refuse to cooperate or you are too far gone to comprehend instructions, and we might as well use you to test the gun. So for the last time—can you understand me?"

"I understand you," she said. "What do you want?" Her accent was impossible to place, like one of those Eurotrash playboys who had lived in so many places that they had picked up something from all of them.

"That's better. We want you to do something for us," he said. "Are you willing to cooperate?"

"You need me for something?" She spoke without emotion.

"You will undergo a magic ritual. You will be required to do this voluntarily and to make the appropriate actions and response when prompted." The man looked at her intently.

"Yes." She licked her lips.

"If you do anything to interrupt or corrupt the ritual then you will be immediately destroyed without a second chance. Do you understand?"

"Yes," she said, again.

"You don't say much, do you?" the interrogator said. She did not answer.

The man got up and left the room but the guards remained watching her.

A woman approached carrying a bag of arcane objects and herbs.

"Witch," whispered Karla. For the first time she looked apprehensive.

The woman set out her magic paraphernalia on the floor. She lit scented candles and dimmed the lights. She put various herbs in a bowl and ground them up in Buxton spring water from a plastic bottle. Closing her eyes the witch recited an incantation, sitting cross-legged on Karla's right.

"I think this is your cue, old boy," said Farley.

"Yah." Jameson opened the door and walked in. He knelt down in front of Karla.

The witch paused while Jameson found a comfortable position, then she started the ceremony proper.

"Tied in chains that can't be seen,

"Tied in chains that can't be parted,

"Tied in chains that bind her being,

"Hecate, Queen of Night,

"Hear me, Hecate, hear my summoning,

"She offers body, mind and heart,

"Come, Hecate, and hear her promise,

"Bind her body, mind and heart,

"He is here and waits possession,

"An open channel for your purpose,

"On his head the geas falls,

"Hear her, Hecate, work the magic,

"Bind her body, mind and heart."

The witch chanted on and on until Karla's eyes dropped. Little will-o'-wisps danced in green and white and blue around the three and the candles flared. It looked like a clip from a soap advert dreamt up by a planner who had pushed too much white powder up his nose. Jameson couldn't move. The witch arched her back and sighed deeply.

"Hecate, Queen of Darkness, she comes, she comes."

Then she slumped forward as if exhausted. The candle flames subsided and the will-o'-wisps faded. There was a long pause and Jameson's hands and feet tingled with pins and needles as if the circulation had been temporarily cut off. The witch sat up and snapped her fingers, waking Karla up. She offered Karla a bowl. Yellow vapor flowed gently from it onto the floor.

"Drink and say, 'With all my heart I offer,'" said the witch.

Karla hesitated, took a sideways look at a guard, then bent her head forward.

The witch put the bowl to her lips and Karla drank. "With all my heart I offer," she said.

Jameson took the bowl in turn and drank. "I accept the responsibility."

The witch blew the candles out slowly and ceremonially. She said a small incantation as each flame was extinguished. When the last was out, she left the room. The guards followed and closed the door.

"Hello, Karla, my name is Jameson. Well, here we are, all alone."

Jameson had done some hairy things for the Commission but this was the most dangerous. He feigned casualness out of some personal sense of pride. There was no real point. He knew Karla could smell his emotions and he must reek of fear.

"We will soon have you out of all those chains." He chatted amiably and pointlessly as he worked.

He unclipped her ankles first, then her arms and wrists. Karla shot out of the chair and moved warily to the back of the room. Jameson stood still, turning to watch her. She tested the armored glass and walls with the heel of her hand. She hit like a pile driver but the room was reinforced. Then she tried the door without success.

"I have the door key." Jameson showed it to her then put it in his pocket.

She walked up to him and opened her mouth, revealing elongated canines. He wanted to run, oh boy, how he wanted to run, but he was locked in with her. There was nowhere to go. She stopped and looked puzzled.

"I feel your fear." She spoke to him for the first time. "I don't . . . I don't like the feeling."

He pulled a rail pistol from under his arm. It was a three-shot weapon that could be easily concealed as a last-ditch defence. Jameson's weapons instructor had always said that if you needed to fire a second time at rail-pistol range then you were already dead. So the three-shot magazine was a luxury.

Jameson held the pistol at arm's length pointed at her heart. "Pay careful attention, Karla. I will kill you if you feed on a human being. I will kill you unless you kill me first."

She made a halfhearted move toward him, claws and teeth extended, but hesitated. He slapped her across the face, causing her to recoil. "What have you done to me?" she whispered.

"I will kill you if you ever feed on a human being unless you kill me first. Do you understand me?"

She then did something utterly unexpected. She backed away from him to the corner, curled up into a ball, and shook. What was he supposed to do now? He squatted down beside her and put his hand on her shoulder. She shrank away.

"It's all right, Karla. It's all right," he said, softly stroking her arm. "You don't want to kill me, the magic won't let you, and I don't want to kill you. You will tell me when you need to feed and I will get you blood." After a while she stopped shaking.

"Come on, get up," he said, cajolingly.

"What have you done to me?" she repeated.

"You've been bound to me," he said gently. "The witch's magic has bound you. Come on, get up."

This was ridiculous; he was treating a man-killing monster as if she was a frightened woman. The trouble was that she looked like a frightened woman, albeit one with metallic green eyes. She allowed him to haul her to her feet.

"Now we are going to leave this place. You will stay close to me and remember: attack a human being and I will kill you."

Jameson unlocked the door and walked out. He didn't look around but he heard her follow him. They walked down a corridor and into another room full of people. Everyone in that room was a volunteer and everyone was scared. They were all dead if she went into a killing frenzy. Jameson held his pistol inconspicuously at his side. Karla looked in and opened her mouth, showing long teeth. She looked at Jameson and then backed out into the corridor.

"It's okay, Karla. Follow me." Jameson grabbed her hand and pulled her behind him. She looked rigidly ahead as he paraded her through the room. He took her to a door that opened out into a courtyard.

"Well, Karla. You passed the test. I guess the spell works, or at least it has so far."

Jameson walked to where his car was parked. The blue Jaguar two-seater sports was his beloved. He clicked the remote and the car chirruped a welcome, flashing its amber indicators. He opened the left-hand door. "Come on, Karla. Get in."

She shrank back. "Smelly, noisy."

Jameson held out his hand to her. "We have to use the car to go home. Come on, I've even fitted darkened windows," he said, encouragingly. Home was too far to walk and it was too late for the tube. The thought of taking her on a tube train was—disconcerting.

She climbed into the Jag and perched on the edge of the seat. Jameson got in the driver's side and clipped his belt on. He tried to attach hers but she stopped him and shook her head. "I guess the seat belt laws don't apply to you," he said. Actually, very little of the United Kingdom's legal code had been written with her in mind.

He started the engine. She seemed fascinated by the parade of lights that flicked across the dashboard. "Karla, have you been in a car before?"

She shook her head.

"I suppose the technology has only been around for a hundred years," said Jameson, with heavy, and wasted, irony.

He pulled out of the bay and up to the security barrier. His chipped identity card lifted the bar. At this time in the morning, even the streets of London were empty and the big Jag ate the miles. Jameson was a fast, confident driver and, as he got into the mood, he swung the car through the wet streets, letting the back step out as he used the accelerator to steer. He flicked the player on.

The Jag had a state-of-the-art MP3 system. Jameson downloaded the latest CDs into it every month. He had the system rigged to "*random mood selection.*" Theoretically, the system analyzed his driving and the weather to select appropriate tracks. Jameson also had set it to favor recent recordings.

Katie Melua's perfect, crystal-clear voice infiltrated their airspace.

"*Piece by piece is how I'll let go of you - Kiss by kiss, will leave my mind one at a time.*"

A hand gripped his thigh.

Karla gripped the roof handhold with one hand and his leg with the other. "Fast," she said. "Go fast."

Good grief, thought Jameson. Jaguar sports cars had a well-deserved reputation as totty magnets but this was ridiculous. But her enthusiasm was infectious, especially to a man who still possessed a strong boy-racer streak.

He pulled the gear selector down and across to drop it two gears and he opened the throttle as they joined the Cromwell Road. The bonnet lifted as the V12 dug the rear wheels into the tarmac. The Jag shot past the gothic cathedral-like building of The Natural History Museum. Not only the dinosaurs watched them pass: a trail of flashing speed cameras winked in their wake, like photographers behind a Hollywood starlet parading up the red carpet. The car was registered with the diplomatic plates of a small African country so the traffic police could only sigh and tear up the tickets.

She gripped him hard as the Jag accelerated. "Um, Karla, you're hurting my leg."

She turned shining emerald eyes on him and released him fractionally. "I can feel your blood pumping."

There was, he thought, no answer to that. He turned off the A4, southwest to Richmond.

Jameson lived at the top of a small, modern block of flats halfway up Richmond Hill. The building was wonderfully tasteless, and quite out of keeping with the rest of the area. He had often thought that the builder must have had serious black on the head clerk of Richmond's Planning Department to get permission for such a monstrosity. Nevertheless, the view from his flat took in the Thames and half of Richmond below. After only fifteen minutes, he found a bay to park the Jag a bare five hundred meters from his flat. It was a good night. Sometimes he needed to get a taxi home from where he parked the car.

The deadlocked door opened with a click and he punched his code into the elaborate security systems. "I will need to teach you how an electronic alarm system works," he said. "What are you waiting for?"

She stood outside. "I can't come in. Something stops me."

"Ah, I forgot the magical shield around the flat. It obviously regards you as hostile. Hang on." He reached out and held her wrist. "You are welcome in my home. That should do it, try again."

She walked in. "The kitchen is here. There are blood bags in the fridge and a microwave." She looked blank. "I will teach you how to use them. The sitting room is in here. My bedroom is at the end and this is yours."

He opened the door on a well-appointed room. "It's a little small, I'm afraid, but you know London prices."

He was gabbling, he knew. How could she possibly understand property prices? But the situation was stressful. He paused but she said nothing. "It'll be dawn soon. The window is double blinded and I have drawn the curtains in the other rooms to give you the run of the flat. I need to sleep, so I'll see you later."

She did not speak or even move as he let himself out. Jameson was tired but sleep eluded him. He had total faith in the Commission's magic geeks when they assured him that Karla couldn't possibly attack him. Yeah, right. They gave the assurances but it was his neck not theirs. How the hell had he volunteered for this? You killed suckers, as quickly and safely as possible, before they killed you. What you didn't do was have them over as houseguests. He listened intently but all he could hear was his heart, *thump, thump, thump*. Come to think of it, she could probably hear it too. Jameson checked his rail pistol was charged and rolled over.

When he woke, it was mid-afternoon. The flat was as silent as the grave. Jameson winced; the metaphor was unattractive. He put his robe on and knocked gently on Karla's door. There was no answer so he pushed it open. The room was just as he had left it, the bed unruffled. There was no evidence that she had ever been in it. Where the hell was she?

He found her in the lounge, sitting cross-legged on the floor, in the darkest corner, to the side of the window. He almost drew the curtains; cursing himself gently, he turned on the light instead. She had a book open on her lap. She must have been reading in the dim light. He made a note that her night vision was extraordinary.

Reading was a good sign. It suggested her mind was functioning. "What attracted your interest, hmm, the complete works of William Shakespeare. You like the Bard, then."

Jameson had read English lit at Cambridge. He had obtained a good rowing blue and a poor third-class degree. Two sorts of people went to Oxford and Cambridge in Jameson's day. The first group was state-school geeks with oversized brains; they generally got firsts. The second group was the public school–educated sons and daughters of the cream of society, that is the thick and the rich. They spent three years networking and clubbing, and got thirds. It was very unfashionable to get a second since it implied that you were too geeky to enjoy the social life and too dim to cut the academic mustard.

He had kept his course books after graduating. Many of them were still unopened, but they filled the spaces on his shelves nicely. His Shakespeare, however, was well thumbed.

"What are you reading? The sonnets? You have a taste for romanticism, then." She did not answer but it was important that he keep communicating with her so he took the book from her hands and read from the open page.

" 'In the old age black was not counted fair, or if it were, it bore not beauty's name; but now is black beauty's successive heir, and beauty slander'd with a bastard's shame.' "

He flicked down the page. "Thou art as tyrannous, so as thou art, as those whose beauties proudly make them cruel; for well thou know'st to my dear doting heart . . . Thy black is fairest in my judgment's place, in nothing art though black save in thy deeds, and hence this slander, as I think, proceeds."

"The Dark Lady sonnets!" he said. Jameson had a soft spot for these poems. His one attempt at amateur dramatics had been a part in Shaw's play based on the Dark Lady of the Sonnets. His girlfriend of the moment had played the Lady so he had been persuaded to play the Beefeater. He had a scant dozen lines of dialogue. The only one he could remember now had been something like "Halt, who goes there?" The girlfriend had dumped him right afterward for the smooth bastard who played the romantic lead, young Will Shakespeare himself. But Jameson's interest in Shakespeare had been awakened and had never quite died.

"He was so young," she said, "but his words hung in the air."

"You were there?" he said. "You heard the Bard?" Jameson gazed at her in astonishment and increasing excitement. The rational side of his mind insisted that coincidences like this did not happen. But the romantic part whispered that it was not impossible.

"Are you really that old, Karla? Could you have met Shakespeare?" he said, doubtfully.

"The poet's words were like quicksilver, like fire in my head," she said, "and he loved me."

"He loved you?" said Jameson, in astonishment. He paced the room, excitement mounting. Could she lie in her current state? Why would she lie? Do suckers fantasize? He knew so little about her kind. Mostly, he just killed them.

"I wish I had paid more attention to Gimpy Harris' lectures," Jameson said. Gimpy Harris was Professor Auberon Harris, an eminent Shakespearean scholar. Jameson had slept off several hangovers through his lectures.

"What did Gimpy say about the Dark Lady?" Jameson ticked the points off on his fingers. "She was older than Shakespeare. She was probably not an aristocrat. He called her black because of both her coloring and the wickedness in her heart. She was devious and unfaithful. Loving her was wrong in some way. The Bard was almost vicious in his denunciation of his love for her and the damage it would do to his soul."

He thumbed through the Dark Lady arc with a new eye. "Then will I swear beauty herself is black, and all they foul that thy complexion lack."

"So shalt thou feed on death, that feeds on men, and death once dead, there's no more dying then."

"Read in one way, that could have come straight out of the *Necronomicon*—the Book of the Dead," whispered Jameson. Oh this surely was not possible.

"For I have sworn thee fair and thought thee bright, who art as black as hell, as dark as night."

"He's talking about the undead, the creatures of the night!" said Jameson, belief starting to overcome skepticism.

"In loving thee thou know'st I am forsworn . . . For I have sworn thee fair; more perjur'd I, to swear against the truth so foul a lie."

"Oh my God, it's all here. The Dark Lady was a black-haired vampire, the undead who feed on death so that they never die, a creature of the night. His soul was foresworn for loving her." Jameson was stunned. He had read these passages a hundred times and seen them simply as the record of an unfortunate love affair. That was the problem with Shakespeare. There were so many ways to interpret the words, depending on the reader's mind-set.

He knelt down beside her and pushed the hair out of her eyes. "What do you remember, Karla? What secrets are locked in your head? Gimpy would have sold his soul for an hour with you." That might have been literally true but Gimpy would still have paid the price.

"It's been so long," she said.

"Do you understand what was happening to you, Karla?" he said. "You were regressing fast. Soon, you would have been completely animal. Then you would have made a fatal mistake. Well, you are going to be kicked out of it now."

Jameson gunned the Jaguar up the North Circular. London's northwestern inner ring road is a driver's delight. Large roundabouts connect stretches of urban dual carriageway, offering a constant challenge. Karla was a particular temptation as speed thrilled her and she urged him on, not that he ever needed much encouragement.

The player had selected Franz Ferdinand. *"You see her, you can't touch her. You hear her, you can't hold her."*

Tonight he was barely getting into his stride when a large Ford attached itself to his tail. Jameson dropped a gear and accelerated away from it. The Ford followed and deployed hidden blue flashing lights and a familiar *bee-boo* noise.

"Damn, I seem to have picked up the only patrol car in London. Let me do the talking," Jameson said.

"You want her, you can't have her. You want to, she won't let you."

He pulled over, killed the player, and lowered the driver's window. "Who do we think we are then, sir, Michael Schumacher?" Only London's Metropolitan Police could make the word "sir" sound so deeply insulting.

"No, officer. I think I'm a diplomat. My passport." Jameson handed it over. The bobby examined it with his torch. It was a perfectly good passport that declared Jameson to be an attaché of the Republic of Hamrandi. "As you see, I have diplomatic immunity to prosecution."

"Where's Hamrandi, when it's at home?" the guardian of the law asked.

"Africa," said Jameson succinctly.

The policeman sniffed, eloquently. "Amazing how diplomats from the poorest countries have the flashiest cars. And what about her? Is she a diplomat too?"

"No, officer. She's just a colleague. And as she is simply sitting there she doesn't need to prove anything, does she?"

The policeman shone his torch at her. "Would you mind removing your sunglasses please, madam?"

She just looked at him.

"Take your glasses off, love," said Jameson.

Karla removed the shades. Her eyes flashed metallic green in the torchlight. She hissed at the policeman, who jumped.

"Amazing what women can do nowadays with colored contact lenses, isn't it?" said Jameson, cheerfully.

The policeman was so rattled that he failed to reprimand Karla for not wearing a belt. Nevertheless, he rallied manfully. "Yes, sir. You may be a diplomat but keep your speed down, or we will find reasons to keep pulling you over and making your life miserable."

"Absolutely, officer. I shall certainly be more careful in future," Jameson assured him.

"See that you do." With that parting shot, the guardian of the law reasserted his dignity and strode back to his motor.

"We had better be more circumspect for the rest of the evening," said Jameson, propelling the Jag at a sedate pace.

"Slow," said Karla, succinctly. She had improved immensely in the last fortnight and now even initiated discourse. But she was still not one would call a sparkling conversationalist.

Jameson pulled into the rear car park at the Brent Cross shopping center, leaving the motor tucked well away in a dimly lit corner. He opened the passenger door for Karla and handed her out. As he wanted her to behave like a lady, he elected to treat her as one. She took his arm, as he had trained her. He had put a lot of effort into training her and the more he tried the faster she learnt. He escorted her to a shop that had one dress in the window, a dress with no price tag. Simpsons was a ladies outfitter, not a dress shop.

"Are you up to this, love? You will have to maintain control out of my sight. Can you do that for me, Karla?"

"I can do it," she said.

"Mr. Jameson?" said the personal shopper. "We are expecting you." The lady—Simpsons does not have shop assistants, they have ladies—looked somewhat askance at Karla's tattered leathers.

"My friend"—Jameson gestured at Karla—"has just flown back from a spiritual odyssey to Nepal. Her luggage is believed to have been rerouted to Bangkok via Istanbul. While the airline looks for it, she will need daywear, business wear, an evening outfit, and something suitable for bike riding; she favors leathers. I expect you to make appropriate suggestions as she is somewhat out of touch, fashionwise. Charming place, Nepal, but somewhat rural." Jameson indicated Karla's outfit, which spoke for itself.

"Does sir require an account?" said the lady. By way of answer, Jameson laid a Coutts Classic card down on the counter. Coutts was the Queen's bank. Liquid assets of one hundred thousand pounds were required to open an account.

"Charge it to that," Jameson said.

"Madam will require underwear to match?" said the lady. From the look on her face, she was estimating her commission on the sale.

"I would imagine so," said Jameson, vaguely. He retreated hastily from what was clearly becoming a male no-go zone.

The lady raised a hand and a younger version materialized at her elbow. "Madam will need luggage to carry away her selection. Go round to V&J and pick up a set."

She seized Karla by the arm and led her determinedly into the racks. Karla gave him a look of desperation over her shoulder so he smiled encouragingly. Jameson, preparing for a long wait, took out a packet of Dunhill. One of the staff frowned at him and pointed to a sign indicating that the whole arcade was a no-smoking zone.

Cursing Blair's nanny government, he trooped out to the car park and joined a small huddle of pariahs camped around the main entrance. The rebellious "enemies of the Blairite state" sucked on their burning weeds and stomped up and down to keep warm. He flirted for four cigarettes with a charming girl from Hackney, any difference in social class submerged in their common exile. They were the dispossessed in the new politically correct society.

Reluctantly, for the young lady from Hackney was a very nice girl who had admitted to certain interesting fantasies regarding Jaguar sports cars, he dragged himself back to the shop to see how the wardrobing of his pet creature of the night was proceeding. The personal shopper was standing outside the changing area talking to Karla, who lurked within where Jameson couldn't see her.

"Madam wears it well. The gentleman wished you to have evening-wear and that is eveningwear. Look, he has returned. Why not show him?" She reached in and hauled Karla out into the shop.

The personal shopper had dressed the Dark Lady in a wisp of a little black dress with matching strappy sandals and clutch bag. "I feel ridiculous," muttered Karla, sulkily.

"You look fabulous," said Jameson, simply. "We'll take it."

Karla elected to wear her new black leathers out of the shop. Jameson let her have her way as he thought she had received enough fashion shocks for one night. She was definitely starting to look mutinous. Jameson insisted on carrying the luggage. He was intellectually aware that she could carry him and the luggage with one hand but, dammit, a gentleman carried the bags for a lady. And back there in that shop, she had looked every inch a lady.

Four youths hung around the Jaguar. "Nice wheels, mate," said the largest. "We've been looking after your motor for you to make sure it don't get damaged. Might still get damaged unless you pay us a pony."

"Sod off," said Jameson, succinctly. "Or I'll set my girlfriend on you."

The youths straightened up and closed on him. Jameson ran through the options in his head. Karla was well fed so shouldn't be hungry. The magic spell would probably force her to intervene if the yobs attacked him. That could rapidly get out of hand. Perhaps better to have a more controlled situation. It would be a good test of how well he could control her and how well she could control herself to please him.

"You have been very patient tonight, Karla, so I give you these four. No killing or maiming but other than that, have fun. Oh and Karla?" She looked at him. "No feeding."

"Really," said Karla, happily. "I can play with them?"

"Sure," said Jameson. "Have a ball." He hoped he wasn't making a terrible error.

"Hold on a min—" a yob started to say.

Karla grabbed him, picked him up, and heaved him horizontally across the car park.

"No," said Jameson, in genuine anguish. "Mind the Jag." Too late: the yob crashed into the wing, leaving a dent.

The gang leader produced a knife and ran at her. He thrust viciously at her face. She caught him by the wrist and twisted. Something broke with a crack. Karla kicked his legs out from under him and rabbit punched him as he fell. The last two made a run for it, but she was on them, like a cheetah running down rabbits. She grabbed them, one hand on each neck, and crashed their heads together. Then she tossed them casually aside.

The leader groaned and rose to his knees attracting her attention. He would have done better to have stayed down. She moved over to him. Jameson noticed that she slid like an ice dancer. She really was extraordinarily graceful, a beautiful man-killer who moved like a tigress. Karla hauled the leader up by the front of his denim jacket. Blood ran down his face and neck. She stared at it in fascination, opening her mouth to reveal long canines. He fainted dead away, becoming limp in her grip.

"No feeding, Karla. Remember," Jameson said softly.

She licked the blood from his face and shuddered. "No feeding," she repeated, retracted her teeth and dropped him.

Lights appeared.

"Oh no, not plod again," said Jameson.

A "jam sandwich" pulled into the car park and made its way unhurriedly toward them.

"Well, well," said the keeper of the Queen's peace, emerging from the police car. "If it isn't the diplomat from . . . where is that place?"

"Hamrandi," said Jameson.

"Hamrandi," repeated the bobby, with satisfaction. "The attaché from Hamrandi."

The gang leader revived and groaned. "As I live and breathe, Chippy Jones," said the policeman, with a grin. "The North Circular's answer to the West Side Boys. Working the old 'guard your wheels for, you, mister', were you, Chippy?"

The policeman applied first aid with the back of his hand across Chippy's face, knocking him fully awake.

"We was attacked," said Chippy.

"No, attacked, eh, how shocking," said the bobby, looking utterly unshocked. "Have you been beating up the local wildlife then, ambassador?"

"Not him, her!" Chippy wailed.

"The young lady." The bobby laughed. "She hammered you! All together Chippy, or did you line up one at a time, like gentlemen?"

"She ain't yuman," said Chippy.

"What would you know about being human, Chippy?" said the policeman, scornfully. "Do you want to press charges, sir?" he asked Jameson.

"Against this shower?" said Jameson. "I can't be bothered."

"You had better be off then." He looked at Karla, thoughtfully. "Interesting bodyguards you Hamrandi people use. Good night, sir."

Jameson noticed that Farley was nervous, very, very nervous. He fidgeted, he sweated, he adjusted his laptop, and he adjusted his tie. He was an analyst not a field operative. His job involved collating, analyzing and interpreting data. He planned operations and briefed the agents. He might have worked for an insurance company or been the bloke who determined the optimum failure rate of lightbulbs to maximize profits but, amongst other things, he was a financial expert.

The Commission still had people who hung out in Gothic cemeteries and ancient temples but in London, you followed the money trail. Farley had antennae sensitive to the smallest sniff of bad money on the move around the merchant banks and clearing houses of the City.

Often, the Commission's analysts found illicit transactions that had no paranormal interest at all. But that was all right too. The Commission could always use additional funds and the original owners of the loot were in no position to complain.

Jameson knew that Farley had briefed too many field teams for the danger aspect of the work that the agents did to bother him. He had acquired the essential knack that all staff officers need, of emotionally disconnecting himself from outcomes. He did his very best to prepare field operatives for their task but if it subsequently went pear-shaped and people died–well, he had done his best. But Jameson was willing to bet that Farley had never sat on a sofa next to a demon, hence the nervousness.

"I first noticed the movement of money through an account at CBJs. Large sums are being laundered from the trade of Aztec grave goods. Someone has access to unknown burial grounds in Mexico."

"And the money is being used for . . . ?" asked Jameson.

"No idea," said Farley. "It's just accumulating at the moment. We traced the movements to a banker and put a watcher team on him."

"What makes you think we have a Code Z?" asked Jameson.

"The people who bought the grave goods. Some just had breakdowns but others . . ." Farley shrugged and pushed a London *Evening Standard* clipping over to Jameson. It read, "Islington dad slaughters baby twins and partner before cutting his own throat."

"There was something else," said Farley. "One of the watchers disappeared, a young woman. She turned up in the Thames, drained of blood."

"The banker?" said Jameson.

"He's taken to working at home during the day and only comes into the office after dark," said Farley.

"So he's been possessed by a sucker. The best time to take him would be at midday, when he's torpid, at his home. Why are you briefing us? Karla is also . . . not at her best in daylight." Jameson smiled at her.

"Oh, I agree with your analysis, Major Jameson. But we don't know where he currently lives."

"The dead watcher," said Jameson.

"Must have followed him to his new lair, yes. We do not want to risk any more watchers, so you will have to take him at night when he leaves the office. He uses a laptop; we want the hard drive."

Farley produced a picture. "We also want him destroyed." He looked at Karla. "Will that present you with a conflict? You are of a type."

"He is not of me," said Karla.

Farley looked at Jameson, who shrugged. He was not exactly sure what Karla meant but there would be little point in asking her. If she wanted to tell them then she would, cross questioning her would be unproductive.

"This laptop has software synched to CBJ's communications. It will tell you when the banker goes online. I suggest you pick him up when he leaves the office."

"Someone will have to shut down the flow of artifacts at the source," said Jameson.

"That is in hand and none of your concern," said Farley, pompously. "The Texas office is sending in a team."

"Oh really, rather them than me. Aztec blood magic is nasty." Jameson shuddered. "Who are the poor saps assigned to that piece of fun?"

"I believe Pitts has taken the job on," said Farley.

Jameson had met Pitts, a tough, slow-talking Texan, whom he remembered as a first-rate shot. "Best of British luck, mate." He whispered a quiet blessing.

"If there's nothing more?" Farley snapped the lid of the laptop down when no one answered. "I'll see myself out," he said, with what could only be described as relief.

The sun was setting as the Jag headed north up the South Circular. The Pagoda at Kew Gardens stood out against the setting sun. The sky was a streak of red as the light filtered through the pollution of twenty million people. Jameson switched on the car player as they crossed the river. Spookily it selected "*When the Sun Goes Down*," the *Arctic Monkeys* hit. The player had been selecting eerily appropriate music lately when he drove with Karla onboard. He suspected he had "a god in the machine"—or at least a small demon in the chip.

"*They said it changes when the sun goes down, over the river going out of town.*"

The song was about Sheffield but it could be London or any British city. The Monkeys sang how the streets change when the sun goes down and the day people hurry home to their TV dinners and suburban warmth of their double-glazed, centrally heated lives. The night people come out. The girls with pinched faces shivering in skirts that are too short and blouses that are too thin. Housewives that need a bit extra to pay the lekky bill, addicts who owe their dealer, or just students whose loans have run out. And then there are the punters, the middle-aged, middle-management, middle-class, middle-of-the-road men slowing down their company Ford Mondeos and Vauxhall Vectras to walking pace, kerb-crawling so that they could assess the talent and hire a friend for an hour. Jameson reflected that he and Karla were in no position to cast stones. They too were of the dark, people as black as night.

Over the river he connected with the A4, to follow it into The City. The player seemed to favor the Monkeys tonight.

"All you people are vampires, all your stories are stale."

Jameson killed the autoselector and manually restricted the machine to old Sixties numbers. It retaliated with "Waterloo Sunset." He sighed and let it run. The damn machine was trying to tell him something.

Relying on his diplomatic plates, Jameson parked on the double yellow lines opposite CBJs. He plugged his iPaq into the car's power supply and jiggled with the software that he had downloaded from the laptop.

"Yeah, our target is definitely in there, doing whatever merchant bankers do to earn their million-quid bonuses."

"A million pounds sounds such a great deal of money," said Karla. "They used to run the whole country on less than that."

"Yah, well. Some day let me explain inflation to you. I'm going to get some sleep. Watch that display and tell me if anything changes."

Jameson pushed the seat back and propped himself against the door. He couldn't get comfortable but must have dozed because Karla was shaking him awake. "He's coming outside."

"What? Why didn't you wake me earlier when he logged off? Oh, I see. Bloody computers." According to his iPaq the banker was still online. Karla gestured to a shadowy figure getting into a BMW. He carried a computer case. "Are you sure that's him, Karla?" She did not answer. "Yes, of course you're sure. You can feel him, can't you?"

The Beamer pulled out of the bay and Jameson followed. The banker drove steadily through the streets east and north, turning into smaller and smaller side streets. Soon they were driving through dimly lit narrow alleys. Jameson hung back as far as he could to avoid detection. Every so often, he changed the pattern of the light array on the front of the Jag, to make it look like a different vehicle in the banker's rearview mirror.

The BMW stopped outside a run-down warehouse. "That's odd," said Jameson, pulling in. "I thought all these old buildings had been pulled down years ago."

The banker locked the Beamer and vanished down the side of the warehouse. "Come on, Karla, we are losing him."

"No," she said. "I know where he is going. Follow close to me."

She followed after the banker. There was a narrow footpath between two buildings. Jameson could hear footsteps in the distance but the lighting was terrible. Karla pushed on. The pavement gave way to cobblestones. Jameson just hated walking on cobblestones. They turned your ankles with every step. As they went deeper into the alley, the buildings closed in on both sides.

"I don't know why they have bothered to put up lights disguised as Victorian gas lamps," said Jameson. "It's not as if this was a prime tourist site. Mind, you could make a great theme park here. See the Whitechapel ripper murders re-enacted," he said theatrically.

Curls of fog drifted along the alley. "Fog, in London?" said Jameson, in astonishment. "I don't remember that being forecast." London was a dry city. Fog was as rare as snow.

Jameson felt that he was on a film set. "Those imitation Victorian gas lights, Karla," he said. "They aren't really imitation, are they?"

"No," she said. "This is a special place for my kind. You must stay close to me, Jameson, or I will lose you."

Jameson heard piano music up ahead through the mist. They entered a small square with a dirt floor. An old pub lined one side. A door opened spilling lamplight out. A man in a top hat pulled a giggling woman in a Victorian dress after him. They kissed and made their way unsteadily out of the square.

"This way," said Karla, pulling Jameson after her.

As they left, Jameson heard a woman scream behind him. He turned to look.

"No!" she warned, pulling him back. "Here things are seldom what they seem." She walked on to a cul-de-sac with another Old London pub at the end. Jameson went to push the door open but Karla stopped him, one hand on his chest. "We have to blend in. In there, you belong to me. You walk directly behind me. You obey me without question. I won't be able to protect you if you don't." There was a pleading element to her voice that he had not heard before.

He touched her face lightly with his fingers. "You're the boss. I'll follow your lead."

They entered.

Inside was a twenty-first-century nightclub, with neon lights, chrome fittings, and giant fish tanks. Modern rock hammered from hidden speakers so loud that he could feel it in his chest. Jameson couldn't understand why the sound did not penetrate outside. She walked down a corridor and out onto an open warehouse-sized area. In the center was a dance floor.

Karla found them a table just off the dance floor. She held out her hand to him and clicked her fingers. Her lips made a small gesture. Taking the hint he pulled out the Dunhills. She leaned forward and he put one in her mouth and then one in his own. Jameson had an old battered steel lighter that he had used in the Guards. It ran on petrol so could be recharged from the nearest Land Rover wherever he happened to be based.

Karla leaned forward so could light her. "The target is sitting at a table on your left."

Jameson lit his own cigarette before glancing casually around the room. The banker was sitting with two men—well, two man-sized things. He had the case open and was trading something.

"Yeah?" A waitress in a 1950s usherette costume appeared at their table and chewed gum.

"Malt whiskey, two large ones," said Karla, without consulting him.

"That'll be eighteen quid," the waitress said, shifting the gum around.

"Pay her twenty," said Karla.

Jameson handed over a twenty-pound note.

"Gee, thanks," said the waitress, with total contempt, before flouncing off.

Karla shrugged. "They can't get the staff these days."

A blonde in an exquisite evening gown sleazed up to their table. She drew deep on a cigarette holder and blew the smoke to the ceiling. "'Lo. Karla. I'd heard you were losing your mind, darling."

"I wonder who starts these rumours," said Karla. "You look well, Rosanna, considering your age."

The two women planted false smiles on their faces and air kissed at least two feet apart. Rosanna stood right in front of Jameson and stared at him. She took him by the chin and moved his head from side to side. "You have a new pet, I see. You do collect waifs and strays, don't you? Mind you, this one's rather cute. I wouldn't mind trying him myself." She parted her lips to show elongated canines.

Jameson let his jacket fall open far enough to show his bolt pistol and grinned back, showing his teeth. They locked eyes.

"He has spirit, Karla. I think he could be dangerous." Rosanna touched his face again. "He has strong bonds to you. I don't understand, magic is involved."

Karla seized her hard by the wrist and pulled her hand away. "I don't share my possessions. You know that, Rosanna. They're too fragile and you like to play rough."

The blonde smiled enigmatically, blew more smoke, and slinked off without another word. Jameson checked out the banker. He was locked in some interminable negotiation. His briefcase was open and the laptop was inside. The waitress brought the drinks. Jameson took a sip. It was good stuff but he couldn't quite place it.

The music poured around them again. The Kaiser Chiefs opened with "*Every Day I Love You Less and Less.*" "Come on," said Karla. "I want to dance."

"*I can't believe once you and me did sex.*"

She strutted to the dance floor in a walk that made Jerry Hall seem introverted. Jameson was a pretty good dancer. He would not win many marks for elegance but he was fit and strong. But Karla was just incredible and she exploited the driving beat of the band with great skill. Her body seemed to bend in ways unknown to man. She danced as if she had not signed up to the law of gravity.

"*It makes me sick to think of you undressed.*"

In the end, Jameson gave up trying to match her and let her use him the way a pole dancer uses the pole. When the song ended, she draped herself on him, wrapping one leg around his.

"I thought you said that we had to be inconspicuous," said Jameson.

"No, I said that we had to blend in," said Karla. "We are blending beautifully, my pet."

Then Katie Melua sang how the man with the power who was a charmer with a snake took her halfway up the Hindu Kush to show her things she had never seen.

Karla held her arms out straight, palm up, and rested them on his shoulders. Then she undulated against him. Jameson kept his mind on the job and watched the banker. He leaned forward and whispered in Karla's ear. "Matey is leaving, so we need to follow. After your performance, what could be more natural than we should leave? But I warn you that I will definitely shoot you if you try to carry me out over your shoulder."

She laughed. The first time he had heard her laugh. She was recovering fast.

They exited, looking unhurried but covering ground quickly. "Okay, Karla, he's on his own. Pick a place to take him."

They followed the banker through the archaic streets, the fog allowing them to keep close. After some minutes, Karla accelerated up to the man and kicked his legs away. Before he hit the ground, she punched him twice more. Once he was down, she put the boot in. It was quick, clinical, and he never laid a finger on her. When Jameson reached the scene, he kicked the briefcase away. Taking the rail pistol from under his arm, he fired one wooden bolt into the banker's heart. The gun thumped, but the slow acceleration of the bolt compared to a bullet made the kick manageable. The banker collapsed in upon himself and his body flowed into dust.

Karla's eyes flashed metallic green and her lips parted to show long canines. She shook with excitement. She pushed Jameson up against a wall and moved her mouth toward him. He jerked back, shocked. She hissed and her eyes flashed. "So I'm good enough to fight for you but not good enough to kiss."

He had the rail pistol between them, muzzle jammed into her heart. She looked down at it. "If you're going to shoot then shoot," she said, calling his bluff. Then she kissed him savagely on the mouth. A tooth cut his lip and she watched the trickle of blood with fascination. She put out her tongue and licked it, shuddering at the sensation. He still did not fire.

"Karla, it's not that you're not attractive," he said. "But we put a love geas on you. I can't take advantage. It wouldn't be right. . . ."

"I know what you did," she said. She let him go and walked away from him. He picked up the briefcase and hurried after her. It seemed to him that her hips swayed far more than was strictly necessary.

The way back seemed much shorter. The streets quickly normalized. They had barely started when Jameson saw the Jaguar on the other side of the road. Somehow they seemed to have come round in a circle. He turned to look back, to see from where they had come, but behind was a high brick wall. He went to check but the wall was real. Karla had reached the car. Jameson took out his electronic card, but before he could trigger it she put her hand on the Jag's roof. It made a friendly chirrup and flashed its amber lights, the doors unlocking with a clunk. How the hell had she done that? That damned car had taken a shine to her.

When he reached the Jag she was already inside. She had dropped the back of her seat down and was curled up on it like a kitten. She flashed metallic green eyes at him when he got in and stretched her legs out. His mouth was suddenly very dry.

❖   ❖   ❖

Farley stood at the front of the small lecture theater operating the PowerPoint display. "The information on the laptop was most helpful," said Farley. "We have an address. The distribution center for the Aztec grave goods is a storage unit in Hackney. You go in, see what you can find, and bug the place."

"Why aren't we doing this in daylight?" said Gaston. "Where there's one sucker there could be more."

"The place is full of workmen during the day. The streets are awash with people. It isn't viable, Gaston, it has to be at night. You do have backup in the event of a Code Z incident." Farley waved vaguely in Karla's direction. "You know her capabilities."

"Oh yes," said Gaston, softly. "We know what she can do."

They all rode in a Commission transit van battered, with the logo of a plumber on the side. These motors looked rough but were mechanically sound. Karla amused herself by playing with the combat team. She yawned and showed her teeth. The troops grasped their rail guns in sweaty hands. She enjoyed feeling their anxiety. Gaston nudged Jameson.

He whispered in her ear. "Behave yourself. Leave the men alone."

"I'm bored." She pouted and closed her eyes.

The wait went on. "Hurry up and wait," said Gaston. "You remember, Major."

Jameson sucked on a Dunhill. Yes, he remembered. Waiting on the Falls Road in support of the police in a Pig, a light armored personal carrier that rode on six wheels. The politicians would not let the army use heavy tracked armor for political reasons. After all, it might look like a real war if they used "tanks." The car bomb went off in front of them, incinerating the drivers instantly. Jameson was right at the back to be first out of the rear troop-deployment doors, in the time-honored way of a British officer. This time the tradition saved him. Half his section was killed, most of the rest horribly burnt. He got away without a scratch.

He inhaled deeply from the Dunhill and blew the smoke up into the van. "Yes, I remember," he said, unemotionally. Karla looked at him, uncertainly; she was sensitive to his moods.

Gaston's phone uttered a soft bleep. He checked the message. "Okay, move out."

He pulled open the door and they jumped out. The team walked quickly to a side door of the building. In the dark, their combat gear might not be noticed but running was the surest way to attract unwelcome attention. The technician knelt down at the lock and inserted the electronic key. Gaston and the technician went in first. Inside was a corridor with an alarm system on the wall. The technician inserted a probe and ran diagnostics. He turned the alarms off within a few seconds.

"A good system," the technician said, "but no match for the software that I threw at it."

"Move back," Gaston said to the technician. "I'll take point."

"Karla and I had better be alongside you," said Jameson.

It was then that the butterfly flapped its wings.

"Okay, you come up front," said Gaston. "But *she* stays at the rear to guard our backs."

Jameson was not sure whether Gaston genuinely thought that they needed a rearguard or whether he simply did not want Karla too close to him. But Gaston was the team leader, so Jameson indicated that she should comply. She did not like being separated from him and expressed her displeasure openly with bared canines. Jameson ignored her.

The team moved down the corridor in single file to a door at the end. Gaston tried the handle; it was unlocked. He pushed the door open with his gun barrel. Nothing moved inside. Jameson slipped in and moved to the right away from the door. He dropped on one knee and covered the interior of the warehouse, while Gaston slipped in and took up a position on the left. Inside was an open area, filled with palettes and boxes. Two forklift trucks stood up against the wall. Nothing stirred.

Gaston stood up warily and signaled that they should move in. He and Jameson led the way; the rest of the team followed in single file through the door. Karla was the last in. The world exploded at the moment that she crossed the threshold.

Jameson saw a bright flash that left him with afterimages on his retinas, like the negative filming that they used in old TV programs to indicate that an alien had fired his ray gun. He had a brief sensation of floating, then something thumped him in the back and it went dark.

He hurt. Jameson hurt all over. His cheek was on concrete and his helmet was missing. The warehouse was lit when he opened his eyes. He could see a wire mesh. He'd lost his helmet. One sat upright the other side of the wire and Jameson wondered if it was his. No, it couldn't be. The helmet opposite still had a head in it. Jameson was fairly certain that he still had his head attached because it hurt like hell.

"I thought that you were a goner," said Gaston. The man helped him sit up.

"What happened?" said Jameson.

"Some sort of bomb went off behind us. Killed everyone but you and me, Major."

"It wasn't a bomb," said Jameson. "There was a flash but no heat. Look, nothing is burnt and the damage is localized."

It was true. Most of the interior of the warehouse was surprisingly undamaged, if you ignored the blood and body parts sprayed around.

"It went off when Karla was entering the room," said Jameson. "There must have been a trigger in the door frame."

"So why didn't we set it off?" said Gaston.

"Because the alarm was there to deter humans. The booby trap was set up to kill something else. Something like Karla, a creature of the night."

"I don't want to worry you," said Gaston. "But someone has put us in a cage."

"Someone like him," said Jameson.

"Yeah," said Gaston.

A man appeared in front of them. He looked Mediterranean, not just in features but in the way he sported moustaches and a wide-brimmed hat. His smile said "insane" the way a letter from the tax office said "gotcha." He casually picked up a large wooden crate and dropped it back on the palette from which it had been blown.

"I suppose your appearance is connected with my banker's sudden disappearance. But I bet that you are keen to tell me everything you know." The man's accent was unplaceable, smeared by many too many regions and times—rather like Karla's, Jameson reflected. Their jailer opened his mouth to show long curved canines.

"Is that what I think it is?" said Gaston.

"Depends," said Jameson. "If you think that it's the tooth fairy then, no. But if you think that it is an evil mad old sucker then I think you could be right."

"Manners," said the man. "You are in no position to annoy me."

"And if we are polite and helpful then you will let us go and all will be well, will it?" said Jameson.

"Well, no actually," conceded the man.

Jameson slipped his hand inside his jacket, looking for the rail pistol.

The man noticed the motion and held it up. "Interesting toy. When did you stop using crossbows? You cattle so love innovation. Every time I turn around, why, you are at something new." He tossed the gun aside.

"Shit," said Jameson. "Go to Plan B."

"What was Plan B?" said Gaston.

"I had hoped that you could tell me," said Jameson.

"You two are such fun," said the man, delightedly. "I wish I could keep you around for a while but duty calls."

He walked to the cage and unlocked the door. Jameson and Gaston shrank back but it was a small cage and there was nowhere to go. The man reached in and effortlessly hauled Jameson out. Jameson tried hitting him but it was like striking iron. His head was pushed aside and the canines descended.

"Would you mind unhanding my property? I don't recall offering you a bite." Karla was just there, head up, hands on her hips, a dark-haired angel in black leather.

"Karla. I heard that you were back. So it was you who set off my little trap. You should have been dissipated to the winds by my little surprise, my sweet."

"I have a strong sense of self-identity," she said.

"I must admit that it was not intended for the likes of you. I would have doubled the power if I had known that you were dropping in." The man looked at her almost fondly.

"You are still holding my pets. Let them go and we'll be off," Karla demanded.

"Karla, get out. Save yourself," Jameson said.

The man slapped Jameson quiet and threw him back in the cage. "I don't think I can let you leave, Karla my love. Not now."

Without warning, the man snarled and threw himself at Karla, clawing with both hands. He moved so very fast. She backed up, blocking his blows, then kicked him in the kneecap. It sounded like a wrecking ball hitting a wall. He didn't move at all.

"You always were a quick little thing," the man said. He swung without warning and backhanded her across the face. Karla spun into a stack of heavy palettes, knocking them over.

Jameson pulled on the cage door, which had self-locked. "We have to help her, Gaston. She can't win."

Karla picked herself up and squared up to the man. He waited for her with that insane grin across his face, apparently content for her to take the initiative. She moved in and caught him with punches and kicks. She was much faster, but her blows weren't hurting him, at least, not hurting him enough. He did not even bother to try to dodge or block her attack but traded punch for punch. She evaded his swings with the speed and grace that she had shown on the dance floor, but her luck ran out in the end. A punch caught her in the side of the head sending her tumbling over the floor.

Jameson and Gaston kicked the cage door but they couldn't break it down.

The man closed with Karla as she tried to get up, hitting powerful blows into her body before she could dodge. She dropped to her knees and he kicked her in the chest. Karla went down and stayed down. He grabbed her by the shoulder and picked her up. His left hand elongated into vicious dinosaur-like claws. He hooked them in her shoulder and slowly ripped down, tearing her body open. Jameson saw her ribs come apart, the broken ends poking out. The man chuckled the whole time, like someone enjoying a really good Mel Brooks comedy.

There was a thump and the man jerked.

"What? No!" he said.

There was a second thump and a third. Jameson saw the head of the third bolt stick out of his back. The man let Karla go and fell over backward. Dissolution started at his hands and feet and spread, until there was nothing but a greasy stain on the floor. The instructor was wrong. Three shots are not a luxury, reflected Gaston. Sometimes you needed backup.

Karla dropped Jameson's rail pistol. The whole front of her body was ripped out. She toppled forward onto the floor.

Jameson knelt at the wire mesh. "Come to me, Karla, come to me," he said.

She was only a few feet from the cage but it took agonizing minutes for her to crawl the distance.

"I can't break the wire, Karla. You have to. One more effort, old girl, come on," Jameson said, gently.

She twisted her hand in the mesh and pulled. It bent out of shape and snapped like cotton. Jameson took hold of the jagged wire in his right hand and slashed his left wrist open. Red blood dripped out.

Gaston grabbed his wrist. "Is this a good idea, Major?"

"Did you learn to leave wounded comrades to die when you were in the Paras, Gaston? In the Guards, we looked after our own."

"The Paras learnt at Arnheim that the Guards aren't much cop in a fight, sir," said Gaston, who, nevertheless, released him. The Parachute Regiment had never forgiven the Guard's Armoured Regiments for failing to relieve them at the bridge at Arnhem in Montgomery's doomed WWII offensive. But this was hardly the place to discuss ancient history so Jameson let the comment pass. He put the bleeding wound on his wrist to Karla's mouth and let his blood run inside. After a few seconds, she began to suck. "That's it, Karla, suck it down."

"Surely, she's too badly gone," said Gaston.

"I don't know," said Jameson. "But I'm hoping that the magic connection between us has made my blood special. She reacts strongly when I cut myself."

Gaston gave him a strange look but held his tongue.

Jameson's wound in his wrist began to clot but she reopened it with her teeth. It didn't hurt him at all. Gradually her body knitted itself back together. Ribs bent down and reformed. Tissue flowed across them to re-create her chest.

"I think that you ought to stop, Major," said Gaston, after some time. "You have lost too much already." He pulled Jameson's wrist back inside the wire mesh. Karla hissed and tried to push her head though the mesh after the blood, then she seemed to catch herself and her teeth retracted.

"Your blood," she said. "It burns in me like fire. I have never tasted anything so—"

She shook her head again. Jameson was feeling giddy. "Can you open the cage, Karla?" said Gaston.

It took her two attempts but she managed to break the lock. Then she sat down with a thump. Jameson opened the door and got out but he was weaving as he tried to keep his balance. Gaston put one arm around Karla and the other around Jameson. He half carried them to the door.

"The Commissions' elite death squad. Huh! What a couple of crocks you two really are. I think it's time I asked for some leave. Fiji, I fancy Fiji. Ever been to Fiji, Major? We had some Fijians in the Paras.

They always said that I should look them up one day. Now seems like a good time to me. What do you think, Major? Major? Come on now, don't pass out on me."

Jameson slept most of the next day and into the night. He rose only to eat and take his iron tablets. It was the early hours before he felt rested enough to take an interest in life again. Karla was nowhere to be found in the flat. She had not gone out because the door was locked and the key still in the lock. That only left one place.

His lease included access to the roof. It was probably intended that he should set up a dinky little roof garden, with shrubs in pots clinging desperately to life in the polluted London air, surrounded by mock hardwood furniture from B&Q. Jameson was hardly the green-fingered type, however.

The door to the roof was unlatched, indicating that she had passed that way, so he mounted the narrow stairs. He had to stop halfway for a rest. His blood fluid had been replaced by means of a drip but it was going to be some time before his body replaced all the red blood cells. He easily became breathless.

When he emerged, it took a few moments for his eyes to adapt to the gloom. Karla was sitting on the edge, legs hanging over the side. He went and sat down beside her.

"His name was Vexillo," she said.

"What?" said Jameson.

"The old one. He was called Vexillo. He was very powerful. He said he would live forever. But I killed him." Her voice rang with satisfaction. "Make sure your people know. Have them record it in their books that I killed him," she said. "You don't need to mention the gun in your files, do you?" she asked, anxiously.

"No," he said. "That's unnecessary detail."

There was a pause before she spoke again.

"Your people are becoming truly dangerous, Jameson," she said. "Once you only had stakes and fire. Now you hunt us with terrible weapons. I am not sure my kind has a future."

Jameson could think of nothing to say so he sat with her in companionable silence for some little time.

"Do you intend to do it yourself?" Karla asked.

"Do what?" he said.

"Will you put the bolt into my heart, yourself?" she said. "You hardly intend to let me go, do you?"

"No, we couldn't do that. You would start killing people again, Karla."

She nodded in acceptance of his analysis. "So would it have been you?"

"Yes. I owe you that. I would have done it myself. How did you work it out?"

"It was easy enough, once you awakened me. I really am quite clever. That was how I lasted so long."

There was another long silence.

"I was nearly finished when you awakened me. The last one to rouse me when I had reached dormancy was the poet. His words filled me with such passion that I lasted another four hundred years. He never forgave himself when he realized what he'd done, but he loved me so much."

"I know," said Jameson. "It's all there in the Dark Lady sonnets, the passion, the love, the hate, and the shame."

They faced east, looking across the city. The dark indigo of the sky was turning blue and the first hint of pink stained the horizon.

"It will be dawn soon. We had better go indoors," Jameson said.

"I have not seen the rising sun for such a long time. This morning I shall," Karla said, with quiet determination.

Jameson looked at her in astonishment.

"What are you talking about? You won't see it. The ultraviolet will burn out your eyes before incinerating your body. Come indoors now." He grabbed at her arm but she easily broke his hold.

"I don't want you to have to destroy me. I want to leave with dignity. Oh, don't look so sad, Jameson. I am long past my time. The poet got me four hundred more years and, thanks to you, I end on a high note. I killed Vexillo," she said, triumphantly. She tilted her head up to the sky and showed her long canines. Her eyes flashed metallic green. She had never looked more like a monster. She had never looked so desirable.

Jameson seized her by the arms. "You are not listening, Karla. I said it *would* have been me, not it *will* be. It took me too long to realize the meaning of my oath but I do now. Come inside with me. I can't promise to save you but I promise to try."

He kissed her hard on the lips. Her razor-sharp teeth lacerated his tongue but he did not care. She did not resist when he lifted her in his arms and carried her off the roof. She was light, no heavier than a

woman of the same size, which was just as well considering his physical condition. Somehow, he had expected her to be heavier.

Jameson knocked and entered the council chamber. Lord Harwood, a senior Commissioner, chaired the meeting.

"Ah, Major Jameson, come in."

"Thank you, my lord." Jameson nodded at the other members of
the room.

"I believe you know Sir James, who heads special operations, Mr.
Benson, and Miss Arnoux of R&D."

Hung on the wall over Lord Harwood's head was a painting of an
Elizabethan race-built galleon, of the sort commanded by Drake or
Hawkins. Lord Harwood was not descended from the old aristocracy.
He had acquired his peerage recently for services to the arts; he had
bailed the Royal Opera House out of an awkward financial hole. That
was for form's sake. In the hallowed traditions of England, his peerage
had really been awarded for substantial campaign contributions to a
political party. However, he had researched his family thoroughly and
had found an ancestor who had sailed with John Hawkins.

"I believe most of you know my secretary, Miss Sonnet." Jameson
indicated the prim woman in a business suit behind him.

Jameson took a seat at the table. Miss Sonnet sat on a seat against
the wall and took a notebook out of her bag. She would record, but
not contribute, to the meeting.

"The purpose of this meeting is to evaluate Project 139 and consider termination procedures," said Lord Harwood. "As this was
essentially an R&D operation perhaps you would start, Miss Arnoux."

"The project was the culmination of a program to test various geas
spells on paranormal entities. It was decided to evaluate a love geas as
a method for binding a paranormal to one of our operatives. R&D is
pleased with the results. The spell worked perfectly, with one small
reservation about the principle of reciprocation that we are still evaluating. As far as we are concerned, the project has been a great
success and can now be shut down. We would like to debrief Major
Jameson, of course."

"Thank you, Miss Arnoux," said Lord Harwood. "Could I have a
summary of your report on the subject's utility for special operations,
Sir James?"

"A bit of a mixed bag, my lord. Leaving out all the bullshit, we ran
into two problems. One is that the operations team found it unsettling

to work in close contact with an unrestrained Code Z. The second is that the main mission was completely compromised by a device set specifically to attack paranormals. That we might have to defend against such an attack had, understandably, escaped the planners. We will have to learn to think differently if we are to utilize paranormals within our combat teams. Other than that it was a success. Our agent, Major Jameson, retained command control of the paranormal at all times. I concur; we have the information we need. The experiment may now be terminated."

"How very neat," said Jameson, who had heard enough. "She has served her purpose so she can be dumped. No matter that she fought and bled for us."

"She's a monster, Jameson. She doesn't matter," said Lord Harwood.

"Yes, she is a monster but she does matter. She is not an unthinking animal. She thinks, she feels, she laughs. She is a person. If you prick her, does she not bleed; if you tickle her, does she not laugh; and if you wrong her will she not take revenge?" Jameson had taken the trouble to look up the quote even if, under the stress of the moment, he did not get it quite right. "I promised, on our behalf, to accept responsibility for her."

"That is what we were worried about," said Miss Arnoux, sighing. "There is reciprocity in the spell. Tell me, Major Jameson, are you sleeping with her yet?"

Miss Arnoux was a dried-up prune. In Jameson's view, having a man would vastly improve the blasted woman. "I don't think my bedroom habits are any of your damn business," Jameson said.

"Yes, I thought you might be. It's the spell, Jameson. Once she is eliminated, we will reverse the spell and you will feel quite differently," Miss Arnoux said.

The woman was so damned smug and sure of herself. Lord Harwood looked puzzled, then he looked at Jameson's secretary and his eyes narrowed. His hand slipped below the table. Jameson casually unclipped the flap on his soft leather briefcase and put his hand inside.

The door opened in response to the silent alarm and Gaston walked in wearing full combat gear followed by three troopers. "Hello, Karla," Gaston said to Miss Sonnet and pointed his rail gun at her. The troopers followed his example.

Miss Arnoux gaped like a fish then looked at Karla and paled. Jameson slowly pulled his briefcase off his hand to reveal an automatic pistol pointed at Lord Harwood. "It seems that we have a situation," he said.

Lord Harwood took his glasses off and polished them. "Gaston's men will gun her down whether you kill me or no, Major. I was very impressed by your stage magician's skills. Most of you know my secretary . . . Neatly done. Actually, none of us in the room knew her but we all assumed that someone else must. Masterful misdirection, my boy, it took me some little while to work it out. How did you disguise her eyes?"

"Dark contact lenses; a policeman gave me the idea," said Jameson.

"Indeed," said Lord Harwood.

"Why not hear me out, my lord? Then Gaston can kill me and Karla right after I kill you," said Jameson. "This is not about a spell or reciprocity. This is about integrity. We either have it or we don't. We can't have a little bit of honor, an integrity constrained only to people we approve of. Once we draw a line and impose limits on our integrity . . . why, then we have none at all."

"We are not talking about how we treat *people*. She's a monster. Think, Jameson," said Lord Harwood. "She will be tied to you all your life if we let her survive. You will never have a girlfriend, a wife, or children. It won't be you she would kill when she got jealous."

"Yes, she is a monster. But we used to think that we did not have to treat some people fairly either, people who were the wrong class, or the wrong nationality, or the wrong color skin. She may be as black as hell, my lord, but once my ancestors despised yours for much the same reason."

Lord Harwood froze. He resumed polishing his glasses with long, dark brown fingers. Lord Harwood's ancestor had sailed with Hawkins to the Americas all right, but not on the deck. Harwood's ancestor had been chained in the hold.

"He has a point, my lord," said Gaston. "And she did save our lives." Gaston had joined the Paras because that regiment was already commissioning black officers when the fashionable Guards Regiments still had a color bar against even black private soldiers. When your mother came from Cameroon, as Gaston's had, then these things mattered.

Harwood sighed. "I know that I am going to regret this but . . . Benson."

"Yes, my lord?" said the Commission's administrator.

"Add Miss Sonnet to the payroll as a secretary."

Jameson relaxed and carefully clicked the pistol's safety back on. "Thank you, my lord."

"A trial period, mark you, Jameson. She's as black as hell."

Jameson looked across at Karla, who gazed back at him with an utter lack of expression. He wished he knew how this was going to turn out. The risks were immense but he just couldn't kill her out of hand so he was stuck with the situation. His lips curled; at least it wouldn't be boring. He looked around the meeting. Gaston grinned at him, gun muzzle pointed at the ground. Miss Arnoux looked as if she had been goosed by a Royal Marine. Jameson made an observation so softly that the others had to strain to hear it. "Let's not kid ourselves, people. She may be as black as hell but all of us in this room, we are as dark as night."

Benny Comes Home

by Esther Friesner

"Crazy, that's what she is," Gertrude Rosenfeld (née Gratz) told everyone on the IRT local. She couldn't help it: Like all the Gratz women, she was possessed of an internal amplification system that was the bane of librarians, movie theater ushers, and sermonizing rabbis everywhere. "My poor sister, she's gone out of her mind. It has to be. There's no other reason for her to be doing something like this. I don't know where to hide my head from shame."

"Why, Ma?" Crammed onto the wickerwork seat between his mother's ample, apple blossom–scented flesh and his father's slumped bulk, little Oscar Rosenfeld looked up eagerly from his *Detective* comic book. He had just turned eleven, old enough to realize that the adventures of the Batman were pretty good entertainment for a dime, but this was better. "What's to be ashamed of?"

Heaven knew *he* wasn't ashamed by the prospect of having a madwoman for an aunt. On the contrary, he found the possibility rather stimulating. If *Tanteh* Rifka was crazy, maybe this Cousins' Club meeting wasn't going to be so boring after all. The Joker was crazy, and he was a criminal mastermind. To Oscar's way of thinking,

Tanteh Rifka already resembled the Joker insofar as her overgenerous application of red lipstick and pallid pancake makeup, to say nothing of her rather gaudy taste in clothes. All she needed was to dye her hair emerald green to complete the picture and then could fabulous jewel theft be too far behind?

"What's to be ashamed of?" his mother echoed. "What's to be ashamed of, he asks? Is this what they teach them in the schools these days, that it's nothing to be ashamed of, having a crazy person in the family?"

"*Sha*, Gertie, *sha*." Gertrude's husband, Abe, spoke with the flat, weary air of a man who knows he has already lost the battle, the war, and the writing of the history books afterward. "He's only a boy, he doesn't know what he's talking about. Let it go."

The Statue of Liberty would turn butterfingers and drop her torch before Gertrude Rosenfeld would let go of an argument. "*This* is how you talk to your wife among people?" she demanded. "*This* is how you teach the boy he should respect his mother? By undermining my authority? Oh, it's easy for you; *you* don't have a sister who's gone crazy!" Her voice broke and cataracts of tears drenched her cheeks. Mrs. Rosenfeld's command of strategic waterworks was deadly.

"Gertie, Gertie, don't." There was a note of genuine panic in Abe's voice. Twenty years of marriage had taught him that his blushing bride had absolutely no qualms about making scenes in public. Scenes? Whole dramas. Grand operas, yet! He still woke up in a cold sweat from dreams of her famous production, *You Want I Should Do WHAT in the Bedroom, You Pervert?!*, which had debuted on their honeymoon, in the lobby of Kutscher's resort, to Standing Room Only and thunderous critical acclaim.

Abe crammed his huge white handkerchief into Gertie's hands. "Shhh, shhh, stop crying, forget I said anything. And *you*—!" He rounded on Oscar. "Who asked for your opinion, you little *pisher*? If your mama says there's something to be ashamed of, you be *ashamed*!"

"Abie, don't yell at the boy!" Gertrude exclaimed. Her eyes went from flood to flint in an instant. She gathered her son to her bosom, nearly smothering him in the process, and glared *fleischig* daggers at her husband. "Is it his fault that Rifka's crazy? Is it?" And answering her own question before her husband could get a word in edgewise (why start a precedent?) she declared: "It is not! It's that no-good boy of hers, that Benny's fault, that's who. Like a bitterness in the mouth, he is, eating out his own mother's heart with anguish. Other boys, the war's over in Europe, they come home. But Benny? He stays! For *over ten years*, he stays. What, Europe's a bargain? Our people couldn't run away fast enough from such a bargain! No wonder Rifka's gone *mishuggeh*! May God take me from this earth if I ever have to know from such a thing!" On that note, she gave her own son a monitory squeeze and released him from her embrace.

Little Oscar fell back against his father, breathing hard, his face lightly dusted with talcum powder, his comic book a crumpled mess. He was both terrified and elated by his recent ordeal and what it foreshadowed. If Ma was this upset by *Tanteh* Rifka's supposed madness, the odds were favorable that the rest of the female Gratzes would be likewise all aflutter. An otherwise tedious evening of family socializing might well be relieved by pyrotechnic outbursts of hoo-hah seldom seen anywhere outside of Greek tragedy.

Plus, there would be herring.

There was herring. There was *always* herring by the Gratz Cousins' Club. The three immortal immutables—the only sacred Trinity in which that extended clan believed—were Death, Taxes, and Herring, with maybe a nice *shtik* prune danish, for after. The imminence of pickled fish enveloped the Rosenfelds like a supernatural presence almost from the minute they stepped off the train at Flatbush Avenue and walked the three blocks to the apartment building where the former Rifka Gratz—now Strauss—lived with her husband, Max.

The Gratz family Cousins' Club met on the third Sunday of every other month because that was the way it had always been from the time that the Gratz brothers, Ludwig and Morris, had brought their families to the *goldineh medina* of America, back in the 1890s. The procedures and underlying organizational *tsimmes* governing the Cousins' Club were originally the brainchild of Chaia Gratz (née Siegel), Ludwig's first wife from back in the Old Country. It was she who decreed that the club should convene when it did. ("So we should have less chance of a meeting falling on the High Holydays, and so I shouldn't have to see that *farbisseneh* sister-in-law of mine more than six times a year, God willing.") It was likewise she who determined that the club should meet only in the afternoons, to give those family members who lived in the farther flung reaches of the New York City area sufficient time to get home at a decent hour. ("You never know what's out there in the dark," she'd say, rolling her eyes meaningly.)

Most important of all, it was she who laid out the plan for rotating the site of club meetings, every household within the family taking its proper turn hosting the event. Only established married couples counted as households. Singles, newlyweds, widows and widowers, and—God forbid!—those who had brought the shame of divorce onto the clan were all excluded from the rotation.

Although she was not a Gratz by blood, Chaia held an unassailably solid claim to authority within the family: Having borne her Ludwig six little female Gratzes like six pearls, and having set down the rules for the Cousins' Club, she died while bringing forth a seventh child, a boy, thus acquiring that most indisputable prerogative to supremacy, martyrdom via male-producing motherhood. This automatically made her the Gratz equivalent of a saint.

Thus it was that Chaia Gratz achieved her own kind of immortality, her familial decisions continuing to carry weight and to annoy people for better than thirty-five years after her death. It was a legacy more deeply carved into the spirits of her descendants and corollary kin than any of the letters chiseled into the old-fashioned brownstone marker on her grave.

So when (in the Year of *Their* Lord, 1958) Mrs. Becky "Rifka" Strauss declared that this time the Cousins' Club would meet on Sunday *night*, it was almost the same as if she'd announced that she would be serving a lovely lobster bisque to go with the ham and cheese sandwiches.

As he walked along the sidewalk en route to his recurring date with Destiny and danish, little Oscar contrived to fall back a few paces from his mother in order to tug at his father's sleeve and ask, "Papa? How come Evie doesn't have to come to this?"

Mr. Rosenfeld sighed. "Your sister will be there," he said, speaking as heavily as he walked. Twenty-three years of his wife's delectable, *schmaltz*-laden cooking had worked their magic, transforming a young man who once resembled Fred Astaire into a replica of Sidney Greenstreet, only not half so nimble. "She had something important to do tonight with her girlfriends—a nice party for the Dreyfus girl, Joanie, she's getting married soon, your sister should only be so lucky already!—but when *Tanteh* Rifka sprang this last-minute nighttime meeting *mishegass* on us, Evie had to go first by the girlfriends, then come here all by herself, and at *this* hour, so your poor mama should drop dead from worry, *cholileh!*"

While Abe went through several ritual gesticulations to avert Gertrude's imaginary death by maternal anxiety, Oscar set to work parsing his father's words. The results were both disappointing and encouraging, a paradox unworkable anywhere else in the real world except *du côté de chez* Gratz.

Point the first: Oscar's sister, Evie, was coming to the Cousins' Club meeting fresh from a bridal shower for Joanie Dreyfus, a young woman who looked like a bundle of throw pillows drenched in vinegar. Everyone at the Cousins' Club meeting must know this beforehand, otherwise Evie's delayed arrival would be sniping fodder. ("So, Gertie, your daughter's now too good to show up on time like the rest of us? What, Miss Big-shot Career Girl can't afford, maybe, a watch?")

Point the second: In the Gratz family culture, it mattered not how pretty, smart, well-educated, refined, creative, or successfully employed a girl was; if she wasn't married, she was nothing. Worse than nothing: A cipher, a nebbish, a humiliation, a living reproach to her parents and, more specifically, irrefutable proof of her own mother's bitter failure as a woman, a matriarch, and a nag. Evie could stand up at the Cousins' Club meeting and announce, "I've just been awarded the Nobel Peace Prize!" only to hear, "And this gets you a husband how?"

Point the third: It was a given that every last female at the Cousins' Club was going to make at least one stinging remark to Evie about her ongoing state of unblessed singleness. This would aggravate Evie. (All the more so because if Evie dared find the gumption to make any sort of retort, it would inevitably be greeted by, "What's wrong with you, you snap at me like that? I only ask how come you're not married yet because I *care*. By you this is a sin, to *care* about your own niece/cousin/obscurely related single female family member? Hmph! With a temper like that, no wonder you still can't get a man!")

It was likewise a constant of the universe that every last female at the Cousins' Club would also manage to needle Gertrude about her daughter's lack of matrimonial success long before Evie showed up. This would get Gertrude worked up to such a degree that when Evie finally did arrive, she would be White Sands to her mother's fifty kiloton why-aren't-you-married-yet-you-want-to-kill-your-own-mother-from-shame A-bomb.

Oscar grinned. Some things were even better than herring!

To Gertie's unspoken relief and Oscar's disappointment, no one at the Cousins' Club meeting mentioned Evie or the bridal shower. Was it for this he had endured the inevitable gauntlet of cheek-pinching and kisses? (Oscar swore up and down that after some Cousins' Club meetings he could remove the layers of lipstick from his face with a trowel. The scraped-off goo displayed distinct cosmetological strata, enabling the careful scholar to figure out the order in which Oscar's aunts, great-aunts, cousins, and other female relations had assailed him.)

Aside from being transformed into a walking color-sampler for Helena Rubinstein, Hazel Bishop, and Max Factor, Oscar's ears rang painfully with countless cries of "*Oy!* Look at him! Looksobighe'sgetting!" followed quickly by "*K'n ein'horeh!* P'too-p'too-p'too!" Who had been the first genius to determine that spitting all over a kid would ward off the Evil Eye? Dripping pints of familial saliva, Oscar bellied up to the buffet and was somewhat placated to see that there was not only herring, but also plates of smoked whitefish, sable, and even—O rapture! O luxury!—lox.

The buffet table chatter centered on repeated declarations that all the platters looked so gorgeous that it would be a pity to touch anything. The Visigoths probably said much the same thing about Rome just before they laid the city waste. Alaric and his hordes had nothing on the Gratz family when confronted by the Seven Hills of Smoked Salmon.

Oscar filled up a plate, then cast about for someplace to sit. This was a toughie. Even the sci-fi comic books he adored could not account for the unearthly, mystifying powers of the Gratzes: Bend the concepts space and time how he might, Oscar simply could not explain how all of his relatives managed to occupy every sofa, armchair, ottoman, rocker, stool, and folding chair in the apartment while at the same time never leaving the buffet.

"Oscar, sweetie, here! Come sit by *Tanteh* Lillian!" A scarlet-clawed hand waved furiously from the far end of the living room as blinding beams of light reflected off a pair of turquoise-colored, rhinestone-studded harlequin eyeglasses. Oscar swallowed hard and wondered if he had time to escape into one of the bedrooms before—

Too late. His mother had overheard. "Oscar, don't stand there like a *goyisher kop*. You don't hear *Tanteh* Lillian calling you? You want the whole family should think *both* my children got no manners? Go! Go!" She backed up her words with an encouraging shove between the shoulder blades, a shove so hard that Oscar was surprised not to see her hand protruding from the center of his chest, helping itself to a nice piece of lox off his platter.

By the time he made his way across the room, *Tanteh* Lillian had forgotten all about summoning him to her side. She was deep in deliciously scandalized conversation with her sisters, Gloria and Greta. (The girls in that movie-mad branch of the family got off much easier than their brothers, Boris, Lon, Valentino, and Chico.) Feeling his mother's eagle eye still heavy upon him, Oscar wriggled himself onto the sofa between two of the ladies and tried to eat in peace.

It was not to be. The conversation going on above his head proved to be far more fascinating than any succulent sliver of dead fish, even unto a slice of Leviathan itself: They were talking about Benny.

"—the reason why Rifka changed the meeting time! The *only* reason."

"Sure, that's what I heard, but why—?"

"Why else? Because she's ashamed. Because she doesn't want any of us to see by the light of day what that ungrateful *momzer* is doing to his own mother! Because maybe this way she hoped a lot of us wouldn't be able to come by, so she wouldn't have so many witnesses to her disgrace, itshouldn'thappentoadog."

"*Momzer*? Rifka's boy, he served in the war! He was made a captain, yet!" There followed a gloriously elaborate spate of Yiddish maledictions where the only words Oscar could recognize were *Hitler, Nazis, mad dog,* and *burn in Hell.*

"Captain, *shmaptain*." *Tanteh* Gloria waved away Cousin Benny's commission and multiple Purple Hearts with one sweep of her cocktail-ringed hand. "He's *how* old and still not married? What, I've got to draw you a picture?"

"Shh! Shh! You want Rifka should maybe hear you and burst a blood vessel?" In the way of the women of her tribe, *Tanteh* Greta sincerely believed that the best way to stifle Gloria was by shushing her loudly. Luckily for the integrity of Rifka's blood vessels, in a room already throbbing with so many other female Gratzes exercising their concept of "indoor voices," Gloria's remark and Greta's cover-up attempt went largely unnoticed.

Oscar, however, did notice. "What kinda picture, *Tanteh* Gloria?" he asked. "I mean, I thought it was only bad if *girls* didn't get married."

The three sisters exchanged a look that spoke volumes, all of them written in the key of *oy.* Before they could come up with an answer or—more likely—shove Oscar back in his mother's direction, the unthinkable happened: A hush fell over the Gratz Cousins' Club.

Benny had arrived.

Benny had not arrived alone.

Looking back, Oscar couldn't put his finger on the exact moment that the whispers began. They were simply *there*, like the brown horsehair sofa under his rump, like the smell of Uncle Max's cigars, like the mustard-and-spinach-patterned wallpaper. They were real whispers, too, not Gratz whispers: whispers fit for a Connecticut country club, whispers proper to an Episcopalian funeral, whispers where you could *not* hear every word clearly from a distance of ten feet away. It was all very frustrating for Oscar, to say nothing of confusing. For the life of him, he couldn't figure out why his extended family was acting so weird.

Cousins' Club Standard Operating Procedure required that when someone showed up accompanied by a non–family member, the sluice gates opened and the women streamed forward, shrieking and clucking and demanding, "So, who's this? When are you two getting married?" No one saw anything pushy or impolitic about the latter question. If you brought someone to Cousins' Club, you wanted to marry them. That, or you wanted to end the affair, and exposing them to the full force of the Gratz women was the coward's way to do it. Either way, it was like the scene in *The Jungle Book* where Mowgli and the new cubs were displayed for the inspection of the wolf pack, only without old Akeela there to declare, "Look well, O Gratzes!"

This time no one moved, no one swept down upon Benny and his escort, no one clamored to know the identity of that charming person in his company nor when the wedding day would be.

How could they? Benny had arrived with another man.

There was something vaguely perturbing about the gentleman in question. Though his pale face, dark eyes, and pitch-black hair were commonplace to the Eastern European branches of the Gratz clan, he carried these as no Gratz had ever done, with a disquieting air of the exotic, the forbidden, the . . . *goyish*. He stood only a little taller than Benny—who at six-foot-one was no slouch in that department, unless he *did* slouch—yet where Benny was robust and well-muscled, this guy was so thin that he seemed to tower over *Tanteh* Rifka's son. He wore his suit like a panther's pelt. Benny was no slob, but next to his companion he looked positively scruffy.

And next to his companion he stayed: Stayed, stood, walked, sat down, you name it. They stuck so close to one another that they might as well have been joined at the hip. It was like watching a sister act.

Oscar didn't get it. Sure, if someone showed up at Cousins' Club accompanied by a person of the same sex, no one could fire off the Marriage Cathechism ("So, when—?" "So, where—?" "So, a ring—?" "So small?") but in those cases the relatives would still surge in to make the newcomer welcome and add him or her to the official family fix-up list ("So, you're Benny's friend? Such a good-looking man like you, and not married? Come, you should meet my daughter."). That wasn't happening either.

In all the seething mass of Gratzes, only Oscar stared. To be fair, the boy had a built-in excuse for such impolite behavior: It was the first time he had ever seen his cousin Benny in the flesh. The man had left to serve his country when Oscar was still an infant in arms. Yet to be honest as well as fair, even if Benny had been more familiar to Oscar than a face from a photograph lovingly displayed on *Tanteh* Rifka's sideboard, his entrance, appearance, escort, and the reactions that these had elicited among the gathered Gratzes still would have made gawking inevitable.

The rest of Oscar's relatives were being incredibly assiduous about *not* staring, not even casting a casual glance in Benny's direction. If concerted inattention could render a person invisible, Benny would have become a phantom on the spot. Oscar was utterly at sea. Why the silence, then the *real* whispers, then—hideously unnatural act for any Gratz!—why the deliberate *minding of their own business*?

Only *Tanteh* Rifka seemed untouched by the plague of intentional indifference. She alone rushed up to Benny and his friend, threw her arms around her son, and embraced him fiercely. "And this must be Kazimir," she said. Her lips curved up in a grimace so taut, so false, so petrified, so downright horrific that green hair or no green hair, in Oscar's eyes *Tanteh* Rifka had clinched her claim to Jokerhood.

If Benny's friend noticed that the warmth of Rifka's welcome was forced, he gave no sign. Bowing, he raised one of her plump hands to his lips, kissed it, then met her eyes. "My pleasure," he said. His smile was cold and brilliant as a winter's midnight sky.

Oscar heard that low, powerful voice, recognized the foreign accent weighing down every word. He snapped to attention where he sat, idle curiosity sharply changed to intense focus, like a fox terrier suddenly catching wind of a rabbit. The man's pallor mirrored Benny's own, except the lips that had just touched *Tanteh* Rifka's hand were so red they might have been rouged. His gaze was cold, hypnotic. When *Tanteh* Rifka urged the two men toward the buffet, Benny ate without relish, like an automaton, but despite a display of succulent foods fit to tempt the prissiest palate, his companion, Kazimir, did not eat at all. In fact, he showed a positive aversion to the acutely fragrant end of the table that proffered platters of salami, pastrami, tongue, and the garlicky delights of *carnatzlach* sausage and *p'tcha*. (He stood in good company as to that lattermost dish: To young Oscar's eyes *p'tcha*—a redolent, translucent, unnerving concoction of calf's foot jelly— looked like something that a Martian would sneeze.) And he did not drink . . . Manischewitz. Or Dr. Brown's cream soda. Or even a nice glass of tea.

All at once, in a revelation worthy of thunderbolts and Wagnerian crescendos, *Oscar knew*!

As to *what* he knew, before he could put down the lox and blurt any word of his epiphany, a thick, stubby finger jammed him in the ribs so hard that it knocked half the breath from his body.

"What, *boychik*, you never seen a *faigeleh* before?"

The question as to whether this were the first time Oscar had seen a man's man (in the Oscar Wilde rather than Ernest Hemingway sense of the term) was rendered almost unintelligible by the low, raspy, carton-of-Camels-a-day voice that uttered it. There could be only one source: *Bubbeh* Gratz.

To speak the name of *Bubbeh* Gratz was to invoke the ageless power of pure, primal, run-screaming-wet-your-pants terror. She was *Bubbeh*, not *bubbeh*: The absolute magnitude of her authority and dominion within the family was more than lowercase letters could bear. She was also *Bubbeh* only by courtesy, for she was no one's grandmother nor, indeed, mother. Born Louisa Claire (aka Leah Chaviva) Gratz, she had *stayed* Louisa Claire Gratz despite the best efforts of the family to drag her down with them into the depths of marital bliss. She had not just proved to be unmarriageable, she had actively fought to stay single with the same zeal she'd brought to all her other battles, whether for workers' unions, women's votes, Colored People's rights, or the reestablishment of a Jewish homeland.

Squat as a trodden toad, with steel-gray hair, steel-gray eyes, steel-rimmed *pince-nez* spectacles, and a body as white and blobby as a ladleful of mashed potatoes, *Bubbeh* Gratz was the oldest living member of the family. She wore contention for her crown and wielded spleen for her scepter. It was foretold by one unnamed member of the Gratz tribe whose hand had strayed to the forbidden art of tea-leaf reading that on the day *Bubbeh* Gratz found anything she *did* approve of in this world, she would depart for the next. Thus she was assured of unnatural immortality.

Again the short, fat finger rammed the boy's rib cage. "You don't talk back, someone talks to you?" Another jab. Oscar could have sworn he heard his young bones give up a faint, pitiful *crack*, but pain was immediately engulfed by panic when he noted that he and *Bubbeh* were the only two people left on the sofa. The assorted aunts had turned terror into transmigration, vanishing from the living room to rematerialize in the safety of the kitchen doorway where they huddled like hens in a thunderstorm. He sat alone, noshing herring with the dragon.

"I—I'm sorry, *Bubbeh*." Oscar borrowed courage from imagining that he was a hero like the Batman or Tarzan or Flash Gordon, though the Joker, the Leopard Men, and Ming the Merciless all rolled into one were still strictly bush league next to *Bubbeh*. "I don't know what that means, *faigeleh*."

"No?" She tilted her head back, looked down her nose at him, and then, without wasting words or one instant's worry about whether the boy's parents wanted him to have the information, she told him. She spoke of the matter casually, as though it were the most natural thing in the world. She didn't even pause in her ongoing task of wrapping up the bounty of her buffet plate in sheet upon sheet of waxed paper and stuffing her cavernous pocketbook with packet after packet of cold cuts and smoked fish. (Whoever hosted the Cousins' Club knew that all the womenfolk came prepared to use purses and coat pockets to cache as many alleged leftovers as they could. "*Fahlaydah*, it shouldn't go to waste." Their hosts budgeted and bought food accordingly.)

Oscar's lower jaw dropped like the parachute ride at Coney Island. "Two *guys*?" His voice cracked as badly as his rib. "*Together*? Doing *that*?" He watched, appalled and fascinated, as Kazimir leaned close to Cousin Benny and whispered something in his ear. Benny nodded dumbly and followed his "friend" down the hall. What might have been a simple request to be shown the toilet became something far more freighted with forbidden meaning as Oscar realized that this was the same hall that led to the bedrooms.

"With *each other*? Benny and that guy are—?" He shook his head. "You're wrong."

"What, you don't believe me?" *Bubbeh* dropped yet another parcel of salami into her purse. "Just because it's not something they write about in that science fiction *drek* you read?"

Now *drek*—a.k.a. manure, either literal or figurative— was one Yiddish word Oscar knew, though customarily applied by his father to the doings of Senator Joseph McCarthy. This was the first time Oscar had heard it used to describe his favorite reading matter. "It's not *drek*! It's— it's real good! Educational! It's all about *ideas* and stuff!"

"*Nu*, what isn't?" *Bubbeh* Gratz chuckled. "Educational is what you tell your parents, they shouldn't stop you from reading it. 'Educational . . .' *Life* is educational, *boychik*. What you read by science fiction, it's all spaceships, bug-eyed monsters, rayguns, alien princesses with a pair *tsatskehs* on them, the poor girls can't hardly stand up straight! It's got nothing to teach you about real life."

For an instant, Oscar had a scary thought: What if *Bubbeh* Gratz conveyed her dangerously anti–sci-fi attitude to his parents? As the oldest living Gratz, her words would carry more weight than her orthopedic shoes already did. If she said that sci-fi was worthless, useless, *drek*, Ma and Dad might very well believe her and then—

No. No, never, *k'n ein' horeh*, *p'too-p'too-p'too*, the accursed outcome did not bear thinking on. Oscar's heart beat faster: Bad enough, what he'd just concluded about Benny and that Kazimir creep, but worse by far the realization that *Bubbeh* Gratz might cause him to lose the one thing that opened up doorways to the stars in a life that was otherwise circumscribed by school, *shul* , and herring.

"Oh, yeah?" He shouted his defiance full in her face. Fear had made him bold. "Well, if sci-fi's not about real life, how come I'm the only one here who knows the difference between a *faigeleh* and a vampire?"

Alas for Oscar, he spoke out at the instant when every other conversation in the Strauss apartment hit a coincidental stop. The fateful words echoed through the sudden silence and promptly turned it into something greater than itself: The hush heard 'round the world, the acoustic equivalent of negative space and antimatter.

The first sound to creep back into the room was a low, thin wail of anguish from *Tanteh* Rifka. This quickly blossomed into racking sobs. The women swarmed over her like ants on a caramel, jabbering wildly as they dragged her into the kitchen. The men, abandoned, turned their attention to Oscar. Even kindly, torpid Uncle Max was glaring at him.

It was at this moment that the doorbell rang. It rang loudly and repeatedly, each peal longer and more emphatic than the one before, until finally the doorknob turned and Oscar's sister, Evie, let herself in.

"Hi, everyone," she said. Her face, her entire body was tense; she was clearly bracing herself for the onslaught of questions about her friend Joanie's bridal shower, followed fast by "well-meaning" comments concerning her own ongoing failure to land a husband. There was really no way to calculate the sheer magnitude of the shock wave she experienced upon entering the Cousins' Club venue and finding her unmarried self most unnaturally ignored, even by her own parents.

"Evie!" Oscar broke away from the ring of scowling menfolk and flung himself on his sister with terrifying enthusiasm. "Boy, am I ever glad to see *you*!"

Evie pried herself free of her little brother's suspiciously eager embrace and held him at arm's length. "Okay, Oscar, what did you do *now*?"

Little did she know it was a loaded question until it went off in her face. The torrent of explanations from all sides swept her to the brink of insensibility before she fought her way back up the narrative stream, gasped, and managed to ask: "So since when is Cousin Benny a queer vampire?"

The sound of one hand clapping itself to a forehead in exasperation was repeated many times throughout the living room. It remained for *Bubbeh* Gratz to step in as the voice of clarification:

"*I* said Benny's a *faigeleh*, him and his friend. *This* little *pisher* said he's a vampire."

"I did not!" Oscar's protest flew free in the face of his father's ineffective attempts to shush the lad. "I said Benny's *friend* was the vampire. I mean, *look* at him! Look how pale he is, how he's all dressed in black, how he couldn't come here unless it was at night. You gotta watch him drink Benny's blood to prove I'm right or what?"

"I would not suggest waiting for that opportunity." Kazimir stood in the hallway leading from the bedrooms, Benny glued to his side as always. The foreigner's face contorted with distaste. "We heard what was said. I bid you . . . good evening."

He was gone so quickly it seemed as if he'd sprouted wings. Benny uttered a low moan, but when he tried to rush after his friend, *Tanteh* Rifka suddenly materialized from the kitchen and laid hold of her son with an unyielding grasp.

"Benny, *zieskeit*, let him go!" she cried. "Such a friend you don't need, believe me!"

"Ma, please," Benny protested. "You've gotta let me go; it'll kill me if you don't."

"Fine, go!" Benny's mother dropped her hold on his arm and clutched her chest. "Better you should tear my heart out and grind it into the dirt than you should listen to me. Who am I to ask you for anything? Only the woman who suffered the tortures of the damned to give birth to you. But go, *go*! I'm only thankful that with my health I won't be around to suffer your ingratitude much longer." She staggered toward the nearest sofa, alternating sobs with coughing fits and groans.

"Oh my God, I can't take this." Evie rolled her eyes. "I have just sat through that snotty Joanie Dreyfus unwrapping thirty-four identical sets of monogrammed guest towels with nothing to eat but dried-out cucumber sandwiches because *Mrs.* Dreyfus thinks that's *refined*, for Lord's sake, and I am *not* going to have my first chance at a decent meal ruined because Cousin Benny's queer friend had a hissy fit and stomped out. You wait right there with your Ma, Benny: I'll bring back your boyfriend." So saying, Evie was out the door.

Oscar took one look at the remaining family faces surrounding him. If life were a comic book, their eyes would be emitting tiny red lightning bolts, symbolizing the emanation of killer Guilt rays. "I'll help you, Evie!" he yelped, and bolted before anyone could stop him.

He hoped to catch up to his sister on the stairs or at least in the lobby of *Tanteh* Rifka's building, but it was not meant to be. Evie had a head start and hunger had given her speed. Oscar hit the sidewalk and cast around for some sight of her, to no avail. The Flatbush streets were well lighted with the yellow radiance of streetlamps, none of which revealed his sister's retreating form. On such a warm evening, kids were still out playing potsy, fathers settled world affairs over a pack of Lucky Strikes and a bottle of Coca-Cola, mothers swapped news, recipes, and beaming brags about their perfect children, while grandmothers enthroned on a row of folding chairs sat in awful judgment without appeal over the whole neighborhood, but that was all. There was no sign of Evie; there was no sign of Kazimir.

Oscar pondered his options: Go back upstairs and face the collective Wrath of Gratz—with the added likelihood that *Bubbeh* would seize this opportunity to blame the recent blowup on "that sci-fi *drek* the *boychik* reads"—or wander aimlessly around the streets until his absence became so terrifying that when he finally did return to the Strauss apartment, all would be forgiven out of sheer relief to have him back again.

It wasn't a hard choice to make: Oscar jammed his hands into the pockets of his good pants and sauntered off in a random direction, whistling the *Davy Crockett* theme song. If he knew his kinfolk—and he did, thanks to all those Cousins' Club meetings—being a Lost Child would trump his Troublemaker status into oblivion.

He was halfway to the corner when he heard a sound that set the short hairs on the nape of his neck on end, a plaintive, high-pitched moan that came from the back of a strange passageway between two large apartment buildings. Five concrete steps led down into a tunnel that served the function of an alley. The lone working lightbulb cast a weak glow over a clutter of trash cans near the stairs, but left the far end shrouded in shadow.

The moan came again, louder, shuddering through the air. For Oscar, there was no mistaking the voice that had uttered it. He'd swear to its identity on a stack of *Detective* comics: "Evie? Evie, is that you? What are you doing down there?" No answer came out of the shades. For a moment he paused on the lip of the passageway, unsure of whether to descend into the gloom or run to *Tanteh* Rifka's apartment for help.

With alacrity worthy of UNIVAC, his young mind blitzed through all the possibilities that might be lurking just beyond the pathetic pool of light, all the consequences that might befall if he didn't do something and do it *now*. Swiftly he weighed his hopes of getting immediate backup from any of the strangers on the sidewalk. He knew how *that* would go:

"Who are you . . .? Rifka's nephew? Rifka Strauss, from 3-C?"

"No, Simon, the Strausses live by 5-C."

"I'm telling you, Shayna, it's 3-C, and may God strike me dead if I'm wrong."

"Fine, so I'll be a widow."

"Little boy, does your *tanteh* Rifka know you're out here like a wild thing, talking nonsense about someone making a big tumult down by where the super keeps the garbage?"

And over this imagined interchange there loomed another image, a gaunt specter of the night—white skin, red lips, arms spread wide like a bat's leathery wings. When those arms closed, they clasped to the monster's bosom that helpless victim of his hideous thirst, Evie. The fantasized Kazimir raised a bloody mouth from his unnatural feast and filled Oscar's head with dreadful, gloating laughter.

That did it. He took a deep breath, clenched his fists, and asked himself *What would the Batman do?* He knew the answer: Oscar Rosenfeld dove into the darkness.

"Evie! Evie, I'm coming!" As he sped past the row of garbage cans, he caught sight of a godsend: Huddled in the space between two of the cans was a busted-up old orange crate. Oscar paused just long enough to wrench free one of the broken wooden slats, then ran on, couching his improvised stake like a lance, ready to send the vampire to his doom.

"Oh my God, Oscar, what are you doing, running with that sharp thing? You want you should poke your eye out, God forbid?" Like a *deus ex* Future Jewish Mothers of America, Evie materialized out of the darkness and intercepted her little brother, yanking the slat from his hands and throwing it far away. Behind her, Kazimir observed the whole business with burning crimson eyes.

"Evie, no!" Oscar hollered, lunging for his do-it-yourself vampire-slayer. Again she thwarted him, pulling him back by the shoulders. He stared at her in horror. He'd read the stories: He understood why his own sister had betrayed him. A faint spill of light came from the rear end of the passageway, where lamp-lit single family homes shared backyard space with the big apartment buildings. The soft glow illuminated the young woman's face, her hair—

—her neck.

"He got you!" Oscar stared spellbound at the dark mark on his sister's dainty throat. "You're his slave for all eternity! Ma's gonna *plotz*!" He began to sniffle, then to sob for his lost sister, the vampire's newest plaything.

"Oscar, why're you crying, a big boy like you?" Evie asked.

" 'Cause I'm too late, and he bit you, and now you're gonna become a vampire, and sleep in a coffin by day, and drink the blood of the living by night, and— and—" Abruptly, Oscar's sobs stopped. He took a long, shaky breath, then a closer look at his sister's neck.

"*That's* no vampire bite," he declared. With dynamism worthy of a young Perry Mason, he leveled an accusatory finger at her. "There's no puncture marks. That's— that's—" He cudgeled his brain for a word he'd learned from some older boys at school—accompanied by salacious winks and snickers—when they spoke of the *mysterium tremendum* that was Brooklyn Woman.

"—a hickey." The glaring beam from the flashlight in Cousin Benny's fist illuminated Evie's throat, then swept over to engulf Kazimir. "I can't leave you alone for a minute, can I?" he said coldly.

"No matter how much I wish you would, no." The vampire drew back his lips in a grimace that began life as a feral snarl but resolved itself into a sheepish grin. "I keep telling you, Benny: I like *girls*."

"So do I. We should talk," said a gravelly voice. *Bubbeh* Gratz shoved Benny aside and lumbered down the concrete steps into the passageway, bearing down upon Oscar, Evie, and Kazimir like an orthopedically shod juggernaut. She did not stop until she stood nose-to-shirtfront with the vampire.

"It's a good thing I followed Benny when he handed his poor mama that *tumel* about going out for a pack cigarettes. For this you need to take a flashlight? Bah. Children. And *you*." She stabbed her pocketbook sharply into Kazimir's belly. "So the little *pisher* was right, after all?" She jerked her head at Oscar. "You're a vampire, like out of that sci-fi *drek*? With the blood-drinking and the coffin-sleeping and the whole undead *mishegass*?"

Kazimir nodded nervously. In all his years on either side of the grave, he had never encountered anything quite so daunting as *Bubbeh* Gratz.

That formidable woman now rounded on Evie. "And *you*," she declared, waving her purse at the trembling maiden. "You aren't gone maybe five minutes from the apartment and already you're making moofkie-foofkie in an alley with *this* piece of work? What are you, a cat? A *bummerke*? A Little Miss Round Heels?"

Evie grabbed *Bubbeh* Gratz's meaty hands. "Please don't tell Ma," she begged. "All I wanted was to talk to Kazimir somewhere away from all the neighborhood *yentas*, so they shouldn't know about him and Benny being . . . you know."

"Except as I told this lovely girl, Benny and I are *not* 'you know,'" Kazimir put in.

"Say it again, louder, I don't think they heard you in Far Rockaway," Benny said bitterly. "For this I got away from Ma, Kaz? For you to give me a slap in the face? *Again*? With my own cousin?"

Evie shushed them both. "I wanted he should come back upstairs, that's all. But then— I don't know what happened, or how it happened so fast or—" She paused, left flummoxed by her own emotions. "There's something about him that's so— so—"

"Sexy?" *Bubbeh* Gratz gave a lecherous chuckle and nudged the girl with one plump elbow. "Like I can't know that word? I'm through playing the game, but I can still keep score."

Benny descended the concrete steps to join the miniature family reunion in the alleyway. He placed one hand on Evie's shoulder and said, "I know what you mean about Kaz. Why do you think I spent ten years of my life trying to get him to change his mind about me? I hope you never have to know what it's like, Evie, when the love of your life won't even give you a chance to— OW!"

The *zetz* that *Bubbeh* Gratz landed on Benny's arm might not have shaken the pillars of heaven, but it probably shook the pillars of Teaneck, New Jersey. "What love? What life? You haven't been paying attention? He says he likes *girls*, stupid!"

"So do you," Oscar spoke up. *Bubbeh* Gratz and the others looked at him as though he'd just proclaimed his vocation for the Catholic priesthood. Oscar responded with a defiant: "Well, that's what you *said*."

"Like you didn't know, already?" *Bubbeh* Gratz inquired. The silence that followed was eloquent. "You *didn't*?" *Bubbeh*'s grizzled eyebrows rose. She looked from Oscar to Evie. "The *boychik*, okay, him I can see not knowing, but you?" Evie shook her head. "And you, the *faigeleh*, nothing?"

Benny shrugged helplessly. "No one in the family ever said anything about you liking—about how you never got married because—about you being a—" His voice trailed off.

"*Oy*." *Bubbeh* Gratz sighed. "This generation, *kasha varnishkes* for brains. You don't need to be *told* things about your family, you big *yutz*: You just *know*! Why do you think we have these Cousins' Club meetings? For our health? It's where we come so we can find out all the family things we need to know but no one wants to talk about."

"You mean like about how you're a girl *faigeleh*?" Oscar asked *Bubbeh* brightly.

Bubbeh Gratz smiled. "You're a smart boy. Here, have a sourball." She flicked open her purse and gave Oscar a piece of unwrapped hard candy so covered in pocket lint that it looked like a dandelion puff. It was either a reward or revenge.

The furry candy came out of the same purse into which *Bubbeh* Gratz had been stuffing salami and its pungent kindred all evening. The gust of garlic-laden air released from the purse's depths hit poor Kazimir like a mallet. He groaned, demonstrated that there was a stage of pallor that went beyond the dead-and-bloodless variety, and fainted.

"Oh my God, what do we do now?" Evie cried, kneeling beside the fallen vampire and cradling his head to her bosom.

"First, *mamaleh*, you stop holding him to your *tsatskehs* like you want he should take a drink," *Bubbeh* Gratz said. "Then, we should all go get one."

Oscar sat in a booth at the back of McNulty's bar making an outline of the Bat Signal out of maraschino cherry stems. The remains of four Shirley Temples stood ranged on the tabletop in front of him. They had all come with extra cherries as a bribe to Oscar's goodwill. It hadn't worked.

"They've got their nerve," he muttered, fiddling with the pattern of scarlet stems. "Turning me into a stupid babysitter." He spared a cold glance for his charge, the still-unconscious vampire. "Boy, I wish you could've seen some of the looks we got from the little old ladies in front of *Tanteh* Rifka's building when Benny walked by with you slung over his shoulder. I thought they were all gonna have a heart attack or something. Wait until they tell his Ma!" Oscar grinned in spite of his displeasure with having been shunted aside to play vampire-tender.

Kazimir was propped up in one corner of the booth, eyes closed, mouth open. He looked like just another drunk, which was exactly how *Bubbeh* Gratz had introduced him to her old friend, Mr. Cullen McNulty, the establishment's owner/barkeep.

"But a drunk with money," she clarified when that worthy man seemed reluctant to let their group enter his place of business. "You wait until he gets his second wind, and then such drinking you'll see—!"

"It's Sunday," McNulty said. "He's not supposed to be drinking on a Sunday."

"And you're not supposed to be serving on a Sunday, you old *gonif*," she countered. "But if someone *knows* you're here today, you pour. It's a public service for the local *shikkers*, those drunks should have some-where safe to get a snootful. Now draw us three beers, give the *boychik* a nice glass soda pop, and don't make every little thing into a big *megillah!*"

Before McNulty could voice any further doubts or demurrals, Benny flashed him a twenty and he saw reason. Now, lined up like birds on a telephone wire, Benny, *Bubbeh*, and Evie sat nursing a trio of beers at the bar while Oscar minded Kazimir in the booth. They were the only people in the place, it being too late for the after-church-drymouth crowd and too early for the real night owls.

From time to time Oscar caught tantalizing scraps of the bar side conversation concerning how Benny had first encountered and fallen hard for Kazimir. The amorous thunderbolt struck him in a café in Germany, in the war's aftermath, when the world was still just a little topsy-turvy and strange things had more of a chance to happen.

Oscar strained his ears, hoping to pick up some clue as to why the vampire had not turned Cousin Benny into a meal from the get-go. What was that Benny was saying, over at the bar? He'd taken Kaz up to his hotel room? Why would anyone need to go up to a hotel room just to keep talking? That was weird.

Weirder was yet to come: "—really did just want to talk . . . to listen, I mean . . . about the family. Funny, right?" Benny raised his Pilsner glass in a mock toast. "He was fascinated. All he wanted to do was listen to me tell him all about—"

—*the family? Our family?* Oscar shook his head. Some things were even more unbelievable than vampires.

And yet, there it was: The few sentence fragments Oscar overheard told how, in his infatuated state, Benny was willing to do anything to keep Kazimir in his company that night. And apparently Kazimir was willing to hold off on drinking Benny's blood if that meant he'd get to hear more about that herring-bearing freak show that was Clan Gratz.

Alas, the dawn was *not* willing to hold off, and so the vampire found himself thrown into peril of his afterlife, marooned in a cheap hotel room, far from the shelter of his coffin. Having no other recourse, he confessed his true nature to his smitten suitor and threw himself on Benny's mercy.

"—word of honor never to harm me," Benny was saying. "To stay by me and protect me forever, as I protected him that day. Forever . . . or until I told him he was free to go."

"Oh, Benny, how noble!" Evie sighed, casting a fond look back to the booth where Kaz still sat in a garlic coma.

"Oy, Benny, how *narrish*!" *Bubbeh* Gratz's sigh was anything but fond. "Other boys, they save coins, stamps, box tops. You save *monsters*?"

"He's *not* a monster!" Benny protested.

"By you he's not a monster, but trust me: Someone who doesn't want to *shtup* him thinks different."

"But I love him! Doesn't that count for *something*?"

"Unless he loves you back, it counts for *bubkes*," *Bubbeh* Gratz replied. "Listen, *boychik*, maybe by some men, hanging on like a leech finally gets them, but that's not love: That's them *shtupping* you so you'll stop with the nagging, already. You've got no class, they've got no backbone, a *nice* bargain! Ten years this one owes you his life and he hasn't let you touch him? *Learn*, already! You can't make gefilte fish from goulash. Get someone who loves *you*! But first, take my advice: Get married. Find a nice girl who wants to get a husband, have a kid or two, and then to be left in peace. Give your poor mother grandchildren instead of aggravation. Trust me, once you make with the grandchildren, you can get away with *anything* in this family."

"Why didn't you take your own advice, then?" Benny demanded.

Bubbeh Gratz grinned. "Because when the egg pops out, it's not the rooster who screams, *fershtais*?"

"So you want me to get married, have kids, and *then* find a man who—?" Benny began.

"Hey, get a load of *that*, guys! Gramma Hettie saw right: Jew-boy's back." A strident voice cut Benny off in mid-sentence and drew all eyes to the doorway of McNulty's. The speaker was a short, boxy man about Benny's age, wearing a cheap suit with the green-on-brown sheen of rancid roast beef. He was attended by a pair of swarthy, lumbering brutes whose forearm hair could have founded a wig-making dynasty. Rumpled trousers and sweat-stained white singlets were their livery and apelike hooting was their best stab at laughter. *Bubbeh* Gratz took the trio's measure calmly, but Evie's cheeks went pale.

Benny's face was ashen too, though not with fear. "Carl Dorst," he said between clenched teeth. "Ten years away, and I see *you* the first night I'm back? Son of a—"

"What's'a matter, Jew-boy, ain't you glad to see me?" Dorst rolled into McNulty's like he owned the place. "Or don't you *care* about me no more? My gramma Hettie, she told me saw you and your boyfriend come in here. Said you was *carrying* him. What is he, your war bride? This your *honeymoon*, ya fag?"

(Thus did Oscar learn that neighborhoods, like families, were full of secrets that were no secret, things known by all and said by none; none except the Carl Dorsts of the world, that is.)

Benny stood up. "If you've got business with me, Carl, let's take it outside."

Dorst showed no sign of wanting to leave the premises. "So you can run? Sure, ain't that just like you kikes: Buncha yellow bastards, always running back to *Maaaa*ma." His lip curled. "We missed you here in the neighborhood since you been gone, Benny. Yeah, Jimmy Gannon missed you most of all. You remember Jimmy, don'cha? *Pretty* Jimmy? The one who *didn't* go into the army because he was nothing but a goddam—"

"Shut your mouth, Dorst!" McNulty stepped out from behind the bar. "You know damn well that Jimmy didn't go into the army because he had the asthma. Is that why *you* didn't enlist? Tell me *that*, if you can! You think I forgot the way you and your goons ganged up on him the last time you was in here, how you busted that poor lad's jaw? Get the hell out of my place! You're not welcome here."

"But kikes and faggots are?" Dorst smirked. Suddenly something sharp glittered in his hand. McNulty saw, and backed away slowly. The dank air in the bar became electric with peril. It was heady stuff, pure catnip to those too young to know better. With all adult eyes on Dorst and his men, no one noticed Oscar slip out of the booth and creep closer for a better view. This beat the heck out of *Detective* comics!

Like a load of wet wash hitting the sidewalk from a great height, *Bubbeh* Gratz slid off her bar stool and stood by Benny. "*Shame* on you, Carl Friedrich Dorst!" she declaimed. "*Big* man. Always with that mouth, your tongue should only shrivel like a prune. Over thirty years I know you and not *once* do you give your poor family a minute they could be proud of you! And *you've* got the gall to call our Benny a coward? You should only be such a coward, you lousy *nogoodnik*—"

The sound of Dorst's free hand connecting with *Bubbeh* Gratz's cheek was almost as shocking as the sight of that penny-ante lowlife slapping the old woman. But this was nothing compared to the thunderous report of another hand cracking across Carl Dorst's own ugly mug so hard that he staggered back against one of his loutish hangers-on.

"Don't you dare touch my *Bubbeh*!" Evie shouted as she raised her hand to give Dorst a second taste of Gratz justice. She wasn't afraid any more.

"Evie, no. They're punks, but they're dangerous." Benny tried to get Evie out of harm's way, but he wasn't fast enough. Dorst gave a curt signal to his goons. They yanked the girl away from Benny before he could react and shoved her at Dorst. He grabbed her by the wrist so hard that she whimpered.

"You want I shouldn't touch your *what*, baby?" He leered. "Y'know, you ain't half bad, for a Jew. A little mouthy, a little outta line, but—OW!"

"Let go of my sister!" Oscar yelled. The command was purely for effect: The instant that Oscar's foot connected with Dorst's shin, the neighborhood bully lost his hold on Evie.

There followed one of those instants when the laws of time altered subtly and many things happened at once: A loud clunk echoed through the bar. Mr. McNulty had brought out a baseball bat and dropped it on the bar. He glared at Dorst and his overmuscled crew. *Bubbeh* Gratz set aside her gargantuan pocketbook in favor of the superior destructive potential of Benny's flashlight. Evie scampered around behind the bar and grabbed a couple of full liquor bottles. She rearmed Benny with one and raised the other by the neck until she looked like the tavern version of a rolling pin–toting housewife straight out of the funny pages. The Gratzes stood ready to do battle.

Unfortunately, that elastic moment also contained Carl Dorst grabbing Oscar by the neck with one hand and bringing his nasty little jackknife right up against the boy's face with the other. "Whaddaya say, Benny?" he drawled. "Wanna see me give this little heeb a *human* nose?"

"*Try it and die.*"

A voice old as dust and hollow as an empty tomb filled McNulty's tavern. Carl Dorst and his pet thugs turned to confront the vampire in full hunting mode, arms high and outstretched, hands like claws, pale face contorted with inhuman fury, and red, red lips pulled back to expose keen, glittering, deadly fangs. Even with a knife less than an inch from his right eye, Oscar forgot to be afraid.

Wow, he thought. *He needs a cape. Then this would* really *be something!*

Cape or no cape, Kazimir's display of the vampire rampant packed more than enough clout to deal with Dorst and his crew. They took one look, screamed like horror-flick sorority girls, and bolted out the back way, leaping the bar and leaving suspicious puddles in the sawdust as they fled.

Kazimir dropped his pose and hurried to *Bubbeh* Gratz's side. "Are you all right?" he asked, studying her reddened cheek solicitously.

"It'll take more than a *patsh* from a little snot like Carl Dorst to bother me," she replied. "But just you wait until I tell his *bubbeh* Hettie what he did, *then* you'll see something!" She chuckled, relishing the grandmotherly retribution to come.

"Kaz, you were *wonderful*," Evie cooed, draping herself over the vampire's shoulders like a mink stole. "Would you really have *killed* them if they'd hurt Oscar?"

Kaz smiled modestly. "In truth, I was relieved that it did not come to that," he said. "I never drink . . . swine."

In the Strauss apartment, all was well. The initial flurry of familial squawking that attended the return of Benny, Oscar, and Evie was quickly swallowed whole by concerted gasps, groans, and ultimate glee when *Bubbeh* Gratz recounted how Kazimir had defended them all in McNulty's. So adept was she at painting a picture of disaster narrowly averted that no one thought to ask what she and the others had been doing in the illicit bar in the first place. She made no bones about the fact that Benny's foreign friend was indeed a creature of the night, for she knew that this was less important to her kin than how he'd given that *shtik drek* Dorst the bum's rush.

"*Nu*, Kazimir, it's like *Bubbeh* says? You're a vampire?" Uncle Max asked affably. And when Kazimir admitted this was so, he added: "And from this, you make a living?"

While Max tried making small talk with the vampire, his wife, Rifka, was both stunned and overjoyed as her beloved Benny told anyone who would listen that his first order of business, now that he was back in the United States, was to find himself a nice girl and get married.

"A nice, *understanding* girl," *Bubbeh* Gratz specified. "One who wants to get married in the worst way." And she sighed.

No sooner had Kazimir managed to excuse himself from Uncle Max's company than Gertrude Rosenfeld cornered him. With little Oscar secured to her bosom by a hammerlock that Haystack Calhoun might envy, she showered tearful blessings on the vampire's head. "How can I ever repay you for saving my children from that *momzer*?

You're a gift, a saint, a blessing! I don't care if you and Benny are . . . *friends*, from now on, you're like family to me, you hear? *Family.*"

"Mrs. Rosenfeld, you have voiced my dearest dream," Kazimir replied. "This family, this wonderful family of yours has enchanted me from the moment I first heard of you. And while Benny and I are indeed friends, though never . . . *friends*, there is someone else in your family with whom I would very much like to become . . . *friends*, and that someone is—"

Gertrude's shriek of horror caused irate neighbors above, below and flanking the Strauss apartment to play Desi Arnaz–style conga drum riffs on the floor, ceiling, and walls. "You want you should date my Evie?" she gasped. "My *daughter*? My *little girl*? My *baby*? My *infant*? My—?"

"Ma, he loves me." Evie spoke up before her mother could reduce her to an embryo. "He told me so on the way back up here. I know we just met, but Kaz and I, we feel that there's something special between us."

"Oh, I know what *he* wants to feel between you, believe me," Mrs. Rosenfeld countered. She turned on Kazimir. "You want I should let you date my Evie? You should live so long!"

"I think he already has, Ma," Oscar said, fighting free of the maternal stranglehold.

"He's a monster!" Gertrude cried. "He drinks blood! He's dead! He's not even Jewish! He—"

"He wants to marry me," Evie said softly. "He said *that* on the way back up here too."

Gertrude stopped dead in mid-rant. A smile bloomed across her face. "*Mazel tov!*" she cried, and buried the vampire in the abyss of her cleavage.

The Cousins' Club burst into congratulations, *fortissimo*. The Gratzes didn't believe in the Romantic nonsense of love at first sight. *Marriage* at first sight, though? That was another story. The women swept Evie off in a flash flood of good wishes, with footnotes:

"Evie, *mazel tov*! So he's monster: You think maybe my Bernie's a saint?"

"You should only live and be well! So he drinks blood: Better that than gin, let me tell you."

"A blessing on your head! So he's dead. Look, you're no spring chicken yourself, and as long as he wants children . . ."

"You should never know from bad things! So he's *goyish*. Eh. Maybe he'll convert. And as long as you raise the kids Jewish—"

"You could do worse."

Oscar slipped away in the midst of the joyous uproar. He wriggled out of the crush of gabbling female bodies, then skirted the clan males as they took turns welcoming Kazimir into the family with the traditional handshake, cigar, pitying gaze, and mournful sigh. He did an end run around *Tanteh* Rifka, *Bubbeh* Gratz, and Benny as the ladies talked matchmaking strategy:

"Find one that's been on the market a while," *Bubbeh* said. "One that's not so much in the looks department, she shouldn't mind when the husband goes out at night so long as he comes home, eventually, and gives her a couple kids and a mink. One that's willing to settle."

"The girl who gets my Benny isn't 'settling' for anything," *Tanteh* Rifka said huffily.

"Maybe not, but she'll be standing for plenty."

Benny gave Oscar a feeble *Help me!* look as the boy scooted by, headed for the bedrooms.

Oscar found the refuge he sought in the room where *Tanteh* Rifka had piled her kinfolks' coats on the bed. The mound wasn't as massive as its wintertime counterpart, but it was still a formidable heap of outerwear. Oscar burrowed into the side of the fabric hill until he found what he was looking for, his much-mangled copy of *Detective* comics.

He settled down for a good, satisfying, peaceful read, but his anticipation swiftly turned to disenchantment. The Batman's exploits had lost their zing. The Joker's insanity failed to amuse. The whole point of escaping a humdrum life through the portal of fantasy crumbled before his eyes. An abrupt, life-altering revelation left him open-mouthed and appalled: *With family like mine, who needs sci-fi?*

Oscar wept for lost childhood dreams.

Then he went to eat more herring, and to ask his ma what *shtup* meant.

Femme Fatale

By Jason D. Wittman

When I first met Molly Flammare, I hadn't heard any of the stories they told about her. She was definitely a dame to tell stories about— later, when it was all over, I heard any number of them told in darkened bars, or around barrel drum fires, by men with nothing better to do than sit with their buddies, or their shot glasses, and spin their dreams—though, when Molly was the subject, the dreams often turned into nightmares. But I was new in Minneapolis, so for me the subject of Molly Flammare was a blank slate. I think that was a blessing: for that reason, I could see her for what she was. And the reality was enough to put any story to shame.

I was fifteen. I'd been orphaned a couple years back, Dad taken by the Germans at Omaha Beach, Mom by tuberculosis. But I wasn't going to any orphanage, so I left Chicago for Minneapolis and took to playing my dad's trumpet at the corner of Lake and Garfield. Apparently I had talent, 'cause people threw me enough coins every day to buy a hamburger at Charlie's Diner, and sometimes a lot more than that. So I kept playing, and things were looking up. But then Johnny Icarus sent some punks to pay me a visit.

They were just kids, high-school dropouts with too much time on their hands. They came to me on a July morning when people had yet to come out in full force, and there were only a few nickels in my hat.

"How you doin', kid?" said one. I looked around, and smelled trouble right away. There were four of them, surrounding me on all sides.

"Who wants to know?" I asked, trying to sound tough.

"Johnny Icarus," said the same kid. "That's who."

"Never heard of him."

The kid shrugged. "He's new to this town. But he wants to make a good impression here, really wants to help people. In fact, he looks at people like you, and he sees someone in need of . . . protection."

I stifled a groan.

"How much?"

The kid smiled. "Cut to the chase. Johnny Icarus likes that. Well, just for today—" He reached for my hat. "—we'll only take what you got right now. But our going rate is ten per—"

I kicked him in the face, picked up my hat, and ran like hell.

Maybe that was stupid. What was really stupid was running away from Charlie's Diner, where Charlie could protect me. But there was nothing I could do about that, and as I ran it became clear I was falling right into their trap.

Three more kids ran up to head me off. I ducked down an alley—where four more kids waited for me.

I stood there, clutching my trumpet. They would probably just rough me up; I could survive that. But they would trash the trumpet too, and that was my only way to make a living. Where would I get a new one? Charlie? I didn't think he could afford it. And what would I do next time this happened?

"Hey," said a voice from the other end of the alley. "Why don't you pick on someone your own size?"

A man stood there, holding a two-by-four. By his clothes, I guessed he was down on his luck. But it looked like he knew how to use that two-by-four, and I was taking any help I could get.

The gang leader whipped out a switchblade. "You think you can take on all of us?"

"What the hell." The newcomer tapped the two-by-four in his palm. "I got nothing to lose."

I braced myself. I still didn't like the odds—but then something happened that made the odds irrelevant.

Suddenly, the sunlight dimmed—looking up, I saw storm clouds that looked like they'd been there forever. A cold wind blew through the alley, and I shivered like it was the dead of winter.

"Leave them alone, boys," said a woman's voice from the other end of the alley, opposite from Mr. Two-by-four.

Peering into the wind, I saw her for the first time.

She was tall. Good God, she was tall, the kind of tall that had to duck through doorways. The way she stood said she knew exactly what she was doing. But her face didn't say much of anything. It was hidden under the brim of her hat.

She stood in the alleyway like the cold and wind weren't even there.

The gang leader hesitated, weighing his options. He decided on the safe route.

"L-look, ma'am, we . . . we don't want any trouble . . ."

"Course not." She had a deep voice that could hold a stadium's attention with a whisper. "The only one who wants trouble is Johnny Icarus. That's his name, right?"

No one said anything.

"Beat it," she said. "And tell Johnny that Molly Flammare sends her regards."

And those kids beat it, like the proverbial bat out of hell.

She just stood where she was. She might not even have been looking at us. The wind still screamed in our faces, and the brim of her hat still kept her face in shadow. Then, without a word to either one of us, she left the alley. And just before she turned the corner, she reached up with one hand, made a sweeping gesture at the sky, and it was sunny again.

Sunny again. Just like that.

I looked at Mr. Two-by-four. We both wore the same expression, like the rug had been pulled out from under us. Then I ran after Molly Flammare.

I'd half expected her to be nowhere in sight when I came onto the street. But there she was, strolling down Lake, her burgundy dress standing out against the gleaming concrete. She walked pretty slow, but the length of her stride meant she was already a long ways down the block.

"Ma'am?" I shouted, running to catch up. Behind me, I heard the footsteps of Mr. Two-by-four. "Ma'am?"

She turned as I practically skidded to a stop beside her.

Her clothes said money. They also said autumn, like she was ready for a walk in a windy park in October. Her burgundy skirt hung below her knees. Her matching jacket had sleeves hanging to her wrists, and she wore black leather gloves. The front of her jacket was unbuttoned to her waist, revealing a black turtleneck sweater. Her hat, wide-brimmed and worn at a tilt, sat on a mane of hair the color and shine of polished wood.

Her face was a mask. Not really a mask, but it didn't show anything to anybody unless it really wanted to. Looking back, I realize that her face was just another part of her clothing. It was a way of protecting herself against the world around her.

"I . . . I just thought I should, uh, thank you for helping us out back there . . . um . . . we really appreciate it. Thanks. Ma'am."

I got the jitters under her gaze, like I was back in school reciting Tennyson to the teachers. But when I was done stammering, she gave me a smile. It was a beautiful smile, warm and honest, but sad, the kind of smile that's directed at memories.

"You play a good trumpet, kid." She reached down and took it from me, turning it over in her hands. "Sometimes I can hear you from my apartment uptown." She looked at me. "What's your name?"

"Tommy," I said. "Tommy Gabriel."

"Gabriel." She smiled at the trumpet. "How appropriate."

I didn't know what she meant by that, but if she was smiling, I was happy.

She gave the trumpet back, and looked at Mr. Two-by-four.

"How about you? What's your name?"

"Blatta, ma'am." A tired voice, dead tired. "Jimmy Blatta."

Something about that name made her look at him long and hard. When she asked, "You play anything?" I got the impression she was buying time to think.

"No, ma'am," said Jimmy Blatta. "I'm just a soldier, back from the war, looking for a job. If you could tell me where to find one, I'd be grateful."

Molly looked him over a moment longer, then made up her mind. "You stood up for the kid. I like that. Here's a little something for your trouble." She handed him a ten-dollar bill, and a box of matches. "I own a supper club on Lyndale. The address is on the matchbox. Go there around five and ask for Louis. He'll set you up with something."

Jimmy Blatta took the matchbox, and the ten-dollar bill, and the clouds left his face just like Molly had waved her hand again. "Thanks," he said.

Molly looked at me. "Might not be a good idea for you to play on the street for a while. How'd you like to play for me?"

I gaped at her like an idiot. "You mean . . . at the club?"

"Sure." She smiled, and handed me another matchbox and ten-dollar bill. She probably guessed I hadn't even seen a whole ten dollars before, and figured what the hell. "Have Jimmy bring you along at five. I'll have Louis set you up too." She tugged the brim of her hat. "Later, boys."

I stopped her. "Ma'am?"

She looked back. "What?"

"How . . ." I shrugged. "How'd you do all that back there?"

She smiled.

"You wouldn't understand, kid. Most of it's just smoke and mirrors anyway. See you at the club."

Then she walked away, slowly, but her legs carried her far with each stride.

I treated Jimmy Blatta to lunch at Charlie's. I figured I owed him that much, even though it was Molly who saved my bacon.

Charlie's Diner was your typical greasy spoon, but it was the closest thing to a home I'd known since leaving Chicago. The first thing you noticed walking in was the smell of burgers on the grill. I never smelled burgers like that anywhere else—Charlie said he had his own special way of cooking them, but he wasn't telling anyone, not even me. The walls were decorated with recruitment posters with leggy dames telling you to join the army, or the navy, or the air corps. ("You know, I joined the navy because of that girl," a guy told me once. "Spent the war on a submarine with ninety other poor slobs.") And the radio was always on. Charlie turned it way up whenever Judy Garland started singing.

From the look Charlie gave me when I paid him, you'd think he never saw a ten-dollar bill either. But when he heard who we got it from, he nearly dropped our burgers.

We watched as Charlie carefully put our plates down, then gripped the counter with both hands. It was a minute before he looked up and asked, "How'd you two get mixed up with her?"

We told him. Hell, we'd been waiting to tell him. When we finished, Charlie nodded like he'd heard that story before. Then he leaned real close and whispered, "Boys? Trust me on this. You don't want to get involved with Molly Flammare."

I wanted to ask why not, but that was a stupid question. I'd seen what she could do with my own eyes; even a kid like me could tell she was dangerous. But Jimmy was older. He knew what questions to ask.

"They tell stories about her, don't they?" he said.

Charlie laughed, but he didn't think the joke was funny. "You better believe it. You hear them mostly at two AM, when people come to the diner for a place to hide. You can't believe all of them, though." He picked up a newspaper, and began paging through it. "Some stories say one thing, others say something else."

"So tell us the one that happened to you," said Jimmy.

Charlie didn't look at him. He didn't look at the newspaper either.

"C'mon! Nobody gets that scared at a bunch of stories! What'd she do to you?"

Charlie stood where he was, not looking at us, or the paper. Finally, he put it down, and took a deep breath.

"You're right," he said. "You're both new here, and you really should know about this. Okay. Here's what happened.

"I had a brother once. His name was Eddie. Wasn't much of a brother, though. Hell, he wasn't much of a human being. Guy just didn't know how to stay out of trouble. And consequences didn't mean a damn thing to him. He was in and out of jail I don't know how many times, and when he got out, he went right back to the same old routine.

"A couple years ago, I heard that he'd raped some girl who wasn't even out of high school yet. The cops came here and asked me where he was. I told them I didn't know, and that was true. I said I would call them if I found out, and *that* was true. And wouldn't you know it, not even two hours after they left, here comes Eddie, parking his car up front and sauntering through the door like he was king of England.

"I told him I was going to call the cops. He knew I wasn't kidding, so he ran back to his car. I reached for the phone, but by then it was too late—for Eddie, I mean. Because Molly was waiting for him.

"That thing you saw her do in the alley? That's nothing. They say lightning won't hit you if you're in a car, but it hit Eddie. Because Molly wanted it to.

"She sprung for the funeral afterward. Nothing fancy, but respectable. But it had to be closed-casket. All that was left of Eddie was some black stuff that looked like it was scraped off a barbecue grill. Parts of that car glowed red an hour after she left."

An eerie silence fell over the diner. It was Jimmy who broke it.

"Look, Charlie, I know he was your brother and everything, but it sounds like he had it coming. I mean, so Molly has a mean streak for those who deserve it. That doesn't make her a monster."

Charlie shook his head. "There's other stories, remember? And not all of the stories are true, but they all . . . *feel* like the truth, you know what I mean? And one thing they all say—" He wagged a finger. "—is that anyone who gets involved with Molly Flammare winds up dead."

Jimmy and I looked at each other, then back at Charlie.

"Maybe not like Eddie," Charlie went on. "But dead is dead. She's like a spider!" He held up a hand with the fingers curled. "Sitting in her web. Waiting for flies to buzz too close."

Then he realized what he was doing, and pulled himself together. He picked up the newspaper again, and paged through it. "Look, what you do is your business," he said. "But I'm giving you free advice here, and I'm advising you to stay away from—"

Then he saw something in the newspaper, and went white as a sheet.

The paper fell from his hands. He stared at us wide-eyed, his mouth opening and closing like a fish.

"Smoke break," he finally got out. "I need a smoke break." He reached under the counter and brought out a pack of cigarettes. Then he took off through the back door like greased lightning.

Jimmy went around the counter and picked up the paper to see what had spooked Charlie.

"Oh, God," Jimmy said. "Look at this."

I saw a full-page ad showing the silhouette of a woman leaning against a wall, a woman who could only be Molly Flammare. The ad read:

> Don't worry about them, Charlie
> They're not the ones I'm after . . .
> . . . and neither were you.
> MOLLY'S
> SUPPER CLUB
> 27th and Lyndale
> open till 2AM

By the way...

... your metaphor's a little off.

In the end, Jimmy and I went to Molly's. The way we saw it, Charlie's brother only got what he deserved, and we hadn't done anything like that. And Jimmy really needed that job.

Not that we didn't have misgivings. Anything that spooked Charlie like that was something to look out for. So Jimmy and I agreed to mind our p's and q's around her.

Molly's Supper Club was about what you'd expect—big and classy, like Molly herself. You felt like you had to be in a tuxedo just to be there. If you stood on the marble floor, you could see your reflection staring right back at you. If you stood on the carpet, you felt your feet sink an inch deep.

A guy came out to meet us, saying his name was Louis. "And you must be Tommy!" he said, ruffling my hair. I hated it when people did that. "Be with you in a second, I gotta set your friend up here." He shook Jimmy's hand. "Mr. Blatta, sir. Molly told me what you did for Tommy here. You're a real stand-up guy."

"I try to be."

"I understand you were a soldier in the war?"

"I was in the Army. Medically discharged."

"Which unit?"

"Eighty-seventh Infantry."

Louis nodded. "My son was in the Fifty-third. Didn't come back."

"I'm very sorry to hear that, sir."

"Yeah, well. Anyway, Molly asked me to set you up with a job. You up to waiting tables?"

"You know what they say about beggars and choosers."

"Good answer. It's not a bad job; you're on your feet most of the time, but the tips are decent. I'll get you into some threads." He pushed Jimmy toward the kitchen door. "Be with you in a minute, Tommy! Go ahead and take a look round!"

So I was all alone with the tables and the chairs and the bandstand on the stage. I hadn't been in a place that quiet in years.

I went up and stood at center stage. They would probably just make me another member of the band, but I could dream, couldn't I? Here I could be the center of attention. No cars roaring by, no talking, just me and my trumpet, and the spotlight.

I stood there, looking around. Then I raised my trumpet, and I played "Moonlight Serenade."

For those few minutes, I was the only person in the world. Playing the trumpet took no effort at all. There's never any effort when you're doing what you want to do, what you're *meant* to do. At least you don't notice it. I closed my eyes, and while the song lasted, there was only me, and the soaring notes.

I let the last note linger, keeping my eyes closed as the memory of the song soaked into the walls, and into me. And when I opened my eyes, there was Molly Flammare standing in a doorway.

The light shone behind her, so I couldn't see her face. But there was a smile in her voice as she said, "You're hired, Tommy."

I ducked my head. "Thanks, ma'am."

Then Louis and Jimmy came in through another doorway, Jimmy decked out in a brand-new monkey suit. "What do you think, Tommy?" he said.

I grinned. "Looking good, Jimmy." In the back of my head, though, I got a little worried. Was I going to have to wear one of those things?

"Kid, was that you playing that trumpet?" Louis asked.

"Course it was," said Molly as she sauntered into the room. "You think I'd tell you to hire just any old bum off the street?" She stopped in front of me, and looked me up and down. Standing on the stage, I was almost at eye level with her.

"You got anything in his size?" she asked Louis.

"No, ma'am. We'll have to buy one custom-made."

Molly smiled, and ruffled my hair. "Don't worry, kid. The suit's on me."

That's how I started my new job at Molly's. I met the band a couple hours later. They listened to me play, and just like that, I was one of the boys.

We played five nights a week, with Sundays and Mondays off. The monkey suit drove me nuts at first, but I got used to it. Having all those people looking at me also took some getting used to, but I learned to shut them out of my head and focus on the song. In time, I learned to enjoy myself.

And boy did Jimmy Blatta's prospects improve. He became the go-to guy on the staff, he worked so hard. He was just glad to be working, able to put money in his pocket and food on his plate. We didn't get much chance to talk during work, but we would nod at each other across the room on occasion. There was one time he seemed a bit under the weather—I found him in the restroom splashing water on his face—but other than that, he was fine.

Molly gave both of us apartments in the same building. This made me a little nervous—I was making more money than I'd ever dreamed of, but could I afford an apartment in *this* building?—but Molly said it was on her. I wondered if she was worried about Johnny Icarus—and then he showed up at our front doorstep.

I'd walked into Jimmy's room one day to say hi, and I saw him at his window, which looked down at the front of the club.

"Hey, Jimmy—"

"Sh!" he said, and beckoned me to the window.

I looked down and saw Molly, standing in front of the entrance like she was guarding it. In front of her, climbing out of a shiny black limousine, stood three men dressed in pinstripe suits and red ties.

The two on either side had fists the size of cement blocks, maybe to compensate for the lack of a neck. The one in the middle was the kind of big that had to step sideways through a door. His huge head swiveled slowly from side to side, looking at everything as if he owned it. But Molly wasn't impressed one bit.

"This is an exclusive club, Johnny," she said. "You're not welcome here."

So that was Johnny Icarus?

"Not welcome here?" Johnny echoed, indicating his limo and his bodyguards with a sweep of his gut. "Am I missing something? Rest assured, madam, I simply come here for mirth and merriment—and let me add that I am a generous tipper."

Molly shook her head. "It's a question of reputation. I don't like the way you operate. Stop muscling in on the mom and pop businesses, and we'll talk. Until then, I'm going to have to ask you to leave."

Johnny glared at her. "Are you telling me how to do business?"

"In this town, you're damn right I am."

Johnny took a step toward. "Now see here—"

Molly thrust her fist into the air, and a thunderclap boomed so close I nearly jumped out of my skin.

"Let's see if that improved your hearing," Molly said as the cold wind blew around her, and storm clouds boiled overhead. "I don't like what people tell me about you. Until I do, you're not getting into my club."

One of Johnny's goons took a step toward Molly, but Johnny waved him back.

"You haven't hurt anybody yet, Johnny, so I'm still going to give you a chance. Either stop leaning on the mom-and-pops, or leave town. The sooner the better."

Johnny Icarus held himself very still. He held his gaze on Molly, but she looked right back at him.

Finally, Molly won the stare-down. Johnny looked to his two goons and jerked his head toward the limo. They entered it, and drove away.

A lot of people were telling that story the next day, believe me. But as time wore on, and nothing happened, we soon forgot about it.

We learned a little more about Molly herself, too. Every so often she would come down to the club, not every night, but enough so we wouldn't miss her. She had this special table reserved just for her; no one could sit there even when she wasn't around. It had a ticker bolted to it, like the kind investors use to keep track of their stocks. Only it didn't keep track of stocks as far as anyone could tell. Most of the time it didn't even work, even when Molly was there. But every two or three days, it would start ticking, and spit out a foot or two of tape.

When Molly wasn't there—usually around the daylight hours—me and Jimmy Blatta would take a look at it. It wasn't any language I'd ever seen. I thought it might be Chinese, but Jimmy said that wasn't it. We even asked Louis about it once, but he said he didn't know either.

When Molly was there—she'd be sitting at her table, listening to the band—she would pick up the tape and look at it. Then she would get up and leave the club. No one knew what she did during those times, not even Louis, or if he did know, he wasn't telling. Me, I liked to think it was that ticker told Molly I was in trouble with those boys in the alley. When she came back, sometimes she was in a real bad mood. And when that happened, me and Jimmy always noticed it was raining outside.

But that only happened once in while. Most of the time Jimmy was happy to have a job, I was happy to play trumpet, and Molly sat at her table.

One night when the place had closed, Jimmy was busy wiping tables, I was sitting on the stage with my trumpet, when Molly walked in. She wore white this time, white skirt and jacket over the black turtleneck and the black gloves, and for no reason I could think of, this seemed like a special occasion. "Evening, ma'am," I said, but she had her eyes fixed on Jimmy.

She walked up to him. He stopped wiping the table, and looked up at her.

"Hi, Jimmy."

"Ma'am."

"Working hard?"

"I suppose so."

She took his hand. "Sometimes you work too hard. Come here."

And she led him onto the dance floor.

I was floored. I'd never seen Molly do anything like this, or heard of it. On their nights off, sometimes the boys in the band would look into their bottles and wonder out loud what sort of man would get hitched up with Molly Flammare. He would have to be Superman or Captain America, or else he'd have to settle for living in Molly's shadow, because more than anything else, Molly had guts—and class. Somebody wondered if Louis was Molly's man, but I'd never seen them look at each other that way.

But then, never in my wildest dreams did I think she would have an interest in Jimmy Blatta.

"Tommy," Molly said. "Play a little something for us."

It took me a moment to pick my jaw up off the floor. Then I raised my trumpet, and began to play.

It was just like my first day at Molly's, only this time, even I wasn't there. It was just the song, and Jimmy Blatta, and Molly Flammare, and it was like they were flying.

You'd think a man dancing with a woman who stood head and shoulders above him would look pretty funny, but not here, not with Molly. It might have been that Jimmy was a pretty good dancer—when the band was doing practice sessions, I'd seen him do some pretty neat moves with a mop, just for laughs—but it might have been Molly too. I wouldn't put it past her to know how to give a man his dignity. Like I said, Molly had class.

When the song was over, I put down my trumpet, only then realizing how tired I was. Molly and Jimmy came down to earth, not saying anything, just looking at each other.

Molly reached up with a gloved hand, and caressed his cheek. "Good night, Jimmy," she said. Then she walked out of the room.

Jimmy stood there for I don't know how long. I watched him. It looked like he was about to cry.

"Jimmy?" I said. "You okay?"

"Yeah," he said. "Yeah, I'm . . . look, kid, no offense, just beat it, okay? I need to be alone for a while."

I said, "Okay, Jimmy," and I left the same way Molly had gone.

When I entered the hallway, I saw Molly waiting at the elevator.

All of a sudden I wondered if this was what Charlie meant when he said everyone who got close to Molly wound up dead. Was she starting on Jimmy now? Was she luring him to her web, only to . . . what?

Maybe I should have done my wondering someplace else. Because Molly turned and saw me.

"What's on your mind, Tommy?"

I stood there with my mouth open, just waiting for any flies who might want to set up shop.

"I . . . uh . . . nothing, ma'am. Good night."

"Tommy." She sat on the leather-cushioned bench behind her. "Come here."

I did. God only knows why. My feet moved like they had minds of their own, and there I was, standing in front of Molly.

"Talk to me."

But I couldn't talk. What the hell could I say?

"Ma'am . . . Look, you really got to Jimmy back there, all right? He can barely think straight. And I consider him a friend, ma'am. And I'd hate to see him . . ."

That's all that would come out. But it seemed to be enough.

"You're right to be worried," said Molly. "Some dames will do that sort of thing just so they can rip a man's heart out. Some guys will go straight through hell and not think twice about it, but get them by the heart, and they wish they were dead. But that's not why I did it, Tommy. Jimmy's come across some hard luck, and I thought he deserved a little more than he's got. He wants to be something, Tommy. More than that, he wants to be the right *kind* of something. And when—"

She stopped herself. I have no idea what she was going to say.

What she said instead was: "Don't worry about it. Whatever's going to happen to Jimmy, it's not going to come from me."

The elevator opened, and Molly stood up.

"Good night, Tommy."

Things went back to normal after that. Well, sort of. To say nothing had changed between Jimmy and Molly would be lying. When they passed each other in the club or in the hallway, she would give him a smile and a "Hi, Jimmy," and he would say, "Ma'am," in tones of hushed reverence. Once I even caught them talking in the elevator lobby. I couldn't hear what they said, but Jimmy's face told me he had something big on his mind. Then Molly reached up and caressed his face with that gloved hand of hers. I heard her say, "Later, Jimmy." Then the elevator opened, and she went up to her apartment.

But on this day in particular, Molly wasn't anywhere in the building. The foot or so of tape hanging from the ticker on her table gave us some clue as to why she'd gone.

"Why do you keep looking at those things?" Jimmy asked me. "Nobody can read them except Molly."

I shrugged. "Just curiosity."

"Hey, we haven't been to Charlie's in a while. What do you say we go and see how he's doing?"

"Sure." It was our day off, and I was itching for something to do. "I'm in the mood for a burger."

We walked, since we weren't in any hurry, and it was a nice day out. We weren't paying that much attention. If we had, we might have noticed somebody following us.

When we came in, Charlie acted like it was Christmas morning. He shook our hands, asking how we were doing and grinning to beat the band. We asked for a couple hamburgers, and he said sure, it was on him. We'd come in the dead hours before the lunchtime rush, and he had nothing better to do.

"So . . . you still working at Molly's?" We could tell it was still a touchy subject with him.

"You bet, Charlie," Jimmy answered. "Nothing's happened to us, either. Life at the diner been treating you good?"

"Can't complain," said Charlie as he plunked a couple Cokes on the counter. "Business has been pretty steady. But I hear—"

The front door jingled, and in came Johnny Icarus and his two goons. Behind Johnny stood a kid. It was the same kid who cornered me in that alley when I first met Molly.

Johnny pointed at me. "This the kid, Joey?"

"Yes sir, Mr. Icarus. That's him."

"Young sir," said Johnny as his gut swiveled to face me. "I will thank you to come with us."

"What do you want with him?" said Jimmy.

"I believe he works at a certain establishment," said Johnny, "called Molly's. I wish to ask him a few questions about the proprietor."

"Then ask them here," said Jimmy, "or ask me. The kid doesn't know anything that I don't."

"Look, gentlemen," said Johnny as he spread his hands, "I'm willing to make it worth the boy's while. I'll give him anything he wants, chocolate bars, baseball cards, I'll even pay for his hamburger—"

"Kid? You want to go with him?"

"No."

"Then he ain't going!" said Charlie as he raised his shotgun.

Poor Charlie didn't stand a chance. He should have known they wouldn't turn tail and run at the sight of a lousy shotgun; he should have just started blasting. But he hesitated, and that gave one of Johnny's boys enough time to take out a gun and shoot Charlie between the eyes.

Jimmy took his Coke bottle by the neck and smashed it on the edge of the counter. Then he jumped at the guy who'd shot Charlie and drove the sharp edges into his throat.

That left the other guy. He had a gun too, and he shot Jimmy in the back.

I felt like I'd been punched in the gut. I ran to Jimmy and shook him, calling his name over and over, crying my eyes out. Then I felt Johnny Icarus's hand on my shoulder.

"As I stated earlier," he said, "I wish to ask you a few questions regarding your employer."

They stuffed me in a car, and kept my head down. The goon Jimmy killed must have been the one who usually drove, because this guy damn near flipped us over a couple times. When we stopped, we were in some sort of warehouse. They took me to a little office in the corner, and sat me on a chair across from some guy reading a newspaper. When he put it down, I found myself looking at a priest.

"Father Jacques," said Johnny Icarus. "Here is young Mr. Gabriel, as promised."

Father Jacques mopped his forehead with a handkerchief. "I'll get to work on him right away," he said.

Now, I've heard of mob lawyers, mob accountants, even mob doctors. But a mob *priest*?

Johnny left, and the priest started asking me questions. What books does Miss Flammare read? What sort of furnishings does she have in her apartment? Have you ever seen a pentagram, either in her building, or on her person? I asked him some of my own questions, like what the hell was a pentagram? He stared at me a moment, then he got up, knocked on the door, and asked for a pencil and paper. When he got them, he sat at the desk and drew a five-pointed star with a circle around it. He was real nervous about it, too.

"That's a pentagram," he said. "Have you seen it?"

I shook my head. "No."

He tore up the drawing, and crossed himself.

Then, there was a knock on the door. Mopping his forehead, Father Jacques got up and answered it. I saw Joey reading a newspaper before the priest shut the door behind him.

Seeing that newspaper gave me an idea. Father Jacques had left his paper on the desk. I grabbed the paper and started looking through it.

There was a full-page ad on page three:

You're finally catching on, kid.

Still got that box of matches I gave you?

MOLLY'S

SUPPER CLUB

27th and Lyndale

open till 2AM

And don't touch anything metal.

A roll of thunder outside drove her point across real good.

I still had the box of matches in my pocket. But before I could figure out what to do, the door handle jiggled. I put the paper back, and sat down.

"Just give me five more minutes with him, Mr. Icarus," said Father Jacques as he came in.

Johnny closed the door without a word.

Father Jacques looked at me. I swear to God his eyeballs were sweating.

"Is there anything you can tell me?" he whispered. "Do you have any idea how she does what she does?"

I spread my hands. "Far as I can tell, she just . . . does it."

"Can you even tell me how she might be found?"

Thunder rumbled again. I jerked my thumb at it. "Sounds to me like she's coming for you."

He looked up like he was expecting lightning to come through the roof.

"Does she . . . treat you well?"

"If you're good to her, she's good to you. I wouldn't want to be the guy who killed Jimmy right now."

He settled down a little, thinking.

Then he asked: "Would holy water work against her?"

Something about the way he said it made me answer: "About as good as anything else."

He nodded, opened the door, and went through. "Mr. Icarus?"

He told Johnny that he had to get some holy water back at the church. Johnny said he would take Father Jacques there himself. I heard them leave in the car.

That left me with Joey and the goon who killed Jimmy.

Well, obviously I was supposed to start a fire. But with what? There was a wastebasket by the desk, but I didn't think that would be big enough. Then I saw the filing cabinet. Oh yeah, there were lots of papers in there. I struck a match and set a fire in all the drawers.

When the papers were good and burning, I called for help. When he heard me, the goon started swearing. He had to know I was up to something, but Johnny wanted me alive. So he opened the door.

"*I'm gonna wring your little neck, kid!*" he bellowed. And I got more than a little nervous. I knew Molly would save me, but I began wondering how. And when.

The goon took one step toward me. Then he stopped.

He looked at me like he was trying to remember something. Then he fell flat on his face.

A switchblade stuck out of his back. I looked up, and saw Joey.

I wondered what made him help me. Then I remembered.

"You were reading the newspaper."

Joey nodded, very slowly, like he was afraid he would fall apart.

"I'm . . . I'm very sorry for what happened to Jimmy and . . . and Charlie."

I didn't know what Molly said to him. Maybe I didn't want to know. I ran through the office door and out of the warehouse.

It was raining. I was just in time to see lightning strike not fifty feet away from me, and when I opened my eyes again, all four tires had been blown out on Johnny Icarus's car. It swerved in the mud, turning around a couple times and almost flipping over before it finally stopped. And there, about fifty feet beyond that, stood Molly, right in the middle of the road, like the wind, and the rain, and the lightning weren't even there.

Johnny climbed out of the car, dragging Father Jacques by his starched collar. He held the priest in front of him with one hand while the other held a tommy gun.

"You crossed the line, Johnny." Even with all the wind and thunder, I could hear every word Molly said. "You shouldn't've done that to Jimmy and Charlie."

Johnny peeked over Father Jacques's shoulder. "You wouldn't hurt a man of the cloth, would you?"

Molly reached out with one hand.

"If I had to."

Father Jacques screamed as the lightning struck, and I flinched away again. But when I looked back, there lay Father Jacques face down in the mud, still screaming, still blubbering, still alive. A flaming pile of flesh was all that remained of Johnny Icarus.

Father Jacques pulled himself up to his knees. He folded his hands and prayed. He blubbered and shook so much he might have been saying "Now I lay me down to sleep" for all I knew. But he stayed there on his knees, still praying, until Molly walked up to him, and he looked at her.

"Get out of here," Molly said. "I don't ever want to see your face in this town again."

He didn't need to be told twice. He got up and ran, never looking back. Last time I saw him, just before he disappeared into the rain, he was still running.

Then I heard somebody else's footsteps. I turned and saw Joey running for it from the warehouse.

"Not you, Joey!" Molly shouted. "Come here!"

He stopped dead in his tracks. I thought he looked terrified before.

"I said come here, Joey!"

Slowly, staring straight at the ground, he turned and shuffled through the mud toward Molly.

Just then it dawned on me that I felt sorry for him. That was probably why I called out to him, "Joey."

He stopped and looked at me.

"If she wanted you dead, you would be."

And I walked with him to where Molly stood.

She knelt down and grabbed his arm.

"You've been hanging out with the wrong crowd, Joey. But that's going to change because you'll be working for me from now on. Meet me at the club at seven tomorrow morning, and I'll set you up with a job. And if you're not there at seven, I'll come looking for you. You got me?"

"Y-yes, m-ma'am."

"Look at me, Joey."

He didn't.

"Look at me!"

Then he did.

"Don't worry about it," Molly said. "Keep your nose clean, and you'll be fine." She stood up. "Now get out of here."

As Joey ran off, the whole thing came flooding back to me, first Charlie's death, then Jimmy's. I started crying again.

"I'm sorry, Molly. Guess we should've checked with you before going to Charlie's."

Molly shook her head.

"*I'm* sorry, Tommy. Even I can't be everywhere at once."

Then we heard a car engine, and we saw a pair of headlights followed by a beautiful silver-gray car with Louis in the driver's seat. Molly opened the door, leaned in, and said, "Take us to the hospital, Louis."

The hospital?

"You mean . . . Jimmy's still alive?"

Molly just said, "Get in, Tommy."

As Louis drove, Molly told me what happened: after Johnny left the diner, Jimmy dragged himself on his stomach, smearing blood all over the place, to the curb, where he managed to hail a cab. The cabbie wanted to take him straight to the hospital, but Jimmy said no, take him to Molly's. So that's what the cabbie did. When they got there, Molly was still gone, but Louis was there, and he knew how to get a hold of her. But he sent Jimmy to the hospital first.

When we arrived, Molly knew exactly where to go. A doctor stood waiting for us outside a hospital room.

"How is he, Danny?" Molly asked.

"He's lost a lot of blood, Molly. He won't last the night." He looked through the door. "Course, he wouldn't have lasted much longer anyway."

"What do you mean?" I said. "What's he talking about, Molly?"

Molly only said, "Tell him, Danny."

Danny looked at me. "You know Mr. Blatta was in the army, right?"

"Yeah. He said he was medically discharged."

"That's right. But he probably didn't tell you that he was diagnosed with terminal cancer. They said he had about six months to live. So they sent him back home from Europe." Danny shrugged. "He never even saw combat."

Molly looked over to where Jimmy lay. "Can we talk to him?"

"Sure."

Jimmy looked even worse than I expected. I had no problem believing he wouldn't live to see the morning. But when he opened his eyes and tried to smile, he mostly succeeded.

"Tommy," he whispered. "You're okay. That's good."

"Yeah, Jimmy," I said. "I'm okay. And Johnny's gone now. Molly took care of him."

He looked at her.

"Molly . . ."

She shook her head. "Oh, Jimmy. You didn't have to prove any-thing. Not to me."

"Not to you, maybe. But there's some things a man's got to prove to himself, you know?"

Molly didn't say anything. It looked like she couldn't say anything.

"Molly . . . whenever I asked you . . . that question . . . you always said, 'later.'" He closed his eyes, and opened them again. "Can 'later' be now?"

Molly stood stock still. It was like time itself had stopped.

Then she said, "Sure, Jimmy. You can have it now."

And she took off her gloves.

This really spooked me, because I had never seen her do that before. She had smooth, milky-white hands that looked like they belonged on a statue. And she leaned over Jimmy Blatta, she placed her milky white hands on either side of his face, she lowered her lips to his, and they shared a long, slow kiss.

I stood there and watched. Again, it was like I wasn't even there. There was only Jimmy Blatta, and Molly Flammare, and they were dancing one last time.

When Molly pulled back, Jimmy's face had changed. He wasn't smiling, but it was really peaceful, like everything was going to be okay. Molly looked at that face, not saying a word. Then she bit her lip, and left the room in a hurry.

The doctor went over to Jimmy, and pulled the sheet over his head.

I looked at him. "Aren't you going to check his pulse or something?"

"He's dead, kid," said the doctor. "Trust me."

I looked at him a moment longer. Then I went into the hallway.

Molly sat on one of a row of chairs standing against the wall. She had her gloves back on. When I sat down next to her, she said, "Poor guy. Never had a chance. Just couldn't win for losing."

I didn't know what to say. But Molly went on talking without me: "And the only thing I could give him was . . ."

She waved a hand at the room we had just left, shaking her head. Then she began to cry.

I was only a kid. What could I say to her? "Come on, Molly. Don't cry," I said, and reached up to wipe away her tears—

Her hand clamped down on my wrist like a steel trap. It almost hurt. No. It did hurt.

"Never touch me, Tommy," she said softly. It was a gentle warning, a friendly warning, but still a warning. "No one can ever touch me."

It wasn't until then that I knew why Molly always wore gloves, why she dressed for autumn in the middle of summer. Only then did I know where those stories Charlie had heard came from. Only then did I understand the gift that she gave Jimmy Blatta.

I pried my wrist from her fingers. Then I took her hand, squeezing it through the glove. "We can do this, though," I said. "Can't we, Molly?"

She didn't say a word. But she did squeeze back.

We sat there forever in the hallway, holding hands, remembering Jimmy as the world went by without us. I have no idea how long we stayed like that, but when she was ready to face life again, Molly gave my hand an extra squeeze.

"Thanks, Tommy."

Joey got a job bussing tables at the club. The first month or so, he tiptoed everywhere, afraid of his own shadow, but then he learned to stop being afraid of Molly and start respecting her. Then he really turned his life around, and now he might actually turn out to be a decent human being.

I still play trumpet with the band. Sure, I could have moved on to bigger and better things. Hell, Armstrong came to town once and asked me if I wanted to play with him. Armstrong, can you believe it? But ever since Jimmy Blatta, I've noticed Molly feeling more and more down, and other than Louis, I'm about the only friend she has. And when I look at her when she's sad, I remember that the only time I've seen her truly happy is when I'm playing trumpet for her. There's no way I could take that away from Molly. So I stay at the club.

Still, I don't want from her what Jimmy did. I'm all right with just flying around her, admiring her for what she is, respecting her for what she does. I told that to Louis once, and he said I got the metaphor right.

Molly still has that ticker on the table, and she still does what it tells her, whatever that is. I think the city is her responsibility, and she's there whenever it needs her. But sometimes she needs something too, and when she does, I'm there for her.

It rains a lot more now in the city. Sometimes, at two AM when the club is closed, Louis and I hear thunder rumbling outside, and we know that Molly needs some cheering up. Then I walk onto the stage with my trumpet, and I wait there until Molly comes in, and she sits at her table without saying a word. Then I put the trumpet to my lips, and I play for Molly until she feels better, and she lets the moon come out from behind the clouds.

Dedicated to the memory of Claude Dziuk (1929–2005), my senior high school English teacher, who is now reading Shakespeare aloud in that big classroom in the sky—Jason D. Wittman

A Hire Power

By J. Simon

Another Monday in the office, and it was going to be a bad one. She could tell. Liz sipped her coffee and grimaced. Stone cold. She didn't know how they did it. The stencil on her door read: "Liz Flaraherty, Inhuman Resources." Her computer had a virus scanner, a firewall, and a jingly bell to ward off demonic possession. Her stapler rarely stayed where she put it, though she never actually *saw* it move. All in a day's work.

The phone rang. She picked up. "Hello?"

"Divination support."

"I don't need support."

"You will."

Liz slammed down the receiver. This was bad. Tech support had a crystal ball, and they only called when something very bad was about to happen. On the other hand, if she avoided talking to them, she could put off the otherwise inevitable disaster . . .

". . . except that you can't," said Devon as he slipped into her office, "since we knew that would be your attitude and only rang the phone as a distraction. Sorry."

"All right. What's going to happen this time?"

He shrugged apologetically. "Sorry. Causality. You've got to actually do it before the me that was in the past can foresee the future you doing it and become the present me waiting for the present you to do what the future you did to summon the past me to fix the problem that hasn't happened yet."

"Did you, perchance, foresee a swift kick in the butt?"

He turned and pointed. There was a pillow stuffed down his backside.

"Damn you."

"Go on. Don't mind me. Go through your normal routine."

Liz reached cautiously toward the computer, eyes never leaving Devon. No reaction. With the delicacy of someone probing for mines, she touched her coffee mug. The stapler. The file cabinet. He just watched her.

"Give me a hint."

"Dinosaurs versus tanks."

"What?"

"You'll see."

"I don't need this," Liz groaned. Still watching Devon, she lifted the mail bin up onto her desk. It was locked seventeen ways with cold iron and had a gilded goat's skull on the top. It rattled ominously. Little paper fingers reached questingly under the lid.

"Isn't there supposed to be a blanket counteranimation on my office?"

"Dunno. Didn't foresee *that* problem. Were any error messages oozing from the walls in pentagrams of blood when you came in?"

"Listen, Devon, résumé golems may be made from paper, but they're *strong*. Just what problem *did* you foresee?"

There was a grating creak, a sudden jolt, and the mail bin's lock snapped right off. Hundreds of résumé golems swarmed out of the box, chortling and cavorting and shouting Employment Objectives in reedy little voices. Devon held up a shiny, brand-new lock. "That one," he said.

Liz rubbed her temples. Such an auspicious start to the day. Dozens of résumé golems danced in a fey ring on her desk, invoking the elder gods of Accounts Receivable. Devon shrugged and went about fixing the mail bin. Animate paper men climbed up her shoulders to whisper salary requirements in her ear.

"All right. That's it. Wally! Pedro!"

The two large paperweights on her desk quivered. At her command, they twisted to look at her, air bubbles pushing up to form bulging froglike "eyes."

"Eliminate all résumés that have not graduated from an accredited hundred-year wizarding college," she decided. "I want archmaster-level experience with large distributed divinations, WIZ-XP, Quik-Fetish, GolemPublisher, oh yes, and twelve years' experience with that time-travel cantrip that's going to be released next month."

The paperweights smiled, exposing ghastly maws dripping with molten glass, their eyes now glowing a dusky demonic red. Slithering along the desk, they began slurping and chomping and chewing their way through the clutter. Devon finished his work, glanced warily at the ongoing carnage, and hastily excused himself from the office. Finally, fourteen quiescent and eminently qualified résumés were in her hand—and one last envelope lay in the middle of the floor. Odd— usually the problem with Wally and Pedro was to *stop* them from eating things. As she watched, the envelope's printed address flowed and shifted into elegant script: "Just add water."

"I don't have time for this. Why," she asked rhetorically, "does everyone think I want to see their clever little tricks and gimmicks? Wally, Pedro! Destroy!"

The paperweights wobbled and gibbered, but did not advance. Liz groaned, dipped her fingers in cold coffee, and flicked a tiny droplet onto the paper.

THOOMP. Just like that, it expanded to the size of a small pillow. Curious despite herself, Liz flicked another drop onto it.

THOOMP-THOOMP-THOOMP. The paper doubled and redoubled in size until it was as big as a bed, and as thick. With a tearing sound, the oversized envelope opened and a blinking, bearded, bespectacled man crawled out.

"Archmage Argentus." He bowed. "Master of the arcane, keeper of dread secrets, proactive efficiency wizard nonpareil at your service."

He drew a glowing glyph in the air, and a little molten man dropped into Liz's coffee and began doing a credible breaststroke through the now-steaming liquid. Argentus snapped his fingers, and the creature vanished. "Kona elemental," he explained.

"Hmph." Liz blew on the coffee, sipped it. Whatever he'd done, it was *good*. Refilled to the top, too. "All right. That was kind of impressive. I don't suppose you have a gigantic expanding résumé in your pocket?"

The wizard shrugged. "That could, ah, be a slight problem. I've spent the past thousand years in a cave in England."

"Traditional. Enchanted sleep?"

He looked offended. "Writing a play, actually."

"A play? Just one? In a thousand years?"

Argentus glowered at her. "It was going magnificently well, thank you very much. A beautiful, poetic work of Old English. Then the vowels shifted. Hell of a thing, actually. Threw me for a loop. You don't know what it's like to labor for ages only to find everyone around you gabbling like buffoons."

"Try me."

"Well. I'd just about mastered the new way of speaking when this Shakespeare twerp came along and just happened to write about the same thing I was working on. Like no one else ever thought of star-crossed lovers getting bunged up in an accidental double suicide! But mine was funnier!"

"Ah," Liz said wisely.

"Anyway," Argentus said, "I kept at it. Reworked the plot and crafted a play of truly masterful quality. By then, of course, Hollywood blockbusters were at their ascendancy and quality no longer mattered. Now I've got this slick little screenplay. Dinosaurs versus, er, tanks. It's a little rough." An addled look came into his eye. "But with a zombie cast and real dinosaurs, it would be amazingly cost-effective!"

Liz shook her head. "As much as I've enjoyed hearing about your personal life . . ."

"I have thirteen starving kids to support, too."

"Really?"

Argentus shrugged. "It could be arranged."

"Ah, right. But I'd rather hear about your powers and training. Why should I hire you?"

"Rather than tell you," the wizard grandly announced, "I will show you! Prepare to witness the mind-searing pleasures of Hell itself!" He pulled himself up to his full height, beard bristling electrically, and shouted a word that seemed to echo to the corners of the universe. Liz blinked. She checked her watch. She glanced from side to side.

"So. Monday morning in my office is Hell. Somehow, I always suspected."

"No, no!" Argentus stamped his foot. "It's those damned bureaucrats! There are so many regulations these days, I can hardly conjure a piece of bread without a dozen forms and permissions. Bah! Like your soul would've been in *that* much danger!"

"I'm sorry, Mr. Argentus, but I simply don't have a place for an enchanter whose knowledge is as out of date as your own."

"I'll start anywhere!" he said desperately. "I'll do anything! Look, I can make copies!"

Her coffee mug made a bubbling *poink* sound and turned into a dozen coffee mugs. Liz put her head in her hands.

"Unless you have four years' experience in an office environment..."

"You think that Argentus, master of stigmata, theurge of Thrain, demiurge of Mystos, couldn't learn to use the fax machine?"

Liz started feeding the spurious coffee mugs to Wally and Pedro. They glowed appreciatively and began to purr. "To be perfectly frank," she said, "I don't think someone who goes around calling himself master of munchkins and bane of the universe—*and means it*— would make the best clerical assistant. Conjuring demons, intimidating customers, and loudly proclaiming one's superiority are expressly forbidden under line thirteen-B of the employee guidelines."

"Oh, really!"

"See for yourself."

Argentus scanned through the pamphlet she gave him. His eyebrows jumped a little. "No stealing souls on company time . . . Internet strictly banned from orc-porn sites . . . Friday is Causal Day and will be time-shifted to occur *before* Thursday . . ."

"Lines seventeen through twenty."

"Oh." He said nothing, but the pamphlet slowly crumpled and turned black in his hand, little bits of ash floating away until there was nothing left.

"I'm sorry, Mr. Argentus, but you're simultaneously over- and underqualified for every position at this company. If you'd just spend a few decades learning NecroJava . . ."

The wizard climbed into the big envelope on the floor and began closing it after him.

"Um . . . begging your pardon," he said apologetically, "but do you have any extremely large stamps?"

A note slipped under the door. It looked like Devon's handwriting. Not good.

"The door, Mr. Argentus. You could try using the door. Lots of wizards use doors."

He sniffed unhappily. "I'll bet your duct wizard doesn't."

"Our *what* wizard?"

"Duct wizard. The ducts and in-between spaces of a major company are far more comfortable than some damned drafty cave in England, and with all the snack machines for forage . . ." His eyes widened. "You mean *you don't have a duct wizard?*"

With a whooping cry, Argentus flew up through the air and smashed right through the ceiling of her office. Broken foam tiles showered onto her desk and, of course, into her coffee. There was a disturbing *scuffle-scuffle-scuffle* and the wizard had vanished somewhere into the guts of the building.

"Oh, by the fuzzy green nuts of . . . !"

Massaging her temples, Liz picked up Devon's note: *"Do not, under any circumstances, let him know we don't have a duct wizard!!"* Underneath, in smaller print: *"P.S.: Now that we have a duct wizard, you'd better start leaving out an offering of Cheez-Lykes every Wednesday. Or else."* Below that, even smaller yet: *"P.P.S.: Don't invest in the zombie-dinosaur flick. Not after what Shakespeare's ghost is gonna put out three years from now."*

Another Monday in the office, and it wasn't even noon yet. Liz coughed experimentally. Sure enough, she felt a sick day coming on. Tuesday would be fine. Tuesday she could handle. But today she was going to stroll through the arboretum, rent a crossbow, and frag a few smurfs.

Come to think of it, she felt better already.

Poga

By John Barnes

Her father always called her "plain old goddam Amy." Then she told him it hurt her feelings, so he started calling her "Poga," his acronym for it, which he explained to other people as her nickname from their travels in San Pantalon, the little Central American country that he made up because he liked to see if he could get people to pretend that they had been there. Being called "Poga" still hurt her feelings but not in a way other people could catch him at.

She could hear his voice now just as if he had not been dead for four years. The eyes of his photograph, dusty and propped beside her coleus on the windowsill, seemed to evade her just like when he was alive.

He would sometimes gaze over her shoulder soulfully and tell her how important she was to him. Probably he hoped she'd share those moments with his fans.

The only time she could remember him looking into her eyes directly, really, had been whenever he got ranting about all the goddam kids who'd rather reread goddam Tolkien for the goddam twentieth time than pick up something new and good and that was why we were so goddam poor all the goddam time. Then—only then—he seemed really to see Amy, just Amy, right there and as she was.

Gah. Thinking about him too much already. She grabbed a paper towel from the rack beside the plant table, spit on his picture, and wiped the dust off. "It's not like I'm trying to avoid you, asshole. I'm going back to The Cabin and all." She set it facedown on the table.

She sighed, a pretty melodramatic sigh for plain old goddam Amy, and got back to packing, which wasn't much because her vacation clothes weren't much different from her working clothes; they were just her going-out in public clothes, elf-made and without blood, paint, and ink stains.

She didn't care much. In the working week, she put on her old-blood-and-fluids-stained Wal-Mart tees and jeans to go in to the lab, photographed dead animals and bits of cadavers on her digital, and brought the pictures back here to do her drawings in her paint-and-ink-spattered sweats.

To go out with friends, she wore her elf-made stuff, which always fit, never wore out, washed clean, and was warm or cool as needed. Colin always teased her about owning

"Five golden rings!

"Four tee shirts,

"three sweatshirts,

"two pairs of jeans,

"and a warm pair of Mithril socks!"

because all they ever saw her in were those. Actually she wore other socks when her Mithril of Wyoming socks were in the wash, but Colin barely noticed her except when he wanted to be funny at her expense, or when it was cool to know her, which was any time Dad came up in conversation around people new to their clique. That was when Colin's arm gripped plain old goddam Amy's plump little shoulders, and felt way too goddam good, and the girl she saw reflected in his pupils was sort of cute, or had been cute once. Cuter anyway. A cuteness had been present and now was absent.

Gah. Making little jokes the way Colin and the crowd did. It seemed like she was inviting everyone—Dad, Colin—that she really didn't want to come along.

But now the tape was running in her head, how things always went when there was a new person in the crowd who kept glancing at Amy, trying to catch her eye, shyly wanting to know who this was. When that happened, and attention began to slip away from him, Colin would tuck her under his arm like a football and start explaining that she was The Amy, The Real Amy, That Amy, yes, Little Amy from Burton Goldsbane's Wonderful Books, and she had grown up in The Cabin, and the capitals would fly thick and fast, even orally.

Anyway she was just going up to The Cabin, as Dad had always pronounced it, capitals and all. (At least Dad had only orally capitalized The Cabin and Little Amy; when he wasn't ignoring her, Colin was a storm of capitals. Or at least a steady soaking drizzle.)

Nobody in Feather Mountain was going to give a fart in a windstorm what she looked like because they hadn't since she'd been sixteen and concentrating on how close she could get to the dress-code line without getting sent home. People there didn't know what she wore all the time in Greeley, anyway.

So she packed what she wanted, just dumped all her elven stuff into her duffel bag (twenty-six years old and she'd never owned a proper suitcase, talk about a perpetual student). That was enough for the week but her thought of Colin and his dumb little song made her feel too much like Poga, so she dutifully looked through her one big drawer of as-yet-unstained human-made clothes, seeing if she could make herself find something to take along and work on getting used to.

Well, no. She couldn't. Too scratchy, too clingy, too warm, deceptively warm-looking but not really warm, not right for eight thousand feet in March. Done. She stuffed the whole scratchy, clingy, chilly pile back in the drawer on top of—

Her soul.

Her hands scrabbled at the coarse fabrics, yanking the sweaters, jeans, and tees back out, tossing them any old way onto the bed behind her, and there it was, lying in the drawer, where she had just glimpsed a corner of it.

Folded away in the corner, small and gray, unpressed, uncared for. They said when you found it you always knew it right then for what it was, and sure enough, she did.

Though it was so much smaller.

And so much dingier than she'd remembered.

In her memory it had been about two yards of fine, patterned raw silk, iridescent, coruscating, "numinous and luminous and voluminous," centered around "a big bold beautiful textured satin valentine heart set in a deep blue diamond," as she had written in her journal yesterday, making her notes for her search of The Cabin. "As long as he was tall, exactly."

As who was tall?

Maybe she had written his name, whoever he was, in her journal. Had she packed her journal? She picked it up from her desk, closed it, and dropped it into her duffel bag.

Was she all packed? No, she needed to put in her toiletry bag and— her soul, right, she had just found her soul. She looked down at her hand and there it was, again.

Not a big piece of beautifully woven raw silk with a textured valentine at the center.

A two-by-two square of gray unhemmed muslin. It was dusty. Really, she thought she had kept her soul cleaner than *this*.

Plus she didn't remember that her soul had been marked in dressmaker's chalk, that weird shade of blue that only came in a Baudie's Dressmaker's Stylus, which you could only get at Mrs. Puttanesca's shop, where Amy had learned to sew.

Dear Mrs. Puttanesca, so patient. Piles of bolts of fabric. Warm summer street air from Feather Mountain drifting through the shop. Just the thought took her back.

You could get a Baudie's at any Wal-Mart.

That thought took her sideways.

Why would she think you could get it at any Wal-Mart?

Of *course* you could only get a Baudie's Dressmakers' Chalk Stylus at Mrs. P's, because the company had been out of business for *decades* but Mrs. Puttanesca had bought four big boxes of them way, way, back before Amy was even *born*. And nothing worked as well as a Baudie's, anyone who had ever tried one knew that, you drew on the fabric as easy and fine as a good dip pen on a nice hard paper with just the right tooth—so why, in her mind's eye, was Amy seeing a big rack of them on sale at Wal-Mart?

Amy *never* went into Wal-Mart.

Except a lot of her scratchiest, clingiest stuff came from Wal-Mart.

Well, that was why she didn't go there, obviously.

Weird wandering thoughts and memories were supposed to be common just after you found your soul. She'd seen that on Oprah or Ricki Lake or one of those shows, they'd brought in a bunch of young women and their mothers with strange tales to tell about acting weird. Amy couldn't remember much of what they'd said but she could see that white sans-serif caption in the corner of the TV screen: "My Daughter Found Her Soul and Now She's Weird."

She didn't need TV to know about it. Every woman in her crowd who had found her soul had gone all weird. Aimee had thrown over a dream job, just walked into her boss's office and said, "I quit" and walked out, and now she was down in Oaxaca painting big-eyed kids. Ami had come by one Friday to The Lowered Bar, where the usual TGIF crowd met, waving her red-and-blue flannel soul over her head, but before they even got a good look at it, she'd said, "My ride is here," and a pegason, ridden by one hell of a hot-looking elf, had lighted on the sidewalk in front of The Lowered Bar in a clatter of hooves and a thunder of feathered wings.

Ami had run out, the TGIF crowd following like puzzled kittens after a ball, and, as the pegason swung a wing forward and up to give her room, bounded into the saddle behind the elf, tying her soul around her waist. With three big flaps and a *galumph, galumph, galumph,* the pegason had taken off, not giving the Greeley cops any time to get there with an illegal-landing citation, and spiraled up a thermal off The Lowered Bar's parking lot.

Ami had shouted a promise to write (Amy thought; it was hard to hear over some wisecrack Colin was making), then the pegason had merged into a bigger thermal shot upward. With an elven sense of drama, Ami and her elf had silhouetted against the full moon.

"So perfectly elvish," Amy had said, and Colin had asked her about why she said that, over and over, and why she stared so hard at the elf, until she had changed the subject and started telling stories about all the different ways she'd gotten suspended from Feather Mountain High School.

In the next few weeks, Ami had sent just a few e-mails from Cody and Billings, and about a year later a jpeg of a much fatter, dumpier Ami proudly holding a pointy-eared golden-eyed baby in front of something that looked for all the world like the Magic Kingdom, and then nothing, not even a thank-you for the baby quilt Amy had made. (She had lied that the rest of the crowd had chipped in materials, though in fact none of them even mentioned Ami after some nasty jokes about the picture of the baby—really nasty jokes, Amy thought, everyone knows you can't take a picture of a half-elven and have it come out, it's the camera that does that, mirrors do it too, it was unfair to Ami and unfair to her child and simply unfair. But she hadn't said anything to Colin and the others. It had been a few months after she'd given up saying anything to them, and had just accepted her usual place in Colin's armpit and her occasional place on his lapel).

And as for Émye—so horrible. And it had happened right after she had found her soul, she'd just shown it to Amy when they had dinner together on Saturday, gone missing the next week, and then the first parts of her had been found the following Monday.

It had taken Amy weeks to persuade Detective Sergeant Derrick de Zoos, he of the sincere puppy-dog look, that she really had no idea what might have become of Émye beyond the ghastly details in the papers. Worse yet, he had needed to keep coming back to break more news to her, as they found Émye's head, then the shallow grave with most of her, and then the rest, and then the place where she had been held and tortured, and so on, place after place, name after name to check with Amy's memory, until finally it had all led to nothing. Amy's memory of things Émye had said or people Émye had introduced her to contained no name they could connect to that old Q-hut above Eagle. None of the stores where the knives had been purchased, or the places Émye's torn body had been disposed of, had rung any bell for Amy, and Amy seemed to have been her only public friend (not counting the rest of the crowd, which had not known her at all except as a girl who sat next to Amy at TGIFs at The Lowered Bar).

In retrospect Émye had been the real star of the crowd as far as Amy could see, far more interesting than the daughter (and favorite character) of Burton Goldsbane, let alone an illustrator for biology and medical textbooks.

Yet Émye, half-elven, supernaturally beautiful, had merely hung around shyly, gracing the clique without the clique ever realizing it had been graced; Amy was the only one who regularly called Émye and made time and room for her. Perhaps that was why, when they found Émye's cell phone in the grave, only Amy's number had been in its memory.

She could only assume that Émye must have had some entirely separate, secret life over the border, that finding her soul (Émye had a bedsheet-sized piece of pure white linen) had made her misbehave somehow in that other world, and something or someone had punished her. Or maybe Émye had been chosen for some dark sacrifice because of something about her soul. Or perhaps that it was all a coincidence and it just happened that shortly after finding her soul, Émye was in the wrong place at the wrong time. But Amy had no way to know which it had been, and just because she had been Émye's only friend in no way implied that they had been close friends.

Eventually she persuaded Detective Sergeant Derrick de Zoos that she knew no more than that, and he stopped calling her—about that.

Unfortunately, by then, Derrick had acquired another interest in Amy entirely.

Derrick really was a very nice guy, and the cards, the flowers, and the invitations were flattering. She just had to constantly remind herself that she was not the sort of woman who dated cops, at least not the kind who got serious about them (and if you were going to date Derrick de Zoos, you'd have to get serious about him—he was that type). She could not imagine herself sending him out every day and wondering if he would be shot at, or having mischievous precocious cop-kids who worshipped their father, or retiring to some beachfront community somewhere where they could spend most of their time barbecuing and going to movies.

She wanted Derrick to give up courting her. But it *had* to be of his own accord, because she couldn't have borne bluntly telling him to go away (oh, those big brown eyes would have been *sad*!) Besides, her few times going out with Derrick had been fun, or at least a welcome break from hanging out with her old college friends at The Lowered Bar.

Plus going out with Derrick upset Colin, who fancied himself a dangerously masculine man of the world, but who was actually (though still handsome-faced in the way that had conquered a dozen nerdy freshman virgins) a soft doughy guy who lived on junk food, wrote software, and watched a lot of movies. Derrick's being a real live masculine cop made Colin get pissy in a way that reminded her of the way Dad had gotten whenever anyone mentioned Tolkien.

A cop's girlfriend, lover, or wife should have a sturdy brown burlap soul, or perhaps a pure white linen one, and hers—well, it wasn't the iridescent raw silk she had thought, now was it? She looked down, again, at the square of unbleached muslin hanging limply from her hand. Little gray dust bunnies drifted down from it onto the floor and the toes of her Bean Snow Sneakers.

She lifted her soul to eye level, grasping a corner with each hand, and shook it out gently, tumbling the remaining dust onto her feet and into her cuffs. That outline in blue chalk was obviously—

Amy's father had a shrub of gray hair on top of his head, desert-sky eyes, and a basketball belly on his otherwise scrawny frame. You noticed him, visually. But when Amy thought of him, most of all she remembered his *clatter:* the bang of the manual typewriter as she played around his feet, which had given way to the squirr-whuck-*chik!* of the electric welcoming her home, along with the Oreos and milk and the silly poems on the kitchen table.

Later, there had been the house-shaking daisy-wheel printer covering the sound of her running downstairs to get into a car with primer on the fender, a sullen boy in the front seat, a case of beer in the trunk, and disappointment in the offing because the boy was never quite how she thought boys should be.

Finally, during her college breaks, after he had the money for a quiet laser printer, she had awakened early every morning in Feather Mountain to the thunder of his clumsy stiff fingers pounding against the uncooperating keys, all precision aged out of his aching hands as they walloped a final three books into the word processor, as if he were regressing back onto the manual typewriter.

The window-shape of late-winter sunlight jumped sideways on the living room floor.

Amy had been in a reverie. Her soul still dangled from her upraised hands. Her arms were sore. Had she really stood here staring into that cloth for half an hour?

She switched on the bright lights over her drawing table and spread the soft cloth on it.

The outline of a heart—not a valentine heart, either. Most people would see only a blob, but Amy recognized a real human heart, lying on its atria, drawn from directly above. The chalk line showed no skips, no sketch marks, no hesitations . . . her soul must have been pinned tight to the table, not to have wrinkled at all as this was drawn. The unbroken chalk line had the assurance of a hard edge in an over-developed photograph. Yet it was just the right width and color to be Baudie's ...

The drawing on the other side was of a human heart, at the same scale, lying on its right ventricle.

She spread her soul out on the light table. Sure enough. The blue lines on one side matched those on the other, as if the Baudie's Dress-maker's Chalk Stylus—had somehow gone right through the fabric.

Could she make her friends understand how strange this was? *Now and then, for some complex patterns, if you're sewing or cutting out, it can be handy to have a mark on both sides,* she would say. They would all look bored. To the guys, sewing was girl stuff. To the girls, it was something authentic for authentic Third World peasant women to do in their authentic culture so that authentic woman entrepreneurs could bring it up here and sell it in little stores that just dripped of authenticity.

Or maybe the real reason they would all look bored was just that a brilliantly drawn chalk line for sewing was the sort of thing that plain old goddam Amy would talk about. But they'd let her talk, so long as she didn't go on too long about it. *See,* she would say, already afraid she was boring them, *it's pretty rare that you mark both sides and, if you do it at all, normally you only make a few marks on one side where it's going to be hard to see what you're doing after you've pinned something.*

For a cut-out line like this, you'd never *mark the whole way round. And most certainly of certainlies*—that had been a favorite phrase of Dad's in his books about Little Amy at the The Cabin, so it might suppress their impatience while she finished explaining that *nobody could possibly trace all the way around in a medium like chalk on muslin, with no bunching or shaking or anything. I've been doing med illo for years and I couldn't do that. Leo-fucking-nardo couldn't do that on a good day.*

They would all nod solemnly, Colin would say something sarcastic, and the clique would go back to quoting television at each other.

Maybe finding your soul made you cynical too.

The rectangles of light from the sunny window distorted further into rhombi, and jumped across the floor again.

Another reverie. Forty-five minutes this time, though she'd had fewer thoughts, at least fewer she could recall.

She wadded up her too-small, colorless, strangely marked soul and tossed it into the duffel bag with her too-large, colorless, perfectly self-maintained elven sweaters.

On top of her soul she put her meager toiletry bag: toothpaste, shampoo, aspirin, and hairbrush. No makeup. What would be the point? There wasn't going to be anyone at The Cabin except her, and she could never get things to come out anyway no matter how long she stood at the mirror.

Or had she invited someone to The Cabin?

She closed up the duffel, shouldered it, and went down to the convertible that she'd inherited, along with too much else, from Dad.

When she turned a different way, the old LeSabre seemed to perk up and sing, as if it didn't have to do something it hated, this one time;

whether it was getting away from The Lowered Bar, or from Greeley, or it was all just her imagination, the car sounded happy.

Going east to west across the Front Range, you point the car's nose down the straight-as-a-bullet two-lane road, stand on the accelerator, and go into that mental groove where you can run down a country road flat-out and wide-eyed, alert and quick enough not to rear-end a frontloader, T-bone a hay truck, or put an antelope through your windshield. You chew up road as the mountains loom, and make sure you stay alert.

The phone rang. She pulled the headset from her neck up onto her ears and said, "Hello?"

"Hey, there, this is Sergeant Derrick de Zoos of the Colorado Bureau of Cute Chick Control—"

"Oh, my dear sweet god, how long did you spend making *that* one up?"

"Hours and hours," his voice said, a warm smiling baritone in her ears. His voice, she thought, was even better than the eyes and the muscles. Now if he could just stop being a cop and lose that sense of humor.

She reminded herself to focus on the road. "Well, maybe it just needed a few more drafts."

"Everyone's a critic. I bet your dad always said that."

"Almost as often as he said, 'Goddam Tolkien.' "

"What did he have against Tolkien?"

"Several million book sales and a vast repeat business. So what are you actually after, here, Detective? Am I charged with anything cool?"

"You're charged with being cool, how's that? Here I am, a detective, all set for major crimes, and no major criminals have turned up, so of course I thought of you."

She saw brake lights far ahead and took her foot off the gas, letting the LeSabre slow down. "Aren't you worried about someone taping your calls to me?"

"They're nothing compared to the calls I make to other girls."

Amy couldn't help smiling; she liked Derrick whether she wanted to or not. "So let me guess. You're soaking up taxpayer time and money on the phone to me because you're finally getting a weekend off?"

"A *three-day* weekend," he said, in a tone approaching religious awe. "So, first question, does it take three days to wash your hair?"

"Day and a half, tops."

The brake lights had been a big old F250 turning off into a dirt road; she put her foot down again and the LeSabre pressed pleasantly against her back.

"Old boyfriends coming to town? Dental appointments?"

"They're rotating a paratroop regiment home from Avalon, and I should see a brain surgeon, but no." She liked bantering with the detective; Derrick *got* banter in a way that none of her crowd did, understanding it was a mutual game and not a public performance.

Belatedly, she realized she had just put herself into a corner, when Derrick asked, "So what lame excuse are you going to give me for not seeing me?"

"Oh, god, I should have seen that coming. There's two reasons it will be tough, but tough is not impossible. One, I'm driving up to The Cabin—right now, actually on the road—to spend a week."

"Your dad's old place?"

"You remember everything I say."

"I heard the capitals, so I recognized the place right away. But I thought that your dad's foundation was putting artists-in-residence into it."

"Right now it's in between. Samantha just left, and Piet isn't due for another six weeks, and I get to use it during in-betweens. So you might have to be willing to drive up to Feather Mountain on one of your days off."

"Deal!"

Doh! Why had she done that? Was she trying to keep Derrick pursuing her? And if so, why? And wouldn't it be awkward with three of them there?

That was, two.

The road lurched a little sideways and her breath caught before she brought the car back into her lane. Thank all the gods for dry pavement and good tires. She must have been off in like a two-second reverie.

"Amy? Are you still there?"

"Still here," she said, thinking, *Good question, Detective.*

"Did I get too pushy?"

"Not at all," she said. "Just had to think and drive and didn't have any brain cells to spare for talking. But yes, come on up to The Cabin this weekend. I want you to. The question is whether you want to, because the other thing is, just this afternoon, I found my soul, so if you come to see me, I might be pretty weird, you know."

"And you're *driving*?"

You weren't supposed to do that, Amy remembered, belatedly. "Derrick, I feel fine."

"It's not a law or anything," he said, "but you are going to be kind of out of it and accident prone, so be a little careful, okay? And you're making me wonder about that long pause on the phone."

She was about to make something up, tell him there was a tractor on the shoulder and cars coming the other way, but the words stuck in her throat, like they always did.

"Or is that sounding too protective?" he asked.

"Maybe a little."

"Well, it's pure self-interest. I want you around to reject me for years to come. How do you feel right now?"

"Weird but not bad and not out of it. I did have a couple of reveries right after I found it. But as far as I can tell, I'm alert now."

"Well, I know this is hovering and I know you hate it, but call me when you get to The Cabin, okay? Just so I know you got there. And then we can figure out whether you really invited me or I just trapped you into it."

"Derrick, sometimes you are too smart for both of our good."

"Whatever. Anyway, call me from The Cabin? Then maybe we'll make plans or not, but I'll know. Call the cell—I don't get off till three AM, but I don't expect I'll be doing much of anything, unless Greeley gets a lot tougher than it's ever been up till now. Can't even really hope for a good stabbing."

"The tough act isn't working, either," she said, smiling into the phone and hoping he heard it as teasing. "All right, I'll call you."

"You will?"

"Actually, yes. I promise. I just realized I probably did worry you some, and besides, I kind of want to have someone looking for me if I don't make it there. But as far as I can tell, I'm fine now, really."

"Okay. 'Preciate it, Amy."

"No problem, Derrick. Have a quiet night."

She crossed 25 into a series of dips and rises, where in dinosaur times the Pacific Plate finished skidding under North America like a piece of cardboard under a tablecloth. Wrinkles and folds in the Earth rise and steepen and cram together to become the Rocky Mountain Front, an area of astonishing beauty populated by elves and fairies illegally squatting below the Wyoming line, Buddhists and anarchists and old tommyknockers who can tolerate the elves, and, south toward Raton, bordersnakes, demons, and Apache ghosts.

Other ghosts are everywhere, silent, unspeaking, forever watching the invaders. Dad had taken her out to watch them gather and dance beside the borrow pit in the moonlight, countless times.

Not the borrow pit!

The lovely dark pool at the foot of the pine-covered slope from The Cabin with a twenty-foot waterfall falling into its north end. The pool that tumbled down the steep bouldery slope to Maggie's Creek in its southeast corner. She remembered vividly. The ghosts, Utes mostly, had come to dance on the flat rock, as broad as a tennis court, by the waterfall, in the moonlight, and she and her father had sat watching them till the sunrise swept them away.

Cops had found Dad floating on his back in the open water around the waterfall, nude, dead of exposure, one bright sunny February day. Pike and ravens had been feeding on him for a few days, and his blue eyes, typing-strong fingers, and sardonic lips were already gone; they had had to identify him by his teeth.

The sheriff's office had been mystified by the $400 cash on the front table but Amy hadn't. She'd had to tell them that that was $300 standard, $50 premium for getting the exact physical type (young, pale, black-haired, size four or smaller, ski-jump nose, fox-faced), plus $50 for driving up from Boulder or Fort Collins. They found a bunch of escort-service phone numbers on his computer and that ended the mystery; they'd even located the girl who had driven all that way to a door that didn't open and lost a night's earnings by it. The time of his call to the service established the last time he'd definitely been alive, six days before he was found.

Amy had always wished she could find a way to apologize to the girl for that. But then she had always wished she could apologize to all the vampire-brunette pixies. Dad liked to say that he drank cheap and hated Tolkien for free, so girls who were born to play the lead in *Peter Pan* were his one expensive vice. He had been saying that ever since Amy was old enough to understand why she was supposed to find somewhere else to be, or stay very quietly in her room, about once a month.

Later on, in her personal finance course, she had sat down and figured out that he had dropped a bit over five K a year on his "one vice." Run that through compound interest by twenty years, think about what they could have had during those years, and the figure had made her eyes water. In her journal she had written, *I am changing my major from business to art and biology so I won't have to look at things that are quite so upsetting.*

How far had she come over the rising wrinkles in the continent? It seemed like only five minutes in the groove, with the seat pushing against her back and the motor tached up past four, but no, it had been almost an hour by the clock. The sun was most of the way down now, the towns farther apart, the mountains close, their shadows already stretching far out behind her so that it was night here and day in the sky. She was almost to Van Buren, at the foot of Maggie's Creek Canyon.

She topped the last rise before Van Buren, and the truck stop's neon island in a sodium-glare pond welcomed her into the dark below. She put her blinker on—she had skipped lunch, her bladder was about to burst, and the needle was near E. She glanced up and had to brake hard to make the last parking lot ramp into the truck stop. Her car fishtailed on the gravel but the passenger side door didn't quite kiss the BP stanchion (after a nervous split second). Then her front tires grabbed pavement and she crunched over the gravel and up to the pump.

No hurt, no foul, as Dad said whenever he fucked up without totally fucking up, which was pretty much the average for Dad.

She gassed up, paid, peed, and then decided to move the car over to the main parking slots and sit down to eat at the counter. Derrick was right. If she was going to be driving within a few hours of finding her soul, she really ought to take some care of herself, for the sake of other drivers if nothing else. Might as well make sure she was comfortable, well-rested, and prepared, since the trip up Maggie's Creek Canyon Road in the dark was going to be stressy.

How had she let it get so late? Then she remembered that she had spent about an hour and a half in reverie. Aimee and Ami and Émye had all said that you forgot things a lot when you first got your soul back, though it seemed to Amy that she had been remembering things rather than forgetting them. Except that whatever she had been remembering, she'd been forgetting again.

Really, it *was* confusing and disorienting. She must've been driving a bit spaced out, but probably awake enough and therefore safe enough. She hoped.

Her usual double-burger-with-nothing had cooled to about room temperature, and the long hand on the clock had jumped halfway round. She wolfed the burger before it could get colder, gulped her slightly warmer chili, and left her lukewarm coffee on the counter, begging a refill with fresh hot stuff for her thermos. Forty minutes for a burger at a counter; life was slipping away just like that.

The last time she had come through here had been with her friends, with Colin sitting in the passenger seat of the red Miata she'd had then, grabbing the door frame as she went up Maggie's Creek Canyon at a perfectly reasonable pace. It had been for Dad's funeral. Behind her there had been two more carloads of her friends, supposedly all there to support her through Dad's funeral, and actually along to be able to say that yes, they had known Little Amy in college, and been to The Cabin, and even been at Burton Goldsbane's funeral. It was the ultimate privilege—or payment—for having consented to be friends with plain old goddam Amy.

Extra privileges, such as actually riding shotgun in Poga's Miata, knowing the real story behind that Poga nickname, and being able to tell people that Little Amy drove like a lunatic, came for agreeing to sleep with her or at least to crash on her couch.

At the funeral she had almost heard her father whispering in her ear what he said often when he was drunk; *Amy, Poga, Amy-Amy-Poga, I deal in lies all the time, little Poga, and the first thing to keep in mind is that to lie well you can't lose what the truth is. Disappear into the jaws of your own lie and it will digest you and leave you as a little pile of mendacious poop by the road. So lie all you want, Poga, but don't let the goddam lie eat you.*

She had kind of enjoyed the shocked look on her friends' faces when they saw Feather Mountain and The Cabin and the waterfall pond the way they were. . . .

Which had been what?

No time to think about that now. She was into the canyon. In daylight this place was gorgeous, at night a scary challenge, though a familiar one. She didn't need to see anything more than what was in her headlights—she felt, or just knew, where things were and where she was. The rock walls, brief pullouts, and steep drop-offs were where they belonged, held in place by her memory, and marked by the sudden flashes of the bright mad dance of stars between the peaks, spires, and canyon lips.

She knew and watched for the game trails across the road. In icy late winter, in the last hour of light and the first hour of darkness, there were often deer and coyote, even elk or bear, heading down for a drink from fast-flowing Maggie's Creek, which never froze all the way over. Or you could see a Ute ghost, or even an elf flying low to follow the road, and be startled just as you came onto black ice, and be into the canyon before you knew it—though as long as some of the drops were, you'd know it for much too long.

A mountain road at night is busy, if you intend to make time and still get there alive. Amy had learned to drive on this road but it still required her full attention. She could never remember every place where shadow lay on the road all day long so that runoff dribbling across the road turned into black ice, suddenly under the tires, quick, thin, slick, invisible, and hard as death itself. Traffic coming the other way compelled her to constantly pop brights on and off, and she was always braking behind locals who saw no reason to hurry, or pulling into turnoffs to let other locals pass, blinking from the bright headlights in the rearview mirror, peering ahead for the not-pulled-over enough car with naked, semidrunk kids in it that could be in any pulloff.

She wondered idly how many of these turnoffs she'd gotten laid in, during high school. Maybe the Burton Goldsbane Foundation would like to put up some small monuments: "Little Amy Was Slept With Here." And by her bedroom window, a statue of Burton Goldsbane himself, rampant with a puzzled expression—

Why by her window?

Approaching the blind curve that often had elk on the road just beyond it, she felt the reverie reaching up for her as if it were big, strong hands with unnaturally long fingers trying to cover her eyes, touch her body, stroke her—*Never mind!* She was driving the goddam canyon and the reverie would just have to leave her alone. The reverie vanished like the blur does when you focus a telescope.

With the very small part of her mind that had time to think, she was glad, almost smug. No reverie was going to shove her around. When she emerged at the head of the canyon, driving across the long truss bridge that leaped the raggy head of the canyon, and up into Feather Mountain Park, she glanced at the clock. As always, it had taken only about half an hour but she felt as if she had been driving all night.

Feather Mountain Park is not terribly impressive, as parks go. When she had gone off to college and met people from other parts of the country for the first time, Amy had forever been explaining that she had not grown up in a national park, that a park is a wide flat space between the mountains with too much wind and not enough rain for trees or crops, but perfect for horses and cattle. "Aryan Masculine Paradise," she used to explain. "Room for many cattle for the Tamer of Horses, and also lots of room for playing with guns and driving drunk real fast. Lots of long views you can snipe at federal agents from. Roadhouses with six country songs, none changed since 1970, on a thousand-year-old jukebox. When the Lord of the Park wants babies, there are local girls, dumb as rocks, blond and well-knockered, drinking underage at every roadhouse, drunk as shit and desperate to move out of their parents' house. And lots of room for a man to build his cabin—or park his double-wide. With all that going for it, what's a few months of below-zero, a wind that never stops whistling, and a little isolation and insanity?"

For some reason that had made people uncomfortable, though redneck jokes were common currency at UNC, especially among people who were afraid that they might not have scraped all the redneck off yet. After a while she made the connection and stopped telling those jokes; the problem wasn't what life in Feather Mountain Park was like, or that people felt bad about laughing at it. The problem was that the kids who had devoured all of Burton Goldsbane's Little Amy books did not want to picture sweet, dreamy Little Amy out on the back roads with older boys. Colin found it a little *too* interesting. Maybe *that* was why she stuck with him, though she never talked about life in Aryan Masculine Paradise anymore around him.

What everyone had wanted, Amy thought, was to claim friendship with Little Amy from the books, with shy bookish good looks and a dreamy artsy iridescent valentine-centered soul; it didn't matter whether they wanted to worship her or win her heart or debauch her, they wanted Little Amy, and while she might have been perfectly happy to be worshipped or loved or debauched—better yet, all three—she just didn't have that iridescent soul.

And that brought her back to the thought of what was in her duffel bag. She had had such a clear picture in her head of her magnificent soul, and here she had a gray rag with a brilliantly drawn technical illustration: a real heart and not a valentine. Why had she ever gone looking for it in the first place, if it was going to turn out like this?

She topped the rise and looked down on the town of Feather Mountain. She'd also tried to make a joke out of the observation that there was a name shortage out here, that towns very often were named after prominent local features and so was everything else within reach, Feather Mountain standing above Feather Mountain Park where the town of Feather Mountain lay at the crossing of Feather Mountain Road and Maggie's Creek Canyon Road; she said when she was little she didn't know that anywhere could be named anything except Feather Mountain and Maggie's Creek. But nobody else thought that was weird, so she gave up on that joke too.

In the night with the miles of blinding-silver snow all around it, Feather Mountain was at least interesting, visually, and maybe even attractive. The sky was spattered with stars; you could see so many up here, down to very dim ones, and the moon had not yet risen.

She crossed the last stretch of Feather Mountain Park on the swooping miles-wide arcs of blacktop as the town popped in and out of view, until finally she came over the last low ridge just above the town and the wild spill of stars vanished in the glare on her windshield.

Two blocks of façade-style buildings with steep pitched roofs behind the façade, the real old-timey places from when this had been a tank town on the narrow gauge. Maybe twenty frame houses, Sears railroad bungalows that the real estate people now called Victorians, clustered around those two blocks, and then around that was the usual sprawl of aluminum-sided fake frame houses, prefabs, and mobile homes on gravel streets. Out on the edge of that disorderly cluster, linked to the downtown by the other well-lighted street, lay a huge sodium-glaring parking lot surrounded by Wal-Mart, McDonald's, KFC, and Gibson's; the glare illuminated the irregular sprawl of mobile homes uphill from the parking lot.

Amy's LeSabre shot by the façade row of Main Street. No light on at Mrs. Puttanesca's—but what would you expect at nine o'clock on a Friday night?

She would have to make some time for a visit. She hadn't talked with Mrs. P since the funeral.

Just beyond the streetlights, as the stars popped back out of the black sky, Amy took the familiar turnoff up the steep winding road to The Cabin. Over the first hill, down into the little draw among the pines, and the friendly dark closed around her; she seemed to drive into that vivid spill of stars as she made the long climb up the main hill.

There were several houses back here, and she passed them all without seeing any sign of life. When she came to the driveway for The Cabin—actually just a place where the road narrowed and a sign announced that this was now private property rather than a public road—she was relieved to find that Bartie Brown had been up there with his snowplow, since when she'd known him in high school he'd only been reliable about getting beer. But when she'd talked to him to arrange the plowing, he'd rather shyly said that nowadays he had four trucks and was growing into a real business, and had asked permission to put up one of his advertising signs beside her private road.

She laughed when she saw his sign; the name of his company was How Now Brown Plow. Possibly there was more to Bartie than she'd realized ten years ago—maybe not being drunk and high all the time had something to do with it.

At The Cabin she parked in the same spot under the built-on carport where she had always parked her old VW Bug during high school, and her red Miata during college. "Plain old goddam Amy, home again," she said, aloud, but somehow it lacked the bitterness and irony she had intended. The car door opened into the expected blast of cold, and she pulled her duffel from the backseat and shouldered it up.

What was she doing here?

The question was what she had been trying to remember. Her whole reason for going up to Feather Mountain and The Cabin had been to look for her soul (a big expanse of vivid iridescence, in raw silk, with the most glorious embroidered ruby-red valentine heart at its center), which she was sure was somewhere in one of the elf-crafted cedar chests along one wall of her bedroom.

But she had found her soul. It was right here in her duffel. What was she doing here?

She had reason enough to want to take some time off, but once she'd found her soul, she could have just turned left on 25, headed down to Denver or Santa Fe or even into Mexico, or picked up 70 in Denver and headed to Vegas or L.A.

She still could. If the weather didn't suit her clothes she could just buy clothes on the way; her job was to keep her busy and because she liked saving money of her own, but she could buy a new wardrobe anytime she wanted one, she just never did. She could head to somewhere sunny and spend the next week in gauzy bits of fabric that cost more than her first car, in a hotel room that cost, for a week, what her apartment cost for three months, and live on umbrella drinks and desserts if she wanted. And she just might want.

No point in running the canyon again, though. Not in the dark when she was tired. Tomorrow could be another day.

Inside the front door, she found six tied-up garbage bags.

The Foundation had said that they had thoroughly checked Samantha out of the place, and yet they'd left these lying around? She had some bones to pick with the manager—

There was a pile of dishes in the sink, too. Had they not cleaned up at all, or—

She opened the refrigerator.

Fresh milk and fruit, bologna that couldn't have been more than a couple days out of the store.

There was some little sound from upstairs. She reached for her cell phone, thought for a second, and dialed.

"Derrick de Zoos."

"Derrick, it's me, Amy. I'm at The Cabin, but I want you to stay on the line with me for a little bit, if you have time and you can. I think there's someone else in here, squatting in The Cabin."

"What?! Get the hell out of there!"

"Easy. I think I know who I'm going to find. And it will be fine. I just want you on the line just in case. If something doesn't sound good, call the Larimer County Sheriff and tell them to send a deputy up here, they'll know the place, but I think it's all fine. I just want a backup plan in place in case this isn't who I think it is."

"I don't like you taking chances—"

"And I don't like you being protective, but we'll both have to live with it. My guess is it's Samantha, and trust me, she's harmless. And a friend. I just want you on the line in case a couple Texas-hunter assholes are squatting in here. But I bet it's just Samantha."

Samantha was a waif-thin, tiny, black-haired girl who churned out picture book scripts at a terrifying rate, showing great promise without ever quite selling one.

Amy carried her duffel up to her room as a way of temporizing. Since whoever was in the house didn't seem to have much furniture, and the only bed was in Amy's room, it seemed like the place to look.

"What are you doing now?"

"Climbing the stairs, Derrick. Going to the only room with a bed."

Amy's room, with the furniture her mother had given her before leaving, and Dad's office were the two rooms the Foundation required to be preserved pretty much as they had been, though Amy's room was a bit neater, and Dad's office phenomenally neater, than they had been when anyone lived there. Not to mention that they had taken down all of Amy's Kurt Cobain posters and dug the Care Bears back out of storage.

She'd kept the same bedroom set—bed, end tables, dressers, chests, and so forth, though. Her mother had returned to Elfland when Amy was too small to remember, but had left that bedroom furniture as a parting gift, and even after the money suddenly poured in following the unexpected success of *Amy and Titania,* that hand-carved elven furniture had been much the nicest stuff in The Cabin.

Dad had bought good things, all leather and oak and very Scandinavian, that were now in storage; he'd left Amy's room alone because it was hers, and his office because he could not bear the thought of changing anything and possibly jeopardizing the amazing luck that had taken him, after fifteen Little Amy books, from a reliable seller for every library's collection, and the recipient of a few fan letters every month, to the *Times* best-seller list.

Probably he had made 99 percent of the money he ever made in the last six years of his life. She wondered what he might have done differently if he had known that those were the last six. Probably written one less Little Amy book to make time for the series finisher he always said he would do some day, spent a little more time traveling, and had hookers up at The Cabin twice a week. And drunk more, laughed more, and eaten more pizza-with-everythings. Dad hadn't been the type to mourn about tomorrow, no matter how inevitably it was closing in. Which had something to do with those times in Amy's childhood when she had been forbidden to answer the phone because it might be "the money bastards," Dad's expression for bill collectors, "they're like goddam Tolkien's goddam orcs but not as well written, Amy, and if you talk to one on the phone he can steal your soul."

The stairs she ascended, and the balustrade were elf-carved, too, part of the list of things Dad had put into the cabin, like replacing the pinewood floors with maple and the plain old thermopane windows with old-fashioned double sashes, to make it more like The Cabin in the Little Amy books. When she'd been nine, there had been a steel utility stair he got for free from a warehouse that was being torn down, and they had rejoiced at getting to spend two weeks installing it, finally replacing the strapped on extension ladder they'd used before then.

"Talk to me, Amy, this is scary."

"*You're* scared? You've got a gun and you're eighty miles away."

At the top of the stairs, she flicked on a light and walked down to her bedroom door, far down at the end of the hall (at least the place had always been big).

When she flipped the light switch, she gasped.

"Amy! Are you okay!" Derrick's voice in her ear was demanding, as if she were a patrolman about to do something fatal.

Her soul—what she thought was her soul—what she *had* thought was her soul—was on the bed, as a quilt. A big, gorgeous, elven-made quilted comforter, with a raw silk face printed and embroidered with the pattern she remembered so well, a very nice one and it would probably have cost a thousand dollars at the gift shops in Cheyenne or Sidney, but nonetheless it was not a soul, it was just your basic shiny elf-quilt, astonishingly warm, eternally durable, fascinating, and elegant.

But a *quilt.* Though the pattern was indeed just as long as he was tall, and—

"Amy, are you okay? Say something. I'm dialing Larimer Sheriff's right now—"

"I'm fine, I was just startled by something that has nothing to do with anything, sorry I worried you, you don't need to send the deputies."

Of course she remembered that quilt vividly, now. She had been tucked under it clear back when she was younger than Little Amy in the books. She had lain on it with her homework open in front of her while she chatted on the phone about keggers and shopping trips down to Boulder or Fort Collins. She'd debated taking it to college with her.

"I know you'll hate my asking, but are you okay?"

"I'm fine," she said, and realized how husky her voice sounded. Her face was wet. "Just one of those finding-my-soul-things. I've got PMS—Perceiving My Soul—okay?"

"I think it's weird you can joke about it."

"Well, I can cry, too."

"Are you?"

"Mind your own business."

Amy just could not believe that she had remembered her fucking *bedspread* as her soul. She had lived so close to the Border for so long—Wyoming was less than half an hour's drive up the highway from here, one low range and you'd be descending into it—and somehow she had managed to make a mistake like—

"H'lo?" The quilt moved. "Hello?" The voice was sleep-drenched and sad. An arm, in a blue flannel sleeve with Han Solo on it, reached out from under the quilt; and a surprisingly alto voice croaked, "Ah shit, ah shit, ah shit," as if it had not been used in months. The quilt flipped back revealing a small, painfully thin woman, big eyes and liver-lips beneath a messy mop of jet-black hair that made her look like a dead dandelion. She groped for her thick horn-rimmed glasses, on the bedside table, like an old drunk feeling around for his bottle, pulled them on with a grimace, and blinked at Amy through a cloud of blear.

"Derrick," Amy said, "it's what I thought, and it's fine, 'kay? I need to talk to Sam now. Thanks for being there and putting up with me and everything."

"All right. Can I call later about maybe—"

"I'll call you. Promise. Gotta go." She clicked off and looked at Sam expectantly, not even considering being angry; this was too perfect and too typical.

"Ah shit, Amy, I guess I should try to explain this or something."

"Well," Amy said, "you're not in much shape to explain anything, but I bet I can. After the fellowship ran out, even though you wrote something like ten picture books while you were on it, you still hadn't sold anything, so you didn't have any money or anywhere to go. The next fellowship person wasn't due for more than two months, so you put your stuff in storage and since you still had a key here, you stay here, sleep in my bed, because it's the only one here, and write at Dad's desk or the kitchen counter, and keep hanging on and hoping your agent will call or something. You're living on mac and cheese and bologna sandwiches. That about cover it?"

"Yeah, I guess it does." Sam sat up. "You're not mad."

"No."

"Why not?"

"Dad's will set up the Foundation to support people who kept swinging at writing no matter what. I think I have pretty good proof the Board was right about you. And I'm probably only here for a day or two, and I know perfectly well you'll take better care of the place than I will. Do you have any money at all?"

"About three hundred in cash. I could give it to you if—"

"Not what I'm thinking about. I just wanted to make sure you're okay. Really. But get dressed anyway. I'm forcing you into slavery—I have a trunkload of groceries, because I had been planning to be here about ten days, and you get to help carry them in."

"But it's *your* house," Samantha said, climbing out of bed, unself-consciously changing into the jeans and sweatshirt from the bedpost. "*I'd* be mad."

"Then I'll never hide in *your* house. Things have been a little weird lately, and I could use having some company, and you probably need some variety in your diet. Let's just get the stuff in and then we'll sort it all out over some frozen pizza and Castles and Fat Tire."

"Is it okay to say I love you forever?"

"Only if that means I can tease you about the *Star Wars* jammies."

Sam shrugged and shook her black bangs out of her eyes, finger-combing her thick mass of hair. "Warm. My size. Clearance at Wal-Mart. Helps me stay in the right spirit for the readers. Besides, Han and Chewie *rock*."

The frozen White Castles went into the microwave at once, while the oven warmed up a Red Baron four-cheese. "This is going to be more calories than I get in a week," Samantha said. "Not that I'd dream of complaining."

The microwave pinged and Amy pulled out the plate of sliders. They huddled over the cold beer and warm Castles, going through both faster than they had intended to. They had become friends almost the instant that the Board chose Samantha (Amy wasn't sup-posed to meet candidates before the choice was made), sharing a morbid sense of humor and the sort of attitude that well-meaning teachers had always taken them aside to talk about.

They balanced each other somehow. Amy drew dead and pickled things with frightening precision. Sam wrote sweet, sentimental sto-ries of very young childhood, which everyone recognized as well done and no one wanted to publish.

The last few months had been the same; a steady drizzle of rejec-tion slips because her work "lacked something." Sam made a face. "Wish I knew what I lacked. Okay, so I've got no plot, but neither does *Goodnight, Moon*. I write about really trivial childhood stuff but so does Beverly Cleary. And I really exaggerate stuff and get really silly, but, well, all I can say is, Shel Silverstein, *Calvin and Hobbes*, Maurice Sendak, *The Phantom Tollbooth*. And of course, Little Amy. Which I hope you'll forgive me for saying."

"I live to be said. I don't know. Dad broke his heart and bank account for most of his life, and two different editors laid their jobs on the line to keep the series going, and about fifty librarians and book sales people created a fan club that could never get up to a hundred members—and then one day, presto, he does a lightning rewrite of *A Midsummer Night's Dream,* Titania strikes back with the genders reversed, Little Amy as the Counter-Puck, and making fun of my first boyfriend by setting him up as Bottom, and zip, bop, bang, he's richer than God."

"I've told you before I started reading those books long before *Amy and Titania.* I got *Amy and the Secret Cave* for Christmas right after it came out because I was already such a big Little Amy fan. Thanks for the food but please don't insist that I crap all over the only good thing in my childhood."

"Sorry. I really do hope whatever made *Amy and Titania* a success wallops you next week."

"Can you stand one question? I really don't want to be nosy—well, I do want to be nosy, but I don't want to offend you."

"If you do I'll just break a plate over your head and get over it."

"Great. Uh, you just said your father was making fun of your first boyfriend in that book—did you hate him for that?"

"Hate him? I don't even remember him. His name started with W—Walt? Wally? something like that—and Dad said, very accurately, that he was the sort of person you wanted to look at until you heard, 'the kind that the phrase *beautiful but dumb* was coined for,' and I was crazy about him then, I guess, but I'd probably have to reread the book. What are you laughing at?"

"Oh, you *really* don't remember *Amy and Titania.*"

"I said I don't."

"Well, he was beautiful and dumb and that was funny, but the idea of him being named Wally, it's just—just so—I mean—"

Once Samantha got going on the wonderfulness of Dad's books, she could go for hours without ever producing an independent clause, giggling and waving her hands into a string of happy "you knows". Amy did her best to look stern. "Come on, take care of yourself, Sam. Make sure you consume enough of all this lovely fat, carbs, and alcohol. You need it a lot more than I do."

"Doing my best. There's only so much of me to go around it." She folded up a drippy piece of pizza and ate it like a sandwich. "Funny thing, for a lot of us, *Amy and Titania* kind of spoiled things. We liked it, but not as much as the earlier ones, and suddenly Little Amy wasn't an inside joke for sad lonely brainos. But it's good that after all that work, your dad got something out of it. That's a good thing, surely?"

"Yeah. He did work hard for what he got."

They decided the first frozen pizza and round of beers would be lonesome without another, and dealt with those in pleasant silence before Samantha finally said, "Um, not that it's necessarily my place to bring up the subject, but what did you have in mind for the sleeping arrangement?"

"Well, ownership has a few privileges attached. I'm taking the bed. Can you be comfortable on the nap couch in Dad's office?"

"I sleep there half the time anyway. I was going to suggest it."

They got blankets and a fresh pillowcase for the nap couch pillow from one of the cedar chests in Amy's room. As Amy turned the light off in the office, she couldn't help feeling that she really ought to have tucked Samantha in. "Good night, Sam."

"Night," the voice under the covers muttered. "Thanks for not bein'ad."

Mad? Sad? Bad? Probably *mad.*

Amy hesitated a moment in the doorway. The big, high triangular window—one of Dad's few really successful building projects—framed Taurus's head, with the Pleiades in the upper right corner and just the tip of Orion's bow in the bottom point. She had seen the same stars framing Dad, slumped asleep over his desk.

She closed the door very softly.

Back in her room, she unpacked her duffel, and there was her stupid soul again, still a lifeless gray rag, with that remarkable drawing on it. She spread it out on her bedspread to look at it a bit more, positioning it carefully—the diamond that enclosed the gaudy valentine heart on the bedspread was the same shape and size as—

Though the lights were on, the floor was dark as it rushed up into her face.

"Come on." A hand was shaking her shoulder, in an annoyingly tentative way. She rolled over on her back, and it was Wolfbriar looking down at her, exactly as he had been when she had been thirteen and he had been whatever age an elf ever is; they are all perpetually newborn, which is the only way they can bear living forever, and they never die, which is the only thing that makes their intense sensory memory endurable. "Come on. Wake up."

"What happened?"

"Your soul became not-in-pieces."

"Whole," Amy said, sitting up and rubbing her head. She'd had hangovers she liked better than this. "Whole," she repeated. Elves were like that with human languages; they would usually only learn one of any pair of antonyms.

"Whole," he said. "Your soul has been not-whole for a not-brief time."

Or then again, who really understood elves?

"Yes, it has. Since . . . oh, my. Since the night in here." Her eyes widened. "We hid you in the trunk because my dad was coming upstairs yelling 'Who is up there with you?' . . ."

Now she remembered the kissing and touching that had gotten more and more exciting; the final wild moments where she had whispered, "Yes, yes, yes . . ."

The never-before-tested bed creaking and squealing in rhythm, betraying them but she hadn't cared—

Then, "What the hell are you doing up there? Is Wolfbriar up there with you?" in a drunken bellow from the front room, and the realization that Dad's little pixie must already have gone home, and the thumps of a big man hurrying up a ladder . . . Wolfbriar hiding in the cedar trunk, willing himself to not-be.

But since he would not exist to terminate the hiding spell, he had had to set a condition. And with Amy's soul newly divided, surely it must have seemed to him that she would repair her soul as soon as possible, so he had made her soul's reunion the trigger for his reappearance, but . . . *well, sometimes you just don't get around to things,* she thought.

She stood up, breathing deeply, and now her vision had cleared and become double again, the way it naturally was for a half-elf. She saw The Cabin as she had known it as Little Amy, and she saw the clumsily modified prefab house by the borrow pit. Her elf-eye delighted in the weave of silver in the walls, and her human eye saw the rough-fitted, stained, and urethaned but never sanded enough number-two pine of the floor, and—

She saw the bridge to her window, that Wolfbriar had sung into existence so long ago. He reached for her hand.

"Let's go," he said, tugging at her hand. If they walked down that bridge together, it would complete what had been begun; she would be off to Wyoming with him, like Ami on her pegason.

"You're in a hurry," she said.

"You would be too, if you'd been not-out of a trunk for thirteen years," he said, and they both began to laugh.

"My friend is asleep in the other room," Amy said. "But if we're quiet, we can go down to the kitchen and talk—"

"Food, yes, and water, and . . . um—"

"Next door down the hall," Amy said. "Then just come downstairs. You *have* been in a trunk for thirteen years, haven't you?"

When Wolfbriar came down to the kitchen there was another bout of figuring things out, because he couldn't touch iron and all of the tableware was stainless steel, but eventually she made a pile of sandwiches for him. "I sought," Wolfbriar said, "to carry off a Singer-of-the-True's daughter. That would have been a not-small not-failure for me to claim, in Elfland, where I have long been thought not-ugly but not-impressive. The deed would have been not-small enough to make not-commoners of us both."

Amy shrugged. "At the time you came, I was very carryoffable. But now I've lived on this side for another thirteen years, and I'm human down to the bone, and, well, it's just different."

"I know," Wolfbriar said sadly. "The ceranin is gone from your soul. I thought the only chance was to lead you over the bridge, right then, and off to Elfland, because I knew your soul would hold you back."

The ceranin?

That gaudy pattern, Amy realized. That picture of all the magic her heart was capable of and of what it might be on the other side—

She ran up the stairs to look. The bedspread was now all gray muslin, but on it was the most amazing layout; in the blue chalk, the same perfect lines depicted every organ of the human body with photographic precision but the clarity that only a line drawing can have. It wasn't gaudy at all; this spoke of precision and of things as they were. She loved it at once.

The bridgehead was at the window, and the long bridge descended across the pool, Little Amy's pool, composed as a mirror in the light of the rising moon; there was the falls, and there the flat rock where the Ute ghosts danced, and there . . .

She let herself see with her other eyes, and there was the frozen spill from the culvert, and the old borrow pit gradually silting up to become the meadow it had been before, and it was just another redneck homestead in the Rockies. Barely perceptible with her human eyes, the bridge glinted as if outlined in faintly glowing spiderwebs.

The gravel along the shore would crunch and there would be no diamonds in it. The borrow pit had some carp and the occasional whitefish, just garbage fish really, and would be deep green in the summer because of the mud that ran into it and because it was warm and shallow. Amy had smoked her first (and last ever, it was nasty) cigarette over there, sitting with Dennis; she had caught some big gross carp and fed them to Rags, her old buddy of a tomcat; she had thrown rocks at the water out of sheer boredom, and gathered jars of pond water and sat for hours at the microscope, one eye on the eyepiece and the other gazing at her drawing.

She had spent one whole summer of her science project, out there with her snorkel, collecting water at one-foot intervals to see how the microbial life changed from top to bottom.

The first human boy she had kissed had been the one that she shot floating bottles with. Dad would save her a case of beer bottles and they'd toss them out in the water and plink until the bottle erupted in a shower of glass shards and went to the bottom, and one day when they'd sunk a bottle after far too many tries, he had carefully set down his pistol, and then hers, muzzles pointed away (they had both had the NRA class), and put his mouth on hers.

"The lakes of Elfland," Wolfbriar said, "do not need glamour to be beautiful. There are no borrow pits in Elfland anymore."

She had been to Elfland; as a Singer-of-the-True Dad had been invited, and had taken her. Every pond there sparkled like a jewel, but it had no hydras, no paramecia, just sapphire-clear water. After sneaking out at night, she had sat in the moonlight with Wolfbriar and the glamour had crawled up around them till it was as beautiful— and as untouchable—as a movie of a smiling face projected onto a cloud. She had walked along the walls of the reconstructed town of Casper, and marveled at the smooth perfection of ivory and mother-of-pearl that went on for miles, and never once seen graffiti, or a water stain.

"Do you know what happened at the end of every one of Dad's books?"

"No," Wolfbriar said. He was standing very close.

She pushed him away. "Little Amy came back to the real world, happy to have been away, but glad to be home."

"Oh," a little voice said.

Amy turned. Samantha was staring at them. "I heard voices and, um—"

"It's all right. Turn on the light, will you? Wolfbriar's glamour is getting to you because of the moonlight."

Samantha reached for the switch and flipped it.

"You're even more beautiful without the glamour," she told Wolfbriar. "I've never met one of your kind before."

Amy suddenly whooped, the reaction and the thought hitting so fast that she wasn't aware that she was reacting until she already had. "Oh, my. Oh, my. Well, it's a petty nasty mean pleasure, but I'm not skipping it for anything. I get to quote Tolkien in Dad's house! 'Yes, Sam, that's an elf!'"

Wolfbriar was staring back at Sam. "You are a Singer-of-the-True."

"Unpublished."

"It does not matter who listens, only who sings. You are a Singer-of-the-True."

"Well, I guess I like to think so."

Amy looked at the clock. Three in the morning. She looked back and from the way Samantha and Wolfbriar were walking toward each other, she realized that the magic that gathered around The Cabin—oh, she'd always known Dad was writing about a reality—had managed everything perfectly. "Why don't you two head down the hall," she said, "and in the morning we'll all catch up. I think you'll find you have a lot to talk about, but I'm all talked out and really sleepy."

They went out holding hands, and she climbed the stairs and slipped into bed, yet again. As she fell asleep, she could see the stars very clearly, and the bridge just barely, and the blue chalk glowed on her bedspread and she realized she might work all her life to be able to draw, just once, as well as what was already on her soul. Tomorrow, perhaps, she would put it in a chest to keep it nice, and then think about how best to take it along home with her, but for tonight, just once more, she wanted to be warmed under it.

As she had figured would happen, just before dawn, they came tiptoeing through, holding hands, as if they had been holding hands for three hours. "Don't go without saying good-bye," she said, rolling out of bed.

Samantha and Wolfbriar permitted her to hug them both, and Samantha said, "I left you a note. Three CDs of finished work and a short letter to mail to my agent. And a box of my personal stuff to send UPS to Coeur d'Alene; across the border it usually takes a couple of weeks but Wolfbriar promises me they'll have everything I need. I left most of my money to cover your trouble and the postage and all. I'll try to write to you but you know how it usually goes."

She watched them walk across the bridge, or float on air above the borrow pit, and eventually they reached the other side. They stepped off the bridge and turned and waved. A big sturdy pegason descended from the swarm of morning stars, and they were off. She waved until the bright white pegason was just another star, moving slowly as a satellite. Then she went back to bed and slept till noon.

After getting a burger at the grill downtown, she put her now-complete soul into her duffel; she realized she could leave behind the elf-clothes, which were floppy and baggy and uniformly gray-ugly. There was a Victoria's Secret in Boulder, or maybe she'd just go a bit further, down to Flatirons Crossing Mall, hit the major department stores and the trendy-girly stores and so on, spend some of that big pile of Dad's money that had been building up for so long. She'd need makeup, and perhaps to find a hairdresser who wouldn't snicker, and . . . well, today was going to be expensive but fun.

She looked at the clock. Even if he had decided to sleep in, Derrick would surely be up by now.

He sounded very pleased to hear from her.

"Just me," she said. "Plain old goddam Amy. You know my Dad used to call me that? He had a pet name for me, the abbreviation for 'plain old goddam Amy,' Poga. No, actually, it sounds terrible, but I'd kind of like it if you'd call me that. We can talk about it when you get here. Now pack a bag, and get up here this evening, but don't be too early—shall we say eightish?" She gave him directions and made him read them back.

"Plan to stay tonight and Sunday night, okay?"

"All right," he said.

"You sound funny."

"Stunned. Very happy, but I'm stunned, Amy."

"Amy?"

"Okay, I'm stunned, Poga."

"I like the way you say 'Poga,' Derrick, it's sweet." She stretched luxuriously, cradling the phone against her ear and neck, rubbing where she planned to have Derrick do a lot of kissing. There was no one there to appreciate it but she tumbled her hair around with her hand in a way she knew made her look cute, exposing one pointed ear. Ditch the brown contacts and show the gold eyes, human guys liked that. Haircut, new clothes, girly shoes, come'n'get it undies, the whole froufy nine yards. Like she hadn't done since high school. "And do *not* show up early. It takes me a while to turn into plain old goddam Amy. But we're both gonna like her."

IN REMEMBRANCE

Jim Baen (1943-2006)

The Legacy of Jim Baen

by Eric Flint

My original plans for the second issue's "The Editor's Page" got swept aside in June by the death of Jim Baen, the man who launched the magazine and whose name is—and will remain—on the masthead. Jim lived just long enough to see the first issue of the magazine come out on June 1. Less than two weeks later, on June 12th, he suffered a massive stroke from which he never recovered consciousness. He died on June 28th.

That's not much of a consolation, but it's some. This magazine was important to Jim for several reasons, one of which I will spend most of this editorial discussing. He was only sixty-two years old when he died, after a life of many accomplishments, of which *Universe* was one.

And by no means the smallest, either. For Jim, the magazine was both a return to his own origins—he was the editor of *Galaxy* back in the mid-seventies, early in his career—and a continuation and expansion of a policy he had made central to Baen Books since the onset of the electronic era. That was his complete and total opposition to so-called Digital Rights Management and all the panoply of laws, regulations and attitudes that surround it. One of the reasons he asked me to be the editor of *Jim Baen's Universe* is because he knew I shared, in full, his hostility toward DRM. He wanted *Universe,* among other things, to be a showcase demonstrating that it was perfectly possible for a commercial publisher to be successful without soiling themselves with DRM. ("Soiling" is the genteel way to put it. Jim was far more likely, in private correspondence and conversation, to use a simpler Anglo-Saxon term.)

There are a lot of ways you can examine Jim Baen's life and his career. I spent some time thinking about how I would handle it, in this editorial. In the end, I decided I would concentrate simply on this one aspect of the man's legacy. Partly that was because I couldn't see where anything I could say in a general obituary would add anything to what David Drake already said in his superb one—which we included in the second issue of the magazine. And partly it's because I think talking about Jim's general accomplishments as an editor and publisher would fall in the category of hauling coal to Newcastle. Even leaving aside Dave Drake's obituary, many other people by now have said or written a great deal on the subject. *Locus* magazine did a cover on Jim's life, with appreciations by people who'd known him for many years and worked with him, such as Tom Doherty, Lois McMaster Bujold, Harry Turtledove, David Weber and others.

So, I decided I would concentrate on just this one aspect of his life.

Jim's hostility to Digital Rights Management, along with the alternative approach to it which he developed as a publisher, will in my opinion eventually be accepted as his single most important legacy. It will take years before we know, but I firmly believe the eventual historical verdict will be that Jim Baen was a central figure in the fight to prevent giant corporations from hijacking humanity's common intellectual heritage in the name of "defending copyright from infringement."

Jim had many other accomplishments to his credit—but this is the one, and the only one, in which he played a unique role. As an editor, he was excellent, true enough. But there are other excellent editors. As a publisher, he carved out his own approach to fantasy and science fiction, which is in many ways quite distinct. But there's a difference between "distinct" and "unique."

There are other excellent F&SF publishers, too, as Jim would be the first to agree. And if none of them had exactly his emphasis, there was always a lot of overlap. Many titles published by Baen Books could easily have been published by another house, and vice versa.

But in his fight against DRM, Jim stood alone as a publisher. No other commercial publisher, so far at least, has done more than slide a toe into the DRM-free waters that Jim cheerfully bathed in for many years—and, in doing so, demonstrated in practice that all the propaganda that its advocates advance to justify the increasingly Draconian nature of DRM is, in addition to everything else, so much hogwash even on the practical level of a publishing house's profits and losses.

Here are the facts. They are simple ones, because Jim Baen made them so:

1) All Baen titles that are produced in electronic format are made available to the public through Baen's Webscription service, cheaply and with no encryption. That policy stands in direct opposition to that of all other commercial publishers, who insist not only on encrypting their e-books but usually making them ridiculously expensive as well.

2) That policy has been maintained now for seven years, uninterrupted, since Webscriptions was launched in September of 1999. Month after month, year after year, Baen has sold e-books through Webscriptions using this simple formula: "We'll sell e-books cheaply and unencrypted."

3) Baen earns more income as a publisher and pays its authors more in the way of royalty payments from Webscriptions than any other outlet for electronic books. Typically, a popular Baen author—I'll use myself as the example—will receive royalties from electronic sales that are well into four figures. Granted, that's still a small percentage of my income as a writer, but that's a given since the electronic market is so small. The fact remains, however, that *as a percentage* of my income, the royalties from electronic sales of my books are higher—considerably higher—than the overall sales of all e-books represent as a percentage of the entire book market.

4) The difference between the level and amount of these royalties and those paid by other publishers, who are still addicted to DRM, is stark. Actually, "stark" is the polite way of putting it. The more accurate way of stating this reality is that the royalties paid by other publishers in the way of e-book sales are derisively low.

I will give you two examples:

In one royalty period, from a major publisher who was not Baen Books—that was Tor Books, generally considered the most important publisher in the field—David Drake once earned $36,000 in royalties for the paper edition of a popular title, *Lord of the Isles*. The electronic royalties from that same book, during that same period, came to $28.

That's right. Twenty-eight dollars. Less than one-tenth of one percent of his paper royalties—where a Baen title, typically, will pay electronic royalties that are somewhere in the range of five percent or more, measured against paper royalties.

Five percent is still small, of course. As I said, that simply reflects the small size of the e-book market. But five percent reflects market reality, where one-tenth of one percent reflects nothing more than the absurdity of DRM—even on the practical level of making money for publishers and authors.

The second example, from my own experience, is not quite as extreme. My novel *1812: The Rivers of War* was published by Del Rey, another of the major F&SF corporate publishing houses. In the first royalty report, Del Rey reported sales of the hardcover edition at slightly over ten thousand copies with earnings for the author of $27,810.65. The electronic sales for the same edition came to one hundred and twenty copies, with earnings of $545.30.

Translating that into percentage terms, again, that means that the electronic sales were two percent of the paper sales, in terms of money, and one percent in terms of actual sales. That's quite a bit below what Baen would have sold, but it begins to approach the ballpark.

I can't prove it, because I don't have access to the detailed records, but I'm pretty sure the difference between my sales and David's were due to the fact that several years elapsed between the two books coming out, over the course of which time other publishers were influenced by Jim Baen's policies. Del Rey agreed, after I requested it, to make at least one version of the electronic edition of *Rivers of War* available in an unencrypted format—something which I'm sure they wouldn't have done a few years earlier. The e-book was still grossly overpriced—they charged $17.95 for it, where Baen would have charged between $2.50 and $5.00—but it wasn't encrypted.

Before I move on, I should take the time to make clear that the problem here doesn't usually lie with the editors and managing staff of other publishing houses. All of these people, who have a hands-on relationship to fantasy and science fiction publishing, knew Jim Baen as a colleague and were often friends of his. In the case of Tom Doherty, who runs Tor Books, a very old and close friend. They followed what he was doing carefully. And, far more than the abstract arguments advanced in this debate by such vocal opponents of DRM as myself or Cory Doctorow or Charlie Stross, it was Jim's ability to demonstrate in practice that his alternative worked that made the key difference.

More and more often, the editors and managing staff of other F&SF publishing houses are starting to turn in Jim's direction. Or trying to, at least. The problem they run into, however, is that where Jim ran his own publishing house, the others are usually owned by large corporations—and, as is almost always the case, at the level of top executives of major corporations, DRM is considered Holy Writ.

Still, it's progress—and all of it was made possible by Jim Baen. It was his position as a commercial publisher that made him unique in the anti-DRM movement. That's because while an individual author who rejects DRM might risk as much as Jim, in the way of lost income, they simply can't *prove* their claim the way he could.

What an individual author does, however valuable, is one thing. What the head of a major publishing house does, is something else entirely. Today, measured in terms of titles produced every month, Baen Books is the second most important paper publisher in science fiction, after Tor Books. (A reality that is recently being reflected in *Locus* polls, I notice, whose readers are now listing Baen as their second most popular publisher.) And it is, easily, the pre-eminent F&SF publisher in the electronic market.

Having *that* publisher on your side of a debate as important to the public and far-ranging in its implications as the fight over DRM makes a huge difference. In fact, it makes a *qualitative* difference. Individual authors can be dismissed; lawyers can be dismissed; political pundits and theorists can be dismissed; anyone can be dismissed—except another publisher. Jim Baen was in a position to *prove* what others like myself could only argue; or, at best, demonstrate by such things as making many of my titles available for free in electronic format.

I've done that for years now, as have a number of Baen authors like David Drake, David Weber, John Ringo and others. Some other authors, who don't publish through Baen, have done much the same. Two examples are Cory Doctorow and Charlie Stross; there are others.

About two-thirds of all my titles are available for free to the public in the Baen Free Library, which we opened in December 2000, not much more than a year after the start of Webscriptions. True enough, I can use that fact to demonstrate that a consistent anti-DRM policy followed by an individual author does not cause the sky to fall. To give perhaps the clearest example, my most popular title is *1632*. It has been available for free in electronic format to the public for five years now—and the book has never suffered *any* decline in sales during that time period. Year after year, despite being available for free as an e-book, the paper edition sells about fifteen thousand copies. That figure fluctuates a bit from one year to the next, of course, but there is no overall downward trend at all. The standard rule of thumb in the industry is that 80% of a book's sales happen in the first three months after publication. But in the case of *1632*, sixty percent of the book's sales have come since the first year it came out—during which period the book was always available to the public for free in electronic format.

Impressive, yes. But, in the end, it's really just a stunt. That's about all an individual author can do. Putting my most popular title up for free to the public was my literary equivalent of Evel Knevel jumping over twenty cars on a motorcycle. I did it to demonstrate, as graphically and daringly as possible, that people who worry about the so-called "threat of online piracy" are being spooked by shadows.

Stunts have the great value of drawing a lot of public attention, but the problem is that most people figure they're just that—stunts.

Who knows? The fact that it worked for one author doesn't mean it would work for others, much less all authors. Just as the fact that people will marvel at Evel Knevel's ability to jump over twenty cars on a motorcycle doesn't make them in the least bit inclined to follow his lead. Many of them also know, after all, that in the course of his daredevil career Evel Knevel broke just about every bone in his body.

But what Jim did *wasn't* a stunt. All the arguments that people can and do marshal against me, such as:

— you're just lucky;

—you would have been popular anyway, regardless of the free e-books; in fact, they may have cut into your sales and you prospered despite them;

—yadda yadda yadda . . .

Simply can't be made against Jim Baen, because what Jim did wasn't a series of stunts, it was a major publishing house's *policy*.

In the end, the Free Library is an excellent demonstration of some truths, but it doesn't prove anything. What does prove something is the much more mundane, even—by now—humdrum, regular sales of all its e-books through Webscriptions done by Baen Books.

Year after year, month after month, Baen Books keeps *proving* that DRM is, in addition to everything else, a liability for a commercial publisher. All the arguments that can be advanced against me—or David Drake, or Cory Doctorow, or Charlie Stross—simply can't be advanced against Baen. That's because it all evens out in the wash, when you're dealing with a major publisher's *policy.*

If someone insists that I probably would have done well anyway, I can point out that *all* of Baen's authors do better in electronic sales through Baen's Webscriptions than anyone else.

What? Are we *all* "lucky"?

If someone insists that Cory Doctorow's policies with regard to DRM prove nothing because Cory doesn't make most of his income as an author, I can simply point out that *all* of Baen's authors do better in the electronic market than other authors do. And not one of them has an equivalent to Cory's very popular Boing Boing web site, and many of them—including me—do in fact depend on writing for their entire income.

For years, I've danced about and done my best to draw public attention to the issue, like a virtual Gene Kelly. Nor was that work unimportant, because it did in fact get a lot of publicity. *Business Week's* online magazine ran an article on me, and I was once invited to attend—all expenses paid—an international conference in London on the subject of electronic publishing.

But I could only do it—and it only made a big difference—because I had Jim Baen at my side. I could dance, but he could hammer. And hammer, and hammer, and hammer, and hammer, like a blacksmith at his trade.

Which, in the end, is what he was. And when the day finally comes, as I believe it will, that the American public decisively repudiates DRM and demands that giant corporations cease and desist from their efforts to lock up society's intellectual heritage for their own private gain, the world will look back and recognize Jim Baen as the man who, more than any other, forged that outcome. Not by words, but by deeds.

One last thing. In a jocular manner, in the course of an email exchange we were having on the subject of DRM, Jim once called me "Baen's bulldog." The reference, to those familiar with the history of evolution, is to Darwin's most forceful and popular advocate, Thomas Henry Huxley.

Jim was joking . . . mostly. And I responded in kind, at the time. But there was an underlying seriousness to the statement, and we both knew it. Leave aside the humor, and it was true.

And still is. Jim Baen is gone. The bulldog remains—and I intend to continue using this magazine the way Jim wanted me to. Among other things, as a bully pulpit for explaining to the public that DRM is a serious and deep threat to the liberties of the American population and that of the world as a whole. And that a clear and practical alternative exists, created and maintained by Jim Baen, that guts all the claims made by DRM advocates that their anti-democratic policies are essential for the preservation of copyright and the livelihood of authors, artists, and other intellectual creators.

The reason I will be able to do that illustrates another part of Jim's legacy. The difference between what an author like myself can advocate and demonstrate, and what a publisher can *do*, is that the latter leaves behind an institutional framework where the former does not.

There will be no change in Baen Books' policy, now that Jim is dead.

First, because there is no reason to change the policy. It works, and it works well.

Secondly, because—like all successful policies—Jim's has left behind a coherent and organized vested interest, in the form of a staff that is accustomed and comfortable with his policies, and, just as important, a large fan base that is also comfortable and accustomed to it.

People usually use the term "vested interest" as a pejorative, but that's just silly. It all depend on whether the interest being vested is a good one or not. Democracy, after all, is also a "vested interest"—and it becomes more difficult to undermine or destroy, the more thoroughly rooted it becomes.

So it is with Jim's anti-DRM policies. By now, even if the incoming management wanted to change those policies—which it has no intention of doing, I can assure you—they would find it so damaging to Baen's financial interests that they would shy away from even thinking about it. The uproar from the very large fan base that Baen Books has created for Jim's policies with regard to electronic publication—which, I will point out, is so far the one and only clearly defined "vested interest" that can be matched against the vested interests of music recording and movie industry executives and their powerful lobbies—would be enormous.

That, too, is Jim's legacy. Thousands of regular readers—and buyers—of electronic books whom he created as a vested interest in the *right* way to handle the challenges of the electronic era for the publishing industry.

I asked Jim to read and approve all of the editorials I wrote in my *Salvoes Against Big Brother* column. I did that because, although I am listed as the author of those essays, I considered Jim to be the co-author of them in all but name.

He was able to read and approve the first three of those essays. With regard to the first, he sent me the following email:

Hi. I've read both. The DRM one has my enthusiastic approval, and you certainly did not say anything I don't agree with.

He gave me his verbal agreement to the second and third essays. That was in the course of a telephone conversation that may have been the last one I ever had with him. If not, certainly one of the last.

He won't be able to read the ones that will come after. I don't believe in an afterlife, and neither did Jim. But if we're both proven wrong, whatever other problems I may face in that life-after-death, I'm not at all worried that Jim's shade won't be pleased by the rest of what I have to say.

Why Die?

By Jim Baen

[Note: The author would like to acknowledge the inestimable help received from conversations with Dr. Lambshead, and for the enthusiastic support of Professor Uglund, whose analysis follows the article. There are probably several persons on the planet who will understand the analysis.]

Many people have suggested that aging is a preprogrammed, genetically controlled function in higher animals. This appears to be confirmed by the research findings of Cynthia Kenyon, an eminently respectable scientist who publishes in peer-reviewed journals, on aging in nematodes. She reported extensions of nematode life span of five times normal, i.e. from around two weeks to ten, with their apparent vigor undiminished until shortly before death. In other words, they don't just drag out old age but function properly for an extended period.

She accomplishes this by selectively blocking the expression of various DAF genes, including DAF-2 and DAF-16. DAF-2 suppresses the action of DAF-16, the latter triggers or suppresses at least six other genes, the end result of which is to promote longevity. DAF-16 seems to influence the production of proteins that protect against free-radical damage. So it could be said that DAF-2 has the function of deliberately limiting a nematode's life span.

Of course, one has to be careful extrapolating from a nematode worm with a life span measured in weeks to something long-lived like a human being. In nematodes, DAF-2 and DAF-16 are associated with moulting. Nematodes are ecdysozoans (moulting animals) and these have the ability to go into a special "shutdown" state, known as *dauer larvae* in the case of the Kenyon's test animal, the nematode *Caenorhabditis elegans.*

Human beings neither moult nor go into a shutdown mode (not even teenagers). However, the DAF-2 gene is similar to a gene in mammals called IGF-1 that is connected with insulin function. Martin Holzenberger created strains of mice in which one or both copies of the rodent gene for the IGF-1 receptor had mutations. Mice lacking any normal copies died as embryos. However, mice with one working copy developed normally and lived, on average, 26 percent longer than did animals with two normal copies of the IGF-1 receptor gene.

For the purposes of this article, let us assume that getting old and dying is a defined process, a process that is controlled by our genes; that our life span is deliberately limited. Why? This seems astonishingly counterevolutionary. The two basic driving forces in evolution are (i) survival and (ii) success in mating (for sexual organisms). Surviving by definition implies extension of life span. However, it is also true that for many organisms that the longer an organism survives the more successful it will be at mating—even geeks will manage to reproduce if given enough chances.

So if our life span is deliberately limited by our genes then there must be some evolutionary advantage. The rest of this article will try and address this point.

One possibility is that we limit our life span by the need for optimal performance up to the time of successful reproduction. This is the racing-car analogy. An engineer designing a Ford or a Peugeot tends to overengineer to give reliability and a decent life span rather than optimize for performance. In contrast, the racing genius Colin Chapman used to examine his cars after a race and any component that was in too good a condition was promptly lightened. An ideal Chapman racing car would fall to pieces one inch after crossing the finish line—but in first place!

The racing-car analogy does not really seem to explain Kenyon's results because when DAF-2 is suppressed the worms stay younger longer; they do not stagger on in senility. It is almost as if the genes do not care how long a worm could live or what condition it might be in through most of that life but just decide it has lived long enough. What evolutionary mechanism could cause this?

In Utah, studies have been done that show that it is possible, in fact surprisingly easy, to track the presence of polygamous marriages by the occurrence of babies with birth defects. It turns out that having a few highly prolific males makes a surprisingly large impact on the occurrence of double recessives in the general population, and that this in turn leads to a surprisingly large number of birth defects; children with Down's syndrome, cleft palate, club feet, various leukodystrophies, and the like occur much more commonly than they would without the prior presence of these males. This observation is anecdotally common human experience. Inbreeding causes an increase in nasty recessive genes in the population, and polygamy inevitably will increase inbreeding.

This is a common problem in conservation. Once a population of an organism drops below a certain level then the species is in terrible trouble. In theory, one could recreate a species from a single male and female. In practice, there are likely to be enormous genetic issues.

For human populations, inbreeding is likely to be especially dangerous for two reasons. The first is that the human genome is particularly messy compared to other mammals such as dogs or rats. The second reason is that reproductive success of males in human beings (who are highly social animals) tends to be correlated with status and status tends to increase with age. As the hypothetical TV interviewer put to the young blonde, "What first attracted you to this elderly, balding, multimillionaire, Miss Smith?" The wealthy middle-aged man with a younger trophy wife is a phenomenon observed in all human society. A long life span in men is more of an issue because one high-status man can impregnate many women. Reason one will tend to accentuate the impact of reason two.

So if a metapopulation (a subgroup) of a species that has mutations that shorten its life span has offspring that are more successful than the offspring of a longer-lived metapopulation, then the former population will replace the latter. An evolutionary mechanism, therefore, exists that could promote death genes.

Just because this is logical and reasonable does not make it true, but I leave you with one final thought. Women commonly live longer than men and, in my model, it is long-lived men that should be more dangerous to the species. If you are male, then nature could have it in for you.

A Genetic Model for Eternal Life as an Evolutionary Strategy

by Karl Inne Ugland

(University of Oslo, Marine Zoology, Pb 1066, 0316 Oslo, Norway)

Introduction

Classical and molecular genetics are concerned with the nature and transmission of genetic information, and how this information is translated into phenotypes. Population genetics theory is most successful when dealing with simply inherited traits—traits whose transmission follows simple Mendelian rules. Yet many of the most interesting and important traits are not so simply inherited: they depend on several genes, which often interact in complex ways with one another and with the environment.

Population genetics includes a large body of mathematical theory; one of the richest and most successful bodies of mathematics in biology. The useful application of this theory has been greatly enhanced in recent years by new molecular techniques.

Usually, the first step is to study the frequency of different genotypes or phenotypes in a sample of the population. The concept **locus** is used to designate a chromosomal location, and the concept **allele** designates an alternative form of the gene occupying the considered position. Usually, we are more interested in the frequencies of the different alleles than in the frequencies of the different genotypes. This is because allele frequency is a more economical way to characterise the population. The number of possible genotypes is enormous. Consider for example 100 loci, each with 4 segregating alleles. With 4 alleles A, B, C, D the total number of possible genotypes at each locus is 10: (1) four homozygotes: AA, BB, CC and DD plus (2) six heterozygotes: AB, AC, AD, BC, BD and CD. For all 100 loci there are thus 10^{100} possible genotypes, i.e. more than the number of atoms in our universe! It is, therefore, much better to stick to allele-frequencies.

The characterisation of a population in terms of allele frequencies rather than genotype frequencies has another advantage. In a Mendelian population, the genotypes are scrambled every generation by segregation and recombination. New combinations are put together only to be taken apart in later generations. If we are to study a population over a time period of more than a few generations, then the stable entity is the gene.

In nature it is the **organism** that **survives** and **reproduces**, so **natural selection** acts on the organisms and it is the **fitness** of the organism that determines the likelihood of survival and reproduction. But what an individual actually transmits to future generations is a random sample of its genes, and those genes that increase fitness will be more represented in future generations. Thus, there is selection of genes determining the properties like vigour and fertility.

Any description of nature, whether verbal or mathematical, will only be a caricature and therefore necessarily incomplete. In the previous century, scientists realised that we cannot ask whether a mathematical model is true, we can only ask if it gives a good or bad description of our data, and so may be used for prediction of future observations and experiments. Some models are only rough caricatures, but the advantage with this class of models is that they are easy to understand. An example is the successful theory of thermodynamics where the gas molecules are regarded as elastic spheres.

The Gene Pool

One of the most useful conventions in population genetics is the model of a **gene pool**. We assume that each parent contributes equally to a large pool of gametes. Each offspring is regarded as a random sample of one egg and one sperm from this pool. Each gene is chosen randomly, as if we were drawing different coloured beans from a bag. This oversimplified model building is called "beanbag genetics" and has a surprisingly strong predictive power. In 1964, the great British geneticist, J.B.S. Haldane, wrote an amusing and spirited article "A Defence of Beanbag Genetics" (Persp. Biol. & Med., 7: 343-359).

Clearly the beanbag model is a crude representation of nature. A real population has individuals of all ages, some dying, some choosing mates, some giving birth, etc, etc. Keeping track of all this information is not only impractical, but often is neither interesting nor important. Most questions of genetic or evolutionary interest do not require minute details. The gene pool model will give us the same kind of insight that simple models in the physical sciences do, and often with predictions that are sufficiently accurate for most uses. Furthermore, it is important to be aware of that departure from the simple models may usually be treated with appropriate modifications.

Suppose now that a population consists of individuals with an extremely long life span. In the tradition of "beanbag genetics", the population is homozygous at the locus determining life span; i.e. all genotypes are AA and code for long-life. However, in any population there will be some random death rate basically determined from outer sources like biological (virus, sickness, predation or accidents due, for example, to natural catastrophes). Thus, rather living forever, the long-lived strategy has to tolerate the operation of a random death rate; that is, the survival rate, S, is close to 1. This strategy is called **evolutionary stable** if the population rejects all kinds of invading alleles that reduce the life span. In order to investigate this stability, we assume that a small fraction ε of the gene pool consists of an allele 'a' such that the genotypes Aa induces a shorter life span via changes in the birth rates and survival rates. We must find the requirement that the new allele will increase in the gene pool.

A Hardy-Weinberg Type Model for Analyzing the Evolutionary Stability of Infinite Long Life

Since we are only interested in the general principles that govern the stability of the long-life strategy, we simplify the population dynamics of the mutant allele as follows: On average they live t years and reproduces b_{Aa} offspring of which l_{Aa} survives the next t years.

The probability of surviving t years for the long-lived individuals is $L = S^t =$ (S multiplied by itself t times). Finally, we ignore the homozygous mutant allele (of genotype aa), since their abundance is of the order $\varepsilon * \varepsilon$ in the gene pool.

Thus the initial genotype frequencies are $(1 - \varepsilon)$ of AA and ε of Aa where the abundant first group of individuals (AA) have a very long life span and the second potential invader group (Aa) only live t years. In the gene pool the frequency of A is $(1 - \varepsilon) * 1 + \varepsilon * (1/2) = 1 - \varepsilon/2$ while the frequency of a is $q = \dfrac{\varepsilon}{2}$.

We shall now try to answer the question: Under what circumstances is the fraction of the allele a expected to increase in the gene pool?

In order to solve this problem we need another assumption: The population size is so large that the mating may be considered as a random mixture of the genes. We must consider all kinds of matings between the genotypes:

(1) Consider first a long-lived female (AA) that mates with a long-lived male (AA). During t years she produces b_{AA} offspring (of genoype AA) that have a chance of l_{AA} to survive the next t years. In the population the probability of such matings is $(1 - \varepsilon)*(1 - \varepsilon)$.

(2) Consider next a long-lived female (AA) that mates with a mutant short-lived male (Aa). During t years she produces b_{AA} offspring of which 50% are long-lived (AA) with a chance of l_{AA} to survive the next t years, and 50% are short-lived (Aa) with a chance of l_{Aa} to survive the next t years . In the population the probability of such matings is $(1 - \varepsilon) * \varepsilon$.

(3) Then consider a mutant short-lived female (Aa) that mates with a long-lived male (AA). During t years she produces b_{Aa} offspring of which 50% are long-lived (AA) with a chance of l_{AA} to survive the next t years, and 50% are short-lived (Aa) with a chance of l_{Aa} to survive the next t years. In the population, the probability of such matings is $\varepsilon * (1 - \varepsilon)$.

(4) Finally consider a mutant short-lived female (Aa) that mates with a mutant short-lived male (Aa). During t years she produces b_{Aa} offspring of which 25% are long-lived (AA) with a chance of l_{AA} to survive the next t years, and 50% are short-lived (Aa) with a chance of l_{Aa} to survive the next t years. In the population the probability of such matings is $\varepsilon * \varepsilon$.

After t years the number of long-lived and short-lived recruits are respectively

$$W_{AA} = (1-\varepsilon)^2 \, b_{AA} \, l_{AA} + (1-\varepsilon) * \varepsilon(1/2) \, b_{AA} \, l_{AA}$$
$$+ \varepsilon * (1-\varepsilon)(1/2) \, b_{Aa} \, l_{AA} + \varepsilon * \varepsilon(1/4) \, b_{Aa} \, l_{AA}$$

$$W_{Aa} = (1-\varepsilon) * \varepsilon \, (1/2) \, b_{AA} \, l_{Aa} + \varepsilon *(1-\varepsilon)(1/2) \, b_{Aa} \, l_{Aa}$$
$$+ \varepsilon * \varepsilon(1/2) \, b_{Aa} \, l_{Aa}$$

Now, the number of adult long-lived individuals surviving a period of t years will be $(1-\varepsilon)N * S$ where N is the total population size. In order to keep the population at a stable size of N individuals, we have to introduce a common death rate m for the recruits of all genotypes:

$$(1-m) * N * W_{AA} + (1-m) * N * W_{Aa} + (1-\varepsilon)N * L = N$$

After t years the new fraction of the short-lived allele a in the gene pool is

$$q' = \frac{(1-m)W_{Aa}}{2[(1-m)W_{Aa} + (1-m)W_{AA} + (1-\varepsilon)L]}$$

Thus we see that the fraction of the allele a will increase in the gene pool if $q' > q = \dfrac{\varepsilon}{2}$, i.e.

$$\frac{(1-m)W_{Aa}}{2(1-m)W_{Aa} + 2(1-m)W_{AA} + 2(1-\varepsilon)L} > \frac{\varepsilon}{2}$$

which is equivalent to

$$\frac{(1-m)(1-\varepsilon)}{2}(b_{Aa}l_{Aa} + (1-\varepsilon)b_{AA}l_{Aa}) > (1-m)W_{AA} + (1-\varepsilon)L$$

Reordering the terms, finally gives the requirement that the mutant allele coding for short-lived may invade the gene pool:

$$\frac{1}{2}(b_{Aa}l_{Aa} + (1-\varepsilon)b_{AA}l_{Aa}) > \frac{W_{AA}}{(1-\varepsilon)} + \frac{L}{(1-m)}$$

Thus, if the mutant allele a codes for a birth rate b_{Aa} and survival rate l_{Aa} such that this inequality is satisfied it will invade the gene pool. But what does this inequality essentially tell us? In order to see the essential requirement for invasion we may use standard techniques in numerical analysis. First, since ε is a small quantity in the order of $1/100$, we may use the standard approximations in the final expressions: $1 - \varepsilon \approx 1$ and $\frac{1}{1-\varepsilon} \approx 1 + \varepsilon + \varepsilon^2 \approx 1$ so the inequality is practically the same as $\frac{1}{2}(b_{Aa}l_{Aa} + b_{AA}l_{Aa}) > W_{AA} + \frac{L}{(1-m)}$

Then we take a closer look at the extra nonspecific mortality rate m that was introduced in order to keep the population at its equilibrium value N. In order to understand the magnitude of this quantity we consider the population without the mutant allele a (that is all genotypes are AA), so the equilibrium equation reduces to $N * W_{AA} + N * L = N$ which is seen to imply

Equilibrium condition: $W_{AA} + L = 1$

The equilibrium equation simply states that in order to stabilise the population, the recruitment to the stock must be balanced with the death rates. Now according to classical Darwinian thinking, successful new mutants only accomplish small changes. In our case, this means that the new allele a will only slightly modify the recruitment, so the final adjustment of the new short-lived recruits will be small. Hence $W_{AA} + \frac{L}{(1-m)} \approx W_{AA} + L = 1$ so we finally obtain the following essential criteria for successful invasion:

Criteria for successful invasion of the gene pool:

$$\frac{b_{Aa} + b_{AA}}{2}l_{Aa} > 1$$

In words, this criteria simply says that the new allele a will successfully invade the gene pool if the number of surviving mutant offspring to adulthood exceeds 1. Note that offspring of genotype Aa is created in two different ways: Either the mother is of genotype AA and mates with a male of genotype Aa in which case 50% of the offspring will be Aa, or the mother is of genotype Aa in which case also 50% of the offspring will be Aa. This explains why it is the average litter size of the two genotypes $\dfrac{b_{Aa} + b_{AA}}{2}$ that enters the invasion criteria. Now the expected number of mutant offspring that reaches adulthood is found by multiplying with their survival rate l_{Aa}. Since the recruitment of the long-lived genotypes exactly matches the adult mortality $1 - L$, the total recruitment to the adult group is exactly 1 (i.e. the equilibrium condition). Note that this is precisely where the long-life enters the equations: the total recruitment is the recruitment of offspring that manage to live up to adulthood **PLUS** the number of adults surviving the period (as mentioned above, only nongenetic accidents cause a small death rate among the long-lived individuals). So the criteria for successful invasion of the gene pool may be restated in words as follows:

Criteria for successful invasion of the gene pool:
The recruitment of the short-lived individuals must exceed 1

Note that this is good classical Darwinism: The genotype with the highest recruitment will at the end fill up the whole gene pool.

It is now easy to see why Jim Baen's hypothesis is supported by this genetic model. The whole issue about why we must die may be formulated as the question of whether a long-lived strategy is evolutionary stable. A simple, first approximation, genetic model says that the long-lived strategy will only be evolutionary stable if it is difficult for mutant alternatives to establish a recruitment larger than 1. But as Jim Baen has pointed out using classical biological knowledge: there are all sorts of difficulties with inbreeding. Therefore, almost any alternative strategy that reduces energy devoted to long-life and put it into clutch size or vitality of offspring will have a better total recruitment than the long-lived. Therefore, the strategy of eternal life is evolutionary unstable. For human beings this has the consequence that 130 years is the maximum age.

Cohort Analysis of the Evolutionary Stability of Infinite Long Life

In this section we derive the same result in an alternative model that takes all the year-classes (cohorts) into account.

Suppose there are M adult long-lived individuals consisting of 1000 year classes, and let the clutch size per individual be b_A, the survival up to maturity is l_m and the survival rate of adults is s_A. At equilibrium Mb_A offspring are produced each year by 1000 year classes:

$$b_A[Mb_A l_A + Mb_A l_A s_A^1 + Mb_A l_A s_A^2 + Mb_A l_A s_A^3 + \ldots + Mb_A l_A s_A^{999}] = Mb_A$$

which is seen to reduce to

Equilibrium condition

$$b_A l_A \frac{1 - s_A^{1000}}{1 - s_A} = 1 \quad \text{which practically states that} \quad b_A l_A = 1 - s_A$$

that is, the population will be in equilibrium if the recruitment to the adult population (i.e., birth rate multiplied by immature survival) balances the adult death rate.

Consider now a potential invading allele a that codes for living only 100 years as adults, i.e., 10% of the prevailing strategy of 1000 years. Initially there are $x_0 = \varepsilon M$ individuals of these new genotypes having a birth rate of b_a, a survivorship of the immature period equal l_a and an adult survivorship of s_a. With these parameters the iteration equation for the adult mutants are

$$x_{k+1} = s_a x_k + \left(\frac{b_A + b_a}{2} x_{k-tm} \right) l_a = s_a x_k + \frac{b_A + b_a}{2} l_a x_{k+1-tm}$$

Substituting a general solution of the form $x_k = r^k x0$ gives the characteristic equation for the growth of the mutant

$$r^{tm} = s_a r^{tm-1} + \frac{b_A + b_a}{2} la$$

In order to see where the root lies, define the two functions

$$f(r)r^{tm} \text{ and } g(r) = s_a r^{tm-1} + \frac{b_A + b_a}{2} l_a$$

and notice that $f(0) = 0 < \frac{b_A + b_a}{2} la = g(0)$, but since $tm > tm - 1$,

$f(r)$ will eventually become greater than $g(r)$. Thus somewhere they intercept, and the crucial question is whether they intercept to the left of $r = 1$, in which case the number of invaders will decline, or to the right of $r = 1$, in which case the number of short lived individuals will increase. Since

$$f(1) = 1 \text{ and } g(1) = s_a + \frac{b_A + b_a}{2} l_a$$

it follows that the condition for interception to the right of $r = 1$, that is, $f(1) < g(1)$, is

$$1 < s_a + \frac{b_A + b_a}{2} l_a \text{ which finally gives}$$

Criteria for successful invasion of the gene pool:

$$\frac{b_A + b_a}{2} l_a > 1 - s_a$$

In words: The recruitment to the mutant short-lived individuals (=average birth rate of long- and short lived genotypes multiplied with the survival probability up to maturity) must be larger than the adult death rate of the short-lived individuals. Note that this condition is equivalent to that found in our previous Hardy-Weinberg type model, so the same discussion applies.

Let us finally see that if the following approximation of the population dynamics of the mutant

$$x_k = \left(s_a + \frac{b_A + b_a}{2} l_a \right)^k \varepsilon M$$

is substituted into the formula of the Hardy-Weinberg model, we arrive at the same criteria for εM mutant to invade a homozygous population of $(1 - \varepsilon)M$ long-lived adults:

$$\frac{\varepsilon}{2} < \frac{\left(s_a + \frac{b_A + b_a}{2}l_a\right)^{100} \varepsilon M}{2\left[\left(s_a + \frac{b_A + b_a}{2}l_a\right)^{100} \varepsilon M + (1 - \varepsilon)Ms_A^{100} + (1 - \varepsilon)Mb_A l_A \frac{1 - s_A^{100}}{1 - s_A}\right]}$$

where the second term in the denominator is the number of long-lived adult that survived the total life span of the short lived (i.e., 100 years) and the third term is the number of adult long-lived that recruits to the adult population of long lived (since these are prevailing we ignore the contribution of long-lived from the short-lived). Using the equilibrium criterion, $b_A l_A = 1 - s_A$, we obtain

$$(1 - \varepsilon)\left(s_a + \frac{b_A + b_a}{2}l_a\right)^{100} < (1 - \varepsilon)$$

which is equivalent to $s_a + \frac{b_A + b_a}{2}l_a > 1$ that is, $\frac{b_A + b_a}{2}l_a > 1 - s_a$

Thus, we arrive at precisely the same inequality, demonstrating an inner consistency in our models.

A Competition Model with Trade-Off Between Reproduction and Survival

While the two previous models started with the assumption that long-life was an evolutionary stable strategy, we now develop a model where the different life history strategies are in direct competition with each other. However, if a new mutant code for better survival we shall now explicitly regard this as a strategy to allocate more energy to survival at the cost of energy devoted to reproduction. The simplest equation for such a trade-off model is

$$bl = b(s)l(s) = (1 - s)^\lambda \text{ where l is a positive real number}$$

A first approximation to the population growth will then be

$$x_{k+1} = [s + (1-s)^\lambda]x_k$$

which has the solution

$$x_k = [s + (1-s)^\lambda]^k x_0$$

From this we see that natural selection will favor a strategy which maximizes the function

$$f(s) = s + (1-s)^\lambda$$

Putting the derivative equal to zero,

$$f'(s) = 1 - \lambda(1-s)^{\lambda-1} = 0,$$

gives the optimum survival rate as $s^* = 1 - \left(\dfrac{1}{\lambda}\right)^{\frac{1}{\lambda-1}}$ implying an evolutionary stable expected life span of $T^* = \dfrac{s^*}{1-s^*}$

So also in this model will the long-lived be selected against because they do not provide the optimal combination of birth rate and survival rate. Another consequence of tremendous importance is that given a strategy near the optimal, there will be no selection against deleterious genes at ages over T^*. This allows death genes, racing-car analogy construction of organs, etc. Now human beings have evolved from species where these mechanisms already have been operating, so this is an evolutionary blind route with respect to long-life unless it is possible to enter our genes directly and reconstruct them. We are an animal that has evolved over many millions of years to be short lived.

A Personal Remembrance of Jim Baen

by John Lambshead

Jim Baen was a genius. I am head of a science research team at London's Natural History Museum, have a visiting chair at Southampton University, and I am a Royal Society Program Manager, so I have met the odd genius in the course of my work.

Other people will tell you about Jim's influence on the publishing industry. I would like to draw attention to his profound grasp of evolutionary biology. Jim had some original ideas on why metazoa age and die—this is still a contentious subject—and he used me as a sounding board. I couldn't find any holes in his logic so I passed his work to Professor Karl Ugland of Oslo University, who subjected Jim's hypothesis to rigorous mathematical analysis using standard genomic theory. "Baen is a clever fellow," Karl concluded. I concur; the chance of a layperson coming up with a new testable hypothesis in evolutionary biology is close to zero but Jim did it. His "Why Die" article and Karl's mathematical test of it are published in the first issue of *Jim Baen's Universe*.

Jim was always fascinated by the wide variety of early hominids. "Our family tree is too bushy at the base," he would say to me. He suggested that maybe our ancestors had interbred back into the ancestral chimp populations and that was the explanation for so many morphotypes. I was deeply skeptical. There are good reasons why fertile hybrids are unlikely between higher vertebrate species, but Jim persisted despite the cold water I poured on him. Then came news that analysis of chimp and human DNA showed that our respective ancestors must have interbred for some considerable time; it is even possible that modern humans are descended from the hybrids rather than "pure" hominid strains. Had Jim lived, he intended to work up a new article on this subject. He had deduced a hypothesis of human evolution before the DNA evidence. This is an exceptional achievement.

Jim Baen was not an easy man. He retained that childlike attitude to the world that one associates with genius. He could be petulant and unreasonable. He was also loyal, decent, and a lifeline to anyone who needed help. I suspect he would have risen to the top of any creative profession that he tackled. Science fiction's gain was science's loss when Jim chose the former. I am very grateful that he was my friend.

London, England, July 2006

Afterword

Jim Baen's Universe had its origins in a series of discussions in the fall of 2005 between Jim Baen, David Drake and myself. All of us were concerned about the dismal state of the market these days for short fiction in science fiction and fantasy. Most people familiar with F&SF know that short form fiction has been declining steadily for decades, in our genre. All four of the major paper magazines still in existence—*Analog, Asimov's, The Magazine of Fantasy and Science Fiction* and *Realms of Fantasy*—have been struggling against declining circulation figures for a long time, with no end in sight. Many smaller magazines have folded altogether. And the one major online F&SF magazine that had been paying the best rates in the industry, the Sci-Fi channel's *SciFiction*, recently closed down.

Our concern wasn't particularly personal, since none of us were directly affected all that much. Baen Books' income as a publishing house comes almost entirely from novels, as does my income and Dave Drake's as writers—and the market for science fiction and fantasy novels is doing quite well nowadays.

Still, these difficult times for F&SF magazines has an impact on everyone in the field, indirectly if not directly. It's extremely damaging, and for two reasons—one which affects authors directly, the other which affects the readership base of the genre and therefore its future.

The absence of a large and vigorous market for short form fiction hammers authors directly. That's because it makes F&SF authors almost completely dependent on the novel market. And, while the novel market is and always will be intrinsically more lucrative than the short form market, it is also an extremely harsh environment for authors.

Why? Well, simplifying a lot, it's because of the fundamental economics involved. Novels, unlike washing machines and toasters and automobiles, are unique, each and every one of them. Not "unique" in the sense that they don't have generic similarities, but unique simply in the obvious fact that each and every story has to be different or nobody is going to want to read it.

When you walk onto the parking lot of an auto dealer, the last thing you want to hear the car dealer tell you is that "this car is unlike any other." Translation: *it's a lemon*. But when you walk into a bookstore, that's exactly what you want. A story that, at least in one way or another, is different from any other.

What that means, however, is that the book market is incredibly opaque. Even in the largest car dealership, there won't be more than a relative handful of models available to choose from. A dozen, let's say. Two dozen, at the most. Whereas any Barnes and Noble or Borders in the country is likely to have 100,000 *different* "models" in stock.

How are you supposed to choose between them? Well, you can't, that's all. What happens in the real world is that almost all book-buyers, except a small percentage of unusually adventurous ones, will stick almost all of the time to buying only those authors they are familiar with.

What this creates, willy-nilly, is a hierarchy among authors in the marketplace that is...

"Extreme," is the only word I can think of.

Everybody familiar with the publishing industry knows the basic facts of life:

All of a publisher's profits and about half of the operating expenses are covered by the sales of a small number of so-called "lead" writers. And it's a very small number of authors. In the case of Baen, not usually more than half a dozen. And even a big corporate publisher won't have more than a dozen or so lead writers.

Midlist writers generally do well to make a small profit for the publisher, or at least break even. Sales of their books—all told—cover the other half of operating expenses.

New writers, and first novels, generally lose money for a publisher.

Those are the cold, hard facts. What it means for authors is that developing a career is a very chancy business nowadays—and it was always chancy to begin with. Because what happens is that even *after* you get a first novel published, you still have to overcome what Mike Resnick calls "the fourth book hurdle."

The hurdle is this: A publisher will generally give a new author an average of three books to demonstrate if they can become lead writers. If they can't, they're out the door and the publisher will try a new writer to see if they might be able to do it.

Yes, it's heartless. But there's an underlying economic reality for that practice, it's not because publishers are being mean for the hell of it. It's simply a fact that, as a purely mathematical exercise in calculating profits, it makes real sense to toss writers overboard—even good ones, selling fairly decently—if doing so might improve your chances of grabbing the lead writer lottery ticket that generates Ye Big Bucks in novel publishing.

Granted, not all publishers are the same, and they don't all follow exactly the same practices. A midlist writer will sometimes find a smaller independent publisher like Baen or DAW a less unforgiving environment than most of the big corporate houses. And there are some big houses that make a genuine effort to cushion midlist writers against the cold realities of the marketplace. Still, for any commercial publisher, the underlying economics of novel publishing remain stark and unforgiving. "Make it big or die on the vine" is still the rule, even if an author can linger on the vine longer at one house than he or she might be able to at another.

Leaving aside issues of unfairness—and, no, it ain't fair, not even close—this reality has a negative impact on the field as a whole.

First, because it's incredibly wasteful. Not all writers develop their talents at a rapid pace, even leaving aside the fact that there's always a certain amount of pure luck involved. For every Heinlein, there's a Frank Herbert, who needed years to make it big. In today's environment, I'm not at all sure Herbert would have had that time—and we'd be short *Dune* as a result.

But it's also detrimental the other way around, because it places such pressure on lead writers that they very often react by becoming extremely conservative in what they write. Not all do, to be sure. I don't, and neither do a number of other lead writers. But even relatively adventurous lead writers stick most of the time to the tried and true approaches—and there are a lot of lead writers out there who are scared to death to vary at all from the type of story that enabled them to become lead writers in the first place.

In short, the situation is lousy—and the steady collapse of the paperback market is making it even worse. Mass market paperback sales today are probably half what they were a few years ago, and there's no sign I can see that that's going to turn around any time in the foreseeable future.

There's no magic in the real world, however much there may be in fantasy novels. The vanishing of SF paperbacks and magazines is due to profound changes in the economic and social structure of the Unites States. (And the rest of the world's industrial countries, to one degree or another.) Put simply, it's just the literary equivalent of the same dynamic that has seen McDonald's and Burger King supplanting thousands of independent little diners and restaurants, and has seen Home Depot and Lowe's replacing thousands of little hardware stores.

What's happened is that the big retail outlets essentially forced what had once been a sprawling distribution industry with almost five hundred separate companies in North America to consolidate into a handful of companies—and then told them they only wanted bestsellers. Within a few years, F&SF magazines began vanishing from everywhere except book superstores, and so did most paperback titles except for those written by bestselling authors.

To put it another way, the sales of most books and specialty magazines have imploded into the superstore book chains (Barnes & Noble, Border's, Books-a-Million, etc.) From the standpoint of *hardcover* sales, especially novels, that's been quite a good development. So if you publish a lot of novels, as is true for lead writers like myself and David Drake, you're doing fine. But it's a terrible situation for most midlist and new writers. Midlist writers working at novel length usually live and die on their ability to show they can do well in paperback, so a publisher will give them a shot at a hardcover. That was never easy at any time, and today it's gotten a lot worse.

In decades past, it was the size and health of the magazines that cushioned all of these problems. They allowed midlist writers a place they could keep getting published, gain perhaps slow but steady public recognition, and improve their skills—without being under the "fourth book" guillotine. And, while it was always very hard even in the salad days of the magazines for an author to make a full-time living as a short fiction writer (at least, unless you could sell to *The Saturday Evening Post*), they could bring in enough of an income to take a day job that allowed them as much freedom to write as possible.

On the flip side, the magazines provided lead writers with a place they could stretch their skills if they wanted to, without running the risk of falling off that precious lead writer sales plateau.

Okay, so much for the writers. Now I want to explain how the decline of short form fiction has been hammering the field as a whole.

It's not complicated. It's what's often called the "graying of science fiction." Put crudely and bluntly, the average age of science fiction and fantasy fans keeps rising. Once the quintessential genre of choice of teenagers, it's now a genre that's developed a great big middle-aged potbelly.

What do you expect—when the *entry* level purchase, nowadays, is likely to be a $25 hardcover? And, to make things worse, you have to drive an average of seven miles to get to a superstore that'll even carry a science fiction title at all? (And that's the national average. In some areas of the country, you have to drive a hundred miles or more.)

That's not how I got introduced to science fiction, as a twelve-year-old, I can tell you that. I got introduced through magazines and cheap Ace Double books on the wire racks of my local drugstore, in a small town in rural California. Which...

Don't exist any more. The books and magazines, I mean. The small town is still there, and so is the drug store—but it no longer carries any SF titles.

The problem isn't even the price of a paperback, as such. That hasn't actually risen any, over the past half a century, measured by the only price criterion that matters. To wit, today a paperback novel costs just about the same as a movie ticket. And, fifty years ago... it cost just about the same as a movie ticket did then.

No, the problem is *availability*. When I was a kid, SF magazines and paperbacks could be found all over the place. Today, with a few exceptions—and those, almost invariably, only a small number of top-selling authors—you can only find F&SF titles in bookstores, especially the chain superstores.

You can think whatever you want about this fundamental transformation of modern society. But facts are facts, and they are stubborn things. If you want to try to turn that situation around, with respect to our genre, you have to figure out a new approach.

Which, we think we have. Out of those discussions between the three of us in the fall of 2005, we developed the basic outline of a new business model for producing a major science fiction and fantasy magazine. The result was *Jim Baen's Universe,* and while we've refined the model in the light of practice since the first issue came out in June of 2006, the basic model has held steady.

Our strategy is to use the free entry and accessibility of the internet to substitute for the ready availability of paper editions of SF magazines in times past. This will be a big challenge, of course, because the electronic fiction market is still very small. But, by combining the advantages of electronic distribution with Baen's longstanding policies with regard to electronic publishing, we think we've got a good shot at pulling it off.

Essentially, what we're trying to do is circumvent the modern barriers to publishing short fiction in F&SF while paying good rates to authors—we pay the best rates in the industry to our writers—by taking advantage of two new factors in the equation:

The first, obviously, is the internet and the possibility for electronic publication. That eliminates, at one stroke, most of the tremendous costs and bottlenecks of distribution.

The second is that we continue with the magazine the same policies that Baen Books developed from the beginning of the internet era with respect to selling electronic books. Baen has always approached online publishing with a very different—almost diametrically opposed— philosophy than all major commercial publishers. The standard wisdom in the industry was that electronic publishing would be crippled by so-called "electronic piracy." As a result, all major commercial publishers except Baen adopted stringent encryption methods—what's generally called DRM, "digital rights management"—in order to combat electronic copyright infringement.

Jim Baen thought that was nonsense, and would have no effect except to strangle the electronic publishing industry while it was still in the crib. Instead, his publishing house adopted the following basic guidelines, from the very beginning:

1) Baen electronic titles would be published with no encryption.

2) Baen electronic titles would be sold cheaply. Depending on the package chosen by the customer—these range from monthly Webscriptions packages to the sale of individual titles—the cost per book would average somewhere between $2.50 and $6.00.

3) Baen would provide a hefty selection of sample chapters for every book, available for free online.

4) Baen would make available a large number of complete titles for free in the Baen Library.

The last two provisions are to enable online customers to do what customers in brick-and-mortar walk-in bookstores take for granted, which is being able to look through a book before buying it.

The end result was exactly what Jim expected. Baen's electronic sales today, adjusting for the number of titles produced, are far greater than those of other commercial publishers—and the royalties from electronic sales earned by Baen's authors are likewise far greater than those earned by authors from electronic titles produced by other publishing houses.

As a magazine, *Jim Baen's Universe* carries over all of those policies—and we added a new one. In order to make the magazine available to various categories of customers who suffer from particular pricing obstacles, we offer the magazine at steeply discounted subscription rates (as low as $6.00 a year for six issues) to the following people:

- the blind and handicapped;
- students;
- soldiers on active duty;
- readers from developing countries.

Jim Baen died in June of 2006, just a few weeks after the first issue of the magazine came out. His ashes were scattered, along with his mother's, at the roots of a southern red oak tree in David Drake's back yard, in a private ceremony that I attended along with a number of other people. By now, those ashes have long since vanished back into the universe that produced the man.

There is no memorial to him anywhere, outside of a small headstone at the base of the tree. But, as editor of the magazine, I like to think *Universe* is, if not a memorial for Jim, certainly something that continues his tradition.

If you enjoyed these stories, please consider subscribing to the magazine—or, better still, buying one or another level of membership in the Universe Club which supports it. You can do so simply by going online to:

www.baens-universe.com

Then, select "Subscribe" from the menu at the top.

You will be able to select from any one of several Club membership, or select just an annual subscription ($30 for six issues), or one of the discounted subscriptions if you qualify.

As I write this afterword, *Jim Baen's Universe* has just successfully completed its first year of publication and we are preparing the June 2007 issue, which will inaugurate our second year. Join us!

Eric Flint
April, 2007

About The Magazine

Jim Baen's Universe has been hailed as the best new science fiction and fantasy magazine in decades. A groundbreaking on-line magazine, in its first year of publication it has published such award winning authors as Mike Resnick, Gene Wolfe, Gregory Benford, David Brin, Esther Friesner, Catherine Asaro, David Weber, David Drake, and more.

Jim Baen's Universe is available in many formats and completely unencrypted, without Digital Rights Management or copy protection schemes. It can be downloaded into a home computer, laptop, palm blackberry, pocket pc, ebook reader, or almost any other electronic device. Subscribers can also simply read the magazine without downloading it, on any Internet-enabled mobile device. Or, if hardcopy is preferred, the PDF version of the magazine is specifically designed for home printing. To subscribe go to www.baens-universe.com.

Editor Flint states, "We don't have the restrictions that traditional paper publication put on a magazine. We can experiment, and allow our authors to experiment with length. This gives our readers a unique experience."

Publisher Toni Weisskopf notes, "This was Jim Baen's last project, and he wanted it to succeed. We are pleased to report that it has."

Readers can subscribe for $30 per year, or they can purchase an upgraded membership in the Universe Club. Universe Club members receive e-books, chances to be tuckerized into new books by famous authors, editorially selected bundled novels (unencrypted e-books) and lots more. The entire list of Universe Club swag is at: www.baens-universe.com